The Willows and Others

July 1st 1889.

Family home . Kent   Algy

ALGERNON BLACKWOOD

The Willows and Others

Collected Short Fiction
Volume 1: 1889–1907

Edited by S. T. Joshi

Hippocampus Press

New York

Published by Hippocampus Press
P.O. Box 641, New York, NY 10156.
www.hippocampuspress.com

Cover illustration and design © 2023 by Jason Van Hollander.
Hippocampus Press logo designed by Anastasia Damianakos.

First edition
1 3 5 7 9 8 6 4 2

ISBN 978-1-61498-432-0 six-volume set
ISBN 978-1-61498-401-6 volume 1
ISBN 978-1-61498-428-3 ebook

Contents

Introduction

The bountiful output of Algernon Blackwood (1869–1951) over a period of more than six decades is a testament to the vigor of his imagination and the deep personal resources from which he drew it. His work is closely related to the events of his life, and it is for that reason regrettable that much of the documentary evidence relating to his life has perished. Some of it was destroyed in 1940 when a German shell destroyed his London home, with Blackwood himself narrowly escaping death. His own autobiography, *Episodes Before Thirty* (1923), is highly illuminating; and this work, along with other material culled from a multiplicity of sources, has allowed Mike Ashley—the leading authority on Blackwood—to fashion a compelling portrait of the writer and his evolving state of mind.[1]

Algernon Henry Blackwood was born on March 14, 1869, at Shooter's Hill, Kent. His father, Sir Stevenson Arthur Blackwood, was a notable figure in Queen Victoria's government; in 1880 he attained the rank of permanent secretary to the Post Office. Algernon was educated privately, then attended Wellington College (1883–84), followed by two years at the school of the Moravian Brotherhood in Königsfeld, Germany. He would write poignantly—but perhaps somewhat exaggeratedly—of the harsh discipline of the Brothers in the recently discovered story "A Strange Adventure in the Black Forest" (1889) as well as in the more celebrated "Secret Worship." He also faced some family difficulties. His father's rigid brand of evangelical Christianity did not sit well with Algernon, who escaped into the world of religious mysticism by way of such works as Patanjali's

---

1. See *Starlight Man: The Extraordinary Life of Algernon Blackwood* (Constable, 2001; published in the US as *Algernon Blackwood: An Extraordinary Life* (Carroll & Graf, 2001); rev. ed. under the former title (Stark House, 2019).

Yoga Aphorisms, a text that fuses Buddhism, Jainism, and other eastern religious doctrines.[2]

Blackwood was soon pursuing other means of expanding his awareness of unusual phenomena, teaming up with Frank Podmore, a central figure in the Society for Psychical Research, in exploring some purported haunted houses. This led to his first known published story, "A Mysterious House" (*Belgravia,* July 1889), based on a visit to Edinburgh in 1888. For all that Blackwood was initially attracted to spiritualism, occultism, and related phenomena, to the point of briefly joining the Order of the Golden Dawn, he ultimately rejected this approach to perceiving reality.

But Blackwood also needed to think of employment. In 1887 his father took him on an extended trip to Canada; in 1890 Blackwood returned to Canada and attempted to establish himself as a dairy farmer. The business failed in 1892, and Blackwood drifted to New York, where he became a reporter—first for the *Sun* and then for the *New York Times.* Later he became the private secretary for a wealthy banker, James Speyer, spending two years at the job (1897–99). By this time, however, Blackwood had become homesick and returned to England. He took a dramatic trip down the Danube in a canoe in 1900, in the company of Wilfred Wilson (transformed into "the Swede" in Blackwood's most celebrated tale, "The Willows")—an adventure he wrote up in a stirring essay, "Down the Danube in a Canadian Canoe" (see Appendix).

While engaged in working for a dried milk company, Blackwood found abundant leisure time to continue his explorations of bizarre phenomena, both with the Society for Psychical Research and the Golden Dawn. These adventures led to his writing a variety of stories during the early years of the twentieth century. A chance meeting with a colleague from New York, Angus Hamilton, resulted in Hamilton reading some of these stories and taking them (without Black-

---

2. Patanjali is a shadowy figure who is believed to have lived between the 2nd and 4th centuries C.E. The translation of *Yoga Aphorisms* Blackwood read was probably the one published in Calcutta in 1883 (Printed by J. W. Thomas, Baptist Mission Press), since Blackwood reports that he was "about seventeen" when he read the book (*Episodes Before Thirty* [New York: E. P. Dutton, 1923], 31).

wood's knowledge) to the publisher Eveleigh Nash, who promptly accepted them and issued them as *The Empty House and Other Ghost Stories* (1906). The book was favorably reviewed, and Nash issued a second collection, *The Listener and Other Stories* (1907). Blackwood's career as a writer of weird fiction was underway.

It can be seen from the stories in this volume that in his early work Blackwood was striving to find his voice as a writer, both in subject matter and in style and tone. For all that he remained a life-long bachelor, he indulged in a few tales of romance, such as "The Story of Karl Ott" and "Testing His Courage." His enthusiasm for the outdoors (and for the emotional life of children) is exemplified in "The Last Egg in the Nest," while his sympathy for the back-breaking and frequently deadly work of Canadian loggers is displayed in "How Garnier Broke the Log-Jam."

But it is his weird tales that are of greatest interest to us—and here again we see how Blackwood drew deeply upon the multifarious activities of his first three decades of life, spanning two continents. His rapture at the untenanted wilderness of Canada, where he under-took numerous camping trips, is embodied in "A Haunted Island." Haunted houses in England and Scotland are the focus of "The Empty House," "Smith: An Episode in a Lodging House," "The Listener," and "The Woman's Ghost Story." Reincarnation—a domi-nant theme in much of Blackwood's later work—finds expression in "The Insanity of Jones" and other stories, while the idea of the ele-mental is exemplified in "May Day Eve." The revenant is the focus of "Keeping His Promise."

And yet, it is of interest to note several tales of non-supernatural horror in this volume—a mode of writing that Blackwood by and large eschewed in his subsequent career. "Max Hensig—Bacteriologist and Murderer" is the signal instance of this mode, and it manifestly draws upon Blackwood's work as a reporter in New York, as does "The Strange Adventures of a Private Secretary in New York."

In the introduction to a late volume of his best stories, *Tales of Algernon Blackwood* (1938), reprinted here in the Appendix, Black-wood makes clear that his aesthetic purpose in writing weird tales is to investigate "questions of extended or expanded consciousness." This does not at all mean that strange phenomena perceived by such a consciousness is merely internal or subjective; rather, Blackwood believes that an expanded consciousness allows for the perception of genuine events. As he states in regard to the novel *The Centaur* (1911), which is something of a spiritual autobiography, the protagonist's "sense of beauty blazed into a realisation of the planetary bodies as superhuman entities."

In other words, Algernon Blackwood's entire corpus of weird fiction is based upon a coherent philosophy of life—an intense and deeply held belief that the world that we grasp through our five senses is only the tip of the iceberg of what actually exists in the world and universe around us. We need not subscribe to this philosophy ourselves to appreciate the high artistry Blackwood brings to his writing, early and late, and the extraordinary insight into human character he displays in his portrayals of those few individuals who find themselves enmeshed in the bizarre and the supernatural.

—S. T. JOSHI

Editor's Note

In establishing the text of Algernon Blackwood's tales, one is hampered by the near-total absence of handwritten or typed manuscripts. Many of these may have perished when Blackwood's London home was bombed by the Germans in 1940, assuming they had not been destroyed by the author at an earlier date. Accordingly, one is dependent on ascertaining Blackwood's stylistic and punctuational preferences by consultation of the magazine, newspaper, and book appearances of his stories.

From these appearances it can be seen that Blackwood generally adhered to the British spelling preferences of his day, with some exceptions; e.g., he preferred "judgment" to "judgement," "acknowledgment" to "acknowledgement," and "connection" to "connexion." He generally placed punctuation inside quotation marks (with standard exceptions such as the semicolon, colon, question-mark, and exclamation-mark); some publications of Blackwood's tales use single quotation marks in accordance with British usage, but this has been systematized and double quotation marks have been used. Blackwood does not omit the period in "Mr.," "Mrs.," "St. [saint]," etc. He overwhelmingly uses the serial or Oxford comma; in instances where it is lacking, it has been inserted.

In terms of individual words, Blackwood appears to prefer "to-day," "to-night," and "to-morrow"; "half-way"; "some one," "every one," and "any one" (but "something" or "somebody"); "camp fire" (but "camp-fire" when adjectival); "for ever"; "towards"; and "round" (as opposed to "around"). In the great majority of cases he inserts a hyphen when using the suffix "-like."

No editor of Blackwood's work can fail to be indebted to the tireless scholarship of Mike Ashley, whose bio-bibliography[3] remains all but definitive. Ashley himself has now located several additional tales that had been previously unknown, and he has graciously provided the editor with the texts of these and other hard-to-find works. In every sense of the term, this edition would not exist without Mike Ashley's decades of research, as well as his kindness and generosity.

---

3. *Algernon Blackwood: A Bio-bibliography* (Greenwood Press, 1987).

A Mysterious House

Explanations are usually very tedious, and so without any introduction or preambulation I will plunge right into the midst of this uncanny story I am about to tell. . . . When, some fifteen years before the time of which I write, I was a schoolboy at Eton I made close friends with a fellow above me in the school, named Pellham. We were very great chums, and later on we went to Cambridge together, where my friend spent money and time in wasting both, while I read for holy orders, though I never actually entered the Church. Since that time I had completely lost sight of him and he of me, and, with the exception of seeing his marriage in the papers, had no news at all of his whereabouts. One morning, however, towards the close of September 1857, I received a letter from him, short, precise, and evidently written in a great hurry, asking me to go down and see him at his family seat just outside Norwich. I packed my bag and went that very same evening. He met me himself at the station and drove me home. We hardly recognised each other at first sight, so much had we changed in appearance, both being on the dark side of thirty-five, but our individual characters had remained much the same and we were still to all appearances the best of friends. My friend was not very talkatively disposed, and I kept up a fire of questions until we drew up at the park gates. Going up the drive to the house he brightened up considerably, and gave me plenty of information about himself and family. He was quite alone, I was surprised to hear, his wife and two daughters with an uncle of his having left for the Continent two days previous. After dinner he seemed quite the old "Cambridge Undergrad" again, and once settled round the old-fashioned hearth, with cheroots and coffee, we talked on over the days spent at Eton and Cambridge. We were just discussing our third edition of tobacco, when Pellham suddenly changed the subject, and said he would tell me now why he had written so shortly to me to pay him this unexpected visit. His face grew grave as he began by asking me if I was still a sceptic as regards ghostly manifestations.

"Indeed I am," was my answer; "I have had no reason to change my views on the subject, and think exactly as I used to at Cambridge, when we so strongly differed; but I remember you then saying that, if ever in after years you should come across an opportunity of proving to me your ideas on the subject, you would write to me at once, and I also recollect giving my word that, if possible, I would come. But during the fifteen years that have since passed by I have bestowed little, if any, thought on the subject."

"Exactly," answered Pellham, with a grave smile that did not please me; "but now I have at last heard of a case which will satisfy us both, I think, so I wrote to you to come down and fulfil your old promise by investigating it."

"Well! let me hear all about it first," I said cautiously. I certainly was not overjoyed to hear this news, for, though a sceptic to all intents and purposes, still "ghosts" was a subject for which I had a certain fear, and the highest ambition of my life was not to investigate haunted houses and the like just because I had years ago promised I would should a chance occur. But I repressed my feelings and tried to look interested, which I was, and delighted, which I certainly was not. Pellham then gave me a long account—thrilling enough too it was—of the case, which I have somewhat condensed in the following form. Some three or four years before, my friend had bought up a house which stood on the moorland about eight miles off. One morning before breakfast the tenant of the house, a Mr. Sherleigh (who was there with his family), suddenly burst into my friend's study without any ceremony, and, in great heat and excitement, shouted out the following words:

"You shall suffer for it, Lord Pellham, my wife mad, and the little boy killed with fright, because you didn't choose to warn us of the room next the drawing-room, but you shall—." Here the footman entered, and at a sign from his master led the excited and evidently cracked old man from the room, but not before he had crashed down some gold pieces on the table, with: "That's the last rent you'll get for that house, as sure as I am the last tenant."

"Well," continued my friend, "that very day, now two years ago, I rode over there myself and the house was empty. The Sherleighs had left it, and since that day I have never been able to let it to anyone. Mr. Sherleigh, who was quite mad, poor fellow, threw himself before a train, and was cut to pieces, and Mrs. Sherleigh spread a report that it was haunted, and now no one will take it or even go near it, though it stands high and is in a very healthy position. Two nights ago," he went on gravely, "I was riding past the road which leads up to it, and through the trees I could see light in one of the upper rooms, and figures, or rather shadows, of a woman's figure, with something in her arms, kept crossing to and fro before the window-blind. I determined to go in and see what on earth it was, and tying my horse just outside I went in. In a minute or two I was close underneath the window where the light was still visible, and the shadow still moving to and fro with a horrible regularity. As I stood there, undecided, a feeling within warned me not to enter the house, so vivid, it was almost a soft voice that whispered in my ear. I heard no noise inside, the night air was moaning gently through the fir trees which surrounded the house on one side and nearly obscured the upper part of the window from view. I stooped down and picked up a large stone—it was a sharp-edged flint—and without any hesitation hurled it with all my might at the window pane, some eight or ten feet from the ground. The stone went straight and struck the window on one of the wooden partitions, smashing the whole framework, glass and all, into a thousand splinters, many of which struck me where I stood. The result was awful and unexpected. The moment the stone touched the glass the lights quite disappeared, and in the blackness in which I was shrouded, the next minute, I could see hiding behind the broken corners of glass a dark face and form for a short instant, and then it went and all was pitch dark again. There I was among those gloomy pine trees hardly knowing which way to turn. The face I had caught a momentary glimpse of was the face of Mr. Sherleigh, whom I knew to be dead! My knees trembled. I tried to grope my way out of the wood, and stumbled from tree to tree, often striking my head against the low branches. In vain. With the weird light in the window as a guide, I had taken but a few minutes to come, but now all was dark and I could not find my way back again. I felt as if the dismal tree trunks were living things, which seemed to move. Suddenly I heard a noise on my left. I stopped and listened. Horror! I was still close to the window, and what I heard was a cracking and splintering of broken glass, as if some one from inside were slowly forcing their way out through the hole made by my stone! Was it he? The fir tree next me suddenly shook violently, as if agitated by a powerful gust of wind, and then in a gleam of weird light I saw a long dark body hanging half-way out of the window, with black hair streaming down the shoulders. It raised one arm and slammed down something at my feet which fell with a rattle, and then hissed out: 'There's the last rent you'll ever have for this house.' I stood literally stupefied with horror, then a cold numb sensation came over me and I fell fainting on my face, but not until I had heard my horse give a prolonged neigh and then his footsteps dying away in the distance on the hard moorland road. . . . When I recovered consciousness it was broad daylight. I was cold and damp; all night I had lain where I fell. I rose and limped, stiff and tired, to the place where I had tied my horse the night before, but no horse was there. And the horrible sound of his hoofs echoing away in the distance came back to me, and I shuddered as I thought of what I had seen. After a terrible trudge of three hours I reached home. A tremendous search had been made for me, of course, but no one dreamt of looking for me where I really was. The horse had found his way home, and I have never found out what frightened him so."

My friend's account was over. He lit his cigar, which had gone out during the narrative, and settling himself comfortably in his chair, said, "Well, old boy, that's a case I don't feel at all inclined to investigate by myself, but I'll do it with your aid. You know, a genuine sceptic is a great addition in such things, so we'll get to the bottom of it somehow."

My feelings at that moment were not difficult to describe. I disliked the whole affair, and wanted heartily to get out of it; and yet something urged me to go through with it and show my friend that the house was all right, that imagination did it all, that the horse may have taken fright at anything, and that very possibly there really was some one in the house all the time, and imagination had done the rest. Such were the somewhat mixed thoughts in my mind at the time. However, in a few moments all was settled and we had agreed to go the following night, search the house first, and then sit up all night in the room next the drawing-room. Then we both went to our separate bedrooms to think the matter over and get a long sleep, as we neither expected to get any the following night.

Next morning at breakfast we both talked cheerfully about the coming night and how best to meet its requirements as regards food, etc. We agreed to take pistols for weapons, horses as a means of conveyance, and abundant food wherewith to fortify ourselves against a possible attack of ghosts.

The day drew on towards its close. It was very hot and sultry weather, and not a breath of wind stirred the murky atmosphere, as at 4.30 P.M. we bestrode our horses and made off in the direction of the "White House." A long gravel road, lonely in the extreme, led us across the wild uncultivated moorland for six or seven miles, then we saw a copse of fir trees which, my friend informed me, were the trees which sheltered one side of the house. In a few minutes we had passed through the front garden gate and were among the dark fir trees, and then as we turned a sharp corner the house burst full upon us. It was square and ugly. Great staring windows in regular rows met our eyes and conveyed an unpleasant impression to the brain—at least, they did to mine. From the very moment we had passed the front gate till I left the house next morning, I felt a nasty sick sensation creep over me, a feeling of numbness and torpor which seemed to make the blood run thick and sluggish in my veins. The events of that night have remained engraven on my brain as with fire, and, though they happened years ago, I can see them now as vividly as then. Only an eye-witness can possibly describe them, should he wish to do justice to them, and so my feeble pen shall make the attempt.

It was about 6.30, and we had settled our horses in a barn outside for the night. There were only two walls to keep the barn in position, and these were simply a row of rotten posts, half-decayed in places, so we securely tied the horses and, with a good supply of hay, left them for the night. We then approached the door and, after fumbling in the lock for some time, Pellham succeeded in opening it. A sickly, musty odour pervaded the hall, and the first thing we did after a thorough search, which revealed nothing, was to open all the doors and windows all over the house, so as to let in what little air there was. Then we went upstairs into the little room next the drawing-room, where, according to Sherleigh, strange things had occurred. But the window was in pieces, and hardly an entire pane of glass was left, and we were forced to select another room on the same floor (i.e. the second) and looking out on the same copse of pine trees, whose branches almost touched the glass, so close were they. It was a very ordinary room; a fireplace, no furniture but a rickety table and three chairs, one of which was broken. The only disagreeable feature we noticed about the room was its gloominess; it was so very dark. The trees outside, as I have already said, were so close that the slightest breath of wind rustled their twigs against the window. We soon had six candles fixed and burning in different parts of the little room, and the blaze of light was still further increased by a roaring fire, on which a kettle was singing for tea, and eggs boiling in a saucepan, and at half-past seven we were in the middle of our first tea in a haunted house. It was, indeed, less luxurious than the dinners I had been used to lately, but otherwise there was nothing to find fault with, and a little later the tea things were cleared away in a heap in a corner (where, by-the-by, they are to this day), and we were sitting round an empty table, smoking in silence. The door out into the passage was fast shut, but the window was wide open. The sun had sunk out of sight in a beautiful sky of wonderful colouring. Small fleecy clouds floating about caught the soft after-glow and looked unearthly as seen through the thick fir branches. The faint red hue of the western sky looked like the reflection of some huge and distant conflagration, growing dimmer and fainter as the dark engines of the night played upon it, extinguishing the leaping flames and suffusing the sky with a red reflected glow. Not a breath of air stirred the trees. My friend had left the window and was poking and arranging the fire, with his back turned towards me. I was standing close to the window, looking at the fast-fading colours, when it seemed to me that the window sash was moving. I looked closer. Yes! I was not mistaken. The lower half was gradually sinking; gradually and very quietly it went down. At first I thought the weight had slipped and gone wrong, and the window was slipping down of its own accord; but when I saw the bolt pulled across and fastened as by an invisible hand, I thought differently. My first impulse was to immediately undo the bolt again and open the window, but on trying to move—good heavens! I found I had lost all power of motion and could not move a muscle of my body. I was literally rooted to the ground. Neither could I move the muscles of my tongue or mouth; I could not speak or utter a sound. Pellham was still doing something to the fire, and I could hear him muttering to himself, though I could not distinguish any words. Suddenly, then, I felt the power of motion returning to me; my muscles were relaxing, and turning, though not without a considerable effort, I walked to the fireplace. Pellham, then, for the first time noticed that the window was shut, and he made a remark about the closeness of the night, asking me why I had closed it.

"Hulloa," he went on, before I had time to answer, "by the gods above! what is happening to that window? Look—why it's moving!"

I turned. *The window was slowly being opened again.*

Yes, sure enough it was. Slowly and steadily it moved or was pushed up.

We could but believe our eyes; in half a minute the window was wide open again. I turned and looked at Pellham and he looked at me, and in dead silence we stared at one another, neither knowing what to say or wishing to break the silence. But at length my friend spoke.

"I wish I were a sceptic, old man, like you are; sceptics are always safer in a place like this."

"Yes," I said, as cheerfully as I could, "I feel safe enough, and what's more, I am convinced that the window was opened by human agency from outside."

Pellham smiled, he knew as well as I that no human fingers could have fastened the bolt from outside. "Well," he said briskly, "perhaps you are right; come, let's examine the window."

We rose and approached it, and my friend put his head and shoulders out into the air. It was very dark, and a strange oppressive stillness reigned outside, only broken by the gentle moaning sound of the night wind as it rustled through the trees and swept their branches like the strings of a lyre. I followed my friend's example, and together we peered out into the night. Soon my eyes rested on the ground below us, and at the base of one of the nearer pines I thought

I could distinguish a black form, clinging, as it seemed, to the tree. I pointed it out to Pellham, who failed to see anything, or at least said so; anyhow, I was glad to believe that my excited imagination was the real cause. We were still leaning out of the window in silence, when several of the trees, especially the one where I imagined I had seen the shape, were most violently agitated, as though by a mighty wind; but we felt not the slightest breath on our faces. At the same instant we heard a subdued shuffling sound in the room behind us, which seemed to come from the direction of the chimney. But neither of us referred to it as we slowly walked back to the fire and took up our places on either side on the two chairs, which were at the best very rickety.

"It isn't wise to leave the window open," said my friend, suddenly, "for if there really is any one outside, they can see all and everything we do; while we, for our part, can see absolutely nothing of what goes on outside."

I agreed, and walked up to the window, shutting it with a bang and firmly drawing the bolt.

"I've brought a book," he went on, "which I thought we might read out aloud in turn to relieve the dulness and the silence."

He stopped speaking and looked at me, and at the same moment I raised my eyes to his face. To my intense horror and surprise I noticed for the first time a long smear of blood, wet and crimson, across his forehead. My horror was so great that for some seconds I could not find my tongue, and sat stupidly staring at him. At last I gasped out:

"My dear fellow, what has happened to you, have you cut yourself?"

"Where? what do you mean?" he replied, looking round him with surprise.

For answer I took out my handkerchief, and wiping his brow, showed him the red stains. But as I stood there showing him this proof and as he was expressing his utter astonishment, I distinctly saw something that for the moment made the blood rush from the extremities and crowd into my head. Something seemed to tighten round my heart. I saw a large, gleaming knife and hand disappear into the air in the direction of the window. It was too much; my nerves failed me, and I dropped fainting to the floor.

*   *   *

When I came to myself I was lying where I fell by the fireplace. Pellham was sitting beside me.

"I thought you were dead," he said, "you've been unconscious for over an hour." He said this in such a queer manner and laughed so fiendishly that I wondered what had happened to him during the interval. Had he seen something awful and gone mad? There was a strange light in his dark eyes and a leer on his lip. Just then he took up his book quite naturally and began to read aloud, every now and then he made a comment on what he was reading, quite sensibly too, and soon I began to think, as I sipped my brandy out of our flask, that I must have had a frightful dream. But there at my feet lay the blood-stained handkerchief, and I could not get over that. I glanced at his face; the smear had disappeared, and no scratch or wound was visible.

Pellham had not been reading long, perhaps some five or ten minutes, when we heard a strange noise outside among the trees, just audible above the death-like stillness of the autumn night. It was a confused voice like the low whispering of several persons, and as I listened, still weak from the last shock, the blood stood still in my veins. Pellham went on reading as usual. This struck me as very curious, for he must have heard the noise plainly; but I said nothing, and glancing at him I saw the same light in his eyes and the evil leer on his mouth, looking ugly in the flickering glare of the candles and fire-light.

Suddenly we heard a tremendous noise outside, altogether drowning the first. The horses had broken loose and were tearing wildly past the house. Long and wild neighs rang out and died away, and we knew our horses were gone. Pellham was still reading, and as I looked at him a sudden and horrid thought flashed through my brain. It was this: had he anything to do with this? Was it possible? Before I had time to answer my question Pellham threw down the book and made for the door, locked it, drew out the key, and opening the window threw it far away among the trees. I then recognised the awful fact that I was alone with a madman. I glanced at my watch, it was a quarter to one. Instead of one hour I must have been unconscious two at least. This was terrible in the extreme. He was a man of far more powerful physique than I. What was to be done?

Pellham strode grinning up to the fire, went down on both knees, and commenced blowing between the bars with all his might. I saw my chance, and quietly walking to the window, without a word I climbed out, and letting myself as far down as my arms would allow I then let go and dropped. It was a distance of four or five feet, but in the darkness I tumbled forward on my face. As I rose, uninjured, I distinctly heard the sound of running feet close to me, but in my bewilderment I could not make out clearly in which direction they were going; they only lasted a moment or two. But what a terrific sight met my gaze as I turned the corner of the house, and saw volumes of smoke pouring steadily out of the windows and roof of the back portion of the house. Now and again a long flame, too, shot up to heaven.

"Good God!" I cried, "the house is on fire."

No wonder the horses had taken flight. But my poor friend, what could I do for him? The window was too high for me to climb in again, and the doors were locked. In a few minutes the flames would spread to this side of the house and the poor fellow would be burnt to death unless he had enough sense left to jump out of the window.

I hurried back to the spot where I had let myself down from the window, just in time to see the last scene of the most ghastly experience I have ever witnessed. Pellham was standing at the window. In his hand was a red-hot poker, and it was pointed at his throat, but the strain was too great for my nervous system and with a violent start *I woke up!*

After our heavy tea we had both fallen asleep, just as we were in our chairs. Pellham was still snoring opposite me, and the light was stealing in through the window. It was morning, about half-past six. All the candles had burnt themselves out, and it was a wonder they had not set fire to the dry wood near them.

Twenty minutes later we had re-lit the fire and were discussing the remnant of eggs and coffee. Half an hour later we were riding home in the bright, crisp, morning air, and an hour and a half later we were in the middle of a second and far superior breakfast, during which I did *not* tell my dream, but during which we *did* agree that it had been the dullest and most uncomfortable night we had ever spent away from home.

A Strange Adventure in the Black Forest

In the southern portion of the Duchy of Baden, situated in the darkest depths of the Black Forest, lies the primitive village of Königsfeld. For some little distance round this lonely collection of houses the land has been considerably cleared of trees, and from certain points of vantage—the village stands 3,000 feet above the sea—one gazes round on the flowing curves of the Black Forest range, ever clothed in the sombre garments of the pines, which give the hills a soft appearance of velvet. On every side hundreds and hundreds of tall pine trees stretch away over hill and vale, until at length, in the far distance, the eye fails to distinguish them, as the sky seems to come down and mingle with their gloomy tints.

This little village of Königsfeld, far away from the world on these wild heights, is a Moravian settlement, and a model one of its kind. Built in a square, with fresh green gardens, and a fountain in the centre, it is complete in itself. On one side rises the church, facing which, on the opposite side of the square, stands a large, ugly building of stone, a little out of keeping, perhaps, with the modest size of the surrounding wooden houses. This is nothing else than the school—the "Knaben-Anstalt." One of those simple, strict, and striking establishments known as "Moravian schools."

It was to this school that, one morning in May, 187—, my father packed me off, for better, for worse, and it was in this lonely hamlet, and among its unsophisticated inhabitants, that I had my first experience of Continental life. But of that I intend to say nothing; it can be of little interest, and, beyond the novelty of living with French, Italian, Russian, and Brazilian youths, all struggling with the German tongue, and the excitement connected with strange customs, fierce winters, hot summers, and wonderfully beautiful surroundings—beyond this, there would be, indeed, little of interest to relate. But what I propose to record is an event that occurred to me before I had been there very long, an event that to me was, and always has been, totally inexplicable on natural grounds.

When I had been an inmate of the said establishment for nearly three months, having sufficiently mastered the language to be able to peer into its deeper mysteries, I was one morning suddenly summoned from my work-table, where I had been poring over a German version of Euclid, half asleep in the heat of the mid-day sun—summoned to the august presence of the Herr Direktor. There he stood behind his high desk, covered with papers, vigorously smoking a long cigar and staring fixedly at me through his strong spectacles, which made his eyes look as big as saucers. In his hand he held a letter, and, before he spoke, I remember puzzling my sleepy brain as to his object in sending for me. Could he have known that my "Euclid" had been upside down, and that I was thinking sadly of my home in Kent? Could he possibly have been aware that, for the half-hour preceding his summons for me, I had slyly been producing from my pocket one fat cherry after another, and, under the pretence of scratching my nose, had introduced them in slow succession to the inside of my cavernous mouth? Impossible! I thought, but my surmises were cut short by his stentorian voice, which woke me once more into life, in spite of the heat of the day. "Blackvood," he began, and then, looking for something on his desk, he paused a moment. "Ja," I gasped, fearing he was hunting for a stick, and then, without rhyme or reason, I added "Ja, bitte!" Though thoroughly accustomed to hear the words of his native tongue put to any use, and made to serve any purpose that might seem fit to the "user," still he smiled a gentle smile at my inane "Ja bitte," and having found what he was looking for, namely, a letter, he proceeded to inform me that my father had written to him to say that my sister, C—, was on a visit to Nüremberg, and that, if his son had been well-behaved, could he—the Herr Direktor—see his way to letting me go to see her for a few days in that town.

I was so delighted at this news, that, forgetting in whose presence I was, I ejaculated "Hurrah!" and, at the same time, gave a sort of jump for joy—modified somewhat by the size of the room I was in. But hardly had I done this iniquitous act when I remembered where I was, and seeing the saucer eyes upon me, I shuffled meekly and again said "Ja bitte," adding this time a modest "Ach! Ach!" But the "Herr Direktor" was in a good mood, and saying that as I had been working well (I thought of the Euclid still lying upside down and I murmured "Jawohl") and the holidays were near, he had no objection to my going and hoped that I should enjoy myself.

So it was all settled, and before evening the whole school knew that "Blackvood" was going. But I kept my counsel and told no one where or wherefore I was going. The consequence was that various reports were spread about. One was that I was expelled, another that I had received bad news, while a third said that I had complained of the living, and having given the Herr Direktor a bit of my mind, I was leaving of my own accord; and this was the version that, by sundry signs and winks, I induced the school to believe.

However, the following morning, before the rest of the place was awake, I was rolling along in a cart, down the broad, white road that led to our nearest station, some five or six miles distant. It was a lovely morning, and as my driver took me along at a brisk pace through the fresh, sweet air I simply revelled in the thought that I was really free from supervision for a whole week. The road lay mostly through the deepest part of the forest. On either side a wall of stately pines shot up to heaven, and their summits gleamed bright in the first rays of the rising sun. The air, redolent of pines and moss, was life itself, and now and then was mingled with it that delicious odour of newly-sawn wood, as we passed the stacks near the roadside.

I was thus taking in the sweet scents and scenery, and forming plans for my visit to Nüremberg, when suddenly the horse reared up as high as the cart would allow it, and began to kick and plunge violently. To my surprise I noticed, on looking round me, that there was nothing that could possibly have frightened the animal. The road was just the same there as it had been for the last two miles, except that on our right a clearing of some fifty yards square had been made. The ground of this clearing was soft and marshy and a small stream ran through it and under the road. Across this stream, dividing the clearing into two halves, ran a high bank, evidently an old mill-dam of some sort.

Meanwhile the driver had left his seat by my side, and was leading his horse, still frightened, past the spot. When he had taken his seat again, I asked him at what the horse could possibly have shied, and he answered mysteriously, in his half dialect I could only just understand, that he never knew a horse that did not take fright on passing that spot, since the "Rothe Mühle" had disappeared. I was by no means superstitiously inclined in those days, but thinking I might hear a genuine Black Forest legend, I further questioned the man, and, after some time, induced him to tell me the following story, which I have since confirmed, and now condense somewhat as follows:—

A good many years previous to the time of which I write, there had stood in that clearing, described above, a tall reddish building of wood, called the Red Mill. It was owned and worked by a peasant, one Hans Binschedler, a man of an evil reputation, which he thoroughly deserved. A slave to drink and a man of frightful passions, he was much feared by the neighbouring peasantry, and few cared to pass his way at night-time alone. Many stories were afloat concerning him, but no one took any steps to stop the man in his supposed course of crime. However, at length the climax was reached. One morning, when the winter's snow lay thick upon the ground, a body was found lying on the road just opposite the Red Mill. It was the corpse of a traveller, and on his neck were marks of violence, whilst all round the snow was much disturbed by the signs of an awful struggle, and down the road for some distance tracks of long strides told of a terrible chase—a chase ending in murder. Before the tracks began to lengthen by running, the traces of a second man came out of the forest; so that it was pretty clear the murderer had followed, or waited for his victim in the shades of the forest, and then rushed out suddenly upon him and accomplished the act. The guilt of the grim deed was easily brought home to the door of Binschedler, for he was discovered two days afterwards at the bottom of his mill pool. So the neighbourhood was freed from his evil presence, but soon a report spread that the mill had disappeared, and on investigation this proved to be the case, the whole structure appearing to have been engulfed by the swampy land on which it had stood.

But, besides this, other reports soon spread far and wide. One man passing there at night—alone of course—had seen the gaunt, red form of the mill standing there in the darkness, as of old. A second man swore he had heard a muffled scream; while a third averred on his life that, while driving past there in the dusk, he had heard footsteps in the forest, keeping even with his trap, at a pace no man could possibly maintain in the dense forest, and what was more, that his horse had heard it and bolted, and had not stopped for miles. Such were the stories afloat, and, at length, things grew to such a pass, that a body of the villagers, with the "Prediger" of the brotherhood at their head, set out to exorcise the unclean spirit that haunted the fatal spot. Having reached the spot, the preacher opened his bible *three times in succession,* it having, on all three occasions, been shut by an invisible hand. After this they returned home discomfited, and ever since the evil reputation has stuck to the place, with a determination that will take long to dispute.

Such was the story my driver told me, and when he had finished, the old gateway of Villingen was in sight, and, the forest once left behind us, I soon forgot the story, which at the time had amused and interested me, in the bustle of getting into the train and the excitement of gleaning what information I could concerning my journey from the railway officials. In due course Nüremberg was reached, that

> "Quaint old town of toil and traffic;
>   Quaint old town of art, and song;
> Memories haunt thy pointed gables
>   Like the rooks that round them throng;
> Memories of the middle ages,
>   When the emperors, rough and bold,
> Had their dwelling in thy castle,
>   Time defying, centuries old."

Oh! what a happy week I spent there, within the precincts of those ancient and massive walls. Each day a blazing sun shone in a deep blue sky and a delicious breeze kept cool the narrow old streets. I was, perhaps, scarcely old enough to fully appreciate the artistic beauties of the wonderful old city, but my sister, who was no tyro with her brush, and who had the eye and soul of a true artist, was enthusiastic to a degree, and certainly I shared her delight. Of course, she had not been staying alone in the town, but had with her a com-

panion—a travelling companion, a female companion! a beautiful
female companion!! and, must I own it?—the society of this beautiful
female companion was much sought by me and served in no little
way to heighten my enjoyment. True, I was always glad to carry my
sister's painting stool and box, when in the calm eventide we would
go and sit on the bridge over the Pegnitz to catch some lovely sunset
tint, or mount the hill, and from the grim old bastions of the fortress,
strive to put faithfully on canvas the shade and form of the "Blue
Franconian Mountains," I was only too pleased to do this, but I was
much more pleased when, my sister once settled on her stool, I
would stroll off to a little distance with the "beautiful travelling companion," and in that most romantic spot talk of the past and of the
future, for I was not afraid to confide anything to—to go to any
length with—even to kissing—one who, although a beautiful travelling companion, could never be anything to me but an elderly and
very favourite *"Aunt"*! But we were a happy trio and we passed a
happy week. Only too quickly the days sped by, and I scarcely realised that one of the pleasantest visits of my early days was over, until
I suddenly woke up in the railway carriage, as the train drew up at
Villingen station, just about the time when my sister and aunt were
arriving at Prague. The delightful dream of the quaint old city had
fled, and as I stood on the platform and watched the train grow
smaller and smaller, till it at length turned a corner and disappeared
into the depths of the forest, I remembered that I had omitted to
send word for a conveyance to meet me. At first I was extremely annoyed and muttered a good deal about "echte Deutsche Dumheit,"
when really it was "echte Englische Dumheit." But on second
thoughts, the prospect of a walk seemed to me not so unpleasant as I
had at first imagined; the distance was nothing, only some five or six
miles, a lovely country, too, to be seen on the way and there was a
good chance of getting a lift *en route* from some peasant's cart returning late to his home. So leaving word that my bag would be sent for
in the course of the next day, I started off on my lonely trudge with
nothing to carry but a walking stick of English holly.

It was about half-past seven, and the sun was just sinking behind
the distant ridge of tall pines which, clearly and sharply defined,
stood out against the golden sky. It was very beautiful indeed; where

the forest was less dense the slanting rays found their way in between the straight, dark trunks, and lit up the carpet of bright mosses, throwing long and curious shadows across the road, which, however, were soon lost in the deep gloom of the closer and denser forest on the other side. The colours of the sky, and the sweet fresh air soon took my memory back to Nüremberg, and I walked on and on, going over again in my mind our various deeds during the past week. At one time my fancy took me back to the hot street glaring beneath our feet and above the deep blue sky. In front of us rose Albrecht Dürer's house, where that evangelist of art lived and laboured. At another time we were slowly pacing the cool aisles of Sainte Lawrence's Church or looking from the height of the walls, across the valley of the Pegnitz, with the blue background of mountains in the far distance.

But though I was little thinking of my actual surroundings there was no fear of my losing the way or taking a wrong path, for there was but one in those days, and that one I was following straight enough and the least deviation from it would have been sufficient warning, for I should have charged the pine tree stems in so doing.

But after some time my thoughts were called back from roving the streets of Nüremberg, as I became aware that it had grown very dark. I abruptly stood still in the middle of the road and looked around me. The sun had long since disappeared and though in the open country it would still have been fairly light, yet here, where the narrow road was walled in on either side by closely-packed tall pine trees, the remaining light of day could not so easily find its way, and the result was that, except straight overhead, where a narrow streak of daylight still remained, it was very dark indeed, and beneath the trees the gloom was so deep that it was with very great difficulty I could distinguish even the nearest trunks from the surrounding darkness. I glanced at my watch and found that it was considerably past eight, so I knew that I must have covered at least three miles, or about half of my distance.

I was in a happy state of mind and in no hurry to get back to the grim establishment of learning, to mix once more with somewhat grimy specimens of other nations, so I started off again at a rather slow pace, thinking that I might possibly get a lift later, though I knew this was only a chance, and a very remote one at that. My mind was now less employed than before, and as I walked lazily along, thinking how far I still had to go, what distance I had come and so forth, for the first time the extreme loneliness of the road struck me. There was not a sign of another living being beside myself, nor even of animal life. There are but few birds in the Black Forest, I mean singing birds, and these had gone to rest. There were no rabbits to dart suddenly across the road, no squirrels to be frightened and seen scuttling up the trees. Not even a moth flew across my path, and, if any had, I should scarcely have been able to see them, unless they had been white ones. Everything was hushed and still; nature was breathing her very gentlest. Only from time to time a large night-beetle would whirr round me, with his metallic buzz, and then whirr heavily away in the darkness. The night wind had risen and gently stirred the topmost branches of the tall trees, but the moaning murmur of that sound, at such an hour and in such a place, was to my mind worse than absolute and awful silence. On I tramped, a little faster than before, and the clack of my boots rang out hard on the dusty road. But there was no echo; the thick trees deadened the sound to such an extent that one might stand and scream, and even if people were near, which is not the case, one's shouts would be sucked in by the hundreds and myriads of trees long before the sound could travel any distance. Still I walked on, but without the confidence of my starting moments. The gloomy surroundings had their effect on me, and my thoughts took a gloomy turn. The fantastic depths of a somewhat morbid, though powerful, imagination were stirred within me. I grasped my stick more firmly and went a little faster. Now and then I glanced behind me, but there, as in front, the white glimmer of the road was soon lost in the all-pervading darkness. I began to long for the friendly lights of Königsfeld village, but I knew that I had at least two miles to go before I could possibly see them.

I earnestly wished that I had a cheery companion with me, and even a rough old woodcutter, with his terrible dialect, would still have been to me pleasant company. But there was no one, neither behind, nor coming to meet me. I was quite alone with trees, hundreds and thousands of them, all alike, all tall, straight, grim and gaunt, and black as ink. Nothing but trees, trees, trees! Their crests, like the plumes on a hearse, swayed mournfully in the moaning breeze, as I passed them in never-ending succession. Suddenly another sound rose sharply on the still night air! It was the sound of a footstep in the forest, as the dry fir needles crackled underneath its tread. A footstep close to me, on my right side, unmistakably. I stopped short, and my heart beat loudly and my breath came short and thick. The sound was not repeated for a second, and as I stood there waiting in suspense, the silence was so deep and awful that I felt I must break it, and in a loud voice, that seemed to rise above the trees and escape their deadening effect, I shouted:

"Wer ist's? Wer geht da?"

Not a sound followed my question! The blood rushed from my heart and an indescribable sensation of fear crept over me. I could stand it no longer and firmly seizing my stout holly stick, I dashed off at a pace that made the road seem to fly past my feet like a flash of light, and the trees seem like a dark paling with a level top. But what was my intense horror to hear, as I madly tore along, the accompanying steps of some one in the forest on my right hand, ever keeping even pace with me, a feat I knew *no man* could accomplish in amongst so dense a growth of trees. I had not been mistaken, then, before, when I imagined I had heard a footfall on the pine needles. These thoughts flashed through my brain in less than a second, and at the same time I suddenly remembered the horrible story that the driver had told me, when a week before I had driven through this way to the station, and which I had since completely forgotten. But now with frightful force it came back to my mind, and maddened with fear I dashed on at a pace I should have thought myself incapable of. But, horror! the terrible steps ever kept even with me. Now sounding heavy and dead on the thick moss, now sharp and clear on the pine needles, they never for a moment slackened, as we gradually drew nearer the scene of the murder—the clearing where the Rothe Mühle once stood. The easy pace I had taken at first now stood me in good stead, and without a sign of failing wind or strength I flew on. But it was useless; in vain I tried to outstrip the sickening thud of the other runner. Suddenly, and before I was fully aware of it, I reached—or, must I say *we* reached?—the dreaded clearing. I knew, or rather I *felt,* that something would happen here, that either I must fail and give in, that the other steps would cease, or else that something, of which I had no idea, would occur to stop the awful flight. I cannot say why I thought this, but I did, and I was not mistaken in my notion. The clearing was on my left, while the "steps" ever sounded on my right. As, faster than ever, I clashed passed the bared spot of the crime, the "steps" suddenly left the softer ground of the forest and, sounding hard and clear on the road, seemed to *pass in front of me,* and crossing the road, I heard a splash, as of a heavy body falling on to the soft marshy ground—and all was still! still as death! At the same instant a cold puff of wind swept across my face, and as I leapt on faster still in my agony of fear, my stick in some unaccountable manner caught between my legs, and tripping, I was thrown forward several feet along the road and fell heavily on my face and hands.

When I came to myself again I was still lying where I had fallen, namely a little to one side of the dusty road. It was darker than ever, and, for a few minutes, I lay there totally unable to think where I was or to recollect what had happened. I made a slight movement, and a sudden pain shot up my leg from my knee-joint. That shock brought back to my scattered senses the earlier events of the evening, and I shuddered to myself as I thought of the chase I had had. But I was neither frightened nor badly hurt. I sat up and found that beyond a bruised knee and torn trowsers, and a few ugly scratches on my hands, I was unhurt; and by an effort—for I was very stiff—I rose to my feet. The blood rushed to my head tumultuously, and, in trying to steady myself, I missed the familiar support of my stick. But it was useless to hunt for it in the dark, so, striking a match, I glanced quickly round me. The match went out almost instantaneously, but not before the flickering light had enabled me to see the straight white line of my holly stick a few feet in front of me on the roadside. After groping a little, I laid my hand on it and slowly resumed my walk.

After twenty minutes' trudge, I suddenly passed out from between the dismal walls of pines and saw the lights of the village before me, and in my whole life, neither before nor since, have I been so glad to see and welcome houses and signs of life. Once out of the forest I was able to see clearly; there was no moon, but myriads of stars studded the vault of heaven, and, after inspecting for some seconds the white face of my watch, I discovered that it was only twenty minutes past nine, so that I could not have been insensible for more than half an hour, if so long. As I drew nearer the village and the school building, I reflected that reasons for my late arrival would have to be forthcoming, and, after some little thought on the subject, I determined that, at all costs, I would conceal the real cause of my delay, for though, undoubtedly, I had received a terrible scare, yet I felt that I should only look ridiculous before the eyes of my schoolfellows, and, to tell the plain truth, I owned to myself that I felt somewhat foolish. The consequence was that, when I did at last arrive within the prison walls of that severe establishment, I somewhat dissembled by saying and repeating with great eagerness that I had spent over half an hour in Villingen town, in a vain search after a vehicle.

But the Herr Direktor did not discover my prevarication and lack of moral courage, and only expressed his pleasure on hearing how I had enjoyed my visit to Nüremberg.

But, whenever I passed that clearing in the forest—which I often did, though never again alone—and heard an ignorant or sceptical remark or a breathless question about the ghost of Binschedler and the haunted mill, I smiled quietly a very superior smile, for, although I might not know the mysteries of German syntax, I had at least been acquainted with a genuine German ghost!

The Story of Karl Ott

Niederwald was a little village situated in a deep valley among the Alps, and it was generally conceded by the inhabitants that Karl Ott was the most obstinate man in it.

He was not only held to be such because his motto in life was "Never give in even if you are wrong," but also because he had for three years proposed to the daughter of the English lady with amazing perseverance, and, in the face of equally persevering refusals, still persisted in renewing his offer.

Karl Ott, eldest and only son of the village pastor, called upon the daughter of the English lady just as regularly as the church-goers went to receive from his father's hands the communion on the first Sunday in every month. Their walk through the village and up the winding path into the dark pine forest was as regularly expected by the simple villagers as was their return an hour or two later; Karl Ott with a set look on his face, and on the lips of the daughter of the English lady an amused and peculiarly sweet smile.

Leaving her at her mother's house—the little wooden one opposite the *Gasthaus* with the creeping vines and the dark-stained pillars—Karl Ott strode down the village street to his father's house, and the following conversation took place regularly.

"Karl, my son, had you a pleasant walk?"

"Yes, father."

"And what did she say, my son?"

"She treated it as a grand joke, father."

"She laughed at you, Karl?"

"Yes, father."

"And did she give you no encouragement, my son?"

"No; that is—*Vielleicht etwas.*"

"Only a very little—perhaps," repeated the pastor, who knew every answer in advance.

There was a little pause here, and then:

"You will try again, my son," more as a statement of fact than a question.

"If she did not love me, father, she could not go with me so freely and often."

"She is not playing with you, Karl?" with his eyes on his son's face.

Karl never answered this last question. He only laughed, and asked a question, himself.

"With me? *Aber was für eine Idee!*"

Karl Ott may have been original, unsophisticated, but he was a dangerous man to be trifled with. He knew it, and thought of course every one else knew it. For was he not acknowledged to be the most obstinate and difficult man in the whole village?

The English lady and her daughter, with an English servant, had lived in the little house with the dark-stained pillars for three years. They were generally known to the village folk as the "English Lady" and the "Beautiful daughter of the English Lady," because the villagers found themselves wholly unable to pronounce their double-barrelled name.

They were in reality very poor, though compared to Herr Stosch, the richest man in the village, they seemed rich, very rich. A small income goes a long way in Niederwald, and the English lady and her daughter had sought the secluded life it afforded because of reverses at home when the husband and father died. At least so they said, and no one questioned the truth of it. Niederwald was a quiet, curious little out-of-the-world spot, and the people who had been bred and born there were equally quiet and far more curious.

It was a lovely place. A stream tumbled from the big mountains behind, and flowed peacefully through the village, till the spring thaws and the winter storms converted it into a raging, racing torrent. Vineyards sloped away, below the village, to a lake, while above it dense pine forests stretched away till they joined the region of rocks and cliffs, and, finally, of everlasting snows. Above all, three lofty white peaks peered over from the clouds into the little village, and reflected the sunset glory long after the village was wrapped in darkness and shadow.

Karl Ott owned a large vineyard, and made money by it. His *Weinlese* were always successful, and his grapes sweeter and juicier even, than those that grew in sunny Italy, on the other side of the great white peaks.

He had seen the English lady and her daughter when they first came to Niederwald, and his father, as pastor, went with him to call upon them. While his father stumbled along in his broken English with the mother, Karl conversed with the beautiful daughter in German. He welcomed her to Niederwald. She had travelled with her father before he died, and had seen much. She had even been in the fair country that lay beyond the three white peaks. She was older than he was, and knew more of the world, he thought. He found that she loved the mountains and the forests, and that she listened eagerly to his descriptions of the gorges, ravines, and vastnesses of the Alps around them. She longed to see them and climb to the great white peaks. And Karl, who knew every boulder and every tree, and had grown up in company with toppling *seracs* and dizzy crevasses, promised to show them to her.

He was not slow to believe what his father told him afterwards: that the proud English lady had sacrificed her daughter's best years to her own pride in coming to live in Niederwald, and bury her poverty where none could see it and sneer.

It was thus their walks began; and the English lady, apparently wrapped up in her pride and disappointments, let them go together.

Karl Ott had been fortunate enough to earn the gratitude of the daughter of the English lady, and it was then he first made up his mind to fall in love with her.

He did everything so deliberately, and his obstinate will held his feelings so under control, that he was not able to fall in love without first thinking the matter over, and then coming to a decision. Such decision was, however, absolutely final, and from it there could be no recall.

The Devil's Rocks formed a steep slope of loose rocks that had crumbled down from the cliffs above, and accumulated. They were not twenty yards long, and terminated abruptly at the edge of a precipice over two thousand feet. The rocks had to be crossed on the way to Wannsee. They were very dangerous, because the slightest disturbance set them all rolling over each other towards the brink. Several persons from the neighbouring villages had been killed in this way by losing their balance when the rocks began to move under their weight, and being swept down over the short distance that lay between the narrow path and the dizzy abyss. They were called the Devil's Rocks—*Teufelsfelsen*—because the devil was said to be concealed beneath them, and to move them with his fingers whenever any one approached.

Karl and the girl were climbing slowly, and the little dog had run on ahead. His weight was more than sufficient to start the treacherous stones in motion. In spite of his struggles, and with much piteous barking, the little fellow was carried to the edge. Karl saved it by going after it, while the girl, speechless with horror, watched them from the path. She was powerless to help, and she knew they must both be carried over, and—and she did so love the dog.

She could hear the rocks that had already leaped over the edge crashing down the face of the cliff, striking here and there its buttresses and projecting ledges. How brave of Karl! He had her darling by the scruff of his neck. Oh! the splendid fellow that he was. Ah! but—horrors! he had slipped again! Her heart stopped beating for a moment, and she hid her eyes in her hand. She heard a rush of wind, and she knew that Karl Ott and the dog had disappeared into the gulf.

The next minute he was standing by her side with the dog in his arms. It was licking his hand, and evidently had no idea of the cruel death it had escaped. How it was done Karl could not tell. Only the rush of loose rocks suddenly ceased, and the one his weight rested on, six inches from the edge, came to a standstill, and he scrambled up again to the path with the doggie panting and frightened in his hands. That was all he could say about it. He watched the girl kiss her dog, and saw her tears drop on to his little brown ears. He heard her thank him; and as her large eyes, with the long, moistened eyelashes, looked so gratefully into his, he experienced a strange sensation in his heart.

He thought the tears were those of gratitude.

He thought of the girl, of her eyes and hair. He thought of the tears that fell on the dog's ears, and he thought of the slender brown hands that held him. A feeling more tender than any he had yet known crept into his heart. He thought of his father, the pastor; of the proud English lady; and then he thought again of her beautiful daughter.

He remembered, too, that he owned a vineyard, which made him rich. And he made up his mind.

The rocks were dropping past him, and plunging downwards over the precipice. He stooped, and picked one up.

"As surely as I have plucked this one from the fingers of the Devil who is moving them from beneath," he said aloud, slowly, "and as surely as it will drop through the air and rest on the ground below,"—here he peered over the edge,—"so surely will I make the daughter of the English lady my wife." He threw the stone upwards and forwards, saw it for a moment against the sky, and then heard it rushing downwards through the air.

A few seconds afterwards it crashed upon the rocks below, and Karl Ott, as soon as the echoes had died away, climbed down again, and went home to bed.

Next day he told his father of his resolve, and the pastor had said, "My son, you have my benediction."

Karl waited a few weeks before he thought it well to speak his mind.

It was winter time, and one day Herr Müller, proprietor of the *Gasthof,* his son Fritz, Pastor Ott, Karl Ott, young Stosch, Frau Müller, and the English girl took their skates and a luncheon basket, and drove six miles in a sleigh to the end of the frozen lake.

Karl slowly and deliberately fastened the shining skates on to the pretty little feet of the daughter of the English lady. They were soon flying together before the wind over the black ice, with the fox terrier racing after them as best he could on the slippery surface. He was barking his little heart out for happiness.

But in Karl Ott's heart there was no sign of fluttering. His big muscular frame, with its mountain-trained sinews, never carried a more confident heart than then. The fact that he was going to ask the English girl to marry him did not make his pulse beat any more quickly than usual; and "usual" was by no means fast.

He felt, as he flew over the ice with the English girl beside him, as if the little gloved hands lying warmly in his own were already his; as if the hair, that escaped from under her fur cap and sometimes blew across his cheeks, was even then his to caress.

His purpose being so single, he had no recourse to beating about the bush, and saw no reason for hesitancy or difficulty in giving expression to so straightforward a proposition.

Karl simply waited for a pause in their talk, turned to the English girl as they were skating out in the middle of the lake, and said in his deep voice, in which was no tremor, nor trace of nervousness:

"Ich liebe Dich. Ich anbiete Dir mein Leben, mein Herz, meine Weinbergen, and meines Vater's Segnung."

As he spoke he looked her steadily in the face. He could not meet her eyes, because, in her desire to choose the best ice, she was looking downwards. But the girl made no answer, and no change came over her face. The wind roared in their ears as it swept past them, and the ring of their skates sounded musically over the lake.

Karl waited some time for an answer, and then came to the conclusion that the girl had not heard him. It was the fault of the wind. He took his eyes from her face, and glanced down at the little feet that shot forward so swiftly and gracefully. He was sure she had not heard him.

There was nothing for him to do but repeat the proposition; and this Karl Ott at once did, in a louder voice, and with an amount of calm deliberation that would have been the envy of all lovers in all lands, could they have seen him.

This time she certainly heard him, for she turned her face up and looked at him. Her eyes were wide open, but on her face, aglow with the wind, there was no evidence of surprise or embarrassment. Her lips were parted in the effort of breathing; her fur cap sat jauntily on her hair, and her hands nestled cosily and warm in his own. Karl kept his eyes on hers, and waited for her to speak. But she did not speak, and Karl began to feel decidedly uncomfortable. He did not know what to make of it.

Then the daughter of the English lady nestled in a little closer to his side, and, with a laugh that showed two rows of gleaming teeth, shouted against the wind,—"What was that you said just now about your father's benediction? If you don't look where you are taking me, it will be given over our drowned and frozen bodies."

Then Karl knew that she could not have heard all that he said. She was shouting her loudest, and he heard her none too distinctly. Dropping his eyes from her face, he looked ahead. They were within fifty yards of the lake proper. The shallow water of the great marsh lay behind them, and they were already skating over the thin, green ice that a little farther on came to an abrupt end in the deep waters. Karl saw their danger at a glance. With a swing he altered his course, pulling the girl round with him, so that she came close up against his side and her hair blew again across his cheek. She laughed merrily, and tucked it under her fur cap.

Talking was an easy matter now. The wind was behind them.

"What was that remark you made about your father's benediction?" she laughed again: "did you mean us to be drowned, or what? It would be a pity, to end our friendship in iced water!"

Something in her voice made Karl feel for a moment that there was between them an immeasurable distance. The thought fled as suddenly as it came, and Karl's phenomenal obstinacy began to assert itself.

He was on the point of repeating, word for word, his twice-made proposition, when there was a sound of skaters behind them, and the next moment Müller and young Stosch raced up and joined them.

Their presence put an end, for the time, to any further avowals of love or proposals of marriage.

They formed a line of skaters hand in hand, the girl between Müller and himself, and sped along to join the rest of the party round a log fire and a luncheon basket.

Karl did not find himself again alone with the daughter of the English lady, until the horse was being harnessed into the sleigh, and the remnants of the luncheon were being packed up. And then it was only for a brief moment, when he had nothing prepared in the way of words. The fact was, he felt nonplussed. Had she vouchsafed some sort of an answer, he would have known what to do and say. But her silence completely outwitted him. He could not understand it, and, for the time being, his obstinacy was met and conquered by the subtler force of silence.

Now that they were alone again for a moment, she asked him to tighten the strap that fastened her skates together.

"Make a neat little bundle of it, Mr. Ott," she said, "so that they won't clash together, and get scratched."

While he was doing her request, the muscles of his great fingers slow from the cold, the girl stood facing him. "And please," she added ever so gently, and looking up into his eyes, "please, Karl, never ask me those sort of questions again, because, if you do, we cannot go together on the mountains. And you know there's nobody else here who can climb like you, and—and I may not go alone. Now, please don't, Karl, for it is quite impossible."

The smile she gave him was gentle enough to melt his obstinacy into slavery. But it only made Karl Ott angry. It was his turn to be silent now, for he knew enough, cold, strange lover that he was, to understand that she looked upon him only as a companion.

The first time she met him after the skating party, she greeted him with an amused smile that, so far as he was concerned, seemed to increase the distance he felt lay between them. It also increased his obstinacy. And this same amused smile was all the answer he got to his many subsequent proposals.

She called him Karl now, and when he had concluded his awkward sentence about offering her his love and his life and his vineyards, there was only this little smile for answer.

If he dared, as he often did, to repeat his words, the little smile broadened out into a laugh, that effectually closed his lips for the moment, because he utterly failed to comprehend the feelings that caused it.

They never got any further than this, and the state of affairs might well have continued for a dozen years.

Meanwhile Karl's love for the daughter of the English lady changed in character. It was beginning to come from his heart instead of from his will. He now and again caught himself wondering what in the world he would do if she died, or—the thought was horrible—if she married some one else!

One day in the early spring, when Karl Ott went to the little post office, he met the English girl there. The snow was still lying low down on the mountain sides. In the air was that indescribable sweetness that is only known in the neighbourhood of pine forests at a certain elevation.

She held some letters in her hand and was stamping them for England. Karl suggested a ramble on the heights of the Kronenberg, and the girl was pleased.

"Yes," she said; "and if you think the snow is sufficiently melted, we will go by way of the Devil's Rocks. I should like to see them once more."

"Once more!" repeated Karl with surprise. "Why! what do you mean?"

"Oh! we are going away," she said simply. "Mother is going back to live in England again. We leave in two days."

Karl fairly gasped. His heart sank within him.

"Wait here a moment," she added: "I will go and put on my nailed boots and climbing skirts. Then I'll tell you all about it!" She had seen the blank look of dismay that had come into his face, and, for the first time, she felt in her heart a feeling of sorrow for him.

"Poor Karl Ott!" she thought; "but he is such a simple boy, and has so much to learn. He surely could not have imagined that I might care for him!"

So they climbed up the lower slopes of the great Kronenberg, these two, who had together explored every foot of the mountains, and knew their most inaccessible parts, who had seen the sun rise from the top of the three white peaks, and watched the last sunset lights linger on the far away snow slopes that seemed to hang in the sky over the village. For nearly five years they had been companions in many a ramble through the deep forests, and had followed the torrents to their sources under the ice of the dangerous, slow-creeping glaciers. And as they followed the winding path, so familiar to them, the English girl told her companion of the impending change in their life.

"We are going back to our old home in Kent," she told him. "Mother's sister is dead, and we shall be better off now. We go to Paris on Saturday, and you must come to the station, Karl, and see us off."

Come to the station and see us off!

Karl listened in silence. He asked no questions, and made no comments. The shock had been so sudden and so unexpected, it had stirred his feelings as they never had been stirred before. He could not define them, much less reduce them to words. Surprise, disappointment, rage, struggled for the mastery with sorrow, pride, and outraged confidence. They rose up in him in such a strength of turmoil, that he felt as if his heart was being torn out and destroyed. He walked as in a dream, not knowing what he would do next. But the feeling that was uppermost was the bitterness that he had been trifled with. Karl Ott was obstinate, and, whatever he felt, there was no indication of it on his face or in his manner. His feelings nevertheless increased in strength the more he tried to repress them. So he just walked on by her side, and listened to her voice, as they climbed up through the fragrant pine woods and then through the belt of stunted mountain oaks that led to the rocks beyond. When she had finished he made an effort to say something.

"I am sorry you are going. I did not expect it," was what he said in a quiet voice.

The girl said she was sorry too, she was so fond of the mountains and forests; but he surely did not think she was going to live in Niederwald for the rest of her life!

Karl had no answer ready; or rather had a thousand ready, but they were all so strong, and he did not know which to choose.

Then the climbing over the rough boulders that formed the long slope at the foot of Kronenberg's great shoulder began, and rendered talking, except in short exclamations, impossible.

They climbed on together, till they reached the final slope, at the top of which began the little path leading to the Devil's Rocks.

"Karl," she laughed, showing her white teeth, "I'm exhausted. You'll have to bury me here, or carry me to the top."

Karl turned his head away and looked for a moment at the view of lake and forest far beneath them, and an expression came into his eyes that the girl did not see. Then he took her in his arms, swung her little body on to his great shoulders, and carried her steadily over the remainder of the trying, soft snow-slope. He did not tremble. He could have carried her, for that matter, over a tight-rope stretched from the peak of the Matterhorn to the Eggischorn. His feet never took false hold, his balance always was true; and, when she laughed aloud and clutched his head with her two arms for safety, he felt his muscles respond to this call on their reserve force, and carry their precious burden with the ease of steel springs.

When they reached the top he let her down gently from his

shoulders. She looked up at him shyly, and told him he was the strongest pack-horse she had ever ridden upon in the Alps, and Karl felt that he wanted to take her in his arms and kiss her.

"And when did you—your mother, I mean—first decide to leave?" he asked, in a voice so quiet that a stranger would have thought him indifferent to whatever answer he got.

"Oh!" she said, with an almost imperceptible start, which did not escape his notice. "Oh! we have known it all along. We—we only came here for five years, you know."

But Karl didn't know; and her matter-of-fact way of announcing this important fact, which he felt should have been told him years ago, when he first proposed to her, came to him as a revelation. It acted as a stimulant too. "Then she does not care for me even as much as she does for one of the little snowdrops that are just coming up with the spring," was the thought that passed through his brain.

"You intended from the beginning to leave Niederwald this spring?" he asked quietly.

She looked at him sweetly, and nodded her head. Karl met her eyes for a moment without a sign of expression on his face, and then turned to look at the view again. It was ever changing, and a great grey cloud was rolling up the opposite rock-walls of Chasseront— gloomy Chasseront, as it was called.

Karl again broke the silence.

"Yet you never told me that," he said, almost gently. "I thought you would always live in Niederwald."

Karl was so simple, so innocent, so honest!

"Live here always!" she cried. "Oh, Karl!" And there came over her face that same smile of amusement that he knew so well. But there was in it something of pity as well, now, and Karl was stung more deeply than ever by it. Poor Karl!

"You allowed me to be always with you on the mountains," he continued, with something like anger in his voice, "and you allowed no one else. You have made and permitted me to grow very fond of you. You have always—"

"Now, Karl," she remonstrated. The smile of amused pity had died out of her eyes, for she felt that her companion was growing unpleasantly earnest. He spoke slowly, but in his voice was an inflection she had never heard there before. The idea of his getting really angry rather frightened her. Slow, deep natures, she knew, were never really angry unless when moved to their very bottom, and Karl Ott's nature was a very slow and a very deep one.

"You have always laughed at my proposals," he went on, in his deep voice, totally ignoring her interruption, "but you never forbade them. You knew I meant what I said, and that, in God's name in heaven, I loved you seriously and for ever!"

"Silly boy!" she laughed with spirit, and looking him full in the face: "how could you possibly imagine anything so impossible?"

Karl did not move a muscle, or take his eyes off hers. He felt his blood leave his heart suddenly in a body, and then rush tumultuously back again. It made his cheeks blaze, and moistened his skin.

"You ought to have known," she went on, emboldened by his silence, which she interpreted as an acknowledgment of defeat. "Our positions are so different; our ages, too; and we belong to different races. Besides, oh, Karl! I told you long ago, when first you spoke, that I could never love any one!"

Never love any one! Suddenly the truth began to dawn on his mind. She loved some one else, then!

The girl suddenly put her hand on his shoulder and looked into his face, moving closer to him, as if about to speak. She kept her hand there, although she was aware that he shrank from her touch as if she had been a leper. She had opened her lips when he interrupted her with raging vehemence.

"And you, damned girl," he cried, "have allowed me all this time to remain in ignorance that you loved some one else; allowed me to pay court to you, and to love you until all my heart and life and future are all yours; to—to love so deeply, that to lose you must mean to die! And you might so easily have told me the truth: a word years ago would have prevented all, instead of letting month after month go by, playing with my life as only women can, who have—who are——"

"Karl, stop!" she cried. "I am married already!"

He stood and looked into the eyes and face he loved so hopelessly. Then he turned, and looked down, and out on to the panorama of distant woods and blue mountains. There was no word between them for a minute or more. Then the girl, who was sobbing now, sought his hand, and in a broken whisper, which could hardly have reached his ear, she moaned,—

"But, Karl, my husband was a criminal—and for five years he has been—has been away. That is, we are going home to meet him when he is released—next week."

He felt the girl draw closer to him, until her heaving breast was against his heart, and he could feel her quick sobs. He felt her arms round his neck; her head, with the golden hair, was on his shoulder.

"Can you never forgive me, Karl?" she whispered, her tears falling fast and hot on his neck.

Karl made no answer. Perhaps he had not heard her. Perhaps his thoughts were still in the cloudy distance where the little patch of blue heaven had disappeared. Perhaps, ah! perhaps, he was wondering, and thinking, and asking himself if, after all, the girl had loved him all along and loved him still.

So they stood together on that lonely mountain path, and the girl's head, radiant in the soft sunshine, sank lower on his shoulder, and the wind played with her beautiful hair.

But Karl Ott moved his feet, and set the Devil's Rocks in motion. Then he seized the girl in his arms and, raising her face to his, covered the tear-stained cheeks and the red mouth and the hair with a thousand kisses.

The stones moved forward, with a hoarse, grinding sound, towards the brink.

She heard the sound; she felt them moving beneath her feet, and she tried to free herself.

But Karl pressed her struggling little body closer to him. He held her to his heart. She was his own at last, and—he loved her. Pressed thus to his heart, the beautiful daughter of the English lady was carried by the shifting rocks to the brink of the abyss.

Her cry of terror was half smothered by his hot lips laid on her own, as they fell backwards into the air.

And the wind heard her cry, and the far white peaks saw them fall.

And the Devil's Rocks, that dropped over the edge for several minutes afterwards, covered their bodies and formed their tombstone.

A Haunted Island

The following events occurred on a small island of isolated position in a large Canadian lake, to whose cool waters the inhabitants of Montreal and Toronto flee for rest and recreation in the hot months. It is only to be regretted that events of such peculiar interest to the genuine student of the psychical should be entirely uncorroborated. Such unfortunately, however, is the case.

Our own party of nearly twenty had returned to Montreal that very day, and I was left in solitary possession for a week or two longer, in order to accomplish some important "reading" for the law which I had foolishly neglected during the summer.

It was late in September, and the big trout and maskinonge were stirring themselves in the depths of the lake, and beginning slowly to move up to the surface waters as the north winds and early frosts lowered their temperature. Already the maples were crimson and gold, and the wild laughter of the loons echoed in sheltered bays that never knew their strange cry in the summer.

With a whole island to oneself, a two-storey cottage, a canoe, and only the chipmunks, and the farmer's weekly visit with eggs and bread, to disturb one, the opportunities for hard reading might be very great. It all depends!

The rest of the party had gone off with many warnings to beware of Indians, and not to stay late enough to be the victim of a frost that thinks nothing of forty below zero. After they had gone, the loneliness of the situation made itself unpleasantly felt. There were no other islands within six or seven miles, and though the mainland forests lay a couple of miles behind me, they stretched for a very great distance unbroken by any signs of human habitation. But, though the island was completely deserted and silent, the rocks and trees that had echoed human laughter and voices almost every hour of the day for two months could not fail to retain some memories of it all; and I was not surprised to fancy I heard a shout or a cry as I passed from rock to rock, and more than once to imagine that I heard my own name called aloud.

In the cottage there were six tiny little bedrooms divided from one another by plain unvarnished partitions of pine. A wooden bedstead, a mattress, and a chair stood in each room, but I only found two mirrors, and one of these was broken.

The boards creaked a good deal as I moved about, and the signs of occupation were so recent that I could hardly believe I was alone. I half expected to find some one left behind, still trying to crowd into a box more than it would hold. The door of one room was stiff, and refused for a moment to open, and it required very little persuasion to imagine some one was holding the handle on the inside, and that when it opened I should meet a pair of human eyes.

A thorough search of the floor led me to select as my own sleeping quarters a little room with a diminutive balcony over the verandah roof. The room was very small, but the bed was large, and had the best mattress of them all. It was situated directly over the sitting-room where I should live and do my "reading," and the miniature window looked out to the rising sun. With the exception of a narrow path which led from the front door and verandah through the trees to the boat-landing, the island was densely covered with maples, hemlocks, and cedars. The trees gathered in round the cottage so closely that the slightest wind made the branches scrape the roof and tap the wooden walls. A few moments after sunset the darkness became impenetrable, and ten yards beyond the glare of the lamps that shone through the sitting-room windows—of which there were four—you could not see an inch before your nose, nor move a step without running up against a tree.

The rest of that day I spent moving my belongings from my tent to the sitting-room, taking stock of the contents of the larder, and chopping enough wood for the stove to last me for a week. After that, just before sunset, I went round the island a couple of times in my canoe for precaution's sake. I had never dreamed of doing this before, but when a man is alone he does things that never occur to him when he is one of a large party.

How lonely the island seemed when I landed again! The sun was down, and twilight is unknown in these northern regions. The darkness comes up at once. The canoe safely pulled up and turned over on her face, I groped my way up the little narrow pathway to the verandah. The six lamps were soon burning merrily in the front room; but in the kitchen, where I "dined," the shadows were so gloomy, and the lamplight was so inadequate, that the stars could be seen peeping through the cracks between the rafters.

I turned in early that night. Though it was calm and there was no wind, the creaking of my bedstead and the musical gurgle of the water over the rocks below were not the only sounds that reached my ears. As I lay awake, the appalling emptiness of the house grew upon me. The corridors and vacant rooms seemed to echo innumerable footsteps, shufflings, the rustle of skirts, and a constant undertone of whispering. When sleep at length overtook me, the breathings and noises, however, passed gently to mingle with the voices of my dreams.

A week passed by, and the "reading" progressed favourably. On the tenth day of my solitude, a strange thing happened. I awoke after a good night's sleep to find myself possessed with a marked repugnance for my room. The air seemed to stifle me. The more I tried to define the cause of this dislike, the more unreasonable it appeared. There was something about the room that made me afraid. Absurd as it seems, this feeling clung to me obstinately while dressing, and more than once I caught myself shivering, and conscious of an inclination to get out of the room as quickly as possible. The more I tried to laugh it away, the more real it became; and when at last I was dressed, and went out into the passage, and downstairs into the kitchen, it was with feelings of relief, such as I might imagine would accompany one's escape from the presence of a dangerous contagious disease.

While cooking my breakfast, I carefully recalled every night spent in the room, in the hope that I might in some way connect the dislike I now felt with some disagreeable incident that had occurred in it. But the only thing I could recall was one stormy night when I suddenly awoke and heard the boards creaking so loudly in the corridor that I was convinced there were people in the house. So certain was I of this, that I had descended the stairs, gun in hand, only to find the doors and windows securely fastened, and the mice and black-beetles in sole possession of the floor. This was certainly not sufficient to account for the strength of my feelings.

The morning hours I spent in steady reading; and when I broke off in the middle of the day for a swim and luncheon, I was very much surprised, if not a little alarmed, to find that my dislike for the room had, if anything, grown stronger. Going upstairs to get a book, I experienced the most marked aversion to entering the room, and while within I was conscious all the time of an uncomfortable feeling that was half uneasiness and half apprehension. The result of it was that, instead of reading, I spent the afternoon on the water paddling and fishing, and when I got home about sundown, brought with me half a dozen delicious black bass for the supper-table and the larder.

As sleep was an important matter to me at this time, I had decided that if my aversion to the room was so strongly marked on my return as it had been before, I would move my bed down into the sitting-room, and sleep there. This was, I argued, in no sense a concession to an absurd and fanciful fear, but simply a precaution to ensure a good night's sleep. A bad night involved the loss of the next day's reading,—a loss I was not prepared to incur.

I accordingly moved my bed downstairs into a corner of the sitting-room facing the door, and was moreover uncommonly glad when the operation was completed, and the door of the bedroom closed finally upon the shadows, the silence, and the strange *fear* that shared the room with them.

The croaking stroke of the kitchen clock sounded the hour of eight as I finished washing up my few dishes, and closing the kitchen door behind me, passed into the front room. All the lamps were lit, and their reflectors, which I had polished up during the day, threw a blaze of light into the room.

Outside the night was still and warm. Not a breath of air was stirring; the waves were silent, the trees motionless, and heavy clouds hung like an oppressive curtain over the heavens. The darkness seemed to have rolled up with unusual swiftness, and not the faintest glow of colour remained to show where the sun had set. There was present in the atmosphere that ominous and overwhelming silence which so often precedes the most violent storms.

I sat down to my books with my brain unusually clear, and in my heart the pleasant satisfaction of knowing that five black bass were lying in the ice-house, and that to-morrow morning the old farmer would arrive with fresh bread and eggs. I was soon absorbed in my books.

As the night wore on the silence deepened. Even the chipmunks were still; and the boards of the floors and walls ceased creaking. I read on steadily till, from the gloomy shadows of the kitchen, came the hoarse sound of the clock striking nine. How loud the strokes sounded! They were like blows of a big hammer. I closed one book and opened another, feeling that I was just warming up to my work.

This, however, did not last long. I presently found that I was reading the same paragraphs over twice, simple paragraphs that did not require such effort. Then I noticed that my mind began to wander to other things, and the effort to recall my thoughts became harder with each digression. Concentration was growing momentarily more difficult. Presently I discovered that I had turned over two pages instead of one, and had not noticed my mistake until I was well down the page. This was becoming serious. What was the disturbing influence? It could not be physical fatigue. On the contrary, my mind was unusually alert, and in a more receptive condition than usual. I made a new and determined effort to read, and for a short time succeeded in giving my whole attention to my subject. But in a very few moments again I found myself leaning back in my chair, staring vacantly into space.

Something was evidently at work in my sub-consciousness. There was something I had neglected to do. Perhaps the kitchen door and windows were not fastened. I accordingly went to see, and found that they were! The fire perhaps needed attention. I went in to see, and found that it was all right! I looked at the lamps, went upstairs into every bedroom in turn, and then went round the house, and even into the ice-house. Nothing was wrong; everything was in its place. Yet something was wrong! The conviction grew stronger and stronger within me.

When I at length settled down to my books again and tried to read, I became aware, for the first time, that the room seemed growing cold. Yet the day had been oppressively warm, and evening had

brought no relief. The six big lamps, moreover, gave out heat enough
to warm the room pleasantly. But a chilliness, that perhaps crept up
from the lake, made itself felt in the room, and caused me to get up
to close the glass door opening on to the verandah.

For a brief moment I stood looking out at the shaft of light that
fell from the windows and shone some little distance down the
pathway, and out for a few feet into the lake.

As I looked, I saw a canoe glide into the pathway of light, and
immediately crossing it, pass out of sight again into the darkness. It
was perhaps a hundred feet from the shore, and it moved swiftly.

I was surprised that a canoe should pass the island at that time of
night, for all the summer visitors from the other side of the lake had
gone home weeks before, and the island was a long way out of any
line of water traffic.

My reading from this moment did not make very good progress,
for somehow the picture of that canoe, gliding so dimly and swiftly
across the narrow track of light on the black waters, silhouetted itself
against the background of my mind with singular vividness. It kept
coming between my eyes and the printed page. The more I thought
about it the more surprised I became. It was of larger build than any
I had seen during the past summer months, and was more like the
old Indian war canoes with the high curving bows and stern and wide
beam. The more I tried to read, the less success attended my efforts;
and finally I closed my books and went out on the verandah to walk
up and down a bit, and shake the chilliness out of my bones.

The night was perfectly still, and as dark as imaginable. I stumbled down the path to the little landing wharf, where the water made
the very faintest of gurgling under the timbers. The sound of a big
tree falling in the mainland forest, far across the lake, stirred echoes
in the heavy air, like the first guns of a distant night attack. No other
sound disturbed the stillness that reigned supreme.

As I stood upon the wharf in the broad splash of light that followed me from the sitting-room windows, I saw another canoe cross
the pathway of uncertain light upon the water, and disappear at once
into the impenetrable gloom that lay beyond. This time I saw more
distinctly than before. It was like the former canoe, a big birch-bark,
with high-crested bows and stern and broad beam. It was paddled by

two Indians, of whom the one in the stern—the steerer—appeared to be a very large man. I could see this very plainly; and though the second canoe was much nearer the island than the first, I judged that they were both on their way home to the Government Reservation, which was situated some fifteen miles away upon the mainland.

I was wondering in my mind what could possibly bring any Indians down to this part of the lake at such an hour of the night, when a third canoe, of precisely similar build, and also occupied by two Indians, passed silently round the end of the wharf. This time the canoe was very much nearer shore, and it suddenly flashed into my mind that the three canoes were in reality one and the same, and that only one canoe was circling the island!

This was by no means a pleasant reflection, because, if it were the correct solution of the unusual appearance of the three canoes in this lonely part of the lake at so late an hour, the purpose of the two men could only reasonably be considered to be in some way connected with myself. I had never known of the Indians attempting any violence upon the settlers who shared the wild, inhospitable country with them; at the same time, it was not beyond the region of possibility to suppose. . . . But then I did not care even to think of such hideous possibilities, and my imagination immediately sought relief in all manner of other solutions to the problem, which indeed came readily enough to my mind, but did not succeed in recommending themselves to my reason.

Meanwhile, by a sort of instinct, I stepped back out of the bright light in which I had hitherto been standing, and waited in the deep shadow of a rock to see if the canoe would again make its appearance. Here I could see, without being seen, and the precaution seemed a wise one.

After less than five minutes the canoe, as I had anticipated, made its fourth appearance. This time it was not twenty yards from the wharf, and I saw that the Indians meant to land. I recognised the two men as those who had passed before, and the steerer was certainly an immense fellow. It was unquestionably the same canoe. There could be no longer any doubt that for some purpose of their own the men had been going round and round the island for some time, waiting for an opportunity to land. I strained my eyes to follow them in the darkness, but the night had completely swallowed them up, and not even the faintest swish of the paddles reached my ears as the Indians plied their long and powerful strokes. The canoe would be round again in a few moments, and this time it was possible that the men might land. It was well to be prepared. I knew nothing of their intentions, and two to one (when the two are big Indians!) late at night on a lonely island was not exactly my idea of pleasant intercourse.

In a corner of the sitting-room, leaning up against the back wall, stood my Marlin rifle, with ten cartridges in the magazine and one lying snugly in the greased breech. There was just time to get up to the house and take up a position of defence in that corner. Without an instant's hesitation I ran up to the verandah, carefully picking my way among the trees, so as to avoid being seen in the light. Entering the room, I shut the door leading to the verandah, and as quickly as possible turned out every one of the six lamps. To be in a room so brilliantly lighted, where my every movement could be observed from outside, while I could see nothing but impenetrable darkness at every window, was by all laws of warfare an unnecessary concession to the enemy. And this enemy, if enemy it was to be, was far too wily and dangerous to be granted any such advantages.

I stood in the corner of the room with my back against the wall, and my hand on the cold rifle-barrel. The table, covered with my books, lay between me and the door, but for the first few minutes after the lights were out the darkness was so intense that nothing could be discerned at all. Then, very gradually, the outline of the room became visible, and the framework of the windows began to shape itself dimly before my eyes.

After a few minutes the door (its upper half of glass), and the two windows that looked out upon the front verandah, became specially distinct; and I was glad that this was so, because if the Indians came up to the house I should be able to see their approach, and gather something of their plans. Nor was I mistaken, for there presently came to my ears the peculiar hollow sound of a canoe landing and being carefully dragged up over the rocks. The paddles I distinctly heard being placed underneath, and the silence that ensued thereupon I rightly interpreted to mean that the Indians were stealthily approaching the house. . . .

While it would be absurd to claim that I was not alarmed—even frightened—at the gravity of the situation and its possible outcome, I speak the whole truth when I say that I was not overwhelmingly afraid for myself. I was conscious that even at this stage of the night I was passing into a psychical condition in which my sensations seemed no longer normal. Physical fear at no time entered into the nature of my feelings; and though I kept my hand upon my rifle the greater part of the night, I was all the time conscious that its assistance could be of little avail against the terrors that I had to face. More than once I seemed to feel most curiously that I was in no real sense a part of the proceedings, nor actually involved in them, but that I was playing the part of a spectator—a spectator, moreover, on a psychic rather than on a material plane. Many of my sensations that night were too vague for definite description and analysis, but the main feeling that will stay with me to the end of my days is the awful horror of it all, and the miserable sensation that if the strain had lasted a little longer than was actually the case my mind must inevitably have given way.

Meanwhile I stood still in my corner, and waited patiently for what was to come. The house was as still as the grave, but the inarticulate voices of the night sang in my ears, and I seemed to hear the blood running in my veins and dancing in my pulses.

If the Indians came to the back of the house, they would find the kitchen door and window securely fastened. They could not get in there without making considerable noise, which I was bound to hear. The only mode of getting in was by means of the door that faced me, and I kept my eyes glued on that door without taking them off for the smallest fraction of a second.

My sight adapted itself every minute better to the darkness. I saw the table that nearly filled the room, and left only a narrow passage on each side. I could also make out the straight backs of the wooden chairs pressed up against it, and could even distinguish my papers and inkstand lying on the white oilcloth covering. I thought of the gay faces that had gathered round that table during the summer, and I longed for the sunlight as I had never longed for it before.

Less than three feet to my left the passage-way led to the kitchen, and the stairs leading to the bedrooms above commenced in this passage-way, but almost in the sitting-room itself. Through the windows I could see the dim motionless outlines of the trees: not a leaf stirred, not a branch moved.

A few moments of this awful silence, and then I was aware of a soft tread on the boards of the verandah, so stealthy that it seemed an impression directly on my brain rather than upon the nerves of hearing. Immediately afterwards a black figure darkened the glass door, and I perceived that a face was pressed against the upper panes. A shiver ran down my back, and my hair was conscious of a tendency to rise and stand at right angles to my head.

It was the figure of an Indian, broad-shouldered and immense; indeed, the largest figure of a man I have ever seen outside of a circus hall. By some power of light that seemed to generate itself in the brain, I saw the strong dark face with the aquiline nose and high cheek-bones flattened against the glass. The direction of the gaze I could not determine; but faint gleams of light as the big eyes rolled round and showed their whites, told me plainly that no corner of the room escaped their searching.

For what seemed fully five minutes the dark figure stood there, with the huge shoulders bent forward so as to bring the head down to the level of the glass; while behind him, though not nearly so large, the shadowy form of the other Indian swayed to and fro like a bent tree. While I waited in an agony of suspense and agitation for their next movement little currents of icy sensation ran up and down my spine and my heart seemed alternately to stop beating and then start off again with terrifying rapidity. They must have heard its thumping and the singing of the blood in my head! Moreover, I was conscious, as I felt a cold stream of perspiration trickle down my face, of a desire to scream, to shout, to bang the walls like a child, to make a noise, or do anything that would relieve the suspense and bring things to a speedy climax.

It was probably this inclination that led me to another discovery, for when I tried to bring my rifle from behind my back to raise it and have it pointed at the door ready to fire, I found that I was powerless to move. The muscles, paralysed by this strange fear, refused to obey the will. Here indeed was a terrifying complication!

There was a faint sound of rattling at the brass knob, and the door was pushed open a couple of inches. A pause of a few seconds, and it was pushed open still further. Without a sound of footsteps that was appreciable to my ears, the two figures glided into the room, and the man behind gently closed the door after him.

They were alone with me between the four walls. Could they see me standing there, so still and straight in my corner? Had they, perhaps, already seen me? My blood surged and sang like the roll of drums in an orchestra; and though I did my best to suppress my breathing, it sounded like the rushing of wind through a pneumatic tube.

My suspense as to the next move was soon at an end—only, however, to give place to a new and keener alarm. The men had hitherto exchanged no words and no signs, but there were general indications of a movement across the room, and whichever way they went they would have to pass round the table. If they came my way they would have to pass within six inches of my person. While I was considering this very disagreeable possibility, I perceived that the smaller Indian (smaller by comparison) suddenly raised his arm and pointed to the ceiling. The other fellow raised his head and followed the direction of his companion's arm. I began to understand at last. They were going upstairs, and the room directly overhead to which they pointed had been until this night my bedroom. It was the room in which I had experienced that very morning so strange a sensation of fear, and but for which I should then have been lying asleep in the narrow bed against the window.

The Indians then began to move silently around the room; they were going upstairs, and they were coming round my side of the table. So stealthy were their movements that, but for the abnormally sensitive state of the nerves, I should never have heard them. As it was, their cat-like tread was distinctly audible. Like two monstrous black cats they came round the table towards me, and for the first time I perceived that the smaller of the two dragged something along the floor behind him. As it trailed along over the floor with a soft, sweeping sound, I somehow got the impression that it was a large dead thing with outstretched wings, or a large, spreading cedar branch. Whatever it was, I was unable to see it even in outline, and I was too terrified, even had I possessed the power over my muscles, to move my neck forward in the effort to determine its nature.

Nearer and nearer they came. The leader rested a giant hand upon the table as he moved. My lips were glued together, and the air
seemed to burn in my nostrils. I tried to close my eyes, so that I
might not see as they passed me; but my eyelids had stiffened, and
refused to obey. Would they never get by me? Sensation seemed also
to have left my legs, and it was as if I were standing on mere sup-
ports of wood or stone. Worse still, I was conscious that I was losing
the power of balance, the power to stand upright, or even to lean
backwards against the wall. Some force was drawing me forward, and
a dizzy terror seized me that I should lose my balance, and topple
forward against the Indians just as they were in the act of passing me.

Even moments drawn out into hours must come to an end some
time, and almost before I knew it the figures had passed me and had
their feet upon the lower step of the stairs leading to the upper bedrooms. There could not have been six inches between us, and yet I
was conscious only of a current of cold air that followed them. They
had not touched me, and I was convinced that they had not seen me.
Even the trailing thing on the floor behind them had not touched my
feet, as I had dreaded it would, and on such an occasion as this I was
grateful even for the smallest mercies.

The absence of the Indians from my immediate neighbourhood
brought little sense of relief. I stood shivering and shuddering in my
corner, and, beyond being able to breathe more freely, I felt no whit
less uncomfortable. Also, I was aware that a certain light, which,
without apparent source or rays, had enabled me to follow their every gesture and movement, had gone out of the room with their departure. An unnatural darkness now filled the room, and pervaded its
every corner so that I could barely make out the positions of the
windows and the glass doors.

As I said before, my condition was evidently an abnormal one.
The capacity for feeling surprise seemed, as in dreams, to be wholly
absent. My senses recorded with unusual accuracy every smallest occurrence, but I was able to draw only the simplest deductions.

The Indians soon reached the top of the stairs, and there they
halted for a moment. I had not the faintest clue as to their next
movement. They appeared to hesitate. They were listening attentive-

ly. Then I heard one of them, who by the weight of his soft tread must have been the giant, cross the narrow corridor and enter the room directly overhead—my own little bedroom. But for the insistence of that unaccountable dread I had experienced there in the morning, I should at that very moment have been lying in the bed with the big Indian in the room standing beside me.

For the space of a hundred seconds there was silence, such as might have existed before the birth of sound. It was followed by a long quivering shriek of terror, which rang out into the night, and ended in a short gulp before it had run its full course. At the same moment the other Indian left his place at the head of the stairs, and joined his companion in the bedroom. I heard the "thing" trailing behind him along the floor. A thud followed, as of something heavy falling, and then all became as still and silent as before.

It was at this point that the atmosphere, surcharged all day with the electricity of a fierce storm, found relief in a dancing flash of brilliant lightning simultaneously with a crash of loudest thunder. For five seconds every article in the room was visible to me with amazing distinctness, and through the windows I saw the tree trunks standing in solemn rows. The thunder pealed and echoed across the lake and among the distant islands, and the flood-gates of heaven then opened and let out their rain in streaming torrents.

The drops fell with a swift rushing sound upon the still waters of the lake, which leaped up to meet them, and pattered with the rattle of shot on the leaves of the maples and the roof of the cottage. A moment later, and another flash, even more brilliant and of longer duration than the first, lit up the sky from zenith to horizon, and bathed the room momentarily in dazzling whiteness. I could see the rain glistening on the leaves and branches outside. The wind rose suddenly, and in less than a minute the storm that had been gathering all day burst forth in its full fury.

Above all the noisy voices of the elements, the slightest sounds in the room overhead made themselves heard, and in the few seconds of deep silence that followed the shriek of terror and pain I was aware that the movements had commenced again. The men were leaving the room and approaching the top of the stairs. A short pause, and they began to descend. Behind them, tumbling from step to step, I could hear that trailing "thing" being dragged along. It had become ponderous!

I awaited their approach with a degree of calmness, almost of apathy, which was only explicable on the ground that after a certain point Nature applies her own anæsthetic, and a merciful condition of numbness supervenes. On they came, step by step, nearer and nearer, with the shuffling sound of the burden behind growing louder as they approached.

They were already half-way down the stairs when I was galvanised afresh into a condition of terror by the consideration of a new and horrible possibility. It was the reflection that if another vivid flash of lightning were to come when the shadowy procession was in the room, perhaps when it was actually passing in front of me, I should see everything in detail, and worse, be seen myself! I could only hold my breath and wait—wait while the minutes lengthened into hours, and the procession made its slow progress round the room.

The Indians had reached the foot of the staircase. The form of the huge leader loomed in the doorway of the passage, and the burden with an ominous thud had dropped from the last step to the floor. There was a moment's pause while I saw the Indian turn and stoop to assist his companion. Then the procession moved forward again, entered the room close on my left, and began to move slowly round my side of the table. The leader was already beyond me, and his companion, dragging on the floor behind him the burden, whose confused outline I could dimly make out, was exactly in front of me, when the cavalcade came to a dead halt. At the same moment, with the strange suddenness of thunderstorms, the splash of the rain ceased altogether, and the wind died away into utter silence.

For the space of five seconds my heart seemed to stop beating, and then the worst came. A double flash of lightning lit up the room and its contents with merciless vividness.

The huge Indian leader stood a few feet past me on my right. One leg was stretched forward in the act of taking a step. His immense shoulders were turned towards his companion, and in all their magnificent fierceness I saw the outline of his features. His gaze was directed upon the burden his companion was dragging along the floor; but his profile, with the big aquiline nose, high cheek-bone, straight black hair and bold chin, burnt itself in that brief instant into my brain, never again to fade.

Dwarfish, compared with this gigantic figure, appeared the proportions of the other Indian, who, within twelve inches of my face, was stooping over the thing he was dragging in a position that lent to his person the additional horror of deformity. And the burden, lying upon a sweeping cedar branch which he held and dragged by a long stem, was the body of a white man. The scalp had been neatly lifted, and blood lay in a broad smear upon the cheeks and forehead.

Then, for the first time that night, the terror that had paralysed my muscles and my will lifted its unholy spell from my soul. With a loud cry I stretched out my arms to seize the big Indian by the throat, and, grasping only air, tumbled forward unconscious upon the ground.

I had recognised the body, *and the face was my own!* . . .

It was bright daylight when a man's voice recalled me to consciousness. I was lying where I had fallen, and the farmer was standing in the room with the loaves of bread in his hands. The horror of the night was still in my heart, and as the bluff settler helped me to my feet and picked up the rifle which had fallen with me, with many questions and expressions of condolence, I imagine my brief replies were neither self-explanatory nor even intelligible.

That day, after a thorough and fruitless search of the house, I left the island, and went over to spend my last ten days with the farmer; and when the time came for me to leave, the necessary reading had been accomplished, and my nerves had completely recovered their balance.

On the day of my departure the farmer started early in his big boat with my belongings to row to the point, twelve miles distant, where a little steamer ran twice a week for the accommodation of hunters. Late in the afternoon I went off in another direction in my canoe, wishing to see the island once again, where I had been the victim of so strange an experience.

In due course I arrived there, and made a tour of the island. I also made a search of the little house, and it was not without a curious sensation in my heart that I entered the little upstairs bedroom. There seemed nothing unusual.

Just after I re-embarked, I saw a canoe gliding ahead of me around the curve of the island. A canoe was an unusual sight at this time of the year, and this one seemed to have sprung from nowhere. Altering my course a little, I watched it disappear around the next projecting point of rock. It had high curving bows, and there were two Indians in it. I lingered with some excitement, to see if it would appear again round the other side of the island; and in less than five minutes it came into view. There were less than two hundred yards between us, and the Indians, sitting on their haunches, were paddling swiftly in my direction.

I never paddled faster in my life than I did in those next few minutes. When I turned to look again, the Indians had altered their course, and were again circling the island.

The sun was sinking behind the forests on the mainland, and the crimson-coloured clouds of sunset were reflected in the waters of the lake, when I looked round for the last time, and saw the big bark canoe and its two dusky occupants still going round the island. Then the shadows deepened rapidly; the lake grew black, and the night wind blew its first breath in my face as I turned a corner, and a projecting bluff of rock hid from my view both island and canoe.

The Listener

Sept. 4.—I have hunted all over London for rooms suited to my income—£120 a year—and have at last found them. Two rooms, without modern conveniences, it is true, and in an old, ramshackle building, but within a stone's throw of P—— Place and in an eminently respectable street. The rent is only £25 a year. I had begun to despair when at last I found them by chance. The chance was a mere chance, and unworthy of record. I had to sign a lease for a year, and I did so willingly. The furniture from our old place in H——shire, which has been stored so long, will just suit them.

Oct. 1.—Here I am in my two rooms, in the centre of London, and not far from the offices of the periodicals where occasionally I dispose of an article or two. The building is at the end of a *cul-de-sac*. The alley is well paved and clean, and lined chiefly with the backs of sedate and institutional-looking buildings. There is a stable in it. My own house is dignified with the title of "Chambers." I feel as if one day the honour must prove too much for it, and it will swell with pride—and fall asunder. It is very old. The floor of my sitting-room has valleys and low hills on it, and the top of the door slants away from the ceiling with a glorious disregard of what is usual. They must have quarrelled—fifty years ago—and have been going apart ever since.

Oct. 2.—My landlady is old and thin, with a faded, dusty face. She is uncommunicative. The few words she utters seem to cost her pain. Probably her lungs are half choked with dust. She keeps my rooms as free from this commodity as possible, and has the assistance of a strong girl who brings up the breakfast and lights the fire. As I have said already, she is not communicative. In reply to pleasant efforts on my part she informed me briefly that I was the only occupant of the house at present. My rooms had not been occupied for some years.

There had been other gentlemen upstairs, but they had left.

She never looks straight at me when she speaks, but fixes her dim eyes on my middle waistcoat button, till I get nervous and begin to think it isn't on straight, or is the wrong sort of button altogether.

Oct. 8.—My week's book is nicely kept, and so far is reasonable. Milk and sugar 7d., bread 6d., butter 8d., marmalade 6d., eggs 1s. 8d., laundress 2s. 9d., oil 6d., attendance 5s.; total 12s. 2d.

The landlady has a son who, she told me, is "somethink on a homnibus." He comes occasionally to see her. I think he drinks, for he talks very loud, regardless of the hour of the day or night, and tumbles about over the furniture downstairs.

All the morning I sit indoors writing—articles; verses for the comic papers; a novel I've been "at" for three years, and concerning which I have dreams; a children's book, in which the imagination has free rein; and another book which is to last as long as myself, since it is an honest record of my soul's advance or retreat in the struggle of life. Besides these, I keep a book of poems which I use as a safety valve, and concerning which I have no dreams whatsoever. Between the lot I am always occupied. In the afternoons I generally try to take a walk for my health's sake, through Regent's Park, into Kensington Gardens, or farther afield to Hampstead Heath.

Oct. 10.—Everything went wrong to-day. I have two eggs for breakfast. This morning one of them was bad. I rang the bell for Emily. When she came in I was reading the paper, and, without look-ing up, I said, "Egg's bad." "Oh, is it, sir?" she said; "I'll get another one," and went out, taking the egg with her. I waited my breakfast for her return, which was in five minutes. She put the new egg on the table and went away. But, when I looked down, I saw that she had taken away the good egg and left the bad one—all green and yel-low—in the slop basin. I rang again.

"You've taken the wrong egg," I said.

"Oh!" she exclaimed; "I thought the one I took down didn't smell so very bad." In due time she returned with the good egg, and I resumed my breakfast with two eggs, but less appetite. It was all very trivial, to be sure, but so stupid that I felt annoyed. The character of that egg influenced everything I did. I wrote a bad article, and tore it up. I got a bad headache. I used bad words—to myself. Everything was bad, so I "chucked" work and went for a long walk.

I dined at a cheap chop-house on my way back, and reached home about nine o'clock.

Rain was just beginning to fall as I came in, and the wind was rising. It promised an ugly night. The alley looked dismal and dreary, and the hall of the house, as I passed through it, felt chilly as a tomb. It was the first stormy night I had experienced in my new quarters. The drafts were awful. They came criss-cross, met in the middle of the room, and formed eddies and whirlpools and cold silent currents that almost lifted the hair of my head. I stuffed up the sashes of the windows with neckties and odd socks, and sat over the smoky fire to keep warm. First I tried to write, but found it too cold. My hand turned to ice on the paper.

What tricks the wind did play with the old place! It came rushing up the forsaken alley with a sound like the feet of a hurrying crowd of people who stopped suddenly at the door. I felt as if a lot of curious folk had arranged themselves just outside and were staring up at my windows. Then they took to their heels again and fled whispering and laughing down the lane, only, however, to return with the next gust of wind and repeat their impertinence. On the other side of my room a single square window opens into a sort of shaft, or well, that measures about six feet across to the back wall of another house. Down this funnel the wind dropped, and puffed and shouted. Such noises I never heard before. Between these two entertainments I sat over the fire in a great-coat, listening to the deep booming in the chimney. It was like being in a ship at sea, and I almost looked for the floor to rise in undulations and rock to and fro.

Oct. 12.—I wish I were not quite so lonely—and so poor. And yet I love both my loneliness and my poverty. The former makes me appreciate the companionship of the wind and rain, while the latter preserves my liver and prevents me wasting time in dancing attendance upon women. Poor, ill-dressed men are not acceptable "attendants."

My parents are dead, and my only sister is—no, not dead exactly, but married to a very rich man. They travel most of the time, he to find his health, she to lose herself. Through sheer neglect on her part she has long passed out of my life. The door closed when, after an absolute silence of five years, she sent me a cheque for £50 at Christmas. It was signed by her husband! I returned it to her in a thousand pieces and in an unstamped envelope. So at least I had the satisfaction of knowing that it cost her something! She wrote back with a broad quill pen that covered a whole page with three lines, "You are evidently as cracked as ever, and rude and ungrateful into the bargain." It had always been my special terror lest the insanity of my father's family should leap across the generations and appear in me. This thought haunted me, and she knew it. So after this little exchange of civilities the door slammed, never to open again. I heard the crash it made, and, with it, the falling from the walls of my heart of many little bits of china with their own peculiar value—rare china, some of it, that only needed dusting. The same walls, too, carried mirrors in which I used sometimes to see reflected the misty lawns of childhood, the daisy chains, the wind-torn blossoms scattered through the orchard by warm rains, the robbers' cave in the long walk, and the hidden store of apples in the hay-loft. She was my inseparable companion then—but, when the door slammed, the mirrors cracked across their entire length, and the visions they held vanished for ever. Now I am quite alone. At forty one cannot begin all over again to build up careful friendships, and all others are comparatively worthless.

Oct. 14.—My bedroom is 10 by 10. It is below the level of the front room, and a step leads down into it. Both rooms are very quiet on calm nights, for there is no traffic down this forsaken alley-way. In spite of the occasional larks of the wind, it is a most sheltered strip. At its upper end, below my windows, all the cats of the neighbourhood congregate as soon as darkness gathers. They lie undisturbed on the long ledge of a blind window of the opposite building, for after the postman has come and gone at 9.30, no footsteps ever dare to interrupt their sinister conclave, no step but my own, or sometimes the unsteady footfall of the son who "is somethink on a homnibus."

Oct. 15.—I dined at an "A.B.C." shop on poached eggs and coffee, and then went for a stroll round the outer edge of Regent's Park. It was ten o'clock when I got home. I counted no less than thirteen cats, all of a dark colour, crouching under the lee side of the alley walls. It was a cold night, and the stars shone like points of ice in a blue-black sky. The cats turned their heads and stared at me in silence as I passed. An odd sensation of shyness took possession of me under the glare of so many pairs of unblinking eyes. As I fumbled with the latch-key they jumped noiselessly down and pressed against my legs, as if anxious to be let in. But I slammed the door in their faces and ran quickly upstairs. The front room, as I entered to grope for the matches, felt as cold as a stone vault, and the air held an unusual dampness.

Oct. 17.—For several days I have been working on a ponderous article that allows no play for the fancy. My imagination requires a judicious rein; I am afraid to let it loose, for it carries me sometimes into appalling places beyond the stars and beneath the world. No one realises the danger more than I do. But what a foolish thing to write here—for there is no one to know, no one to realise! My mind of late has held unusual thoughts, thoughts I have never had before, about medicines and drugs and the treatment of strange illnesses. I cannot imagine their source. At no time in my life have I dwelt upon such ideas as now constantly throng my brain. I have had no exercise lately, for the weather has been shocking; and all my afternoons have been spent in the reading-room of the British Museum, where I have a reader's ticket.

I have made an unpleasant discovery: there are rats in the house. At night from my bed I have heard them scampering across the hills and valleys of the front room, and my sleep has been a good deal disturbed in consequence.

Oct. 19.—The landlady, I find, has a little boy with her, probably her son's child. In fine weather he plays in the alley, and draws a wooden cart over the cobbles. One of the wheels is off, and it makes a most distracting noise. After putting up with it as long as possible, I found it was getting on my nerves, and I could not write. So I rang the bell. Emily answered it.

"Emily, will you ask the little fellow to make less noise? It's impossible to work."

The girl went downstairs, and soon afterwards the child was called in by the kitchen door. I felt rather a brute for spoiling his play. In a few minutes, however, the noise began again, and I felt that he was the brute. He dragged the broken toy with a string over the stones till the rattling noise jarred every nerve in my body. It became unbearable, and I rang the bell a second time.

"That noise *must* be put a stop to!" I said to the girl, with decision.

"Yes, sir," she grinned, "I know; but one of the wheels is hoff. The men in the stable offered to mend it for 'im, but he wouldn't let them. He says he likes it that way."

"I can't help what he likes. The noise must stop. I can't write."

"Yes, sir; I'll tell Mrs. Monson."

The noise stopped for the day then.

Oct. 23.—Every day for the past week that cart has rattled over the stones, till I have come to think of it as a huge carrier's van with four wheels and two horses; and every morning I have been obliged to ring the bell and have it stopped. The last time Mrs. Monson herself came up, and said she was sorry I had been annoyed; the sounds should not occur again. With rare discursiveness she went onto ask if I was comfortable, and how I liked the rooms. I replied cautiously. I mentioned the rats. She said they were mice. I spoke of the drafts. She said, "Yes, it were a drafty 'ouse." I referred to the cats, and she said they had been as long as she could remember. By way of conclusion, she informed me that the house was over two hundred years old, and that the last gentleman who had occupied my rooms was a painter who "'ad real Jimmy Bueys and Raffles 'anging all hover the walls." It took me some moments to discern that Cimabue and Raphael were in the woman's mind.

Oct. 24.—Last night the son who is "somethink on a homnibus" came in. He had evidently been drinking, for I heard loud and angry voices below in the kitchen long after I had gone to bed. Once, too, I caught the singular words rising up to me through the floor, "Burning from top to bottom is the only thing that'll ever make this 'ouse right." I knocked on the floor, and the voices ceased suddenly, though later I again heard their clamour in my dreams.

These rooms are very quiet, almost too quiet sometimes. On windless nights they are silent as the grave, and the house might be miles in the country. The roar of London's traffic reaches me only in heavy, distant vibrations. It holds an ominous note sometimes, like that of an approaching army, or an immense tidal-wave very far away thundering in the night.

Oct. 27.—Mrs. Monson, though admirably silent, is a foolish, fussy woman. She does such stupid things. In dusting the room she puts all my things in the wrong places. The ash-trays, which should be on the writing-table, she sets in a silly row on the mantelpiece. The pen-tray, which should be beside the inkstand, she hides away cleverly among the books on my reading-desk. My gloves she arranges daily in idiotic array upon a half-filled book-shelf, and I always have to rearrange them on the low table by the door. She places my arm-chair at impossible angles between the fire and the light, and the tablecloth—the one with Trinity Hall stains—she puts on the table in such a fashion that when I look at it I feel as if my tie and all my clothes were on crooked and awry. She exasperates me. Her very silence and meekness are irritating. Sometimes I feel inclined to throw the inkstand at her, just to bring an expression into her watery eyes and a squeak from those colourless lips. Dear me! What violent expressions I am making use of! How very foolish of me! And yet it almost seems as if the words were not my own, but had been spoken into my ear—I mean, I never make use of such terms naturally.

Oct. 30.—I have been here a month. The place does not agree with me, I think. My headaches are more frequent and violent, and my nerves are a perpetual source of discomfort and annoyance.

I have conceived a great dislike for Mrs. Monson, a feeling I am certain she reciprocates. Somehow, the impression comes frequently to me that there are goings on in this house of which I know nothing, and which she is careful to hide from me.

Last night her son slept in the house, and this morning as I was standing at the window I saw him go out. He glanced up and caught my eye. It was a loutish figure and a singularly repulsive face that I saw, and he gave me the benefit of a very unpleasant leer. At least, so I imagined.

Evidently I am getting absurdly sensitive to trifles, and I suppose it is my disordered nerves making themselves felt. In the British Museum this afternoon I noticed several people at the readers' table staring at me and watching every movement I made. Whenever I looked up from my books I found their eyes upon me. It seemed to me unnecessary and unpleasant, and I left earlier than was my custom. When I reached the door I threw back a last look into the room, and saw every head at the table turned in my direction. It annoyed me very much, and yet I know it is foolish to take note of such things. When I am well they pass me by. I must get more regular exercise. Of late I have had next to none.

Nov. 2.—The utter stillness of this house is beginning to oppress me. I wish there were other fellows living upstairs. No footsteps ever sound overhead, and no tread ever passes my door to go up the next flight of stairs. I am beginning to feel some curiosity to go up myself and see what the upper rooms are like. I feel lonely here and isolated, swept into a deserted corner of the world and forgotten. . . . Once I actually caught myself gazing into the long, cracked mirrors, trying to see the sunlight dancing beneath the trees in the orchard. But only deep shadows seemed to congregate there now, and I soon desisted.

It has been very dark all day, and no wind stirring. The fogs have begun. I had to use a reading-lamp all this morning. There was no cart to be heard today. I actually missed it. This morning, in the gloom and silence, I think I could almost have welcomed it. After all, the sound is a very human one, and this empty house at the end of the alley holds other noises that are not quite so satisfactory.

I have never once seen a policeman in the lane, and the postmen always hurry out with no evidence of a desire to loiter.

10 P.M.—As I write this I hear no sound but the deep murmur of the distant traffic and the low sighing of the wind. The two sounds melt into one another. Now and again a cat raises its shrill, uncanny cry upon the darkness. The cats are always there under my windows

when the darkness falls. The wind is dropping into the funnel with a noise like the sudden sweeping of immense distant wings. It is a dreary night. I feel lost and forgotten.

Nov. 3.—From my windows I can see arrivals. When any one comes to the door I can just see the hat and shoulders and the hand on the bell. Only two fellows have been to see me since I came here two months ago. Both of them I saw from the window before they came up, and heard their voices asking if I was in. Neither of them ever came back.

I have finished the ponderous article. On reading it through, however, I was dissatisfied with it, and drew my pencil through almost every page. There were strange expressions and ideas in it that I could not explain, and viewed with amazement, not to say alarm. They did not sound like my *very own,* and I could not remember having written them. Can it be that my memory is beginning to be affected?

My pens are never to be found. That stupid old woman puts them in a different place each day. I must give her due credit for finding so many new hiding places; such ingenuity is wonderful. I have told her repeatedly, but she always says, "I'll speak to Emily, sir." Emily always says, "I'll tell Mrs. Monson, sir." Their foolishness makes me irritable and scatters all my thoughts. I should like to stick the lost pens into them and turn them out, blind-eyed, to be scratched and mauled by those thousand hungry cats. Whew! What a ghastly thought! Where in the world did it come from? Such an idea is no more my own than it is the policeman's. Yet I felt I *had* to write it. It was like a voice singing in my head, and my pen wouldn't stop till the last word was finished. What ridiculous nonsense! I must and will restrain myself. I must take more regular exercise; my nerves and liver plague me horribly.

Nov. 4.—I attended a curious lecture in the French quarter on "Death," but the room was so hot and I was so weary that I fell asleep. The only part I heard, however, touched my imagination vividly. Speaking of suicides, the lecturer said that self-murder was no escape from the miseries of the present, but only a preparation of greater sorrow for the future. Suicides, he declared, cannot shirk their responsibilities so easily. They must return to take up life exactly where they laid it so violently down, but with the added pain and punishment of their weakness. Many of them wander the earth in unspeakable misery till they can *reclothe* themselves in the body of some one else—generally a lunatic, or weak-minded person, who cannot resist the hideous obsession. This is their only means of escape. Surely a weird and horrible idea! I wish I had slept all the time and not heard it at all. My mind is morbid enough without such ghastly fancies. Such mischievous propaganda should be stopped by the police. I'll write to the *Times* and suggest it. Good idea!

I walked home through Greek Street, Soho, and imagined that a hundred years had slipped back into place and De Quincey was still there, haunting the night with invocations to his "just, subtle, and mighty" drug. His vast dreams seemed to hover not very far away. Once started in my brain, the pictures refused to go away; and I saw him sleeping in that cold, tenantless mansion with the strange little waif who was afraid of its ghosts, both together in the shadows under a single horseman's cloak; or wandering in the companionship of the spectral Anne; or, later still, on his way to the eternal rendezvous at the foot of Great Titchfield Street, the rendezvous she never was able to keep. What an unutterable gloom, what an untold horror of sorrow and suffering comes over me as I try to realise something of what that man—boy he then was—must have taken into his lonely heart.

As I came up the alley I saw a light in the top window, and a head and shoulders thrown in an exaggerated shadow upon the blind. I wondered what the son could be doing up there at such an hour.

Nov. 5.—This morning, while writing, some one came up the creaking stairs and knocked cautiously at my door. Thinking it was the landlady, I said, "Come in!" The knock was repeated, and I cried louder, "Come in, come in!" But no one turned the handle, and I continued my writing with a vexed "Well, stay out, then!" under my breath. Went on writing? I tried to, but my thoughts had suddenly dried up at their source. I could not set down a single word. It was a dark, yellow-fog morning, and there was little enough inspiration in the air as it was, but that stupid woman standing just outside my door waiting to be told again to come in roused a spirit of vexation that filled my head to the exclusion of all else. At last I jumped up and opened the door myself.

"What do you want, and why in the world don't you come in?" I cried out. But the words dropped into empty air. There was no one there. The fog poured up the dingy staircase in deep yellow coils, but there was no sign of a human being anywhere.

I slammed the door, with imprecations upon the house and its noises, and went back to my work. A few minutes later Emily came in with a letter.

"Were you or Mrs. Monson outside a few minutes ago knocking at my door?"

"No, sir."

"Are you sure?"

"Mrs. Monson's gone to market, and there's no one but me and the child in the 'ole 'ouse, and I've been washing the dishes for the last hour, sir."

I fancied the girl's face turned a shade paler. She fidgeted towards the door with a glance over her shoulder.

"Wait, Emily," I said, and then told her what I had heard. She stared stupidly at me, though her eyes shifted now and then over the articles in the room.

"Who was it?" I asked when I had come to the end.

"Mrs. Monson says it's honly mice," she said, as if repeating a learned lesson.

"Mice!" I exclaimed; "it's nothing of the sort. Some one was feeling about outside my door. Who was it? Is the son in the house?"

Her whole manner changed suddenly, and she became earnest instead of evasive. She seemed anxious to tell the truth.

"Oh no, sir; there's no one in the house at all but you and me and the child, and there couldn't 'ave been nobody at your door. As for them knocks—" She stopped abruptly, as though she had said too much.

"Well, what about the knocks?" I said more gently.

"Of course," she stammered, "the knocks isn't mice, nor the footsteps neither, but then—" Again she came to a full halt.

"Anything wrong with the house?"

"Lor', no, sir; the drains is splendid!"

"I don't mean drains, girl. I mean, did anything—anything bad ever happen here?"

She flushed up to the roots of her hair, and then turned suddenly pale again. She was obviously in considerable distress, and there was something she was anxious, yet afraid to tell—some forbidden thing she was not allowed to mention.

"I don't mind what it was, only I should like to know," I said encouragingly.

Raising her frightened eyes to my face, she began to blurt out something about "that which 'appened once to a gentleman that lived hupstairs," when a shrill voice calling her name sounded below.

"Emily, Emily!" It was the returning landlady, and the girl tumbled downstairs as if pulled backwards by a rope, leaving me full of conjectures as to what in the world could have happened to a gentleman *upstairs* that could in so curious a manner affect my ears *downstairs*.

Nov. 10.—I have done capital work; have finished the ponderous article and had it accepted for the —— *Review,* and another one ordered. I feel well and cheerful, and have had regular exercise and good sleep; no headaches, no nerves, no liver! Those pills the chemist recommended are wonderful. I can watch the child playing with his cart and feel no annoyance; sometimes I almost feel inclined to join him. Even the grey-faced landlady rouses pity in me; I am sorry for her: so worn, so weary, so oddly put together, just like the building. She looks as if she had once suffered some shock of terror, and was momentarily dreading another. When I spoke to her to-day very gently about not putting the pens in the ashtray and the gloves on the book-shelf she raised her faint eyes to mine for the first time, and said with the ghost of a smile, "I'll try and remember, sir." I felt inclined to pat her on the back and say, "Come, cheer up and be jolly. Life's not so bad after all." Oh! I am much better. There's nothing like open air and success and good sleep. They build up as if by magic the portions of the heart eaten down by despair and unsatisfied yearnings. Even to the cats I feel friendly. When I came in at eleven o'clock to-night they followed me to the door in a stream, and I stooped down to stroke the one nearest to me. Bah! The brute hissed and spat, and struck at me with her paws. The claw caught my hand and drew blood in a thin line. The others danced sideways into the darkness, screeching, as though I had done them an injury. I believe these cats really hate me. Perhaps they are only waiting to be reinforced. Then they will attack me. Ha, ha! In spite of the momentary annoyance, this fancy sent me laughing upstairs to my room.

The fire was out, and the room seemed unusually cold. As I groped my way over to the mantelpiece to find the matches I realised all at once that there was another person standing beside me in the darkness. I could, of course, see nothing, but my fingers, feeling along the ledge, came into forcible contact with something that was at once withdrawn. It was cold and moist. I could have sworn it was somebody's hand. My flesh began to creep instantly.

"Who's that?" I exclaimed in a loud voice.

My voice dropped into the silence like a pebble into a deep well. There was no answer, but at the same moment I heard some one moving away from me across the room in the direction of the door. It was a confused sort of footstep, and the sound of garments brushing the furniture on the way. The same second my hand stumbled upon the matchbox, and I struck a light. I expected to see Mrs. Monson, or Emily, or perhaps the son who is something on an omnibus. But the flare of the gas jet illumined an empty room; there was not a sign of a person anywhere. I felt the hair stir upon my head, and instinctively I backed up against the wall, lest something should approach me from behind. I was distinctly alarmed. But the next minute I recovered myself. The door was open onto the landing, and I crossed the room, not without some inward trepidation, and went out. The light from the room fell upon the stairs, but there was no one to be seen anywhere, nor was there any sound on the creaking wooden staircase to indicate a departing creature.

I was in the act of turning to go in again when a sound overhead caught my ear. It was a very faint sound, not unlike the sigh of wind; yet it could not have been the wind, for the night was still as the grave. Though it was not repeated, I resolved to go upstairs and see for myself what it all meant. Two senses had been affected—touch and hearing—and I could not believe that I had been deceived. So, with a lighted candle, I went stealthily forth on my unpleasant journey into the upper regions of this queer little old house.

On the first landing there was only one door, and it was locked. On the second there was also only one door, but when I turned the handle it opened. There came forth to meet me the chill musty air that is characteristic of a long unoccupied room. With it there came an indescribable odour. I use the adjective advisedly. Though very faint, diluted as it were, it was nevertheless an odour that made my gorge rise. I had never smelt anything like it before, and I cannot describe it.

The room was small and square, close under the roof, with a sloping ceiling and two tiny windows. It was cold as the grave, without a shred of carpet or a stick of furniture. The icy atmosphere and the nameless odour combined to make the room abominable to me, and, after lingering a moment to see that it contained no cupboards or corners into which a person might have crept for concealment, I made haste to shut the door, and went downstairs again to bed. Evidently I had been deceived after all as to the noise.

In the night I had a foolish but very vivid dream. I dreamed that the landlady and another person, dark and not properly visible, entered my room on all fours, followed by a horde of immense cats. They attacked me as I lay in bed, and murdered me, and then dragged my body upstairs and deposited it on the floor of that cold little square room under the roof.

Nov. 11.—Since my talk with Emily—the unfinished talk—I have hardly once set eyes on her. Mrs. Monson now attends wholly to my wants. As usual, she does everything exactly as I don't like it done. It is all too utterly trivial to mention, but it is exceedingly irritating. Like small doses of morphine often repeated, she has finally a cumulative effect.

Nov. 12.—This morning I woke early, and came into the front room to get a book, meaning to read in bed till it was time to get up. Emily was laying the fire.

"Good morning!" I said cheerfully. "Mind you make a good fire. It's very cold."

The girl turned and showed me a startled face. It was not Emily at all!

"Where's Emily?" I exclaimed.

"You mean the girl as was 'ere before me?"

"Has Emily left?"

"I came on the 6th," she replied sullenly, "and she'd gone then." I got my book and went back to bed. Emily must have been sent away almost immediately after our conversation. This reflection kept coming between me and the printed page. I was glad when it was time to get up. Such prompt energy, such merciless decision, seemed to argue something of importance—to somebody.

Nov. 13.—The wound inflicted by the cat's claw has swollen, and causes me annoyance and some pain. It throbs and itches. I'm afraid my blood must be in poor condition, or it would have healed by now. I opened it with a penknife soaked in an antiseptic solution, and cleansed it thoroughly. I have heard unpleasant stories of the results of wounds inflicted by cats.

Nov. 14.—In spite of the curious effect this house certainly exercises upon my nerves, I like it. It is lonely and deserted in the very heart of London, but it is also for that reason quiet to work in. I wonder why it is so cheap. Some people might be suspicious, but I did not even ask the reason. No answer is better than a lie. If only I could remove the cats from the outside and the rats from the inside. I feel that I shall grow accustomed more and more to its peculiarities, and shall die here. Ah, that expression reads queerly and gives a wrong impression: I meant *live and die* here. I shall renew the lease from year to year till one of us crumbles to pieces. From present indications the building will be the first to go.

Nov. 16.—It is abominable the way my nerves go up and down with me—and rather discouraging. This morning I woke to find my clothes scattered about the room, and a cane chair overturned beside the bed. My coat and waistcoat looked just as if they had been *tried on* by some one in the night. I had horribly vivid dreams, too, in which some one covering his face with his hands kept coming close up to me, crying out as if in pain. "Where can I find covering? Oh, who will clothe me?" How silly, and yet it frightened me a little. It was so dreadfully real. It is now over a year since I last walked in my sleep and woke up with such a shock on the cold pavement of Earl's Court Road, where I then lived. I thought I was cured, but evidently not. This discovery has rather a disquieting effect upon me. To-night I shall resort to the old trick of tying my toe to the bed-post.

Nov. 17.—Last night I was again troubled by most oppressive dreams. Some one seemed to be moving in the night up and down my room, sometimes passing into the front room, and then returning to stand beside the bed and stare intently down upon me. I was being watched by this person all night long. I never actually awoke, though I was often very near it. I suppose it was a nightmare from indigestion, for this morning I have one of my old vile headaches. Yet all my clothes lay about the floor when I awoke, where they had evidently been flung (had I so tossed them?) during the dark hours, and my trousers trailed over the step into the front room.

Worse than this, though—I fancied I noticed about the room in the morning that strange, fetid odour. Though very faint, its mere suggestion is foul and nauseating. What in the world can it be, I wonder?. . . In future I shall lock my door.

Nov. 26.—I have accomplished a lot of good work during this past week, and have also managed to get regular exercise. I have felt well and in an equable state of mind. Only two things have occurred to disturb my equanimity. The first is trivial in itself, and no doubt to be easily explained. The upper window where I saw the light on the night of November 4, with the shadow of a large head and shoulders upon the blind, is one of the windows in the square room under the roof. In reality it has *no blind at all!*

Here is the other thing. I was coming home last night in a fresh fall of snow about eleven o'clock, my umbrella low down over my head. Half-way up the alley, where the snow was wholly untrodden, I saw a man's legs in front of me. The umbrella hid the rest of his figure, but on raising it I saw that he was tall and broad and was walking, as I was, towards the door of my house. He could not have been four feet ahead of me. I had thought the alley was empty when I entered it, but might of course have been mistaken very easily.

A sudden gust of wind compelled me to lower the umbrella, and when I raised it again, not half a minute later, there was no longer any man to be seen. With a few more steps I reached the door. It was closed as usual. I then noticed with a sudden sensation of dismay that the surface of the freshly fallen snow was *unbroken*. My own footmarks were the only ones to be seen anywhere, and though I retraced my way to the point where I had first seen the man, I could find no slightest impression of any other boots. Feeling creepy and uncomfortable, I went upstairs, and was glad to get into bed.

Nov. 28.—With the fastening of my bedroom door the disturbances ceased. I am convinced that I walked in my sleep. Probably I untied my toe and then tied it up again. The fancied security of the locked door would alone have been enough to restore sleep to my troubled spirit and enable me to rest quietly.

Last night, however, the annoyance was suddenly renewed in another and more aggressive form. I woke in the darkness with the impression that some one was standing outside my bedroom door *listening*. As I became more awake the impression grew into positive knowledge. Though there was no appreciable sound of moving or breathing, I was so convinced of the propinquity of a listener that I crept out of bed and approached the door. As I did so there came faintly from the next room the unmistakable sound of some one retreating stealthily across the floor. Yet, as I heard it, it was neither the tread of a man nor a regular footstep, but rather, it seemed to me, a confused sort of crawling, almost as of some one on his hands and knees.

I unlocked the door in less than a second, and passed quickly into the front room, and I could feel, as by the subtlest imaginable vibrations upon my nerves, that the spot I was standing in had just that instant been vacated! The Listener had moved; he was now behind the other door, standing in the passage. Yet this door was also closed. I moved swiftly, and as silently as possible, across the floor, and turned the handle. A cold rush of air met me from the passage and sent shiver after shiver down my back. There was no one in the doorway; there was no one on the little landing; there was no one moving down the staircase. Yet I had been so quick that this midnight Listener could not be very far away, and I felt that if I persevered I should eventually come face to face with him. And the courage that came so opportunely to overcome my nervousness and horror seemed born of the unwelcome conviction that it was somehow necessary for my safety as well as my sanity that I should find this intruder and force his secret from him. For was it not the intent action of his mind upon my own, in concentrated listening, that had awakened me with such a vivid realisation of his presence?

Advancing across the narrow landing, I peered down into the well of the little house. There was nothing to be seen; no one was moving in the darkness. How cold the oilcloth was to my bare feet.

I cannot say what it was that suddenly drew my eyes upwards. I only know that, without apparent reason, I looked up and saw a person about half-way up the next turn of the stairs, leaning forward over the balustrade and staring straight into my face. It was a man. He appeared to be clinging to the rail rather than standing on the stairs. The gloom made it impossible to see much beyond the general outline, but the head and shoulders were seemingly enormous, and stood sharply silhouetted against the skylight in the roof immediately above. The idea flashed into my brain in a moment that I was looking into the visage of something monstrous. The huge skull, the mane-like hair, the wide-humped shoulders, suggested, in a way I did not pause to analyse, that which was scarcely human; and for some seconds, fascinated by horror, I returned the gaze and stared into the dark, inscrutable countenance above me, without knowing exactly where I was or what I was doing.

Then I realised in quite a new way that I was face to face with the secret midnight Listener, and I steeled myself as best I could for what was about to come.

The source of the rash courage that came to me at this awful moment will ever be to me an inexplicable mystery. Though shivering with fear, and my forehead wet with an unholy dew, I resolved to advance. Twenty questions leaped to my lips: What are you? What do you want? Why do you listen and watch? Why do you come into my room? But none of them found articulate utterance.

I began forthwith to climb the stairs, and with the first signs of my advance *he* drew himself back into the shadows and began to move. He retreated as swiftly as I advanced. I heard the sound of his crawling motion a few steps ahead of me, ever maintaining the same distance. When I reached the landing he was half-way up the next flight, and when I was half-way up the next flight he had already arrived at the top landing. I then heard him open the door of the little square room under the roof and go in. Immediately, though the door did not close after him, the sound of his moving entirely ceased.

At this moment I longed for a light, or a stick, or any weapon whatsoever; but I had none of these things, and it was impossible to go back. So I marched steadily up the rest of the stairs, and in less than a minute found myself standing in the gloom face to face with the door through which this creature had just entered.

For a moment I hesitated. The door was about half-way open, and the Listener was standing evidently in his favourite attitude just behind it—listening. To search through that dark room for him seemed hopeless; to enter the same small space where he was seemed horrible. The very idea filled me with loathing, and I almost decided to turn back.

It is strange at such times how trivial things impinge on the consciousness with a shock as of something important and immense. Something—it may have been a beetle or a mouse—scuttled over the bare boards behind me. The door moved a quarter of an inch, closing. My decision came back with a sudden rush, as it were, and thrusting out a foot, I kicked the door so that it swung sharply back to its full extent, and permitted me to walk forward slowly into the aperture of profound blackness beyond. What a queer soft sound my bare feet made on the boards! How the blood sang and buzzed in my head!

I was inside. The darkness closed over me, hiding even the windows. I began to grope my way round the walls in a thorough search; but in order to prevent all possibility of the other's escape, I first of all *closed the door.*

There we were, we two, shut in together between four walls, within a few feet of one another. But with what, with whom, was I thus momentarily imprisoned? A new light flashed suddenly over the affair with a swift, illuminating brilliance—and I knew I was a fool, an utter fool! I was wide awake at last, and the horror was evaporating. My cursed nerves again; a dream, a nightmare, and the old result—walking in my sleep. The figure was a dream-figure. Many a time before had the actors in my dreams stood before me for some moments after I was awake. . . . There was a chance match in my pyjamas' pocket, and I struck it on the wall. The room was utterly empty. It held not even a shadow. I went quickly down to bed, cursing my wretched nerves and my foolish, vivid dreams. But as soon as ever I was asleep again, the same uncouth figure of a man crept back to my bedside, and bending over me with his immense head close to my ear, whispered repeatedly in my dreams, "I want your body; I want its covering. I'm waiting for it, and listening always." Words scarcely less foolish than the dream.

But I wonder what that queer odour was up in the square room. I noticed it again, and stronger than ever before, and it seemed to be also in my bedroom when I woke this morning.

Nov. 29.—Slowly, as moonbeams rise over a misty sea in June, the thought is entering my mind that my nerves and somnambulistic dreams do not adequately account for the influence this house exercises upon me. It holds me as with a fine, invisible net. I cannot escape if I would. It draws me, and it means to keep me.

Nov. 30.—The post this morning brought me a letter from Aden, forwarded from my old rooms in Earl's Court. It was from Chapter, my former Trinity chum, who is on his way home from the East, and asks for my address. I sent it to him at the hotel he mentioned, "to await arrival."

As I have already said, my windows command a view of the alley, and I can see an arrival without difficulty. This morning, while I was busy writing, the sound of footsteps coming up the alley filled me with a sense of vague alarm that I could in no way account for. I went over to the window, and saw a man standing below waiting for the door to be opened. His shoulders were broad, his top-hat glossy, and his overcoat fitted beautifully round the collar. All this I could see, but no more. Presently the door was opened, and the shock to my nerves was unmistakable when I heard a man's voice ask, "Is Mr. —— still here?" mentioning my name. I could not catch the answer, but it could only have been in the affirmative, for the man entered the hall and the door shut to behind him. But I waited in vain for the sound of his steps on the stairs. There was no sound of any kind. It seemed to me so strange that I opened my door and looked out. No one was anywhere to be seen. I walked across the narrow landing, and looked through the window that commands the whole length of the alley. There was no sign of a human being, coming or going. The lane was deserted. Then I deliberately walked downstairs into the kitchen, and asked the grey-faced landlady if a gentleman had just that minute called for me.

The answer, given with an odd, weary sort of smile, was *"No!"*

Dec. 1.—I feel genuinely alarmed and uneasy over the state of my nerves. Dreams are dreams, but never before have I had dreams in broad daylight.

I am looking forward very much to Chapter's arrival. He is a capital fellow, vigorous, healthy, with no nerves, and even less imagination; and he has £2,000 a year into the bargain. Periodically he makes me offers—the last was to travel round the world with him as secretary, which was a delicate way of paying my expenses and giving me some pocket-money—offers, however, which I invariably decline. I prefer to keep his friendship. Women could not come between us; money might—therefore I give it no opportunity. Chapter always laughed at what he called my "fancies," being himself possessed only of that thin-blooded quality of imagination which is ever associated with the prosaic-minded man. Yet, if taunted with this obvious lack, his wrath is deeply stirred. His psychology is that of the crass materialist—always a rather funny article. It will afford me genuine relief, nonetheless, to hear the cold judgment his mind will have to pass upon the story of this house as I shall have it to tell.

Dec. 2.—The strangest part of it all I have not referred to in this brief diary. Truth to tell, I have been afraid to set it down in black and white. I have kept it in the background of my thoughts, preventing it as far as possible from taking shape. In spite of my efforts, however, it has continued to grow stronger.

Now that I come to face the issue squarely it is harder to express than I imagined. Like a half-remembered melody that trips in the head but vanishes the moment you try to sing it, these thoughts form a group in the background of my mind, behind my mind, as it were, and refuse to come forward. They are crouching ready to spring, but the actual leap never takes place.

In these rooms, except when my mind is strongly concentrated on my own work, I find myself suddenly dealing in thoughts and ideas that are not my own! New, strange conceptions, wholly foreign to my temperament, are for ever cropping up in my head. What precisely they are is of no particular importance. The point is that they are entirely apart from the channel in which my thoughts have hitherto been accustomed to flow. Especially they come when my mind is at rest, unoccupied; when I'm dreaming over the fire, or sitting with a book which fails to hold my attention. Then these thoughts which are not mine spring into life and make me feel exceedingly uncomfortable. Sometimes they are so strong that I almost feel as if some one were in the room beside me, thinking aloud.

Evidently my nerves and liver are shockingly out of order. I must work harder and take more vigorous exercise. The horrid thoughts never come when my mind is much occupied. But they are always there—waiting and as it were *alive*.

What I have attempted to describe above came first upon me gradually after I had been some days in the house, and then grew steadily in strength. The other strange thing has come to me only twice in all these weeks. *It appals me.* It is the consciousness of the propinquity of some deadly and loathsome disease. It comes over me like a wave of fever heat, and then passes off, leaving me cold and trembling. The air seems for a few seconds to become tainted. So penetrating and convincing is the thought of this sickness, that on both occasions my brain has turned momentarily dizzy, and through my mind, like flames of white heat, have flashed the ominous names of all the dangerous illnesses I know. I can no more explain these visitations than I can fly, yet I know there is no dreaming about the clammy skin and palpitating heart which they always leave as witnesses of their brief visit.

Most strongly of all was I aware of this nearness of a mortal sickness when, on the night of the 28th, I went upstairs in pursuit of the listening figure. When we were shut in together in that little square room under the roof, I felt that I was face to face with the actual essence of this invisible and malignant disease. Such a feeling never entered my heart before, and I pray to God it never may again.

There! Now I have confessed. I have given some expression at least to the feelings that so far I have been afraid to see in my own writing. For—since I can no longer deceive myself—the experiences of that night (28th) were no more a dream than my daily breakfast is a dream; and the trivial entry in this diary by which I sought to explain away an occurrence that caused me unutterable horror was due solely to my desire not to acknowledge in words what I really felt and believed to be true. The increase that would have accrued to my horror by so doing might have been more than I could stand.

Dec. 3.—I wish Chapter would come. My facts are all ready marshalled, and I can see his cool, grey eyes fixed incredulously on my face as I relate them: the knocking at my door, the well-dressed caller, the light in the upper window and the shadow upon the blind, the man who preceded me in the snow, the scattering of my clothes at night, Emily's arrested confession, the landlady's suspicious reticence, the midnight listener on the stairs, and those awful subsequent words in my sleep; and above all, and hardest to tell, the presence of the abominable sickness, and the stream of thoughts and ideas that are not my own.

I can see Chapter's face, and I can almost hear his deliberate words, "You've been at the tea again, and underfeeding, I expect, as usual. Better see my nerve doctor, and then come with me to the south of France." For this fellow, who knows nothing of disordered liver or high-strung nerves, goes regularly to a great nerve specialist with the periodical belief that his nervous system is beginning to decay.

Dec. 5.—Ever since the incident of the Listener, I have kept a night-light burning in my bedroom, and my sleep has been undisturbed. Last night, however, I was subjected to a far worse annoyance. I woke suddenly, and saw a man in front of the dressing-table regarding himself in the mirror. The door was locked, as usual. I knew at once it was the Listener, and the blood turned to ice in my veins. Such a wave of horror and dread swept over me that it seemed to turn me rigid in the bed, and I could neither move nor speak. I noted, however, that the odour I so abhorred was strong in the room.

The man seemed to be tall and broad. He was stooping forward over the mirror. His back was turned to me, but in the glass I saw the reflection of a huge head and face illumined fitfully by the flicker of the night-light. The spectral grey of very early morning stealing in round the edges of the curtains lent an additional horror to the picture, for it fell upon hair that was tawny and mane-like, hanging loosely about a face whose swollen, rugose features bore the once seen never forgotten leonine expression of— I dare not write down that awful word. But, by way of corroborative proof, I saw in the faint mingling of the two lights that there were several bronze-coloured blotches on the cheeks which the man was evidently examining with great care in the glass. The lips were pale and very thick and large. One hand I could not see, but the other rested on the ivory back of my hairbrush. Its muscles were strangely contracted, the fingers thin to emaciation, the back of the hand closely puckered up. It was like a big grey spider crouching to spring, or the claw of a great bird.

The full realisation that I was alone in the room with this nameless creature, almost within arm's reach of him, overcame me to such a degree that, when he suddenly turned and regarded me with small beady eyes, wholly out of proportion to the grandeur of their massive setting, I sat bolt upright in bed, uttered a loud cry, and then fell back in a dead swoon of terror upon the bed.

Dec. 6.— . . . When I came to this morning, the first thing I noticed was that my clothes were strewn all over the floor. . . . I find it difficult to put my thoughts together, and have sudden accesses of violent trembling. I determined that I would go at once to Chapter's hotel and find out when he is expected. I cannot refer to what happened in the night; it is too awful, and I have to keep my thoughts rigorously away from it. I feel light-headed and queer, couldn't eat any breakfast, and have twice vomited with blood. While dressing to go out, a hansom rattled up noisily over the cobbles, and a minute later the door opened, and to my great joy in walked the very subject of my thoughts.

The sight of his strong face and quiet eyes had an immediate effect upon me, and I grew calmer again. His very handshake was a sort of tonic. But, as I listened eagerly to the deep tones of his reassuring voice, and the visions of the night time paled a little, I began to realise how very hard it was going to be to tell him my wild intangible tale. Some men radiate an animal vigour that destroys the delicate woof of a vision and effectually prevents its reconstruction. Chapter was one of these men.

We talked of incidents that had filled the interval since we last met, and he told me something of his travels. He talked and I listened. But, so full was I of the horrid thing I had to tell, that I made a poor listener. I was for ever watching my opportunity to leap in and explode it all under his nose.

Before very long, however, it was borne in upon me that he too was merely talking for time. He too held something of importance in the background of his mind, something too weighty to let fall till the right moment presented itself. So that during the whole of the first half-hour we were both waiting for the psychological moment in which properly to release our respective bombs; and the intensity of our minds' action set up opposing forces that merely sufficed to hold one another in check—and nothing more. As soon as I realised this, therefore, I resolved to yield. I renounced for the time my purpose of telling my story, and had the satisfaction of seeing that his mind, released from the restraint of my own, at once began to make preparations for the discharge of its momentous burden. The talk grew less and less magnetic; the interest waned; the descriptions of his travels became less alive. There were pauses between his sentences. Presently he repeated himself. His words clothed no living thoughts. The pauses grew longer. Then the interest dwindled altogether and went out like a candle in the wind. His voice ceased, and he looked up squarely into my face with serious and anxious eyes.

The psychological moment had come at last!

"I say—" he began, and then stopped short.

I made an unconscious gesture of encouragement, but said no

word. I dreaded the impending disclosure exceedingly. A dark shadow seemed to precede it.

"I say," he blurted out at last, "what in the world made you ever come to this place—to these rooms, I mean?"

"They're cheap, for one thing," I began, "and central and—"

"They're too cheap," he interrupted. "Didn't you ask what made 'em so cheap?"

"It never occurred to me at the time."

There was a pause in which he avoided my eyes.

"For God's sake, go on, man, and tell it!" I cried, for the suspense was getting more than I could stand in my nervous condition.

"This was where Blount lived so long," he said quietly, "and where he—died. You know, in the old days I often used to come here and see him, and do what I could to alleviate his—" He stuck fast again.

"Well!" I said with a great effort. "*Please* go on—faster."

"But," Chapter went on, turning his face to the window with a perceptible shiver, "he finally got so terrible I simply couldn't stand it, though I always thought I could stand anything. It got on my nerves and made me dream, and haunted me day and night."

I stared at him, and said nothing. I had never heard of Blount in my life, and didn't know what he was talking about. But, all the same, I was trembling, and my mouth had become strangely dry.

"This is the first time I've been back here since," he said almost in a whisper, "and, 'pon my word, it gives me the creeps. I swear it isn't fit for a man to live in. I never saw you look so bad, old man."

"I've got it for a year," I jerked out, with a forced laugh; "signed the lease and all. I thought it was rather a bargain."

Chapter shuddered, and buttoned his overcoat up to his neck. Then he spoke in a low voice, looking occasionally behind him as though he thought some one was listening. I too could have sworn some one else was in the room with us.

"He did it himself, you know, and no one blamed him a bit; his sufferings were awful. For the last two years he used to wear a veil when he went out, and even then it was always in a closed carriage. Even the attendant who had nursed him for so long was at length obliged to leave. The extremities of both the lower limbs were gone, dropped off, and he moved about the ground on all fours with a sort of crawling motion. The odour, too, was—"

I was obliged to interrupt him here. I could hear no more details of that sort. My skin was moist, I felt hot and cold by turns, for at last I was beginning to understand.

"Poor devil," Chapter went on; "I used to keep my eyes closed as much as possible. He always begged to be allowed to take his veil off, and asked if I minded very much. I used to stand by the open window. He never touched me, though. He rented the whole house. Nothing would induce him to leave it."

"Did he occupy—these very rooms?"

"No. He had the little room on the top floor, the square one just under the roof. He preferred it because it was dark. These rooms were too near the ground, and he was afraid people might see him through the windows. A crowd had been known to follow him up to the very door, and then stand below the windows in the hope of catching a glimpse of his face."

"But there were hospitals."

"He wouldn't go near one, and they didn't like to force him. You know, they say it's not contagious, so there was nothing to prevent his staying here if he wanted to. He spent all his time reading medical books, about drugs and so on. His head and face were something appalling, just like a lion's."

I held up my hand to arrest further description.

"He was a burden to the world, and he knew it. One night I suppose he realised it too keenly to wish to live. He had the free use of drugs—and in the morning he was found dead on the floor. Two years ago, that was, and they said then he had still several years to live."

"Then, in heaven's name!" I cried, unable to bear the suspense any longer, "tell me what it was he had, and be quick about it."

"I thought you knew!" he exclaimed, with genuine surprise. "I thought you knew!"

He leaned forward and our eyes met. In a scarcely audible whisper I caught the words his lips seemed almost afraid to utter:

"He was a leper!"

A Case of Eavesdropping

Jim Shorthouse was the sort of fellow who always made a mess of things. Everything with which his hands or mind came into contact issued from such contact in an unqualified and irremediable state of mess. His college days were a mess: he was twice rusticated. His schooldays were a mess: he went to half a dozen, each passing him on to the next with a worse character and in a more developed state of mess. His early boyhood was the sort of mess that copybooks and dictionaries spell with a big "M," and his babyhood—ugh! Was the embodiment of howling, yowling, screaming mess.

At the age of forty, however, there came a change in his troubled life, when he met a girl with half a million in her own right, who consented to marry him, and who very soon succeeded in reducing his most messy existence into a state of comparative order and system.

Certain incidents, important and otherwise, of Jim's life would never have come to be told here but for the fact that in getting into his "messes" and out of them again he succeeded in drawing himself into the atmosphere of peculiar circumstances and strange happenings. He attracted to his path the curious adventures of life as unfailingly as meat attracts flies, and jam wasps. It is to the meat and jam of his life, so to speak, that he owes his experiences; his after-life was all pudding, which attracts nothing but greedy children. With marriage the interest of his life ceased for all but one person, and his path became regular as the sun's instead of erratic as a comet's.

The first experience in order of time that he related to me shows that somewhere latent behind his disarranged nervous system there lay psychic perceptions of an uncommon order. About the age of twenty-two—I think after his second rustication—his father's purse and patience had equally given out, and Jim found himself stranded high and dry in a large American city. High and dry! And the only

90

clothes that had no holes in them safely in the keeping of his uncle's wardrobe.

Careful reflection on a bench in one of the city parks led him to the conclusion that the only thing to do was to persuade the city editor of one of the daily journals that he possessed an observant mind and a ready pen, and that he could "do good work for your paper, sir, as a reporter." This, then, he did, standing at a most unnatural angle between the editor and the window to conceal the whereabouts of the holes.

"Guess we'll have to give you a week's trial," said the editor, who, ever on the lookout for good chance material, took on shoals of men in that way and retained on the average one man per shoal. Anyhow it gave Jim Shorthouse the wherewithal to sew up the holes and relieve his uncle's wardrobe of its burden.

Then he went to find living quarters; and in this proceeding his unique characteristics already referred to—what theosophists would call his Karma—began unmistakably to assert themselves, for it was in the house he eventually selected that this sad tale took place.

There are no "diggings" in American cities. The alternatives for small incomes are grim enough—rooms in a boarding-house where meals are served, or in a room-house where no meals are served— not even breakfast. Rich people live in palaces, of course, but Jim had nothing to do with "sich-like." His horizon was bounded by boarding-houses and room-houses; and, owing to the necessary irregularity of his meals and hours, he took the latter.

It was a large, gaunt-looking place in a side street, with dirty windows and a creaking iron gate, but the rooms were large, and the one he selected and paid for in advance was on the top floor. The landlady looked gaunt and dusty as the house, and quite as old. Her eyes were green and faded, and her features large.

"Waal," she twanged, with her electrifying Western drawl, "that's the room, if you like it, and that's the price I said. Now, if you want it, why, just say so; and if you don't, why, it don't hurt me any."

Jim wanted to shake her, but he feared the clouds of long-accumulated dust in her clothes, and as the price and size of the room suited him, he decided to take it.

"Anyone else on this floor?" he asked.

She looked at him queerly out of her faded eyes before she answered.

"None of my guests ever put such questions to me before," she said; "but I guess you're different. Why, there's no one at all but an old gent that's stayed here every bit of five years. He's over thar," pointing to the end of the passage.

"Ah! I see," said Shorthouse feebly. "So I'm alone up here?"

"Reckon you are, pretty near," she twanged out, ending the conversation abruptly by turning her back on her new "guest," and going slowly and deliberately downstairs.

The newspaper work kept Shorthouse out most of the night. Three times a week he got home at 1 A.M., and three times at 3 A.M. The room proved comfortable enough, and he paid for a second week. His unusual hours had so far prevented his meeting any inmates of the house, and not a sound had been heard from the "old gent" who shared the floor with him. It seemed a very quiet house.

One night, about the middle of the second week, he came home tired after a long day's work. The lamp that usually stood all night in the hall had burned itself out, and he had to stumble upstairs in the dark. He made considerable noise in doing so, but nobody seemed to be disturbed. The whole house was utterly quiet, and probably everybody was asleep. There were no lights under any of the doors. All was in darkness. It was after two o'clock.

After reading some English letters that had come during the day, and dipping for a few minutes into a book, he became drowsy and got ready for bed. Just as he was about to get in between the sheets, he stopped for a moment and listened. There rose in the night, as he did so, the sound of steps somewhere in the house below. Listening attentively, he heard that it was somebody coming upstairs—a heavy tread, and the owner taking no pains to step quietly. On it came up the stairs, tramp, tramp, tramp—evidently the tread of a big man, and one in something of a hurry.

At once thoughts connected somehow with fire and police flashed through Jim's brain, but there were no sounds of voices with the steps, and he reflected in the same moment that it could only be the old gentleman keeping late hours and tumbling upstairs in the darkness. He was in the act of turning out the gas and stepping into bed, when the house resumed its former stillness by the footsteps suddenly coming to a dead stop immediately outside his own room.

With his hand on the gas, Shorthouse paused a moment before turning it out to see if the steps would go on again, when he was startled by a loud knocking on his door. Instantly, in obedience to a curious and unexplained instinct, he turned out the light, leaving himself and the room in total darkness.

He had scarcely taken a step across the room to open the door, when a voice from the other side of the wall, so close it almost sounded in his ear, exclaimed in German, "Is that you, father? Come in."

The speaker was a man in the next room, and the knocking, after all, had not been on his own door, but on that of the adjoining chamber, which he had supposed to be vacant.

Almost before the man in the passage had time to answer in German, "Let me in at once," Jim heard some one cross the floor and unlock the door. Then it was slammed to with a bang, and there was audible the sound of footsteps about the room, and of chairs being drawn up to a table and knocking against furniture on the way. The men seemed wholly regardless of their neighbour's comfort, for they made noise enough to waken the dead.

"Serves me right for taking a room in such a cheap hole," reflected Jim in the darkness. "I wonder whom she's let the room to!"

The two rooms, the landlady had told him, were originally one. She had put up a thin partition—just a row of boards—to increase her income. The doors were adjacent, and only separated by the massive upright beam between them. When one was opened or shut the other rattled.

With utter indifference to the comfort of the other sleepers in the house, the two Germans had meanwhile commenced to talk both at once and at the top of their voices. They talked emphatically, even angrily. The words "Father" and "Otto" were freely used. Shorthouse understood German, but as he stood listening for the first minute or two, an eavesdropper in spite of himself, it was difficult to make head or tail of the talk, for neither would give way to the other, and the jumble of guttural sounds and unfinished sentences was wholly unintelligible. Then, very suddenly, both voices dropped together; and, after a moment's pause, the deep tones of one of them, who seemed to be the "father," said, with the utmost distinctness—

"You mean, Otto, that you refuse to get it?"

There was a sound of someone shuffling in the chair before the answer came. "I mean that I don't know how to get it. It is so much, father. It is *too* much. A part of it—"

"A part of it!" cried the other, with an angry oath, "a part of it, when ruin and disgrace are already in the house, is worse than useless. If you can get half you can get all, you wretched fool. Half-measures only damn all concerned."

"You told me last time—" began the other firmly, but was not allowed to finish. A succession of horrible oaths drowned his sentence, and the father went on, in a voice vibrating with anger—

"You know she will give you anything. You have only been married a few months. If you ask and give a plausible reason you can get all we want and more. You can ask it temporarily. All will be paid back. It will re-establish the firm, and she will never know what was done with it. With that amount, Otto, you know I can recoup all these terrible losses, and in less than a year all will be repaid. But without it . . . You must get it, Otto. Hear me, you must. Am I to be arrested for the misuse of trust moneys? Is our honoured name to be cursed and spat on?" The old man choked and stammered in his anger and desperation.

Shorthouse stood shivering in the darkness and listening in spite of himself. The conversation had carried him along with it, and he had been for some reason afraid to let his neighbourhood be known. But at this point he realised that he had listened too long and that he must inform the two men that they could be overheard to every single syllable. So he coughed loudly, and at the same time rattled the handle of his door. It seemed to have no effect, for the voices continued just as loudly as before, the son protesting and the father growing more and more angry. He coughed again persistently, and also contrived purposely in the darkness to tumble against the partition, feeling the thin boards yield easily under his weight, and making a considerable noise in so doing. But the voices went on unconcernedly, and louder than ever. Could it be possible they had not heard?

By this time Jim was more concerned about his own sleep than the morality of overhearing the private scandals of his neighbours, and he went out into the passage and knocked smartly at their door. Instantly, as if by magic, the sounds ceased. Everything dropped into utter silence. There was no light under the door and not a whisper could be heard within. He knocked again, but received no answer.

"Gentlemen," he began at length, with his lips close to the key-hole and in German, "please do not talk so loud. I can overhear all you say in the next room. Besides, it is very late, and I wish to sleep."

He paused and listened, but no answer was forthcoming. He turned the handle and found the door was locked. Not a sound broke the stillness of the night except the faint swish of the wind over the sky-light and the creaking of a board here and there in the house below. The cold air of a very early morning crept down the passage, and made him shiver. The silence of the house began to impress him disagreeably. He looked behind him and about him, hoping, and yet fearing, that something would break the stillness. The voices still seemed to ring on in his ears; but that sudden silence, when he knocked at the door, affected him far more unpleasantly than the voices, and put strange thoughts in his brain—thoughts he did not like or approve.

Moving stealthily from the door, he peered over the banisters into the space below. It was like a deep vault that might conceal in its shadows anything that was not good. It was not difficult to fancy he saw an indistinct moving to-and-fro below him. Was that a figure sitting on the stairs peering up obliquely at him out of hideous eyes? Was that a sound of whispering and shuffling down there in the dark halls and forsaken landings? Was it something more than the inarticulate murmur of the night?

The wind made an effort overhead, singing over the sky-light, and the door behind him rattled and made him start. He turned to go back to his room, and the draught closed the door slowly in his face as if there were some one pressing against it from the other side. When he pushed it open and went in, a hundred shadowy forms seemed to dart swiftly and silently back to their corners and hiding-places. But in the adjoining room the sounds had entirely ceased, and Shorthouse soon crept into bed, and left the house with its inmates, waking or sleeping, to take care of themselves, while he entered the region of dreams and silence.

Next day, strong in the common sense that the sunlight brings, he determined to lodge a complaint against the noisy occupants of the next room and make the landlady request them to modify their voices at such late hours of the night and morning. But it so happened that she was not to be seen that day, and when he returned from the office at midnight it was, of course, too late.

Looking under the door as he came up to bed he noticed that there was no light, and concluded that the Germans were not in. So much the better. He went to sleep about one o'clock, fully decided that if they came up later and woke him with their horrible noises he would not rest till he had roused the landlady and made her reprove them with that authoritative twang, in which every word was like the lash of a metallic whip.

However, there proved to be no need for such drastic measures, for Shorthouse slumbered peacefully all night, and his dreams—chiefly of the fields of grain and flocks of sheep on the far-away farms of his father's estate—were permitted to run their fanciful course unbroken.

Two nights later, however, when he came home tired out, after a difficult day, and wet and blown about by one of the wickedest storms he had ever seen, his dreams—always of the fields and sheep—were not destined to be so undisturbed.

He had already dozed off in that delicious glow that follows the removal of wet clothes and the immediate snuggling under warm blankets, when his consciousness, hovering on the borderland between sleep and waking, was vaguely troubled by a sound that rose indistinctly from the depths of the house, and, between the gusts of wind and rain, reached his ears with an accompanying sense of uneasiness and discomfort. It rose on the night air with some pretence of regularity, dying away again in the roar of the wind to reassert itself distantly in the deep, brief hushes of the storm.

For a few minutes Jim's dreams were coloured only—tinged, as it were, by this impression of fear approaching from somewhere insensibly upon him. His consciousness, at first, refused to be drawn back from that enchanted region where it had wandered, and he did not immediately awaken. But the nature of his dreams changed unpleasantly. He saw the sheep suddenly run huddled together, as though frightened by the neighbourhood of an enemy, while the fields of waving corn became agitated as though some monster were moving uncouthly among the crowded stalks. The sky grew dark, and in his dream an awful sound came somewhere from the clouds. It was in reality the sound downstairs growing more distinct.

Shorthouse shifted uneasily across the bed with something like a groan of distress. The next minute he awoke, and found himself sitting straight up in bed—listening. Was it a nightmare? Had he been dreaming evil dreams, that his flesh crawled and the hair stirred on his head?

The room was dark and silent, but outside the wind howled dismally and drove the rain with repeated assaults against the rattling windows. How nice it would be—the thought flashed through his mind—if all winds, like the west wind, went down with the sun! They made such fiendish noises at night, like the crying of angry voices. In the daytime they had such a different sound. If only—

Hark! It was no dream after all, for the sound was momentarily growing louder, and its *cause* was coming up the stairs. He found himself speculating feebly what this cause might be, but the sound was still too indistinct to enable him to arrive at any definite conclusion.

The voice of a church clock striking two made itself heard above the wind. It was just about the hour when the Germans had commenced their performance three nights before. Shorthouse made up his mind that if they began it again he would not put up with it for very long. Yet he was already horribly conscious of the difficulty he would have of getting out of bed. The clothes were so warm and comforting against his back. The sound, still steadily coming nearer, had by this time become differentiated from the confused clamour of the elements, and had resolved itself into the footsteps of one or more persons.

"The Germans, hang 'em!" thought Jim. "But what on earth is the matter with me? I never felt so queer in all my life."

He was trembling all over, and felt as cold as though he were in a freezing atmosphere. His nerves were steady enough, and he felt no diminution of physical courage, but he was conscious of a curious sense of malaise and trepidation, such as even the most vigorous men have been known to experience when in the first grip of some horrible and deadly disease. As the footsteps approached this feeling of weakness increased. He felt a strange lassitude creeping over him, a sort of exhaustion, accompanied by a growing numbness in the extremities, and a sensation of dreaminess in the head, as if perhaps the consciousness were leaving its accustomed seat in the brain and preparing to act on another plane. Yet, strange to say, as the vitality was slowly withdrawn from his body, his senses seemed to grow more acute.

Meanwhile the steps were already on the landing at the top of the stairs, and Shorthouse, still sitting upright in bed, heard a heavy body brush past his door and along the wall outside, almost immediately afterwards the loud knocking of someone's knuckles on the door of the adjoining room.

Instantly, though so far not a sound had proceeded from within, he heard, through the thin partition, a chair pushed back and a man quickly cross the floor and open the door.

"Ah! it's you," he heard in the son's voice. Had the fellow, then, been sitting silently in there all this time, waiting for his father's arrival? To Shorthouse it came not as a pleasant reflection by any means.

There was no answer to this dubious greeting, but the door was closed quickly, and then there was a sound as if a bag or parcel had been thrown on a wooden table and had slid some distance across it before stopping.

"What's that?" asked the son, with anxiety in his tone.

"You may know before I go," returned the other gruffly. Indeed his voice was more than gruff: it betrayed ill-suppressed passion.

Shorthouse was conscious of a strong desire to stop the conversation before it proceeded any further, but somehow or other his will was not equal to the task, and he could not get out of bed. The conversation went on, every tone and inflection distinctly audible above the noise of the storm.

In a low voice the father continued. Jim missed some of the words at the beginning of the sentence. It ended with: ". . . but now they've all left, and I've managed to get up to you. You know what I've come for." There was distinct menace in his tone.

"Yes," returned the other; "I have been waiting."

"And the money?" asked the father impatiently.

No answer.

"You've had three days to get it in, and I've contrived to stave off the worst so far—but to-morrow is the end."

No answer.

"Speak, Otto! What have you got for me? Speak, my son; for God's sake, tell me."

There was a moment's silence, during which the old man's vibrating accents seemed to echo through the rooms. Then came in a low voice the answer—

"I have nothing."

"Otto!" cried the other with passion, "nothing!"

"I can get nothing," came almost in a whisper.

"You lie!" cried the other, in a half-stifled voice. "I swear you lie. Give me the money."

A chair was heard scraping along the floor. Evidently the men had been sitting over the table, and one of them had risen. Shorthouse heard the bag or parcel drawn across the table, and then a step as if one of the men was crossing to the door.

"Father, what's in that? I must know," said Otto, with the first signs of determination in his voice. There must have been an effort on the son's part to gain possession of the parcel in question, and on the father's to retain it, for between them it fell to the ground. A curious rattle followed its contact with the floor. Instantly there were sounds of a scuffle. The men were struggling for the possession of the box. The elder man with oaths, and blasphemous imprecations, the other with short gasps that betokened the strength of his efforts. It was of short duration, and the younger man had evidently won, for a minute later was heard his angry exclamation.

"I knew it. Her jewels! You scoundrel, you shall never have them. It is a crime."

The elder man uttered a short, guttural laugh, which froze Jim's blood and made his skin creep. No word was spoken, and for the space of ten seconds there was a living silence. Then the air trembled with the sound of a thud, followed immediately by a groan and the crash of a heavy body falling over on to the table. A second later there was a lurching from the table on to the floor and against the partition that separated the rooms. The bed quivered an instant at the shock, but the unholy spell was lifted from his soul and Jim Shorthouse sprang out of bed and across the floor in a single bound. He knew that ghastly murder had been done—the murder by a father of his son.

With shaking fingers but a determined heart he lit the gas, and the first thing in which his eyes corroborated the evidence of his ears was the horrifying detail that the lower portion of the partition bulged unnaturally into his own room. The glaring paper with which it was covered had cracked under the tension and the boards beneath it bent inwards towards him. What hideous load was behind them, he shuddered to think.

All this he saw in less than a second. Since the final lurch against the wall not a sound had proceeded from the room, not even a groan or a footstep. All was still but the howl of the wind, which to his ears had in it a note of triumphant horror.

Shorthouse was in the act of leaving the room to rouse the house and send for the police—in fact his hand was already on the door-knob—when something in the room arrested his attention. Out of the corner of his eyes he thought he caught sight of something moving. He was sure of it, and turning his eyes in the direction, he found he was not mistaken.

Something was creeping slowly towards him along the floor. It was something dark and serpentine in shape, and it came from the place where the partition bulged. He stooped down to examine it with feelings of intense horror and repugnance, and he discovered that it was moving toward him from the *other side* of the wall. His eyes were fascinated, and for the moment he was unable to move. Silently, slowly, from side to side like a thick worm, it crawled forward into the room beneath his frightened eyes, until at length he could stand it no longer and stretched out his arm to touch it. But at the instant of contact he withdrew his hand with a suppressed scream. It was sluggish—and it was warm! And he saw that his fingers were stained with living crimson.

A second more, and Shorthouse was out in the passage with his hand on the door of the next room. It was locked. He plunged forward with all his weight against it, and, the lock giving way, he fell headlong into a room that was pitch dark and very cold. In a moment he was on his feet again and trying to penetrate the blackness. Not a sound, not a movement. Not even the sense of a presence. It was empty, miserably empty!

Across the room he could trace the outline of a window with rain streaming down the outside, and the blurred lights of the city beyond. But the room was empty, appallingly empty; and so still. He stood there, cold as ice, staring, shivering, listening. Suddenly there was a step behind him and a light flashed into the room, and when he turned quickly with his arm up as if to ward off a terrific blow he found himself face to face with the landlady. Instantly the reaction began to set in.

It was nearly three o'clock in the morning, and he was standing there with bare feet and striped pyjamas in a small room, which in the merciful light he perceived to be absolutely empty, carpetless, and without a stick of furniture, or even a window-blind. There he stood staring at the disagreeable landlady. And there she stood too, staring and silent, in a black wrapper, her head almost bald, her face white as chalk, shading a sputtering candle with one bony hand and peering over it at him with her blinking green eyes. She looked positively hideous.

"Waal?" she drawled at length, "I heard yer right enough. Guess you couldn't sleep! Or just prowlin' round a bit—is that it?"

The empty room, the absence of all traces of the recent tragedy, the silence, the hour, his striped pyjamas and bare feet—everything together combined to deprive him momentarily of speech. He stared at her blankly without a word.

"Waal?" clanked the awful voice.

"My dear woman," he burst out finally, "there's been something awful—" So far his desperation took him, but no farther. He positively stuck at the substantive.

"Oh! there hasn't been nothin'," she said slowly, still peering at him. "I reckon you've only seen and heard what the others did. I never can keep folks on this floor long. Most of 'em catch on sooner or later—that is, the ones that's kind of quick and sensitive. Only you being an Englishman I thought you wouldn't mind. Nothin' really happens; it's only thinkin' like."

Shorthouse was beside himself. He felt ready to pick her up and drop her over the banisters, candle and all.

"Look there," he said, pointing at her within an inch of her blinking eyes with the fingers that had touched the oozing blood; "look there, my good woman. Is that only thinking?"

She stared a minute, as if not knowing what he meant.

"I guess so," she said at length.

He followed her eyes, and to his amazement saw that his fingers were as white as usual, and quite free from the awful stain that had been there ten minutes before. There was no sign of blood. No amount of staring could bring it back. Had he gone out of his mind? Had his eyes and ears played such tricks with him? Had his senses become false and perverted? He dashed past the landlady, out into the passage, and gained his own room in a couple of strides. Whew! . . . the partition no longer bulged. The paper was not torn. There was no creeping, crawling thing on the faded old carpet.

"It's all over now," drawled the metallic voice behind him. "I'm going to bed again."

He turned and saw the landlady slowly going downstairs again, still shading the candle with her hand and peering up at him from time to time as she moved. A black, ugly, unwholesome object, he thought, as she disappeared into the darkness below, and the last flicker of her candle threw a queer-shaped shadow along the wall and over the ceiling.

Without hesitating a moment, Shorthouse threw himself into his clothes and went out of the house. He preferred the storm to the horrors of that top floor, and he walked the streets till daylight. In the evening he told the landlady he would leave next day, in spite of her assurances that nothing more would happen.

"It never comes back," she said—"that is, not after he's killed."

Shorthouse gasped.

"You gave me a lot for my money," he growled.

"Waal, it aren't my show," she drawled. "I'm no spirit medium. You take chances. Some'll sleep right along and never hear nothin'. Others, like yourself, are different and get the whole thing."

"Who's the old gentleman?—does he hear it?" asked Jim.

"There's no old gentleman at all," she answered coolly. "I just told you that to make you feel easy like in case you did hear anythin'. You were all alone on the floor."

"Say now," she went on, after a pause in which Shorthouse could think of nothing to say but unpublishable things, "say now, do tell, did you feel sort of cold when the show was on, sort of tired and weak, I mean, as if you might be going to die?"

"How can I say?" he answered savagely; "what I felt God only knows."

"Waal, but He won't tell," she drawled out. "Only I was wonderin' how you really did feel, because the man who had that room last was found one morning in bed—"

"In bed?"

"He was dead. He was the one before you. Oh! You don't need to get rattled so. You're all right. And it all really happened, they do say. This house used to be a private residence some twenty-five years ago, and a German family of the name of Steinhardt lived here. They had a big business in Wall Street, and stood 'way up in things."

"Ah!" said her listener.

"Oh yes, they did, right at the top, till one fine day it all bust and the old man skipped with the boodle—"

"Skipped with the boodle?"

"That's so," she said; "got clear away with all the money, and the son was found dead in his house, committed soocide it was thought. Though there was some as said he couldn't have stabbed himself and fallen in that position. They said he was murdered. The father died in prison. They tried to fasten the murder on him, but there was no motive, or no evidence, or no somethin'. I forget now."

"Very pretty," said Shorthouse.

"I'll show you somethin' mighty queer anyways," she drawled, "if you'll come upstairs a minute. I've heard the steps and voices lots of times; they don't pheaze me any. I'd just as lief hear so many dogs barkin'. You'll find the whole story in the newspapers if you look it up—not what goes on here, but the story of the Germans. My house would be ruined if they told all, and I'd sue for damages."

They reached the bedroom, and the woman went in and pulled up the edge of the carpet where Shorthouse had seen the blood soaking in the previous night.

"Look thar, if you feel like it," said the old hag. Stooping down, he saw a dark, dull stain in the boards that corresponded exactly to the shape and position of the blood as he had seen it.

That night he slept in a hotel, and the following day sought new quarters. In the newspapers on file in his office after a long search he found twenty years back the detailed story, substantially as the woman had said, of Steinhardt & Co.'s failure, the absconding and subsequent arrest of the senior partner, and the suicide, or murder, of his son Otto. The landlady's room-house had formerly been their private residence.

The Last Egg in the Nest

A Climbing Adventure

The three Ransom boys were home for the holidays, and all the household knew it. The household included four dogs, a pony, two pet cats, a very talkative parrot, and several white mice, which had been trained to do all sorts of wonderful tricks.

Of course there were others in the household—two sisters, a father, and a mother—but, at times, it seemed as if the animals were by far its most important section.

The Ransom boys—Harry, George, and Edwin, aged respectively ten, twelve, and sixteen—were as fine a trio of manly schoolboys as you could find anywhere, even if they were sometimes up to larks that their father was not supposed to know about in general, and certainly did not know about in particular.

"Has Fred been over yet?" asked Edwin, the first night after dinner.

"Not yet," answered his sister, a pretty girl of eighteen; "but I expect he will come over to-night."

"You ought to know best, May," said George, with a wink at his brothers.

The blush that rose to May's fair cheeks was scarcely noticeable in the lamplight, and George was such a persistent tease that this particular stab drew no special degree of attention. May went on sewing placidly, and let the boys ramble on with their talk and plans for the holidays.

Fred Winter was a neighbour's son, who had been at the same school with the Ransoms, but had just gone up to Cambridge. He was specially high in the brothers' estimation, because, among other claims to their esteem, he possessed a very complete collection of birds' eggs, which he had accumulated with great pains, and to which his elder brother, who travelled widely, had brought home valuable foreign additions. Harry and George Ransom, just at this period of their lives, thought that a large and complete collection of birds' eggs was about *the* most desirable possession in the world. At least two-thirds of their holidays were spent in looking for specimens with which to enlarge their collection; and Edwin, the youngest of the three, who had always joined their expeditions as a sort of golf "caddie" (to carry the bag and climbing irons), was now for the first time admitted seriously into the partnership.

"Mr. Winter has added a wonderful new hawk's egg to his collection, I believe," May continued quietly, after a pause. "He told me the other day that he bought it from a man who climbed down Farmer Mutton's cliffs to the nest and—"

"Farmer Mutton's cliffs!"

"A new hawk's egg!"

"What hawk is it?"

"What kind of egg—speckled or plain?"

"How did he get it? Did the birds attack him?"

"How did he get down the cliffs?"

May dropped her sewing in dismay at the sudden storm the simple remark had raised, but she had the boys in her power now, because, if they teased her, she could hold them in check by refusing to satisfy their curiosity.

"He climbed down to the nest with ropes," she said, answering the last question first, probably because it was the only one she was able to answer. "They let him down from above, and he was so glad to get back again to the ground that he dropped some of the eggs and broke them."

"Silly idiot!" said Edwin.

"What an ass!" sneered George.

"Humph!" grunted Harry, who was too disgusted even to find words.

"There was a straight drop of three hundred feet beneath him," May went on, "and the rope began to split, or creek, or something, just as they hauled him back over the edge."

A fresh storm of questions that broke out here was interrupted by the arrival of Freddy Winter himself. The boys at once surrounded him and took him prisoner, and their sister, who was the real object of his visit, enjoyed very little personal conversation with Mr. Winter that evening. She recognised that a judicious concession to the enemy might save her much subsequent teasing, and, being of a naturally sweet disposition, she contrived that the boys should have their egg-collecting hero all to themselves for the greater part of the evening.

Winter was a good-natured fellow into the bargain, so he allowed himself to be taken prisoner, and made no effort to escape until his captors had forced from him all the secrets concerning the hawk's nest in Farmer Mutton's cliffs. Then, by a judicious invitation to "the trio" to come over morning, for the hundredth time, to inspect his collection, and particularly to view the new-found treasure, he saw his opportunity to get away.

"And now I must say good-night to your sister and be getting home," he said, at last making his escape, while the boys fled to their special den where they could be alone to discuss the exceedingly important matters that had been brought to their consideration that evening.

The conference turned out to be a very curious one. It appeared from Fred's account that the hawk's nest in Farmer Mutton's cliffs was not actually a new discovery. The hawks had nested there for years and years, but the dangerous character of the cliffs, combined with the fact that the farmer was very fond of his hawk's nest and had threatened to shoot any boys he caught attempting to rob it, had effectually guarded the birds from invasion and attack. The cliffs rose in a sheer wall of more than four hundred feet, and offered very little foothold. From below they were absolutely inaccessible, but their summit could be reached by a roundabout pathway, and the trees that grew along the edge provided natural posts to which a rope with any amount of weight at the end of it could be safely fastened. Then it was simply a matter of having the necessary nerve to make the descent, dangling at the end of a rope, with two angry, sharp-beaked birds screaming round your head. Dick Ormsby, who worked on the farm that adjoined old Mutton's, had accomplished this feat, and had found two nests. With four eggs in a little bag tied round his neck, his companions had pulled him slowly up the dizzy distance, and landed him safely over the edge of the cliff. In his frantic efforts to ward off the blows of the parent birds, however, and prevent himself at the same time from swinging out too much from the rocks and fraying the rope on which his life depended, he had struck the eggs a blow that had smashed two of them beyond all power of mending.

Fred had bought one of the remaining sound ones at the stiff price of a guinea, for, as Dick said, "it was a specerlative venture; the eggs is rare anyway, and I risked my life. Now, ef that don't constitute value, I don't know nuthin'. The eggs is preshus stones—that's what they is, an' I'll let 'em go at a guinea apiece, or I won't let 'em go at all."

So Dick got his price, and, according to what Fred told the "trio," the other egg was still to be had at the same figure.

How to get possession of that egg, then, was the momentous subject under consideration of the boys. It had taken very little time and effort to show that funds were reprehensibly low, and that the purchase of the egg from Dick at his own price was for the moment out of the question.

"The figure is a prohibitive one," announced Edwin slowly, and with a deep breath to help him over the long word. "I haven't a sixpence to my name, and my next pocket-money isn't due for a week."

"Nor have I," sighed Harry.

"I have a *very* little," said George, in his turn, "but it's May's birthday next Monday, and I wanted to buy her a present with it."

"May will have other birthdays, I suppose," suggested Edwin; but the idea did not "catch on."

Mr. Ransom was not a rich man. He made his boys a weekly allowance of pocket-money, which he intended should be enough to enable them to hold their own with other boys in their set, and yet was not enough to let them get into mischief. As a matter of fact, however, they were too independent to care two straws whether they could hold their own with other boys, and their allowances were accordingly just sufficient to allow them to get comfortably into mischief. This they did at regular intervals.

The net result of their conference now was the decision that the egg could not be bought, and that the only way to obtain so valuable a specimen for their collection was to climb down to the nest themselves and get one.

The dangers of the undertaking only served to whet their appetite for the adventure.

"I'll go down at the end of a rope," said Edwin, the youngest, "if you fellows are sure you can pull me up again."

"Oh, we can pull you up all right," said Harry authoritatively; "but I think I'd better be the one to go down. I'll wear a fencing mask in case the birds attack me."

"Bring up the eggs in your mouth, remember," said Edwin wisely, "or you'll break them as Dick did. Besides, you've got the largest mouth of us all, and the only one that will hold two eggs at once."

At any other time Edwin might have got a cuff over the head for this gratuitous piece of information, but on this occasion it was so obviously a compliment that his elder brother only smiled complacently, and replied with a consciousness of superior power in his tone.

"Oh, trust me not to break them, once I get my hands on them. No one knows how to carry birds' eggs in his mouth without breaking them better than I do."

"Well, now," slowly began George, who had not been heard from at all since the bold project of robbing the nest had been under discussion, "don't you fellows think it is rather a cruel trick to play? One of the nests is already empty. It only had two eggs in it, and Fred said that Dick took them both. The other one can only have one or two left in it."

"It only has one," interrupted Harry, "because Dick divided the two eggs, and put one in the empty nest."

"Then there's only an egg apiece for each nest," George went on, "and if we take those the birds will have no young ones at all. I hate to do a thing like that. Why not ask Dick to hold his egg for us until we can afford to get it, or, for that matter, we might wait just as well till next year. The hawks are pretty sure to nest again in the same spot, and then we can get two eggs, or as many as we want, for that matter."

"If we got there first," growled Harry. "I don't see anything cruel in it, George; the birds don't seem to mind much. They'll lay a lot more eggs at once. Birds are like our old hens, and never know the difference."

"This is in the interest of science," announced Edwin, with a solemn face, throwing out his chest. "It's an opportunity not to be lost. I think you're afraid you will have to do the climbing."

Edwin evidently did not show to his elder brothers the respect they demanded of him, and this retort would inevitably have led to a scuffle and a chase round the room had not Harry interposed in his most determined way, and ordered his brothers to "shut up" at once.

So George, who was a tender-hearted little chap where dumb animals were concerned, was overruled on the question of cruelty, and when the trio at length fell asleep, long after midnight, it had been finally decided that a raid was to be made upon the hawks' nest, with the aid of ropes, from the top of the cliffs, and in spite of the alleged terrors of Farmer Mutton's gun.

For various reasons the date of the attack was postponed several days. One reason was that the yearly fair was in progress in the neighbouring town, and the boys were waiting to learn if Farmer Mutton was not going in to see it. Another reason was that a hundred feet of strong reliable rope was not so easily procured as they had imagined. In the meantime, however, they had been over to see Fred's specimen, and the sight had been almost too much for them. They had also paid a secret visit of inspection to the cliffs, and Fred Winter had pointed out to them, without any idea that they intended to reach it, the exact spot where the nests were.

The cliffs rose very abruptly out of the farmer's fields. They formed the end of a range of hills that showed nowhere so grand and rugged an appearance as here. A stream flowed at their base, and watered the farm, and from time to time huge blocks of stone, loosened by the frost and rains, came thundering down to terrify the cows in old Mutton's meadows and find a resting-place in the muddy bottom of the stream.

"A nasty piece of climbing, in my opinion," declared Fred, as he pointed out to the trio how Dick had accomplished his feat. "If that rope had had any weak spot in it, the man would have been dashed to pieces on those sharp rocks after a pleasant little drop of about two hundred feet."

"He'd have been dead long before he got to the bottom, wouldn't he?" observed Edwin, while the others laughed in chorus.

High up against the skyline Fred showed them the tree to which the rope had been tied. Close behind it, but not visible from where they were standing, was a big angular rock round which the men had thrown the slack rope in loops as they pulled Dick higher and higher. In this way, in case the weight had become too much for them and the rope had slipped through their hands, there was never more than a few spare inches to go. The boys listened attentively to all the details Fred had to give, sometimes not without a shudder, and exchanged many looks that were full of meaning and significance.

About a hundred feet from the summit, on a narrow ledge formed by the dislodgment, years before, of some heavy mass of rock, the hawks had built their clumsy nests of sticks and twigs. Far above their heads, as the boys stood in Farmer Mutton's meadow and shaded their eyes to look upwards, they could just make out the two fierce birds, mere specks in the sky, circling round and round, many hundred feet above the summit of the cliffs. From time to time their shrill cry, that had something plaintive in it, dropped downward to them.

"They can see us far better than we can see them," said Fred; "and you can be sure they are watching us too. Their eyes are as sharp and quick as eagles'."

"Poor things," said George; "perhaps they are crying for the stolen eggs."

"You are too tender-hearted to be an egg-collector," laughed Fred. "It's a good thing the farmers are not, or we should never have hens' eggs for breakfast."

"I don't mind taking one egg from a nest, or even two, if there are plenty left, and the bird won't miss them," replied George; "but it seems rather a shame to take all."

"They have probably laid a lot more by this time," remarked Edwin, who knew nothing whatever of the habits of hawks, and little of any other birds.

Two days after this preliminary visit to the scene of action, Farmer Mutton hitched up his best team and drove with his wife and daughter to the fair. The boys, who had been watching his movements narrowly, heaved collectively a sigh of relief, and, with enough rope to lower a dozen men into the crater of Vesuvius, started in the early afternoon along the pathway that led by a roundabout route to the summit of the cliff.

It had been decided, as a wise alteration in their plans, to lower George down to the nest, because Harry's greater strength would be far more needed in hauling up than in warding off the possible attacks of the enraged birds. George accepted the position with becoming gravity, and paid no attention whatever to Edwin's remark that it was only right the least valuable member of the party should be the one to run most risk of breaking his neck.

Far below, when they reached the top of the cliffs, they could see Farmer Mutton's cosy house nestling among the apple trees, and his cows grazing in the fields, looking about the size of Newfoundland dogs. The wind rushed up the sides of the precipice with a shriek, and laughed in their faces.

"Ugh! What a height!" they said in one breath, as they lay down flat on their faces and peered cautiously over the dizzy brink.

So far there had been no signs of the hawks, and Edwin's statements that they were probably on their nests was about the most likely remark to which he gave utterance that day.

George, without a word, took off his coat, put on the fencing mask, and tied the rope securely round his waist and under his arms. The other end was made fast to the trunk of a big pine tree that stood a yard or so from the edge, and the boys then proceeded to haul George over a branch of the tree, so as to test the tying of the rope and see if it hurt him anywhere. A round piece of wood was fixed between two stones on the edge of the cliff to prevent the rope fraying, and the boys, with clenched teeth, next proceeded to lower George slowly over the brink of the precipice.

"Remember, old fellow, two pulls mean you are ready to come up, and three that you have safely reached the ledge. Don't forget the signal, and we'll haul you up whenever you want to come," cried Harry, as his brother disappeared from view and swung into space with three hundred feet of air between him and Farmer Mutton's meadows.

Slowly, foot by foot, Harry and Edwin let out the rope, which had been carefully looped round the angle of the big boulder. The strain did not seem too great for them at first, and sometimes, when

George found a chance foothold on the face of the cliff, there was no weight at all. A hundred feet is a long way, though, when a boy, and a brother at that, is hanging at the other end of a rope that can only move a foot at a time. The work soon began to tell on the two boys, as their hard breathing well testified.

"Brace yourself well against the rock, Edwin, and move exactly when I do."

"Right you are," gasped the youngest.

Steadily the rope passed over the edge, and the boys began to wonder how soon George would reach the ledge and find a resting-place. The only way they could tell would be by the slackening of the rope.

"Think he's all right?" asked Edwin, puffing and blowing, but working with every muscle like a little man.

"Of course he is. George is the pluckiest chap I ever knew."

"If he misses that ledge and passes it, how shall we know? He can't signal with his full weight on the rope."

Harry saw the force of this remark, and, before unwinding another coil of the rope from the boulder, he told his brother to go to the edge and look over.

Edwin crept cautiously along the ground and peered over the brink. Harry watched his face anxiously, and saw his cheek suddenly turn pale under the flush of the exercise.

"Harry," he said quietly, turning to his brother a white face, "he's missed the ledge. He's dangling several feet below it, and the beastly hawks are at him, I do believe!"

"Shout that we'll pull him up at once," cried Harry. "Up to the nests, I mean—quick!"

Once, twice, three times, Edwin put his hands to his mouth, trumpet-wise, and hallooed to his brother, a hundred and twenty feet below. The wind sweeping round the bare rocks caught his voice and dived with it into the depths. George made no sign—and Edwin did not know whether he had heard or not.

"Come and pull," roared Harry. "That's the only thing to do."

The boys had never before realised how dear their brother was to them. He had never seemed such a good fellow as at this moment, when he was swinging in the wind against the face of that awful cliff.

It was one thing to let him down, foot by foot, but it was quite another thing to pull him up, inch by inch. The weight seemed twice as great. The brothers strained every muscle, and hauled till the rope cut into their hands and the perspiration poured in streams down their faces. Loop by loop they passed the rope round the rock, inch by inch it crept up toward them over the brink, and at last they had the satisfaction and relief of feeling the signal which meant that George was on the ledge and able to give the three pulls.

"Run and see, quick, while I hold on," cried Harry excitedly.

But Edwin had dropped to the ground exhausted. The strain of the last few minutes had been too much for him, and the effort that would have been no easy matter even for two men had laid him panting and tired out upon his back.

Seeing his brother's predicament. Harry, who himself was not far from being "done," crawled to the edge and craned his head out to see. The height made him dizzy for a moment, but he was immensely relieved to see his brother standing safe, for the moment at least, upon one end of the narrow ledge of rock. He shouted to him some words of encouragement, in a lull of the wind, and his heart gave a bound when he saw George wave his arm in return.

The nests were at the other end of the ledge, perhaps twenty feet away from where George was standing, and it was a very difficult matter to crawl along near enough to get the eggs. The distance was too great for Harry to see the nests themselves, much less to make out if there were eggs in them or not. But he plainly saw the birds, which, frightened and angry, were flying in swift circles in the neighbourhood of their home. Sometimes they seemed above and sometimes below the spot where George was perched, but, so far at least as Harry could see, they had no intention of actually attacking him.

With his hand on the rope to feel the slightest signal from George, Harry lay down beside his brother to recover strength and wind.

"I wouldn't be in George's place for a good deal," he said. "I had no idea it was such dizzy work climbing down a cliff. The rocks bulge out a little above the nests and you have to dangle out there with nothing between you and Mutton's fields until you can swing in and get your feet on the ledge. Hullo! the rope's moving!"

Sure enough the rope was sliding sideways across the piece of wood that was fixed on the edge of the cliff to prevent the rocks cutting it. Edwin, who had by this time recovered his breath, ran at once to look over and see what was the matter.

"George is creeping along the ledge," he cried; "he's within a few feet of the nest, and the birds are screaming and flapping their wings like fury just over his head. Oh, they are monsters!"

While his brothers had so anxiously been watching his progress from the top of the cliff, George, whose head was never affected by dizziness, had been calmly facing the terrors of his position. The rocks above the ledge overhung it in such a way that he had to make considerable swing to get his feet in upon the projection. The first time he had missed it by about six inches, and before he could gather himself together for another attempt he had been lowered too far below it. The frightened hawks had risen screaming from their nests and shot up into the air, where they circled and dropped and rose again with a power and swiftness that were amazing.

As he felt himself being still lowered, George began to think that his brothers would not stop until the rope gave out, which he calculated would be just in time to leave him dangling half-way down the face of the precipice.

Meanwhile, the force of the wind made him swing to and fro more than was pleasant, and the rope, moreover, began to pinch and hurt under his arms.

The wind rushed up, cold and strong, round his legs, and brought with it the faint mooing of the cows far below. It made a peculiar swishing sound as it swept across the rocks above his head.

When at length his brothers began to haul him up again to the ledge, he realised for the first time that they were going to find it very hard work indeed. He rose so slowly, inch by inch, with little jerks, and he knew by the motion that his brothers had all they could manage. It was fully ten minutes before he found himself opposite the ledge, with the coveted nests, and this time he was moving so slowly that he found no great difficulty in landing himself upon the rock. With feelings of thankfulness and relief he gave the signal, by three pulls, that he had arrived upon the ledge; and when, a moment later, he heard Harry's voice shouting to him from above, he waved his arm in return and wished devoutly that he was upon the top of the cliff by his side.

After a few moments' rest he began to crawl along the ledge, which was nowhere so much as two feet wide, in the direction of the nests. His brothers above saw the rope move, and were watching him.

It was ticklish work. He clung to the face of the cliff with his fingers, and moved, inch by inch, the rope still under his arms in case of a slip. After a while he was obliged to go down on his knees with his face close against the wall of rock and his heels hanging over into space. At last he got within arm's reach of the first nest and saw that there was only one egg in it. The birds were flapping their big grey wings close to his head, uttering piteous cries, but they did not seem inclined to attack him. Sometimes they swept so close past him that he could feel the wind their wings made upon his face. George listened to their cries, and to him they seemed to say, "Leave us something, at least! Don't take *all* our precious eggs. They are our children and we love them."

The little fellow's heart turned sick within him as he listened to their wild cries of appeal. He interpreted them only too well. What should he do? They were only wild birds—wild, fierce birds too, that preyed on other inoffensive lives. His hand was outstretched to take the egg. There was nothing to prevent him. "To come all this way, with the danger and the trouble, for nothing," he thought to himself—"and what will Harry and Edwin say?" It was hard to decide.

Just then the mother-bird did an amazing thing. Under his very nose, as it were, she swooped down, folded her broad wings, tucked in her claws under her and entered her nest. It was the mother's devotion in the very face of the enemy; and George, boy though he was, could not fail to be touched the bird's courage.

The balance was turned, and he withdrew his hand that had almost touched her long feathers, and began to retrace his steps carefully along the ledge.

"I don't care what they say; I can't do it," he said to himself. "I'll save up my pocket-money and buy the egg from Dick, and May must wait for her birthday present after all."

Then he gave the signal to hoist.

Harry and Edwin from above had watched their brother's perilous journey with much anxiety. They could not see the nest itself because a rock jutted out and concealed it; but they saw the big bird swoop in at him, and they were afraid it had attacked him.

"It can't hurt him," said Harry, "with that fencing mask over his face. The only thing I'm afraid of is that it may strike the rope with its beak and cut it."

The boys were glad at length when they saw George crawling back along the ledge, and still gladder to feel the hoisting signal.

They began, with renewed strength, the terrible pull up the hundred feet to the ledge. Neither of them said anything, but, at the end of the first five minutes, so severe was the strain that Edwin dropped on his knees, exhausted. George was not then a quarter of the way up. Harry held on like grim death till his brother was able to get up and help him again, and by this means they slowly hauled George up the face of the precipice.

How it would all have ended is hard to say, for Harry too was nearly exhausted, and the rope had begun to slip backward through their weakening grasp. The boys' hearts were in their mouths, for they knew that if the rope got beyond their control and fell the distance they had already hoisted it, the jerk would either break it in two, or it would slip from their brother's body and let him drop upon the rocks, three hundred feet below. The predicament was a terrible one.

"Hullo, boys! What are you doing here, and what in the world is that rope for?"

It was May's voice, and Fred Winter with her.

By the happiest of strange coincidences Fred had called that afternoon to take her for a walk, and she asked to see the place where Dick had climbed down to the hawk's nest. She little expected to find her brothers there.

"George is at the other end of the rope," cried Harry, with a gasp.

May uttered a scream of horror, and Fred, who had taken in the situation at a glance, at once lent his powerful strength to the rope with such effect that in a very few minutes George's face appeared, ghastly white below the network of the mask, above the edge of the cliff. His shoulders and legs followed in very short order, and his brothers seized him and dragged him away from the dangerous brink.

As soon as the rope was untied, May's tears had been dried, and the worst of the explanations were over:

"I thought you would never get me up," George said at length; "but I'm awfully glad to be here again. I haven't got any eggs," he added slowly. "There was only one in the nest, so I didn't take it."

"Quite right," said Fred, with a glance at Miss Ransom's eyes, which were still half sunshine, half tears.

Harry and Edwin were so glad to have their brother safely with them again that they said nothing at all, and the party, still excited over the adventure that had involved so narrow an escape, made their way home again. They followed the winding pathway through the woods, and the boys, with the rope over their arms, tired and subdued, went on ahead and left Fred Winter to follow slowly with their sister.

What he said to her and what she replied in turn, of course, they never knew, but when she said good-night to them that evening she announced as a great secret that Fred had proposed to her that very afternoon and that she had accepted him.

Next day Fred came over with a present for the boys; and what do you think it was? It was a speckled hawk's egg for their collection.

The House of the Past

One night a Dream came to me and brought with her an old and rusty key. She led me across fields and sweet smelling lanes, where the hedges were already whispering to one another in the dark of the spring, till we came to a huge, gaunt house with staring windows and lofty roof half hidden in the shadows of very early morning. I noticed that the blinds were of heavy black, and that the house seemed wrapped in absolute stillness.

"This," she whispered in my ear, "is the House of the Past. Come with me and we will go through some of its rooms and passages; but quickly, for I have not the key for long, and the night is very nearly over. Yet, perchance, you shall remember!"

The key made a dreadful noise as she turned it in the lock, and when the great door swung open into an empty hall and we went in, I heard sounds of whispering and weeping, and the rustling of clothes, as of people moving in their sleep and about to wake. Then, instantly, a spirit of intense sadness came over me, drenching me to the soul; my eyes began to burn and smart, and in my heart I became aware of a strange sensation as of the uncoiling of something that had been asleep for ages. My whole being, unable to resist, at once surrendered itself to the spirit of deepest melancholy, and the pain of my heart, as the Things moved and woke, became in a moment of time too strong for words. . . .

As we advanced, the faint voices and sobbings fled away before us into the interior of the House, and I became conscious that the air was full of hands held aloft, of swaying garments, of drooping tresses, and of eyes so sad and wistful that the tears, which were already brimming in my own, held back for wonder at the sight of such intolerable yearning.

"Do not allow all this sadness to overwhelm you," whispered the

Dream at my side. "It is not often They wake. They sleep for years and years and years. The chambers are all full, and unless visitors such as we come to disturb them, they will never wake of their own accord. But, when one stirs, the sleep of the others is troubled, and they too awake, till the motion is communicated from one room to another and thus finally throughout the whole House. . . . Then, sometimes, the sadness is too great to be borne, and the mind weakens. For this reason Memory gives to them the sweetest and deepest sleep she has, and she keeps this old key rusty from little use. But, listen now," she added, holding up her hand: "do you not hear all through the House that trembling of the air like the distant murmur of falling water? And do you not now. . . perhaps . . . *remember?*"

Even before she spoke, I had already caught faintly the beginning of a new sound; and, now, deep in the cellars beneath our feet, and from the upper regions of the great House as well, I heard the whispering, and the rustling and the inward stirring of the sleeping Shadows. It rose like a chord swept softly from huge unseen strings stretched somewhere among the foundations of the House, and its tremblings ran gently through its walls and ceilings. And I knew that I heard the slow awakening of the Ghosts of the Past.

Ah, me, with what terrible inrushing of sadness I stood with brimming eyes and listened to the faint dead voices of the long ago. . . . For, indeed, the whole House was awakening; and there presently rose to my nostrils the subtle, penetrating perfume of Age: of letters, long preserved, with ink faded and ribbons pale; of scented tresses, golden and brown, laid away, ah, how tenderly! among pressed flowers that still held the inmost delicacy of their forgotten fragrance; the scented presence of lost memories—the intoxicating incense of the past. My eyes o'erflowed, my heart tightened and expanded, as I yielded myself up without reserve to these old, old influences of sound and smell. These Ghosts of the Past—forgotten in the tumult of more recent memories—thronged round me, took my hands in theirs, and, ever whispering of what I had so long forgot, ever sighing, shaking from their hair and garments the ineffable odours of the dead ages, led me through the vast House, from room to room, from floor to floor.

And the Ghosts—were not all equally clear to me. Some had indeed but the faintest life, and stirred me so little that they left only an indistinct, blurred impression in the air; while others gazed half reproachfully at me out of faded, colourless eyes, as if longing to recall themselves to my recollection; and then, seeing they were not recognised, floated back gently into the shadows of their room, to sleep again undisturbed till the Final Day, when I should not fail to know them.

"Many of them have slept so long," said the Dream beside me, "that they wake only with the greatest difficulty. Once awake, however, they know and remember *you* even though you fail to remember them. For it is the rule in this House of the Past that, unless you recall them distinctly, remembering precisely when you knew them and with what particular causes in your past evolution they were associated, they cannot stay awake. Unless you remember them when your eyes meet, unless their look of recognition is returned by you, they are obliged to go back to their sleep, silent and sorrowful, their hands unpressed, their voices unheard, to sleep and dream, deathless and patient, till . . ."

At this moment, her words died away suddenly into the distance, and I became conscious of an overpowering sensation of delight and happiness. Something had touched me on the lips, and a strong, sweet fire flashed down into my heart and sent the blood rushing tumultuously through my veins. My pulses beat wildly, my skin glowed, my eyes grew tender, and the terrible sadness of the place was instantly dispelled as if by magic. Turning with a cry of joy, that was at once swallowed up in the chorus of weeping and sighing round me, I looked . . . and instinctively stretched forth my arms in a rapture of happiness towards . . . towards a vision of a Face . . . hair, lips, eyes; a cloth of gold lay about the fair neck, and the old, old perfume of the East—ye stars, how long ago—was in her breath. Her lips were again on mine; her hair over my eyes; her arms about my neck, and the love of her ancient soul pouring into mine out of eyes still starry and undimmed. Oh, the fierce tumult, the untold wonder, if I could only remember! . . . That subtle, mist-dispelling odour of many ages ago, once so familiar . . . before the Hills of Atlantis were above the blue sea, or the sands had begun to form the bed of the Sphinx. Yet wait; it comes back; I begin to remember. Curtain upon curtain rises in my soul, and I can almost see beyond. But that hideous stretch of the years, awful and sinister, thousands upon thousands. . . . My heart shakes, and I am afraid. Another curtain rises and a new vista, farther than the others, comes into view, interminable, running to a point among thick mists. Lo, they too are moving, rising, lightening. At last, I shall see . . . already I begin to recall . . . the dusky skin . . . the Eastern grace, the wondrous eyes that held the knowledge of Buddha and the wisdom of Christ before these had even dreamed of attainment. As a dream within a dream, it steals over me again, taking compelling possession of my whole being . . . the slender form . . . the stars in that magical Eastern sky . . . the whispering winds among the palm trees . . . the murmur of the river's waves and the music of the reeds where they bend and sigh in the shallows on the golden sand. Thousands of years ago in some æonian distance. It fades a little and begins to pass; then seems again to rise. Ah me, that smile of the shining teeth . . . those lace-veined lids. Oh, who will help me to recall, for it is too far away, too dim, and I cannot wholly remember; though my lips are still tingling, and my arms still outstretched, it again begins to fade. Already there is a look of sadness too deep for words, as she realises that she is unrecognised . . . she, whose mere presence could once extinguish for me the entire universe . . . and she goes back slowly, mournfully, silently to her dim, tremendous sleep, to dream and dream of the day when I *must* remember her and she *must* come where she belongs. . . .

She peers at me from the end of the room where the Shadows already cover her and win her back with outstretched arms to her age-long sleep in the House of the Past.

Trembling all over, with the strange odour still in my nostrils and the fire in my heart, I turned away and followed my Dream up a broad staircase into another part of the House.

As we entered the upper corridors I heard the wind pass singing over the roof. Its music took possession of me until I felt as though my whole body were a single heart, aching, straining, throbbing as if it would break; and all because I heard the wind singing round this House of the Past.

"But, remember," whispered the Dream, answering my unspoken wonder, "that you are listening to the song it has sung for untold ages into untold myriad ears. It carries back so appallingly far; and in that simple dirge, profound in its terrible monotony, are the associations and recollections of the joys, griefs, and struggles of all your previous existence. The wind, like the sea, speaks to the inmost memory," she added, "and that is why its voice is one of such deep spiritual sadness. It is the song of things for ever incomplete, unfinished, unsatisfying."

As we passed through the vaulted rooms, I noticed that no one stirred. There was no actual sound, only a general impression of deep, collective breathing, like the heave of a muffled ocean. But the rooms, I knew at once, were full to the walls, crowded, rows upon rows. . . . And, from the floors below, rose ever the murmur of the weeping Shadows as they returned to their sleep, and settled down again in the silence, the darkness, and the dust. The dust . . . Ah, the dust that floated in this House of the Past, so thick, so penetrating; so fine, it filled the throat and eyes without pain; so fragrant, it soothed the senses and stilled the aching of the heart; so soft, it parched the tongue, without offence; yet so silently falling, gathering, settling over everything, that the air held it like a fine mist and the sleeping Shadows wore it for their shrouds.

"And these are the oldest," said my Dream, "the longest asleep," pointing to the crowded rows of silent sleepers. "None here have wakened for ages too many to count; and even if they woke you would not know them. They are, like the others, all your own, but they are the memories of your earliest stages along the great Path of Evolution. Some day, though, they will awake, and you must know them, and answer their questions, for they cannot die till they have exhausted themselves again through you who gave them birth."

"Ah me," I thought, only half listening to or understanding these last words, "what mothers, fathers, brothers may then be asleep in this room; what faithful lovers, what true friends, what ancient enemies! And to think that some day they will step forth and confront me, and I shall meet their eyes again, claim them, know them, forgive, and be forgiven . . . the memories of all my Past. . . ."

I turned to speak to the Dream at my side, but she was already fading into dimness, and, as I looked again, the whole House melted away into the flush of the eastern sky, and I heard the birds singing and saw the clouds overhead veiling the stars in the light of coming day.

Testing His Courage

The Story of a Quaint Device

Julia Mansfield went disconsolately to her ball that night. She was learning, bit by bit, to pay the price that inevitably must be paid by a great heiress, and in the process she was coming to the conclusion that a little money—enough—is better than a lot.

Already, though she was barely twenty-three, cynical lines had traced their bitter story round the corners of her mouth, and in her eyes there occasionally shone a shrewd light which was certainly not there when she first carne out. The fact was she was passing through that most swiftly disillusioning of all life's processes—finding out the opposite sex.

Julia was not, strictly speaking, pretty. She possessed that intelligent sort of face which earnest men adore, but which bores the majority and alarms most of the rest. Hence, as we have said, she was going to the ball without the enthusiasm of the illusioned young girl. There was, however, one man she hoped to see there. Mark Lister had never paid her a compliment or shown the least desire to make love. She had always liked and respected him and, though he made no sign, her intuition persuaded her that it was a mutual liking, and that it was her money that made him keep aloof.

The ball commenced at ten, but it was considerably after midnight when Mark Lister entered the room.

He was an engineer; good-looking, big, strong, but with only his pay to live on. He was just leaving to take up a rather good appointment in India and he had come to this ball solely to see Miss Mansfield and to confess his love.

He did not intend to ask her to marry him, but yet he wished her at the last to know his secret. It could not possibly hurt her, he argued, and in after life it would always be a source of pleasure to him to think that she knew.

Mark Lister's mind was simple, direct, and without subtlety or guile, and the possible result of his rather selfish expedient did not cross his mind.

It did not take him long to find the girl he sought, and when, later, the time arrived to claim his dance he came at once to the point without hesitation.

"I have come to this ball simply and solely to see you," he said. "I have something to say to you. No, do not be alarmed, there's no question at the end of it. It's a mere statement of fact. If you will sit out this dance, I'll tell you."

He led her to a secluded corner and began at once.

"I'm going to India in three days, but before I go I wanted to tell you—if I may—that I've been in love with you ever since I saw you first at your coming-out ball in this very house three years ago. I tell you this because—I don't quite know why—I fear my reason's very selfish—because it will always be such a pleasure to me to feel that you know. It can do you no harm. I wanted you to know it. There, that's all—and—well, that's the longest speech I ever made in my life!"

He half rose to go, as the music was beginning again, but she held out a hand and stopped him.

"Wait," she said peremptorily. "I'll give you this dance too. I am interested in your declaration. It is unusual. You put no question at the end of it—that customary question I'm so tired of hearing."

"No; I think you are fitted for a better—a bigger career than I could hope to give you. Besides, I love my profession, and could not allow myself to dream of giving it up, even if I dared to think you cared for me. Therefore, I have never permitted myself to think further than this: that I love you, and I want you to know it."

"Evidently, we are both unusual people," she laughed, but in a tone that made his heart leap. "Now, suppose I put a question to you, will you answer it truly?"

"Yes."

"Do you want to marry me?"

"Yes."

"Would you have asked me if I were poor?"

"Yes."

There was a long pause. He felt the girl drawing him with terrific force, but he made no sign. The fragrance of her hair and breath rose to his brain. Again he made a move, and again she stopped him with her hand.

"Mr. Lister," she said—and the personality of the girl robbed the words of any reproach and unmaidenliness—"you have told me the truth without humiliating me. Now, I'll tell you something, too. You have won my love. I love you, and have loved you for a long time."

"You *really* mean that?" he cried.

"You want to marry me—I want to marry you," she continued quietly. "There's only one thing I want you first to prove to me— your courage. No, not your physical courage; that's a mere matter of nerves and imagination. I mean your moral courage, which is a matter of character."

"How?"

"Go and ask my aunt for my hand in marriage. You know, she has the disposal of me. I am her ward."

She watched his face, but he did not flinch. Her aunt had the reputation of being a veritable dragon, a woman to dread, a woman with a bitter and merciless tongue, a sayer of brutal things—usually true!

"All right, I'll go," he said without hesitation. "Only, she's never seen me, or heard of me."

"That makes no difference. This is my test. Do you accept it?" He bowed his head.

"Then go to-morrow at four o'clock. I shall tell her another suit- or is coming to ask for me. She hates the very name of 'suitor.' It's like a red rag to a bull."

This was her parting shot. Mark Lister handed her over to Lord de Pennylesse to go down to supper, and left the ball room.

Next day at the appointed hour he presented himself at the door of the great mansion in Grosvenor Square, but before going up to the dragon's den he asked to see Miss Mansfield alone.

"Miss Mansfield is out, sir, and will not return till evening," was the footman's reply to his question, and with rather a sinking heart he then sent up his card to the aunt, Lady Hester. In due course he was shown into a severe little upstairs drawing-room where, at once as he entered the room, he saw the figure of the much-dreaded old lady seated in an arm-chair by the fire. She looked very prim and severe, and the high fashion of wearing her hair, and the dark spectacles, certainly did not tend to soften the general aspect of severity with which she acidly welcomed him. Her attitude at once seemed to put him in the wrong. She motioned him to a chair, and without delay, in a thin, bored voice, plunged into her subject. Evidently her intention was to conclude the interview as soon as possible and get back to her novel. She sat up stiffly, facing him, yet never once actually taking the trouble to look at him; her back was to the light.

"I believe you wish to marry my niece, Mr—er—"

"Lister," he supplied. Her voice was like the cracking of an icicle just before it drops.

"Mr. Lister," she went on. "Well, sir, as she is also my ward, it is, of course, my duty to ask you if you are in a position to support her—"

"I am an engineer, with a salary of £400 and excellent prospects."

"*Please* don't interrupt," she went on testily. "I was about to say, if you can support her in the way she has been accustomed to?"

"No; I certainly cannot at present give her the luxury she has been accustomed to," he answered frankly, "but she can supply all that unnecessary sort of thing with her own money."

"Her own money, my dear sir! Are you aware that she has no money, practically speaking, of her own? Her fortune is entirely at my disposal, and if she marries a man of whom I disapprove she won't have a penny."

"This is news to me, and very good news," he answered quite calmly, "for if she loves me really she will not mind what—"

"Fiddlesticks, fiddlesticks!" ejaculated the old lady, kicking her footstool viciously. "You don't know what you're talking about, young man. Are you selfish enough to tempt the girl to lose her fortune? Don't you know that money is one's only real friend in this world and that—"

Mark Lister had a good deal of self-control, but he interrupted here.

"Lady Hester," he said, quietly but firmly, "I have come here to

make a formal demand for your ward's hand. If you disapprove of
me as her husband, and will kindly tell me so plainly, I shall then feel
free to ask her if she will have me without your consent. If she pre-
fers her fortune I shall know how to value her love. But not for one
minute do I believe that she loves her wretched money better than
me."

"That's delightfully plain talk, Mr. Lister," snapped the old lady,
"and I'll meet you on equal terms. I refuse my consent. There! Now
you can write and tell her so. If she marries you she shan't have a
penny except the £100 a year she has in her own right."

"I'm delighted with your decision," he said with some heat. "If
she won't marry me on what I've got, I don't want her."

"You'll find a table with writing paper behind you," wheezed the
old lady, burying herself in her book without even looking up to see
what he was doing.

Mark Lister turned to the table and began a letter. He did not
hesitate for a minute. He believed the girl loved him. The decision
was for her to make.

It was not that he valued himself so highly, but that he felt the
right thing for him to do was to give her the chance. He would play
the game. At least it would prove that he wanted herself, not her
money.

He was half-way through his epistle when he suddenly felt a hand
clapped over both his eyes. Good heavens! What was the old cat up
to now? He struggled an instant to free himself, but the fingers only
tightened their grasp. Then he seized the wrist to force it away, and
half rose in his chair as he did so. Surely that tender little hand he felt
so soft and yielding beneath his own was not that of the severe, prim,
bony old maid he had been just arguing with! It seemed incredible.
He wrenched himself free, and turned upon his blindfolder.

Julia Mansfield stood before him, her face crimson with blushes,
her eyes sparkling with happiness. Upon the floor at her feet lay a
bundle of false hair, a pair of blue spectacles, a shawl, and other par-
aphernalia. Lady Hester's arm-chair was empty; her book lay upon
the floor. The disguise had been perfect and complete.

"Mark!" she cried. "Then you do love me for myself. Oh, if you
knew the number of men that have failed to pass that test! I never

really doubted you, but it was sweet to hear it from your own lips—and in such a temper, too! Of course, my fortune is my own, and, what's more to the point, you are, too!"

"You—little—minx—you!" he cried, kissing her between each word. "You don't deserve to have a husband at all."

"Am I forgiven?"

For reply he kissed her again.

"What about your aunt?" he asked presently.

"I am my aunt," replied Julia, "and a very convenient relative I have always found myself. But this is the last of her. I must at once announce that Lady Hester is travelling on the Continent for an indefinite period."

How Garnier Broke the Log-Jam

A Camp-Fire Story

A log-jam is a mighty serious thing, an' don't you forgit it," said Hank Davis, as he carefully selected a burning ember from the camp fire with his naked fingers and held it to the ash of a half-smoked cigar.

We others, sitting cleaning our guns by the fitful light, said nothing, for we knew this was Hank's preface to a yarn. All day long we had tramped the woods and marshes on the trail of the elusive moose, and, after a big supper of venison, trout, and coffee, we were just in the mood for a story. We felt, too, that Hank—this picturesque, dirty, hard-faced son of the woods—was just the fellow to tell it.

There he sat opposite to us, leaning against a fallen tree, his face smeared, his slouch hat over one eye, and his big fingers toying with the gleaming barrel that always carried true when it rested against his shoulder and had his fierce eye looking down it.

"An' I never hunt through these pairts and see the runnin' water," he went on as though to himself, "without calling to mind that thar frog-eatin' Canuck, Jean Garnier, an' how 'twas he broke the jam way back in the sixties."

Behind us the tents shone white and ghostly in the firelight, and the stars peeped down through a tangle of pine-branches that just stirred in the night breeze. On our left the big lake stretched for many miles, and there was not a habitable bit of land in any direction under a two days' journey.

So we learned (in language that will not bear faithful reproduction) that Jean Garnier hailed originally from a little village near Montreal, named Ste. Rose. He had lived there all his life, more or less, and "a mighty wet life it was too." For Garnier was very fond of the white whisky of French Canada—that powerful fiery liquid made from corn and found all through Upper Canada—and was more often under its influence than otherwise. But, in spite of his bad habits, he had won the love of a very charming girl in the village, and he loved her too, he told himself, better than anything else in the world.

"With a single exception," she said to him one day. "That horrid whisky—you love that better than you love me. Otherwise you'd give it up for me."

"But you wouldn't cast away a man just because of a drop of whisky."

"Jean, Jean! It's because I love you so much, that's why I say I won't marry you till you give over swallowing that vile white fire." The girl looked up with a loving appeal in her brown eyes, but she saw the deepening frown on his face, and her heart misgave her.

"Jean, dear, you were a strong-built man a while ago, and I was mighty proud when you came that day and put your arm round my waist and said you loved me—me, a weakly bit of a thing, and you standing up six feet of beautiful strength. The girls were all wild you chose me. Now they laugh instead. And it's all that dreadful drink—"

The man drew closer, interrupting her with a fierce gesture. "Marry me straight away, Lucie, and I'll swear never to touch another drop. I'll give it up altogether."

He bent his dark head down to the level of her face and stretched out his arms to catch her to his heart. But she slipped past him, white to the lips, and her heart thumping. She knew this was a last struggle, and her mind was made up. Her courage must not fail her now after all those hours of prayer and sleeplessness. He had broken a hundred promises for the drink; but she believed in his love, and was determined not to spare herself if she could only save him.

Jean was dimly conscious of the nobility of her love, and her great force of character worked subtly upon him and overcame him. His arms dropped to his side, and he fell back a pace or two. The longing rose in him eagerly, triumphantly, as it had risen many a time before, to become the true man again, to fight with his whole being and win at last. A stray gleam of sunshine fell from the clouds just then, and threw into vivid contrast the strength of his face and the signs of weakness born of long indulgence. The double revelation smote the girl anew. She drew to his side again.

"Oh, Jean, I cannot argue, but"—her voice broke—"but tell me again that you do love me, more than anything else in the whole world. Give me your promise once again. I'll believe it—"

There was a deep silence between them. The sun was hidden by a passing cloud. The wind stirred mournfully in the clustering Golden Rod behind them, as if the sighs their hearts would not hold had passed out together and mingled in the air of heaven before them.

The man's eyes were fixed upon the ground. The moments passed, and he showed no sign that he had even heard her appeal. Then a low sob from the girl broke the silence. Jean suddenly straightened and shook himself. He squared his splendid shoulders, and his great chest heaved with the breathing of strong emotion.

"Lucie, child," he said simply—but his voice was very low and tense—"I love you better than anything else in heaven or earth, and I cannot lose you. I give you my promise, and this time *le bon Dieu* will help me to keep it."

She looked up gratefully, with swimming eyes.

"But first," he went on, "I shall go away. You will wait for me; it will not be long—a few months at most; but when I come back I shall be your old Jean again—a man—and worthy of your splendid love. And, remember always, I love you."

It was late autumn when this conversation took place, and a large lumber camp was then in process of formation. Garnier saw the chance to get away from his old companions into a vigorous open-air life that would give his system strength for the great battle. He joined the camp and went away into the far lonely region of forest near the head-waters of the Ottawa River (where we were moose-hunting when Hank told us the story), and for six months the snow and ice cut them off from civilisation as completely as if they had gone to the moon.

The little world of a lumber camp, shut in by the snows and the frozen lakes, surrounded by bleak hills and leagues of pathless forest, has a peculiar interest all its own. A winter that brings a snowfall of ten feet, with thirty-foot drifts and a temperature of forty degrees below zero, is a very serious winter indeed. The life in the camp is almost martial, and necessarily so. In an average-sized camp there are some fifty men, rough, vigorous, often desperate fellows, and they are ruled with a rod of iron by the Shanty Boss—*i.e.* he who rules over the shanty. For there is one huge pine-log shanty in which they eat, and another in which they sleep. The latter has several large stoves burning night and day, and hardly any ventilation. Wooden bunks, three deep, with blankets, and moss or cedar-branches for mattresses, line the walls all the way round. A cook and a "cookee" (assistant cook) rule over the eating shanty, and provide the men with four tremendous meals a day—salt pork, crushed apples, coffee, brown sugar, and a rough kind of bread. The camp rises long before it is light, and at once, after breakfast, the men go out to chop down the trees. At ten o'clock a meal is brought out to them. At two o'clock it is repeated. At six o'clock they come home, dog tired, for the fourth meal, and by eight o'clock they are in bed and asleep. No "shooting-irons" are allowed to be brought into camp, and another rule (which seems to an outsider who has seen the sleepy, tired crew trudge home, almost unnecessary), very strictly enforced, forbids a single spoken word in the sleeping shanty.

The work is extremely hard, and there is little energy left over for fighting or quarrelling, although some Shanty Bosses run their commandoes with more success than others.

The "axeing" of the big trees is all done while there is snow on the ground, for without its slippery assistance it would be impossible to draw the huge logs to the water's edge. One set of men make a roadway to the nearest lake or stream, consisting of a main artery with smaller trails running into it and taking in all the big trees on the way. Saplings and undergrowth are cut away from the surface of the snow so that the horses may have a clear skidway along which to draw the great logs. In the summer these skidways are recognisable as faint vistas through the forest, always leading to water.

Once the logs reach the lake or stream they are piled up in stacks twenty feet high along the shore, and, when the ice melts in the spring, are tumbled over into the water and floated in immense "booms" acres in extent, for many weeks, across lakes and down streams till they reach the swift waters of the Ottawa River, and thence are guided to the saw-mills many miles farther to the south-wards.

In the spring these booms choke up many a good fishing stream. Perhaps some unwieldy log gets caught by a projection in the bank at a sharp corner. Instantly the others, ever crowding on behind, pile up upon its back, and in a short time a towering heap of logs dams the river from bank to bank, forms an ever-changing waterfall, floods the surrounding "bush," and, in short, forms a log-jam. To start the logs on their journey again is to "break a jam," and it may easily be imagined that the task of disentangling these massive tree-trunks one from another and setting loose the heap of ill-balanced monsters is one fraught with the greatest personal danger. In fact, to break a jam is to lead a forlorn hope, and the honour is pressed upon no one. The Gangman of the boom asks for volunteers from among the single men; and more than one fine fellow whose sweetheart is waiting in some far village of the St. Lawrence to marry him when the camp breaks up in the early summer has lost her prospective husband in this manner.

Guiding the booms, even in clear water, is a dangerous matter. With spiked boots and a balancing-pole that is also a thrusting-pole, the men run along the logs, jumping from one to the other and keeping their balance with amazing agility. Here and there, however, it may be a man slips in and the logs close over him and make it impossible for him to rise to the surface again.

For these, and other reasons, the pay is good—$40 a month (8*l.*). It is paid in a lump sum at the end of the six months—nearly 50*l.* a head. The men at once close with the boss for an engagement in the autumn, and then rush off into civilisation as fast as ever canoes can take them. Many of them, alas! drink up their money in a week or two, and are then penniless for the remainder of the summer. In these circumstances there are little "hotels" on the borders of the timber limits that take them in and board them, first making an arrangement with the Shanty Boss to pay their expenses direct out of the next camp's wages. Many lumbermen, alas! do this year in and year out for the greater part of their lives.

Hank gave us all this information, much adorned with unnecessary expletives, by way of explaining what happened subsequently to Garnier, for Hank and Garnier were members of the same camp, and when it broke up to follow the logs in the spring, they chanced also to be assigned to the same boom.

The men were half-way down a little rushing stream, called, if I remember rightly, the Sabbatis River, when the jam came upon them.

The water was unusually high, full of melted snow and lumps of ice. The journey across the open lakes had been cold and dangerous, and the moment the boom headed into the narrow stream it started off in a wild rush, with a clumsy galloping motion of its great logs that filled the woods round with deep echoes. This headlong career down stream of an army of tree-trunks has something uncanny, even horrible, about it. They seem almost alive, like some antediluvian monsters escaping from the lake in preconcerted onslaught, their ribs black and shining, snorting as they go, irresistible, terrific. As they crash together in the foaming water, leaping away from the impact, half climbing upon one another's shoulders, and slipping back with a roar into the waves, to thrust their blunt noses again skywards the next moment, it is difficult to believe that they are merely so much dead wood racing on as fast as ever they can go to the whizzing saws of the mills.

The men knew the dangers that lay ahead, increasing every moment; but none of them flinched. Personal courage in a lumber camp is at a discount, or, as Hank put it more picturesquely, "You kin bet your sweet life there ain't no white-livered skulkers in a lumber camp outfit." So that, when the inevitable jam came and the logs began piling up upon each other, with that dreadful thunderous sound which must be heard to be appreciated, it was certainly through no fault of theirs; and, having done all they could to prevent it, they sprang, dived, swam, or wriggled for the shore, each as best he could, and fortunately with no accidents and no lives lost.

There, in mid-stream, the logs banged and crashed together. The massive wall grew more and more solid. The water hissed through it in places, gurgling up underneath it, and pouring in little torrents over it, wherever it could find a way. A black barrier had suddenly barred the river's course. Logs stuck out at all possible angles, like huge pencils in a heap of children's toys. Some stood upright, others lurched sideways, and the whole mass heaved and swayed and groaned as the weight increased and the water pressed up against it.

And, meanwhile, the burden of the water grew steadily behind, and the river began to rise perceptibly.

The time had come to call for volunteers. Some one must break the jam.

Standing behind a clump of hemlock trees, out of sight of the rest of the men, Jean Garnier was wrestling with his thoughts. Here was the chance he had been looking for—the chance of proving beyond a doubt to the girl he loved that he was a man once more, that his courage had returned, his nerves grown steady, and that he was master of himself. No man of intemperate habits and shaken nerve could hope to break a log-jam successfully. Everybody knew that. The girls should no longer laugh at her, or the men sneer at him. He could hold up his head again in the village, for she would be proud of him, and he would have proved that he had once for all, and finally, turned over a new leaf. This was only a single act, true, but it was the culmination of many, many weeks of self-restraint, and she would know and realise this, and her respect would come back for him.

He weighed swiftly the awful risk of losing her, and perhaps of breaking her heart, if he failed and was killed. But he cast them aside in the balance. Somehow he felt sure he would get through all right. His old confidence in himself had returned. There were many offers even in the first five minutes, but no one could stand against Jean Garnier. His experience, his strength, his length of limb and arm, and his undoubted skill, all combined to favour him.

He shook hands with a few pals and laughed when the Shanty Boss, a man of proved courage himself, gave him a word of final advice, and added to it—a strange phrase in such company—"may God bring you safe through it."

Only one man can break a jam. Others can help from the shore, or from whatever vantage-points there may be; but one mind, and above all *one man's weight*, must decide the awful course of the loosening mass.

Before starting, he crossed over to speak to his friend Hank Davis. "You know why I'm doing this, Hank," he said in his Canuck French. "It's simply to show *her* that I've got back my nerve and courage, and that I'm not the loafer I used to be. If anything happens, give her my wages, and tell her why I did it. See?"

Hank gave him a characteristic blessing, and Garnier looked over his shoulder and laughed as he said, "I'll get through all right; don't you worry yourself."

The next moment he was gone. A crowd of silent men stood in the shadow of the great trees and watched. Garnier carried his pole easily and approached the jam from the rear, springing from log to log where they lay tightly packed and ever rising on the swollen river. A strange silence descended upon the crowd in the wood. The roar of the water became a thing apart. Every eye was fixed on Garnier— a tall, sinewy figure, passing lightly through the spray from log to log; springing with unerring judgment across foaming gaps; leaving one log just before it turned; landing on another, and leaping from it again to a third a second before it was sucked endways, first rising like a pillar, into a vortex of whirling waves.

He soon reached the summit of the barrier and began to use his spiked pole with a will. He thrust here and there; dislodged a log on his left, helped forward one on his right, and toppled over another in front of him. The judgment of the man never failed. It became an awful fight between the river and the logs, seeking to destroy him, and the skilful courageous woodsman—a fight in which the slightest miscalculation, or false distribution of a few pounds' weight, meant a terrible death.

"If anyone can do it, he can," murmured the boss, cold-blooded, and without excitement, leaning against a tree on the shore and smoking his pipe. It was not the first time he had seen jams broken by a long way.

"Oh, I guess he'll fix it all right," said another, a personal pal of Garnier's, and whose eyes never left the leaping, shifting figure out in mid-stream.

Just then there rose on the air a terrifying sound. It seemed to come from under the ground, and the very earth shook. The next minute the whole solid barrier of logs melted away like summer mist before the men's eyes. The jam was broken. It collapsed with an appalling shout of sound. Water spurted up in a hundred fountains to the sky. Whole groups of logs rose on end, wet and shaking, and fell crashing against one another. Then a mighty wave rolled down the river from the wall of water accumulated behind the jam, and the entire mass slid in a broad seething of water past the watching crowd of men and into a bank of enveloping spray beyond.

On the crest of this great wave, erect and calm amid the leaping logs, stood the figure of Garnier. He still held his pole as he swept past them and vanished into the fierce confusion of mist and foam below. A second later, at the bottom of the fall, the logs could be heard crashing and smashing together with a fiendish uproar in the swirling waters. The men turned to look at one another, and the Shanty Boss looked *up* the river instead of *down.*

A second later, and the men were flying down the banks to gather the logs into a new boom, and, if possible, to find the body of Jean Garnier. It would, of course, be in pieces, perhaps even unrecognisable; but still they could put him in a decent grave, with a wooden cross and the date, and the Shanty Boss could mumble a prayer over it while they stood round and bared their heads beneath "the murmuring pines and the hemlocks."

But, as they were searching the shore a quarter of a mile or so lower down, a faint voice was heard calling across the river—

"I'm all right, boys; but get a hustle on and come over to me."

It seemed incredible, but, following the direction of the sound with their eyes, they saw a man's figure crouching on the shore just beyond the reach of the still swollen river. It was indeed Garnier. His face was scarcely recognisable as a human countenance, and both his arms turned out to be broken, but apparently he had escaped serious internal injury in the most marvellous manner.

No one ever knew how he escaped, least of all the man himself.

"I saw you all standing under the trees like a streak of black," he said, "as I was carried past, and the next minute a tree jumped up an' caught me such a smack in the face that I thought the whole of my skull had gone off with it. That's all I remember."

But the chance wave that swept him into safety on the shore had also brought him back a helpless, disfigured man for life. No girl would care to marry him now, and the courage of this rough woodsman was again shown—even if it was mistaken courage—in his decision to live for the rest of his broken life in the woods, and to show himself no more in the village of Ste. Rose, a burden to his parents and a perpetual source of horror and regret to the girl he loved.

"Take her my wages, Hank, old pard, and tell her—tell her I broke the jam. You know—she'll understand. There's lots of fellers buried up in these woods," he added, "that's broke jams before me."

"It'll break her heart as well," Hank observed. "Lucie's almighty fond of you." But Garnier held to his decision, and those among the men who were returning to Ste. Rose agreed to conceal the fact that he was alive.

The arms were set in due course by the camp doctor, the wounds in the face healed gradually; and two months later the man entered into a partnership with a fishing Indian of those parts, and prepared to spend the rest of his life in the woods.

When Hank returned to Ste. Rose he went at once to fulfil the promise he had given to his comrade. It was an odious and difficult task. Moreover, it was not the whole truth. His long face betrayed the nature of his message.

"What is your news of him?" she asked quickly. "Tell me at once. Oh! is it bad? You look so dreadful—?"

"He broke the jam," Hank said huskily, for he did not understand roundabout methods of breaking bad news. Quickest was best, he thought. "And, there—I never seen any man do a grander thing. He was the bravest chap of the lot, and that cool over it all—"

"Is he—gone then?" she asked in a breathless whisper and with so awful a face that Hank cut short the description he had imagined she would like, and hurried on to his message and the money.

"Here's his wages I was to give you," he said, with the feeling that he was doing a most shameful thing, "and I was particular to tell you that he did it so you might know he was a man again, and—" But Hank's sentence remained unfinished, for the girl had fallen in a faint at his feet. He picked her up and laid her on the sofa, and in the time he had to collect himself before she came round again he made up his mind, after his own method, that his promise to Jean was a bad one, and that he was blessed if he'd keep it.

"He ain't gone at all only you don't give a feller time to answer," he said as soon as she opened her eyes. "He's only a bit mussed up, that's all. He's waiting for you, if you'll only listen instead of faintin'."

"But I made him do it," she murmured despairingly. "I sent him away. He did it for me. Oh! take me to him at once, or bring him to me. I *must* see him. I can't live without him."

Bit by bit the girl learned the exact truth, and the story so set her heart aflame that there was nothing for it but to go after her lover into the woods and seek till she found him. He had originally gone up with the camp in November. He broke the jam in April, and the news was brought to her in the end of July. It was thus nine months since she had seen him, and her heart ached unspeakably.

A week or so after Hank's revelation he started up into the woods again to search for Garnier and the Indian. Lucie and her brother went with him. But the Indian kept a moving camp, and it was some time before they got upon his tracks.

"It was well on in September," said Hank, as he finished the story, "when we found the trail of the fishing Indian and put up with his old squaw. Garnier and the Indian were out on a fishing boat, and wouldn't be back for a week or more. One evening at sunset, as we were sitting on the shore parin' cedar ribs for the canoes, we heard some one singing far out on the lake, and there, sure 'nough, was the big fishing-canoe with Pete, the Indian, in the bows, and Garnier, in the stern seat, steering. His arms were as good as ever, and his voice—well it kinder made the tears rise in yer throat somehow to hear it.

"And Lucie, she jumped up and couldn't settle herself to doin' anything except runnin' along the shore and calling to him across the water. I think old Pete had an idea his wigwam was being attacked, because he stopped paddling one time, and made as if he was sheerin' round to land somewhar else. But at last they come close enough to see who it was, and then—well, I never seen a canoe nearer upsettin' in the whole of my life. For Garnier, he stood up an' stared, and then sot down again, and then got up again, just as if he was on shore instead of in a bark canoe loaded with fish.

"Then, when they landed, Lucie's brother an' I, we took old Pete, the Indian, aside to show him something in the bush. He wasn't exactly lookin' for it, that's true, but then we wanted him out of the way whar he couldn't stare in that foolish Indian way. An' they two—well, Pete's old squaw followed us out also—and they two had the dirty old wigwam all to themselves to do their fist-shakin' in.

"Yes, an' it all happened not over a mile away from this here very spot whar we're now settin'," he observed, looking round into the woods where the silence and the shadows were growing every minute deeper, "an' I do b'lieve the old Indian's still lamenting his luck at losing such a good, honest fishing partner to this very day."

The Empty House

Certain houses, like certain persons, manage somehow to proclaim at once their character for evil. In the case of the latter, no particular feature need betray them; they may boast an open countenance and an ingenuous smile; and yet a little of their company leaves the unalterable conviction that there is something radically amiss with their being: that they are evil. Willy nilly, they seem to communicate an atmosphere of secret and wicked thoughts which makes those in their immediate neighbourhood shrink from them as from a thing diseased.

And, perhaps, with houses the same principle is operative, and it is the aroma of evil deeds committed under a particular roof, long after the actual doers have passed away, that makes the gooseflesh come and the hair rise. Something of the original passion of the evil-doer, and of the horror felt by his victim, enters the heart of the innocent watcher, and he becomes suddenly conscious of tingling nerves, creeping skin, and a chilling of the blood. He is terror-stricken without apparent cause.

There was manifestly nothing in the external appearance of this particular house to bear out the tales of the horror that was said to reign within. It was neither lonely nor unkempt. It stood, crowded into a corner of the square, and looked exactly like the houses on either side of it. It had the same number of windows as its neighbours; the same balcony overlooking the gardens; the same white steps leading up to the heavy black front door; and, in the rear, there was the same narrow strip of green, with neat box borders, running up to the wall that divided it from the backs of the adjoining houses. Apparently, too, the number of chimney pots on the roof was the same; the breadth and angle of the eaves; and even the height of the dirty area railings.

And yet this house in the square, that seemed precisely similar to its fifty ugly neighbours, was as a matter of fact entirely different—horribly different.

Wherein lay this marked, invisible difference is impossible to say. It cannot be ascribed wholly to the imagination, because persons who had spent some time in the house, knowing nothing of the facts, had declared positively that certain rooms were so disagreeable they would rather die than enter them again, and that the atmosphere of the whole house produced in them symptoms of a genuine terror; while the series of innocent tenants who had tried to live in it and been forced to decamp at the shortest possible notice, was indeed little less than a scandal in the town.

When Shorthouse arrived to pay a "week-end" visit to his Aunt Julia in her little house on the seafront at the other end of the town, he found her charged to the brim with mystery and excitement. He had only received her telegram that morning, and he had come anticipating boredom; but the moment he touched her hand and kissed her apple-skin wrinkled cheek, he caught the first wave of her electrical condition. The impression deepened when he learned that there were to be no other visitors, and that he had been telegraphed for with a very special object.

Something was in the wind, and the "something" would doubtless bear fruit; for this elderly spinster aunt, with a mania for psychical research, had brains as well as will power, and by hook or by crook she usually managed to accomplish her ends. The revelation was made soon after tea, when she sidled close up to him as they paced slowly along the sea-front in the dusk.

"I've got the keys," she announced in a delighted, yet half awesome voice. "Got them till Monday!"

"The keys of the bathing-machine, or—?" he asked innocently, looking from the sea to the town. Nothing brought her so quickly to the point as feigning stupidity.

"Neither," she whispered. "I've got the keys of the haunted house in the square—and I'm going there to-night."

Shorthouse was conscious of the slightest possible tremor down his back. He dropped his teasing tone. Something in her voice and manner thrilled him. She was in earnest.

"But you can't go alone—" he began.

"That's why I wired for you," she said with decision.

He turned to look at her. The ugly, lined, enigmatical face was alive with excitement. There was the glow of genuine enthusiasm round it like a halo. The eyes shone. He caught another wave of her excitement, and a second tremor, more marked than the first, accompanied it.

"Thanks, Aunt Julia," he said politely; "thanks awfully."

"I should not dare to go quite alone," she went on, raising her voice; "but with you I should enjoy it immensely. You're afraid of nothing, I know."

"Thanks so much," he said again. "Er—is anything likely to happen?"

"A great deal *has* happened," she whispered, "though it's been most cleverly hushed up. Three tenants have come and gone in the last few months, and the house is said to be empty for good now."

In spite of himself Shorthouse became interested. His aunt was so very much in earnest.

"The house is very old indeed," she went on, "and the story—an unpleasant one—dates a long way back. It has to do with a murder committed by a jealous stableman who had some affair with a servant in the house. One night he managed to secrete himself in the cellar, and when everyone was asleep, he crept upstairs to the servants' quarters, chased the girl down to the next landing, and before anyone could come to the rescue threw her bodily over the banisters into the hall below."

"And the stableman—?"

"Was caught, I believe, and hanged for murder; but it all happened a century ago, and I've not been able to get more details of the story."

Shorthouse now felt his interest thoroughly aroused; but, though he was not particularly nervous for himself, he hesitated a little on his aunt's account.

"On one condition," he said at length.

"Nothing will prevent my going," she said firmly; "but I may as well hear your condition."

"That you guarantee your power of self-control if anything really horrible happens. I mean—that you are sure you won't get too frightened."

"Jim," she said scornfully, "I'm not young, I know, nor are my nerves; but *with you* I should be afraid of nothing in the world!"

This, of course, settled it, for Shorthouse had no pretensions to being other than a very ordinary young man, and an appeal to his vanity was irresistible. He agreed to go.

Instinctively, by a sort of sub-conscious preparation, he kept himself and his forces well in hand the whole evening, compelling an accumulative reserve of control by that nameless inward process of gradually putting all the emotions away and turning the key upon them—a process difficult to describe, but wonderfully effective, as all men who have lived through severe trials of the inner man well understand. Later, it stood him in good stead.

But it was not until half-past ten, when they stood in the hall, well in the glare of friendly lamps and still surrounded by comforting human influences, that he had to make the first call upon this store of collected strength. For, once the door was closed, and he saw the deserted silent street stretching away white in the moonlight before them, it came to him clearly that the real test that night would be in dealing with *two fears* instead of one. He would have to carry his aunt's fear as well as his own. And, as he glanced down at her sphinx-like countenance and realised that it might assume no pleasant aspect in a rush of real terror, he felt satisfied with only one thing in the whole adventure—that he had confidence in his own will and power to stand against any shock that might come.

Slowly they walked along the empty streets of the town; a bright autumn moon silvered the roofs, casting deep shadows; there was no breath of wind; and the trees in the formal gardens by the sea-front watched them silently as they passed along. To his aunt's occasional remarks Shorthouse made no reply, realising that she was simply surrounding herself with mental buffers—saying ordinary things to prevent herself thinking of extra-ordinary things. Few windows showed lights, and from scarcely a single chimney came smoke or sparks. Shorthouse had already begun to notice everything, even the smallest details. Presently they stopped at the street corner and looked up at the name on the side of the house full in the moonlight, and with one accord, but without remark, turned into the square and crossed over to the side of it that lay in shadow.

"The number of the house is thirteen," whispered a voice at his side; and neither of them made the obvious reference, but passed across the broad sheet of moonlight and began to march up the pavement in silence.

It was about half-way up the square that Shorthouse felt an arm slipped quietly but significantly into his own, and knew then that their adventure had begun in earnest, and that his companion was already yielding imperceptibly to the influences against them. She needed support.

A few minutes later they stopped before a tall, narrow house that rose before them into the night, ugly in shape and painted a dingy white. Shutterless windows, without blinds, stared down upon them, shining here and there in the moonlight. There were weather streaks in the wall and cracks in the paint, and the balcony bulged out from the first floor a little unnaturally. But, beyond this generally forlorn appearance of an unoccupied house, there was nothing at first sight to single out this particular mansion for the evil character it had most certainly acquired.

Taking a look over their shoulders to make sure they had not been followed, they went boldly up the steps and stood against the huge black door that fronted them forbiddingly. But the first wave of nervousness was now upon them, and Shorthouse fumbled a long time with the key before he could fit it into the lock at all. For a moment, if truth were told, they both hoped it would not open, for they were a prey to various unpleasant emotions as they stood there on the threshold of their ghostly adventure. Shorthouse, shuffling with the key and hampered by the steady weight on his arm, certainly felt the solemnity of the moment. It was as if the whole world—for all experience seemed at that instant concentrated in his own consciousness—were listening to the grating noise of that key. A stray puff of wind wandering down the empty street woke a momentary rustling in the trees behind them, but otherwise this rattling of the key was the only sound audible; and at last it turned in the lock and the heavy door swung open and revealed a yawning gulf of darkness beyond.

With a last glance at the moonlit square, they passed quickly in, and the door slammed behind them with a roar that echoed prodigiously through empty halls and passages. But, instantly, with the echoes, another sound made itself heard, and Aunt Julia leaned suddenly so heavily upon him that he had to take a step backwards to save himself from falling.

A man had coughed close beside them—so close that it seemed they must have been actually by his side in the darkness.

With the possibility of practical jokes in his mind, Shorthouse at once swung his heavy stick in the direction of the sound; but it met nothing more solid than air. He heard his aunt give a little gasp beside him.

"There's someone here," she whispered; "I heard him."

"Be quiet!" he said sternly. "It was nothing but the noise of the front door."

"Oh! get a light—quick!" she added, as her nephew, fumbling with a box of matches, opened it upside down and let them all fall with a rattle on to the stone floor.

The sound, however, was not repeated; and there was no evidence of retreating footsteps. In another minute they had a candle burning, using an empty end of a cigar case as a holder; and when the first flare had died down he held the impromptu lamp aloft and surveyed the scene. And it was dreary enough in all conscience, for there is nothing more desolate in all the abodes of men than an unfurnished house dimly lit, silent, and forsaken, and yet tenanted by rumour with the memories of evil and violent histories.

They were standing in a wide hall-way; on their left was the open door of a spacious dining-room, and in front the hall ran, ever narrowing, into a long, dark passage that led apparently to the top of the kitchen stairs. The broad uncarpeted staircase rose in a sweep before them, everywhere draped in shadows, except for a single spot about half-way up where the moonlight came in through the window and fell on a bright patch on the boards. This shaft of light shed a faint radiance above and below it, lending to the objects within its reach a misty outline that was infinitely more suggestive and ghostly than complete darkness. Filtered moonlight always seems to paint faces on the surrounding gloom, and as Shorthouse peered up into the well of darkness and thought of the countless empty rooms and passages in the upper part of the old house, he caught himself longing again for the safety of the moonlit square, or the cosy, bright drawing-room they had left an hour before. Then realising that these thoughts were dangerous, he thrust them away again and summoned all his energy for concentration on the present.

"Aunt Julia," he said aloud, severely, "we must now go through the house from top to bottom and make a thorough search."

The echoes of his voice died away slowly all over the building, and in the intense silence that followed he turned to look at her. In the candle-light he saw that her face was already ghastly pale; but she dropped his arm for a moment and said in a whisper, stepping close in front of him—

"I agree. We must be sure there's no one hiding. That's the first thing."

She spoke with evident effort, and he looked at her with admiration.

"You feel quite sure of yourself? It's not too late—"

"I think so," she whispered, her eyes shifting nervously toward the shadows behind. "Quite sure, only one thing—"

"What's that?"

"You must never leave me alone for an instant."

"As long as you understand that any sound or appearance must be investigated at once, for to hesitate means to admit fear. That is fatal."

"Agreed," she said, a little shakily, after a moment's hesitation. "I'll try—"

Arm in arm, Shorthouse holding the dripping candle and the stick, while his aunt carried the cloak over her shoulders, figures of utter comedy to all but themselves, they began a systematic search.

Stealthily, walking on tiptoe and shading the candle lest it should betray their presence through the shutterless windows, they went first into the big dining-room. There was not a stick of furniture to be seen. Bare walls, ugly mantelpieces, and empty grates stared at them. Everything, they felt, resented their intrusion, watching them, as it were, with veiled eyes; whispers followed them; shadows flitted noiselessly to right and left; something seemed ever at their back, watching, waiting an opportunity to do them injury. There was the inevitable sense that operations which went on when the room was empty had been temporarily suspended till they were well out of the way again. The whole dark interior of the old building seemed to become a malignant Presence that rose up, warning them to desist and mind their own business; every moment the strain on the nerves increased.

Out of the gloomy dining-room they passed through large folding doors into a sort of library or smoking-room, wrapt equally in silence, darkness, and dust; and from this they regained the hall near the top of the back stairs.

Here a pitch black tunnel opened before them into the lower regions, and—it must be confessed—they hesitated. But only for a minute. With the worst of the night still to come it was essential to turn from nothing. Aunt Julia stumbled at the top step of the dark descent, ill lit by the flickering candle, and even Shorthouse felt at least half the decision go out of his legs.

"Come on!" he said peremptorily, and his voice ran on and lost itself in the dark, empty spaces below.

"I'm coming," she faltered, catching his arm with unnecessary violence.

They went a little unsteadily down the stone steps, a cold, damp air meeting them in the face, close and malodorous. The kitchen, into which the stairs led along a narrow passage, was large, with a lofty ceiling. Several doors opened out of it—some into cupboards with empty jars still standing on the shelves, and others into horrible little ghostly back offices, each colder and less inviting than the last. Black beetles scurried over the floor, and once, when they knocked against a deal table standing in a corner, something about the size of a cat jumped down with a rush and fled, scampering across the stone floor into the darkness. Everywhere there was a sense of recent occupation, an impression of sadness and gloom.

Leaving the main kitchen, they next went towards the scullery. The door was standing ajar, and as they pushed it open to its full extent Aunt Julia uttered a piercing scream, which she instantly tried to stifle by placing her hand over her mouth. For a second Shorthouse stood stock-still, catching his breath. He felt as if his spine had suddenly become hollow and someone had filled it with particles of ice.

Facing them, directly in their way between the doorposts, stood the figure of a woman. She had dishevelled hair and wildly staring eyes, and her face was terrified and white as death.

She stood there motionless for the space of a single second. Then the candle flickered and she was gone—gone utterly—and the door framed nothing but empty darkness.

"Only the beastly jumping candle-light," he said quickly, in a voice that sounded like some one else's and was only half under control. "Come on, aunt. There's nothing there."

He dragged her forward. With a clattering of feet and a great appearance of boldness they went on, but over his body the skin moved as if crawling ants covered it, and he knew by the weight on his arm that he was supplying the force of locomotion for two. The scullery was cold, bare, and empty; more like a large prison cell than anything else. They went round it, tried the door into the yard, and the windows, but found them all fastened securely. His aunt moved beside him like a person in a dream. Her eyes were tightly shut, and she seemed merely to follow the pressure of his arm. Her courage filled him with amazement. At the same time he noticed that a certain odd change had come over her face, a change which somehow evaded his power of analysis.

"There's nothing here, aunty," he repeated aloud quickly. "Let's go upstairs and see the rest of the house. Then we'll choose a room to wait up in."

She followed him obediently, keeping close to his side, and they locked the kitchen door behind them. It was a relief to get up again. In the hall there was more light than before, for the moon had travelled a little further down the stairs. Cautiously they began to go up into the dark vault of the upper house, the boards creaking under their weight.

On the first floor they found the large double drawing-rooms, a search of which revealed nothing. Here also was no sign of furniture or recent occupancy; nothing but dust and neglect and shadows. They opened the big folding doors between front and back drawing-rooms and then came out again to the landing and went on upstairs.

They had not gone up more than a dozen steps when they both simultaneously stopped to listen, looking into each other's eyes with

a new apprehension across the flickering candle flame. From the
room they had left hardly ten seconds before came the sound of
doors quietly closing. It was beyond all question; they heard the
booming noise that accompanies the shutting of heavy doors, followed by the sharp catching of the latch.

"We must go back and see," said Shorthouse briefly, in a low
tone, and turning to go downstairs again.

Somehow she managed to drag after him, her feet catching in her
dress, her face livid.

When they entered the front drawing-room it was plain that the
folding doors had been closed—half a minute before. Without hesitation Shorthouse opened them. He almost expected to see someone
facing him in the back room; but only darkness and cold air met him.
They went through both rooms, finding nothing unusual. They tried
in every way to make the doors close of themselves, but there was
not wind enough even to set the candle flame flickering. The doors
would not move without strong pressure. All was silent as the grave.
Undeniably the rooms were utterly empty, and the house utterly still.

"It's beginning," whispered a voice at his elbow which he hardly
recognised as his aunt's.

He nodded acquiescence, taking out his watch to note the time.
It was fifteen minutes before midnight; he made the entry of exactly
what had occurred in his notebook, setting the candle in its case upon the floor in order to do so. It took a moment or two to balance it
safely against the wall.

Aunt Julia always declared that at this moment she was not actually watching him, but had turned her head towards the inner room,
where she fancied she heard something moving; but, at any rate, both
positively agreed that there came a sound of rushing feet, heavy and
very swift—and the next instant the candle was out!

But to Shorthouse himself had come more than this, and he has
always thanked his fortunate stars that it came to him alone and not
to his aunt too. For, as he rose from the stooping position of balanc-
ing the candle, and before it was actually extinguished, a face thrust
itself forward so close to his own that he could almost have touched
it with his lips. It was a face working with passion; a man's face, dark,
with thick features, and angry, savage eyes. It belonged to a common

man, and it was evil in its ordinary normal expression, no doubt, but as he saw it, alive with intense, aggressive emotion, it was a malignant and terrible human countenance.

There was no movement of the air; nothing but the sound of rushing feet—stockinged or muffled feet; the apparition of the face; and the almost simultaneous extinguishing of the candle.

In spite of himself, Shorthouse uttered a little cry, nearly losing his balance as his aunt clung to him with her whole weight in one moment of real, uncontrollable terror. She made no sound, but simply seized him bodily. Fortunately, however, she had seen nothing, but had only heard the rushing feet, for her control returned almost at once, and he was able to disentangle himself and strike a match.

The shadows ran away on all sides before the glare, and his aunt stooped down and groped for the cigar case with the precious candle. Then they discovered that the candle had not been *blown* out at all; it had been *crushed* out. The wick was pressed down into the wax, which was flattened as if by some smooth, heavy instrument.

How his companion so quickly overcame her terror, Shorthouse never properly understood; but his admiration for her self-control increased tenfold, and at the same time served to feed his own dying flame—for which he was undeniably grateful. Equally inexplicable to him was the evidence of physical force they had just witnessed. He at once suppressed the memory of stories he had heard of "physical mediums" and their dangerous phenomena; for if these were true, and either his aunt or himself was unwittingly a physical medium, it meant that they were simply aiding to focus the forces of a haunted house already charged to the brim. It was like walking with unprotected lamps among uncovered stores of gunpowder.

So, with as little reflection as possible, he simply relit the candle and went up to the next floor. The arm in his trembled, it is true, and his own tread was often uncertain, but they went on with thoroughness, and after a search revealing nothing they climbed the last flight of stairs to the top floor of all.

Here they found a perfect nest of small servants' rooms, with broken pieces of furniture, dirty cane-bottomed chairs, chests of drawers, cracked mirrors, and decrepit bedsteads. The rooms had low sloping ceilings already hung here and there with cobwebs, small windows, and badly plastered walls—a depressing and dismal region which they were glad to leave behind.

It was on the stroke of midnight when they entered a small room on the third floor, close to the top of the stairs, and arranged to make themselves comfortable for the remainder of their adventure. It was absolutely bare, and was said to be the room—then used as a clothes closet—into which the infuriated groom had chased his victim and finally caught her. Outside, across the narrow landing, began the stairs leading up to the floor above, and the servants' quarters where they had just searched.

In spite of the chilliness of the night there was something in the air of this room that cried for an open window. But there was more than this. Shorthouse could only describe it by saying that he felt less master of himself here than in any other part of the house. There was something that acted directly on the nerves, tiring the resolution, en-feebling the will. He was conscious of this result before he had been in the room five minutes, and it was in the short time they stayed there that he suffered the wholesale depletion of his vital forces, which was, for himself, the chief horror of the whole experience.

They put the candle on the floor of the cupboard, leaving the door a few inches ajar, so that there was no glare to confuse the eyes, and no shadow to shift about on walls and ceiling. Then they spread the cloak on the floor and sat down to wait, with their backs against the wall.

Shorthouse was within two feet of the door on to the landing; his position commanded a good view of the main staircase leading down into the darkness, and also of the beginning of the servants' stairs go-ing to the floor above; the heavy stick lay beside him within easy reach.

The moon was now high above the house. Through the open window they could see the comforting stars like friendly eyes watch-ing in the sky. One by one the clocks of the town struck midnight, and when the sounds died away the deep silence of a windless night fell again over everything. Only the boom of the sea, far away and lugubrious, filled the air with hollow murmurs.

Inside the house the silence became awful; awful, he thought, be-cause any minute now it might be broken by sounds portending terror. The strain of waiting told more and more severely on the nerves; they talked in whispers when they talked at all, for their voices aloud sounded queer and unnatural. A chilliness, not altogether due to the night air, invaded the room, and made them cold. The influences against them, whatever these might be, were slowly robbing them of self-confidence, and the power of decisive action; their forces were on the wane, and the possibility of real fear took on a new and terrible meaning. He began to tremble for the elderly woman by his side, whose pluck could hardly save her beyond a certain extent.

He heard the blood singing in his veins. It sometimes seemed so loud that he fancied it prevented his hearing properly certain other sounds that were beginning very faintly to make themselves audible in the depths of the house. Every time he fastened his attention on these sounds, they instantly ceased. They certainly came no nearer. Yet he could not rid himself of the idea that movement was going on somewhere in the lower regions of the house. The drawing-room floor, where the doors had been so strangely closed, seemed too near; the sounds were further off than that. He thought of the great kitchen, with the scurrying black-beetles, and of the dismal little scullery; but, somehow or other, they did not seem to come from there either. Surely they were not *outside* the house!

Then, suddenly, the truth flashed into his mind, and for the space of a minute he felt as if his blood had stopped flowing and turned to ice.

The sounds were not downstairs at all; they were *upstairs*—upstairs, somewhere among those horrid gloomy little servants' rooms with their bits of broken furniture, low ceilings, and cramped windows—upstairs where the victim had first been disturbed and stalked to her death.

And the moment he discovered where the sounds were, he began to hear them more clearly. It was the sound of feet, moving stealthily along the passage overhead, in and out among the rooms, and past the furniture.

He turned quickly to steal a glance at the motionless figure seated beside him, to note whether she had shared his discovery. The faint candle-light coming through the crack in the cupboard door, threw her strongly-marked face into vivid relief against the white of the wall. But it was something else that made him catch his breath and stare again. An extraordinary something had come into her face and seemed to spread over her features like a mask; it smoothed out the deep lines and drew the skin everywhere a little tighter so that the wrinkles disappeared; it brought into the face—with the sole exception of the old eyes—an appearance of youth and almost of childhood.

He stared in speechless amazement—amazement that was dangerously near to horror. It was his aunt's face indeed, but it was her face of forty years ago, the vacant innocent face of a girl. He had heard stories of that strange effect of terror which could wipe a human countenance clean of other emotions, obliterating all previous expressions; but he had never realised that it could be literally true, or could mean anything so simply horrible as what he now saw. For the dreadful signature of overmastering fear was written plainly in that utter vacancy of the girlish face beside him; and when, feeling his intense gaze, she turned to look at him, he instinctively closed his eyes tightly to shut out the sight.

Yet, when he turned a minute later, his feelings well in hand, he saw to his intense relief another expression; his aunt was smiling, and though the face was deathly white, the awful veil had lifted and the normal look was returning.

"Anything wrong?" was all he could think of to say at the moment. And the answer was eloquent, coming from such a woman.

"I feel cold—and a little frightened," she whispered.

He offered to close the window, but she seized hold of him and begged him not to leave her side even for an instant.

"It's upstairs, I know," she whispered, with an odd half laugh; "but I can't possibly go up."

But Shorthouse thought otherwise, knowing that in action lay their best hope of self-control.

He took the brandy flask and poured out a glass of neat spirit, stiff enough to help anybody over anything. She swallowed it with a little shiver. His only idea now was to get out of the house before her collapse became inevitable; but this could not safely be done by turning tail and running from the enemy. Inaction was no longer possible; every minute he was growing less master of himself, and desperate, aggressive measures were imperative without further delay. Moreover, the action must be taken *towards* the enemy, not away from it; the climax, if necessary and unavoidable, would have to be faced boldly. He could do it now; but in ten minutes he might not have the force left to act for himself, much less for both!

Upstairs, the sounds were meanwhile becoming louder and closer, accompanied by occasional creaking of the boards. Some one was moving stealthily about, stumbling now and then awkwardly against the furniture.

Waiting a few moments to allow the tremendous dose of spirits to produce its effect, and knowing this would last but a short time under the circumstances, Shorthouse then quietly got on his feet, saying in a determined voice—

"Now, Aunt Julia, we'll go upstairs and find out what all this noise is about. You must come too. It's what we agreed."

He picked up his stick and went to the cupboard for the candle. A limp form rose shakily beside him breathing hard, and he heard a voice say very faintly something about being "ready to come." The woman's courage amazed him; it was so much greater than his own; and, as they advanced, holding aloft the dripping candle, some subtle force exhaled from this trembling, white-faced old woman at his side that was the true source of his inspiration. It held something really great that shamed him and gave him the support without which he would have proved far less equal to the occasion.

They crossed the dark landing, avoiding with their eyes the deep black space over the banisters. Then they began to mount the narrow staircase to meet the sounds which, minute by minute, grew louder and nearer. About half-way up the stairs Aunt Julia stumbled and Shorthouse turned to catch her by the arm, and just at that moment there came a terrific crash in the servants' corridor overhead. It was instantly followed by a shrill, agonised scream that was a cry of terror and a cry for help melted into one.

Before they could move aside, or go down a single step, some one came rushing along the passage overhead, blundering horribly, racing madly, at full speed, three steps at a time, down the very staircase where they stood. The steps were light and uncertain; but close behind them sounded the heavier tread of another person, and the staircase seemed to shake.

Shorthouse and his companion just had time to flatten themselves against the wall when the jumble of flying steps was upon them, and two persons, with the slightest possible interval between them, dashed past at full speed. It was a perfect whirlwind of sound breaking in upon the midnight silence of the empty building.

The two runners, pursuer and pursued, had passed clean through them where they stood, and already with a thud the boards below had received first one, then the other. Yet they had seen absolutely nothing—not a hand, or arm, or face, or even a shred of flying clothing.

There came a second's pause. Then the first one, the lighter of the two, obviously the pursued one, ran with uncertain footsteps into the little room which Shorthouse and his aunt had just left. The heavier one followed. There was a sound of scuffling, gasping, and smothered screaming; and then out on to the landing came the step—of a single person *treading weightily.*

A dead silence followed for the space of half a minute, and then was heard a rushing sound through the air. It was followed by a dull, crashing thud in the depths of the house below—on the stone floor of the hall.

Utter silence reigned after. Nothing moved. The flame of the candle was steady. It had been steady the whole time, and the air had been undisturbed by any movement whatsoever. Palsied with terror, Aunt Julia, without waiting for her companion, began fumbling her way downstairs; she was crying gently to herself, and when Shorthouse put his arm round her and half carried her he felt that she was trembling like a leaf. He went into the little room and picked up the cloak from the floor, and, arm in arm, walking very slowly, without speaking a word or looking once behind them, they marched down the three flights into the hall.

In the hall they saw nothing, but the whole way down the stairs they were conscious that someone followed them; step by step; when they went faster IT was left behind, and when they went more slowly IT caught them up. But never once did they look behind to see; and at each turning of the staircase they lowered their eyes for fear of the following horror they might see upon the stairs above.

With trembling hands Shorthouse opened the front door, and they walked out into the moonlight and drew a deep breath of the cool night air blowing in from the sea.

Keeping His Promise

It was eleven o'clock at night, and young Marriott was locked into his room, cramming as hard as he could cram. He was a "Fourth Year Man" at Edinburgh University and he had been ploughed for this particular examination so often that his parents had positively declared they could no longer supply the funds to keep him there.

His rooms were cheap and dingy, but it was the lecture fees that took the money. So Marriott pulled himself together at last and definitely made up his mind that he would pass or die in the attempt, and for some weeks now he had been reading as hard as mortal man can read. He was trying to make up for lost time and money in a way that showed conclusively he did not understand the value of either. For no ordinary man—and Marriott was in every sense an ordinary man—can afford to drive the mind as he had lately been driving his, without sooner or later paying the cost.

Among the students he had few friends or acquaintances, and these few had promised not to disturb him at night, knowing he was at last reading in earnest. It was, therefore, with feelings a good deal stronger than mere surprise that he heard his door-bell ring on this particular night and realised that he was to have a visitor. Some men would simply have muffled the bell and gone on quietly with their work. But Marriott was not this sort. He was nervous. It would have bothered and pecked at his mind all night long not to know who the visitor was and what he wanted. The only thing to do, therefore, was to let him in—and out again—as quickly as possible.

The landlady went to bed at ten o'clock punctually, after which hour nothing would induce her to pretend she heard the bell, so Marriott jumped up from his books with an exclamation that augured ill for the reception of his caller, and prepared to let him in with his own hand.

157

The streets of Edinburgh town were very still at this late hour—it was late for Edinburgh—and in the quiet neighbourhood of F——Street, where Marriott lived on the third floor, scarcely a sound broke the silence. As he crossed the floor, the bell rang a second time, with unnecessary clamour, and he unlocked the door and passed into the little hallway with considerable wrath and annoyance in his heart at the insolence of the double interruption.

"The fellows all know I'm reading for this exam. Why in the world do they come to bother me at such an unearthly hour?"

The inhabitants of the building, with himself, were medical students, general students, poor Writers to the Signet, and some others whose vocations were perhaps not so obvious. The stone staircase, dimly lighted at each floor by a gas-jet that would not turn above a certain height, wound down to the level of the street with no pretence at carpet or railing. At some levels it was cleaner than at others. It depended on the landlady of the particular level.

The acoustic properties of a spiral staircase seem to be peculiar. Marriott, standing by the open door, book in hand, thought every moment the owner of the footsteps would come into view. The sound of the boots was so close and so loud that they seemed to travel disproportionately in advance of their cause. Wondering who it could be, he stood ready with all manner of sharp greetings for the man who dared thus to disturb his work. But the man did not appear. The steps sounded almost under his nose, yet no one was visible.

A sudden queer sensation of fear passed over him—a faintness and a shiver down the back. It went, however, almost as soon as it came, and he was just debating whether he would call aloud to his invisible visitor, or slam the door and return to his books, when the cause of the disturbance turned the corner very slowly and came into view.

It was a stranger. He saw a youngish man short of figure and very broad. His face was the colour of a piece of chalk and the eyes, which were very bright, had heavy lines underneath them. Though the cheeks and chin were unshaven and the general appearance unkempt, the man was evidently a gentleman, for he was well dressed and bore himself with a certain air. But, strangest of all, he wore no hat, and carried none in his hand; and although rain had been falling steadily all the evening, he appeared to have neither overcoat nor umbrella.

A hundred questions sprang up in Marriott's mind and rushed to his lips, chief among which was something like "Who in the world are you?" and "What in the name of heaven do you come to me for?" But none of these questions found time to express themselves in words, for almost at once the caller turned his head a little so that the gas light in the hall fell upon his features from a new angle. Then in a flash Marriott recognised him.

"Field! Man alive! Is it you?" he gasped.

The Fourth Year Man was not lacking in intuition, and he perceived at once that here was a case for delicate treatment. He divined, without any actual process of thought, that the catastrophe often predicted had come at last, and that this man's father had turned him out of the house. They had been at a private school together years before, and though they had hardly met once since, the news had not failed to reach him from time to time with considerable detail, for the family lived near his own and between certain of the sisters there was great intimacy. Young Field had gone wild later, he remembered hearing about it all—drink, a woman, opium, or something of the sort—he could not exactly call to mind.

"Come in," he said at once, his anger vanishing. "There's been something wrong, I can see. Come in, and tell me all about it and perhaps I can help—" He hardly knew what to say, and stammered a lot more besides. The dark side of life, and the horror of it, belonged to a world that lay remote from his own select little atmosphere of books and dreamings. But he had a man's heart for all that.

He led the way across the hall, shutting the front door carefully behind him, and noticed as he did so that the other, though certainly sober, was unsteady on his legs, and evidently much exhausted. Marriott might not be able to pass his examinations, but he at least knew the symptoms of starvation—acute starvation, unless he was much mistaken—when they stared him in the face.

"Come along," he said cheerfully, and with genuine sympathy in his voice. "I'm glad to see you. I was going to have a bite of something to eat, and you're just in time to join me."

The other made no audible reply, and shuffled so feebly with his feet that Marriott took his arm by way of support. He noticed for the first time that the clothes hung on him with pitiful looseness. The broad frame was literally hardly more than a frame. He was as thin as a skeleton. But, as he touched him, the sensation of faintness and dread returned. It only lasted a moment, and then passed off, and he ascribed it not unnaturally to the distress and shock of seeing a former friend in such a pitiful plight.

"Better let me guide you. It's shamefully dark—this hall. I'm always complaining," he said lightly, recognising by the weight upon his arm that the guidance was sorely needed, "but the old cat never does anything except promise." He led him to the sofa, wondering all the time where he had come from and how he had found out the address. It must be at least seven years since those days at the private school when they used to be such close friends.

"Now, if you'll forgive me for a minute," he said, "I'll get supper ready—such as it is. And don't bother to talk. Just take it easy on the sofa. I see you're dead tired. You can tell me about it afterwards, and we'll make plans."

The other sat down on the edge of the sofa and stared in silence, while Marriott got out the brown loaf, scones, and huge pot of marmalade that Edinburgh students always keep in their cupboards. His eyes shone with a brightness that suggested drugs, Marriott thought, stealing a glance at him from behind the cupboard door. He did not like yet to take a full square look. The fellow was in a bad way, and it would have been so like an examination to stare and wait for explanations. Besides, he was evidently almost too exhausted to speak. So, for reasons of delicacy—and for another reason as well which he could not exactly formulate to himself—he let his visitor rest apparently unnoticed, while he busied himself with the supper. He lit the spirit lamp to make cocoa, and when the water was boiling he drew up the table with the good things to the sofa, so that Field need not have even the trouble of moving to a chair.

"Now, let's tuck in," he said, "and afterwards we'll have a pipe and a chat. I'm reading for an exam, you know, and I always have something about this time. It's jolly to have a companion."

He looked up and caught his guest's eyes directed straight upon his own. An involuntary shudder ran through him from head to foot. The face opposite him was deadly white and wore a dreadful expression of pain and mental suffering.

"By Gad!" he said, jumping up, "I quite forgot. I've got some whisky somewhere. What an ass I am. I never touch it myself when I'm working like this."

He went to the cupboard and poured out a stiff glass which the other swallowed at a single gulp and without any water. Marriott watched him while he drank it, and at the same time noticed something else as well—Field's coat was all over dust, and on one shoulder was a bit of cobweb. It was perfectly dry; Field arrived on a soaking wet night without hat, umbrella, or overcoat, and yet perfectly dry, even dusty. Therefore he had been under cover. What did it all mean? Had he been hiding in the building? . . .

It was very strange. Yet he volunteered nothing; and Marriott had pretty well made up his mind by this time that he would not ask any questions until he had eaten and slept. Food and sleep were obviously what the poor devil needed most and first—he was pleased with his powers of ready diagnosis—and it would not be fair to press him till he had recovered a bit.

They ate their supper together while the host carried on a running one-sided conversation, chiefly about himself and his exams and his "old cat" of a landlady, so that the guest need not utter a single word unless he really wished to—which he evidently did not! But, while he toyed with his food, feeling no desire to eat, the other ate voraciously. To see a hungry man devour cold scones, stale oatcake, and brown bread laden with marmalade was a revelation to this inexperienced student who had never known what it was to be without at least three meals a day. He watched in spite of himself, wondering why the fellow did not choke in the process.

But Field seemed to be as sleepy as he was hungry. More than once his head dropped and he ceased to masticate the food in his mouth. Marriott had positively to shake him before he would go on with his meal. A stronger emotion will overcome a weaker, but this struggle between the sting of real hunger and the magical opiate of overpowering sleep was a curious sight to the student, who watched it with mingled astonishment and alarm. He had heard of the pleasure it was to feed hungry men, and watch them eat, but he had never actually witnessed it, and he had no idea it was like this. Field ate like an animal—gobbled, stuffed, gorged. Marriott forgot his reading, and began to feel something very much like a lump in his throat.

"Afraid there's been awfully little to offer you, old man," he managed to blurt out when at length the last scone had disappeared, and the rapid, one-sided meal was at an end. Field still made no reply, for he was almost asleep in his seat. He merely looked up wearily and gratefully.

"Now you must have some sleep, you know," he continued, "or you'll go to pieces. I shall be up all night reading for this blessed exam. You're more than welcome to my bed. To-morrow we'll have a late breakfast and—and see what can be done—and make plans— I'm awfully good at making plans, you know," he added with an attempt at lightness.

Field maintained his "dead sleepy" silence, but appeared to acquiesce, and the other led the way into the bedroom, apologising as he did so to this half-starved son of a baronet—whose own home was almost a palace—for the size of the room. The weary guest, however, made no pretence of thanks or politeness. He merely steadied himself on his friend's arm as he staggered across the room, and then, with all his clothes on, dropped his exhausted body on the bed. In less than a minute he was to all appearances sound asleep.

For several minutes Marriott stood in the open door and watched him; praying devoutly that he might never find himself in a like predicament, and then fell to wondering what he would do with his unbidden guest on the morrow. But he did not stop long to think, for the call of his books was imperative, and happen what might, he must see to it that he passed that examination.

Having again locked the door into the hall, he sat down to his books and resumed his notes on *materia medica* where he had left off when the bell rang. But it was difficult for some time to concentrate his mind on the subject. His thoughts kept wandering to the picture of that white-faced, strange-eyed fellow, starved and dirty, lying in his clothes and boots on the bed. He recalled their schooldays together before they had drifted apart, and how they had vowed eternal friendship—and all the rest of it. And now! What horrible straits to be in. How could any man let the love of dissipation take such hold upon him?

But one of their vows together Marriott, it seemed, had completely forgotten. Just now, at any rate, it lay too far in the background of his memory to be recalled.

Through the half-open door—the bedroom led out of the sitting-room and had no other door—came the sound of deep, long-drawn breathing, the regular, steady breathing of a tired man, so tired that, even to listen to it made Marriott almost want to go to sleep himself.

"He needed it," reflected the student, "and perhaps it came only just in time!"

Perhaps so; for outside the bitter wind from across the Forth howled cruelly and drove the rain in cold streams against the window-panes, and down the deserted streets. Long before Marriott settled down again properly to his reading, he heard distantly, as it were, through the sentences of the book, the heavy, deep breathing of the sleeper in the next room.

A couple of hours later, when he yawned and changed his books, he still heard the breathing, and went cautiously up to the door to look round.

At first the darkness of the room must have deceived him, or else his eyes were confused and dazzled by the recent glare of the reading lamp. For a minute or two he could make out nothing at all but dark lumps of furniture, the mass of the chest of drawers by the wall, and the white patch where his bath stood in the centre of the floor.

Then the bed came slowly into view. And on it he saw the outline of the sleeping body gradually take shape before his eyes, growing up strangely into the darkness, till it stood out in marked relief—the long black form against the white counterpane.

He could hardly help smiling. Field had not moved an inch. He watched him a moment or two and then returned to his books. The night was full of the singing voices of the wind and rain. There was no sound of traffic; no hansoms clattered over the cobbles, and it was still too early for the milk carts. He worked on steadily and conscientiously, only stopping now and again to change a book, or to sip some of the poisonous stuff that kept him awake and made his brain so active, and on these occasions Field's breathing was always distinctly audible in the room. Outside, the storm continued to howl, but inside the house all was stillness. The shade of the reading lamp threw all the light upon the littered table, leaving the other end of the room in comparative darkness. The bedroom door was exactly opposite him where he sat. There was nothing to disturb the worker, nothing but an occasional rush of wind against the windows, and a slight pain in his arm.

This pain, however, which he was unable to account for, grew once or twice very acute. It bothered him; and he tried to remember how, and when, he could have bruised himself so severely, but without success.

At length the page before him turned from yellow to grey, and there were sounds of wheels in the street below. It was four o'clock. Marriott leaned back and yawned prodigiously. Then he drew back the curtains. The storm had subsided and the Castle Rock was shrouded in mist. With another yawn he turned away from the dreary outlook and prepared to sleep the remaining four hours till breakfast on the sofa. Field was still breathing heavily in the next room, and he first tiptoed across the floor to take another look at him.

Peering cautiously round the half-opened door his first glance fell upon the bed now plainly discernible in the grey light of morning. He stared hard. Then he rubbed his eyes. Then he rubbed his eyes again and thrust his head farther round the edge of the door. With fixed eyes he stared harder still, and harder.

But it made no difference at all. He was staring into an empty room.

The sensation of fear he had felt when Field first appeared upon the scene returned suddenly, but with much greater force. He became conscious, too, that his left arm was throbbing violently and causing him great pain. He stood wondering, and staring, and trying to collect his thoughts. He was trembling from head to foot.

By a great effort of the will he left the support of the door and walked forward boldly into the room.

There, upon the bed, was the impress of a body, where Field had lain and slept. There was the mark of the head on the pillow, and the slight indentation at the foot of the bed where the boots had rested on the counterpane. And there, plainer than ever—for he was closer to it—was *the breathing!*

Marriott tried to pull himself together. With a great effort he found his voice and called his friend aloud by name!

"Field! Is that you? Where are you?"

There was no reply; but the breathing continued without interruption, coming directly from the bed. His voice had such an unfamiliar sound that Marriott did not care to repeat his questions, but he went down on his knees and examined the bed above and below, pulling the mattress off finally, and taking the coverings away separately one by one. But though the sounds continued there was no visible sign of Field, nor was there any space in which a human being, however small, could have concealed itself. He pulled the bed out from the wall, but the sound *stayed where it was.* It did not move with the bed.

Marriott, finding self-control a little difficult in his weary condition, at once set about a thorough search of the room. He went through the cupboard, the chest of drawers, the little alcove where the clothes hung—everything. But there was no sign of any one. The small window near the ceiling was closed; and, anyhow, was not large enough to let a cat pass. The sitting-room door was locked on the inside; he could not have got out that way. Curious thoughts began to trouble Marriott's mind, bringing in their train unwelcome sensations. He grew more and more excited; he searched the bed again till it resembled the scene of a pillow fight; he searched both rooms, knowing all the time it was useless,—and then he searched again. A cold perspiration broke out all over his body; and the sound of heavy breathing, all this time, never ceased to come from the corner where Field had lain down to sleep.

Then he tried something else. He pushed the bed back exactly into its original position—and himself lay down upon it just where his guest had lain. But the same instant he sprang up again in a single bound. The breathing was close beside him, almost on his cheek, and between him and the wall! Not even a child could have squeezed into the space.

He went back into his sitting-room, opened the windows, welcoming all the light and air possible, and tried to think the whole matter over quietly and clearly. Men who read too hard, and slept too little, he knew were sometimes troubled with very vivid hallucinations. Again he calmly reviewed every incident of the night; his accurate sensations; the vivid details; the emotions stirred in him; the dreadful feast—no single hallucination could ever combine all these and cover so long a period of time. But with less satisfaction he thought of the recurring faintness, and curious sense of horror that had once or twice come over him, and then of the violent pains in his arm. These were quite unaccountable.

Moreover, now that he began to analyse and examine, there was one other thing that fell upon him like a sudden revelation: *During the whole time Field had not actually uttered a single word!* Yet, as though in mockery upon his reflections, there came ever from that inner room the sound of the breathing, long-drawn, deep, and regular. The thing was incredible. It was absurd.

Haunted by visions of brain fever and insanity, Marriott put on his cap and macintosh and left the house. The morning air on Arthur's Seat would blow the cobwebs from his brain; the scent of the heather, and above all, the sight of the sea. He roamed over the wet slopes above Holyrood for a couple of hours, and did not return until the exercise had shaken some of the horror out of his bones, and given him a ravening appetite into the bargain.

As he entered he saw that there was another man in the room, standing against the window with his back to the light. He recognised his fellow-student Greene, who was reading for the same examination.

"Read hard all night, Marriott," he said, "and thought I'd drop in here to compare notes and have some breakfast. You're out early?" he added, by way of a question. Marriott said he had a headache and a walk had helped it, and Greene nodded and said "Ah!" But when the girl had set the steaming porridge on the table and gone out again, he went on with rather a forced tone, "Didn't know you had any friends who drank, Marriott?"

This was obviously tentative, and Marriott replied drily that he did not know it either.

"Sounds just as if some chap were 'sleeping it off' in there, doesn't it, though?" persisted the other, with a nod in the direction of the bedroom, and looking curiously at his friend. The two men stared steadily at each other for several seconds, and then Marriott said earnestly—

"Then you hear it too, thank God!"

"Of course I hear it. The door's open. Sorry if I wasn't meant to."

"Oh, I don't mean that," said Marriott, lowering his voice. "But I'm awfully relieved. Let me explain. Of course, if you hear it too, then it's all right; but really it frightened me more than I can tell you. I thought I was going to have brain fever, or something, and you know what a lot depends on this exam. It always begins with sounds, or visions, or some sort of beastly hallucination, and I—"

"Rot!" ejaculated the other impatiently. "What are you talking about?"

"Now, listen to me, Greene," said Marriott, as calmly as he could, for the breathing was still plainly audible, "and I'll tell you what I mean, only don't interrupt." And thereupon he related exactly what had happened during the night, telling everything, even down to the pain in his arm. When it was over he got up from the table and crossed the room.

"You hear the breathing now plainly, don't you?" he said. Greene said he did. "Well, come with me, and we'll search the room together." The other, however, did not move from his chair.

"I've been in already," he said sheepishly; "I heard the sounds and thought it was you. The door was ajar—so I went in."

Marriott made no comment, but pushed the door open as wide as it would go. As it opened, the sound of breathing grew more and more distinct.

"*Some one* must be in there," said Greene under his breath.

"*Some one* is in there, but *where?*" said Marriott. Again he urged his friend to go in with him. But Greene refused point-blank; said he had been in once and had searched the room and there was nothing there. He would not go in again for a good deal.

They shut the door and retired into the other room to talk it all over with many pipes. Greene questioned his friend very closely, but without illuminating result, since questions cannot alter facts.

"The only thing that ought to have a proper, a logical, explanation is the pain in my arm," said Marriott, rubbing that member with an attempt at a smile. "It hurts so infernally and aches all the way up. I can't remember bruising it, though."

"Let me examine it for you," said Greene. "I'm awfully good at

bones in spite of the examiners' opinion to the contrary." It was a
relief to play the fool a bit, and Marriott took his coat off and rolled
up his sleeve.

"By George, though, I'm bleeding!" he exclaimed. "Look here!
What on earth's this?"

On the forearm, quite close to the wrist, was a thin red line.
There was a tiny drop of apparently fresh blood on it. Greene came
over and looked closely at it for some minutes. Then he sat back in
his chair, looking curiously at his friend's face.

"You've scratched yourself without knowing it," he said presently.

"There's no sign of a bruise. It must be something else that made
the arm ache."

Marriott sat very still, staring silently at his arm as though the solution of the whole mystery lay there actually written upon the skin.

"What's the matter? I see nothing very strange about a scratch,"
said Greene, in an unconvincing sort of voice. "It was your cuff links
probably. Last night in your excitement—"

But Marriott, white to the very lips, was trying to speak. The
sweat stood in great beads on his forehead. At last he leaned forward
close to his friend's face.

"Look," he said, in a low voice that shook a little. "Do you see
that red mark? I mean *underneath* what you call the scratch?"

Greene admitted he saw something or other, and Marriott wiped
the place clean with his handkerchief and told him to look again
more closely.

"Yes, I see," returned the other, lifting his head after a moment's
careful inspection. "It looks like an old scar."

"It *is* an old scar," whispered Marriott, his lips trembling. "*Now* it
all comes back to me."

"All what?" Greene fidgeted on his chair. He tried to laugh, but
without success. His friend seemed bordering on collapse.

"Hush! Be quiet, and—I'll tell you," he said. *"Field made that scar."*

For a whole minute the two men looked each other full in the
face without speaking.

"Field made that scar!" repeated Marriott at length in a louder
voice.

"Field! You mean—last night?"

"No, not last night. Years ago—at school, with his knife. And I made a scar in his arm with mine." Marriott was talking rapidly now.

"We exchanged drops of blood in each other's cuts. He put a drop into my arm and I put one into his—"

"In the name of heaven, what for?"

"It was a boys' compact. We made a sacred pledge, a bargain. I remember it all perfectly now. We had been reading some dreadful book and we swore to appear to one another—I mean, whoever died first swore to show himself to the other. And we sealed the compact with each other's blood. I remember it all so well—the hot summer afternoon in the playground, seven years ago—and one of the masters caught us and confiscated the knives—and I have never thought of it again to this day—"

"And you mean—" stammered Greene.

But Marriott made no answer. He got up and crossed the room and lay down wearily upon the sofa, hiding his face in his hands.

Greene himself was a bit non-plussed. He left his friend alone for a little while, thinking it all over again. Suddenly an idea seemed to strike him. He went over to where Marriott still lay motionless on the sofa and roused him. In any case it was better to face the matter, whether there was an explanation or not. Giving in was always the silly exit.

"I say, Marriott," he began, as the other turned his white face up to him. "There's no good being so upset about it. I mean—if it's all an hallucination we know what to do. And if it isn't—well, we know what to think, don't we?"

"I suppose so. But it frightens me horribly for some reason," returned his friend in a hushed voice. "And that poor devil—"

"But, after all, if the worst is true and—and that chap *has* kept his promise—well, he has, that's all, isn't it?"

Marriott nodded.

"There's only one thing that occurs to me," Greene went on, "and that is, are you quite sure that—that he really ate like that—I mean that he actually *ate anything at all?*" he finished, blurting out all his thought.

Marriott stared at him for a moment and then said he could easily make certain. He spoke quietly. After the main shock no lesser surprise could affect him.

"I put the things away myself," he said, "after we had finished. They are on the third shelf in that cupboard. No one's touched 'em since."

He pointed without getting up, and Greene took the hint and went over to look.

"Exactly," he said, after a brief examination; "just as I thought. It was partly hallucination, at any rate. The things haven't been touched. Come and see for yourself."

Together they examined the shelf. There was the brown loaf, the plate of stale scones, the oatcake, all untouched. Even the glass of whisky Marriott had poured out stood there with the whisky still in it.

"You were feeding—no one," said Greene. "Field ate and drank nothing. He was not there at all!"

"But the breathing?" urged the other in a low voice, staring with a dazed expression on his face.

Greene did not answer. He walked over to the bedroom, while Marriott followed him with his eyes. He opened the door, and listened. There was no need for words. The sound of deep, regular breathing came floating through the air. There was no hallucination about that, at any rate. Marriott could hear it where he stood on the other side of the room.

Greene closed the door and came back. "There's only one thing to do," he declared with decision. "Write home and find out about him, and meanwhile come and finish your reading in my rooms. I've got an extra bed."

"Agreed," returned the Fourth Year Man; "there's no hallucination about that exam; I must pass that whatever happens."

And this was what they did.

It was about a week later when Marriott got the answer from his sister. Part of it he read out to Greene—

"It is curious," she wrote, "that in your letter you should have enquired after Field. It seems a terrible thing, but you know only a short while ago Sir John's patience became exhausted, and he turned him out of the house, they say without a penny. Well, what do you think? He has killed himself. At least, it looks like suicide. Instead of leaving the house, he went down into the cellar and simply starved himself to death. . . . They're trying to suppress it, of course, but I heard it all from my maid, who got it from their footman. . . . They found the body on the 14th and the doctor said he had died about twelve hours before. . . . He was dreadfully thin. . . ."

"Then he died on the 13th," said Greene.

Marriott nodded.

"That's the very night he came to see you."

Marriott nodded again.

With Intent to Steal

To sleep in a lonely barn when the best bedrooms in the house were at our disposal, seemed, to say the least, unnecessary, and I felt that some explanation was due to our host.

But Shorthouse, I soon discovered, had seen to all that; our enterprise would be tolerated, not welcomed, for the master kept this sort of thing down with a firm hand. And then, how little I could get this man, Shorthouse, to tell me. There was much I wanted to ask and hear, but he surrounded himself with impossible barriers. It was ludicrous; he was surely asking a good deal of me, and yet he would give so little in return, and his reason—that it was for my good—may have been perfectly true, but did not bring me any comfort in its train. He gave me sops now and then, however, to keep up my curiosity, till I soon was aware that there were growing up side by side within me a genuine interest and an equally genuine fear; and something of both these is probably necessary to all real excitement.

The barn in question was some distance from the house, on the side of the stables, and I had passed it on several of my journeyings to and fro wondering at its forlorn and untarred appearance under a regime where everything was so spick and span; but it had never once occurred to me as possible that I should come to spend a night under its roof with a comparative stranger, and undergo there an experience belonging to an order of things I had always rather ridiculed and despised.

At the moment I can only partially recall the process by which Shorthouse persuaded me to lend him my company. Like myself, he was a guest in this autumn house-party, and where there were so many to chatter and to chaff, I think his taciturnity of manner had appealed to me by contrast, and that I wished to repay something of what I owed. There was, no doubt, flattery in it as well, for he was more than twice my age, a man of amazingly wide experience, an ex-

172

plorer of all the world's corners where danger lurked, and—most subtle flattery of all—by far the best shot in the whole party, our host included.

At first, however, I held out a bit.

"But surely this story you tell," I said, "has the parentage common to all such tales—a superstitious heart and an imaginative brain—and has grown now by frequent repetition into an authentic ghost story? Besides, this head gardener of half a century ago," I added, seeing that he still went on cleaning his gun in silence, "who was he, and what positive information have you about him beyond the fact that he was found hanging from the rafters, dead?"

"He was no mere head gardener, this man who passed as such," he replied without looking up, "but a fellow of splendid education who used this curious disguise for his own purposes. Part of this very barn, of which he always kept the key, was found to have been fitted up as a complete laboratory, with athanor, alembic, cucurbite, and other appliances, some of which the master destroyed at once—perhaps for the best—and which I have only been able to guess at—"

"Black Arts," I laughed.

"Who knows?" he rejoined quietly. "The man undoubtedly possessed knowledge—dark knowledge—that was most unusual and dangerous, and I can discover no means by which he came to it—no ordinary means, that is. But I *have* found many facts in the case which point to the exercise of a most desperate and unscrupulous will; and the strange disappearances in the neighbourhood, as well as the bones found buried in the kitchen garden, though never actually traced to him, seem to me full of dreadful suggestion."

I laughed again, a little uncomfortably perhaps, and said it reminded one of the story of Giles de Rays, maréchal of France, who was said to have killed and tortured to death in a few years no less than one hundred and sixty women and children for the purposes of necromancy, and who was executed for his crimes at Nantes. But Shorthouse would not "rise," and only returned to his subject.

"His suicide seems to have been only just in time to escape arrest," he said.

"A magician of no high order then," I observed sceptically, "if suicide was his only way of evading the country police."

"The police of London and St. Petersburg rather," returned Shorthouse; "for the headquarters of this pretty company was somewhere in Russia, and his apparatus all bore the marks of the most skilful foreign make. A Russian woman then employed in the household—governess, or something—vanished, too, about the same time and was never caught. She was no doubt the cleverest of the lot. And, remember, the object of this appalling group was not mere vulgar gain, but a kind of knowledge that called for the highest qualities of courage and intellect in the seekers."

I admit I was impressed by the man's conviction of voice and manner, for there is something very compelling in the force of an earnest man's belief, though I still affected to sneer politely.

"But, like most Black Magicians, the fellow only succeeded in compassing his own destruction—that of his tools, rather, and of escaping himself."

"So that he might better accomplish his objects *elsewhere and otherwise*," said Shorthouse, giving, as he spoke, the most minute attention to the cleaning of the lock.

"Elsewhere and otherwise," I gasped.

"As if the shell he left hanging from the rafter in the barn in no way impeded the man's spirit from continuing his dreadful work under new conditions," he added quietly, without noticing my interruption. "The idea being that he sometimes revisits the garden and the barn, chiefly the barn—"

"The barn!" I exclaimed; "for what purpose?"

"Chiefly the barn," he finished, as if he had not heard me, "that is, when there is anybody in it."

I stared at him without speaking, for there was a wonder in me how he would add to this.

"When he wants fresh material, that is—he comes to steal from the living."

"Fresh material!" I repeated aghast. "To steal from the living!" Even then, in broad daylight, I was foolishly conscious of a creeping sensation at the roots of my hair, as if a cold breeze were passing over my skull.

"The strong vitality of the living is what this sort of creature is supposed to need most," he went on imperturbably, "and where he has worked and thought and struggled before is the easiest place for him to get it in. The former conditions are in some way more easily reconstructed—" He stopped suddenly, and devoted all his attention to the gun. "It's difficult to explain, you know, rather," he added presently, "and, besides, it's much better that you should not know till afterwards."

I made a noise that was the beginning of a score of questions and of as many sentences, but it got no further than a mere noise, and Shorthouse, of course, stepped in again.

"Your scepticism," he added, "is one of the qualities that induce me to ask you to spend the night there with me."

"In those days," he went on, in response to my urging for more information, "the family were much abroad, and often travelled for years at a time. This man was invaluable in their absence. His wonderful knowledge of horticulture kept the gardens—French, Italian, English—in perfect order. He had carte blanche in the matter of expense, and of course selected all his own underlings. It was the sudden, unexpected return of the master that surprised the amazing stories of the countryside before the fellow, with all his cleverness, had time to prepare or conceal."

"But is there no evidence, no more recent evidence, to show that something is likely to happen if we sit up there?" I asked, pressing him yet further, and I think to his liking, for it showed at least that I was interested. "Has anything happened there lately, for instance?"

Shorthouse glanced up from the gun he was cleaning so assiduously, and the smoke from his pipe curled up into an odd twist between me and the black beard and oriental, sun-tanned face. The magnetism of his look and expression brought more sense of conviction to me than I had felt hitherto, and I realised that there had been a sudden little change in my attitude and that I was now much more inclined to go in for the adventure with him. At least, I thought, with such a man, one would be safe in any emergency; for he is determined, resourceful, and to be depended upon.

"There's the point," he answered slowly; "for there has apparently been a fresh outburst—an attack almost, it seems,—quite recently. There is evidence, of course, plenty of it, or I should not feel the interest I do feel, but—" he hesitated a moment, as though considering how much he ought to let me know, "but the fact is that three men this summer, on separate occasions, who have gone into that barn after nightfall, have been *accosted*—"

"Accosted?" I repeated, betrayed into the interruption by his choice of so singular a word.

"And one of the stablemen—a recent arrival and quite ignorant of the story—who had to go in there late one night, saw a dark substance hanging down from one of the rafters, and when he climbed up, shaking all over, to cut it down—for he said he felt sure it was a corpse—the knife passed through nothing but air, and he heard a sound up under the eaves as if someone were laughing. Yet, while he slashed away, and afterwards too, the thing went on swinging there before his eyes and turning slowly with its own weight, like a huge joint on a spit. The man declares, too, that it had a large bearded face, and that the mouth was open and drawn down like the mouth of a hanged man."

"Can we question this fellow?"

"He's gone—gave notice at once, but not before I had questioned him myself very closely."

"Then this was quite recent?" I said, for I knew Shorthouse had not been in the house more than a week.

"Four days ago," he replied. "But, more than that, only three days ago a couple of men were in there together in full daylight when one of them suddenly turned deadly faint. He said that he felt an overmastering impulse to hang himself; and he looked about for a rope and was furious when his companion tried to prevent him—"

"But he did prevent him?"

"Just in time, but not before he had clambered on to a beam. He was very violent."

I had so much to say and ask that I could get nothing out in time, and Shorthouse went on again.

"I've had a sort of watching brief for this case," he said with a smile, whose real significance, however, completely escaped me at the time, "and one of the most disagreeable features about it is the deliberate way the servants have invented excuses to go out to the place, and always after dark; some of them who have no right to go there, and no real occasion at all—have never been there in their lives before probably—and now all of a sudden have shown the keenest desire and determination to go out there about dusk, or soon after, and with the most paltry and foolish excuses in the world. Of course," he added, "they have been prevented, but the desire, stronger than their superstitious dread, and which they cannot explain, is very curious."

"Very," I admitted, feeling that my hair was beginning to stand up again.

"You see," he went on presently, "it all points to volition—in fact to deliberate arrangement. It is no mere family ghost that goes with every ivied house in England of a certain age; it is something real, and something very malignant."

He raised his face from the gun barrel, and for the first time his eye caught mine in the full. Yes, he was very much in earnest. Also, he knew a great deal more than he meant to tell.

"It's worth tempting—and fighting, *I* think," he said; "but I want a companion with me. Are you game?" His enthusiasm undoubtedly caught me, but I still wanted to hedge a bit.

"I'm very sceptical," I pleaded.

"All the better," he said, almost as if to himself. "You have the pluck; I have the knowledge—"

"The knowledge?"

He looked round cautiously as if to make sure that there was no one within earshot.

"I've been in the place myself," he said in a lowered voice, "quite lately—in fact only three nights ago—the day the man turned queer."

I stared.

"But—I was obliged to come out—"

Still I stared.

"Quickly," he added significantly.

"You've gone into the thing pretty thoroughly," was all I could find to say, for I had almost made up my mind to go with him, and was not sure that I wanted to hear too much beforehand.

He nodded. "It's a bore, of course, but I must do everything thoroughly—or not at all."

"That's why you clean your own gun, I suppose?"

"That's why, when there's any danger, I take as few chances as possible," he said, with the same enigmatical smile I had noticed before; and then he added with emphasis, "And that is also why I ask you to keep me company now."

Of course, the shaft went straight home, and I gave my promise without further ado.

Our preparations for the night—a couple of rugs and a flask of black coffee—were not elaborate, and we found no difficulty, about ten o'clock, in absenting ourselves from the billiard-room without attracting curiosity. Shorthouse met me by arrangement under the cedar on the back lawn, and I at once realised with vividness what a difference there is between making plans in the daytime and carrying them out in the dark. One's common-sense—at least in matters of this sort—is reduced to a minimum, and imagination with all her attendant sprites usurps the place of judgment. Two and two no longer make four—they make a mystery, and the mystery loses no time in growing into a menace. In this particular case, however, my imagination did not find wings very readily, for I knew that my companion was the most *unmovable* of men—an unemotional, solid block of a man who would never lose his head, and in any conceivable state of affairs would always take the right as well as the strong course. So my faith in the man gave me a false courage that was nevertheless very consoling, and I looked forward to the night's adventure with a genuine appetite.

Side by side, and in silence, we followed the path that skirted the East Woods, as they were called, and then led across two hay fields, and through another wood, to the barn, which thus lay about half a mile from the Lower Farm. To the Lower Farm, indeed, it properly belonged; and this made us realise more clearly how very ingenious must have been the excuses of the Hall servants who felt the desire to visit it.

It had been raining during the late afternoon, and the trees were still dripping heavily on all sides, but the moment we left the second wood and came out into the open, we saw a clearing with the stars overhead, against which the barn outlined itself in a black, lugubrious shadow. Shorthouse led the way—still without a word—and we crawled in through a low door and seated ourselves in a soft heap of hay in the extreme corner.

"Now," he said, speaking for the first time, "I'll show you the inside of the barn, so that you may know where you are, and what to do, in case anything happens."

A match flared in the darkness, and with the help of two more that followed I saw the interior of a lofty and somewhat rickety-looking barn, erected upon a wall of grey stones that ran all round and extended to a height of perhaps four feet. Above this masonry rose the wooden sides, running up into the usual vaulted roof, and supported by a double tier of massive oak rafters, which stretched across from wall to wall and were intersected by occasional uprights. I felt as if we were inside the skeleton of some antediluvian monster whose huge black ribs completely enfolded us. Most of this, of course, only sketched itself to my eye in the uncertain light of the flickering matches, and when I said I had seen enough, and the matches went out, we were at once enveloped in an atmosphere as densely black as anything that I have ever known. And the silence equalled the darkness.

We made ourselves comfortable and talked in low voices. The rugs, which were very large, covered our legs; and our shoulders sank into a really luxurious bed of softness. Yet neither of us apparently felt sleepy. I certainly didn't, and Shorthouse, dropping his customary brevity that fell little short of gruffness, plunged into an easy run of talking that took the form after a time of personal reminiscences. This rapidly became a vivid narration of adventure and travel in far countries, and at any other time I should have allowed myself to become completely absorbed in what he told. But, unfortunately, I was never able for a single instant to forget the real purpose of our enterprise, and consequently I felt all my senses more keenly on the alert than usual, and my attention accordingly more or less distracted. It was, indeed, a revelation to hear Shorthouse unbosom himself in this fashion, and to a young man it was of course doubly fascinating; but the little sounds that always punctuate even the deepest silence out of doors claimed some portion of my attention, and as the night grew on I soon became aware that his tales seemed somewhat disconnected and abrupt—and that, in fact, I heard really only part of them.

It was not so much that I actually heard other sounds, but that I *expected* to hear them; this was what stole the other half of my listening. There was neither wind nor rain to break the stillness, and certainly there were no physical presences in our neighbourhood, for we were half a mile even from the Lower Farm; and from the Hall and stables, at least a mile. Yet the stillness was being continually broken—perhaps *disturbed* is a better word—and it was to these very remote and tiny disturbances that I felt compelled to devote at least half my listening faculties.

From time to time, however, I made a remark or asked a question, to show that I was listening and interested; but, in a sense, my questions always seemed to bear in one direction and to make for one issue, namely, my companion's previous experience in the barn when he had been obliged to come out "quickly."

Apparently I could not help myself in the matter, for this was really the one consuming curiosity I had; and the fact that it was better for me not to know it made me the keener to know it all, even the worst.

Shorthouse realised this even better than I did. I could tell it by the way he dodged, or wholly ignored, my questions, and this subtle sympathy between us showed plainly enough, had I been able at the time to reflect upon its meaning, that the nerves of both of us were in a very sensitive and highly-strung condition. Probably, the complete confidence I felt in his ability to face whatever might happen, and the extent to which also I relied upon him for my own courage, prevented the exercise of my ordinary powers of reflection, while it left my senses free to a more than usual degree of activity.

Things must have gone on in this way for a good hour or more, when I made the sudden discovery that there was something unusual in the conditions of our environment. This sounds a roundabout mode of expression, but I really know not how else to put it. The discovery almost rushed upon me. By rights, we were two men waiting in an alleged haunted barn for something to happen; and, as two men who trusted one another implicitly (though for very different reasons), there should have been two minds keenly alert, with the ordinary senses in active co-operation. Some slight degree of nervousness, too, there might also have been, but beyond this, nothing. It was therefore with something of dismay that I made the sudden discovery that there *was* something more, and something that I ought to have noticed very much sooner than I actually did notice it.

The fact was—Shorthouse's stream of talk was wholly unnatural. He was talking with a purpose. He did not wish to be cornered by my questions, true, but he had another and a deeper purpose still, and it grew upon me, as an unpleasant deduction from my discovery, that this strong, cynical, unemotional man by my side was talking— and had been talking all this time—to gain a particular end. And this end, I soon felt clearly, was to *convince himself.* But, of what?

For myself, as the hours wore on towards midnight, I was not anxious to find the answer; but in the end it became impossible to avoid it, and I knew as I listened, that he was pouring forth this steady stream of vivid reminiscences of travel—South Seas, big game, Russian exploration, women, adventures of all sorts—*because he wished the past to reassert itself to the complete exclusion of the present.* He was taking his precautions. He was afraid.

I felt a hundred things, once this was clear to me, but none of them more than the wish to get up at once and leave the barn. If Shorthouse was afraid already, what in the world was to happen to me in the long hours that lay ahead? . . . I only know that, in my fierce efforts to deny to myself the evidence of his partial collapse, the strength came that enabled me to play my part properly, and I even found myself helping him by means of animated remarks upon his stories, and by more or less judicious questions. I also helped him by dismissing from my mind any desire to enquire into the truth of his former experience; and it was good I did so, for had he turned it loose on me, with those great powers of convincing description that he had at his command, I verily believe that I should never have crawled from that barn alive. So, at least, I felt at the moment. It was the instinct of self-preservation, and it brought sound judgment.

Here, then, at least, with different motives, reached, too, by opposite ways, we were both agreed upon one thing, namely, that temporarily we would forget. Fools we were, for a dominant emotion is not so easily banished, and we were for ever recurring to it in a hundred ways direct and indirect. A real fear cannot be so easily trifled with, and while we toyed on the surface with thousands and thousands of words—mere words—our sub-conscious activities were steadily gaining force, and would before very long have to be properly acknowledged. We could not get away from it. At last, when he had finished the recital of an adventure which brought him near enough to a horrible death, I admitted that in my uneventful life I had never yet been face to face with a real fear. It slipped out inadvertently, and, of course, without intention, but the tendency in him at the time was too strong to be resisted. He saw the loophole, and made for it full tilt.

"It is the same with all the emotions," he said. "The experiences of others never give a complete account. Until a man has deliberately turned and faced for himself the fiends that chase him down the years, he has no knowledge of what they really are, or of what they can do. Imaginative authors may write, moralists may preach, and scholars may criticise, but they are dealing all the time in a coinage of which they know not the actual value. Their listener gets a sensation—but not the true one. Until you have faced these emotions," he went on, with the same race of words that had come from him the whole evening, "and made them your own, your slaves, you have no idea of the power that is in them—hunger, that shows lights beckoning beyond the grave; thirst, that fills with mingled ice and fire; passion, love, loneliness, revenge, and—" He paused for a minute, and though I knew we were on the brink I was powerless to hold him. ". . . and fear," he went on—"fear . . . I think that death from fear, or madness from fear, must sum up in a second of time the total of all the most awful sensations it is possible for a man to know."

"Then you have yourself felt something of this fear," I interrupted; " for you said just now—"

"I do not mean physical fear," he replied; "for that is more or less a question of nerves and will, and it is imagination that makes men cowards. I mean an *absolute* fear, a physical fear one might call it, that reaches the soul and withers every power one possesses."

He said a lot more, for he, too, was wholly unable to stem the torrent once it broke loose; but I have forgotten it; or, rather, mercifully I did not hear it, for I stopped my ears and only heard the occasional words when I took my fingers out to find if he had come to an end. In due course he did come to an end, and there we left it, for I then knew positively what he already knew: that somewhere here in the night, and within the walls of this very barn where we were sitting, there was waiting Something of dreadful malignancy and of great power, Something that we might both have to face ere morning, and Something that he had already tried to face once and failed in the attempt.

The night wore slowly on; and it gradually became more and more clear to me that I could not dare to rely as at first upon my companion, and that our positions were undergoing a slow process of reversal. I thank heaven this was not borne in upon me too suddenly; and that I had at least the time to readjust myself somewhat to the new conditions. Preparation was possible, even if it was not much, and I sought by every means in my power to gather up all the shreds of my courage, so that they might together make a decent rope that would stand the strain when it came. The strain would come, that was certain, and I was thoroughly well aware—though for my life I cannot put into words the reasons for my knowledge—that the massing of the material against us was proceeding somewhere in the darkness with determination and a horrible skill besides.

Shorthouse meanwhile talked without ceasing. The great quantity of hay opposite—or straw, I believe it actually was—seemed to deaden the sound of his voice, but the silence, too, had become so oppressive that I welcomed his torrent and even dreaded the moment when it would stop. I heard, too, the gentle ticking of my watch. Each second uttered its voice and dropped away into a gulf, as if starting on a journey whence there was no return. Once a dog barked somewhere in the distance, probably on the Lower Farm; and once an owl hooted close outside and I could hear the swishing of its wings as it passed overhead. Above me, in the darkness, I could just make out the outline of the barn, sinister and black, the rows of rafters stretching across from wall to wall like wicked arms that pressed upon the hay. Shorthouse, deep in some involved yarn of the South Seas that was meant to be full of cheer and sunshine, and yet only succeeded in making a ghastly mixture of unnatural colouring, seemed to care little whether I listened or not. He made no appeal to me, and I made one or two quite irrelevant remarks which passed him by and proved that he was merely uttering sounds. He, too, was afraid of the silence.

I fell to wondering how long a man could talk without stopping. . . . Then it seemed to me that these words of his went falling into the same gulf where the seconds dropped, only they were heavier and fell faster. I began to chase them. Presently one of them fell much faster than the rest, and I pursued it and found myself almost immediately in a land of clouds and shadows. They rose up and enveloped me, pressing on the eyelids. . . . It must have been just here that I actually fell asleep, somewhere between twelve and one o'clock, because, as I chased this word at tremendous speed through space, I knew that I had left the other words far, very far behind me, till, at last, I could no longer hear them at all. The voice of the storyteller was beyond the reach of hearing; and I was falling with ever increasing rapidity through an immense void.

A sound of whispering roused me. Two persons were talking under their breath close beside me. The words in the main escaped me, but I caught every now and then bitten-off phrases and half sentences, to which, however, I could attach no intelligible meaning. The words were quite close—at my very side in fact—and one of the voices sounded so familiar, that curiosity overcame dread, and I turned to look. I was not mistaken; *it was Shorthouse whispering.* But the other person, who must have been just a little beyond him, was lost in the darkness and invisible to me. It seemed then that Shorthouse at once turned up his face and looked at me and, by some means or other that caused me no surprise at the time, I easily made out the features in the darkness. They wore an expression I had never seen there before; he seemed distressed, exhausted, worn out, and as though he were about to give in after a long mental struggle. He looked at me, almost beseechingly, and the whispering of the other person died away.

"They're at me," he said.

I found it quite impossible to answer; the words stuck in my throat. His voice was thin, plaintive, almost like a child's.

"I shall have to go. I'm not as strong as I thought. They'll call it suicide, but, of course, it's really murder." There was real anguish in his voice, and it terrified me.

A deep silence followed these extraordinary words, and I somehow understood that the Other Person was just going to carry on the conversation—I even fancied I saw lips shaping themselves just over my friend's shoulder—when I felt a sharp blow in the ribs and a voice, this time a deep voice, sounded in my ear. I opened my eyes, and the wretched dream vanished. Yet it left behind it an impression of a strong and quite unusual reality.

"*Do* try not to go to sleep again," he said sternly. "You seem exhausted. Do you feel so?" There was a note in his voice I did not welcome,—less than alarm, but certainly more than mere solicitude.

"I do feel terribly sleepy all of a sudden," I admitted, ashamed.

"So you may," he added very earnestly; "but I rely on you to keep awake, if only to watch. You have been asleep for half an hour at least—and you were so still—I thought I'd wake you—"

"Why?" I asked, for my curiosity and nervousness were altogether too strong to be resisted. "Do you think we are in danger?"

"I think *they* are about here now. I feel my vitality going rapidly—that's always the first sign. You'll last longer than I, remember. Watch carefully."

The conversation dropped. I was afraid to say all I wanted to say. It would have been too unmistakably a confession; and intuitively I realised the danger of admitting the existence of certain emotions until positively forced to. But presently Shorthouse began again. His voice sounded odd, and as if it had lost power. It was more like a woman's or a boy's voice than a man's, and recalled the voice in my dream.

"I suppose you've got a knife?" he asked.

"Yes—a big clasp knife; but why?" He made no answer. "You don't think a practical joke likely? No one suspects we're here," I went on. Nothing was more significant of our real feelings this night than the way we toyed with words, and never dared more than to skirt the things in our mind.

"It's just as well to be prepared," he answered evasively. "Better be quite sure. See which pocket it's in—so as to be ready."

I obeyed mechanically, and told him. But even this scrap of talk proved to me that he was getting further from me all the time in his mind. He was following a line that was strange to me, and, as he distanced me, I felt that the sympathy between us grew more and more strained. *He knew more;* it was not that I minded so much—but that he was willing to *communicate less.* And in proportion as I lost his support, I dreaded his increasing silence. Not of words—for he talked more volubly than ever, and with a fiercer purpose—but his silence in giving no hint of what he must have known to be really going on the whole time.

The night was perfectly still. Shorthouse continued steadily talking, and I jogged him now and again with remarks or questions in order to keep awake. He paid no attention, however, to either.

About two in the morning a short shower fell, and the drops rattled sharply on the roof like shot. I was glad when it stopped, for it completely drowned all other sounds and made it impossible to hear anything else that might be going on. Something *was* going on, too, all the time, though for the life of me I could not say what. The outer world had grown quite dim—the house-party, the shooters, the billiard-room, and the ordinary daily incidents of my visit. All my energies were concentrated on the present, and the constant strain of watching, waiting, listening, was excessively telling.

Shorthouse still talked of his adventures, in some Eastern country now, and less connectedly. These adventures, real or imaginary, had quite a savour of the Arabian Nights, and did not by any means make it easier for me to keep my hold on reality. The lightest weight will affect the balance under such circumstances, and in this case the weight of his talk was on the wrong scale. His words were very rapid, and I found it overwhelmingly difficult not to follow them into that great gulf of darkness where they all rushed and vanished. But that, I knew, meant sleep again. Yet, it was strange I should feel sleepy when at the same time all my nerves were fairly tingling. Every time I heard what seemed like a step outside, or a movement in the hay opposite, the blood stood still for a moment in my veins. Doubtless, the unremitting strain told upon me more than I realised, and this was doubly great now that I knew Shorthouse was a source of weakness instead of strength, as I had counted. Certainly, a curious sense of languor grew upon me more and more, and I was sure that the man beside me was engaged in the same struggle. The feverishness of his talk proved this, if nothing else. It was dreadfully hard to keep awake.

But this time, instead of dropping into the gulf, I saw something come up out of it! It reached our world by a door in the side of the barn furthest from me, and it came in cautiously and silently and moved into the mass of hay opposite. There, for a moment, I lost it, but presently I caught it again higher up. It was clinging, like a great bat, to the side of the barn. Something trailed behind it, I could not make out what. . . . It crawled up the wooden wall and began to move out along one of the rafters. A numb terror settled down all over me as I watched it. The thing trailing behind it was apparently a rope.

The whispering began again just then, but the only words I could catch seemed without meaning; it was almost like another language. The voices were above me, under the roof. Suddenly I saw signs of active movement going on just beyond the place where the thing lay upon the rafter. There was something else up there with it! Then followed panting, like the quick breathing that accompanies effort, and the next minute a black mass dropped through the air and dangled at the end of the rope.

Instantly, it all flashed upon me. I sprang to my feet and rushed headlong across the floor of the barn. How I moved so quickly in the darkness I do not know; but, even as I ran, it flashed into my mind that I should never get at my knife in time to cut the thing down, or else that I should find it had been taken from me. Somehow or other—the Goddess of Dreams knows how—I climbed up by the hay bales and swung out along the rafter. I was hanging, of course, by my arms, and the knife was already between my teeth, though I had no recollection of how it got there. It was open. The mass, hanging like a side of bacon, was only a few feet in front of me, and I could plainly see the dark line of rope that fastened it to the beam. I then noticed for the first time that it was swinging and turning in the air, and that as I approached it seemed to move along the beam, so that the same distance was always maintained between us. The only thing I could do—for there was no time to hesitate—was to jump at it through the air and slash at the rope as I dropped.

I seized the knife with my right hand, gave a great swing of my body with my legs, and leaped forward at it through the air. Horrors! It was closer to me than I knew, and I plunged full into it, and the arm with the knife missed the rope and cut deeply into some substance that was soft and yielding. But, as I dropped past it, the thing had time to turn half its width so that it swung round and faced me—and I could have sworn as I rushed past it through the air, that it had the features of Shorthouse.

The shock of this brought the vile nightmare to an abrupt end, and I woke up a second time on the soft hay-bed to find that the grey dawn was stealing in, and that I was exceedingly cold. After all I had failed to keep awake, and my sleep, since it was growing light, must have lasted at least an hour. A whole hour off my guard!

There was no sound from Shorthouse, to whom, of course, my first thoughts turned; probably his flow of words had ceased long ago, and he too had yielded to the persuasions of the seductive god. I turned to wake him and get the comfort of companionship for the horror of my dream, when to my utter dismay I saw that the place where he had been was vacant. He was no longer beside me.

It had been no little shock before to discover that the ally in whom lay all my faith and dependence was really frightened, but it is quite impossible to describe the sensations I experienced when I real-ised he had gone altogether and that I was alone in the barn. For a minute or two my head swam and I felt a prey to a helpless terror. The dream, too, still seemed half real, so vivid had it been! I was thoroughly frightened—hot and cold by turns—and I clutched the hay at my side in handfuls, and for some moments had no idea in the world what I should do.

This time, at least, I was unmistakably awake, and I made a great effort to collect myself and face the meaning of the disappearance of my companion. In this I succeeded so far that I decided upon a thorough search of the barn, inside and outside. It was a dreadful undertaking, and I did not feel at all sure of being able to bring it to a conclusion, but I knew pretty well that unless something was done at once, I should simply collapse.

But, when I tried to move, found that the cold, and fear, and I know not what else unholy besides, combined to make it almost im-possible. I suddenly realised that a tour of inspection, during the whole of which my back would be open to attack, was not to be thought of. My will was not equal to it. Anything might spring upon me any moment from the dark corners, and the growing light was just enough to reveal every movement I made to any who might be watching. For, even then, and while I was still half dazed and stupid,

I knew perfectly well that some one was watching me all the time with the utmost intentness. I had not merely awakened; I had *been* awakened.

I decided to try another plan; I called to him. My voice had a thin weak sound, far away and quite unreal, and there was no answer to it. Hark, though! There was something that might have been a very faint voice near me!

I called again, this time with greater distinctness, "Shorthouse, where are you? can you hear me?"

There certainly was a sound, but it was not a voice. Something was moving. It was some one shuffling along, and it seemed to be outside the barn. I was afraid to call again, and the sound continued. It was an ordinary sound enough, no doubt, but it came to me just then as something unusual and unpleasant. Ordinary sounds remain ordinary only so long as one is not listening to them; under the influence of intense listening they become unusual, portentous, and therefore extra-ordinary. So, this common sound came to me as something uncommon, disagreeable. It conveyed, too, an impression of stealth. And with it there was another, a slighter sound.

Just at this minute the wind bore faintly over the field the sound of the stable clock, a mile away. It was three o'clock; the hour when life's pulses beat lowest; when poor souls lying between life and death find it hardest to resist. Vividly I remember this thought crashing through my brain with a sound of thunder, and I realised that the strain on my nerves was nearing the limit, and that something would have to be done at once if I was to reclaim my self-control at all.

When thinking over afterwards the events of this dreadful night, it has always seemed strange to me that my second nightmare, so vivid in its terror and its nearness, should have furnished me with no inkling of what was really going on all this while; and that I should not have been able to put two and two together, or have discovered sooner than I did *what* this sound was and *where* it came from. I can well believe that the vile scheming which lay behind the whole experience found it an easy trifle to direct my hearing amiss; though, of course, it may equally well have been due to the confused condition of my mind at the time and to the general nervous tension under which I was undoubtedly suffering.

But, whatever the cause for my stupidity at first in failing to trace the sound to its proper source, I can only say here that it was with a shock of unexampled horror that my eye suddenly glanced upwards and caught sight of the figure moving in the shadows above my head among the rafters. Up to this moment I had thought that it was somebody outside the barn, crawling round the walls till it came to a door; and the rush of horror that froze my heart when I looked up and saw that it was Shorthouse creeping stealthily along a beam, is something altogether beyond the power of words to describe.

He was staring intently down upon me, and I knew at once that it was he who had been watching me.

This point was, I think, for me the climax of feeling in the whole experience; I was incapable of any further sensation—that is any further sensation in the same direction. But here the abominable character of the affair showed itself most plainly, for it suddenly presented an entirely new aspect to me. The light fell on the picture from a new angle, and galvanised me into a fresh ability to feel when I thought a merciful numbness had supervened. It may not sound a great deal in the printed letter, but it came to me almost as if it had been an extension of consciousness, for the Hand that held the pencil suddenly touched in with ghastly effect of contrast the element of the ludicrous. Nothing could have been worse just then. Shorthouse, the masterful spirit, so intrepid in the affairs of ordinary life, whose power increased rather than lessened in the face of danger—this man, creeping on hands and knees along a rafter in a barn at three o'clock in the morning, watching me all the time as a cat watches a mouse! Yes, it was distinctly ludicrous, and while it gave me a measure with which to gauge the dread emotion that caused his aberration, it stirred somewhere deep in my interior the strings of an empty laughter.

One of those moments then came to me that are said to come sometimes under the stress of great emotion, when in an instant the mind grows dazzlingly clear. An abnormal lucidity took the place of my confusion of thought, and I suddenly understood that the two dreams which I had taken for nightmares must really have been sent me, and that I had been allowed for one moment to look over the edge of what was to come; the Good was helping, even when the Evil was most determined to destroy.

I saw it all clearly now. Shorthouse had overrated his strength. The terror inspired by his first visit to the barn (when he had failed) had roused the man's whole nature to win, and he had brought me to divert the deadly stream of evil. That he had again underrated the power against him was apparent as soon as he entered the barn, and his wild talk, and refusal to admit what he felt, were due to this desire not to acknowledge the insidious fear that was growing in his heart. But, at length, it had become too strong. He had left my side in my sleep—had been overcome himself, perhaps, first in *his* sleep, by the dreadful impulse. He knew that I should interfere, and with every movement he made, he watched me steadily, for the mania was upon him and he was *determined to hang himself.* He pretended not to hear me calling, and I knew that anything coming between him and his purpose would meet the full force of his fury—the fury of a maniac, of one, for the time being, truly possessed.

For a minute or two I sat there and stared. I saw then for the first time that there was a bit of rope trailing after him, and that this was what made the rustling sound I had noticed. Shorthouse, too, had come to a stop. His body lay along the rafter like a crouching animal. He was looking hard at me. That whitish patch was his face.

I can lay claim to no courage in the matter, for I must confess that in one sense I was frightened almost beyond control. But at the same time the necessity for decided action, if I was to save his life, came to me with an intense relief. No matter what animated him for the moment, Shorthouse was only a *man;* it was flesh and blood I had to contend with and not the intangible powers. Only a few hours before I had seen him cleaning his gun, smoking his pipe, knocking the billiard balls about with very human clumsiness, and the picture flashed across my mind with the most wholesome effect.

Then I dashed across the floor of the barn and leaped upon the hay bales as a preliminary to climbing up the sides to the first rafter. It was far more difficult than in my dream. Twice I slipped back into the hay, and as I scrambled up for the third time I saw that Shorthouse, who thus far had made no sound or movement, was now busily doing something with his hands upon the beam. He was at its further end, and there must have been fully fifteen feet between us. Yet I saw plainly what he was doing; he was fastening the rope to the rafter. *The other end, I saw, was already round his neck!*

This gave me at once the necessary strength, and in a second I had swung myself on to a beam, crying aloud with all the authority I could put into my voice—

"You fool, man! What in the world are you trying to do? Come down at once!"

My energetic actions and words combined had an immediate effect upon him for which I blessed heaven; for he looked up from his horrid task, stared hard at me for a second or two, and then came wriggling along like a great cat to intercept me. He came by a series of leaps and bounds and at an astonishing pace, and the way he moved somehow inspired me with a fresh horror, for it did not seem the natural movement of a human being at all, but more, as I have said, like that of some lithe wild animal.

He was close upon me. I had no clear idea of what exactly I meant to do. I could see his face plainly now; he was grinning cruelly; the eyes were positively luminous, and the menacing expression of the mouth was most distressing to look upon. Otherwise it was the face of a chalk man, white and dead, with all the semblance of the living human drawn out of it. Between his teeth he held my clasp knife, which he must have taken from me in my sleep, and with a flash I recalled his anxiety to know exactly which pocket it was in.

"Drop that knife!" I shouted at him, "and drop after it yourself—"

"Don't you dare to stop me!" he hissed, the breath coming between his lips across the knife that he held in his teeth. "Nothing in the world can stop me now—I have promised—and I must do it. I can't hold out any longer."

"Then drop the knife and I'll help you," I shouted back in his face. "I promise—"

"No use," he cried, laughing a little, "I must do it and you can't stop me."

I heard a sound of laughter, too, somewhere in the air behind me. The next second Shorthouse came at me with a single bound.

To this day I cannot quite tell how it happened. It is still a wild confusion and a fever of horror in my mind, but from somewhere I drew more than my usual allowance of strength, and before he could well have realised what I meant to do, I had his throat between my fingers. He opened his teeth and the knife dropped at once, for I gave him a squeeze he need never forget. Before, my muscles had felt like so much soaked paper; now they recovered their natural strength, and more besides. I managed to work ourselves along the rafter until the hay was beneath us, and then, completely exhausted, I let go my hold and we swung round together and dropped on to the hay, he clawing at me in the air even as we fell.

The struggle that began by my fighting for his life ended in a wild effort to save my own, for Shorthouse was quite beside himself, and had no idea what he was doing. Indeed, he has always averred that he remembers nothing of the entire night's experiences after the time when he first woke me from sleep. A sort of deadly mist settled over him, he declares, and he lost all sense of his own identity. The rest was a blank until he came to his senses under a mass of hay with me on the top of him.

It was the hay that saved us, first by breaking the fall and then by impeding his movements so that I was able to prevent his choking me to death.

The Wood of the Dead

One summer, in my wanderings with a knapsack, I was at luncheon in the room of a wayside inn in the western country, when the door opened and there entered an old rustic, who crossed close to my end of the table and sat himself down very quietly in the seat by the bow window. We exchanged glances, or, properly speaking, nods, for at the moment I did not actually raise my eyes to his face, so concerned was I with the important business of satisfying an appetite gained by tramping twelve miles over a difficult country.

The fine warm rain of seven o'clock, which had since risen in a kind of luminous mist about the tree tops, now floated far overhead in a deep blue sky, and the day was settling down into a blaze of golden light. It was one of those days peculiar to Somerset and North Devon, when the orchards shine and the meadows seem to add a radiance of their own, so brilliantly soft are the colourings of grass and foliage.

The inn-keeper's daughter, a little maiden with a simple country loveliness, presently entered with a foaming pewter mug, enquired after my welfare, and went out again. Apparently she had not noticed the old man sitting in the settle by the bow window, nor had he, for his part, so much as once turned his head in our direction.

Under ordinary circumstances I should probably have given no thought to this other occupant of the room; but the fact that it was supposed to be reserved for my private use, and the singular thing that he sat looking aimlessly out of the window, with no attempt to engage me in conversation, drew my eyes more than once somewhat curiously upon him, and I soon caught myself wondering why he sat there so silently, and always with averted head.

He was, I saw, a rather bent old man in rustic dress, and the skin of his face was wrinkled like that of an apple; corduroy trousers were caught up with a string below the knee, and he wore a sort of brown fustian jacket that was very much faded. His thin hand rested upon a stoutish stick. He wore no hat and carried none, and I noticed that his head, covered with silvery hair, was finely shaped and gave the impression of something noble.

Though rather piqued by his studied disregard of my presence, I came to the conclusion that he probably had something to do with the little hostel and had a perfect right to use this room with freedom, and I finished my luncheon without breaking the silence and then took the settle opposite to smoke a pipe before going on my way.

Through the open window came the scents of the blossoming fruit trees; the orchard was drenched in sunshine and the branches danced lazily in the breeze; the grass below fairly shone with white and yellow daisies, and the red roses climbing in profusion over the casement mingled their perfume with the sweetly penetrating odour of the sea.

It was a place to dawdle in, to lie and dream away a whole afternoon, watching the sleepy butterflies and listening to the chorus of birds which seemed to fill every corner of the sky. Indeed, I was already debating in my mind whether to linger and enjoy it all instead of taking the strenuous pathway over the hills, when the old rustic in the settle opposite suddenly turned his face towards me for the first time and began to speak.

His voice had a quiet dreamy note in it that was quite in harmony with the day and the scene, but it sounded far away, I thought, almost as though it came to me from outside where the shadows were weaving their eternal tissue of dreams upon the garden floor. Moreover, there was no trace in it of the rough quality one might naturally have expected, and, now that I saw the full face of the speaker for the first time, I noted with something like a start that the deep, gentle eyes seemed far more in keeping with the timbre of the voice than with the rough and very countrified appearance of the clothes and manner. His voice set pleasant waves of sound in motion towards me, and the actual words, if I remember rightly, were—

"You are a stranger in these parts?" or "Is not this part of the country strange to you?"

There was no "sir," nor any outward and visible sign of the def-
erence usually paid by real country folk to the town-bred visitor, but
in its place a gentleness, almost a sweetness, of polite sympathy that
was far more of a compliment than either.

I answered that I was wandering on foot through a part of the
country that was wholly new to me, and that I was surprised not to
find a place of such idyllic loveliness marked upon my map.

"I have lived here all my life," he said, with a sigh, "and am never
tired of coming back to it again."

"Then you no longer live in the immediate neighbourhood?"

"I have moved," he answered briefly, adding after a pause in
which his eyes seemed to wander wistfully to the wealth of blossoms
beyond the window; "but I am almost sorry, for nowhere else have I
found the sunshine lie so warmly, the flowers smell so sweetly, or the
winds and streams make such tender music. . . ."

His voice died away into a thin stream of sound that lost itself in
the rustle of the rose-leaves climbing in at the window, for he turned
his head away from me as he spoke and looked out into the garden.
But it was impossible to conceal my surprise, and I raised my eyes in
frank astonishment on hearing so poetic an utterance from such a
figure of a man, though at the same time realising that it was not in
the least inappropriate, and that, in fact, no other sort of expression
could have properly been expected from him.

"I am sure you are right," I answered at length, when it was clear
he had ceased speaking; "for there is something of enchantment
here—of real fairy-like enchantment—that makes me think of the
visions of childhood days, before one knew anything of—of—"

I had been oddly drawn into his vein of speech, some inner force
compelling me. But here the spell passed and I could not catch the
thoughts that had a moment before opened a long vista before my
inner vision.

"To tell you the truth," I concluded lamely, "the place fascinates
me and I am in two minds about going further—"

Even at this stage I remember thinking it odd that I should be
talking like this with a stranger whom I met in a country inn, for it
has always been one of my failings that to strangers my manner is
brief to surliness. It was as though we were figures meeting in a

dream, speaking without sound, obeying laws not operative in the everyday working world, and about to play with a new scale of space and time perhaps. But my astonishment passed quickly into an entirely different feeling when I became aware that the old man opposite had turned his head from the window again, and was regarding me with eyes so bright they seemed almost to shine with an inner flame. His gaze was fixed upon my face with an intense ardour, and his whole manner had suddenly become alert and concentrated. There was something about him I now felt for the first time that made little thrills of excitement run up and down my back. I met his look squarely, but with an inward tremor.

"Stay, then, a little while longer," he said in a much lower and deeper voice than before; "stay, and I will teach you something of the purpose of my coming."

He stopped abruptly. I was conscious of a decided shiver.

"You have a special purpose then—in coming back?" I asked, hardly knowing what I was saying.

"To call away some one," he went on in the same thrilling voice, "some one who is not quite ready to come, but who is needed elsewhere for a worthier purpose." There was a sadness in his manner that mystified me more than ever.

"You mean—?" I began, with an unaccountable access of trembling.

"I have come for some one who must soon move, even as I have moved."

He looked me through and through with a dreadfully piercing gaze, but I met his eyes with a full straight stare, trembling though I was, and I was aware that something stirred within me that had never stirred before, though for the life of me I could not have put a name to it, or have analysed its nature. Something lifted and rolled away. For one single second I understood clearly that the past and the future exist actually side by side in one immense Present; that it was *I* who moved to and fro among shifting, protean appearances.

The old man dropped his eyes from my face, and the momentary glimpse of a mightier universe passed utterly away. Reason regained its sway over a dull, limited kingdom.

"Come to-night," I heard the old man say, "come to me to-night into the Wood of the Dead. Come at midnight—"

Involuntarily I clutched the arm of the settle for support, for I then felt that I was speaking with some one who knew more of the real things that are and will be, than I could ever know while in the body, working through the ordinary channels of sense—and this curious half-promise of a partial lifting of the veil had its undeniable effect upon me.

The breeze from the sea had died away outside, and the blossoms were still. A yellow butterfly floated lazily past the window. The song of the birds hushed—I smelt the sea—I smelt the perfume of heated summer air rising from fields and flowers, the ineffable scents of June and of the long days of the year—and with it, from countless green meadows beyond, came the hum of myriad summer life, children's voices, sweet pipings, and the sound of water falling.

I knew myself to be on the threshold of a new order of experience—of an ecstasy. Something drew me forth with a sense of inexpressible yearning towards the being of this strange old man in the window seat, and for a moment I knew what it was to taste a mighty and wonderful sensation, and to touch the highest pinnacle of joy I have ever known. It lasted for less than a second, and was gone; but in that brief instant of time the same terrible lucidity came to me that had already shown me how the past and future exist in the present, and I realised and understood that pleasure and pain are one and the same force, for the joy I had just experienced included also all the pain I ever had felt, or ever could feel. . . .

The sunshine grew to dazzling radiance, faded, passed away. The shadows paused in their dance upon the grass, deepened a moment, and then melted into air. The flowers of the fruit trees laughed with their little silvery laughter as the wind sighed over their radiant eyes the old, old tale of its personal love. Once or twice a voice called my name. A wonderful sensation of lightness and power began to steal over me.

Suddenly the door opened and the inn-keeper's daughter came in. By all ordinary standards, hers was a charming country loveliness, born of the stars and wild-flowers, of moonlight shining through autumn mists upon the river and the fields; yet, by contrast with the higher order of beauty I had just momentarily been in touch with, she seemed almost ugly. How dull her eyes, how thin her voice, how vapid her smile, and insipid her whole presentment.

For a moment she stood between me and the occupant of the window seat while I counted out the small change for my meal and for her services; but when, an instant later, she moved aside, I saw that the settle was empty and that there was no longer any one in the room but our two selves.

This discovery was no shock to me; indeed, I had almost expected it, and the man had gone just as a figure goes out of a dream, causing no surprise and leaving me as part and parcel of the same dream without breaking of continuity. But, as soon as I had paid my bill and thus resumed in very practical fashion the thread of my normal consciousness, I turned to the girl and asked her if she knew the old man who had been sitting in the window seat, and what he had meant by the Wood of the Dead.

The maiden started visibly, glancing quickly round the empty room, but answering simply that she had seen no one. I described him in great detail, and then, as the description grew clearer, she turned a little pale under her pretty sunborn and said very gravely that it must have been the ghost.

"Ghost! What ghost?"

"Oh, the village ghost," she said quietly, coming closer to my chair with a little nervous movement of genuine alarm, and adding in a lower voice, "He comes before a death, they say!"

It was not difficult to induce the girl to talk, and the story she told me, shorn of the superstition that had obviously gathered with the years round the memory of a strangely picturesque figure, was an interesting and peculiar one.

The inn, she said, was originally a farmhouse, occupied by a yeoman farmer, evidently of a superior, if rather eccentric, character, who had been very poor until he reached old age, when a son died suddenly in the Colonies and left him an unexpected amount of money, almost a fortune.

The old man thereupon altered no whit his simple manner of living, but devoted his income entirely to the improvement of the village and to the assistance of its inhabitants; he did this quite regardless of his personal likes and dislikes, as if one and all were absolutely alike to him, objects of a genuine and impersonal benevolence. People had always been a little afraid of the man, not understanding his eccentricities, but the simple force of this love for humanity changed all that in a very short space of time; and before he died he came to be known as the Father of the Village and was held in great love and veneration by all.

A short time before his end, however, he began to act queerly. He spent his money just as usefully and wisely, but the shock of sudden wealth after a life of poverty, people said, had unsettled his mind. He claimed to see things that others did not see, to hear voices, and to have visions. Evidently, he was not of the harmless, foolish, visionary order, but a man of character and of great personal force, for the people became divided in their opinions, and the vicar, good man, regarded and treated him as a "special case." For many, his name and atmosphere became charged almost with a spiritual influence that was not of the best. People quoted texts about him; kept when possible out of his way, and avoided his house after dark. None understood him, but though the majority loved him, an element of dread and mystery became associated with his name, chiefly owing to the ignorant gossip of the few.

A grove of pine trees behind the farm—the girl pointed them out to me on the slope of the hill—he said was the Wood of the Dead, because just before any one died in the village he saw them walk into that wood, singing. None who went in ever came out again. He often mentioned the names to his wife, who usually published them to all the inhabitants within an hour of her husband's confidence; and it was found that the people he had seen enter the wood—died. On warm summer nights he would sometimes take an old stick and wander out, hatless, under the pines, for he loved this wood, and used to say he met all his old friends there, and would one day walk in there never to return. His wife tried to break him gently off this habit, but he always had his own way; and once, when she followed and found him standing under a great pine in the thickest portion of the grove, talking earnestly to some one she could not see, he turned and rebuked her very gently, but in such a way that she never repeated the experiment, saying—

"You should never interrupt me, Mary, when I am talking with the others; for they teach me, remember, wonderful things, and I must learn all I can before I go to join them."

This story went like wild-fire through the village, increasing with every repetition, until at length every one was able to give an accurate description of the great veiled figures the woman declared she had seen moving among the trees where her husband stood. The innocent pine-grove now became positively haunted, and the title of "Wood of the Dead" clung naturally as if it had been applied to it in the ordinary course of events by the compilers of the Ordnance Survey.

On the evening of his ninetieth birthday the old man went up to his wife and kissed her. His manner was loving, and very gentle, and there was something about him besides, she declared afterwards, that made her slightly in awe of him and feel that he was almost more of a spirit than a man.

He kissed her tenderly on both cheeks, but his eyes seemed to look right through her as he spoke. "Dearest wife," he said, "I am saying good-bye to you, for I am now going into the Wood of the Dead, and I shall not return. Do not follow me, or send to search, but be ready soon to come upon the same journey yourself."

The good woman burst into tears and tried to hold him, but he easily slipped from her hands, and she was afraid to follow him. Slowly she saw him cross the field in the sunshine, and then enter the cool shadows of the grove, where he disappeared from her sight.

That same night, much later, she woke to find him lying peacefully by her side in bed, with one arm stretched out towards her, *dead.* Her story was half believed, half doubted at the time, but in a very few years afterwards it evidently came to be accepted by all the countryside. A funeral service was held to which the people flocked in great numbers, and every one approved of the sentiment which led the widow to add the words, "The Father of the Village," after the usual texts which appeared upon the stone over his grave.

This, then, was the story I pieced together of the village ghost as the little inn-keeper's daughter told it to me that afternoon in the parlour of the inn.

"But you're not the first to say you've seen him," the girl concluded; "and your description is just what we've always heard, and that window, they say, was just where he used to sit and think, and think, when he was alive, and sometimes, they say, to cry for hours together."

"And would you feel afraid if you had seen him?" I asked, for the girl seemed strangely moved and interested in the whole story.

"I think so," she answered timidly. "Surely, if he spoke to me. He did speak to you, didn't he, sir?" she asked after a slight pause.

"He said he had come for some one."

"Come for some one," she repeated. "Did he say—" she went on falteringly.

"No, he did not say for whom," I said quickly, noticing the sudden shadow on her face and the tremulous voice.

"Are you really sure, sir?"

"Oh, quite sure," I answered cheerfully. "I did not even ask him." The girl looked at me steadily for nearly a whole minute as though there were many things she wished to tell me or to ask. But she said nothing, and presently picked up her tray from the table and walked slowly out of the room.

Instead of keeping to my original purpose and pushing on to the next village over the hills, I ordered a room to be prepared for me at the inn, and that afternoon I spent wandering about the fields and lying under the fruit trees, watching the white clouds sailing out over the sea. The Wood of the Dead I surveyed from a distance, but in the village I visited the stone erected to the memory of the "Father of the Village"—who was thus, evidently, no mythical personage— and saw also the monuments of his fine unselfish spirit: the school-house he built, the library, the home for the aged poor, and the tiny hospital.

That night, as the clock in the church tower was striking half-past eleven, I stealthily left the inn and crept through the dark orchard and over the hayfield in the direction of the hill whose southern slope was clothed with the Wood of the Dead. A genuine interest impelled me to the adventure, but I also was obliged to confess to a certain sinking in my heart as I stumbled along over the field in the darkness, for I was approaching what might prove to be the birth-place of a real country myth, and a spot already lifted by the imaginative thoughts of a considerable number of people into the region of the haunted and ill-omened.

The inn lay below me, and all round it the village clustered in a soft black shadow unrelieved by a single light. The night was moonless, yet distinctly luminous, for the stars crowded the sky. The silence of deep slumber was everywhere; so still, indeed, that every time my foot kicked against a stone I thought the sound must be heard below in the village and waken the sleepers.

I climbed the hill slowly, thinking chiefly of the strange story of the noble old man who had seized the opportunity to do good to his fellows the moment it came his way, and wondering why the causes that operate ceaselessly behind human life did not always select such admirable instruments. Once or twice a night-bird circled swiftly over my head, but the bats had long since gone to rest, and there was no other sign of life stirring.

Then, suddenly, with a singular thrill of emotion, I saw the first trees of the Wood of the Dead rise in front of me in a high black wall. Their crests stood up like giant spears against the starry sky; and though there was no perceptible movement of the air on my cheek I heard a faint, rushing sound among their branches as the night breeze passed to and fro over their countless little needles. A remote, hushed murmur rose overhead and died away again almost immediately; for in these trees the wind seems to be never absolutely at rest, and on the calmest day there is always a sort of whispering music among their branches.

For a moment I hesitated on the edge of this dark wood, and listened intently. Delicate perfumes of earth and bark stole out to meet me. Impenetrable darkness faced me. Only the consciousness that I was obeying an order, strangely given, and including a mighty privilege, enabled me to find the courage to go forward and step in boldly under the trees.

Instantly the shadows closed in upon me and "something" came forward to meet me from the centre of the darkness. It would be easy enough to meet my imagination half-way with fact, and say that a cold hand grasped my own and led me by invisible paths into the unknown depths of the grove; but at any rate, without stumbling, and always with the positive knowledge that I was going straight towards the desired object, I pressed on confidently and securely into the wood. So dark was it that, at first, not a single star-beam pierced the roof of branches overhead; and, as we moved forward side by side, the trees shifted silently past us in long lines, row upon row, squadron upon squadron, like the units of a vast, soundless army.

And, at length, we came to a comparatively open space where the trees halted upon us for a while, and, looking up, I saw the white river of the sky beginning to yield to the influence of a new light that now seemed spreading swiftly across the heavens.

"It is the dawn coming," said the voice at my side that I certainly recognised, but which seemed almost like a whispering from the trees, "and we are now in the heart of the Wood of the Dead."

We seated ourselves on a moss-covered boulder and waited the coming of the sun. With marvellous swiftness, it seemed to me, the light in the east passed into the radiance of early morning, and when the wind awoke and began to whisper in the tree tops, the first rays of the risen sun fell between the trunks and rested in a circle of gold at our feet.

"Now, come with me," whispered my companion in the same deep voice, "for time has no existence here, and that which I would show you is already *there!*"

We trod gently and silently over the soft pine needles. Already the sun was high over our heads, and the shadows of the trees coiled closely about their feet. The wood became denser again, but occasionally we passed through little open bits where we could smell the hot sunshine and the dry, baked pine needles. Then, presently, we came to the edge of the grove, and I saw a hayfield lying in the blaze of day, and two horses basking lazily with switching tails in the shafts of a laden hay-waggon.

So complete and vivid was the sense of reality, that I remember the grateful realisation of the cool shade where we sat and looked out upon the hot world beyond.

The last pitchfork had tossed up its fragrant burden, and the great horses were already straining in the shafts after the driver, as he walked slowly in front with one hand upon their bridles. He was a stalwart fellow, with sunburned neck and hands. Then, for the first time, I noticed, perched aloft upon the trembling throne of hay, the figure of a slim young girl. I could not see her face, but her brown hair escaped in disorder from a white sun-bonnet, and her still browner hands held a well-worn hay rake. She was laughing and talking with the driver, and he, from time to time, cast up at her ardent glances of admiration—glances that won instant smiles and soft blushes in response.

The cart presently turned into the roadway that skirted the edge of the wood where we were sitting. I watched the scene with intense interest and became so much absorbed in it that I quite forgot the manifold, strange steps by which I was permitted to become a spectator.

"Come down and walk with me," cried the young fellow, stopping a moment in front of the horses and opening wide his arms. "Jump! and I'll catch you!"

"Oh, oh," she laughed, and her voice sounded to me as the happiest, merriest laughter I had ever heard from a girl's throat. "Oh, oh! that's all very well. But remember I'm Queen of the Hay, and I must ride!"

"Then I must come and ride beside you," he cried, and began at once to climb up by way of the driver's seat. But, with a peal of silvery laughter, she slipped down easily over the back of the hay to escape him, and ran a little way along the road. I could see her quite clearly, and noticed the charming, natural grace of her movements, and the loving expression in her eyes as she looked over her shoulder to make sure he was following. Evidently, she did not wish to escape for long, certainly not for ever.

In two strides the big, brown swain was after her, leaving the horses to do as they pleased. Another second and his arms would have caught the slender waist and pressed the little body to his heart. But, just at that instant, the old man beside me uttered a peculiar cry. It was low and thrilling, and it went through me like a sharp sword.

HE had called her by her own name—and she had heard.

For a second she halted, glancing back with frightened eyes. Then, with a brief cry of despair, the girl swerved aside and dived in swiftly among the shadows of the trees.

But the young man saw the sudden movement and cried out to her passionately—

"Not that way, my love! Not that way! It's the Wood of the Dead!"

She threw a laughing glance over her shoulder at him, and the wind caught her hair and drew it out in a brown cloud under the sun. But the next minute she was close beside me, lying on the breast of my companion, and I was certain I heard the words repeatedly uttered with many sighs: "Father, you called, and I have come. And I come willingly, for I am very, very tired."

At any rate, so the words sounded to me, and mingled with them I seemed to catch the answer in that deep, thrilling whisper I already knew: "And you shall sleep, my child, sleep for a long, long time, until it is time for you to begin the journey again."

In that brief second of time I had recognised the face and voice of the inn-keeper's daughter, but the next minute a dreadful wail broke from the lips of the young man, and the sky grew suddenly as dark as night, the wind rose and began to toss the branches about us, and the whole scene was swallowed up in a wave of utter blackness.

Again the chill fingers seemed to seize my hand, and I was guided by the way I had come to the edge of the wood, and crossing the hayfield still slumbering in the starlight, I crept back to the inn and went to bed.

A year later I happened to be in the same part of the country, and the memory of the strange summer vision returned to me with the added softness of distance. I went to the old village and had tea under the same orchard trees at the same inn.

But the little maid of the inn did not show her face, and I took occasion to enquire of her father as to her welfare and her whereabouts.

"Married, no doubt," I laughed, but with a strange feeling that clutched at my heart.

"No, sir," replied the inn-keeper sadly, "not married—though she was just going to be—but dead. She got a sunstroke in the hayfields, just a few days after you were here, if I remember rightly, and she was gone from us in less than a week."

Smith: An Episode in a Lodging House

W hen I was a medical student," began the doctor, half turning towards his circle of listeners in the firelight, "I came across one or two very curious human beings; but there was one fellow I remember particularly, for he caused me the most vivid, and I think the most uncomfortable, emotions I have ever known.

"For many months I knew Smith only by name as the occupant of the floor above me. Obviously his name meant nothing to me. Moreover I was busy with lectures, reading, cliniques, and the like, and had little leisure to devise plans for scraping acquaintance with any of the other lodgers in the house. Then chance brought us curiously together, and this fellow Smith left a deep impression upon me as the result of our first meeting. At the time the strength of this first impression seemed quite inexplicable to me, but looking back at the episode now from a standpoint of greater knowledge I judge the fact to have been that he stirred my curiosity to an unusual degree, and at the same time awakened my sense of horror—whatever that may be in a medical student—about as deeply and permanently as these two emotions were capable of being stirred at all in the particular system and set of nerves called Me.

"How he knew that I was interested in the study of languages was something I could never explain, but one day, quite unannounced, he came quietly into my room in the evening and asked me point-blank if I knew enough Hebrew to help him in the pronunciation of certain words.

"He caught me along the line of least resistance, and I was greatly flattered to be able to give him the desired information; but it was only when he had thanked me and was gone that I realised I had been in the presence of an unusual individuality. For the life of me I could not quite seize and label the peculiarities of what I felt to be a very striking personality, but it was borne in upon me that he was a man apart from his fellows, a mind that followed a line leading away from ordinary human intercourse and human interests, and into regions that left in his atmosphere something remote, rarefied, chilling.

"The moment he was gone I became conscious of two things—an intense curiosity to know more about this man and what his real interests were, and secondly, the fact that my skin was crawling and that my hair had a tendency to rise."

The doctor paused a moment here to puff hard at his pipe, which, however, had gone out beyond recall without the assistance of a match; and in the deep silence, which testified to the genuine interest of his listeners, some one poked the fire up into a little blaze, and one or two others glanced over their shoulders into the dark distances of the big hall.

"On looking back," he went on, watching the momentary flames in the grate, "I see a short, thick-set man of perhaps forty-five, with immense shoulders and small, slender hands. The contrast was noticeable, for I remember thinking that such a giant frame and such slim finger bones hardly belonged together. His head, too, was large and very long, the head of an idealist beyond all question, yet with an unusually strong development of the jaw and chin. Here again was a singular contradiction, though I am better able now to appreciate its full meaning, with a greater experience in judging the values of physiognomy. For this meant, of course, an enthusiastic idealism balanced and kept in check by will and judgment—elements usually deficient in dreamers and visionaries.

"At any rate, here was a being with probably a very wide range of possibilities, a machine with a pendulum that most likely had an unusual length of swing.

"The man's hair was exceedingly fine, and the lines about his nose and mouth were cut as with a delicate steel instrument in wax. His eyes I have left to the last. They were large and quite changeable, not in colour only, but in character, size, and shape. Occasionally they seemed the eyes of some one else, if you can understand what I mean, and at the same time, in their shifting shades of blue, green, and a nameless sort of dark grey, there was a sinister light in them that lent to the whole face an aspect almost alarming. Moreover, they were the most luminous optics I think I have ever seen in any human being.

"There, then, at the risk of a wearisome description, is Smith as I saw him for the first time that winter's evening in my shabby student's rooms in Edinburgh. And yet the real part of him, of course, I have left untouched, for it is both indescribable and un-get-at-able. I have spoken already of an atmosphere of warning and aloofness he carried about with him. It is impossible further to analyse the series of little shocks his presence always communicated to my being; but there was that about him which made me instantly on the *qui vive* in his presence, every nerve alert, every sense strained and on the watch. I do not mean that he deliberately suggested danger, but rather that he brought forces in his wake which automatically warned the nervous centres of my system to be on their guard and alert.

"Since the days of my first acquaintance with this man I have lived through other experiences and have seen much I cannot pretend to explain or understand; but, so far in my life, I have only once come across a human being who suggested a disagreeable familiarity with unholy things, and who made me feel uncanny and 'creepy' in his presence; and that unenviable individual was Mr. Smith.

"What his occupation was during the day I never knew. I think he slept until the sun set. No one ever saw him on the stairs, or heard him move in his room during the day. He was a creature of the shadows, who apparently preferred darkness to light. Our landlady either knew nothing, or would say nothing. At any rate she found no fault, and I have since wondered often by what magic this fellow was able to convert a common landlady of a common lodging-house into a discreet and uncommunicative person. This alone was a sign of genius of some sort.

"'He's been here with me for years—long before you come, an' I don't interfere or ask no questions of what doesn't concern me, as long as people pays their rent,' was the only remark on the subject that I ever succeeded in winning from that quarter, and it certainly told me nothing nor gave me any encouragement to ask for further information.

"Examinations, however, and the general excitement of a medical student's life for a time put Mr. Smith completely out of my head.

For a long period he did not call upon me again, and for my part, I felt no courage to return his unsolicited visit.

"Just then, however, there came a change in the fortunes of those who controlled my very limited income, and I was obliged to give up my ground-floor and move aloft to more modest chambers on the top of the house. Here I was directly over Smith, and had to pass his door to reach my own.

"It so happened that about this time I was frequently called out at all hours of the night for the maternity cases which a fourth-year student takes at a certain period of his studies, and on returning from one of these visits at about two o'clock in the morning I was surprised to hear the sound of voices as I passed his door. A peculiar sweet odour, too, not unlike the smell of incense, penetrated into the passage.

"I went upstairs very quietly, wondering what was going on there at this hour of the morning. To my knowledge Smith never had visitors. For a moment I hesitated outside the door with one foot on the stairs. All my interest in this strange man revived, and my curiosity rose to a point not far from action. At last I might learn something of the habits of this lover of the night and the darkness.

"The sound of voices was plainly audible, Smith's predominating so much that I never could catch more than points of sound from the other, penetrating now and then the steady stream of his voice. Not a single word reached me, at least, not a word that I could understand, though the voice was loud and distinct, and it was only afterwards that I realised he must have been speaking in a foreign language.

"The sound of footsteps, too, was equally distinct. Two persons were moving about the room, passing and re-passing the door, one of them a light, agile person, and the other ponderous and somewhat awkward. Smith's voice went on incessantly with its odd, monotonous droning, now loud, now soft, as he crossed and re-crossed the floor. The other person was also on the move, but in a different and less regular fashion, for I heard rapid steps that seemed to end sometimes in stumbling, and quick sudden movements that brought up with a violent lurching against the wall or furniture.

"As I listened to Smith's voice, moreover, I began to feel afraid.

There was something in the sound that made me feel intuitively he was in a tight place, and an impulse stirred faintly in me—very faintly, I admit—to knock at the door and enquire if he needed help.

"But long before the impulse could translate itself into an act, or even before it had been properly weighed and considered by the mind, I heard a voice close beside me in the air, a sort of hushed whisper which I am certain was Smith speaking, though the sound did not seem to have come to me through the door. It was close in my very ear, as though he stood beside me, and it gave me such a start, that I clutched the banisters to save myself from stepping backwards and making a clatter on the stairs.

"'There is nothing you can do to help me,'" it said distinctly, 'and you will be much safer in your own room.'

"I am ashamed to this day of the pace at which I covered the flight of stairs in the darkness to the top floor, and of the shaking hand with which I lit my candles and bolted the door. But, there it is, just as it happened.

"This midnight episode, so odd and yet so trivial in itself, fired me with more curiosity than ever about my fellow-lodger. It also made me connect him in my mind with a sense of fear and distrust. I never saw him, yet I was often, and uncomfortably, aware of his presence in the upper regions of that gloomy lodging-house. Smith and his secret mode of life and mysterious pursuits, somehow contrived to awaken in my being a line of reflection that disturbed my comfortable condition of ignorance. I never saw him, as I have said, and exchanged no sort of communication with him, yet it seemed to me that his mind was in contact with mine, and some of the strange forces of his atmosphere filtered through into my being and disturbed my equilibrium. Those upper floors became haunted for me after dark, and, though outwardly our lives never came into contact, I became unwillingly involved in certain pursuits on which his mind was centred. I felt that he was somehow making use of me against my will, and by methods which passed my comprehension.

"I was at that time, moreover, in the heavy, unquestioning state of materialism which is common to medical students when they begin to understand something of the human anatomy and nervous system, and jump at once to the conclusion that they control the universe and hold in their forceps the last word of life and death. I 'knew it all,' and regarded a belief in anything beyond matter as the wanderings of weak, or at best, untrained minds. And this condition of mind, of course, added to the strength of this upsetting fear which emanated from the floor below and began slowly to take possession of me.

"Though I kept no notes of the subsequent events in this matter, they made too deep an impression for me ever to forget the sequence in which they occurred. Without difficulty I can recall the next step in the adventure with Smith, for adventure it rapidly grew to be."

The doctor stopped a moment and laid his pipe on the table behind him before continuing. The fire had burned low, and no one stirred to poke it. The silence in the great hall was so deep that when the speaker's pipe touched the table the sound woke audible echoes at the far end among the shadows.

"One evening, while I was reading, the door of my room opened and Smith came in. He made no attempt at ceremony. It was after ten o'clock and I was tired, but the presence of the man immediately galvanised me into activity. My attempts at ordinary politeness he thrust on one side at once, and began asking me to vocalise, and then pronounce for him, certain Hebrew words; and when this was done he abruptly enquired if I was not the fortunate possessor of a very rare Rabbinical Treatise, which he named.

"How he knew that I possessed this book puzzled me exceedingly; but I was still more surprised to see him cross the room and take it out of my book-shelf almost before I had had time to answer in the affirmative. Evidently he knew exactly where it was kept. This excited my curiosity beyond all bounds, and I immediately began asking him questions; and though, out of sheer respect for the man, I put them very delicately to him, and almost by way of mere conversation, he had only one reply for the lot. He would look up at me from the pages of the book with an expression of complete comprehension on his extraordinary features, would bow his head a little and say very gravely—

"'That, of course, is a perfectly proper question,'—which was absolutely all I could ever get out of him.

"On this particular occasion he stayed with me perhaps ten or fifteen minutes. Then he went quickly downstairs to his room with my Hebrew Treatise in his hand, and I heard him close and bolt his door.

"But a few moments later, before I had time to settle down to my book again, or to recover from the surprise his visit had caused me, I heard the door open, and there stood Smith once again beside my chair. He made no excuse for his second interruption, but bent his head down to the level of my reading lamp and peered across the flame straight into my eyes.

"'I hope,' he whispered, 'I hope you are never disturbed at night?'

"'Eh?' I stammered, 'disturbed at night? Oh no, thanks, at least, not that I know of—'

"'I'm glad,' he replied gravely, appearing not to notice my confusion and surprise at his question. 'But, remember, should it ever be the case, please let me know at once.'

"And he was gone down the stairs and into his room again.

"For some minutes I sat reflecting upon his strange behaviour. He was not mad, I argued, but was the victim of some harmless delusion that had gradually grown upon him as a result of his solitary mode of life; and from the books he used, I judged that it had something to do with mediæval magic, or some system of ancient Hebrew mysticism. The words he asked me to pronounce for him were probably 'Words of Power,' which, when uttered with the vehemence of a strong will behind them, were supposed to produce physical results, or set up vibrations in one's own inner being that had the effect of a partial lifting of the veil.

"I sat thinking about the man, and his way of living, and the probable effects in the long-run of his dangerous experiments, and I can recall perfectly well the sensation of disappointment that crept over me when I realised that I had labeled his particular form of aberration, and that my curiosity would therefore no longer be excited.

"For some time I had been sitting alone with these reflections— it may have been ten minutes or it may have been half an hour— when I was aroused from my reverie by the knowledge that some one was again in the room standing close beside my chair. My first thought was that Smith had come back again in his swift, unaccountable manner, but almost at the same moment I realised that this could not be the case at all. For the door faced my position, and it certainly had not been opened again.

"Yet, some one was in the room, moving cautiously to and fro, watching me, almost touching me. I was as sure of it as I was of myself, and though at the moment I do not think I was actually afraid, I am bound to admit that a certain weakness came over me and that I felt that strange disinclination for action which is probably the beginning of the horrible paralysis of real terror. I should have been glad to hide myself, if that had been possible, to cower into a corner, or behind a door, or anywhere so that I could not be watched and observed.

"But, overcoming my nervousness with an effort of the will, I got up quickly out of my chair and held the reading lamp aloft so that it shone into all the corners like a searchlight.

"The room was utterly empty! It was utterly empty, at least, to the *eye,* but to the nerves, and especially to that combination of sense perception which is made up by all the senses acting together, and by no one in particular, there was a person standing there at my very elbow.

"I say 'person,' for I can think of no appropriate word. For, if it *was* a human being, I can only affirm that I had the overwhelming conviction that it was *not,* but that it was some form of life wholly unknown to me both as to its essence and its nature. A sensation of gigantic force and power came with it, and I remember vividly to this day my terror on realising that I was close to an invisible being who could crush me as easily as I could crush a fly, and who could see my every movement while itself remaining invisible.

"To this terror was added the certain knowledge that the 'being' kept in my proximity for a definite purpose. And that this purpose had some direct bearing upon my well-being, indeed upon my life, I was equally convinced; for I became aware of a sensation of growing lassitude as though the vitality were being steadily drained out of my body. My heart began to beat irregularly at first, then faintly. I was conscious, even within a few minutes, of a general drooping of the powers of life in the whole system, an ebbing away of self-control, and a distinct approach of drowsiness and torpor.

"The power to move, or to think out any mode of resistance, was fast leaving me, when there rose, in the distance as it were, a tremendous commotion. A door opened with a clatter, and I heard the peremptory and commanding tones of a human voice calling aloud in a language I could not comprehend. It was Smith, my fellow-lodger, calling up the stairs; and his voice had not sounded for more than a few seconds, when I felt something withdrawn from my presence, from my person, indeed from my *very skin*. It seemed as if there was a rushing of air and some large creature swept by me at about the level of my shoulders. Instantly the pressure on my heart was relieved, and the atmosphere seemed to resume its normal condition.

"Smith's door closed quietly downstairs, as I put the lamp down with trembling hands. What had happened I do not know; only, I was alone again and my strength was returning as rapidly as it had left me.

"I went across the room and examined myself in the glass. The skin was very pale, and the eyes dull. My temperature, I found, was a little below normal and my pulse faint and irregular. But these smaller signs of disturbance were as nothing compared with the feeling I had—though no outward signs bore testimony to the fact—that I had narrowly escaped a real and ghastly catastrophe. I felt shaken, somehow, shaken to the very roots of my being."

The doctor rose from his chair and crossed over to the dying fire, so that no one could see the expression on his face as he stood with his back to the grate, and continued his weird tale.

"It would be wearisome," he went on in a lower voice, looking over our heads as though he still saw the dingy top floor of that haunted Edinburgh lodging-house; "it would be tedious for me at this length of time to analyse my feelings, or attempt to reproduce for you the thorough examination to which I endeavoured then to subject my whole being, intellectual, emotional, and physical. I need only mention the dominant emotion with which this curious episode left me—the indignant anger against myself that I could ever have lost my self-control enough to come under the sway of so gross and absurd a delusion. This protest, however, I remember making with all the emphasis possible. And I also remember noting that it brought me very little satisfaction, for it was the protest of my reason only, when all the rest of my being was up in arms against its conclusions.

"My dealings with the 'delusion,' however, were not yet over for the night; for very early next morning, somewhere about three o'clock, I was awakened by a curiously stealthy noise in the room, and the next minute there followed a crash as if all my books had been swept bodily from their shelf on to the floor.

"But this time I was not frightened. Cursing the disturbance with all the resounding and harmless words I could accumulate, I jumped out of bed and lit the candle in a second, and in the first dazzle of the flaring match—but before the wick had time to catch—I was certain I *saw* a dark grey shadow, of ungainly shape, and with something more or less like a human head, drive rapidly past the side of the wall farthest from me and disappear into the gloom by the angle of the door.

"I waited one single second to be sure the candle was alight, and then dashed after it, but before I had gone two steps, my foot stumbled against something hard piled up on the carpet and I only just saved myself from falling headlong. I picked myself up and found that all the books from what I called my 'language shelf' were strewn across the floor. The room, meanwhile, as a minute's search revealed, was quite empty. I looked in every corner and behind every stick of furniture, and a student's bedroom on a top floor, costing twelve shillings a week, did not hold many available hiding-places, as you may imagine.

"The crash, however, was explained. Some very practical and physical force had thrown the books from their resting-place. That, at least, was beyond all doubt. And as I replaced them on the shelf and noted that not one was missing, I busied myself mentally with the sore problem of how the agent of this little practical joke had gained access to my room, and then escaped again. *For my door was locked and bolted.*

"Smith's odd question as to whether I was disturbed in the night, and his warning injunction to let him know at once if such were the case, now of course returned to affect me as I stood there in the early morning, cold and shivering on the carpet; but I realised at the same moment how impossible it would be for me to admit that a more than usually vivid nightmare could have any connection with himself. I would rather stand a hundred of these mysterious visitations than consult such a man as to their possible cause.

"A knock at the door interrupted my reflections, and I gave a start that sent the candle grease flying.

"'Let me in,' came in Smith's voice.

"I unlocked the door. He came in fully dressed. His face wore a curious pallor. It seemed to me to be under the skin and to shine through and almost make it luminous. His eyes were exceedingly bright.

"I was wondering what in the world to say to him, or how he would explain his visit at such an hour, when he closed the door behind him and came close up to me—uncomfortably close.

"'You should have called me at once,' he said in his whispering voice, fixing his great eyes on my face.

"I stammered something about an awful dream, but he ignored my remark utterly, and I caught his eye wandering next—if any movement of those optics can be described as 'wandering'—to the book-shelf. I watched him, unable to move my gaze from his person. The man fascinated me horribly for some reason. Why, in the devil's name, was he up and dressed at three in the morning? How did he know anything unusual had happened in my room? Then his whisper began again.

"'It's your amazing vitality that causes you this annoyance,' he said, shifting his eyes back to mine.

"I gasped. Something in his voice or manner turned my blood into ice.

"'That's the real attraction,' he went on. 'But if this continues one of us will have to leave, you know.'

"I positively could not find a word to say in reply. The channels of speech dried up within me. I simply stared and wondered what he would say next. I watched him in a sort of dream, and as far as I can remember, he asked me to promise to call him sooner another time, and then began to walk round the room, uttering strange sounds, and making signs with his arms and hands until he reached the door. Then he was gone in a second, and I had closed and locked the door behind him.

"After this, the Smith adventure drew rapidly to a climax. It was a week or two later, and I was coming home between two and three in the morning from a maternity case, certain features of which for the time being had very much taken possession of my mind, so much so, indeed, that I passed Smith's door without giving him a single thought.

"The gas jet on the landing was still burning, but so low that it made little impression on the waves of deep shadow that lay across the stairs. Overhead, the faintest possible gleam of grey showed that the morning was not far away. A few stars shone down through the sky-light. The house was still as the grave, and the only sound to break the silence was the rushing of the wind round the walls and over the roof. But this was a fitful sound, suddenly rising and as suddenly falling away again, and it only served to intensify the silence.

"I had already reached my own landing when I gave a violent start. It was automatic, almost a reflex action in fact, for it was only when I caught myself fumbling at the door handle and thinking where I could conceal myself quickest that I realised a voice had sounded close beside me in the air. It was the same voice I had heard before, and it seemed to me to be calling for help. And yet the very same minute I pushed on into the room, determined to disregard it, and seeking to persuade myself it was the creaking of the boards under my weight or the rushing noise of the wind that had deceived me.

"But hardly had I reached the table where the candles stood when the sound was unmistakably repeated: 'Help! help!' And this time it was accompanied by what I can only describe as a vivid tactile hallucination. I was touched: the *skin* of my arm was clutched by fingers.

"Some compelling force sent me headlong downstairs as if the haunting forces of the whole world were at my heels. At Smith's door I paused. The force of his previous warning injunction to seek his aid without delay acted suddenly and I leant my whole weight against the panels, little dreaming that I should be called upon to give help rather than to receive it.

"The door yielded at once, and I burst into a room that was so full of a choking vapour, moving in slow clouds, that at first I could distinguish nothing at all but a set of what seemed to be huge shadows passing in and out of the mist. Then, gradually, I perceived that a red lamp on the mantelpiece gave all the light there was, and that the room which I now entered for the first time was almost empty of furniture.

"The carpet was rolled back and piled in a heap in the corner, and upon the white boards of the floor I noticed a large circle drawn in black of some material that emitted a faint glowing light and was apparently smoking. Inside this circle, as well as at regular intervals outside it, were curious-looking designs, also traced in the same black, smoking substance. These, too, seemed to emit a feeble light of their own.

"My first impression on entering the room had been that it was full of—*people,* I was going to say; but that hardly expresses my meaning. *Beings,* they certainly were, but it was borne in upon me beyond the possibility of doubt, that they were not human beings. That I had caught a momentary glimpse of living, intelligent entities I can never doubt, but I am equally convinced, though I cannot prove it, that these entities were from some other scheme of evolution altogether, and had nothing to do with the ordinary human life, either incarnate or discarnate.

"But, whatever they were, the visible appearance of them was exceedingly fleeting. I no longer saw anything, though I still felt convinced of their immediate presence. They were, moreover, of the same order of life as the visitant in my bedroom of a few nights before, and their proximity to my atmosphere in numbers, instead of singly as before, conveyed to my mind something that was quite terrible and overwhelming. I fell into a violent trembling, and the perspiration poured from my face in streams.

"They were in constant motion about me. They stood close to my side; moved behind me; brushed past my shoulder; stirred the hair on my forehead; and circled round me without ever actually touching me, yet always pressing closer and closer. Especially in the air just over my head there seemed ceaseless movement, and it was accompanied by a confused noise of whispering and sighing that threatened every moment to become articulate in words. To my intense relief, however, I heard no distinct words, and the noise continued more like the rising and falling of the wind than anything else I can imagine.

"But the characteristic of these 'Beings' that impressed me most strongly at the time, and of which I have carried away the most permanent recollection, was that each one of them possessed what seemed to be a *vibrating centre* which impelled it with tremendous force and caused a rapid whirling motion of the atmosphere as it passed me. The air was full of these little vortices of whirring, rotating force, and whenever one of them pressed me too closely I felt as if the nerves in that particular portion of my body had been literally drawn out, absolutely depleted of vitality, and then immediately replaced—but replaced dead, flabby, useless.

"Then, suddenly, for the first time my eyes fell upon Smith. He was crouching against the wall on my right, in an attitude that was obviously defensive, and it was plain he was in extremities. The terror on his face was pitiable, but at the same time there was another expression about the tightly clenched teeth and mouth which showed that he had not lost all control of himself. He wore the most resolute expression I have ever seen on a human countenance, and, though for the moment at a fearful disadvantage, he looked like a man who had confidence in himself, and, in spite of the working of fear, was waiting his opportunity.

"For my part, I was face to face with a situation so utterly beyond my knowledge and comprehension, that I felt as helpless as a child, and as useless.

"'Help me back—quick—into that circle,' I heard him half cry, half whisper to me across the moving vapours.

"My only value appears to have been that I was not afraid to act. Knowing nothing of the forces I was dealing with I had no idea of the deadly perils risked, and I sprang forward and caught him by the arms. He threw all his weight in my direction, and by our combined efforts his body left the wall and lurched across the floor towards the circle.

"Instantly there descended upon us, out of the empty air of that smoke-laden room, a force which I can only compare to the pushing, driving power of a great wind pent up within a narrow space. It was almost explosive in its effect, and it seemed to operate upon all parts of my body equally. It fell upon us with a rushing noise that filled my ears and made me think for a moment the very walls and roof of the building had been torn asunder. Under its first blow we staggered back against the wall, and I understood plainly that its purpose was to prevent us getting back into the circle in the middle of the floor.

"Pouring with perspiration, and breathless, with every muscle strained to the very utmost, we at length managed to get to the edge of the circle, and at this moment, so great was the opposing force, that I felt myself actually torn from Smith's arms, lifted from my feet, and twirled round in the direction of the windows as if the wheel of some great machine had caught my clothes and was tearing me to destruction in its revolution.

"But, even as I fell, bruised and breathless, against the wall, I saw Smith firmly upon his feet in the circle and slowly rising again to an upright position. My eyes never left his figure once in the next few minutes.

"He drew himself up to his full height. His great shoulders squared themselves. His head was thrown back a little, and as I looked I saw the expression on his face change swiftly from fear to one of absolute command. He looked steadily round the room and then his voice began to *vibrate*. At first in a low tone, it gradually rose till it assumed the same volume and intensity I had heard that night when he called up the stairs into my room.

"It was a curiously increasing sound, more like the swelling of an instrument than a human voice; and as it grew in power and filled the room, I became aware that a great change was being effected slowly and surely. The confusion of noise and rushings of air fell into the roll of long, steady vibrations not unlike those caused by the deeper pedals of an organ. The movements in the air became less violent, then grew decidedly weaker, and finally ceased altogether. The whisperings and sighings became fainter and fainter, till at last I could not hear them at all; and, strangest of all, the light emitted by the circle, as well as by the designs round it, increased to a steady glow, casting their radiance upwards with the weirdest possible effect upon his features. Slowly, by the power of his voice, behind which lay undoubtedly a genuine knowledge of the occult manipulation of sound, this man dominated the forces that had escaped from their proper sphere, until at length the room was reduced to silence and perfect order again.

"Judging by the immense relief which also communicated itself to my nerves I then felt that the crisis was over and Smith was wholly master of the situation.

"But hardly had I begun to congratulate myself upon this result, and to gather my scattered senses about me, when, uttering a loud cry, I saw him leap out of the circle and fling himself into the air—as it seemed to me, into the empty air. Then, even while holding my breath for dread of the crash he was bound to make upon the floor, I saw him strike with a dull thud against a solid body in mid-air, and the next instant he was wrestling with some ponderous thing that was absolutely invisible to me, and the room shook with the struggle.

"To and fro *they* swayed, sometimes lurching in one direction, sometimes in another, and always in horrible proximity to myself, as I leaned trembling against the wall and watched the encounter.

"It lasted at most but a short minute or two, ending as suddenly as it had begun. Smith, with an unexpected movement, threw up his arms with a cry of relief. At the same instant there was a wild, tearing shriek in the air beside me and something rushed past us with a noise like the passage of a flock of big birds. Both windows rattled as if they would break away from their sashes. Then a sense of emptiness and peace suddenly came over the room, and I knew that all was over.

"Smith, his face exceedingly white, but otherwise strangely composed, turned to me at once.

"'God!—if you hadn't come— You deflected the stream; broke it up—' he whispered. 'You saved me.'"

The doctor made a long pause. Presently he felt for his pipe in the darkness, groping over the table behind us with both hands. No one spoke for a bit, but all dreaded the sudden glare that would come when he struck the match. The fire was nearly out and the great hall was pitch dark.

But the story-teller did not strike that match. He was merely gaining time for some hidden reason of his own. And presently he went on with his tale in a more subdued voice.

"I quite forget," he said, "how I got back to my own room. I only know that I lay with two lighted candles for the rest of the night, and the first thing I did in the morning was to let the landlady know I was leaving her house at the end of the week.

"Smith still has my Rabbinical Treatise. At least he did not return it to me at the time, and I have never seen him since to ask for it."

A Suspicious Gift

Blake had been in very low water for months—almost under water part of the time—due to circumstances he was fond of saying were no fault of his own; and as he sat writing in his room on "third floor back" of a New York boarding-house, part of his mind was busily occupied in wondering when his luck was going to turn again.

It was his room only in the sense that he paid the rent. Two friends, one a little Frenchman and the other a big Dane, shared it with him, both hoping eventually to contribute something towards expenses, but so far not having accomplished this result. They had two beds only, the third being a mattress they slept upon in turns, a week at a time. A good deal of their irregular "feeding" consisted of oatmeal, potatoes, and sometimes eggs, all of which they cooked on a strange utensil they had contrived to fix into the gas jet. Occasionally, when dinner failed them altogether, they swallowed a little raw rice and drank hot water from the bathroom on the top of it, and then made a wild race for bed so as to get to sleep while the sensation of false repletion was still there. For sleep and hunger are slight acquaintances as they well knew. Fortunately all New York houses are supplied with hot air, and they only had to open a grating in the wall to get a plentiful, if not a wholesome amount of heat.

Though loneliness in a big city is a real punishment, as they had severally learnt to their cost, their experiences, three in a small room for several months, had revealed to them horrors of quite another kind, and their nerves had suffered according to the temperament of each. But, on this particular evening, as Blake sat scribbling by the only window that was not cracked, the Dane and the Frenchman, his companions in adversity, were in wonderful luck. They had both been asked out to a restaurant to dine with a friend who also held out to one of them a chance of work and remuneration. They would not be back till late, and when they did come they were pretty sure to bring in supplies of one kind or another. For the Frenchman never could resist the offer of a glass of absinthe, and this meant that he would be able to help himself plentifully from the free-lunch counters, with which all New York bars are furnished, and to which any purchaser of a drink is entitled to help himself and devour on the spot or carry away casually in his hand for consumption elsewhere. Thousands of unfortunate men get their sole subsistence in this way in New York, and experience soon teaches where, for the price of a single drink, a man can take away almost a meal of chip potatoes, sausage, bits of bread, and even eggs. The Frenchman and the Dane knew their way about, and Blake looked forward to a supper more or less substantial before pulling his mattress out of the cupboard and turning in upon the floor for the night.

Meanwhile he could enjoy a quiet and lonely evening with the room all to himself.

In the daytime he was a reporter on an evening newspaper of sensational and lying habits. His work was chiefly in the police courts; and in his spare hours at night, when not too tired or too empty, he wrote sketches and stories for the magazines that very rarely saw the light of day on their printed and paid-for sentences. On this particular occasion he was deep in a most involved tale of a psychological character, and had just worked his way into a sentence, or set of sentences, that completely baffled and muddled him.

He was fairly out of his depth, and his brain was too poorly supplied with blood to invent a way out again. The story would have been interesting had he written it simply, keeping to facts and feelings, and not diving into difficult analysis of motive and character which was quite beyond him. For it was largely autobiographical, and was meant to describe the adventures of a young Englishman who had come to grief in the usual manner on a Canadian farm, had then subsequently become bar-keeper, sub-editor on a Methodist magazine, a teacher of French and German to clerks at twenty-five cents per hour, a model for artists, a super on the stage, and, finally, a wanderer to the goldfields.

Blake scratched his head, and dipped the pen in the inkpot,

stared out through the blindless windows, and sighed deeply. His thoughts kept wandering to food, beefsteak and steaming vegetables. The smell of cooking that came from a lower floor through the broken windows was a constant torment to him. He pulled himself together and again attacked the problem.

". . . for with some people," he wrote, "the imagination is so vivid as to be almost an extension of consciousness. . . ." But here he stuck absolutely. He was not quite sure what he meant by the words, and how to finish the sentence puzzled him into blank inaction. It was a difficult point to decide, for it seemed to come in appropriately at this point in his story, and he did not know whether to leave it as it stood, change it round a bit, or take it out altogether. It might just spoil its chances of being accepted: editors were such clever men. But, to rewrite the sentence was a grind, and he was so tired and sleepy. After all, what did it matter? People who were clever would force a meaning into it; people who were not clever would pretend— he knew of no other classes of readers. He would let it stay, and go on with the action of the story. He put his head in his hands and began to think hard.

His mind soon passed from thought to reverie. He fell to wondering when his friends would find work and relieve him of the burden—he acknowledged it as such—of keeping them, and of letting another man wear his best clothes on alternate Sundays. He wondered when his "luck" would turn. There were one or two influential people in New York whom he could go and see if he had a dress suit and the other conventional uniforms. His thoughts ran on far ahead, and at the same time, by a sort of double process, far behind as well. His home in the "old country" rose up before him; he saw the lawn and the cedars in sunshine; he looked through the familiar windows and saw the clean, swept rooms. His story began to suffer; the psychological masterpiece would not make much progress unless he pulled up and dragged his thoughts back to the treadmill. But he no longer cared; once he had got as far as that cedar with the sunshine on it, he never could get back again. For all he cared, the troublesome sentence might run away and get into some one else's pages, or be snuffed out altogether.

There came a gentle knock at the door, and Blake started. The knock was repeated louder. Who in the world could it be at this late hour of the night? On the floor above, he remembered, there lived another Englishman, a foolish, second-rate creature, who sometimes came in and made himself objectionable with endless and silly chatter. But he was an Englishman for all that, and Blake always tried to treat him with politeness, realising that he was lonely in a strange land. But to-night, of all people in the world, he did not want to be bored with Perry's cackle, as he called it, and the "Come in" he gave in answer to the second knock had no very cordial sound of welcome in it.

However, the door opened in response, and the man came in. Blake did not turn round at once, and the other advanced to the centre of the room, but *without speaking*. Then Blake knew it was not his enemy, Perry, and turned round.

He saw a man of about forty standing in the middle of the carpet, but standing sideways so that he did not present a full face. He wore an overcoat buttoned up to the neck, and on the felt hat which he held in front of him fresh rain-drops glistened. In his other hand he carried a small black bag. Blake gave him a good look, and came to the conclusion that he might be a secretary, or a chief clerk, or a confidential man of sorts. He was a shabby-respectable-looking person. This was the sum-total of the first impression, gained the moment his eyes took in that it was *not* Perry; the second impression was less pleasant, and reported at once that something was wrong.

Though otherwise young and inexperienced, Blake—thanks, or curses, to the police court training—knew more about common criminal blackguardism than most men of fifty, and he recognised that there was somewhere a suggestion of this undesirable world about the man. But there was more than this. There was something singular about him, something far out of the common, though for the life of him Blake could not say wherein it lay. The fellow was out of the ordinary, and in some very undesirable manner.

All this, that takes so long to describe, Blake saw with the first and second glance. The man at once began to speak in a quiet and respectful voice.

"Are you Mr. Blake?" he asked.

"I am."

"Mr. Arthur Blake?"

"Yes."

"Mr. Arthur *Herbert* Blake?" persisted the other, with emphasis on the middle name.

"That is my full name," Blake answered simply, adding, as he remembered his manners; "but won't you sit down, first, please?"

The man advanced with a curious sideways motion like a crab and took a seat on the edge of the sofa. He put his hat on the floor at his feet, but still kept the bag in his hand.

"I come to you from a well-wisher," he went on in oily tones, without lifting his eyes. Blake, in his mind, ran quickly over all the people he knew in New York who might possibly have sent such a man, while waiting for him to supply the name. But the man had come to a full stop and was waiting too.

"A well-wisher of *mine?*" repeated Blake, not knowing quite what else to say.

"Just so," replied the other, still with his eyes on the floor. "A well-wisher of yours."

"A man or—" he felt himself blushing, "or a woman?"

"That," said the man shortly, "I cannot tell you."

"You can't tell me!" exclaimed the other, wondering what was coming next, and who in the world this mysterious well-wisher could be who sent so discreet and mysterious a messenger.

"I cannot tell you the name," replied the man firmly. "Those are my instructions. But I bring you something from this person, and I am to give it to you, to take a receipt for it, and then to go away without answering any questions."

Blake stared very hard. The man, however, never raised his eyes above the level of the second china knob on the chest of drawers opposite. The giving of a receipt sounded like money. Could it be that some of his influential friends had heard of his plight? There were possibilities that made his heart beat. At length, however, he found his tongue, for this strange creature was determined apparently to say nothing more until he had heard from him.

"Then, what have you got for me, please?" he asked bluntly.

By way of answer the man proceeded to open the bag. He took out a parcel wrapped loosely in brown paper, and about the size of a large book. It was tied with string, and the man seemed unnecessarily long untying the knot. When at last the string was off and the paper unfolded, there appeared a series of smaller packages inside. The man took them out very carefully, almost as if they had been alive, Blake thought, and set them in a row upon his knees. They were dollar bills. Blake, all in a flutter, craned his neck forward a little to try and make out their denomination. He read plainly the figures 100.

"There are ten thousand dollars here," said the man quietly.

The other could not suppress a little cry.

"And they are for you."

Blake simply gasped. "Ten thousand dollars!" he repeated, a queer feeling growing up in his throat. "*Ten thousand.* Are you sure? I mean—you mean they are for *me?*" he stammered. He felt quite silly with excitement, and grew more so with every minute, as the man maintained a perfect silence. Was it not a dream? Wouldn't the man put them back in the bag presently and say it was a mistake, and they were meant for somebody else? He could not believe his eyes or his ears. Yet, in a sense, it was possible. He had read of such things in books, and even come across them in his experience of the courts—the erratic and generous philanthropist who is determined to do his good deed and to get no thanks or acknowledgment for it. Still, it seemed almost incredible. His troubles began to melt away like bubbles in the sun; he thought of the other fellows when they came in, and what he would have to tell them; he thought of the German landlady and the arrears of rent, of regular food and clean linen, and books and music, of the chance of getting into some respectable business, of—well, of as many things as it is possible to think of when excitement and surprise fling wide open the gates of the imagination.

The man, meanwhile, began quietly to count over the packages aloud from one to ten, and then to count the bills in each separate packet, also from one to ten. Yes, there were ten little heaps, each containing ten bills of a hundred-dollar denomination. That made ten thousand dollars. Blake had never seen so much money in a single lump in his life before; and for many months of privation and discomfort he had not known the "feel" of a twenty-dollar note, much less of a hundred-dollar one. He heard them crackle under the man's fingers, and it was like crisp laughter in his ears. The bills were evidently new and unused.

But, side by side with the excitement caused by the shock of such an event, Blake's caution, acquired by a year of vivid New York experience, was meanwhile beginning to assert itself. It all seemed just a little too much out of the likely order of things to be quite right. The police courts had taught him the amazing ingenuity of the criminal mind, as well as something of the plots and devices by which the unwary are beguiled into the dark places where blackmail may be levied with impunity. New York, as a matter of fact, just at that time was literally undermined with the secret ways of the blackmailers, the green-goods men, and other police-protected abominations; and the only weak point in the supposition that this was part of some such proceeding was the selection of himself—a poor newspaper reporter—as a victim. It did seem absurd, but then the whole thing was so out of the ordinary, and the thought once having entered his mind, was not so easily got rid of. Blake resolved to be very cautious.

The man meanwhile, though he never appeared to raise his eyes from the carpet, had been watching him closely all the time.

"If you will give me a receipt I'll leave the money at once," he said, with just a vestige of impatience in his tone, as if he were anxious to bring the matter to a conclusion as soon as possible.

"But you say it is quite impossible for you to tell me the name of my well-wisher, or why *she* sends me such a large sum of money in this extraordinary way?"

"The money is sent to you because you are in need of it," returned the other; "and it is a present without conditions of any sort attached. You have to give me a receipt only to satisfy the sender that it has reached your hands. The money will never be asked of you again."

Blake noticed two things from this answer: first, that the man was not to be caught into betraying the sex of the well-wisher; and secondly, that he was in some hurry to complete the transaction. For he was now giving reasons, attractive reasons, why he should accept the money and make out the receipt.

Suddenly it flashed across his mind that if he took the money and gave the receipt *before a witness*, nothing very disastrous could come of the affair. It would protect him against blackmail, if this was, after all, a plot of some sort with blackmail in it; whereas, if the man were a madman, or a criminal who was getting rid of a portion of his ill-gotten gains to divert suspicion, or if any other improbable explanation turned out to be the true one, there was no great harm done, and he could hold the money till it was claimed, or advertised for in the newspapers. His mind rapidly ran over these possibilities, though, of course, under the stress of excitement, he was unable to weigh any of them properly; then he turned to his strange visitor again and said quietly—

"I will take the money, although I must say it seems to me a very unusual transaction, and I will give you for it such a receipt as I think proper under the circumstances."

"A proper receipt is all I want," was the answer.

"I mean by that a receipt before a proper witness—"

"Perfectly satisfactory," interrupted the man, his eyes still on the carpet. "Only, it must be dated, and headed with your address here in the correct way."

Blake could see no possible objection to this, and he at once proceeded to obtain his witness. The person he had in his mind was a Mr. Barclay, who occupied the room above his own; an old gentleman who had retired from business and who, the landlady always said, was a miser, and kept large sums secreted in his room. He was, at any rate, a perfectly respectable man and would make an admirable witness to a transaction of this sort. Blake made an apology and rose to fetch him, crossing the room in front of the sofa where the man sat, in order to reach the door. As he did so, he saw for the first time the *other side* of his visitor's face, the side that had been always so carefully turned away from him.

There was a broad smear of blood down the skin from the ear to the neck. It glistened in the gaslight.

Blake never knew how he managed to smother the cry that sprang to his lips, but smother it he did. In a second he was at the door, his knees trembling, his mind in a sudden and dreadful turmoil.

His main object, so far as he could recollect afterwards, was to escape from the room as if he had noticed nothing, so as not to arouse the other's suspicions. The man's eyes were always on the carpet, and probably, Blake hoped, he had not noticed the consternation that must have been written plainly on his face. At any rate he had uttered no cry.

In another second he would have been in the passage, when suddenly he met a pair of wicked, staring eyes fixed intently and with a cunning smile upon his own. It was the other's face in the mirror calmly watching his every movement.

Instantly, all his powers of reflection flew to the winds, and he thought only upon the desirability of getting help at once. He tore upstairs, his heart in his mouth. Barclay must come to his aid. This matter was serious—perhaps horribly serious. Taking the money, or giving a receipt, or having anything at all to do with it became an impossibility. Here was crime. He felt certain of it.

In three bounds he reached the next landing and began to hammer at the old miser's door as if his very life depended on it. For a long time he could get no answer. His fists seemed to make no noise. He might have been knocking on cotton wool, and the thought dashed through his brain that it was all just like the terror of a nightmare.

Barclay, evidently, was still out, or else sound asleep. But the other simply could not wait a minute longer in suspense. He turned the handle and walked into the room. At first he saw nothing for the darkness, and made sure the owner of the room was out; but the moment the light from the passage began a little to disperse the gloom, he saw the old man, to his immense relief, lying asleep on the bed.

Blake opened the door to its widest to get more light and then walked quickly up to the bed. He now saw the figure more plainly, and noted that it was dressed and lay only upon the outside of the bed. It struck him, too, that he was sleeping in a very odd, almost an unnatural, position.

Something clutched at his heart as he looked closer. He stumbled over a chair and found the matches. Calling upon Barclay the whole time to wake up and come downstairs with him, he blundered across the floor, a dreadful thought in his mind, and lit the gas over the table. It seemed strange that there was no movement or reply to his shouting. But it no longer seemed strange when at length he turned, in the full glare of the gas, and saw the old man lying huddled up into a ghastly heap on the bed, his throat cut across from ear to ear.

And all over the carpet lay new dollar bills, crisp and clean like those he had left downstairs, and strewn about in little heaps.

For a moment Blake stood stock-still, bereft of all power of movement. The next, his courage returned, and he fled from the room and dashed downstairs, taking five steps at a time. He reached the bottom and tore along the passage to his room, determined at any rate to seize the man and prevent his escape till help came.

But when he got to the end of the little landing he found that his door had been closed. He seized the handle, fumbling with it in his violence. It felt slippery and kept turning under his fingers without opening the door, and fully half a minute passed before it yielded and let him in headlong.

At the first glance he saw the room was empty, and the man gone!

Scattered upon the carpet lay a number of the bills, and beside them, half hidden under the sofa where the man had sat, he saw a pair of gloves—thick, leathern gloves—and a butcher's knife. Even from the distance where he stood the blood-stains on both were easily visible.

Dazed and confused by the terrible discoveries of the last few minutes, Blake stood in the middle of the room, overwhelmed and unable to think or move. Unconsciously he must have passed his hand over his forehead in the natural gesture of perplexity, for he noticed that the skin felt wet and sticky. His hand was covered with blood! And when he rushed in terror to the looking-glass, he saw that there was a broad red smear across his face and forehead. Then he remembered the slippery handle of the door and knew that it had been carefully moistened!

In an instant the whole plot became clear as daylight, and he was so spellbound with horror that a sort of numbness came over him and he came very near to fainting. He was in a condition of utter helplessness, and had anyone come into the room at that minute and called him by name he would simply have dropped to the floor in a heap.

"If the police were to come in now!" The thought crashed through his brain like thunder, and at the same moment, almost before he had time to appreciate a quarter of its significance, there came a loud knocking at the front door below. The bell rang with a dreadful clamour; men's voices were heard talking excitedly, and presently heavy steps began to come up the stairs in the direction of his room.

It *was* the police!

And all Blake could do was to laugh foolishly to himself—and wait till they were upon him. He could not move nor speak. He stood face to face with the evidence of his horrid crime, his hands and face smeared with the blood of his victim, and there he was standing when the police burst open the door and came noisily into the room.

"Here it is!" cried a voice he knew. "Third floor back! And the fellow caught red-handed!"

It was the man with the bag leading in the two policemen.

Hardly knowing what he was doing in the fearful stress of conflicting emotions, he made a step forward. But before he had time to make a second one, he felt the heavy hand of the law descend upon both shoulders at once as the two policemen moved up to seize him. At the same moment a voice of thunder cried in his ear—

"Wake up, man! Wake up! Here's the supper, and good news too!"

Blake turned with a start in his chair and saw the Dane, very red in the face, standing beside him, a hand on each shoulder, and a little further back he saw the Frenchman leering happily at him over the end of the bed, a bottle of beer in one hand and a paper package in the other.

He rubbed his eyes, glancing from one to the other, and then got up sleepily to fix the wire arrangement on the gas jet to boil water for cooking the eggs which the Frenchman was in momentary danger of letting drop upon the floor.

The Strange Adventures of a Private Secretary in New York

I

It was never quite clear to me how Jim Shorthouse managed to get his private secretaryship; but, once he got it, he kept it, and for some years he led a steady life and put money in the savings bank.

One morning his employer sent for him into the study, and it was evident to the secretary's trained senses that there was something unusual in the air.

"Mr. Shorthouse," he began, somewhat nervously, "I have never yet had the opportunity of observing whether or not you are possessed of personal courage."

Shorthouse gasped, but he said nothing. He was growing accustomed to the eccentricities of his chief. Shorthouse was a Kentish man; Sidebotham was "raised" in Chicago; New York was the present place of residence.

"But," the other continued, with a puff at his very black cigar, "I must consider myself a poor judge of human nature in future, if it is not one of your strongest qualities."

The private secretary made a foolish little bow in modest appreciation of so uncertain a compliment. Mr. Jonas B. Sidebotham watched him narrowly, as the novelists say, before he continued his remarks.

"I have no doubt that you are a plucky fellow and—" He hesitated, and puffed at his cigar as if his life depended upon it keeping alight.

"I don't think I'm afraid of anything in particular, sir—except women," interposed the young man, feeling that it was time for him

234

to make an observation of some sort, but still quite in the dark as to his chief's purpose.

"Humph!" he grunted. "Well, there are no women in this case so far as I know. But there may be other things that—that hurt more."

"Wants a special service of some kind, evidently," was the secretary's reflection. "Personal violence?" he asked aloud.

"Possibly (puff), in fact (puff, puff) probably."

Shorthouse smelt an increase of salary in the air. It had a stimulating effect.

"I've had some experience of that article, sir," he said shortly; "but I'm ready to undertake anything in reason."

"I can't say how much reason or unreason there may prove to be in this particular case. It all depends."

Mr. Sidebotham got up and locked the door of his study and drew down the blinds of both windows. Then he took a bunch of keys from his pocket and opened a black tin box. He ferreted about among blue and white papers for a few seconds, enveloping himself as he did so in a cloud of blue tobacco smoke.

"I feel like a detective already," Shorthouse laughed.

"Speak low, please," returned the other, glancing round the room. "We must observe the utmost secrecy. Perhaps you would be kind enough to close the registers," he went on in a still lower voice. "Open registers have betrayed conversations before now."

Shorthouse began to enter into the spirit of the thing. He tiptoed across the floor and shut the two iron gratings in the wall that in American houses supply hot air and are termed "registers." Mr. Sidebotham had meanwhile found the paper he was looking for. He held it in front of him and tapped it once or twice with the back of his right hand as if it were a stage letter and himself the villain of the melodrama.

"This is a letter from Joel Garvey, my old partner," he said at length. "You have heard me speak of him."

The other bowed. He knew that many years before Garvey & Sidebotham had been well known in the Chicago financial world. He knew that the amazing rapidity with which they accumulated a fortune had only been surpassed by the amazing rapidity with which they had immediately afterwards disappeared into space. He was further aware—his position afforded facilities—that each partner was still to some extent in the other's power, and that each wished most devoutly that the other would die.

The sins of his employer's early years did not concern him, however. The man was kind and just, if eccentric; and Shorthouse, being in New York, did not probe to discover more particularly the sources whence his salary was so regularly paid. Moreover, the two men had grown to like each other and there was a genuine feeling of trust and respect between them.

"I hope it's a pleasant communication, sir;" he said in a low voice.

"Quite the reverse," returned the other, fingering the paper nervously as he stood in front of the fire.

"Blackmail, I suppose."

"Precisely." Mr. Sidebotham's cigar was not burning well; he struck a match and applied it to the uneven edge, and presently his voice spoke through clouds of wreathing smoke.

"There are valuable papers in my possession bearing his signature. I cannot inform you of their nature; but they are extremely valuable *to me*. They belong, as a matter of fact, to Garvey as much as to me. Only I've got them—"

"I see."

"Garvey writes that he wants to have his signature removed—wants to cut it out with his own hand. He gives reasons which incline me to consider his request—"

"And you would like me to take him the papers and see that he does it?"

"And bring them back again with you," he whispered, screwing up his eyes into a shrewd grimace.

"And bring them back again with me," repeated the secretary. "I understand perfectly."

Shorthouse knew from unfortunate experience more than a little of the horrors of blackmail. The pressure Garvey was bringing to bear upon his old enemy must be exceedingly strong. That was quite clear. At the same time, the commission that was being entrusted to him seemed somewhat quixotic in its nature. He had already "enjoyed" more than one experience of his employer's eccentricity, and he now caught himself wondering whether this same eccentricity did not sometimes go—further than eccentricity.

"I cannot read the letter to you," Mr. Sidebotham was explaining, "but I shall give it into your hands. It will prove that you are my—er—my accredited representative. I shall also ask you not to read the package of papers. The signature in question you will find, of course, on the last page, at the bottom."

There was a pause of several minutes during which the end of the cigar glowed eloquently.

"Circumstances compel me," he went on at length almost in a whisper, "or I should never do this. But you understand, of course, the thing is a ruse. Cutting out the signature is a mere pretence. It is nothing. *What Garvey wants are the papers themselves.*"

The confidence reposed in the private secretary was not misplaced. Shorthouse was as faithful to Mr. Sidebotham as a man ought to be to the wife that loves him.

The commission itself seemed very simple. Garvey lived in solitude in the remote part of Long Island. Shorthouse was to take the papers to him, witness the cutting out of the signature, and to be specially on his guard against any attempt, forcible or otherwise, to gain possession of them. It seemed to him a somewhat ludicrous adventure, but he did not know all the facts and perhaps was not the best judge.

The two men talked in low voices for another hour, at the end of which Mr. Sidebotham drew up the blinds, opened the registers, and unlocked the door.

Shorthouse rose to go. His pockets were stuffed with papers and his head with instructions; but when he reached the door he hesitated and turned.

"Well?" said his chief.

Shorthouse looked him straight in the eye and said nothing.

"The personal violence, I suppose?" said the other. Shorthouse bowed.

"I have not seen Garvey for twenty years," he said; "all I can tell you is that I believe him to be occasionally of unsound mind. I have heard strange rumours. He lives alone, and in his lucid intervals studies chemistry. It was always a hobby of his. But the chances are twenty to one against his attempting violence. I only wished to warn you—in case—I mean, so that you may be on the watch."

He handed his secretary a Smith and Wesson revolver as he spoke. Shorthouse slipped it into his hip pocket and went out of the room.

A drizzling cold rain was falling on fields covered with half-melted snow when Shorthouse stood, late in the afternoon, on the platform of the lonely little Long Island station and watched the train he had just left vanish into the distance.

It was a bleak country that Joel Garvey, Esq., formerly of Chicago, had chosen for his residence, and on this particular afternoon it presented a more than usually dismal appearance. An expanse of flat fields covered with dirty snow stretched away on all sides till the sky dropped down to meet them. Only occasional farm buildings broke the monotony, and the road wound along muddy lanes and beneath dripping trees swathed in the cold raw fog that swept in like a pall of the dead from the sea.

It was six miles from the station to Garvey's house, and the driver of the rickety buggy Shorthouse had found at the station was not communicative. Between the dreary landscape and the drearier driver he fell back upon his own thoughts, which, but for the spice of adventure that was promised, would themselves have been even drearier than either. He made up his mind that he would waste no time over the transaction. The moment the signature was cut out he would pack up and be off. The last train back to Brooklyn was 7.15; and he would have to walk the six miles of mud and snow, for the driver of the buggy had refused point-blank to wait for him.

For purposes of safety, Shorthouse had done what he flattered himself was rather a clever thing. He had made up a second packet of papers identical in outside appearance with the first. The inscription, the blue envelope, the red elastic band, and even a blot in the lower left-hand corner had been exactly reproduced. Inside, of course, were only sheets of blank paper. It was his intention to change the packets and to let Garvey see him put the sham one into the bag. In case of violence the bag would be the point of attack, and he intended to lock it and throw away the key. Before it could be forced open and the deception discovered there would be time to increase his chances of escape with the real packet.

It was five o'clock when the silent Jehu pulled up in front of a half-broken gate and pointed with his whip to a house that stood in its own grounds among trees and was just visible in the gathering gloom. Shorthouse told him to drive up to the front door but the man refused.

"I ain't runnin' no risks," he said; "I've got a family."

This cryptic remark was not encouraging, but Shorthouse did not pause to decipher it. He paid the man, and then pushed open the rickety old gate swinging on a single hinge, and proceeded to walk up the drive that lay dark between close-standing trees. The house soon came into full view. It was tall and square and had once evidently been white, but now the walls were covered with dirty patches and there were wide yellow streaks where the plaster had fallen away. The windows stared black and uncompromising into the night. The garden was overgrown with weeds and long grass, standing up in ugly patches beneath their burden of wet snow. Complete silence reigned over all. There was not a sign of life. Not even a dog barked. Only, in the distance, the wheels of the retreating carriage could be heard growing fainter and fainter.

As he stood in the porch, between pillars of rotting wood, listening to the rain dripping from the roof into the puddles of slushy snow, he was conscious of a sensation of utter desertion and loneliness such as he had never before experienced. The forbidding aspect of the house had the immediate effect of lowering his spirits. It might well have been the abode of monsters or demons in a child's wonder tale, creatures that only dared to come out under cover of darkness. He groped for the bell-handle, or knocker, and finding neither, he raised his stick and beat a loud tattoo on the door. The sound echoed away in an empty space on the other side and the wind moaned past him between the pillars as if startled at his audacity. But there was no sound of approaching footsteps and no one came to open the door. Again he beat a tattoo, louder and longer than the first one; and, having done so, waited with his back to the house and stared across the unkempt garden into the fast gathering shadows.

Then he turned suddenly, and saw that the door was standing

ajar. It had been quietly opened and a pair of eyes were peering at him round the edge. There was no light in the hall beyond and he could only just make out the shape of a dim human face.

"Does Mr. Garvey live here?" he asked in a firm voice.

"Who are you?" came in a man's tones.

"I'm Mr. Sidebotham's private secretary. I wish to see Mr. Garvey on important business."

"Are you expected?"

"I suppose so," he said impatiently, thrusting a card through the opening. "Please take my name to him at once, and say I come from Mr. Sidebotham on the matter Mr. Garvey wrote about."

The man took the card, and the face vanished into the darkness, leaving Shorthouse standing in the cold porch with mingled feelings of impatience and dismay. The door, he now noticed for the first time, was on a chain and could not open more than a few inches. But it was the manner of his reception that caused uneasy reflections to stir within him—reflections that continued for some minutes before they were interrupted by the sound of approaching footsteps and the flicker of a light in the hall.

The next instant the chain fell with a rattle, and gripping his bag tightly, he walked into a large ill-smelling hall of which he could only just see the ceiling. There was no light but the flickering taper held by the man, and by its uncertain glimmer Shorthouse turned to examine him. He saw an undersized man of middle age with brilliant, shifting eyes, a curling black beard, and a nose that at once proclaimed him a Jew. His shoulders were bent, and, as he watched him replacing the chain, he saw that he wore a peculiar black gown like a priest's cassock reaching to the feet. It was altogether a lugubrious figure of a man, sinister and funereal, yet it seemed in perfect harmony with the general character of its surroundings. The hall was devoid of furniture of any kind, and against the dingy walls stood rows of old picture frames, empty and disordered, and odd-looking bits of woodwork that appeared doubly fantastic as their shadows danced queerly over the floor in the shifting light.

"If you'll come this way, Mr. Garvey will see you presently," said the Jew gruffly, crossing the floor and shielding the taper with a bony hand. He never once raised his eyes above the level of the visitor's waistcoat, and, to Shorthouse, he somehow suggested a figure from the dead rather than a man of flesh and blood. The hall smelt decidedly ill.

All the more surprising, then, was the scene that met his eyes when the Jew opened the door at the further end and he entered a room brilliantly lit with swinging lamps and furnished with a degree of taste and comfort that amounted to luxury. The walls were lined with handsomely bound books, and arm-chairs were arranged round a large mahogany desk in the middle of the room. A bright fire burned in the grate and neatly framed photographs of men and women stood on the mantelpiece on either side of an elaborately carved clock. French windows that opened like doors were partially concealed by warm red curtains, and on a sideboard against the wall stood decanters and glasses, with several boxes of cigars piled on top of one another. There was a pleasant odour of tobacco about the room. Indeed, it was in such glowing contrast to the chilly poverty of the hall that Shorthouse already was conscious of a distinct rise in the thermometer of his spirits.

Then he turned and saw the Jew standing in the doorway with his eyes fixed upon him, somewhere about the middle button of his waistcoat. He presented a strangely repulsive appearance that somehow could not be attributed to any particular detail, and the secretary associated him in his mind with a monstrous black bird of prey more than anything else.

"My time is short," he said abruptly; "I hope Mr. Garvey will not keep me waiting."

A strange flicker of a smile appeared on the Jew's ugly face and vanished as quickly as it came. He made a sort of deprecating bow by way of reply. Then he blew out the taper and went out, closing the door noiselessly behind him.

Shorthouse was alone. He felt relieved. There was an air of obsequious insolence about the old Jew that was very offensive. He began to take note of his surroundings. He was evidently in the library of the house, for the walls were covered with books almost up to the ceiling. There was no room for pictures. Nothing but the shining backs of well-bound volumes looked down upon him. Four brilliant lights hung from the ceiling and a reading lamp with a polished reflector stood among the disordered masses of papers on the desk.

The lamp was not lit, but when Shorthouse put his hand upon it he found it was *warm*. The room had evidently only just been vacated.

Apart from the testimony of the lamp, however, he had already felt, without being able to give a reason for it, that the room had been occupied a few moments before he entered. The atmosphere over the desk seemed to retain the disturbing influence of a human being; an influence, moreover, so recent that he felt as if the cause of it were still in his immediate neighbourhood. It was difficult to realise that he was quite alone in the room and that somebody was not in hiding. The finer counterparts of his senses warned him to act as if he were being observed; he was dimly conscious of a desire to fidget and look round, to keep his eyes in every part of the room at once, and to conduct himself generally as if he were the object of careful human observation.

How far he recognised the cause of these sensations it is impossible to say; but they were sufficiently marked to prevent his carrying out a strong inclination to get up and make a search of the room. He sat quite still, staring alternately at the backs of the books, and at the red curtains; wondering all the time if he was really being watched, or if it was only the imagination playing tricks with him.

A full quarter of an hour passed, and then twenty rows of volumes suddenly shifted out towards him, and he saw that a door had opened in the wall opposite. The books were only sham backs after all, and when they moved back again with the sliding door, Shorthouse saw the figure of Joel Garvey standing before him.

Surprise almost took his breath away. He had expected to see an unpleasant, even a vicious apparition with the mark of the beast unmistakably upon its face; but he was wholly unprepared for the elderly, tall, fine-looking man who stood in front of him—well-groomed, refined, vigorous, with a lofty forehead, clear grey eyes, and a hooked nose dominating a clean shaven mouth and chin of considerable character—a distinguished looking man altogether.

"I'm afraid I've kept you waiting, Mr. Shorthouse," he said in a pleasant voice, but with no trace of a smile in the mouth or eyes. "But the fact is, you know, I've a mania for chemistry, and just when you were announced I was at the most critical moment of a problem and was really compelled to bring it to a conclusion."

Shorthouse had risen to meet him, but the other motioned him to resume his seat. It was borne in upon him irresistibly that Mr. Joel Garvey, for reasons best known to himself, was deliberately lying, and he could not help wondering at the necessity for such an elaborate misrepresentation. He took off his overcoat and sat down.

"I've no doubt, too, that the door startled you," Garvey went on, evidently reading something of his guest's feelings in his face. "You probably had not suspected it. It leads into my little laboratory. Chemistry is an absorbing study to me, and I spend most of my time there." Mr. Garvey moved up to the arm-chair on the opposite side of the fireplace and sat down.

Shorthouse made appropriate answers to these remarks, but his mind was really engaged in taking stock of Mr. Sidebotham's old-time partner. So far there was no sign of mental irregularity and there was certainly nothing about him to suggest violent wrong-doing or coarseness of living. On the whole, Mr. Sidebotham's secretary was most pleasantly surprised, and, wishing to conclude his business as speedily as possible, he made a motion towards the bag for the purpose of opening it, when his companion interrupted him quickly—

"You are Mr. Sidebotham's *private* secretary, are you not?" he asked.

Shorthouse replied that he was. "Mr. Sidebotham," he went on to explain, "has entrusted me with the papers in the case and I have the honour to return to you your letter of a week ago." He handed the letter to Garvey, who took it without a word and deliberately placed it in the fire. He was not aware that the secretary was ignorant of its contents, yet his face betrayed no signs of feeling. Shorthouse noticed, however, that his eyes never left the fire until the last morsel had been consumed. Then he looked up and said, "You are familiar then with the facts of this most peculiar case?"

Shorthouse saw no reason to confess his ignorance.

"I have all the papers, Mr. Garvey," he replied, taking them out of the bag, "and I should be very glad if we could transact our business as speedily as possible. If you will cut out your signature—"

"One moment, please," interrupted the other. "I must, before we proceed further, consult some papers in my laboratory. If you will allow me to leave you alone a few minutes for this purpose we can conclude the whole matter in a very short time."

Shorthouse did not approve of this further delay, but he had no option than to acquiesce, and when Garvey had left the room by the private door he sat and waited with the papers in his hand. The minutes went by and the other did not return. To pass the time he thought of taking the false packet from his coat to see that the papers were in order, and the move was indeed almost completed, when something—he never knew what—warned him to desist. The feeling again came over him that he was being watched, and he leaned back in his chair with the bag on his knees and waited with considerable impatience for the other's return. For more than twenty minutes he waited, and when at length the door opened and Garvey appeared, with profuse apologies for the delay, he saw by the clock that only a few minutes still remained of the time he had allowed himself to catch the last train.

"Now I am completely at your service," he said pleasantly; "you must, of course, know, Mr. Shorthouse, that one cannot be too careful in matters of this kind—especially," he went on, speaking very slowly and impressively, "in dealing with a man like my former partner, whose mind, as you doubtless may have discovered, is at times very sadly affected."

Shorthouse made no reply to this. He felt that the other was watching him as a cat watches a mouse.

"It is almost a wonder to me," Garvey added, "that he is still at large. Unless he has greatly improved it can hardly be safe for those who are closely associated with him."

The other began to feel uncomfortable. Either this was the other side of the story, or it was the first signs of mental irresponsibility.

"All business matters of importance require the utmost care in my opinion, Mr. Garvey," he said at length, cautiously.

"Ah! then, as I thought, you have had a great deal to put up with from him," Garvey said, with his eyes fixed on his companion's face. "And, no doubt, he is still as bitter against me as he was years ago when the disease first showed itself?"

Although this last remark was a deliberate question and the questioner was waiting with fixed eyes for an answer, Shorthouse elected to take no notice of it. Without a word he pulled the elastic band from the blue envelope with a snap and plainly showed his desire to conclude the business as soon as possible. The tendency on the other's part to delay did not suit him at all.

"But never personal violence, I trust, Mr. Shorthouse," he added. "Never."

"I'm glad to hear it," Garvey said in a sympathetic voice, "very glad to hear it. And now," he went on, "if you are ready we can transact this little matter of business before dinner. It will only take a moment."

He drew a chair up to the desk and sat down, taking a pair of scissors from a drawer. His companion approached with the papers in his hand, unfolding them as he came. Garvey at once took them from him, and after turning over a few pages he stopped and cut out a piece of writing at the bottom of the last sheet but one.

Holding it up to him Shorthouse read the words "Joel Garvey" in faded ink.

"There! That's my signature," he said, "and I've cut it out. It must be nearly twenty years since I wrote it, and now I'm going to burn it."

He went to the fire and stooped over to burn the little slip of paper, and while he watched it being consumed Shorthouse put the real papers in his pocket and slipped the imitation ones into the bag. Garvey turned just in time to see this latter movement.

"I'm putting the papers hack," Shorthouse said quietly; "you've done with them, I think."

"Certainly," he replied as, completely deceived, he saw the blue envelope disappear into the black bag and watched Shorthouse turn the key. "They no longer have the slightest interest for me." As he spoke he moved over to the sideboard, and pouring himself out a small glass of whisky asked his visitor if he might do the some for him. But the visitor declined and was already putting on his overcoat when Garvey turned with genuine surprise on his face.

"You surely are not going back to New York to-night, Mr. Shorthouse?" he said, in a voice of astonishment.

"I've just time to catch the 7.15 if I'm quick."

"But I never heard of such a thing," Garvey said. "Of course I took it for granted that you would stay the night."

"It's kind of you," said Shorthouse, "but really I must return to-night. I never expected to stay."

The two men stood facing each other. Garvey pulled out his watch.

"I'm exceedingly sorry," he said; "but, upon my word, I took it for granted you would stay. I ought to have said so long ago. I'm such a lonely fellow and so little accustomed to visitors that I fear I forgot my manners altogether. But in any case, Mr. Shorthouse, you cannot catch the 7.15, for it's already after six o'clock, and that's the last train to-night." Garvey spoke very quickly, almost eagerly, but his voice sounded genuine.

"There's time if I walk quickly," said the young man with decision, moving towards the door. He glanced at his watch as he went. Hitherto he had gone by the clock on the mantelpiece. To his dismay he saw that it was, as his host had said, long after six. The clock was half an hour slow, and he realised at once that it was no longer possible to catch the train.

Had the hands of the clock been moved back intentionally? Had he been purposely detained? Unpleasant thoughts flashed into his brain and made him hesitate before taking the next step. His employer's warning rang in his ears. The alternative was six miles along a lonely road in the dark, or a night under Garvey's roof. The former seemed a direct invitation to catastrophe, if catastrophe there was planned to be. The latter—well, the choice was certainly small. One thing, however, he realised, was plain—he must show neither fear nor hesitancy.

"My watch must have gained," he observed quietly, turning the hands back without looking up. "It seems I have certainly missed that train and shall be obliged to throw myself upon your hospitality. But, believe me, I had no intention of putting you out to any such extent."

"I'm delighted," the other said. "Defer to the judgment of an older man and make yourself comfortable for the night. There's a bitter storm outside, and you don't put me out at all. On the contrary it's a great pleasure. I have so little contact with the outside world that it'll really a god-send to have you."

The man's face changed as he spoke. His manner was cordial and sincere. Shorthouse began to feel ashamed of his doubts and to read between the lines of his employer's warning. He took off his coat and the two men moved to the arm-chairs beside the fire.

"You see," Garvey went on in a lowered voice, "I understand your hesitancy perfectly. I didn't know Sidebotham all those years without knowing good deal about him—perhaps more than you do. I've no doubt, now, he filled your mind with all sorts of nonsense about me—probably told you that I was the greatest villain unhung, eh? and all that sort of thing? Poor fellow! He was a fine sort before his mind became unhinged. One of his fancies used to be that everybody else was insane, or just about to become insane. Is he still as bad as that?"

"Few men," replied Shorthouse, with the manner of making a great confidence, but entirely refusing to be drawn, "go through his experiences and reach his age without entertaining delusions of one kind or another."

"Perfectly true," said Garvey. "Your observation is evidently keen."

"Very keen indeed," Shorthouse replied, taking his cue neatly; "but, of course, there are some things"—and here he looked cautiously over his shoulder—"there are some things one cannot talk about too circumspectly."

"I understand perfectly and respect your reserve."

There was a little more conversation and then Garvey got up and excused himself on the plea of superintending the preparation of the bedroom.

"It's quite an event to have a visitor in the house, and I want to make you as comfortable as possible," he said. "Marx will do better for a little supervision. And," he added with a laugh as he stood in the doorway, "I want you to carry back a good account to Sidebotham."

II

The tall form disappeared and the door was shut.

The conversation of the past few minutes had come somewhat as a revelation to the secretary. Garvey seemed in full possession of normal instincts. There was no doubt as to the sincerity of his manner and intentions. The suspicions of the first hour began to vanish like mist before the sun. Sidebotham's portentous warnings and the mystery with which he surrounded the whole episode had been allowed to unduly influence his mind. The loneliness of the situation and the bleak nature of the surroundings had helped to complete the illusion. He began to be ashamed of his suspicions and a change commenced gradually to be wrought in his thoughts. Anyhow a dinner and a bed were preferable to six miles in the dark, no dinner, and a cold train into the bargain.

Garvey returned presently. "We'll do the best we can for you," he said, dropping into the deep arm-chair on the other side of the fire. "Marx is a good servant if you watch him all the time. You must always stand over a Jew, though, if you want things done properly. They're tricky and uncertain unless they're working for their own interest. But Marx might be worse, I'll admit. He's been with me for nearly twenty years—cook, valet, housemaid, and butler all in one. In the old days, you know, he was a clerk in our office in Chicago."

Garvey rattled on and Shorthouse listened with occasional remarks thrown in. The former seemed pleased to have somebody to talk to and the sound of his own voice was evidently sweet music in his ears. After a few minutes, he crossed over to the sideboard and again took up the decanter of whisky, holding it to the light. "You will join me this time," he said pleasantly, pouring out two glasses, "it will give us an appetite for dinner," and this time Shorthouse did not refuse. The liquor was mellow and soft and the men took two glasses apiece.

"Excellent," remarked the secretary.

"Glad you appreciate it," said the host, smacking his lips. "It's very old whisky, and I rarely touch it when I'm alone. But this," he added, "is a special occasion, isn't it?"

Shorthouse was in the act of putting his glass down when something drew his eyes suddenly to the other's face. A strange note in the man's voice caught his attention and communicated alarm to his nerves. A new light shone in Garvey's eyes and there flitted momentarily across his strong features the shadow of something that set the secretary's nerves tingling. A mist spread before his eyes and the unaccountable belief rose strong in him that he was staring into the visage of an untamed animal. Close to his heart there was something that was wild, fierce, savage. An involuntary shiver ran over him and seemed to dispel the strange fancy as suddenly as it had come. He met the other's eye with a smile, the counterpart of which in his heart was vivid horror.

"It *is* a special occasion," he said, as naturally as possible, "and, allow me to add, very special whisky."

Garvey appeared delighted. He was in the middle of a devious tale describing how the whisky came originally into his possession when the door opened behind them and a grating voice announced that dinner was ready. They followed the cassocked form of Marx across the dirty hall, lit only by the shaft of light that followed them from the library door, and entered a small room where a single lamp stood upon a table laid for dinner. The walls were destitute of pictures, and the windows had venetian blinds without curtains. There was no fire in the grate, and when the men sat down facing each other Shorthouse noticed that, while his own cover was laid with its due proportion of glasses and cutlery, his companion had nothing before him but a soup plate, without fork, knife, or spoon beside it.

"I don't know what there is to offer you," he said; "but I'm sure Marx has done the best he can at such short notice. I only eat one course for dinner, but pray take your time and enjoy your food."

Marx presently set a plate of soup before the guest, yet so loathsome was the immediate presence of this old Hebrew servitor, that the spoonfuls disappeared somewhat slowly. Garvey sat and watched him.

Shorthouse said the soup was delicious and bravely swallowed another mouthful. In reality his thoughts were centred upon his companion, whose manners were giving evidence of a gradual and curious change. There was a decided difference in his demeanour, a difference that the secretary *felt* at first, rather than saw. Garvey's quiet self-possession was giving place to a degree of suppressed excitement that seemed so far inexplicable. His movements became quick and nervous, his eye shifting and strangely brilliant, and his voice, when he spoke, betrayed an occasional deep tremor. Something unwonted was stirring within him and evidently demanding every moment more vigorous manifestation as the meal proceeded.

Intuitively Shorthouse was afraid of this growing excitement, and while negotiating some uncommonly tough pork chops he tried to lead the conversation on to the subject of chemistry, of which in his Oxford days he had been an enthusiastic student. His companion, however, would none of it. It seemed to have lost interest for him, and he would barely condescend to respond. When Marx presently returned with a plate of steaming eggs and bacon the subject dropped of its own accord.

"An inadequate dinner dish," Garvey said, as soon as the man was gone; "but better than nothing, I hope."

Shorthouse remarked that he was exceedingly fond of bacon and eggs, and, looking up with the last word, saw that Garvey's face was twitching convulsively and that he was almost wriggling in his chair. He quieted down, however, under the secretary's gaze and observed, though evidently with an effort—

"Very good of you to say so. Wish I could join you, only I never eat such stuff. I only take one course for dinner."

Shorthouse began to feel some curiosity as to what the nature of this one course might be, but he made no further remark and contented himself with noting mentally that his companion's excitement seemed to be rapidly growing beyond his control. There was something uncanny about it, and he began to wish he had chosen the alternative of the walk to the station.

"I'm glad to see you never speak when Marx is in the room," said Garvey presently. "I'm sure it's better not. Don't you think so?"

He appeared to wait eagerly for the answer.

"Undoubtedly," said the puzzled secretary.

"Yes," the other went on quickly. "He's an excellent man, but he has one drawback—a really horrid one. You may—but, no, you could hardly have noticed it yet."

"Not drink, I trust," said Shorthouse, who would rather have discussed any other subject than the odious Jew.

"Worse than that a great deal," Garvey replied, evidently expecting the other to draw him out. But Shorthouse was in no mood to hear anything horrible, and he declined to step into the trap.

"The best of servants have their faults," he said coldly.

"I'll tell you what it is if you like," Garvey went on, still speaking very low and leaning forward over the table so that his face came close to the flame of the lamp, "only we must speak quietly in case he's listening. I'll tell you what it is—if you think you won't be frightened."

"Nothing frightens me," he laughed. (Garvey must understand that at all events.) "Nothing can frighten me," he repeated.

"I'm glad of that; for it frightens *me* a good deal sometimes."

Shorthouse feigned indifference. Yet he was aware that his heart was beating a little quicker and that there was a sensation of chilliness in his back. He waited in silence for what was to come.

"He has a horrible predilection for vacuums," Garvey went on presently in a still lower voice and thrusting his face farther forward under the lamp.

"Vacuums!" exclaimed the secretary in spite of himself. "What in the world do you mean?"

"What I say of course. He's always tumbling into them, so that I can't find him or get at him. He hides there for hours at a time, and for the life of me I can't make out what he does there."

Shorthouse stared his companion straight in the eyes. What in the name of heaven was he talking about?

"Do you suppose he goes there for a change of air, or—or to escape?" he went on in a louder voice.

Shorthouse could have laughed outright but for the expression of the other's face.

"I should not think there was much air of any sort in a vacuum," he said quietly.

"That's exactly what *I* feel," continued Garvey with ever growing excitement. "That's the horrid part of it. How the devil does he live there? You see—"

"Have you ever followed him there?" interrupted the secretary. The other leaned back in his chair and drew a deep sigh.

"Never! It's impossible. You see I can't follow him. There's not room for two. A vacuum only holds one comfortably. Marx knows that. He's out of my reach altogether once he's fairly inside. He knows the best side of a bargain. He's a regular Jew."

"That is a drawback to a servant, of course—" Shorthouse spoke slowly, with his eyes on his plate.

"A drawback," interrupted the other with an ugly chuckle, "I call it a draw-in, that's what I call it."

"A draw-in does seem a more accurate term," assented Shorthouse. "But," he went on, "I thought that nature abhorred a vacuum. She used to, when I was at school—though perhaps—it's so long ago—"

He hesitated and looked up. Something in Garvey's face—something he had *felt* before he looked up—stopped his tongue and froze the words in his throat. His lips refused to move and became suddenly dry. Again the mist rose before his eyes and the appalling shadow dropped its veil over the face before him. Garvey's features began to burn and glow. Then they seemed to coarsen and somehow slip confusedly together. He stared for a second—it seemed only for a second—into the visage of a ferocious and abominable animal; and then, as suddenly as it had come, the filthy shadow of the beast passed off, the mist melted out, and with a mighty effort over his nerves he forced himself to finish his sentence.

"You see it's so long since I've given attention to such things," he stammered. His heart was beating rapidly, and a feeling of oppression was gathering over it.

"It's my peculiar and special study on the other hand," Garvey resumed. "I've not spent all these years in my laboratory to no purpose, I can assure you. Nature, I know for a fact," he added with unnatural warmth, "does *not* abhor a vacuum. On the contrary, she's uncommonly fond of 'em, much too fond, it seems, for the comfort of my little household. If there were fewer vacuums and more abhorrence we should get on better—a damned sight better in my opinion."

"Your special knowledge, no doubt, enables you to speak with authority," Shorthouse said, curiosity and alarm warring with other mixed feelings in his mind; "but how *can* a man tumble into a vacuum?"

"You may well ask. That's just it. How can he? It's preposterous and I can't make it out at all. Marx knows, but he won't tell me. Jews know more than we do. For my part I have reason to believe—" He stopped and listened. "Hush! here he comes," he added, rubbing his hands together as if in glee and fidgeting in his chair.

Steps were heard coming down the passage, and as they approached the door Garvey seemed to give himself completely over to an excitement he could not control. His eyes were fixed on the door and he began clutching the tablecloth with both hands. Again his face was screened by the loathsome shadow. It grew wild, wolfish. As through a mask, that concealed, and yet was thin enough to let through a suggestion of, the beast crouching behind, there leaped into his countenance the strange look of the animal in the human—the expression of the were-wolf, the monster. The change in all its loathsomeness came rapidly over his features, which began to lose their outline. The nose flattened, dropping with broad nostrils over thick lips. The face rounded, filled, and became squat. The eyes, which, luckily for Shorthouse, no longer sought his own, glowed with the light of untamed appetite and bestial greed. The hands left the cloth and grasped the edges of the plate, and then clutched the cloth again.

"This is *my* course coming now," said Garvey, in a deep guttural voice. He was shivering. His upper lip was partly lifted and showed the teeth, white and gleaming.

A moment later the door opened and Marx hurried into the room and set a dish in front of his master. Garvey half rose to meet him, stretching out his hands and grinning horribly. With his mouth he made a sound like the snarl of an animal. The dish before him was steaming, but the slight vapour rising from it betrayed by its odour that it was not born of a fire of coals. It was the natural heat of flesh warmed by the fires of life only just expelled. The moment the dish rested on the table Garvey pushed away his own plate and drew the other up close under his mouth. Then he seized the food in both hands and commenced to tear it with his teeth, grunting as he did so. Shorthouse closed his eyes, with a feeling of nausea. When he looked up again the lips and jaw of the man opposite were stained with crimson. The whole man was transformed. A feasting tiger, starved and ravenous, but without a tiger's grace—this was what he watched for several minutes, transfixed with horror and disgust.

Marx had already taken his departure, knowing evidently what was not good for the eyes to look upon, and Shorthouse knew at last that he was sitting face to face with a madman.

The ghastly meal was finished in an incredibly short time and nothing was left but a tiny pool of red liquid rapidly hardening. Garvey leaned back heavily in his chair and sighed. His smeared face, withdrawn now from the glare of the lamp, began to resume its normal appearance. Presently he looked up at his guest and said in his natural voice—

"I hope you've had enough to eat. You wouldn't care for this, you know," with a downward glance.

Shorthouse met his eyes with an inward loathing, and it was impossible not to show some of the repugnance he felt. In the other's face, however, he thought he saw a subdued, cowed expression. But he found nothing to say.

"Marx will be in presently," Garvey went on. "He's either listening, or in a vacuum."

"Does he choose any particular time for his visits?" the secretary managed to ask.

"He generally goes after dinner; just about this time, in fact. But he's not gone yet," he added, shrugging his shoulders, "for I think I hear him coming."

Shorthouse wondered whether vacuum was possibly synonymous with wine cellar, but gave no expression to his thoughts. With chills of horror still running up and down his back, he saw Marx come in with a basin and towel, while Garvey thrust up his face just as an animal puts up its muzzle to be rubbed.

"Now we'll have coffee in the library, if you're ready," he said, in the tone of a gentleman addressing his guests after a dinner party.

Shorthouse picked up the bag, which had lain all this time between his feet, and walked through the door his host held open for him. Side by side they crossed the dark hall together, and, to his disgust, Garvey linked an arm in his, and with his face so close to the secretary's ear that he felt the warm breath, said in a thick voice—

"You're uncommonly careful with that bag, Mr. Shorthouse. It surely must contain something more than the bundle of papers."

"Nothing but the papers," he answered, feeling the hand burning upon his arm and wishing he were miles away from the house and its abominable occupants.

"Quite sure?" asked the other with an odious and suggestive chuckle. "Is there any meat in it, fresh meat—raw meat?"

The secretary felt, somehow, that at the least sign of fear the beast on his arm would leap upon him and tear him with his teeth.

"Nothing of the sort," he answered vigorously. "It wouldn't hold enough to feed a cat."

"True," said Garvey with a vile sigh, while the other felt the hand upon his arm twitch up and down as if feeling the flesh. "True, it's too small to be of any real use. As you say, it wouldn't hold enough to feed a cat."

Shorthouse was unable to suppress a cry. The muscles of his fingers, too, relaxed in spite of himself and he let the black bag drop with a bang to the floor. Garvey instantly withdrew his arm and turned with a quick movement. But the secretary had regained his control as suddenly as he had lost it, and he met the maniac's eyes with a steady and aggressive glare.

"There, you see, it's quite light. It makes no appreciable noise when I drop it." He picked it up and let it fall again, as if he had dropped it for the first time purposely. The ruse was successful.

"Yes. You're right," Garvey said, still standing in the doorway and staring at him. "At any rate it wouldn't hold enough for two," he laughed. And as he closed the door the horrid laughter echoed in the empty hall.

They sat down by a blazing fire and Shorthouse was glad to feel its warmth. Marx presently brought in coffee. A glass of the old whisky and a good cigar helped to restore equilibrium. For some minutes the men sat in silence staring into the fire. Then, without looking up, Garvey said in a quiet voice—

"I suppose it was a shock to you to see me eat raw meat like that. I must apologise if it was unpleasant to you. But it's all I can eat and it's the only meal I take in the twenty-four hours."

"Best nourishment in the world, no doubt; though I should think it might be a trifle strong for some stomachs."

He tried to lead the conversation away from so unpleasant a subject, and went on to talk rapidly of the values of different foods, of vegetarianism and vegetarians, and of men who had gone for long periods without any food at all. Garvey listened apparently without interest and had nothing to say. At the first pause he jumped in eagerly.

"When the hunger is really great on me," he said, still gazing into the fire, "I simply cannot control myself. I must have raw meat—the first I can get—" Here he raised his shining eyes and Shorthouse felt his hair beginning to rise.

"It comes upon me so suddenly too. I never can tell when to expect it. A year ago the passion rose in me like a whirlwind and Marx was out and I couldn't get meat. I had to get something or I should have bitten myself. Just when it was getting unbearable my dog ran out from beneath the sofa. It was a spaniel."

Shorthouse responded with an effort. He hardly knew what he was saying and his skin crawled as if a million ants were moving over it.

There was a pause of several minutes.

"I've bitten Marx all over," Garvey went on presently in his strange quiet voice, and as if he were speaking of apples; "but he's bitter. I doubt if the hunger could ever make me do it again. Probably that's what first drove him to take shelter in a vacuum." He chuckled hideously as he thought of this solution of his attendant's disappearances.

Shorthouse seized the poker and poked the fire as if his life depended on it. But when the banging and clattering was over Garvey continued his remarks with the same calmness. The next sentence, however, was never finished. The secretary had got upon his feet suddenly.

"I shall ask your permission to retire," he said in a determined voice; "I'm tired to-night; will you be good enough to show me to my room?"

Garvey looked up at him with a curious cringing expression behind which there shone the gleam of cunning passion.

"Certainly," he said, rising from his chair. "You've had a tiring journey. I ought to have thought of that before."

He took the candle from the table and lit it, and the fingers that held the match trembled.

"We needn't trouble Marx," he explained. "That beast's in his vacuum by this time."

III

They crossed the hall and began to ascend the carpetless wooden stairs. They were in the well of the house and the air cut like ice. Garvey, the flickering candle in his hand throwing his face into strong outline, led the way across the first landing and opened a door near the mouth of a dark passage. A pleasant room greeted the visitor's eyes, and he rapidly took in its points while his host walked over and lit two candles that stood on a table at the foot of the bed. A fire burned brightly in the grate. There were two windows, opening like doors, in the wall opposite, and a high canopied bed occupied most of the space on the right. Panelling ran all round the room reaching nearly to the ceiling and gave a warm and cosy appearance to the whole; while the portraits that stood in alternate panels suggested somehow the atmosphere of an old country house in England. Shorthouse was agreeably surprised.

"I hope you'll find everything you need," Garvey was saying in the doorway. "If not, you have only to ring that bell by the fireplace. Marx won't hear it of course, but it rings in my laboratory, where I spend most of the night."

Then, with a brief good-night, he went out and shut the door after him. The instant he was gone Mr. Sidebotham's private secretary did a peculiar thing. He planted himself in the middle of the room with his back to the door, and drawing the pistol swiftly from his hip pocket levelled it across his left arm at the window. Standing motionless in this position for thirty seconds he then suddenly swerved right round and faced in the other direction, pointing his pistol straight at the keyhole of the door. There followed immediately a sound of shuffling outside and of steps retreating across the landing.

"On his knees at the keyhole," was the secretary's reflection. "Just as I thought. But he didn't expect to look down the barrel of a pistol and it made him jump a little."

As soon as the steps had gone downstairs and died away across the hall, Shorthouse went over and locked the door, stuffing a piece of crumpled paper into the second keyhole which he saw immediately above the first. After that, he made a thorough search of the room. It hardly repaid the trouble, for he found nothing unusual. Yet he was glad he had made it. It relieved him to find no one was in hiding under the bed or in the deep oak cupboard; and he hoped sincerely it was not the cupboard in which the unfortunate spaniel had come to its vile death. The French windows, he discovered, opened on to a little balcony. It looked on to the front, and there was a drop of less than twenty feet to the ground below. The bed was high and wide, soft as feathers and covered with snowy sheets—very inviting to a tired man; and beside the blazing fire were a couple of deep arm-chairs.

Altogether it was very pleasant and comfortable; but, tired though he was, Shorthouse had no intention of going to bed. It was impossible to disregard the warning of his nerves. They had never failed him before, and when that sense of distressing horror lodged in his bones he knew there was something in the wind and that a red flag was flying over the immediate future. Some delicate instrument in his being, more subtle than the senses, more accurate than mere presentiment, had seen the red flag and interpreted its meaning.

Again it seemed to him, as he sat in an arm-chair over the fire, that his movements were being carefully watched from somewhere; and, not knowing what weapons might be used against him, he felt that his real safety lay in a rigid control of his mind and feelings and a stout refusal to admit that he was in the least alarmed.

The house was very still. As the night wore on the wind dropped. Only occasional bursts of sleet against the windows reminded him that the elements were awake and uneasy. Once or twice the windows rattled and the rain hissed in the fire, but the roar of the wind in the chimney grew less and less and the lonely building was at last lapped in a great stillness. The coals clicked, settling themselves deeper in the grate, and the noise of the cinders dropping with a tiny report into the soft heap of accumulated ashes was the only sound that punctuated the silence.

In proportion as the power of sleep grew upon him the dread of the situation lessened; but so imperceptibly, so gradually, and so in-sinuatingly that he scarcely realised the change. He thought he was as wide awake to his danger as ever. The successful exclusion of horri-ble mental pictures of what he had seen he attributed to his rigorous control, instead of to their true cause, the creeping over him of the soft influences of sleep. The faces in the coals were so soothing; the arm-chair was so comfortable; so sweet the breath that gently pressed upon his eyelids; so subtle the growth of the sensation of safety. He settled down deeper into the chair and in another moment would have been asleep when the red flag began to shake violently to and fro and he sat bolt upright as if he had been stabbed in the back.

Someone was coming up the stairs. The boards creaked beneath a stealthy weight.

Shorthouse sprang from the chair and crossed the room swiftly, taking up his position beside the door, but out of range of the keyhole. The two candles flared unevenly on the table at the foot of the bed. The steps were slow and cautious—it seemed thirty seconds between each one—but the person who was taking them was very close to the door. Already he had topped the stairs and was shuffling almost silently across the bit of landing.

The secretary slipped his hand into his pistol pocket and drew back further against the wall, and hardly had he completed the movement when the sounds abruptly ceased and he knew that somebody was standing just outside the door and preparing for a careful observation through the keyhole.

He was in no sense a coward. In action he was never afraid. It was the waiting and wondering and the uncertainty that might have loosened his nerves a little. But, somehow, a wave of intense horror swept over him for a second as he thought of the bestial maniac and his attendant Jew; and he would rather have faced a pack of wolves than have to do with either of these men.

Something brushing gently against the door set his nerves tingling afresh and made him tighten his grasp on the pistol. The steel was cold and slippery in his moist fingers. What an awful noise it would make when he pulled the trigger! If the door were to open how close he would be to the figure that came in! Yet he knew it was locked on the inside and could not possibly open. Again something brushed against the panel beside him and a second later the piece of crumpled paper fell from the keyhole to the floor, while the piece of thin wire that had accomplished this result showed its point for a moment in the room and was then swiftly withdrawn.

Somebody was evidently peering now through the keyhole, and

realising this fact the spirit of attack entered into the heart of the be-
leaguered man. Raising aloft his right hand he brought it suddenly
down with a resounding crash upon the panel of the door next the
keyhole—a crash that, to the crouching eavesdropper, must have
seemed like a clap of thunder out of a clear sky. There was a gasp and
a slight lurching against the door and the midnight listener rose startled and alarmed, for Shorthouse plainly heard the tread of feet
across the landing and down the stairs till they were lost in the silenc-
es of the hall. Only, this time, it seemed to him there were four feet
instead of two.

Quickly stuffing the paper back into the keyhole, he was in the
act of walking back to the fireplace when, over his shoulder, he
caught sight of a white face pressed in outline against the outside of
the window. It was blurred in the streams of sleet, but the white of
the moving eyes was unmistakable. He turned instantly to meet it,
but the face was withdrawn like a flash, and darkness rushed in to fill
the gap where it had appeared

"Watched on both sides," he reflected.

But he was not to be surprised into any sudden action, and quietly walking over to the fireplace as if he had seen nothing unusual he
stirred the coals a moment and then strolled leisurely over to the
window. Steeling his nerves, which quivered a moment in spite of his
will, he opened the window and stepped out on to the balcony. The
wind, which he thought had dropped, rushed past him into the room
and extinguished one of the candles, while a volley of fine cold rain
burst all over his face. At first he could see nothing, and the darkness
came close up to his eyes like a wall. He went a little farther on to the
balcony and drew the window after him till it clashed. Then he stood
and waited.

But nothing touched him. No one seemed to be there. His eyes
got accustomed to the blackness and he was able to make out the
iron railing, the dark shapes of the trees beyond, and the faint light
coming from the other window. Through this he peered into the
room, walking the length of the balcony to do so. Of course he was
standing in a shaft of light and whoever was crouching in the darkness below could plainly see him. *Below?*—That there should be anyone *above* did not occur to him until, just as he was preparing to go in

again, he became aware that something was moving in the darkness over his head. He looked up, instinctively raising a protecting arm, and saw a long black line swinging against the dim wall of the house. The shutters of the window on the next floor, whence it depended, were thrown open and moving backwards and forwards in the wind. The line was evidently a thickish cord, for as he looked it was pulled in and the end disappeared in the darkness.

Shorthouse, trying to whistle to himself, peered over the edge of the balcony as if calculating the distance he might have to drop, and then calmly walked into the room again and closed the window behind him, leaving the latch so that the lightest touch would cause it to fly open. He relit the candle and drew a straight-backed chair up to the table. Then he put coal on the fire and stirred it up into a royal blaze. He would willingly have folded the shutters over the staring windows at his back. But that was out of the question. It would have been to cut off his way of escape.

Sleep, for the time, was at a disadvantage. His brain was full of blood and every nerve was tingling. He felt as if countless eyes were upon him and scores of stained hands were stretching out from the corners and crannies of the house to seize him. Crouching figures, figures of hideous Jews, stood everywhere about him where shelter was, creeping forward out of the shadows when he was not looking and retreating swiftly and silently when he turned his head. Wherever he looked, other eyes met his own, and though they melted away under his steady, confident gaze, he knew they would wax and draw in upon him the instant his glances weakened and his will wavered.

Though there were no sounds, he knew that in the well of the house there was movement going on, *and preparation*. And this knowledge, inasmuch as it came to him irresistibly and through other and more subtle channels than those of the senses, kept the sense of horror fresh in his blood and made him alert and awake.

But, no matter how great the dread in the heart, the power of sleep will eventually overcome it. Exhausted nature is irresistible, and as the minutes wore on and midnight passed, he realised that nature was vigorously asserting herself and sleep was creeping upon him from the extremities.

To lessen the danger he took out his pencil and began to draw the articles of furniture in the room. He worked into elaborate detail the cupboard, the mantelpiece, and the bed, and from these he passed on to the portraits. Being possessed of genuine skill, he found the occupation sufficiently absorbing. It kept the blood in his brain, and that kept him awake. The pictures, moreover, now that he considered them for the first time, were exceedingly well painted. Owing to the dim light, he centred his attention upon the portraits beside the fireplace. On the right was a woman, with a sweet, gentle face and a figure of great refinement; on the left was a full-size figure of a big handsome man with a full beard and wearing a hunting costume of ancient date.

From time to time he turned to the windows behind him, but the vision of the face was not repeated. More than once, too, he went to the door and listened, but the silence was so profound in the house that he gradually came to believe the plan of attack had been abandoned. Once he went out on to the balcony, but the sleet stung his face and he only had time to see that the shutters above were closed, when he was obliged to seek the shelter of the room again.

In this way the hours passed. The fire died down and the room grew chilly. Shorthouse had made several sketches of the two heads and was beginning to feel overpoweringly weary. His feet and his hands were cold and his yawns were prodigious. It seemed ages and ages since the steps had come to listen at his door and the face had watched him from the window. A feeling of safety had somehow come to him. In reality he was exhausted. His one desire was to drop upon the soft white bed and yield himself up to sleep without any further struggle.

He rose from his chair with a series of yawns that refused to be stifled and looked at his watch. It was close upon three in the morning. He made up his mind that he would lie down with his clothes on and get some sleep. It was safe enough, the door was locked on the inside and the window was fastened. Putting the bag on the table near his pillow he blew out the candles and dropped with a sense of careless and delicious exhaustion upon the soft mattress. In five minutes he was sound asleep.

There had scarcely been time for the dreams to come when he found himself lying side-ways across the bed with wide open eyes staring into the darkness. Some one had touched him, and he had writhed away in his sleep as from something unholy. The movement had awakened him.

The room was simply black. No light came from the windows and the fire had gone out as completely as if water had been poured upon it. He gazed into a sheet of impenetrable darkness that came close up to his face like a wall.

His first thought was for the papers in his coat and his hand flew to the pocket. They were safe; and the relief caused by this discovery left his mind instantly free for other reflections.

And the realisation that at once came to him with a touch of dismay was, that during his sleep some definite *change* had been effected in the room. He felt this with that intuitive certainty which amounts to positive knowledge. The room was utterly still, but the corroboration that was speedily brought to him seemed at once to fill the darkness with a whispering, secret life that chilled his blood and made the sheet feel like ice against his cheek.

Hark! This was it; there reached his ears, in which the blood was already buzzing with warning clamour, a dull murmur of something that rose indistinctly from the well of the house and became audible to him without passing through walls or doors. There seemed no solid surface between him, lying on the bed, and the landing; between the landing and the stairs, and between the stairs and the hall beyond.

He knew that the door of the room *was standing open!* Therefore it had been opened from the *inside*. Yet the window was fastened, also on the inside.

Hardly was this realised when the conspiring silence of the hour was broken by another and a more definite sound. A step was coming along the passage. A certain bruise on the hip told Shorthouse that the pistol in his pocket was ready for use and he drew it out quickly and cocked it. Then he just had time to slip over the edge of the bed and crouch down on the floor when the step halted on the threshold of the room. The bed was thus between him and the open door. The window was at his back.

He waited in the darkness. What struck him as peculiar about the steps was that there seemed no particular desire to move stealthily. There was no extreme caution. They moved along in rather a slipshod way and sounded like soft slippers or feet in stockings. There was something clumsy, irresponsible, almost reckless about the movement.

For a second the steps paused upon the threshold, but only for a second. Almost immediately they came on into the room, and as they passed from the wood to the carpet Shorthouse noticed that they became wholly noiseless. He waited in suspense, not knowing whether the unseen walker was on the other side of the room or was close upon him. Presently he stood up and stretched out his left arm in front of him, groping, searching, feeling in a circle; and behind it he held the pistol, cocked and pointed, in his right hand. As he rose a bone cracked in his knee, his clothes rustled as if they were newspapers, and his breath seemed loud enough to be heard all over the room. But not a sound came to betray the position of the invisible intruder.

Then, just when the tension was becoming unbearable, a noise relieved the gripping silence. It was wood knocking against wood, and it came from the farther end of the room. The steps had moved over to the fireplace. A sliding sound almost immediately followed it and then silence closed again over everything like a pall.

For another five minutes Shorthouse waited, and then the suspense became too much. He could not stand that open door! The candles were close beside him and he struck a match and lit them, expecting in the sudden glare to receive at least a terrific blow. But nothing happened, and he saw at once that the room was entirely empty. Walking over with the pistol cocked he peered out into the darkness of the landing and then closed the door and turned the key. Then he searched the room—bed, cupboard, table, curtains, everything that could have concealed a man; but found no trace of the intruder. The owner of the footsteps had disappeared like a ghost into the shadows of the night. But for one fact he might have imagined that he had been dreaming: *the bag had vanished!*

There was no more sleep for Shorthouse that night. His watch pointed to 4 A.M. and there were still three hours before daylight. He sat down at the table and continued his sketches. With fixed determination he went on with his drawing and began a new outline of the man's head. There was something in the expression that continually evaded him. He had no success with it, and this time it seemed to him that it was the eyes that brought about his discomfiture. He held up his pencil before his face to measure the distance between the nose and the eyes, and to his amazement he saw that a change had come over the features. The eyes were no longer open. *The lids had closed!*

For a second he stood in a sort of stupefied astonishment. A push would have toppled him over. Then he sprang to his feet and held a candle close up to the picture. The eye-lids quivered, the eye-lashes trembled. Then, right before his gaze, the eyes opened and looked straight into his own. Two holes were cut in the panel and this pair of eyes, human eyes, just fitted them.

As by a curious effect of magic, the strong fear that had governed him ever since his entry into the house disappeared in a second. Anger rushed into his heart and his chilled blood rose suddenly to boiling point. Putting the candle down, he took two steps back into the room and then flung himself forward with all his strength against the painted panel. Instantly, and before the crash came, the eyes were withdrawn, and two black spaces showed where they had been. The old huntsman was eyeless. But the panel cracked and split inwards like a sheet of thin cardboard; and Shorthouse, pistol in hand, thrust an arm through the jagged aperture and, seizing a human leg, dragged out into the room—the Jew!

Words rushed in such a torrent to his lips that they choked him. The old Hebrew, white as chalk, stood shaking before him, the bright pistol barrel opposite his eyes, when a volume of cold air rushed into the room, and with it a sound of hurried steps. Shorthouse felt his arm knocked up before he had time to turn, and the same second Garvey, who had somehow managed to burst open the window, came between him and the trembling Marx. His lips were parted and his eyes rolled strangely in his distorted face.

"Don't shoot him! Shoot in the air!" he shrieked. He seized the Jew by the shoulders.

"You damned hound," he roared, hissing in his face. "So I've got you at last. That's where your vacuum is, is it? I know your vile hiding-place at last." He shook him like a dog. "I've been after him all night," he cried, turning to Shorthouse, "all night, I tell you, and I've got him at last."

Garvey lifted his upper lip as he spoke and showed his teeth. They shone like the fangs of a wolf. The Jew evidently saw them too, for he gave a horrid yell and struggled furiously.

Before the eyes of the secretary a mist seemed to rise. The hideous shadow again leaped into Garvey's face. He foresaw a dreadful battle, and covering the two men with his pistol he retreated slowly to the door. Whether they were both mad, or both criminal, he did not pause to enquire. The only thought present in his mind was that the sooner he made his escape the better.

Garvey was still shaking the Jew when he reached the door and turned the key, but as he passed out on to the landing both men stopped their struggling and turned to face him. Garvey's face, bestial, loathsome, livid with anger; the Jew's white and grey with fear and horror;—both turned towards him and joined in a wild, horrible yell that woke the echoes of the night. The next second they were after him at full speed.

Shorthouse slammed the door in their faces and was at the foot of the stairs, crouching in the shadow, before they were out upon the landing. They tore shrieking down the stairs and past him, into the hall; and, wholly unnoticed, Shorthouse whipped up the stairs again, crossed the bedroom, and dropped from the balcony into the soft snow.

As he ran down the drive he heard behind him in the house the yells of the maniacs; and when he reached home several hours later Mr. Sidebotham not only raised his salary but also told him to buy a new hat and overcoat, and send in the bill to him.

Skeleton Lake: An Episode in Camp

The utter loneliness of our moose-camp on Skeleton Lake had impressed us from the beginning—in the Quebec backwoods, five days by trail and canoe from civilisation—and perhaps the singular name contributed a little to the sensation of eeriness that made itself felt in the camp circle when once the sun was down and the late October mists began rising from the lake and winding their way in among the tree trunks.

For, in these regions, all names of lakes and hills and islands have their origin in some actual event, taking either the name of a chief participant, such as Smith's Ridge, or claiming a place in the map by perpetuating some special feature of the journey or the scenery, such as Long Island, Deep Rapids, or Rainy Lake.

All names thus have their meaning and are usually pretty recently acquired, while the majority are self-explanatory and suggest human and pioneer relations. Skeleton Lake, therefore, was a name full of suggestion, and though none of us knew the origin or the story of its birth, we all were conscious of a certain lugubrious atmosphere that haunted its shores and islands, and but for the evidences of recent moose tracks in its neighbourhood we should probably have pitched our tents elsewhere.

For several hundred miles in any direction we knew of only one other party of whites. They had journeyed up on the train with us, getting in at North Bay, and hailing from Boston way. A common goal and object had served by way of introduction. But the acquaintance had made little progress. This noisy, aggressive Yankee did not suit our fancy much as a possible neighbour, and it was only a slight intimacy between his chief guide, Jake the Swede, and one of our men that kept the thing going at all. They went into camp on Beaver Creek, fifty miles and more to the west of us.

But that was six weeks ago, and seemed as many months, for days and nights pass slowly in these solitudes and the scale of time changes wonderfully. Our men always seemed to know by instinct pretty well "whar them other fellows was movin'," but in the interval no one had come across their trails, or once so much as heard their rifle shots.

Our little camp consisted of the professor, his wife, a splendid shot and keen woods-woman, and myself. We had a guide apiece, and hunted daily in pairs from before sunrise till dark.

It was our last evening in the woods, and the professor was lying in my little wedge tent, discussing the dangers of hunting alone in couples in this way. The flap of the tent hung back and let in fragrant odours of cooking over an open wood fire; everywhere there were bustle and preparation, and one canoe already lay packed with moose horns, her nose pointing southwards.

"If an accident happened to one of them," he was saying, "the survivor's story when he returned to camp would be entirely unsupported evidence, wouldn't it? Because, you see—"

And he went on laying down the law after the manner of professors, until I became so bored that my attention began to wander to pictures and memories of the scenes we were just about to leave: Garden Lake, with its hundred islands; the rapids out of Round Pond; the countless vistas of forest, crimson and gold in the autumn sunshine; and the starlit nights we had spent watching in cold, cramped positions for the wary moose on lonely lakes among the hills. The hum of the professor's voice in time grew more soothing. A nod or a grunt was all the reply he looked for. Fortunately, he loathed interruptions. I think I could almost have gone to sleep under his very nose; perhaps I did sleep for a brief interval.

Then it all came about so quickly, and the tragedy of it was so unexpected and painful, throwing our peaceful camp into momentary confusion, that now it all seems to have happened with the uncanny swiftness of a dream.

First, there was the abrupt ceasing of the droning voice, and then the running of quick little steps over the pine needles, and the confusion of men's voices; and the next instant the professor's wife was at the tent door, hatless, her face white, her hunting bloomers bagging at the wrong places, a rifle in her hand, and her words running into one another anyhow.

"Quick, Harry! It's Rushton. I was asleep and it woke me. Something's happened. You must deal with it!"

In a second we were outside the tent with our rifles.

"My God!" I heard the professor exclaim, as if he had first made the discovery. "It is Rushton!"

I saw the guides helping—dragging—a man out of a canoe. A brief space of deep silence followed in which I heard only the waves from the canoe washing up on the sand; and then, immediately after, came the voice of a man talking with amazing rapidity and with odd gaps between his words. It was Rushton telling his story, and the tones of his voice, now whispering, now almost shouting, mixed with sobs and solemn oaths and frequent appeals to the Deity, somehow or other struck the false note at the very start, and before any of us guessed or knew anything at all. Something moved secretly between his words, a shadow veiling the stars, destroying the peace of our little camp, and touching us all personally with an undefinable sense of horror and distrust.

I can see that group to this day, with all the detail of a good photograph: standing half-way between the firelight and the darkness, a slight mist rising from the lake, the frosty stars, and our men, in silence that was all sympathy, dragging Rushton across the rocks towards the camp fire. Their moccasins crunched on the sand and slipped several times on the stones beneath the weight of the limp, exhausted body, and I can still see every inch of the pared cedar branch he had used for a paddle on that lonely and dreadful journey.

But what struck me most, as it struck us all, was the limp exhaustion of his body compared to the strength of his utterance and the tearing rush of his words. A vigorous driving-power was there at work, forcing out the tale, red-hot and throbbing, full of discrepancies and the strangest contradictions; and the nature of this driving-power I first began to appreciate when they had lifted him into the circle of firelight and I saw his face, grey under the tan, terror in the eyes, tears too, hair and beard awry, and listened to the wild stream of words pouring forth without ceasing.

I think we all understood then, but it was only after many years that anyone dared to confess what he thought.

There was Matt Morris, my guide; Silver Fizz, whose real name was unknown, and who bore the title of his favourite drink; and huge Hank Milligan—all ears and kind intention; and there was Rushton, pouring out his ready-made tale, with ever-shifting eyes, turning from face to face, seeking confirmation of details none had witnessed but himself—and *one other*.

Silver Fizz was the first to recover from the shock of the thing, and to realise, with the natural sense of chivalry common to most genuine back-woodsmen, that the man was at a terrible disadvantage. At any rate, he was the first to start putting the matter to rights.

"Never mind telling it just now," he said in a gruff voice, but with real gentleness; "get a bite t'eat first and then let her go afterwards. Better have a horn of whisky too. It ain't all packed yet, I guess."

"Couldn't eat or drink a thing," cried the other. "Good Lord, don't you see, man, I want to talk to someone first? I want to get it out of me to someone who can answer—answer. I've had nothing but trees to talk with for three days, and I can't carry it alone any longer. Those cursed, silent trees—I've told it 'em a thousand times. Now, just see here, it was this way. When we started out from camp—"

He looked fearfully about him, and we realised it was useless to stop him. The story was bound to come, and come it did.

Now, the story itself was nothing out of the way; such tales are told by the dozen round any camp fire where men who have knocked about in the woods are in the circle. It was the way he told it that made our flesh creep. He was near the truth all along, but he was skimming it, and the skimming took off the cream that might have saved his soul.

Of course, he smothered it in words—odd words, too— melodramatic, poetic, out-of-the-way words that lie just on the edge of frenzy. Of course, too, he kept asking us each in turn, scanning our faces with those restless, frightened eyes of his, "What would *you* have done?" "What else could I do?" and "Was that *my* fault?" But that was nothing, for he was no milk-and-water fellow who dealt in hints and suggestions; he told his story boldly, forcing his conclu-

sions upon us as if we had been so many wax cylinders of a phonograph that would repeat accurately what had been told us, and these
questions I have mentioned he used to emphasise any special point
that he seemed to think required such emphasis.

The fact was, however, the picture of what had actually happened was so vivid still in his own mind that it reached ours by a
process of telepathy which he could not control or prevent. All
through his true-false words this picture stood forth in fearful detail
against the shadows behind him. He could not veil, much less obliterate, it. We knew; and, I always thought, *he knew that we knew.*

The story itself, as I have said, was sufficiently ordinary. Jake and
himself, in a nine-foot canoe, had upset in the middle of a lake, and
had held hands across the upturned craft for several hours, eventually
cutting holes in her ribs to stick their arms through and grasp hands
lest the numbness of the cold water should overcome them. They
were miles from shore, and the wind was drifting them down upon a
little island. But when they got within a few hundred yards of the island, they realised to their horror that they would after all drift past it.

It was then the quarrel began. Jake was for leaving the canoe and
swimming. Rushton believed in waiting till they actually had passed
the island and were sheltered from the wind. Then they could make
the island easily by swimming, canoe and all. But Jake refused to give
in, and after a short struggle—Rushton admitted there was a struggle—got free from the canoe—and disappeared *without a single cry.*

Rushton held on and proved the correctness of his theory, and
finally made the island, canoe and all, after being in the water over
five hours. He described to us how he crawled up on to the shore,
and fainted at once, with his feet lying half in the water; how lost and
terrified he felt upon regaining consciousness in the dark; how the
canoe had drifted away and his extraordinary luck in finding it caught
again at the end of the island by a projecting cedar branch. He told us
that the little axe—another bit of real luck—had caught in the thwart
when the canoe turned over, and how the little bottle in his pocket
holding the emergency matches was whole and dry. He made a blazing fire and searched the island from end to end, calling upon Jake in
the darkness, but getting no answer; till, finally, so many half-
drowned men seemed to come crawling out of the water on to the

rocks, and vanish among the shadows when he came up with them, that he lost his nerve completely and returned to lie down by the fire till the daylight came.

He then cut a bough to replace the lost paddles, and after one more useless search for his lost companion, he got into the canoe, fearing every moment he would upset again, and crossed over to the mainland. He knew roughly the position of our camping place, and after paddling day and night, and making many weary portages, without food or covering, he reached us two days later.

This, more or less, was the story, and we, knowing whereof he spoke, knew that every word was literally true, and at the same time went to the building up of a hideous and prodigious lie.

Once the recital was over, he collapsed, and Silver Fizz, after a general expression of sympathy from the rest of us, came again to the rescue.

"But now, Mister, you jest *got* to eat and drink whether you've a mind to, or no."

And Matt Morris, cook that night, soon had the fried trout and bacon, and the wheat cakes and hot coffee passing round a rather silent and oppressed circle. So we ate round the fire, ravenously, as we had eaten every night for the past six weeks, but with this difference: that there was one among us who was more than ravenous—and he gorged.

In spite of all our devices he somehow kept himself the centre of observation. When his tin mug was empty, Morris instantly passed the tea-pail; when he began to mop up the bacon grease with the dough on his fork, Hank reached out for the frying pan; and the can of steaming boiled potatoes was always by his side. And there was another difference as well: he was sick, terribly sick before the meal was over, and this sudden nausea after food was more eloquent than words of what the man had passed through on his dreadful, foodless, ghost-haunted journey of forty miles to our camp. In the darkness he thought he would go crazy, he said. There were voices in the trees, and figures were always lifting themselves out of the water, or from behind boulders, to look at him and make awful signs. Jake constantly peered at him through the underbrush, and everywhere the shadows were moving, with eyes, footsteps, and following shapes.

We tried hard to talk of other things, but it was no use, for he was bursting with the rehearsal of his story and refused to allow himself the chances we were so willing and anxious to grant him. After a good night's rest he might have had more self-control and better judgment, and would probably have acted differently. But, as it was, we found it impossible to help him.

Once the pipes were lit, and the dishes cleared away, it was useless to pretend any longer. The sparks from the burning logs zigzagged upwards into a sky brilliant with stars. It was all wonderfully still and peaceful, and the forest odours floated to us on the sharp autumn air. The cedar fire smelt sweet and we could just hear the gentle wash of tiny waves along the shore. All was calm, beautiful, and remote from the world of men and passion. It was, indeed, a night to touch the soul, and yet, I think, none of us heeded these things. A bull-moose might almost have thrust his great head over our shoulders and have escaped unnoticed. The death of Jake the Swede, with its sinister setting, was the real presence that held the centre of the stage and compelled attention.

"You won't p'raps care to come along, Mister," said Morris, by way of a beginning; "but I guess I'll go with one of the boys here and have a hunt for it."

"Sure," said Hank. "Jake an' I done some biggish trips together in the old days, and I'll do that much for'm."

"It's deep water, they tell me, round them islands," added Silver Fizz; "but we'll find it, sure pop,—if it's thar."

They all spoke of the body as "it."

There was a minute or two of heavy silence, and then Rushton again burst out with his story in almost the identical words he had used before. It was almost as if he had learned it by heart. He wholly failed to appreciate the efforts of the others to let him off.

Silver Fizz rushed in, hoping to stop him, Morris and Hank closely following his lead.

"I once knew another travellin' partner of his," he began quickly; "used to live down Moosejaw Rapids way—"

"Is that so?" said Hank.

"Kind o' useful sort er feller," chimed in Morris.

All the idea the men had was to stop the tongue wagging before the discrepancies became so glaring that we should be forced to take notice of them, and ask questions. But, just as well try to stop an angry bull-moose on the run, or prevent Beaver Creek freezing in midwinter by throwing in pebbles near the shore. Out it came! And, though the discrepancy this time was insignificant, it somehow brought us all in a second face to face with the inevitable and dreaded climax.

"And so I tramped all over that little bit of an island, hoping he might somehow have gotten in without my knowing it, and always thinking I *heard that awful last cry of his* in the darkness—and then the night dropped down impenetrably, like a damn thick blanket out of the sky, and—"

All eyes fell away from his face. Hank poked up the logs with his boot, and Morris seized an ember in his bare fingers to light his pipe, although it was already emitting clouds of smoke. But the professor caught the ball flying.

"I thought you said he sank without a cry," he remarked quietly, looking straight up into the frightened face opposite, and then riddling mercilessly the confused explanation that followed.

The cumulative effect of all these forces, hitherto so rigorously repressed, now made itself felt, and the circle spontaneously broke up, everybody moving at once by a common instinct. The professor's wife left the party abruptly, with excuses about an early start next morning. She first shook hands with Rushton, mumbling something about his comfort in the night.

The question of his comfort, however, devolved by force of circumstances upon myself, and he shared my tent. Just before wrapping up in my double blankets—for the night was bitterly cold—he turned and began to explain that he had a habit of talking in his sleep and hoped I would wake him if he disturbed me by doing so.

Well, he did talk in his sleep—and it disturbed me very much indeed. The anger and violence of his words remain with me to this day, and it was clear in a minute that he was living over again some portion of the scene upon the lake. I listened, horror-struck, for a moment or two, and then understood that I was face to face with one of two alternatives: I must continue an unwilling eavesdropper, or I must waken him. The former was impossible for me, yet I shrank from the latter with the greatest repugnance; and in my dilemma I saw the only way out of the difficulty and at once accepted it.

Cold though it was, I crawled stealthily out of my warm sleeping-bag and left the tent, intending to keep the old fire alight under the stars and spend the remaining hours till daylight in the open.

As soon as I was out I noticed at once another figure moving silently along the shore. It was Hank Milligan, and it was plain enough what he was doing: he was examining the holes that had been cut in the upper ribs of the canoe. He looked half ashamed when I came up with him, and mumbled something about not being able to sleep for the cold. But, there, standing together beside the over-turned canoe, we both saw that the holes were far too small for a man's hand and arm and could not possibly have been cut by two men hanging on for their lives in deep water. Those holes had been made afterwards.

Hank said nothing to me and I said nothing to Hank, and presently he moved off to collect logs for the fire, which needed replenishing, for it was a piercingly cold night and there were many degrees of frost.

Three days later Hank and Silver Fizz followed with stumbling footsteps the old Indian trail that leads from Beaver Creek to the southwards. A hammock was slung between them, and it weighed heavily. Yet neither of the men complained; and, indeed, speech between them was almost nothing. Their thoughts, however, were exceedingly busy, and the terrible secret of the woods which formed their burden weighed far more heavily than the uncouth, shifting mass that lay in the swinging hammock and tugged so severely at their shoulders.

They had found "it" in four feet of water not more than a couple of yards from the lee shore of the island. And in the back of the head was a long, terrible wound which no man could possibly have inflicted upon himself.

Max Hensig—Bacteriologist and Murderer

A Story of New York

I

Besides the departmental men on the New York *Vulture,* there were about twenty reporters for general duty, and Williams had worked his way up till he stood easily among the first half-dozen; for, in addition to being accurate and painstaking, he was able to bring to his reports of common things that touch of imagination and humour which just lifted them out of the rut of mere faithful recording. Moreover, the city editor *(anglice* news editor) appreciated his powers, and always tried to give him assignments that did himself and the paper credit, and he was justified now in expecting to be relieved of the hack jobs that were usually allotted to new men.

He was therefore puzzled and a little disappointed one morning as he saw his inferiors summoned one after another to the news desk to receive the best assignments of the day, and when at length his turn came, and the city editor asked him to cover the "Hensig story," he gave a little start of vexation that almost betrayed him into asking what the devil the "Hensig story" was. For it is the duty of every morning newspaper man—in New York at least—to have made himself familiar with all the news of the day before he shows himself at the office, and though Williams had already done this, he could not recall either the name or the story.

"You can run to a hundred or a hundred and fifty, Mr. Williams. Cover the trial thoroughly, and get good interviews with Hensig and the lawyers. There'll be no night assignment for you till the case is over."

Williams was going to ask if there were any private "tips" from the District Attorney's office, but the editor was already speaking

276

with Weekes, who wrote the daily "weather story," and he went back slowly to his desk, angry and disappointed, to read up the Hensig case and lay his plans for the day accordingly. At any rate, he reflected, it looked like "a soft job," and as there was to be no second assignment for him that night, he would get off by eight o'clock, and be able to dine and sleep for once like a civilised man. And that was something.

It took him some time, however, to discover that the Hensig case was only a murder story. And this increased his disgust. It was tucked away in the corners of most of the papers, and little importance was attached to it. A murder trial is not first-class news unless there are very special features connected with it, and Williams had already covered scores of them. There was a heavy sameness about them that made it difficult to report them interestingly, and as a rule they were left to the tender mercies of the "flimsy" men—the Press Associations—and no paper sent a special man unless the case was distinctly out of the usual. Moreover, a hundred and fifty meant a column and a half, and Williams, not being a space man, earned the same money whether he wrote a stickful or a page; so that he felt doubly aggrieved, and walked out into the sunny open spaces opposite Newspaper Row heaving a deep sigh and cursing the boredom of his trade.

Max Hensig, he found, was a German doctor accused of murdering his second wife by injecting arsenic. The woman had been buried several weeks when the suspicious relatives got the body exhumed, and a quantity of the poison had been found in her. Williams recalled something about the arrest, now he came to think of it; but he felt no special interest in it, for ordinary murder trials were no longer his legitimate work, and he scorned them. At first, of course, they had thrilled him horribly, and some of his interviews with the prisoners, especially just before execution, had deeply impressed his imagination and kept him awake o' nights. Even now he could not enter the gloomy Tombs Prison, or cross the Bridge of Sighs leading from it to the courts, without experiencing a real sensation, for its huge Egyptian columns and massive walls closed round him like death; and the first time he walked down Murderers' Row, and came in view of the cell doors, his throat was dry, and he had almost turned and run out of the building.

The first time, too, that he covered the trial of a negro and listened to the man's hysterical speech before sentence was pronounced, he was absorbed with interest, and his heart leaped. The wild appeals to the Deity, the long invented words, the ghastly pallor under the black skin, the rolling eyes, and the torrential sentences all seemed to him to be something tremendous to describe for his sensational sheet; and the stickful that was eventually printed—written by the flimsy man too—had given him quite a new standard of the relative value of news and of the quality of the satiated public palate. He had reported the trials of a Chinaman, stolid as wood; of an Italian who had been too quick with his knife; and of a farm girl who had done both her parents to death in their beds, entering their room stark naked, so that no stains should betray her; and at the beginning these things haunted him for days.

But that was all months ago, when he first came to New York. Since then his work had been steadily in the criminal courts, and he had grown a second skin. An execution in the electric chair at Sing Sing could still unnerve him somewhat, but mere murder no longer thrilled or excited him, and he could be thoroughly depended on to write a good "murder story"—an account that his paper could print without blue pencil.

Accordingly he entered the Tombs Prison with nothing stronger than the feeling of vague oppression that gloomy structure always stirred in him, and certainly with no particular emotion connected with the prisoner he was about to interview; and when he reached the second iron door, where a warder peered at him through a small grating, he heard a voice behind him, and turned to find the *Chronicle* man at his heels.

"Hullo, Senator! What good trail are you following down here?" he cried, for the other got no small assignments, and never had less than a column on the *Chronicle* front page at space rates.

"Same as you, I guess—Hensig," was the reply.

"But there's no space in Hensig," said Williams with surprise. "Are you back on salary again? "

"Not much," laughed the Senator—no one knew his real name, but he was always called Senator. "But Hensig's good for two hundred easy. There's a whole list of murders behind him, we hear, and this is the first time he's been caught."

"Poison?"

The Senator nodded in reply, turning to ask the warder some question about another case, and Williams waited for him in the corridor, impatiently rather, for he loathed the musty prison odour. He watched the Senator as he talked, and was distinctly glad he had come. They were good friends: he had helped Williams when he first joined the small army of newspaper men and was not much welcomed, being an Englishman. Common origin and good-heartedness mixed themselves delightfully in his face, and he always made Williams think of a friendly, honest cart-horse—stolid, strong, with big and simple emotions.

"Get a hustle on, Senator," he said at length impatiently.

The two reporters followed the warder down the flagged corridor, past a row of dark cells, each with its occupant, until the man, swinging his keys in the direction indicated, stopped and pointed:

"Here's your gentleman," he said, and then moved on down the corridor, leaving them staring through the bars at a tall, slim young man, pacing to and fro. He had flaxen hair and very bright blue eyes; his skin was white, and his face wore so open and innocent an expression that one would have said he could not twist a kitten's tail without wincing.

"From the *Chronicle* and *Vulture,*" explained Williams, by way of introduction, and the talk at once began in the usual way.

The man in the cell ceased his restless pacing up and down, and stopped opposite the bars to examine them. He stared straight into Williams's eyes for a moment, and the reporter noted a very different expression from the one he had first seen. It actually made him shift his position and stand a little to one side. But the movement was wholly instinctive. He could not have explained why he did it.

"Guess you vish me to say I did it, and then egsplain to you *how* I did it," the young doctor said coolly, with a marked German accent. "But I haf no copy to gif you shust now. You see at the trial it is nothing but spite—and shealosy of another woman. I lofed my vife. I vould not haf gilled her for anything in the vorld——"

"Oh, of course, of course, Dr. Hensig," broke in the Senator, who was more experienced in the ways of difficult interviewing. "We quite understand that. But, you know, in New York the newspapers try a man as much as the courts, and we thought you might like to make a statement to the public which we should be very glad to print for you. It may help your case——"

"Nothing can help my case in this tamned country where shustice is to be pought mit tollars!" cried the prisoner, with a sudden anger and an expression of face still further belying the first one; "nothing except a lot of money. But I tell you now two things you may write for your public: One is, no motive can be shown for the murder, because I lofed Zinka and vished her to live alvays. And the other is——" He stopped a moment and stared steadily at Williams making shorthand notes—"that with my knowledge—my egceptional knowledge—of poisons and pacteriology I could have done it in a dozen ways without pumping arsenic into her body. That is a fool's way of killing. It is clumsy and childish and sure of discofery! See?"

He turned away, as though to signify that the interview was over, and sat down on his wooden bench.

"Seems to have taken a fancy to you," laughed the Senator, as they went off to get further interviews with the lawyers. "He never looked at me once."

"He's got a bad face—the face of a devil. I don't feel complimented," said Williams shortly. "I'd hate to be in his power."

"Same here," returned the other. "Let's go into Silver Dollars and wash the dirty taste out."

So, after the custom of reporters, they made their way up the Bowery and went into a saloon that had gained a certain degree of fame because the Tammany owner had let a silver dollar into each stone of the floor. Here they washed away most of the "dirty taste" left by the Tombs atmosphere and Hensig, and then went on to Steve Brodie's, another saloon a little higher up the same street.

"There'll be others there," said the Senator, meaning drinks as well as reporters, and Williams, still thinking over their interview, silently agreed.

Brodie was a character; there was always something lively going on in his place. He had the reputation of having once jumped from the Brooklyn Bridge and reached the water alive. No one could actually deny it, and no one could prove that it really happened; and anyhow, he had enough imagination and personality to make the myth live and to sell much bad liquor on the strength of it. The walls of his saloon were plastered with lurid oil-paintings of the bridge, the height enormously magnified, and Steve's body in mid-air, an expression of a happy puppy on his face.

Here, as expected, they found "Whitey" Fife, of the *Recorder,* and Galusha Owen, of the *World.* "Whitey," as his nickname implied, was an albino, and clever. He wrote the daily "weather story" for his paper, and the way he spun a column out of rain, wind, and temperature was the envy of every one except the Weather Clerk, who objected to being described as "Farmer Dunne, cleaning his rat-tail file," and to having his dignified office referred to in the public press as "a down-country farm." But the public liked it, and laughed, and "Whitey" was never really spiteful.

Owen, too, when sober, was a good man who had long passed the rubicon of hack assignments. Yet both these men were also on the Hensig story. And Williams, who had already taken an instinctive dislike to the case, was sorry to see this, for it meant frequent interviewing and the possession, more or less, of his mind and imagination. Clearly, he would have much to do with this German doctor. Already, even at this stage, he began to hate him.

The four reporters spent an hour drinking and talking. They fell at length to discussing the last time they had chanced to meet on the same assignment—a private lunatic asylum owned by an incompetent quack without a licence, and where most of the inmates, not mad in the first instance, and all heavily paid for by relatives who wished them out of the way, had gone mad from ill-treatment. The place had been surrounded before dawn by the Board of Health officers, and the quasi-doctor arrested as he opened his front door. It was a splendid newspaper "story," of course.

"My space bill ran to sixty dollars a day for nearly a week," said Whitey Fife thickly, and the others laughed, because Whitey wrote most of his stuff by cribbing it from the evening papers.

"A dead cinch," said Galusha Owen, his dirty flannel collar poking up through his long hair almost to his ears. "I 'faked' the whole of the second day without going down there at all."

He pledged Whitey for the tenth time that morning, and the albino leered happily across the table at him, and passed him a thick compliment before emptying his glass.

"Hensig's going to be good, too," broke in the Senator, ordering a round of gin-fizzes, and Williams gave a little start of annoyance to hear the name brought up again. "He'll make good stuff at the trial. I never saw a cooler hand. You should've heard him talk about poisons and bacteriology, and boasting he could kill in a dozen ways without fear of being caught. I guess he was telling the truth right enough!"

"That so?" cried Galusha and Whitey in the same breath, not having done a stroke of work so far on the case.

"Rundown totheTombsh angetaninerview," added Whitey, turning with a sudden burst of enthusiasm to his companion. His white eyebrows and pink eyes fairly shone against the purple of his tipsy face. "No, no," cried the Senator; "don't spoil a good story. You're both as full as ticks. I'll match with Williams which of us goes. Hensig knows us already, and we'll all 'give up' in this story right along. No 'beats.'"

So they decided to divide news till the case was finished, and to keep no exclusive items to themselves; and Williams, having lost the toss, swallowed his gin-fizz and went back to the Tombs to get a further talk with the prisoner on his knowledge of expert poisoning and bacteriology.

Meanwhile his thoughts were very busy elsewhere. He had taken no part in the noisy conversation in the bar-room, because something lay at the back of his mind, bothering him, and claiming attention with great persistence. Something was at work in his deeper consciousness, something that had impressed him with a vague sense of unpleasantness and nascent fear, reaching below that second skin he had grown.

And, as he walked slowly through the malodorous slum streets that lay between the Bowery and the Tombs, dodging the pullers-in outside the Jew clothing stores, and nibbling at a bag of pea-nuts he caught up off an Italian push-cart *en route*, this "something" rose a little higher out of its obscurity, and began to play with the roots of the ideas floating higgledy-piggledy on the surface of his mind. He thought he knew what it was, but could not make quite sure. From the roots of his thoughts it rose a little higher, so that he clearly felt it as something disagreeable. Then, with a sudden rush, it came to the surface, and poked its face before him so that he fully recognised it.

The blond visage of Dr. Max Hensig rose before him, cool, smiling, and implacable.

Somehow, he had expected it would prove to be Hensig—this unpleasant thought that was troubling him. He was not really surprised to have labelled it, because the man's personality had made an unwelcome impression upon him at the very start. He stopped nervously in the street, and looked round. He did not expect to see anything out of the way, or to find that he was being followed. It was not that exactly. The act of turning was merely the outward expression of a sudden inner discomfort, and a man with better nerves, or nerves more under control, would not have turned at all.

But what caused this tremor of the nerves? Williams probed and searched within himself. It came, he felt, from some part of his inner being he did not understand; there had been an intrusion, an incongruous intrusion, into the stream of his normal consciousness. Messages from this region always gave him pause; and in this particular case he saw no reason why he should think specially of Dr. Hensig with alarm—this light-haired stripling with blue eyes and drooping moustache. The faces of other murderers had haunted him once or twice because they were more than ordinarily bad, or because their case possessed unusual features of horror. But there was nothing so very much out of the way about Hensig—at least, if there was, the reporter could not seize and analyse it. There seemed no adequate reason to explain his emotion. Certainly, it had nothing to do with the fact that he was merely a murderer, for that stirred no thrill in him at all, except a kind of pity, and a wonder how the man would meet his execution. It must, he argued, be something to do with the *personality* of the man, apart from any particular deed or characteristic.

Puzzled, and still a little nervous, he stood in the road, hesitating. In front of him the dark walls of the Tombs rose in massive steps of granite. Overhead white summer clouds sailed across a deep blue sky; the wind sang cheerfully among the wires and chimney-pots, making him think of fields and trees; and down the street surged the usual cosmopolitan New York crowd of laughing Italians, surly negroes,

Hebrews chattering Yiddish, tough-looking hooligans with that fighting lurch of the shoulders peculiar to New York roughs, Chinamen, taking little steps like boys—and every other sort of nondescript imaginable. It was early June, and there were faint odours of the sea and of sea-beaches in the air. Williams caught himself shivering a little with delight at the sight of the sky and scent of the wind.

Then he looked back at the great prison, rightly named the Tombs, and the sudden change of thought from the fields to the cells, from life to death, somehow landed him straight into the discovery of what caused this attack of nervousness:

Hensig was no ordinary murderer! That was it. There was something quite out of the ordinary about him. The man was a horror, pure and simple, standing apart from normal humanity. The knowledge of this rushed over him like a revelation, bringing unalterable conviction in its train. Something of it had reached him in that first brief interview, but without explaining itself sufficiently to be recognised, and since then it had been working in his system, like a poison, and was now causing a disturbance, not having been assimilated. A quicker temperament would have labelled it long before.

Now, Williams knew well that he drank too much, and had more than a passing acquaintance with drugs; his nerves were shaky at the best of times. His life on the newspapers afforded no opportunity of cultivating pleasant social relations, but brought him all the time into contact with the seamy side of life—the criminal, the abnormal, the unwholesome in human nature. He knew, too, that strange thoughts, *idées fixes* and what not, grew readily in such a soil as this, and, not wanting these, he had formed a habit—peculiar to himself—of deliberately sweeping his mind clean once a week of all that had haunted, obsessed, or teased him, of the horrible or unclean, during his work; and his eighth day, his holiday, he invariably spent in the woods, walking, building fires, cooking a meal in the open, and getting all the country air and the exercise he possibly could. He had in this way kept his mind free from many unpleasant pictures that might otherwise have lodged there abidingly, and the habit of thus cleansing his imagination had proved more than once of real value to him.

So now he laughed to himself, and turned on those whizzing brooms of his, trying to forget these first impressions of Hensig, and simply going in, as he did a hundred other times, to get an ordinary interview with an ordinary prisoner. This habit, being nothing more nor less than the practice of suggestion, was more successful sometimes than others. This time—since fear is less susceptible to suggestion than other emotions—it was less so.

Williams got his interview, and came away fairly creeping with horror. Hensig was all that he had felt, and more besides. He belonged, the reporter felt convinced, to that rare type of deliberate murderer, cold-blooded and calculating, who kills for a song, delights in killing, and gives its whole intellect to the consideration of each detail, glorying in evading detection and revelling in the notoriety of the trial, if caught. At first he had answered reluctantly, but as Williams plied his questions intelligently, the young doctor warmed up and became enthusiastic with a sort of cold intellectual enthusiasm, till at last he held forth like a lecturer, pacing his cell, gesticulating, explaining with admirable exposition how easy murder could be to a man who knew his business.

And *he* did know his business! No man, in these days of inquests and post-mortem examination, would inject poisons that might be found weeks afterwards in the viscera of the victim. No man who knew his business!

"What is more easy," he said, holding the bars with his long white fingers and gazing into the reporter's eyes, "than to take a disease germ ['cherm' he pronounced it] of typhus, plague, or any cherm you blease, and make so virulent a culture that no medicine in the vorld could counteract it; a really powerful microbe—and then scratch the skin of your victim with a pin? And who could drace it to you, or accuse you of murder?"

Williams, as he watched and heard, was glad the bars were between them; but, even so, something invisible seemed to pass from the prisoner's atmosphere and lay an icy finger on his heart. He had come into contact with every possible kind of crime and criminal, and had interviewed scores of men who, for jealousy, greed, passion, or other comprehensible emotion, had killed and paid the penalty of killing. He understood that. Any man with strong passions was a potential killer. But never before had he met a man who in cold blood, deliberately, under no emotion greater than boredom, would destroy a human life and then boast of his ability to do it. Yet this, he felt sure, was what Hensig had done, and what his vile words shadowed forth and betrayed. Here was something outside humanity, something terrible, monstrous; and it made him shudder. This young doctor, he felt, was a fiend incarnate, a man who thought less of human life than of the lives of flies in summer, and who would kill with as steady a hand and cool a brain as though he were performing a common operation in the hospital.

Thus the reporter left the prison gates with a vivid impression in his mind, though exactly how his conclusion was reached was more than he could tell. This time the mental brooms failed to act. The horror of it remained.

On the way out into the street he ran against Policeman Dowling of the ninth precinct, with whom he had been fast friends since the day he wrote a glowing account of Dowling's capture of a "green-goods-man," when Dowling had been so drunk that he nearly lost his prisoner altogether. The policeman had never forgotten the good turn; it had promoted him to plain clothes; and he was always ready to give the reporter any news he had.

"Know of anything good to-day?" he asked by way of habit.

"Bet your bottom dollar I do," replied the coarse-faced Irish policeman; "one of the best, too. I've got Hensig!"

Dowling spoke with pride and affection. He was mighty pleased, too, because his name would be in the paper every day for a week or more, and a big case helped the chances of promotion.

Williams cursed inwardly. Apparently there was no escape from this man Hensig.

"Not much of a case, is it?" he asked.

"It's a jim dandy, that's what it is," replied the other, a little offended. "Hensig may miss the Chair because the evidence is weak, but he's the worst I've ever met. Why, he'd poison you as soon as spit in your eye, and if he's got a heart at all he keeps it on ice."

"What makes you think that?"

"Oh, they talk pretty freely to us sometimes," the policeman said, with a significant wink. "Can't be used against them at the trial, and it kind o' relieves their mind, I guess. But I'd just as soon not have heard most of what that guy told me—see? Come in," he added, looking round cautiously; "I'll set 'em up and tell you a bit."

Williams entered the side-door of a saloon with him, but not too willingly.

"A glarss of Scotch for the Englishman," ordered the officer facetiously, "and I'll take a horse's collar with a dash of peach bitters in it—just what you'd notice, no more." He flung down a half-dollar, and the bar-tender winked and pushed it back to him across the counter.

"What's yours, Mike?" he asked him.

"I'll take a cigar," said the bar-tender, pocketing the proffered dime and putting a cheap cigar in his waistcoat pocket, and then moving off to allow the two men elbow-room to talk in.

They talked in low voices with heads close together for fifteen minutes, and then the reporter set up another round of drinks. The bar-tender took *his* money. Then they talked a bit longer, Williams rather white about the gills and the policeman very much in earnest.

"The boys are waiting for me up at Brodie's," said Williams at length. "I must be off."

"That's so," said Dowling, straightening up. "We'll just liquor up again to show there's no ill-feeling. And mind you see me every morning before the case is called. Trial begins to-morrow."

They swallowed their drinks, and again the bar-tender took a ten-cent piece and pocketed a cheap cigar.

"Don't print what I've told you, and don't give it up to the other reporters," said Dowling as they separated. "And if you want confirmation jest take the cars and run down to Amityville, Long Island, and you'll find what I've said is O.K. every time."

Williams went back to Steve Brodie's, his thoughts whizzing about him like bees in a swarm. What he had heard increased tenfold his horror of the man. Of course, Dowling may have lied or exaggerated, but he thought not. It was probably all true, and the newspaper offices knew something about it when they sent good men to cover the case. Williams wished to heaven he had nothing to do with the thing; but meanwhile he could not write what he had heard, and all the other reporters wanted was the result of his interview. That was good for half a column, even expurgated.

He found the Senator in the middle of a story to Galusha, while

Whitey Fife was knocking cocktail glasses off the edge of the table and catching them just before they reached the floor, pretending they were Steve Brodie jumping from the Brooklyn Bridge. He had promised to set up the drinks for the whole bar if he missed, and just as Williams entered a glass smashed to atoms on the stones, and a roar of laughter went up from the room. Five or six men moved up to the bar and took their liquor, Williams included, and soon after Whitey and Galusha went off to get some lunch and sober up, having first arranged to meet Williams later in the evening and get the "story" from him.

"Get much?" asked the Senator.

"More than I care about," replied the other, and then told his friend the story.

The Senator listened with intense interest, making occasional notes from time to time, and asking a few questions. Then, when Williams had finished, he said quietly:

"I guess Dowling's right. Let's jump on a car and go down to Amityville, and see what they think about him down there."

Amityville was a scattered village some twenty miles away on Long Island, where Dr. Hensig had lived and practised for the last year or two, and where Mrs. Hensig No. 2 had come to her suspicious death. The neighbours would be sure to have plenty to say, and though it might not prove of great value, it would be certainly interesting. So the two reporters went down there, and interviewed any one and every one they could find, from the man in the drug-store to the parson and the undertaker, and the stories they heard would fill a book.

"Good stuff," said the Senator, as they journeyed back to New York on the steamer, "but nothing we can use, I guess." His face was very grave, and he seemed troubled in his mind.

"Nothing the District Attorney can use either at the trial," observed Williams.

"It's simply a devil—not a man at all," the other continued, as if talking to himself. "Utterly unmoral! I swear I'll make McSweater put me on another job."

For the stories they had heard showed Dr. Hensig as a man who openly boasted that he could kill without detection; that no enemy of his lived long; that, as a doctor, he had, or ought to have, the right over life and death; and that if a person was a nuisance, or a trouble to him, there was no reason he should not put them away, provided he did it without rousing suspicion. Of course he had not shouted these views aloud in the market-place, but he had let people know that he held them, and held them seriously. They had fallen from him in conversation, in unguarded moments, and were clearly the natural expression of his mind and views. And many people in the village evidently had no doubt that he had put them into practice more than once.

"There's nothing to give up to Whitey or Galusha, though," said the Senator decisively, "and there's hardly anything we can use in our story."

"I don't think I should care to use it anyhow," Williams said, with rather a forced laugh.

The Senator looked round sharply by way of question.

"Hensig *may be acquitted and get out,*" added Williams.

"Same here. I guess you're dead right," he said slowly, and then added more cheerfully, "Let's go and have dinner in Chinatown, and write our copy together."

So they went down Pell Street, and turned up some dark wooden stairs into a Chinese restaurant, smelling strongly of opium and of cooking not Western. Here at a little table on the sanded floor they ordered chou chop suey and chou om dong in brown bowls, and washed it down with frequent doses of the fiery white whisky, and then moved into a corner and began to cover their paper with pencil writing for the consumption of the great American public in the morning.

"There's not much to choose between Hensig and *that,*" said the Senator, as one of the degraded white women who frequent Chinatown entered the room and sat down at an empty table to order whisky. For, with four thousand Chinamen in the quarter, there is not a single Chinese woman.

"All the difference in the world," replied Williams, following his glance across the smoky room. "She's been decent once, and may be again some day, but that damned doctor has never been anything but what he is—a soulless, intellectual devil. He doesn't belong to humanity at all. I've got a horrid idea that———"

"How do you spell 'bacteriology,' two r's or one?" asked the Senator, going on with his scrawly writing of a story that would be read with interest by thousands next day.

"Two *r's* and one *k,*" laughed the other. And they wrote on for another hour, and then went to turn it in to their respective offices in Park Row.

II

The trial of Max Hensig lasted two weeks, for his relations supplied money, and he got good lawyers and all manner of delays. From a newspaper point of view it fell utterly flat, and before the end of the fourth day most of the papers had shunted their big men on to other jobs more worthy of their powers.

From Williams's point of view, however, it did not fall flat, and he was kept on it till the end. A reporter, of course, has no right to indulge in editorial remarks, especially when a case is still *sub judice,* but in New York journalism and the dignity of the law have a standard all their own, and into his daily reports there crept the distinct flavour of his own conclusions. Now that new men, with whom he had no agreement to "give up," were covering the story for the other papers, he felt free to use any special knowledge in his possession, and a good deal of what he had heard at Amityville and from officer Dowling somehow managed to creep into his writing. Something of the horror and loathing he felt for this doctor also betrayed itself, more by inference than actual statement, and no one who read his daily column could come to any other conclusion than that Hensig was a calculating, cool-headed murderer of the most dangerous type.

This was a little awkward for the reporter, because it was his duty every morning to interview the prisoner in his cell, and get his views on the conduct of the case in general and on his chances of escaping the Chair in particular.

Yet Hensig showed no embarrassment. All the newspapers were supplied to him, and he evidently read every word that Williams wrote. He must have known what the reporter thought about him, at least so far as his guilt or innocence was concerned, but he expressed no opinion as to the fairness of the articles, and talked freely of his chances of ultimate escape. The very way in which he glorified in being the central figure of a matter that bulked so large in the public eye seemed to the reporter an additional proof of the man's perversity. His vanity was immense. He made most careful toilets, appearing every day in a clean shirt and a new tie, and never wearing the same suit on two consecutive days. He noted the descriptions of his personal appearance in the Press, and was quite offended if his clothes and bearing in court were not referred to in detail. And he was unusually delighted and pleased when any of the papers stated that he looked smart and self-possessed, or showed great self-control—which some of them did.

"They make a hero of me," he said one morning when Williams went to see him as usual before court opened, "and if I go to the Chair—which I tink I not do, you know—you shall see something fine. Berhaps they electrocute a corpse only!"

And then, with dreadful callousness, he began to chaff the reporter about the tone of his articles—for the first time.

"I only report what is said and done in court," stammered Williams, horribly uncomfortable, "and I am always ready to write anything you care to say——"

"I haf no fault to find," answered Hensig, his cold blue eyes fixed on the reporter's face through the bars, "none at all. You tink I haf killed, and you show it in all your sendences. Haf you ever seen a man in the Chair, I ask you?"

Williams was obliged to say he had.

"*Ach was!* You haf indeed!" said the doctor coolly.

"It's instantaneous, though," the other added quickly, "and must be quite painless." This was not exactly what he thought, but what else could he say to the poor devil who might presently be strapped down into it with that horrid band across his shaved head!

Hensig laughed, and turned away to walk up and down the narrow cell. Suddenly he made a quick movement and sprang like a panther close up to the bars, pressing his face between them with an expression that was entirely new. Williams started back a pace in spite of himself.

"There are worse ways of dying than that," he said in a low voice, with a diabolical look in his eyes; "slower ways that are bainful much more. I shall get oudt. I shall not be conficted. I shall get oudt, and then perhaps I come and tell you apout them!'

The hatred in his voice and expression was unmistakable, but almost at once the face changed back to the cold pallor it usually wore, and the extraordinary doctor was laughing again and quietly discussing his lawyers and their good or bad points.

After all, then, that skin of indifference was only assumed, and the man really resented bitterly the tone of his articles. He liked the publicity, but was furious with Williams for having come to a conclusion and for letting that conclusion show through his reports.

The reporter was relieved to get out into the fresh air. He walked briskly up the stone steps to the court-room, still haunted by the memory of that odious white face pressing between the bars and the dreadful look in the eyes that had come and gone so swiftly. And what did those words mean exactly? Had he heard them right? Were they a threat?

"There are slower and more painful ways of dying, and if I get out I shall perhaps come and tell you about them."

The work of reporting the evidence helped to chase the disagreeable vision, and the compliments of the city editor on the excellence of his "story," with its suggestion of a possible increase of salary, gave his mind quite a different turn; yet always at the back of his consciousness there remained the vague, unpleasant memory that he had roused the bitter hatred of this man, and, as he thought, of a man who was a veritable monster.

There may have been something hypnotic, a little perhaps, in this obsessing and haunting idea of the man's steely wickedness, intellectual and horribly skilful, moving freely through life with something like a god's power and with a list of unproved and unprovable murders behind him. Certainly it impressed his imagination with very vivid force, and he could not think of this doctor, young, with unusual knowledge and out-of-the-way skill, yet utterly unmoral, free to work his will on men and women who displeased him, and almost safe from detection—he could not think of it all without a shudder and a crawling of the skin. He was exceedingly glad when the last day of the trial was reached and he no longer was obliged to seek the daily interview in the cell, or to sit all day in the crowded court watching the detestable white face of the prisoner in the dock and listening to the web of evidence closing round him, but just failing to hold him tight enough for the Chair. For Hensig was acquitted, though the jury sat up all night to come to a decision, and the final interview Williams had with the man immediately before his release into the street was the pleasantest and yet the most disagreeable of all.

"I knew I get oudt all right," said Hensig with a slight laugh, but without showing the real relief he must have felt. "No one peliefed me guilty but my vife's family and yourself, Mr. *Vulture* reporter. I read efery day your repordts. You chumped to a conglusion too quickly, I tink——"

"Oh, we write what we're told to write——"

"Berhaps some day you write anozzer story, or berhaps you read the story some one else write of your own trial. Then you understand better what you make me feel."

Williams hurried on to ask the doctor for his opinion of the conduct of the trial, and then enquired what his plans were for the future. The answer to the question caused him genuine relief.

"Ach! I return of course to Chermany," he said. "People here are now afraid of me a liddle. The newpapers haf killed me instead of the Chair. Goot bye, Mr. *Vulture* reporter, goot-bye!"

And Williams wrote out his last interview with as great a relief, probably, as Hensig felt when he heard the foreman of the jury utter the words "Not guilty"; but the line that gave him most pleasure was the one announcing the intended departure of the acquitted man for Germany.

III

The New York public want sensational reading in their daily life, and they get it, for the newspaper that refused to furnish it would fail in a week, and New York newspaper proprietors do not pose as philanthropists. Horror succeeds horror, and the public interest is never for one instant allowed to faint by the way.

Like any other reporter who betrayed the smallest powers of description, Williams realised this fact with his very first week on the *Vulture*. His daily work became simply a series of sensational reports of sensational happenings; he lived in a perpetual whirl of exciting arrests, murder trials, cases of blackmail, divorce, forgery, arson, corruption, and every other kind of wickedness imaginable. Each case thrilled him a little less than the preceding one; excess of sensation had simply numbed him; he became, not callous, but irresponsive, and had long since reached the stage when excitement ceases to betray judgment, as with inexperienced reporters it was apt to do.

The Hensig case, however, for a long time lived in his imagination and haunted him. The bald facts were buried in the police files at Mulberry Street headquarters and in the newspaper office "morgues," while the public, thrilled daily by fresh horrors, forgot the very existence of the evil doctor a couple of days after the acquittal of the central figure.

But for Williams it was otherwise. The personality of the heartless and calculating murderer—the intellectual poisoner, as he called him—had made a deep impression on his imagination, and for many weeks his memory kept him alive as a moving and actual horror in his life. The words he had heard him utter, with their covert threats and ill-concealed animosity, helped, no doubt, to vivify the recollection and to explain why Hensig stayed in his thoughts and haunted his dreams with a persistence that reminded him of his very earliest cases on the paper.

With time, however, even Hensig began to fade away into the confused background of piled up memories of prisoners and prison scenes, and at length the memory became so deeply buried that it no longer troubled him at all.

The summer passed, and Williams came back from his hard-earned holiday of two weeks in the Maine backwoods. New York was at its best, and the thousands who had been forced to stay and face its torrid summer heats were beginning to revive under the spell of the brilliant autumn days. Cool sea breezes swept over its burnt streets from the Lower Bay, and across the splendid flood of the Hudson River the woods on the Palisades of New Jersey had turned to crimson and gold. The air was electric, sharp, sparkling, and the life of the city began to pulse anew with its restless and impetuous energy. Bronzed faces from sea and mountains thronged the streets, health and light-heartedness showed in every eye, for autumn in New

York wields a potent magic not to be denied, and even the East Side slums, where the unfortunates crowd in their squalid thousands, had the appearance of having been swept and cleansed. Along the water-fronts especially the powers of sea and sun and scented winds combined to work an irresistible fever in the hearts of all who chafed within their prison walls.

And in Williams, perhaps more than in most, there was something that responded vigorously to the influences of hope and cheerfulness everywhere abroad. Fresh with the vigour of his holiday and full of good resolutions for the coming winter he felt released from the evil spell of irregular living, and as he crossed one October morning to Staten Island in the big double-ender ferry-boat, his heart was light, and his eye wandered to the blue waters and the hazy line of woods beyond with feelings of pure gladness and delight.

He was on his way to Quarantine to meet an incoming liner for the *Vulture*. A Jew-baiting member of the German Reichstag was coming to deliver a series of lectures in New York on his favourite subject, and the newspapers who deemed him worthy of notice at all were sending him fair warning that his mission would be tolerated perhaps, but not welcomed. The Jews were good citizens and America a "free country," and his meetings in the Cooper Union Hall would meet with derision certainly, and violence possibly.

The assignment was a pleasant one, and Williams had instructions to poke fun at the officious and interfering German, and advise him to return to Bremen by the next steamer without venturing among flying eggs and dead cats on the platform. He entered fully into the spirit of the job and was telling the Quarantine doctor about it as they steamed down the bay in the little tug to meet the huge liner just anchoring inside Sandy Hook.

The decks of the ship were crowded with passengers watching the arrival of the puffing tug, and just as they drew alongside in the shadow Williams suddenly felt his eyes drawn away from the swinging rope ladder to some point about half-way down the length of the vessel. There, among the intermediate passengers on the lower deck, he saw a face staring at him with fixed intentness. The eyes were bright blue, and the skin, in that row of bronzed passengers, showed remarkably white. At once, and with a violent rush of blood from the heart, he recognised Hensig.

In a moment everything about him changed: the blue waters of the bay turned black, the light seemed to leave the sun, and all the old sensations of fear and loathing came over him again like the memory of some great pain. He shook himself, and clutched the rope ladder to swing up after the Health Officer, angry, yet genuinely alarmed at the same time, to realise that the return of this man could so affect him. His interview with the Jew-baiter was of the briefest possible description, and he hurried through to catch the Quarantine tug back to Staten Island, instead of steaming up the bay with the great liner into dock, as the other reporters did. He had caught no second glimpse of the hated German, and he even went so far as to harbour a faint hope that he might have been deceived, and that some trick of resemblance in another face had caused a sort of subjective hallucination. At any rate, the days passed into weeks, and October slipped into November, and there was no recurrence of the distressing vision. Perhaps, after all, it was a stranger only; or, if it was Hensig, then he had forgotten all about the reporter, and his return had no connection necessarily with the idea of revenge.

None the less, however, Williams felt uneasy. He told his friend Dowling, the policeman.

"Old news," laughed the Irishman. "Headquarters are keeping an eye on him as a suspect. Berlin wants a man for two murders—goes by the name of Brunner—and from their description we think it's this feller Hensig. Nothing certain yet, but we're on his trail. *I'm* on his trail," he added proudly, "and don't you forget it! I'll let you know anything when the time comes, but mum's the word just now!"

One night, not long after this meeting, Williams and the Senator were covering a big fire on the West Side docks. They were standing on the outskirts of the crowd watching the immense flames that a shouting wind seemed to carry half-way across the river. The surrounding shipping was brilliantly lit up and the roar was magnificent. The Senator, having come out with none of his own, borrowed his friend's overcoat for a moment to protect him from spray and flying cinders while he went inside the fire lines for the latest information obtainable. It was after midnight, and the main story had been telephoned to the office; all they had now to do was to send in the latest details and corrections to be written up at the news desk.

"I'll wait for you over at the corner!" shouted Williams, moving off through a scene of indescribable confusion and taking off his fire badge as he went. This conspicuous brass badge, issued to reporters by the Fire Department, gave them the right to pass within the police cordon in the pursuit of information, and at their own risk. Hardly had he unpinned it from his coat when a hand dashed out of the crowd surging up against him and made a determined grab at it. He turned to trace the owner, but at that instant a great lurching of the mob nearly carried him off his feet, and he only just succeeded in seeing the arm withdrawn, having failed of its object, before he was landed with a violent push upon the pavement he had been aiming for.

The incident did not strike him as particularly odd, for in such a crowd there are many who covet the privilege of getting closer to the blaze. He simply laughed and put the badge safely in his pocket, and then stood to watch the dying flames until his friend came to join him with the latest details.

Yet, though time was pressing and the Senator had little enough to do, it was fully half an hour before he came lumbering up through the darkness. Williams recognised him some distance away by the check ulster he wore—his own.

But *was* it the Senator, after all? The figure moved oddly and with a limp, as though injured. A few feet off it stopped and peered at Williams through the darkness.

"That you, Williams?" asked a gruff voice.

"I thought you were some one else for a moment," answered the reporter, relieved to recognise his friend, and moving forward to meet him. "But what's wrong? Are you hurt?"

The Senator looked ghastly in the lurid glow of the fire. His face was white, and there was a little trickle of blood on the forehead.

"Some fellow nearly did for me," he said; "deliberately pushed me clean off the edge of the dock. If I hadn't fallen on to a broken pile and found a boat, I'd have been drowned sure as God made little apples. Think I know who it was, too. *Think!* I mean I *know,* because I saw his damned white face and heard what he said."

"Who in the world was it? What did he want?" stammered the other.

The Senator took his arm, and lurched into the saloon behind them for some brandy. As he did so he kept looking over
his shoulder.

"Quicker we're off from this dirty neighbourhood, the better,"
he said.

Then he turned to Williams, looking oddly at him over the glass,
and answering his questions.

"Who was it?—why, it was Hensig! And what did he want?—
well, he wanted *you!*"

"Me! Hensig!" gasped the other.

"Guess he mistook me for you," went on the Senator, looking
behind him at the door. "The crowd was so thick I cut across by the
edge of the dock. It was quite dark. There wasn't a soul near me. I
was running. Suddenly what I thought was a stump got up in front of
me, and, Gee whiz, man! I tell you it was Hensig, or I'm a drunken
Dutchman. I looked bang into his face. 'Good-pye, Mr. *Vulture* reporter,' he said, with a damned laugh, and gave me a push that sent
me backwards clean over the edge."

The Senator paused for breath, and to empty his second glass.

"*My* overcoat!" exclaimed Williams faintly.

"Oh, he'd been following you right enough, I guess."

The Senator was not really injured, and the two men walked back
towards Broadway to find a telephone, passing through a region of
dimly-lighted streets known as Little Africa, where the negroes lived,
and where it was safer to keep the middle of the road, thus avoiding
sundry dark alley-ways opening off the side. They talked hard all the
way.

"He's after you, no doubt," repeated the Senator. "I guess he
never forgot your report of his trial. Better keep your eye peeled!" he
added with a laugh.

But Williams didn't feel a bit inclined to laugh, and the thought
that it certainly *was* Hensig he had seen on the steamer, and that he
was following him so closely as to mark his check ulster and make an
attempt on his life, made him feel horribly uncomfortable, to say the
least. To be stalked by such a man was terrible. To realise that he was
marked down by that white-faced, cruel wretch, merciless and implacable, skilled in the manifold ways of killing by stealth—that

somewhere in the crowds of the great city he was watched and waited for, hunted, observed: here was an obsession really to torment and
become dangerous. Those light-blue eyes, that keen intelligence, that
mind charged with revenge, had been watching him ever since the
trial, even from across the sea. The idea terrified him. It brought
death into his thoughts for the first time with a vivid sense of nearness and reality—far greater than anything he had experienced when
watching others die.

That night, in his dingy little room in the East Nineteenth Street
boarding-house, Williams went to bed in a blue funk, and for days
afterwards he went about his business in a continuation of the same
blue funk. It was useless to deny it. He kept his eyes everywhere,
thinking he was being watched and followed. A new face in the office, at the boarding-house table, or anywhere on his usual beat,
made him jump. His daily work was haunted; his dreams were all
nightmares; he forgot all his good resolutions, and plunged into the
old indulgences that helped him to forget his distress. It took twice as
much liquor to make him jolly, and four times as much to make him
reckless.

Not that he really was a drunkard, or cared to drink for its own
sake, but he moved in a thirsty world of reporters, policemen, reckless and loose-living men and women, whose form of greeting was
"What'll you take?" and method of reproach "Oh, he's sworn off!"
Only now he was more careful how much he took, counting the
cocktails and fizzes poured into him during the course of his day's
work, and was anxious never to lose control of himself. He must be
on the watch. He changed his eating and drinking haunts, and altered
any habits that could give a clue to the devil on his trail. He even
went so far as to change his boarding-house. His emotion—the emotion of fear—changed everything. It tinged the outer world with
gloom, draping it in darker colours, stealing something from the sunlight, reducing enthusiasm, and acting as a heavy drag, as it were, upon all the normal functions of life.

The effect upon his imagination, already diseased by alcohol and
drugs, was, of course, exceedingly strong. The doctor's words about
developing a germ until it became too powerful to be touched by any
medicine, and then letting it into the victim's system by means of a

pin-scratch—this possessed him more than anything else. The idea dominated his thoughts; it seemed so clever, so cruel, so devilish. The "accident" at the fire had been, of course, a real accident, conceived on the spur of the moment—the result of a chance meeting and a foolish mistake. Hensig had no need to resort to such clumsy methods. When the right moment came he would adopt a far simpler, *safer* plan.

Finally, he became so obsessed by the idea that Hensig was following him, waiting for his opportunity, that one day he told the news editor the whole story. His nerves were so shaken that he could not do his work properly.

"That's a good story. Make two hundred of it," said the editor at once. "Fake the name, of course. Mustn't mention Hensig, or there'll be a libel suit."

But Williams was in earnest, and insisted so forcibly that Treherne, though busy as ever, took him aside into his room with the glass door.

"Now, see here, Williams, you're drinking too much," he said; "that's about the size of it. Steady up a bit on the wash, and Hensig's face will disappear." He spoke kindly, but sharply. He was young himself, awfully keen, with much knowledge of human nature and a rare "nose for news." He understood the abilities of his small army of men with intuitive judgment. That they drank was nothing to him, provided they did their work. Everybody in that world drank, and the man who didn't was looked upon with suspicion.

Williams explained rather savagely that the face was no mere symptom of delirium tremens, and the editor spared him another two minutes before rushing out to tackle the crowd of men waiting for him at the news desk.

"That so? You don't say!" he asked, with more interest. "Well, I guess Hensig's simply trying to razzle-dazzle you. You tried to kill him by your reports, and he wants to scare you by way of revenge. But he'll never dare *do* anything. Throw him a good bluff, and he'll give in like a baby. Everything's pretence in this world. But I rather like the idea of the germs. That's original!"

Williams, a little angry at the other's flippancy, told the story of the Senator's adventure and the changed overcoat.

"May be, may be," replied the hurried editor; "but the Senator drinks Chinese whisky, and a man who does that might imagine anything on God's earth. Take a tip, Williams, from an old hand, and let up a bit on the liquor. Drop cocktails and keep to straight whisky, and never drink on an empty stomach. Above all, *don't mix!*"

He gave him a keen look and was off.

"Next time you see this German," cried Treherne from the door, "go up and ask him for an interview on what it feels like to escape from the Chair—just to show him you don't care a red cent. Talk about having him watched and followed—suspected man—and all that sort of flim-flam. Pretend to warn him. It'll turn the tables and make him digest a bit. See?"

Williams sauntered out into the street to report a meeting of the Rapid Transit Commissioners, and the first person he met as he ran down the office steps was—Max Hensig.

Before he could stop, or swerve aside, they were face to face. His head swam for a moment and he began to tremble. Then some measure of self-possession returned, and he tried instinctively to act on the editor's advice. No other plan was ready, so he drew on the last force that had occupied his mind. It was that—or running.

Hensig, he noticed, looked prosperous; he wore a fur overcoat and cap. His face was whiter than ever, and his blue eyes burned like coals.

"Why! Dr. Hensig, you're back in New York!" he exclaimed. "When did you arrive? I'm glad—I suppose—I mean—er—will you come and have a drink?" he concluded desperately. It was very foolish, but for the life of him he could think of nothing else to say. And the last thing in the world he wished was that his enemy should know that he was afraid.

"I tink not, Mr. *Vulture* reporder, tanks," he answered coolly; "but I sit py and vatch you drink." His self-possession was perfect, as it always was.

But Williams, more himself now, seized on the refusal and moved on, saying something about having a meeting to go to.

"I walk a liddle way with you, berhaps," Hensig said, following him down the pavement.

It was impossible to prevent him, and they started side by side across City Hall Park towards Broadway. It was after four o'clock; the dusk was falling; the little park was thronged with people walking in all directions, every one in a terrific hurry as usual. Only Hensig seemed calm and unmoved among that racing, tearing life about them. He carried an atmosphere of ice about with him: it was his voice and manner that produced this impression; his mind was alert, watchful, determined, always sure of itself.

Williams wanted to run. He reviewed swiftly in his mind a dozen ways of getting rid of him quickly, yet knowing well they were all futile. He put his hands in his overcoat pockets—the check ulster—and watched sideways every movement of his companion.

"Living in New York again, aren't you?" he began.

"Not as a doctor any more," was the reply. "I now teach and study. Also I write sciendific books a liddle——"

"What about?"

"Cherms," said the other, looking at him and laughing. "Disease cherms, their culture and development." He put the accent on the "op."

Williams walked more quickly. With a great effort he tried to put Treherne's advice into practice.

"You care to give me an interview any time—on your special subjects?" he asked, as naturally as he could.

"Oh yes; with much bleasure. I lif in Harlem now, if you will call von day——"

"Our office is best," interrupted the reporter. "Paper, desks, library, all handy for use, you know."

"If you're afraid——" began Hensig. Then, without finishing the sentence, he added with a laugh, "I haf no arsenic there. You not tink me any more a pungling boisoner? You haf changed your mind about all dat?"

Williams felt his flesh beginning to creep. How could he speak of such a matter! His own wife, too!

He turned quickly and faced him, standing still for a moment so that the throng of people deflected into two streams past them. He felt it absolutely imperative upon him to say something that should convince the German he was not afraid.

"I suppose you are aware, Dr. Hensig, that the police know you have returned, and that you are being watched probably?" he said in a low voice, forcing himself to meet the odious blue eyes.

"And why not, bray?" he asked imperturbably.

"They may suspect something—"

"Susbected—already again? *Ach was!*" said the German.

"I only wished to warn you—" stammered Williams, who always found it difficult to remain self-possessed under the other's dreadful stare.

"No boliceman see what I do—or catch me again," he laughed quite horribly. "But I tank you all the same."

Williams turned to catch a Broadway car going at full speed. He could not stand another minute with this man, who affected him so disagreeably.

"I call at the office one day to gif you interview!" Hensig shouted as he dashed off, and the next minute he was swallowed up in the crowd, and Williams, with mixed feelings and a strange inner trembling, went to cover the meeting of the Rapid Transit Board.

But, while he reported the proceedings mechanically, his mind was busy with quite other thoughts. Hensig was at his side the whole time. He felt quite sure, however unlikely it seemed, that there was no fancy in his fears, and that he had judged the German correctly. Hensig hated him, and would put him out of the way if he could. He would do it in such a way that detection would be almost impossible. He would not shoot or poison in the ordinary way, or resort to any clumsy method. He would simply follow, watch, wait his opportunity, and then act with utter callousness and remorseless determination. And Williams already felt pretty certain of the means that would be employed: *"Cherms!"*

This meant proximity. He must watch every one who came close to him in trains, cars, restaurants—anywhere and everywhere. It could be done in a second: only a slight scratch would be necessary, and the disease would be in his blood with such strength that the chances of recovery would be slight. And what could he do? He could not have Hensig watched or arrested. He had no story to tell to a magistrate, or to the police, for no one would listen to such a tale. And, if he were stricken down by sudden illness, what was more likely than to say he had caught the fever in the ordinary course of his work, since he was always frequenting noisome dens and the haunts of the very poor, the foreign and filthy slums of the East Side, and the hospitals, morgues, and cells of all sorts and conditions of men? No; it was a disagreeable situation, and Williams, young, shaken in nerve, and easily impressionable as he was, could not prevent its obsession of his mind and imagination.

"If I get suddenly ill," he told the Senator, his only friend in the whole city, "and send for you, look carefully for a scratch on my body. Tell Dowling, and tell the doctor the story."

"You think Hensig goes about with a little bottle of plague germs in his vest pocket," laughed the other reporter, "ready to scratch you with a pin?"

"Some damned scheme like that, I'm sure."

"Nothing could be proved anyway. He wouldn't keep the evidence in his pocket till he was arrested, would he?"

During the next week or two Williams ran against Hensig twice—accidentally. The first time it happened just outside his own boarding-house—the *new one*. Hensig had his foot on the stone steps as if just about to come up, but quick as a flash he turned his face away and moved on down the street. This was about eight o'clock in the evening, and the hall light fell through the opened door upon his face. The second time it was not so clear: the reporter was covering a case in the courts, a case of suspicious death in which a woman was chief prisoner, and he thought he saw the doctor's white visage watching him from among the crowd at the back of the court-room. When he looked a second time, however, the face had disappeared, and there was no sign afterwards of its owner in the lobby or corridor.

That same day he met Dowling in the building; he was promoted now, and was always in plain clothes. The detective drew him aside into a corner. The talk at once turned upon the German.

"We're watching him too," he said. "Nothing you can use yet, but he's changed his name again, and never stops at the same address for more than a week or two. I guess he's Brunner right enough, the man Berlin's looking for. He's a holy terror if ever there was one."

Dowling was happy as a schoolboy to be in touch with such a promising case.

"What's he up to now in particular?" asked the other.

"Something pretty black," said the detective. "But I can't tell you yet awhile. He calls himself Schmidt now, and he's dropped the 'Doctor.' We may take him any day—just waiting for advices from Germany."

Williams told his story of the overcoat adventure with the Senator, and his belief that Hensig was waiting for a suitable opportunity to catch him alone.

"That's dead likely too," said Dowling, and added carelessly, "I guess we'll have to make some kind of a case against him anyway, just to get him out of the way. He's too dangerous to be around huntin' on the loose."

IV

So gradual sometimes are the approaches of fear that the processes by which it takes possession of a man's soul are often too insidious to be recognised, much less to be dealt with, until their object has been finally accomplished and the victim has lost the power to act. And by this time the reporter, who had again plunged into excess, felt so nerveless that, if he met Hensig face to face, he could not answer for what he might do. He might assault his tormentor violently—one result of terror—or he might find himself powerless to do anything at all but yield, like a bird fascinated before a snake.

He was always thinking now of the moment when they would meet, and of what would happen; for he was just as certain that they must meet eventually, and that Hensig would try to kill him, as that his next birthday would find him twenty-five years old. That meeting, he well knew, could be delayed only, not prevented, and his changing again to another boarding-house, or moving altogether to a different city, could only postpone the final accounting between them. It was bound to come.

A reporter on a New York newspaper has one day in seven to himself. Williams's day off was Monday, and he was always glad when it came. Sunday was especially arduous for him, because in addition to the unsatisfactory nature of the day's assignments, involving private interviewing which the citizens pretended to resent on their day of rest, he had the task in the evening of reporting a difficult sermon in a Brooklyn church. Having only a column and a half at his disposal, he had to condense as he went along, and the speaker was so rapid, and so fond of lengthy quotations, that the reporter found his shorthand only just equal to the task. It was usually after half-past nine o'clock when he left the church, and there was still the labour of transcribing his notes in the office against time.

The Sunday following the glimpse of his tormentor's face in the court-room he was busily condensing the wearisome periods of the preacher, sitting at a little table immediately under the pulpit, when he glanced up during a brief pause and let his eye wander over the congregation and up to the crowded galleries. Nothing was farther at the moment from his much-occupied brain than the doctor of Amityville, and it was such an unexpected shock to encounter his fixed stare up there among the occupants of the front row, watching him with an evil smile, that his senses temporarily deserted him. The next sentence of the preacher was wholly lost, and his shorthand during the brief remainder of the sermon was quite illegible, he found, when he came to transcribe it at the office.

It was after one o'clock in the morning when he finished, and he went out feeling exhausted and rather shaky. In the all-night drug store at the corner he indulged accordingly in several more glasses of whisky than usual, and talked a long time with the man who guarded the back room and served liquor to the few who knew the pass-word, since the shop had really no licence at all. The true reason for this delay he recognised quite plainly: he was afraid of the journey home along the dark and emptying streets. The lower end of New York is practically deserted after ten o'clock: it has no residences, no theatres, no *cafés,* and only a few travellers from late ferries share it with reporters, a sprinkling of policemen, and the ubiquitous ne'er- do-wells who haunt the saloon doors. The newspaper world of Park Row was, of course, alive with light and movement, but once outside that narrow zone and the night descended with an effect of general darkness.

Williams thought of spending three dollars on a cab, but dismissed the idea because of its extravagance. Presently Galusha Owens came in—too drunk to be of any use, though, as a companion. Besides, he lived in Harlem, which was miles beyond Nineteenth

Street, where Williams had to go. He took another rye whisky—his fourth—and looked cautiously through the coloured glass windows into the street. No one was visible. Then he screwed up his nerves another twist or two, and made a bolt for it, taking the steps in a sort of flying leap—and running full tilt into a man whose figure seemed almost to have risen out of the very pavement.

He gave a cry and raised his fists to strike.

"Where's your hurry?" laughed a familiar voice. "Is the Prince of Wales dead?" It was the Senator, most welcome of all possible appearances.

"Come in and have a horn," said Williams, "and then I'll walk home with you." He was immensely glad to see him, for only a few streets separated their respective boarding-houses.

"But he'd never sit out a long sermon just for the pleasure of watching you," observed the Senator after hearing his friend's excited account.

"That man'll take any trouble in the world to gain his end," said the other with conviction. "He's making a study of all my movements and habits. He's not the sort to take chances when it's a matter of life and death. I'll bet he's not far away at this moment."

"Rats!" exclaimed the Senator, laughing in rather a forced way. "You're getting the jumps with your Hensig and death. Have another rye."

They finished their drinks and went out together, crossing City Hall Park diagonally towards Broadway, and then turning north. They crossed Canal and Grand Streets, deserted and badly lighted. Only a few drunken loiterers passed them. Occasionally a policeman on the corner, always close to the side-door of a saloon, of course, recognised one or other of them and called good-night. Otherwise there was no one, and they seemed to have this part of Manhattan Island pretty well to themselves. The presence of the Senator, ever cheery and kind, keeping close to his friend all the way, the effect of the half-dozen whiskies, and the sight of the guardians of the law, combined to raise the reporter's spirits somewhat; and when they reached Fourteenth Street, with its better light and greater traffic, and saw Union Square lying just beyond, close to his own street, he felt a distinct increase of courage and no objection to going on alone.

"Good-night!" cried the Senator cheerily. "Get home safe; I turn off here anyway." He hesitated a moment before turning down the street, and then added, "You feel O.K., don't you?"

"You may get double rates for an exclusive bit of news if you come on and see me assaulted," Williams replied, laughing aloud, and then waiting to see the last of his friend.

But the moment the Senator was gone the laughter disappeared. He went on alone, crossing the square among the trees and walking very quickly. Once or twice he turned to see if anybody were following him, and his eyes scanned carefully as he passed every occupant of the park benches where a certain number of homeless loafers always find their night's lodging. But there was nothing apparently to cause him alarm, and in a few minutes more he would be safe in the little back bedroom of his own house. Over the way he saw the lights of Burbacher's saloon, where respectable Germans drank Rhine wine and played chess till all hours. He thought of going in for a night-cap, hesitating for a moment, but finally going on. When he got to the end of the square, however, and saw the dark opening of East Eighteenth Street, he thought after all he would go back and have another drink. He hovered for a moment on the kerbstone and then turned; his will often slipped a cog now in this way.

It was only when he was on his way back that he realised the truth: that his real reason for turning back and avoiding the dark open mouth of the street was because he was afraid of something its shadows might conceal. This dawned upon him quite suddenly. If there had been a light at the corner of the street he would never have turned back at all. And as this passed through his mind, already somewhat fuddled with what he had drunk, he became aware that the figure of a man had slipped forward out of the dark space he had just refused to enter, and was following him down the street. The man was pressing, too, close into the houses, using any protection of shadow or railing that would enable him to move unseen.

But the moment Williams entered the bright section of pavement opposite the wine-room windows he knew that this man had come close up behind him, with a little silent run, and he turned at once to face him. He saw a slim man with dark hair and blue eyes, and recognised him instantly.

"It's very late to be coming home," said the man at once. "I thought I recognised my reporder friend from the *Vulture*." These were the actual words, and the voice was meant to be pleasant, but what Williams thought he heard, spoken in tones of ice, was something like, "At last I've caught you! You are in a state of collapse nervously, and you are exhausted. I can do what I please with you." For the face and the voice were those of Hensig the Tormentor, and the dyed hair only served to emphasise rather grotesquely the man's features and make the pallor of the skin greater by contrast.

His first instinct was to turn and run, his second to fly at the man and strike him. A terror beyond death seized him. A pistol held to his head, or a waving bludgeon, he could easily have faced; but this odious creature, slim, limp, and white of face, with his terrible suggestion of cruelty, literally appalled him so that he could think of nothing intelligent to do or to say. This accurate knowledge of his movements, too, added to his distress—this waiting for him at night when he was tired and foolish from excess. At that moment he knew all the sensations of the criminal a few hours before his execution: the bursts of hysterical terror, the inability to realise his position, to hold his thoughts steady, the helplessness of it all. Yet, in the end, the reporter heard his own voice speaking with a rather weak and unnatural kind of tone and accompanied by a gulp of forced laughter—heard himself stammering the ever-ready formula: "I was going to have a drink before turning in—will you join me?"

The invitation, he realised afterwards, was prompted by the one fact that stood forth clearly in his mind at the moment—the thought, namely, that whatever he did or said, he must never let Hensig for one instant imagine that he felt afraid and was so helpless a victim.

Side by side they moved down the street, for Hensig had acquiesced in the suggestion, and Williams already felt dazed by the strong, persistent will of his companion. His thoughts seemed to be flying about somewhere outside his brain, beyond control, scattering wildly. He could think of nothing further to say, and had the smallest diversion furnished the opportunity he would have turned and run for his life through the deserted streets.

"A glass of lager," he heard the German say, "I take berhaps that with you. You know me in spite of—" he added, indicating by a movement the changed colour of his hair and moustache. "Also, I gif you now the interview you asked for, if you like."

The reporter agreed feebly, finding nothing adequate to reply. He turned helplessly and looked into his face with something of the sensations a bird may feel when it runs at last straight into the jaws of the reptile that has fascinated it. The fear of weeks settled down upon him, focussing about his heart. It was, of course, an effect of hypnotism, he remembered thinking vaguely through the befuddlement of his drink—this culminating effect of an evil and remorseless personality acting upon one that was diseased and extra receptive. And while he made the suggestion and heard the other's acceptance of it, he knew perfectly well that he was falling in with the plan of the doctor's own making, a plan that would end in an assault upon his person, perhaps a technical assault only—a mere touch—still, an assault that would be at the same time an attempt at murder. The alcohol buzzed in his ears. He felt strangely powerless. He walked steadily to his doom, side by side with his executioner.

Any attempt to analyse the psychology of the situation was utterly beyond him. But, amid the whirl of emotion and the excitement of the whisky, he dimly grasped the importance of *two fundamental things*.

And the first was that, though he was now muddled and frantic, yet a moment would come when his will would be capable of one supreme effort to escape, and that therefore it would be wiser for the present to waste no atom of volition on temporary half-measures. He would play dead dog. The fear that now paralysed him would accumulate till it reached the point of saturation: that would be the time to strike for his life. For just as the coward may reach a stage where he is capable of a sort of frenzied heroism that no ordinarily brave man could compass, so the victim of fear, at a point varying with his balance of imagination and physical vigour, will reach a state where fear leaves him and he becomes numb to its effect from sheer excess of feeling it. It is the point of saturation. He may then turn suddenly calm and act with a judgment and precision that simply bewilder the object of the attack. It is, of course, the inevitable swing of the pendulum, the law of equal action and reaction.

Hazily, tipsily perhaps, Williams was conscious of this potential power deep within him, below the superficial layers of smaller emotions—could he but be *sufficiently terrified to reach it* and bring it to the surface where it must result in action.

And, as a consequence of this foresight of his sober subliminal self, he offered no opposition to the least suggestion of his tormentor, but made up his mind instinctively to agree to all that he proposed. Thus he lost no atom of the force he might eventually call upon, by friction over details which in any case he would yield in the end. And at the same time he felt intuitively that his utter weakness might even deceive his enemy a little and increase the chances of his single effort to escape when the right moment arrived.

That Williams was able to "imagine" this true psychology, yet wholly unable to analyse it, simply showed that on occasion he could be psychically active. His deeper subliminal self, stirred by the alcohol and the stress of emotion, was guiding him, and would continue to guide him in proportion as he let his fuddled normal self slip into the background without attempt to interfere.

And the second fundamental thing he grasped—due even more than the first to psychic intuition—was the certainty that he could drink more, up to a certain point, with distinct advantage to his power and lucidity—but up to a given point only. After that would come unconsciousness, a single sip too much and he would cross the frontier—a very narrow one. It was as though he knew intuitively that "the drunken consciousness is one bit of the mystic consciousness." At present he was only fuddled and fearful, but additional stimulant would inhibit the effects of the other emotions, give him unbounded confidence, clarify his judgment, and increase his capacity to a stage far beyond the normal. Only—he must stop in time.

His chances of escape, therefore, so far as he could understand, depended on these two things: he must drink till he became self-confident and arrived at the abnormally clear-minded stage of drunkenness; and he must wait for the moment when Hensig had so filled him up with fear that he no longer could react to it. Then would be the time to strike. Then his will would be free and have judgment behind it.

These were the two things standing up clearly somewhere behind that great confused turmoil of mingled fear and alcohol.

Thus for the moment, though with scattered forces and rather wildly feeble thoughts, he moved down the street beside the man who hated him and meant to kill him. He had no purpose at all but to agree and to wait. Any attempt he made now could end only in failure.

They talked a little as they went, the German calm, chatting as though he were merely an agreeable acquaintance, but behaving with the obvious knowledge that he held his victim secure, and that his struggles would prove simply rather amusing. He even laughed about his dyed hair, saying by way of explanation that he had done it to please a woman who told him it would make him look younger. Williams knew this was a lie, and that the police had more to do with the change than a woman; but the man's vanity showed through the explanation, and was a vivid little self-revelation.

He objected to entering Burbacher's, saying that he (Burbacher) paid no blackmail to the police, and might be raided for keeping open after hours.

"I know a nice quiet blace on T'ird Avenue. We go there," he said.

Williams, walking unsteadily and shaking inwardly, still groping, too, feebly after a way of escape, turned down the side street with him. He thought of the men he had watched walking down the short corridor from the cell to the "Chair" at Sing Sing, and wondered if they felt as he did. It was just like going to his own execution.

"I haf a new disgovery in bacteriology—in cherms," the doctor went on, "and it will make me famous, for it is very imbortant. I gif it you egsclusive for the *Vulture*, as you are a friend." He became technical, and the reporter's mind lost itself among such words as "toxins," "alkaloids," and the like. But he realised clearly enough that Hensig was playing with him and felt absolutely sure of his victim. When he lurched badly, as he did more than once, the German took his arm by way of support, and at the vile touch of the man it was all Williams could do not to scream or strike out blindly.

They turned up Third Avenue and stopped at the side door of a cheap saloon. He noticed the name of Schumacher over the porch, but all lights were out except a feeble glow that came through the glass fanlight. A man pushed his face cautiously round the half-opened door, and after a brief examination let them in with a whispered remark to be quiet. It was the usual formula of the Tammany

saloon-keeper, who paid so much a month to the police to be allowed to keep open all night, provided there was no noise or
fighting. It was now well after one o'clock in the morning, and the
streets were deserted.

The reporter was quite at home in the sort of place they had entered; otherwise the sinister aspect of a drinking "joint" after hours,
with its gloom and general air of suspicion, might have caused him
some extra alarm. A dozen men, unpleasant of countenance, were
standing at the bar, where a single lamp gave just enough light to enable them to see their glasses. The bar-tender gave Hensig a swift
glance of recognition as they walked along the sanded floor.

"Come," whispered the German; "we go to the back room, I
know the bass-word," he laughed, leading the way.

They walked to the far end of the bar and opened a door into a
brightly lit room with about a dozen tables in it, at most of which
men sat drinking with highly painted women, talking loudly, quarrelling, singing, and the air thick with smoke. No one took any notice of
them as they went down the room to a table in the corner farthest
from the door—Hensig chose it; and when the single waiter came up
with "Was nehmen die Herren?" and a moment later brought the rye
whisky they both asked for, Williams swallowed his own without the
"chaser" of soda water, and ordered another on the spot.

"It'sh awfully watered," he said rather thickly to his companion,
"and I'm tired."

"Cocaine, under the circumstances, would help you quicker, berhaps!" replied the German with an expression of amusement. Good
God! was there nothing about him the man had not found out? He
must have been shadowing him for days; it was at least a week since
Williams had been to the First Avenue drug store to get the wicked
bottle refilled. Had he been on his trail every night when he left the
office to go home? This idea of remorseless persistence made him
shudder.

"Then we finish quickly if you are tired," the doctor continued,
"and to-morrow you can show me your repordt for gorrections if
you make any misdakes berhaps. I gif you the address to-night pefore
we leave."

The increased ugliness of his speech and accent betrayed his growing excitement. Williams drank his whisky, again without water, and called for yet another, clinking glasses with the murderer opposite, and swallowing half of this last glass, too, while Hensig merely tasted his own, looking straight at him over the performance with his evil eyes.

"I can write shorthand," began the reporter, trying to appear at his ease.

"*Ach,* I know, of course."

There was a mirror behind the table, and he took a quick glance round the room while the other began searching in his coat pocket for the papers he had with him. Williams lost no single detail of his movements, but at the same time managed swiftly to get the "note" of the other occupants of the tables. Degraded and besotted faces he saw, almost without exception, and not one to whom he could appeal for help with any prospect of success. It was a further shock, too, to realise that he preferred the more or less bestial countenances round him to the intellectual and ascetic face opposite. They were at least human, whereas *he* was something quite outside the pale; and this preference for the low creatures, otherwise loathsome to him, brought his mind by sharp contrast to a new and vivid realisation of the personality before him. He gulped down his drink, and again ordered it to be refilled.

But meanwhile the alcohol was beginning to key him up out of the dazed and negative state into which his first libations and his accumulations of fear had plunged him. His brain became a shade clearer. There was even a faint stirring of the will. He had already drunk enough under normal circumstances to be simply reeling, but to-night the emotion of fear inhibited the effects of the alcohol, keeping him singularly steady. Provided he did not exceed a given point, he could go on drinking till he reached the moment of high power when he could combine all his forces into the single consummate act of cleverly calculated escape. If he missed this psychological moment he would collapse.

A sudden crash made him jump. It was behind him against the other wall. In the mirror he saw that a middle-aged man had lost his balance and fallen off his chair, foolishly intoxicated, and that two women were ostensibly trying to lift him up, but really were going swiftly through his pockets as he lay in a heap on the floor. A big man who had been asleep the whole evening in the corner stopped snoring and woke up to look and laugh, but no one interfered. A man must take care of himself in such a place and with such company, or accept the consequences. The big man composed himself again for sleep, sipping his glass a little first, and the noise of the room continued as before. It was a case of "knock-out drops" in the whisky, put in by the women, however, rather than by the saloon-keeper. Williams remembered thinking he had nothing to fear of that kind. Hensig's method would be far more subtle and clever—*cherms!* A scratch with a pin and a germ!

"I haf zome notes here of my disgovery," he went on, smiling significantly at the interruption, and taking some papers out of an inner pocket. "But they are written in Cherman, so I dranslate for you. You haf paper and benzil?"

The reporter produced the sheaf of office copy paper he always carried about with him, and prepared to write. The rattle of the elevated trains outside and the noisy buzz of drunken conversation inside formed the background against which he heard the German's steely insistent voice going on ceaselessly with the "dranslation and egsplanation." From time to time people left the room, and new customers reeled in. When the clatter of incipient fighting and smashed glasses became too loud, Hensig waited till it was quiet again. He watched every new arrival keenly. They were very few now, for the night had passed into early morning and the room was gradually emptying. The waiter took snatches of sleep in his chair by the door; the big man still snored heavily in the angle of the wall and window. When he was the only one left, the proprietor would certainly close up. He had not ordered a drink for an hour at least. Williams, however, drank on steadily, always aiming at the point when he would be at the top of his power, full of confidence and decision. That moment was undoubtedly coming nearer all the time. Yes, but so was the moment Hensig was waiting for. He, too, felt absolutely confident, encouraging his companion to drink more, and watching his gradual collapse with unmasked glee. He betrayed his gloating quite plainly now: he held his victim too securely to feel anxious; when the big man reeled out they would be alone for a brief minute or two unobserved—and meanwhile he allowed himself to become a little too *careless* from over-confidence. And Williams noted that too.

For slowly the will of the reporter began to assert itself, and with this increase of intelligence he of course appreciated his awful position more keenly, and therefore, *felt more fear.* The two main things he was waiting for were coming perceptibly within reach: to reach the saturation point of terror and the culminating moment of the alcohol. Then, action and escape!

Gradually, thus, as he listened and wrote, he passed from the stage of stupid, negative terror into that of active, positive terror. The alcohol kept driving hotly at those hidden centres of imagination within, which, once touched, begin to reveal; in other words, he became observant, critical, alert. Swiftly the power grew. His lucidity increased till he became almost conscious of the workings of the other man's mind, and it was like sitting opposite a clock whose wheels and needles he could just hear clicking. His eyes seemed to spread their power of vision all over his skin; he could see what was going on without actually looking. In the same way he heard all that passed in the room without turning his head. Every moment he became clearer in mind. He almost touched clairvoyance. The presentiment earlier in the evening that this stage would come was at last being actually fulfilled.

From time to time he sipped his whisky, but more cautiously than at first, for he knew that this keen psychical activity was the forerunner of helpless collapse. Only for a minute or two would he be at the top of his power. The frontier was a dreadfully narrow one, and already he had lost control of his fingers, and was scrawling a shorthand that bore no resemblance to the original system of its inventor.

As the white light of this abnormal perceptiveness increased, the horror of his position became likewise more and more vivid. He knew that he was fighting for his life with a soulless and malefic being who was next door to a devil. The sense of fear was being magnified now with every minute that passed. Presently the power of *perceiving* would pass into *doing;* he would strike the blow for his life, whatever form that blow might take.

Already he was sufficiently master of himself to act—to act in the sense of deceiving. He exaggerated his drunken writing and thickness of speech, his general condition of collapse; and this power of *hearing* the workings of the other man's mind showed him that he was successful. Hensig was a little deceived. He proved this by increased carelessness, and by allowing the expression of his face to become plainly exultant.

Williams's faculties were so concentrated upon the causes operating in the terrible personality opposite to him, that he could spare no part of his brain for the explanations and sentences that came from his lips. He did not hear or understand a hundredth part of what the doctor was saying, but occasionally he caught up the end of a phrase and managed to ask a blundering question out of it; and Hensig, obviously pleased with his increasing obfuscation, always answered at some length, quietly watching with pleasure the reporter's foolish hieroglyphics upon the paper.

The whole thing, of course, was an utter blind. Hensig had no discovery at all. He was talking scientific jargon, knowing full well that those shorthand notes would never be transcribed, and that he himself would be out of harm's way long before his victim's senses had cleared sufficiently to tell him that he was in the grasp of a deadly sickness which no medicines could prevent ending in death.

Williams saw and felt all this clearly. It somehow came to him, rising up in that clear depth of his mind that was stirred by the alcohol, and yet beyond the reach, so far, of its deadly confusion. He understood perfectly well that Hensig was waiting for a moment to act; that he would do nothing violent, but would carry out his murderous intention in such an innocent way that the victim would have no suspicions at the moment, and would only realise later that he had been poisoned and—

Hark! What was that? There was a change. Something had happened. It was like the sound of a gong, and the reporter's fear suddenly doubled. Hensig's scheme had moved forward a step. There was no sound actually, but his senses seemed grouped together into one, and for some reason his perception of the change came by way of audition. Fear brimmed up perilously near the breaking point. But the moment for action had not quite come yet, and he luckily saved himself by the help of another and contrary emotion. He emptied his glass, spilling half of it purposely over his coat, and burst out laughing in Hensig's face. The vivid picture rose before him of Whitey Fife catching cocktail glasses off the edge of Steve Brodie's table.

The laugh was admirably careless and drunken, but the German was startled and looked up suspiciously. He had not expected this, and through lowered eyelids Williams observed an expression of momentary uncertainty on his features, as though he felt he was not absolutely master of the situation after all, as he imagined.

"Su'nly thought of Whitey Fife knocking Steve-brodie off'sh Brooklyn Bridsh in a co—cock'tail glashh—" Williams explained in a voice hopelessly out of control. "You know Whhhiteyfife, of coursh, don't you?—ha, ha, ha!"

Nothing could have helped him more in putting Hensig off the scent. His face resumed its expression of certainty and cold purpose. The waiter, wakened by the noise, stirred uneasily in his chair, and the big man in the corner indulged in a gulp that threatened to choke him as he sat with his head sunk upon his chest. But otherwise the empty room became quiet again. The German resumed his confident command of the situation. Williams, he saw, was drunk enough to bring him easily into his net.

None the less, the reporter's perception had not been at fault. There *was* a change. Hensig was about to do something, and his mind was buzzing with preparations.

The victim, now within measuring distance of his supreme moment—the point where terror would release his will, and alcohol would inspire him beyond possibility of error—saw everything as in the clear light of day. Small things led him to the climax: the emptied room; the knowledge that shortly the saloon would close; the grey light of day stealing under the chinks of door and shutter; the increased vileness of the face gleaming at him opposite in the paling gas glare. Ugh! how the air reeked of stale spirits, the fumes of cigar smoke, and the cheap scents of the vanished women. The floor was strewn with sheets of paper, absurdly scrawled over. The table had patches of wet, and cigarette ashes lay over everything. His hands and feet were icy, his eyes burning hot. His heart thumped like a soft hammer.

Hensig was speaking in quite a changed voice now. He had been leading up to this point for hours. No one was there to see, even if anything was to be seen—which was unlikely. The big man still snored; the waiter was asleep too. There was silence in the outer room, and between the walls of the inner there was—*Death*.

"Now, Mr. *Vulture* reporder, I *show* you what I mean all this time to egsplain," he was saying in his most metallic voice.

He drew a blank sheet of the reporter's paper towards him across the little table, avoiding carefully the wet splashes.

"Lend me your bencil von moment, please. Yes?"

Williams, simulating almost total collapse, dropped the pencil and shoved it over the polished wood as though the movement was about all he could manage. With his head sunk forward upon his chest he watched stupidly. Hensig began to draw some kind of outline; his touch was firm, and there was a smile on his lips.

"Here, you see, is the human arm," he said, sketching rapidly; "and here are the main nerves, and here the artery. Now, my discovery, as I haf peen egsplaining to you, is simply—" He dropped into a torrent of meaningless scientific phrases, during which the other purposely allowed his hand to lie relaxed upon the table, knowing perfectly well that in a moment Hensig would seize it—for the purposes of illustration.

His terror was so intense that, for the first time this awful night, he was within an ace of action. The point of saturation had been almost reached. Though apparently sodden drunk, his mind was really at the highest degree of clear perception and judgment, and in another moment—the moment Hensig actually began his final assault—the terror would provide the reporter with the extra vigour and decision necessary to strike his one blow. Exactly how he would do it, or what precise form it would take, he had no idea; that could be left to the inspiration of the moment; he only knew that his strength would last just long enough to bring this about, and that then he would collapse in utter intoxication upon the floor.

Hensig dropped the pencil suddenly: it clattered away to a corner of the room, showing it had been propelled with force, not merely allowed to fall, and he made no attempt to pick it up. Williams, to test his intention, made a pretended movement to stoop after it, and the other, as he imagined he would, stopped him in a second.

"I haf another," he said quickly, diving into his inner pocket and producing a long dark pencil. Williams saw in a flash, through his half-closed eyes, that it was sharpened at one end, while the other end was covered by a little protective cap of transparent substance like glass, a third of an inch long. He heard it click as it struck a button of the coat, and also saw that by a very swift motion of the fingers, impossible to be observed by a drunken man, Hensig removed the cap so that the end was free. Something gleamed there for a moment, something like a point of shining metal—the point of a pin.

"Gif me your hand von minute and I drace the nerve up the arm I speak apout," the doctor continued in that steely voice that showed no sign of nervousness, though he was on the edge of murder. "So, I show you much petter vot I mean."

Without a second's hesitation—for the moment for action had not quite come—he lurched forward and stretched his arm clumsily across the table. Hensig seized the fingers in his own and turned the palm uppermost. With his other hand he pointed the pencil at the wrist, and began moving it a little up towards the elbow, pushing the sleeve back for the purpose. His touch was the touch of death. On the point of the black pin, engrafted into the other end of the pencil, Williams knew there clung the germs of some deadly disease, germs unusually powerful from special culture; and that within the next few seconds the pencil would turn and the pin would *accidentally* scratch his wrist and let the virulent poison into his blood.

He knew this, yet at the same time he managed to remain master of himself. For he also realised that at last, just in the nick of time, the moment he had been waiting for all through these terrible hours had actually arrived, and he was ready to act.

And the little unimportant detail that furnished the extra quota of fear necessary to bring him to this point was—*touch*. It was the touch of Hensig's hand that did it, setting every nerve a-quiver to its utmost capacity, filling him with a black horror that reached the limits of sensation.

In that moment Williams regained his self-control and became absolutely sober. Terror removed its paralysing inhibitions, having led him to the point where numbness succeeds upon excess, and sensation ceases to register in the brain. The emotion of fear was dead, and he was ready to act with all the force of his being—that force, too, raised to a higher power after long repression.

Moreover, he could make no mistake, for at the same time he had reached the culminating effect of the alcohol, and a sort of white light filled his mind, showing him clearly what to do and how to do it. He felt master of himself, confident, capable of anything. He followed blindly that inner guidance he had been dimly conscious of the whole night, and what he did he did instinctively, as it were, without deliberate plan.

He was *waiting for the pencil to turn* so that the pin pointed at his vein. Then, when Hensig was wholly concentrated upon the act of murder, and thus oblivious of all else, he would find his opportunity. For at this supreme moment the German's mind would be focussed on the one thing. He would notice nothing else round him. He would be open to successful attack. But this supreme moment would hardly last more than five seconds at most!

The reporter raised his eyes and stared for the first time steadily into his opponent's eyes, till the room faded out and he saw only the white skin in a blaze of its own light. Thus staring, he caught in himself the full stream of venom, hatred, and revenge that had been pouring at him across the table for so long—caught and held it for one instant, and then returned it into the other's brain with all its original force and the added impetus of his own recovered will behind it.

Hensig felt this, and for a moment seemed to waver; he was surprised out of himself by the sudden change in his victim's attitude. The same instant, availing himself of a diversion caused by the big man in the corner waking noisily and trying to rise, he slowly *turned the pencil round* so that the point of the pin was directed at the hand lying in his. The sleepy waiter was helping the drunken man to cross to the door, and the diversion was all in his favour.

But Williams knew what he was doing. He did not even tremble.

"When that pin scratches me," he said aloud in a firm, sober voice, "it means—death."

The German could not conceal his surprise on hearing the change of voice, but he still felt sure of his victim, and clearly wished to enjoy his revenge thoroughly. After a moment's hesitation he replied, speaking very low:

"You tried, I tink, to get me conficted, and now I punish you, dat is all."

His fingers moved, and the point of the pin descended a little lower. Williams felt the faintest imaginable prick on his skin—or thought he did. The German had lowered his head again to direct the movement of the pin properly. But the moment of Hensig's concentration was also the moment of his own attack. And it had come.

"But the alcohol will counteract it!" he burst out, with a loud and startling laugh that threw the other completely off his guard. The doctor lifted his face in amazement. That same instant the hand that lay so helplessly and tipsily in his turned like a flash of lightning, and, before he knew what had happened, their positions were reversed. Williams held his wrist, pencil and all, in a grasp of iron. And from the reporter's other hand the German received a terrific smashing blow in the face that broke his glasses and dashed him back with a howl of pain against the wall.

There was a brief passage of scramble and wild blows, during which both table and chairs were sent flying, and then Williams was aware that a figure behind him had stretched forth an arm and was holding a bright silvery thing close to Hensig's bleeding face. Another glance showed him that it was a pistol, and that the man holding it was the big drunken man who had apparently slept all night in the corner of the room. Then, in a flash, he recognised him as Dowling's partner—a headquarters detective.

The reporter stepped back, his head swimming again. He was very unsteady on his feet.

"I've been watching your game all the evening," he heard the headquarters man saying as he slipped the handcuffs over the German's unresisting wrists. "We have been on your trail for weeks, and I might jest as soon have taken you when you left the Brooklyn church a few hours ago, only I wanted to see what you were up to—see? You're wanted in Berlin for one or two little dirty tricks, but our advices only came last night. Come along now."

"You'll get nozzing," Hensig replied very quietly, wiping his bloody face with the corner of his sleeve. "See, I have scratched myself!"

The detective took no notice of this remark, not understanding it, probably, but Williams noticed the direction of the eyes, and saw a scratch on his wrist, slightly bleeding. Then he understood that in the struggle the pin had accidentally found another destination than the one intended for it.

But he remembered nothing more after that, for the reaction set in with a rush. The strain of that awful night left him utterly limp, and the accumulated effect of the alcohol, now that all was past, overwhelmed him like a wave, and he sank in a heap upon the floor, unconscious.

The illness that followed was simply "nerves," and he got over it in a week or two, and returned to his work on the paper. He at once made enquiries, and found that Hensig's arrest had hardly been noticed by the papers. There was no interesting feature about it, and New York was already in the throes of a new horror.

But Dowling, that enterprising Irishman—always with an eye to promotion and the main chance—Dowling had something to say about it.

"No luck, Mr. English," he said ruefully, "no luck at all. It would have been a mighty good story, but it never got in the papers. That damned German, Schmidt, alias Brunner, alias Hensig, died in the prison hospital before we could even get him remanded for further enquiries—"

"What did he die of?" interrupted the reporter quickly.

"Black typhus, I think they call it. But it was terribly swift, and he was dead in four days. The doctor said he'd never known such a case."

"I'm glad he's out of the way," observed Williams.

"Well, yes," Dowling said hesitatingly; "but it was a jim dandy of a story, an' he might have waited a little bit longer jest so as I got something out of it for meself."

The Willows

I

After leaving Vienna, and long before you come to Buda-Pesth, the Danube enters a region of singular loneliness and desolation, where its waters spread away on all sides regardless of a main channel, and the country becomes a swamp for miles upon miles, covered by a vast sea of low willow-bushes. On the big maps this deserted area is painted in a fluffy blue, growing fainter in colour as it leaves the banks, and across it may be seen in large straggling letters the word *Sümpfe*, meaning marshes.

In high flood this great acreage of sand, shingle-beds, and willow-grown islands is almost topped by the water, but in normal seasons the bushes bend and rustle in the free winds, showing their silver leaves to the sunshine in an ever-moving plain of bewildering beauty. These willows never attain to the dignity of trees; they have no rigid trunks; they remain humble bushes, with rounded tops and soft outline, swaying on slender stems that answer to the least pressure of the wind; supple as grasses, and so continually shifting that they somehow give the impression that the entire plain is moving and alive. For the wind sends waves rising and falling over the whole surface, waves of leaves instead of waves of water, green swells like the sea, too, until the branches turn and lift, and then silvery white as their under-side turns to the sun.

Happy to slip beyond the control of stern banks, the Danube here wanders about at will among the intricate network of channels intersecting the islands everywhere with broad avenues down which the waters pour with a shouting sound; making whirlpools, eddies, and foaming rapids; tearing at the sandy banks; carrying away masses of shore and willow-clumps; and forming new islands innumerable which shift daily in size and shape and possess at best an impermanent life, since the flood-time obliterates their very existence.

Properly speaking, this fascinating part of the river's life begins soon after leaving Pressburg, and we, in our Canadian canoe, with gipsy tent and frying-pan on board, reached it on the crest of a rising flood about mid-July. That very same morning, when the sky was reddening before sunrise, we had slipped swiftly through still-sleeping Vienna, leaving it a couple of hours later a mere patch of smoke against the blue hills of the Wienerwald on the horizon; we had breakfasted below Fischeramend under a grove of birch trees roaring in the wind; and had then swept up on the tearing current past Orth, Hainburg, Petronell (the old Roman Carnuntum of Marcus Aurelius), and so under the frowning heights of Theben on a spur of the Carpathians, where the March steals in quietly from the left and the frontier is crossed between Austria and Hungary.

Racing along at twelve kilometres an hour soon took us well into Hungary, and the muddy waters—sure sign of flood—sent us aground on many a shingle-bed, and twisted us like a cork in many a sudden belching whirlpool before the towers of Pressburg (Hungarian, Pozsóny) showed against the sky; and then the canoe, leaping like a spirited horse, flew at top speed under the grey walls, negotiated safely the sunken chain of the Fliegende Brücke ferry, turned the corner sharply to the left, and plunged on yellow foam into the wilderness of islands, sand-banks, and swamp-land beyond—the land of the willows.

The change came suddenly, as when a series of bioscope pictures snaps down on the streets of a town and shifts without warning into the scenery of lake and forest. We entered the land of desolation on wings, and in less than half an hour there was neither boat nor fishing-hut nor red roof, nor any single sign of human habitation and civilisation within sight. The sense of remoteness from the world of humankind, the utter isolation, the fascination of this singular world of willows, winds, and waters, instantly laid its spell upon us both, so that we allowed laughingly to one another that we ought by rights to have held some special kind of passport to admit us, and that we had, somewhat audaciously, come without asking leave into a separate little kingdom of wonder and magic—a kingdom that was reserved for the use of others who had a right to it, with everywhere unwritten warnings to trespassers for those who had the imagination to discover them.

Though still early in the afternoon, the ceaseless buffetings of a most tempestuous wind made us feel weary, and we at once began casting about for a suitable camping-ground for the night. But the bewildering character of the islands made landing difficult; the swirling flood carried us in-shore and then swept us out again; the willow branches tore our hands as we seized them to stop the canoe, and we pulled many a yard of sandy bank into the water before at length we shot with a great sideways blow from the wind into a backwater and managed to beach the bows in a cloud of spray. Then we lay panting and laughing after our exertions on hot yellow sand, sheltered from the wind, and in the full blaze of a scorching sun, a cloudless blue sky above, and an immense army of dancing, shouting willow bushes, closing in from all sides, shining with spray and clapping their thousand little hands as though to applaud the success of our efforts.

"What a river!" I said to my companion, thinking of all the way we had travelled from the source in the Black Forest, and how we had often been obliged to wade and push in the upper shallows at the beginning of June.

"Won't stand much nonsense now, will it?" he said, pulling the canoe a little farther into safety up the sand, and then composing himself for a nap.

I lay by his side, happy and peaceful in the bath of the elements—water, wind, sand, and the great fire of the sun—thinking of the long journey that lay behind us, and of the great stretch before us to the Black Sea, and how lucky I was to have such a delightful and charming travelling companion as my friend, the Swede.

We had made many similar journeys together, but the Danube, more than any other river I knew, impressed us from the very beginning with its aliveness. From its tiny bubbling entry into the world among the pinewood gardens of Donaueschingen, until this moment when it began to play the great river-game of losing itself among the deserted swamps, unobserved, unrestrained, it had seemed to us like following the growth of some living creature. Sleepy at first, but later developing violent desires as it became conscious of its deep soul, it rolled, like some huge fluid being, through all the countries we had passed, holding our little craft on its mighty shoulders, playing roughly with us sometimes, yet always friendly and well-meaning, till at length we had come inevitably to regard it as a Great Personage.

How, indeed, could it be otherwise, since it told us so much of its secret life? At night we heard it singing to the moon as we lay in our tent, uttering that odd sibilant note peculiar to itself and said to be caused by the rapid tearing of the pebbles along its bed, so great is its hurrying speed. We knew, too, the voice of its gurgling whirlpools, suddenly bubbling up on a surface previously quite calm; the roar of its shallows and swift rapids; its constant steady thundering below all mere surface sounds; and that ceaseless tearing of its icy waters at the banks. How it stood up and shouted when the rains fell flat upon its face! And how its laughter roared out when the wind blew upstream and tried to stop its growing speed! We knew all its sounds and voices, its tumblings and foamings, its unnecessary splashing against the bridges; that self-conscious chatter when there were hills to look on; the affected dignity of its speech when it passed through the little towns, far too important to laugh; and all these faint, sweet whisperings when the sun caught it fairly in some slow curve and poured down upon it till the steam rose.

It was full of tricks, too, in its early life before the great world knew it. There were places in the upper reaches among the Swabian forests, when yet the first whispers of its destiny had not reached it, where it elected to disappear through holes in the ground, to appear again on the other side of the porous limestone hills and start a new river with another name; leaving, too, so little water in its own bed that we had to climb out and wade and push the canoe through miles of shallows!

And a chief pleasure, in those early days of its irresponsible youth, was to lie low, like Brer Fox, just before the little turbulent tributaries came to join it from the Alps, and to refuse to acknowledge them when in, but to run for miles side by side, the dividing line well marked, the very levels different, the Danube utterly declining to recognise the newcomer. Below Passau, however, it gave up this particular trick, for there the Inn comes in with a thundering power impossible to ignore, and so pushes and incommodes the parent river that there is hardly room for them in the long twisting gorge that follows, and the Danube is shoved this way and that against the cliffs, and forced to hurry itself with great waves and much dashing to and fro in order to get through in time. And during the fight our canoe slipped down from its shoulder to its breast, and had the time of its life among the struggling waves. But the Inn taught the old river a lesson, and after Passau it no longer pretended to ignore new arrivals.

This was many days back, of course, and since then we had come to know other aspects of the great creature, and across the Bavarian wheat plain of Straubing she wandered so slowly under the blazing June sun that we could well imagine only the surface inches were water, while below there moved, concealed as by a silken mantle, a whole army of Undines, passing silently and unseen down to the sea, and very leisurely too, lest they be discovered.

Much, too, we forgave her because of her friendliness to the birds and animals that haunted the shores. Cormorants lined the banks in lonely places in rows like short black palings; grey crows crowded the shingle-beds; storks stood fishing in the vistas of shallower water that opened up between the islands, and hawks, swans, and marsh birds of all sorts filled the air with glinting wings and singing, petulant cries. It was impossible to feel annoyed with the river's vagaries after seeing a deer leap with a splash into the water at sunrise and swim past the bows of the canoe; and often we saw fawns peering at us from the underbrush, or looked straight into the brown eyes of a stag as we charged full tilt round a corner and entered another reach of the river. Foxes, too, everywhere haunted the banks, tripping daintily among the driftwood and disappearing so suddenly that it was impossible to see how they managed it.

But now, after leaving Pressburg, everything changed a little, and the Danube became more serious. It ceased trifling. It was half-way to the Black Sea, within scenting distance almost of other, stranger countries where no tricks would be permitted or understood. It became suddenly grown-up, and claimed our respect and even our awe. It broke out into three arms, for one thing, that only met again a hundred kilometres farther down, and for a canoe there were no indications which one was intended to be followed.

"If you take a side channel," said the Hungarian officer we met in the Pressburg shop while buying provisions, "you may find yourselves, when the flood subsides, forty miles from anywhere, high and dry, and you may easily starve. There are no people, no farms, no fishermen. I warn you not to continue. The river, too, is still rising, and this wind will increase."

The rising river did not alarm us in the least, but the matter of being left high and dry by a sudden subsidence of the waters might be serious, and we had consequently laid in an extra stock of provisions. For the rest, the officer's prophecy held true, and the wind, blowing down a perfectly clear sky, increased steadily till it reached the dignity of a westerly gale.

It was earlier than usual when we camped, for the sun was a good hour or two from the horizon, and leaving my friend still asleep on the hot sand, I wandered about in desultory examination of our hotel. The island, I found, was less than an acre in extent, a mere sandy bank standing some two or three feet above the level of the river. The far end, pointing into the sunset, was covered with flying spray which the tremendous wind drove off the crests of the broken waves. It was triangular in shape, with the apex up stream.

I stood there for several minutes, watching the impetuous crimson flood bearing down with a shouting roar, dashing in waves against the bank as though to sweep it bodily away, and then swirling by in two foaming streams on either side. The ground seemed to shake with the shock and rush, while the furious movement of the willow bushes as the wind poured over them increased the curious illusion that the island itself actually moved. Above, for a mile or two, I could see the great river descending upon me; it was like looking up the slope of a sliding hill, white with foam, and leaping up everywhere to show itself to the sun.

The rest of the island was too thickly grown with willows to make walking pleasant, but I made the tour, nevertheless. From the lower end the light, of course, changed, and the river looked dark and angry. Only the backs of the flying waves were visible, streaked with foam, and pushed forcibly by the great puffs of wind that fell upon them from behind. For a short mile it was visible, pouring in and out among the islands, and then disappearing with a huge sweep into the willows, which closed about it like a herd of monstrous antediluvian creatures crowding down to drink. They made me think of gigantic sponge-like growths that sucked the river up into themselves. They caused it to vanish from sight. They herded there together in such overpowering numbers.

Altogether it was an impressive scene, with its utter loneliness, its bizarre suggestion; and as I gazed, long and curiously, a singular emotion began to stir somewhere in the depths of me. Midway in my delight of the wild beauty, there crept, unbidden and unexplained, a curious feeling of disquietude, almost of alarm.

A rising river, perhaps, always suggests something of the ominous; many of the little islands I saw before me would probably have been swept away by the morning; this resistless, thundering flood of water touched the sense of awe. Yet I was aware that my uneasiness lay deeper far than the emotions of awe and wonder. It was not that I felt. Nor had it directly to do with the power of the driving wind— this shouting hurricane that might almost carry up a few acres of willows into the air and scatter them like so much chaff over the landscape. The wind was simply enjoying itself, for nothing rose out of the flat landscape to stop it, and I was conscious of sharing its great game with a kind of pleasurable excitement. Yet this novel emotion had nothing to do with the wind. Indeed, so vague was the sense of distress I experienced, that it was impossible to trace it to its source and deal with it accordingly, though I was aware somehow that it had to do with my realisation of our utter insignificance before this unrestrained power of the elements about me. The huge-grown river had something to do with it too—a vague, unpleasant idea that we had somehow trifled with these great elemental forces in whose power we lay helpless every hour of the day and night. For here, indeed, they were gigantically at play together, and the sight appealed to the imagination.

But my emotion, so far as I could understand it, seemed to attach itself more particularly to the willow bushes, to these acres and acres of willows, crowding, so thickly growing there, swarming everywhere the eye could reach, pressing upon the river as though to suffocate it, standing in dense array mile after mile beneath the sky, watching, waiting, listening. And, apart quite from the elements, the willows connected themselves subtly with my malaise, attacking the mind insidiously somehow by reason of their vast numbers, and contriving in some way or other to represent to the imagination a new and mighty power, a power, moreover, not altogether friendly to us.

Great revelations of nature, of course, never fail to impress in one way or another, and I was no stranger to moods of the kind. Mountains overawe and oceans terrify, while the mystery of great forests exercises a spell peculiarly its own. But all these, at one point or another, somewhere link on intimately with human life and human experience. They stir comprehensible, even if alarming, emotions. They tend on the whole to exalt.

With this multitude of willows, however, it was something far different, I felt. Some essence emanated from them that besieged the heart. A sense of awe awakened, true, but of awe touched somewhere by a vague terror. Their serried ranks, growing everywhere darker about me as the shadows deepened, moving furiously yet softly in the wind, woke in me the curious and unwelcome suggestion that we had trespassed here upon the borders of an alien world, a world where we were intruders, a world where we were not wanted or invited to remain—where we ran grave risks perhaps!

The feeling, however, though it refused to yield its meaning entirely to analysis, did not at the time trouble me by passing into menace. Yet it never left me quite, even during the very practical business of putting up the tent in a hurricane of wind and building a fire for the stew-pot. It remained, just enough to bother and perplex, and to rob a most delightful camping-ground of a good portion of its charm. To my companion, however, I said nothing, for he was a man I considered devoid of imagination. In the first place, I could never have explained to him what I meant, and in the second, he would have laughed stupidly at me if I had.

There was a slight depression in the centre of the island, and here we pitched the tent. The surrounding willows broke the wind a bit.

"A poor camp," observed the imperturbable Swede when at last the tent stood upright; "no stones and precious little firewood. I'm for moving on early to-morrow—eh? This sand won't hold anything."

But the experience of a collapsing tent at midnight had taught us many devices, and we made the cosy gipsy house as safe as possible, and then set about collecting a store of wood to last till bedtime. Willow bushes drop no branches, and driftwood was our only source of supply. We hunted the shores pretty thoroughly. Everywhere the banks were crumbling as the rising flood tore at them and carried away great portions with a splash and a gurgle.

"The island's much smaller than when we landed," said the accurate Swede. "It won't last long at this rate. We'd better drag the canoe close to the tent, and be ready to start at a moment's notice. I shall sleep in my clothes."

He was a little distance off, climbing along the bank, and I heard his rather jolly laugh as he spoke.

"By Jove!" I heard him call, a moment later, and turned to see what had caused his exclamation. But for the moment he was hidden by the willows, and I could not find him.

"What in the world's this?" I heard him cry again, and this time his voice had become serious.

I ran up quickly and joined him on the bank. He was looking over the river, pointing at something in the water.

"Good heavens, it's a man's body!" he cried excitedly. "Look!"

A black thing, turning over and over in the foaming waves, swept rapidly past. It kept disappearing and coming up to the surface again. It was about twenty feet from the shore, and just as it was opposite to where we stood it lurched round and looked straight at us. We saw its eyes reflecting the sunset, and gleaming an odd yellow as the body turned over. Then it gave a swift, gulping plunge, and dived out of sight in a flash.

"An otter, by gad!" we exclaimed in the same breath, laughing.

It was an otter, alive, and out on the hunt; yet it had looked exactly like the body of a drowned man turning helplessly in the current. Far below it came to the surface once again, and we saw its black skin, wet and shining in the sunlight.

Then, too, just as we turned back, our arms full of driftwood, another thing happened to recall us to the river bank. This time it really was a man, and what was more, a man in a boat. Now a small boat on the Danube was an unusual sight at any time, but here in this deserted region, and at flood time, it was so unexpected as to constitute a real event. We stood and stared.

Whether it was due to the slanting sunlight, or the refraction from the wonderfully illumined water, I cannot say, but, whatever the cause, I found it difficult to focus my sight properly upon the flying apparition. It seemed, however, to be a man standing upright in a sort of flat-bottomed boat, steering with a long oar, and being carried down the opposite shore at a tremendous pace. He apparently was looking across in our direction, but the distance was too great and the light too uncertain for us to make out very plainly what he was about. It seemed to me that he was gesticulating and making signs at us. His voice came across the water to us shouting something furiously, but the wind drowned it so that no single word was audible. There was something curious about the whole appearance—man, boat, signs, voice—that made an impression on me out of all proportion to its cause.

"He's crossing himself!" I cried. "Look, he's making the sign of the Cross!"

"I believe you're right," the Swede said, shading his eyes with his hand and watching the man out of sight. He seemed to be gone in a moment, melting away down there into the sea of willows where the sun caught them in the bend of the river and turned them into a great crimson wall of beauty. Mist, too, had begun to rise, so that the air was hazy.

"But what in the world is he doing at night-fall on this flooded river?" I said, half to myself. "Where is he going at such a time, and what did he mean by his signs and shouting? D'you think he wished to warn us about something?"

"He saw our smoke, and thought we were spirits probably," laughed my companion. "These Hungarians believe in all sorts of rubbish: you remember the shopwoman at Pressburg warning us that no one ever landed here because it belonged to some sort of beings outside man's world! I suppose they believe in fairies and elementals, possibly demons too. That peasant in the boat saw people on the islands for the first time in his life," he added, after a slight pause, "and it scared him, that's all."

The Swede's tone of voice was not convincing, and his manner lacked something that was usually there. I noted the change instantly while he talked, though without being able to label it precisely.

"If they had enough imagination," I laughed loudly—I remember trying to make as much noise as I could—"they might well people a place like this with the old gods of antiquity. The Romans must have haunted all this region more or less with their shrines and sacred groves and elemental deities."

The subject dropped and we returned to our stew-pot, for my friend was not given to imaginative conversation as a rule. Moreover, just then I remember feeling distinctly glad that he was not imaginative; his stolid, practical nature suddenly seemed to me welcome and comforting. It was an admirable temperament, I felt: he could steer down rapids like a red Indian, shoot dangerous bridges and whirlpools better than any white man I ever saw in a canoe. He was a grand fellow for an adventurous trip, a tower of strength when untoward things happened. I looked at his strong face and light curly hair as he staggered along under his pile of driftwood (twice the size of mine!), and I experienced a feeling of relief. Yes, I was distinctly glad just then that the Swede was—what he was, and that he never made remarks that suggested more than they said.

"The river's still rising, though," he added, as if following out some thoughts of his own, and dropping his load with a gasp. "This island will be under water in two days if it goes on."

"I wish the *wind* would go down," I said. "I don't care a fig for the river."

The flood, indeed, had no terrors for us; we could get off at ten minutes' notice, and the more water the better we liked it. It meant an increasing current and the obliteration of the treacherous shingle-beds that so often threatened to tear the bottom out of our canoe.

Contrary to our expectations, the wind did not go down with the sun. It seemed to increase with the darkness, howling overhead and shaking the willows round us like straws. Curious sounds accompanied it sometimes, like the explosion of heavy guns, and it fell upon the water and the island in great flat blows of immense power. It made me think of the sounds a planet must make, could we only hear it, driving along through space.

But the sky kept wholly clear of clouds, and soon after supper the full moon rose up in the east and covered the river and the plain of shouting willows with a light like the day.

We lay on the sandy patch beside the fire, smoking, listening to the noises of the night round us, and talking happily of the journey we had already made, and of our plans ahead. The map lay spread in the door of the tent, but the high wind made it hard to study, and presently we lowered the curtain and extinguished the lantern. The firelight was enough to smoke and see each other's faces by, and the sparks flew about overhead like fireworks. A few yards beyond, the river gurgled and hissed, and from time to time a heavy splash announced the falling away of further portions of the bank.

Our talk, I noticed, had to do with the far-away scenes and incidents of our first camps in the Black Forest, or of other subjects altogether remote from the present setting, for neither of us spoke of the actual moment more than was necessary—almost as though we had agreed tacitly to avoid discussion of the camp and its incidents. Neither the otter nor the boatman, for instance, received the honour of a single mention, though ordinarily these would have furnished discussion for the greater part of the evening. They were, of course, distinct events in such a place.

The scarcity of wood made it a business to keep the fire going, for the wind, that drove the smoke in our faces wherever we sat, helped at the same time to make a forced draught. We took it in turn to make some foraging expeditions into the darkness, and the quantity the Swede brought back always made me feel that he took an absurdly long time finding it; for the fact was I did not care much about being left alone, and yet it always seemed to be my turn to grub about among the bushes or scramble along the slippery banks in the moonlight. The long day's battle with wind and water—such wind and such water!—had tired us both, and an early bed was the obvious programme. Yet neither of us made the move for the tent. We lay there, tending the fire, talking in desultory fashion, peering about us into the dense willow bushes, and listening to the thunder of wind and river. The loneliness of the place had entered our very bones, and silence seemed natural, for after a bit the sound of our voices became a trifle unreal and forced; whispering would have been the fitting mode of communication, I felt, and the human voice, always rather absurd amid the roar of the elements, now carried with it something almost illegitimate. It was like talking out loud in church, or in some place where it was not lawful, perhaps not quite *safe,* to be overheard.

The eeriness of this lonely island, set among a million willows, swept by a hurricane, and surrounded by hurrying deep waters, touched us both, I fancy. Untrodden by man, almost unknown to man, it lay there beneath the moon, remote from human influence, on the frontier of another world, an alien world, a world tenanted by willows only and the souls of willows. And we, in our rashness, had dared to invade it, even to make use of it! Something more than the power of its mystery stirred in me as I lay on the sand, feet to fire, and peered up through the leaves at the stars. For the last time I rose to get firewood.

"When this has burnt up," I said firmly, "I shall turn in," and my companion watched me lazily as I moved off into the surrounding shadows.

For an unimaginative man I thought he seemed unusually receptive that night, unusually open to suggestion of things other than sensory. He too was touched by the beauty and loneliness of the place. I was not altogether pleased, I remember, to recognise this slight change in him, and instead of immediately collecting sticks, I made my way to the far point of the island where the moonlight on plain and river could be seen to better advantage. The desire to be alone had come suddenly upon me; my former dread returned in force; there was a vague feeling in me I wished to face and probe to the bottom.

When I reached the point of sand jutting out among the waves, the spell of the place descended upon me with a positive shock. No mere "scenery" could have produced such an effect. There was something more here, something to alarm.

I gazed across the waste of wild waters; I watched the whispering *willows;* I heard the ceaseless beating of the tireless wind; and, one and all, each in its own way, stirred in me this sensation of a strange distress. But the willows especially; for ever they went on chattering and talking among themselves, laughing a little, shrilly crying out, sometimes sighing—but what it was they made so much to-do about belonged to the secret life of the great plain they inhabited. And it was utterly alien to the world I knew, or to that of the wild yet kindly elements. They made me think of a host of beings from another plane of life, another evolution altogether, perhaps, all discussing a mystery known only to themselves. I watched them moving busily together, oddly shaking their big bushy heads, twirling their myriad leaves even when there was no wind. They moved of their own will as though alive, and they touched, by some incalculable method, my own keen sense of the *horrible*.

There they stood in the moonlight, like a vast army surrounding our camp, shaking their innumerable silver spears defiantly, formed all ready for an attack.

The psychology of places, for some imaginations at least, is very vivid; for the wanderer, especially, camps have their "note" either of welcome or rejection. At first it may not always be apparent, because the busy preparations of tent and cooking prevent, but with the first pause—after supper usually—it comes and announces itself. And the note of this willow-camp now became unmistakably plain to me: we were interlopers, trespassers; we were not welcomed. The sense of unfamiliarity grew upon me as I stood there watching. We touched the frontier of a region where our presence was resented. For a night's lodging we might perhaps be tolerated; but for a prolonged and inquisitive stay— No! by all the gods of the trees and wilderness, no! We were the first human influences upon this island, and we were not wanted. *The willows were against us.*

Strange thoughts like these, bizarre fancies, borne I know not whence, found lodgment in my mind as I stood listening. What, I thought, if, after all, these crouching willows proved to be alive; if suddenly they should rise up, like a swarm of living creatures, marshalled by the gods whose territory we had invaded, sweep towards us off the vast swamps, booming overhead in the night—and then *settle down!* As I looked it was so easy to imagine they actually moved, crept nearer, retreated a little, huddled together in masses, hostile, waiting for the great wind that should finally start them a-running. I could have sworn their aspect changed a little, and their ranks deepened and pressed more closely together.

The melancholy shrill cry of a night-bird sounded overhead, and suddenly I nearly lost my balance as the piece of bank I stood upon fell with a great splash into the river, undermined by the flood. I stepped back just in time, and went on hunting for firewood again, half laughing at the odd fancies that crowded so thickly into my mind and cast their spell upon me. I recalled the Swede's remark about moving on next day, and I was just thinking that I fully agreed with him, when I turned with a start and saw the subject of my thoughts standing immediately in front of me. He was quite close. The roar of the elements had covered his approach.

"You've been gone so long," he shouted above the wind, "I thought something must have happened to you."

But there was that in his tone, and a certain look in his face as well, that conveyed to me more than his usual words, and in a flash I understood the real reason for his coming. It was because the spell of the place had entered his soul too, and he did not like being alone.

"River still rising," he cried, pointing to the flood in the moonlight, "and the wind's simply awful."

He always said the same things, but it was the cry for companionship that gave the real importance to his words.

"Lucky," I cried back, "our tent's in the hollow. I think it'll hold all right." I added something about the difficulty of finding wood, in order to explain my absence, but the wind caught my words and flung them across the river, so that he did not hear, but just looked at me through the branches, nodding his head.

"Lucky if we get away without disaster!" he shouted, or words to that effect; and I remember feeling half angry with him for putting the thought into words, for it was exactly what I felt myself. There was disaster impending somewhere, and the sense of presentiment lay unpleasantly upon me.

We went back to the fire and made a final blaze, poking it up with our feet. We took a last look round. But for the wind the heat would have been unpleasant. I put this thought into words, and I remember my friend's reply struck me oddly: that he would rather have the heat, the ordinary July weather, than this "diabolical wind."

Everything was snug for the night; the canoe lying turned over beside the tent, with both yellow paddles beneath her; the provision sack hanging from a willow-stem, and the washed-up dishes removed to a safe distance from the fire, all ready for the morning meal.

We smothered the embers of the fire with sand, and then turned in. The flap of the tent door was up, and I saw the branches and the stars and the white moonlight. The shaking willows and the heavy buffetings of the wind against our taut little house were the last things I remembered as sleep came down and covered all with its soft and delicious forgetfulness.

II

Suddenly I found myself lying awake, peering from my sandy mattress through the door of the tent. I looked at my watch pinned against the canvas, and saw by the bright moonlight that it was past twelve o'clock—the threshold of a new day—and I had therefore slept a couple of hours. The Swede was asleep still beside me; the wind howled as before; something plucked at my heart and made me feel afraid. There was a sense of disturbance in my immediate neighbourhood.

I sat up quickly and looked out. The trees were swaying violently to and fro as the gusts smote them, but our little bit of green canvas lay snugly safe in the hollow, for the wind passed over it without meeting enough resistance to make it vicious. The feeling of disquietude did not pass, however, and I crawled quietly out of the tent to see if our belongings were safe. I moved carefully so as not to waken my companion. A curious excitement was on me.

I was half-way out, kneeling on all fours, when my eye first took in that the tops of the bushes opposite, with their moving tracery of leaves, made shapes against the sky. I sat back on my haunches and stared. It was incredible, surely, but there, opposite and slightly above me, were shapes of some indeterminate sort among the willows, and as the branches swayed in the wind they seemed to group themselves about these shapes, forming a series of monstrous outlines that shifted rapidly beneath the moon. Close, about fifty feet in front of me, I saw these things.

My first instinct was to waken my companion, that he too might see them, but something made me hesitate—the sudden realisation, probably, that I should not welcome corroboration; and meanwhile I crouched there staring in amazement with smarting eyes. I was wide awake. I remember saying to myself that I was *not* dreaming.

They first became properly visible, these huge figures, just within the tops of the bushes—immense, bronze-coloured, moving, and wholly independent of the swaying of the branches. I saw them plainly and noted, now I came to examine them more calmly, that they were very much larger than human, and indeed that something in their appearance proclaimed them to be *not human* at all. Certainly they were not merely the moving tracery of the branches against the moonlight. They shifted independently. They rose upwards in a continuous stream from earth to sky, vanishing utterly as soon as they reached the dark of the sky. They were interlaced one with another, making a great column, and I saw their limbs and huge bodies melting in and out of each other, forming this serpentine line that bent and swayed and twisted spirally with the contortions of the wind-tossed trees. They were nude, fluid shapes, passing up the bushes, *within* the leaves almost—rising up in a living column into the heavens. Their faces I never could see. Unceasingly they poured upwards, swaying in great bending curves, with a hue of dull bronze upon their skins.

I stared, trying to force every atom of vision from my eyes. For a long time I thought they *must* every moment disappear and resolve themselves into the movements of the branches and prove to be an optical illusion. I searched everywhere for a proof of reality, when all the while I understood quite well that the standard of reality had changed. For the longer I looked the more certain I became that these figures were real and living, though perhaps not according to the standards that the camera and the biologist would insist upon.

Far from feeling fear, I was possessed with a sense of awe and wonder such as I have never known. I seemed to be gazing at the personified elemental forces of this haunted and primeval region. Our intrusion had stirred the powers of the place into activity. It was we who were the cause of the disturbance, and my brain filled to bursting with stories and legends of the spirits and deities of places that have been acknowledged and worshipped by men in all ages of the world's history. But, before I could arrive at any possible explanation, something impelled me to go farther out, and I crept forward on to the sand and stood upright. I felt the ground still warm under my bare feet; the wind tore at my hair and face; and the sound of the river burst upon my ears with a sudden roar. These things, I knew, were real, and proved that my senses were acting normally. Yet the figures still rose from earth to heaven, silent, majestically, in a great spiral of grace and strength that overwhelmed me at length with a genuine deep emotion of worship. I felt that I must fall down and worship—absolutely worship.

Perhaps in another minute I might have done so, when a gust of wind swept against me with such force that it blew me sideways, and I nearly stumbled and fell. It seemed to shake the dream violently out of me. At least it gave me another point of view somehow. The figures still remained, still ascended into heaven from the heart of the night, but my reason at last began to assert itself. It must be a subjective experience, I argued—none the less real for that, but still subjective. The moonlight and the branches combined to work out these pictures upon the mirror of my imagination, and for some reason I projected them outwards and made them appear objective. I knew this must be the case, of course. I took courage, and began to move forward across the open patches of sand. By Jove, though, was it all hallucination? Was it merely subjective? Did not my reason argue in the old futile way from the little standard of the known?

I only know that great column of figures ascended darkly into the sky for what seemed a very long period of time, and with a very complete measure of reality as most men are accustomed to gauge reality. Then suddenly they were gone!

And, once they were gone and the immediate wonder of their great presence had passed, fear came down upon me with a cold rush. The esoteric meaning of this lonely and haunted region suddenly flamed up within me, and I began to tremble dreadfully. I took a quick look round—a look of horror that came near to panic—calculating vainly ways of escape; and then, realising how helpless I was to achieve anything really effective, I crept back silently into the tent and lay down again upon my sandy mattress, first lowering the door-curtain to shut out the sight of the willows in the moonlight, and then burying my head as deeply as possible beneath the blankets to deaden the sound of the terrifying wind.

III

As though further to convince me that I had not been dreaming, I remember that it was a long time before I fell again into a troubled and restless sleep; and even then only the upper crust of me slept, and underneath there was something that never quite lost consciousness, but lay alert and on the watch.

But this second time I jumped up with a genuine start of terror. It was neither the wind nor the river that woke me, but the slow approach of something that caused the sleeping portion of me to grow smaller and smaller till at last it vanished altogether, and I found myself sitting bolt upright—listening.

Outside there was a sound of multitudinous little patterings. They had been coming, I was aware, for a long time, and in my sleep they had first become audible. I sat there nervously wide awake as though I had not slept at all. It seemed to me that my breathing came with difficulty, and that there was a great weight upon the surface of my body. In spite of the hot night, I felt clammy with cold and shivered. Something surely was pressing steadily against the sides of the tent and weighing down upon it from above. Was it the body of the wind? Was this the pattering rain, the dripping of the leaves? The spray blown from the river by the wind and gathering in big drops? I thought quickly of a dozen things.

Then suddenly the explanation leaped into my mind: a bough from the poplar, the only large tree on the island, had fallen with the wind. Still half caught by the other branches, it would fall with the next gust and crush us, and meanwhile its leaves brushed and tapped upon the tight canvas surface of the tent. I raised a loose flap and rushed out, calling to the Swede to follow.

But when I got out and stood upright I saw that the tent was free. There was no hanging bough; there was no rain or spray; nothing approached.

A cold, grey light filtered down through the bushes and lay on the faintly gleaming sand. Stars still crowded the sky directly overhead, and the wind howled magnificently, but the fire no longer gave out any glow, and I saw the east reddening in streaks through the trees. Several hours must have passed since I stood there before watching the ascending figures, and the memory of it now came back to me horribly, like an evil dream. Oh, how tired it made me feel, that ceaseless raging wind! Yet, though the deep lassitude of a sleepless night was on me, my nerves were tingling with the activity of an equally tireless apprehension, and all idea of repose was out of the question. The river I saw had risen further. Its thunder filled the air, and a fine spray made itself felt through my thin sleeping shirt.

Yet nowhere did I discover the slightest evidences of anything to cause alarm. This deep, prolonged disturbance in my heart remained wholly unaccounted for.

My companion had not stirred when I called him, and there was no need to waken him now. I looked about me carefully, noting everything: the turned-over canoe; the yellow paddles—two of them, I'm certain; the provision sack and the extra lantern hanging together from the tree; and, crowding everywhere about me, enveloping all, the willows, those endless, shaking willows. A bird uttered its morning cry, and a string of duck passed with whirring flight overhead in the twilight. The sand whirled, dry and stinging, about my bare feet in the wind.

I walked round the tent and then went out a little way into the bush, so that I could see across the river to the farther landscape, and the same profound yet indefinable emotion of distress seized upon me again as I saw the interminable sea of bushes stretching to the horizon, looking ghostly and unreal in the wan light of dawn. I walked softly here and there, still puzzling over that odd sound of infinite pattering, and of that pressure upon the tent that had wakened me. It *must* have been the wind, I reflected—the wind beating upon the loose, hot sand, driving the dry particles smartly against the taut canvas—the wind dropping heavily upon our fragile roof.

Yet all the time my nervousness and malaise increased appreciably.

I crossed over to the farther shore and noted how the coast-line had altered in the night, and what masses of sand the river had torn away. I dipped my hands and feet into the cool current, and bathed my forehead. Already there was a glow of sunrise in the sky and the exquisite freshness of coming day. On my way back I passed purposely beneath the very bushes where I had seen the column of figures rising into the air, and midway among the clumps I suddenly found myself overtaken by a sense of vast terror. From the shadows a large figure went swiftly by. Some one passed me, as sure as ever man did. . . .

It was a great staggering blow from the wind that helped me forward again, and once out in the more open space, the sense of terror diminished strangely. The winds were about and walking, I remember saying to myself; for the winds often move like great presences under the trees. And altogether the fear that hovered about me was such an unknown and immense kind of fear, so unlike anything I had ever felt before, that it woke a sense of awe and wonder in me that did much to counteract its worst effects; and when I reached a high point in the middle of the island from which I could see the wide stretch of river, crimson in the sunrise, the whole magical beauty of it all was so overpowering that a sort of wild yearning woke in me and almost brought a cry up into the throat.

But this cry found no expression, for as my eyes wandered from the plain beyond to the island round me and noted our little tent half hidden among the willows, a dreadful discovery leaped out at me, compared to which my terror of the walking winds seemed as nothing at all.

For a change, I thought, had somehow come about in the arrangement of the landscape. It was not that my point of vantage gave me a different view, but that an alteration had apparently been effected in the relation of the tent to the willows, and of the willows to the tent. Surely the bushes now crowded much closer—unnecessarily, unpleasantly close. *They had moved nearer.*

Creeping with silent feet over the shifting sands, drawing imperceptibly nearer by soft, unhurried movements, the willows had come closer during the night. But had the wind moved them, or had they moved of themselves? I recalled the sound of infinite small patterings and the pressure upon the tent and upon my own heart that caused me to wake in terror. I swayed for a moment in the wind like a tree, finding it hard to keep my upright position on the sandy hillock. There was a suggestion here of personal agency, of deliberate intention, of aggressive hostility, and it terrified me into a sort of rigidity.

Then the reaction followed quickly. The idea was so bizarre, so absurd, that I felt inclined to laugh. But the laughter came no more readily than the cry, for the knowledge that my mind was so receptive to such dangerous imaginings brought the additional terror that it was through our minds and not through our physical bodies that the attack would come, and was coming.

The wind buffeted me about, and, very quickly it seemed, the sun came up over the horizon, for it was after four o'clock, and I must have stood on that little pinnacle of sand longer than I knew, afraid to come down at close quarters with the willows. I returned quietly, creepily, to the tent, first taking another exhaustive look round and— yes, I confess it—making a few measurements. I paced out on the warm sand the distances between the willows and the tent, making a note of the shortest distance particularly.

I crawled stealthily into my blankets. My companion, to all appearances, still slept soundly, and I was glad that this was so. Provided my experiences were not corroborated, I could find strength somehow to deny them, perhaps. With the daylight I could persuade myself that it was all a subjective hallucination, a fantasy of the night, a projection of the excited imagination.

Nothing further came in to disturb me, and I fell asleep almost at once, utterly exhausted, yet still in dread of hearing again that weird sound of multitudinous pattering, or of feeling the pressure upon my heart that had made it difficult to breathe.

IV

The sun was high in the heavens when my companion woke me from a heavy sleep and announced that the porridge was cooked and there was just time to bathe. The grateful smell of frizzling bacon entered the tent door.

"River still rising," he said, "and several islands out in mid-stream have disappeared altogether. Our own island's much smaller."

"Any wood left?" I asked sleepily.

"The wood and the island will finish to-morrow in a dead heat," he laughed, "but there's enough to last us till then."

I plunged in from the point of the island, which had indeed altered a lot in size and shape during the night, and was swept down in a moment to the landing place opposite the tent. The water was icy, and the banks flew by like the country from an express train. Bathing under such conditions was an exhilarating operation, and the terror of the night seemed cleansed out of me by a process of evaporation in the brain. The sun was blazing hot; not a cloud showed itself anywhere; the wind, however, had not abated one little jot.

Quite suddenly then the implied meaning of the Swede's words flashed across me, showing that he no longer wished to leave post-haste, and had changed his mind. "Enough to last till to-morrow"—he assumed we should stay on the island another night. It struck me as odd. The night before he was so positive the other way. How had the change come about?

Great crumblings of the banks occurred at breakfast, with heavy splashings and clouds of spray which the wind brought into our frying-pan, and my fellow-traveller talked incessantly about the difficulty the Vienna-Pesth steamers must have to find the channel in flood. But the state of his mind interested and impressed me far more than the state of the river or the difficulties of the steamers. He had changed somehow since the evening before. His manner was different—a trifle excited, a trifle shy, with a sort of suspicion about his voice and gestures. I hardly know how to describe it now in cold blood, but at the time I remember being quite certain of one thing, viz., that he had become frightened!

He ate very little breakfast, and for once omitted to smoke his pipe. He had the map spread open beside him, and kept studying its markings.

"We'd better get off sharp in an hour," I said presently, feeling for an opening that must bring him indirectly to a partial confession at any rate. And his answer puzzled me uncomfortably: "Rather! If they'll let us."

"Who'll let us? The elements?" I asked quickly, with affected indifference.

"The powers of this awful place, whoever they are," he replied, keeping his eyes on the map. "The gods are here, if they are anywhere at all in the world."

"The elements are always the true immortals," I replied, laughing as naturally as I could manage, yet knowing quite well that my face reflected my true feelings when he looked up gravely at me and spoke across the smoke:

"We shall be fortunate if we get away without further disaster."

This was exactly what I had dreaded, and I screwed myself up to the point of the direct question. It was like agreeing to allow the dentist to extract the tooth; it *had* to come anyhow in the long run, and the rest was all pretence.

"Further disaster! Why, what's happened?"

"For one thing—the steering paddle's gone," he said quietly.

"The steering paddle gone!" I repeated, greatly excited, for this was our rudder, and the Danube in flood without a rudder was suicide. "But what—"

"And there's a tear in the bottom of the canoe," he added, with a genuine little tremor in his voice.

I continued staring at him, able only to repeat the words in his face somewhat foolishly. There, in the heat of the sun, and on this burning sand, I was aware of a freezing atmosphere descending round us. I got up to follow him, for he merely nodded his head gravely and led the way towards the tent a few yards on the other side of the fireplace. The canoe still lay there as I had last seen her in the night, ribs uppermost, the paddles, or rather, *the* paddle, on the sand beside her.

"There's only one," he said, stooping to pick it up. "And here's the rent in the base-board."

It was on the tip of my tongue to tell him that I had clearly noticed *two* paddles a few hours before, but a second impulse made me think better of it, and I said nothing. I approached to see.

There was a long, finely-made tear in the bottom of the canoe where a little slither of wood had been neatly taken clean out; it looked as if the tooth of a sharp rock or snag had eaten down her length, and investigation showed that the hole went through. Had we launched out in her without observing it we must inevitably have foundered. At first the water would have made the wood swell so as to close the hole, but once out in mid-stream the water must have poured in, and the canoe, never more than two inches above the surface, would have filled and sunk very rapidly.

"There, you see, an attempt to prepare a victim for the sacrifice," I heard him saying, more to himself than to me, "two victims rather," he added as he bent over and ran his fingers along the slit.

I began to whistle—a thing I always do unconsciously when utterly nonplussed—and purposely paid no attention to his words. I was determined to consider them foolish.

"It wasn't there last night," he said presently, straightening up from his examination and looking anywhere but at me.

"We must have scratched her in landing, of course," I stopped whistling to say. "The stones are very sharp—"

I stopped abruptly, for at that moment he turned round and met my eye squarely. I knew just as well as he did how impossible my explanation was. There were no stones, to begin with.

"And then there's this to explain too," he added quietly, handing me the paddle and pointing to the blade.

A new and curious emotion spread freezingly over me as I took and examined it. The blade was scraped down all over, beautifully scraped, as though some one had sand-papered it with care, making it so thin that the first vigorous stroke must have snapped it off at the elbow.

"One of us walked in his sleep and did this thing," I said feebly, "or—or it has been filed by the constant stream of sand particles blown against it by the wind, perhaps."

"Ah," said the Swede, turning away, laughing a little, "you can explain everything!"

"The same wind that caught the steering paddle and flung it so near the bank that it fell in with the next lump that crumbled," I called out after him, absolutely determined to find an explanation for everything he showed me.

"I see," he shouted back, turning his head to look at me before disappearing among the willow bushes.

Once alone with these perplexing evidences of personal agency, I think my first thought took the form of "One of us must have done this thing, and it certainly was not I." But my second thought decided how impossible it was to suppose, under all the circumstances, that either of us had done it. That my companion, the trusted friend of a dozen similar expeditions, could have knowingly had a hand in it, was a suggestion not to be entertained for a moment. Equally absurd seemed the explanation that this imperturbable and densely practical nature had suddenly become insane and was busied with insane purposes.

Yet the fact remained that what disturbed me most, and kept my fear actively alive even in this blaze of sunshine and wild beauty, was the clear certainty that some curious alteration had come about in his *mind*—that he was nervous, timid, suspicious, aware of goings on he did not speak about, watching a series of secret and hitherto unmentionable events—waiting, in a word, for a climax that he expected, and, I thought, expected very soon. This grew up in my mind intuitively—I hardly knew how.

I made a hurried examination of the tent and its surroundings, but the measurements of the night remained the same. There were deep hollows formed in the sand, I now noticed for the first time, basin-shaped and of various depths and sizes, varying from that of a tea-cup to a large bowl. The wind, no doubt, was responsible for these miniature craters, just as it was for lifting the paddle and tossing it towards the water. The rent in the canoe was the only thing that seemed quite inexplicable; and, after all, it *was* conceivable that a sharp point had caught it when we landed. The examination I made of the shore did not assist this theory, but all the same I clung to it with that diminishing portion of my intelligence which I called my "reason." An explanation of some kind was an absolute necessity, just as some working explanation of the universe is necessary—however absurd—to the happiness of every individual who seeks to do his duty in the world and face the problems of life. The simile seemed to me at the time an exact parallel.

I at once set the pitch melting, and presently the Swede joined me at the work, though under the best conditions in the world the canoe could not be safe for travelling till the following day. I drew his attention casually to the hollows in the sand.

"Yes," he said, "I know. They're all over the island. But *you* can explain them, no doubt!"

"Wind, of course," I answered without hesitation. "Have you never watched those little whirlwinds in the street that twist and twirl everything into a circle? This sand's loose enough to yield, that's all."

He made no reply, and we worked on in silence for a bit. I watched him surreptitiously all the time, and I had an idea he was watching me. He seemed, too, to be always listening attentively to something I could not hear, or perhaps for something that he expected to hear, for he kept turning about and staring into the bushes, and up into the sky, and out across the water where it was visible through the openings among the willows. Sometimes he even put his hand to his ear and held it there for several minutes. He said nothing to me, however, about it, and I asked no questions. And meanwhile, as he mended that torn canoe with the skill and address of a red Indian, I was glad to notice his absorption in the work, for there was a vague dread in my heart that he would speak of the changed aspect of the willows. And, if he had noticed that, my imagination could no longer be held a sufficient explanation of it.

At length, after a long pause, he began to talk.

"Queer thing," he added in a hurried sort of voice, as though he wanted to say something and get it over. "Queer thing, I mean, about that otter last night."

I had expected something so totally different that he caught me with surprise, and I looked up sharply.

"Shows how lonely this place is. Otters are awfully shy things—"

"I don't mean that, of course," he interrupted. "I mean—do you think—did you think it really *was* an otter?"

"What else, in the name of heaven, what else?"

"You know, I saw it before you did, and at first it seemed—so *much* bigger than an otter."

"The sunset as you looked up-stream magnified it, or something," I replied.

He looked at me absently a moment, as though his mind were busy with other thoughts.

"It had such extraordinary yellow eyes," he went on half to himself.

"That was the sun too," I laughed, a trifle boisterously. "I suppose you'll wonder next if that fellow in the boat—"

I suddenly decided not to finish the sentence. He was in the act again of listening, turning his head to the wind, and something in the expression of his face made me halt. The subject dropped, and we went on with our caulking. Apparently he had not noticed my unfinished sentence. Five minutes later, however, he looked at me across the canoe, the smoking pitch in his hand, his face exceedingly grave.

"I *did* rather wonder, if you want to know," he said slowly, "what that thing in the boat was. I remember thinking at the time it was not a man. The whole business seemed to rise quite suddenly out of the water."

I laughed again boisterously in his face, but this time there was impatience, and a strain of anger too, in my feeling.

"Look here now," I cried, "this place is quite queer enough without going out of our way to imagine things! That boat was an ordinary boat, and the man in it was an ordinary man, and they were both going down stream as fast as they could lick. And that otter *was* an otter, so don't let's play the fool about it!"

He looked steadily at me with the same grave expression. He was not in the least annoyed. I took courage from his silence.

"And, for heaven's sake," I went on, "don't keep pretending you hear things, because it only gives me the jumps, and there's nothing to hear but the river and this cursed old thundering wind."

"You *fool!*" he answered in a low, shocked voice, "you utter fool. That's just the way all victims talk. As if you didn't understand just as well as I do!" he sneered with scorn in his voice, and a sort of resignation. "The best thing you can do is to keep quiet and try to hold your mind as firm as possible. This feeble attempt at self-deception only makes the truth harder when you're forced to meet it."

My little effort was over, and I found nothing more to say, for I knew quite well his words were true, and that *I* was the fool, not *he*. Up to a certain stage in the adventure he kept ahead of me easily, and I think I felt annoyed to be out of it, to be thus proved less psychic, less sensitive than himself to these extraordinary happenings, and half ignorant all the time of what was going on under my very nose. *He knew* from the very beginning, apparently. But at the moment I wholly missed the point of his words about the necessity of there being a victim, and that we ourselves were destined to satisfy the want. I dropped all pretence thenceforward, but thenceforward likewise my fear increased steadily to the climax.

"But you're quite right about one thing," he added, before the subject passed, "and that is that we're wiser not to talk about it, or even to think about it, because what one *thinks* finds expression in words, and what one *says*, happens."

That afternoon, while the canoe dried and hardened, we spent trying to fish, testing the leak, collecting wood, and watching the enormous flood of rising water. Masses of driftwood swept near our shores sometimes, and we fished for them with long willow branches. The island grew perceptibly smaller as the banks were torn away with great gulps and splashes. The weather kept brilliantly fine till about four o'clock, and then for the first time for three days the wind showed signs of abating. Clouds began to gather in the south-west, spreading thence slowly over the sky.

This lessening of the wind came as a great relief, for the incessant roaring, banging, and thundering had irritated our nerves. Yet the silence that came about five o'clock with its sudden cessation was in a manner quite as oppressive. The booming of the river had everything its own way then: it filled the air with deep murmurs, more musical than the wind noises, but infinitely more monotonous. The wind held many notes, rising, falling, always beating out some sort of great elemental tune; whereas the river's song lay between three notes at most—dull pedal notes, that held a lugubrious quality foreign to the wind, and somehow seemed to me, in my then nervous state, to sound wonderfully well the music of doom.

It was extraordinary, too, how the withdrawal suddenly of bright sunlight took everything out of the landscape that made for cheerfulness; and since this particular landscape had already managed to convey the suggestion of something sinister, the change of course was all the more unwelcome and noticeable. For me, I know, the darkening outlook became distinctly more alarming, and I found myself more than once calculating how soon after sunset the full moon would get up in the east, and whether the gathering clouds would greatly interfere with her lighting of the little island.

With this general hush of the wind—though it still indulged in occasional brief gusts—the river seemed to me to grow blacker, the willows to stand more densely together. The latter, too, kept up a sort of independent movement of their own, rustling among themselves when no wind stirred, and shaking oddly from the roots upwards. When common objects in this way become charged with the suggestion of horror, they stimulate the imagination far more than things of unusual appearance; and these bushes, crowding huddled about us, assumed for me in the darkness a bizarre *grotesquerie* of appearance that lent to them somehow the aspect of purposeful and living creatures. Their very ordinariness, I felt, masked what was malignant and hostile to us. The forces of the region drew nearer with the coming of night. They were focussing upon our island, and more particularly upon ourselves. For thus, somehow, in the terms of the imagination, did my really indescribable sensations in this extraordinary place present themselves.

I had slept a good deal in the early afternoon, and had thus recovered somewhat from the exhaustion of a disturbed night, but this only served apparently to render me more susceptible than before to the obsessing spell of the haunting. I fought against it, laughing at my feelings as absurd and childish, with very obvious physiological explanations, yet, in spite of every effort, they gained in strength upon me so that I dreaded the night as a child lost in a forest must dread the approach of darkness.

The canoe we had carefully covered with a waterproof sheet during the day, and the one remaining paddle had been securely tied by the Swede to the base of a tree, lest the wind should rob us of that too. From five o'clock onwards I busied myself with the stew-pot and preparations for dinner, it being my turn to cook that night. We had potatoes, onions, bits of bacon fat to add flavour, and a general thick residue from former stews at the bottom of the pot; with black bread broken up into it the result was most excellent, and it was followed by a stew of plums with sugar and a brew of strong tea with dried milk. A good pile of wood lay close at hand, and the absence of wind made my duties easy. My companion sat lazily watching me, dividing his attentions between cleaning his pipe and giving useless advice— an admitted privilege of the off-duty man. He had been very quiet all the afternoon, engaged in re-caulking the canoe, strengthening the tent ropes, and fishing for driftwood while I slept. No more talk about undesirable things had passed between us, and I think his only remarks had to do with the gradual destruction of the island, which he declared was now fully a third smaller than when we first landed.

The pot had just begun to bubble when I heard his voice calling to me from the bank, where he had wandered away without my noticing. I ran up.

"Come and listen," he said, "and see what you make of it." He held his hand cupwise to his ear, as so often before.

"*Now* do you hear anything?" he asked, watching me curiously.

We stood there, listening attentively together. At first I heard only the deep note of the water and the hissings rising from its turbulent surface. The willows, for once, were motionless and silent. Then a sound began to reach my ears faintly, a peculiar sound—something like the humming of a distant gong. It seemed to come across to us in the darkness from the waste of swamps and willows opposite. It was repeated at regular intervals, but it was certainly neither the sound of a bell nor the hooting of a distant steamer. I can liken it to nothing so much as to the sound of an immense gong, suspended far up in the sky, repeating incessantly its muffled metallic note, soft and musical, as it was repeatedly struck. My heart quickened as I listened.

"I've heard it all day," said my companion. "While you slept this afternoon it came all round the island. I hunted it down, but could never get near enough to see—to localise it correctly. Sometimes it was overhead, and sometimes it seemed under the water. Once or twice, too, I could have sworn it was not outside at all, but *within myself*—you know—the way a sound in the fourth dimension is supposed to come."

I was too much puzzled to pay much attention to his words. I listened carefully, striving to associate it with any known familiar sound I could think of, but without success. It changed in the direction, too, coming nearer, and then sinking utterly away into remote distance. I cannot say that it was ominous in quality, because to me it seemed distinctly musical, yet I must admit it set going a distressing feeling that made me wish I had never heard it.

"The wind blowing in those sand-funnels," I said, determined to find an explanation, "or the bushes rubbing together after the storm perhaps."

"It comes off the whole swamp," my friend answered. "It comes from everywhere at once." He ignored my explanations. "It comes from the willow bushes somehow—"

"But now the wind has dropped," I objected. "The willows can hardly make a noise by themselves, can they?"

His answer frightened me, first because I had dreaded it, and secondly, because I knew intuitively it was true.

"It is *because* the wind has dropped we now hear it. It was drowned before. It is the cry, I believe, of the——"

I dashed back to my fire, warned by the sound of bubbling that the stew was in danger, but determined at the same time to escape further conversation. I was resolute, if possible, to avoid the exchanging of views. I dreaded, too, that he would begin again about the gods, or the elemental forces, or something else disquieting, and I wanted to keep myself well in hand for what might happen later. There was another night to be faced before we escaped from this distressing place, and there was no knowing yet what it might bring forth.

"Come and cut up bread for the pot," I called to him, vigorously stirring the appetising mixture. That stew-pot held sanity for us both, and the thought made me laugh.

He came over slowly and took the provision sack from the tree, fumbling in its mysterious depths, and then emptying the entire contents upon the ground-sheet at his feet.

"Hurry up!" I cried; "it's boiling."

The Swede burst out into a roar of laughter that startled me. It was forced laughter, not artificial exactly, but mirthless.

"There's nothing here!" he shouted, holding his sides.

"Bread, I mean."

"It's gone. There is no bread. They've taken it!"

I dropped the long spoon and ran up. Everything the sack had contained lay upon the ground-sheet, but there was no loaf.

The whole dead weight of my growing fear fell upon me and shook me. Then I burst out laughing too. It was the only thing to do: and the sound of my laughter also made me understand his. The strain of psychical pressure caused it—this explosion of unnatural laughter in both of us; it was an effort of repressed forces to seek relief; it was a temporary safety valve. And with both of us it ceased quite suddenly.

"How criminally stupid of me!" I cried, still determined to be consistent and find an explanation. "I clean forgot to buy a loaf at Pressburg. That chattering woman put everything out of my head, and I must have left it lying on the counter or—"

"The oatmeal, too, is much less than it was this morning," the Swede interrupted.

Why in the world need he draw attention to it? I thought angrily.

"There's enough for to-morrow," I said, stirring vigorously, "and we can get lots more at Komorn or Gran. In twenty-four hours we shall be miles from here."

"I hope so—to God," he muttered, putting the things back into the sack, "unless we're claimed first as victims for the sacrifice," he added with a foolish laugh. He dragged the sack into the tent, for safety's sake, I suppose, and I heard him mumbling to himself, but so indistinctly that it seemed quite natural for me to ignore his words.

Our meal was beyond question a gloomy one, and we ate it almost in silence, avoiding one another's eyes, and keeping the fire bright. Then we washed up and prepared for the night, and, once smoking, our minds unoccupied with any definite duties, the apprehension I had felt all day long became more and more acute. It was not then active fear, I think, but the very vagueness of its origin distressed me far more than if I had been able to ticket and face it squarely. The curious sound I have likened to the note of a gong became now almost incessant, and filled the stillness of the night with a faint, continuous ringing rather than a series of distinct notes. At one time it was behind and at another time in front of us. Sometimes I fancied it came from the bushes on our left, and then again from the clumps on our right. More often it hovered directly overhead like the whirring of wings. It was really everywhere at once, behind, in front, at our sides and over our heads, completely surrounding us. The sound really defies description. But nothing within my knowledge is like that ceaseless muffled humming rising off the deserted world of swamps and willows.

We sat smoking in comparative silence, the strain growing every minute greater. The worst feature of the situation seemed to me that we did not know what to expect, and could therefore make no sort of preparation by way of defence. We could anticipate nothing. My explanations made in the sunshine, moreover, now came to haunt me with their foolish and wholly unsatisfactory nature, and it was more and more clear to us that some kind of plain talk with my companion was inevitable, whether I liked it or not. After all, we had to spend the night together, and to sleep in the same tent side by side. I saw that I could not get along much longer without the support of his mind, and for that, of course, plain talk was imperative. As long as possible, however, I postponed this little climax, and tried to ignore or laugh at the occasional sentences he flung into the emptiness.

Some of these sentences, moreover, were confoundedly disquieting to me, coming as they did to corroborate much that I felt myself: corroboration, too—which made it so much more convincing—from a totally different point of view. He composed such curious sentences, and hurled them at me in such an inconsequential sort of way, as though his main line of thought was secret to himself, and these fragments were the bits he found it impossible to digest. He got rid of them by uttering them. Speech relieved him. It was like being sick.

"There are things about us, I'm sure, that make for disorder, disintegration, destruction, *our* destruction," he said once, while the fire blazed between us. "We've strayed out of a safe line somewhere."

And, another time, when the gong sounds had come nearer, ringing much louder than before, and directly over our heads, he said as though talking to himself:

"I don't think a phonograph would show any record of that. The sound doesn't come to me by the ears at all. The vibrations reach me in another manner altogether, and seem to be within me, which is precisely how a fourth dimensional sound might be supposed to make itself heard."

I purposely made no reply to this, but I sat up a little closer to the fire and peered about me into the darkness. The clouds were massed all over the sky and no trace of moonlight came through. Very still, too, everything was, so that the river and the frogs had things all their own way.

"It has that about it," he went on, "which is utterly out of common experience. It is *unknown*. Only one thing describes it really: it is a non-human sound; I mean a sound outside humanity."

Having rid himself of this indigestible morsel, he lay quiet for a time; but he had so admirably expressed my own feeling that it was a relief to have the thought out, and to have confined it by the limitation of words from dangerous wandering to and fro in the mind.

The solitude of that Danube camping-place, can I ever forget it? The feeling of being utterly alone on an empty planet! My thoughts ran incessantly upon cities and the haunts of men. I would have given my soul, as the saying is, for the "feel" of those Bavarian villages we had passed through by the score; for the normal, human commonplaces: peasants drinking beer, tables beneath the trees, hot sunshine, and a ruined castle on the rocks behind the red-roofed church. Even the tourists would have been welcome.

Yet what I felt of dread was no ordinary ghostly fear. It was infinitely greater, stranger, and seemed to arise from some dim ancestral sense of terror more profoundly disturbing than anything I had known or dreamed of. We had "strayed," as the Swede put it, into some region or some set of conditions where the risks were great, yet unintelligible to us; where the frontiers of some unknown world lay close about us. It was a spot held by the dwellers in some outer space, a sort of peep-hole whence they could spy upon the earth, themselves unseen, a point where the veil between had worn a little thin. As the final result of too long a sojourn here, we should be carried over the border and deprived of what we called "our lives," yet by mental, not physical, processes. In that sense, as he said, we should be the victims of our adventure—a sacrifice.

It took us in different fashion, each according to the measure of his sensitiveness and powers of resistance. I translated it vaguely into a personification of the mightily disturbed elements, investing them with the horror of a deliberate and malefic purpose, resentful of our audacious intrusion into their breeding-place; whereas my friend threw it into the unoriginal form at first of a trespass on some ancient shrine, some place where the old gods still held sway, where the emotional forces of former worshippers still clung, and the ancestral portion of him yielded to the old pagan spell.

At any rate, here was a place unpolluted by men, kept clean by the winds from coarsening human influences, a place where spiritual agencies were within reach and aggressive. Never, before or since, have I been so attacked by indescribable suggestions of a "beyond region," of another scheme of life, another evolution not parallel to the human. And in the end our minds would succumb under the weight of the awful spell, and we should be drawn across the frontier into *their* world.

Small things testified to this amazing influence of the place, and now in the silence round the fire they allowed themselves to be noted by the mind. The very atmosphere had proved itself a magnifying medium to distort every indication: the otter rolling in the current, the hurrying boatman making signs, the shifting willows, one and all had been robbed of its natural character, and revealed in something of its other aspect—as it existed across the border in that other region. And this changed aspect I felt was new not merely to me, but to the race. The whole experience whose verge we touched was unknown to humanity at all. It was a new order of experience, and in the true sense of the word *unearthly*.

"It's the deliberate, calculating purpose that reduces one's courage to zero," the Swede said suddenly, as if he had been actually following my thoughts. "Otherwise imagination might count for much. But the paddle, the canoe, the lessening food—"

"Haven't I explained all that once?" I interrupted viciously.

"You have," he answered dryly; "you have indeed."

He made other remarks too, as usual, about what he called the "plain determination to provide a victim"; but, having now arranged my thoughts better, I recognised that this was simply the cry of his frightened soul against the knowledge that he was being attacked in a vital part, and that he would be somehow taken or destroyed. The situation called for a courage and calmness of reasoning that neither of us could compass, and I have never before been so clearly conscious of two persons in me—the one that explained everything, and the other that laughed at such foolish explanations, yet was horribly afraid.

Meanwhile, in the pitchy night the fire died down and the wood pile grew small. Neither of us moved to replenish the stock, and the darkness consequently came up very close to our faces. A few feet beyond the circle of firelight it was inky black. Occasionally a stray puff of wind set the willows shivering about us, but apart from this not very welcome sound a deep and depressing silence reigned, broken only by the gurgling of the river and the humming in the air overhead.

We both missed, I think, the shouting company of the winds.

At length, at a moment when a stray puff prolonged itself as though the wind were about to rise again, I reached the point for me of saturation, the point where it was absolutely necessary to find relief in plain speech, or else to betray myself by some hysterical extravagance that must have been far worse in its effect upon both of us. I kicked the fire into a blaze, and turned to my companion abruptly. He looked up with a start.

"I can't disguise it any longer," I said; "I don't like this place, and the darkness, and the noises, and the awful feelings I get. There's something here that beats me utterly. I'm in a blue funk, and that's the plain truth. If the other shore was—different, I swear I'd be inclined to swim for it!"

The Swede's face turned very white beneath the deep tan of sun and wind. He stared straight at me and answered quietly, but his voice betrayed his huge excitement by its unnatural calmness. For the moment, at any rate, he was the strong man of the two. He was more phlegmatic, for one thing.

"It's not a physical condition we can escape from by running away," he replied, in the tone of a doctor diagnosing some grave disease; "we must sit tight and wait. There are forces close here that could kill a herd of elephants in a second as easily as you or I could squash a fly. Our only chance is to keep perfectly still. Our insignificance perhaps may save us."

I put a dozen questions into my expression of face, but found no words. It was precisely like listening to an accurate description of a disease whose symptoms had puzzled me.

"I mean that so far, although aware of our disturbing presence, they have not found us—not 'located' us, as the Americans say," he went on. "They're blundering about like men hunting for a leak of gas. The paddle and canoe and provisions prove that. I think they *feel* us, but cannot actually see us. We must keep our minds quiet—it's our minds they feel. We must control our thoughts, or it's all up with us."

"Death, you mean?" I stammered, icy with the horror of his suggestion.

"Worse—by far," he said. "Death, according to one's belief, means either annihilation or release from the limitations of the senses, but it involves no change of character. *You* don't suddenly alter just because the body's gone. But this means a radical alteration, a complete change, a horrible loss of oneself by substitution—far worse than death, and not even annihilation. We happen to have camped in a spot where their region touches ours, where the veil between has worn thin"—horrors! he was using my very own phrase, my actual words—"so that they are aware of our being in their neighbourhood."

"But *who* are aware?" I asked.

I forgot the shaking of the willows in the windless calm, the humming overhead, everything except that I was waiting for an answer that I dreaded more than I can possibly explain.

He lowered his voice at once to reply, leaning forward a little over the fire, an indefinable change in his face that made me avoid his eyes and look down upon the ground.

"All my life," he said, "I have been strangely, vividly conscious of another region—not far removed from our own world in one sense, yet wholly different in kind—where great things go on unceasingly, where immense and terrible personalities hurry by, intent on vast purposes compared to which earthly affairs, the rise and fall of nations, the destinies of empires, the fate of armies and continents, are all as dust in the balance; vast purposes, I mean, that deal directly with the soul, and not indirectly with mere expressions of the soul—"

"I suggest just now—" I began, seeking to stop him, feeling as though I was face to face with a madman. But he instantly overbore me with his torrent that *had* to come.

"You think," he said, "it is the spirits of the elements, and I thought perhaps it was the old gods. But I tell you now it is—*neither*. These would be comprehensible entities, for they have relations with men, depending upon them for worship or sacrifice, whereas these beings who are now about us have absolutely nothing to do with mankind, and it is mere chance that their space happens just at this spot to touch our own."

The mere conception, which his words somehow made so convincing, as I listened to them there in the dark stillness of that lonely island, set me shaking a little all over. I found it impossible to control my movements.

"And what do you propose?" I began again.

"A sacrifice, a victim, might save us by distracting them until we could get away," he went on, "just as the wolves stop to devour the dogs and give the sleigh another start. But—I see no chance of any other victim now."

I stared blankly at him. The gleam in his eye was dreadful. Presently he continued.

"It's the willows, of course. The willows *mask* the others, but the others are feeling about for us. If we let our minds betray our fear, we're lost, lost utterly." He looked at me with an expression so calm, so determined, so sincere, that I no longer had any doubts as to his sanity. He was as sane as any man ever was. "If we can hold out through the night," he added, "we may get off in the daylight unnoticed, or rather, *undiscovered.*"

"But you really think a sacrifice would—"

That gong-like humming came down very close over our heads as I spoke, but it was my friend's scared face that really stopped my mouth.

"Hush!" he whispered, holding up his hand. "Do not mention them more than you can help. Do not refer to them *by name.* To name is to reveal: it is the inevitable clue, and our only hope lies in ignoring them, in order that they may ignore us."

"Even in thought?" He was extraordinarily agitated.

"Especially in thought. Our thoughts make spirals in their world. We must keep them *out of our minds* at all costs if possible."

I raked the fire together to prevent the darkness having everything its own way. I never longed for the sun as I longed for it then in the awful blackness of that summer night.

"Were you awake all last night?" he went on suddenly.

"I slept badly a little after dawn," I replied evasively, trying to follow his instructions, which I knew instinctively were true, "but the wind, of course—"

"I know. But the wind won't account for all the noises."

"Then you heard it too?"

"The multiplying countless little footsteps I heard," he said, adding, after a moment's hesitation, "and that other sound—"

"You mean above the tent, and the pressing down upon us of something tremendous, gigantic?"

He nodded significantly.

"It was like the beginning of a sort of inner suffocation?" I said.

"Partly, yes. It seemed to me that the weight of the atmosphere had been altered—had increased enormously, so that we should be crushed."

"And *that,*" I went on, determined to have it all out, pointing upwards where the gong-like note hummed ceaselessly, rising and falling like wind. "What do you make of that?"

"It's their sound," he whispered gravely. "It's the sound of *their* world, the humming in their region. The division here is so thin that it leaks through somehow. But, if you listen carefully, you'll find it's not above so much as around us. It's in the willows. It's the willows themselves humming, because here the willows have been made symbols of the forces that are against us."

I could not follow exactly what he meant by this, yet the thought and idea in my mind were beyond question the thought and idea in his. I realised what he realised, only with less power of analysis than his. It was on the tip of my tongue to tell him at last about my hallucination of the ascending figures and the moving bushes, when he suddenly thrust his face again close into mine across the firelight and began to speak in a very earnest whisper. He amazed me by his calmness and pluck, his apparent control of the situation. This man I had for years deemed unimaginative, stolid!

"Now listen," he said. "The only thing for us to do is to go on as though nothing had happened, follow our usual habits, go to bed, and so forth; pretend we feel nothing and notice nothing. It is a question wholly of the mind, and the less we think about them the better our chance of escape. Above all, don't *think*, for what you think happens!"

"All right," I managed to reply, simply breathless with his words and the strangeness of it all; "all right, I'll try, but tell me one more thing first. Tell me what you make of those hollows in the ground all about us, those sand-funnels?"

"No!" he cried, forgetting to whisper in his excitement. "I dare not, simply dare not, put the thought into words. If you have not guessed I am glad. Don't try to. *They* have have put it into my mind; try your hardest to prevent their putting it into yours."

He sank his voice again to a whisper before he finished, and I did not press him to explain. There was already just about as much horror in me as I could hold. The conversation came to an end, and we smoked our pipes busily in silence.

Then something happened, something unimportant apparently, as the way is when the nerves are in a very great state of tension, and this small thing for a brief space gave me an entirely different point of view. I chanced to look down at my sand-shoe—the sort we used for the canoe—and something to do with the hole at the toe suddenly recalled to me the London shop where I had bought them, the difficulty the man had in fitting me, and other details of the uninteresting but practical operation. At once, in its train, followed a wholesome view of the modern sceptical world I was accustomed to move in at home. I thought of roast beef, and ale, motor-cars, policemen, brass bands, and a dozen other things that proclaimed the soul of ordinariness or utility. The effect was immediate and astonishing even to myself. Psychologically, I suppose, it was simply a sudden and violent reaction after the strain of living in an atmosphere of things that to the normal consciousness must seem impossible and incredible. But, whatever the cause, it momentarily lifted the spell from my heart, and left me for the short space of a minute feeling free and utterly unafraid. I looked up at my friend opposite.

"You damned old pagan!" I cried, laughing aloud in his face. "You imaginative idiot! You superstitious idolator! You—"

I stopped in the middle, seized anew by the old horror. I tried to smother the sound of my voice as something sacrilegious. The Swede, of course, heard it too—the strange cry overhead in the darkness—and that sudden drop in the air as though something had come nearer.

He had turned ashen white under the tan. He stood bolt upright in front of the fire, stiff as a rod, staring at me.

"After that," he said in a sort of helpless, frantic way, "we must go! We can't stay now; we must strike camp this very instant and go on—down the river."

He was talking, I saw, quite wildly, his words dictated by abject terror—the terror he had resisted so long, but which had caught him at last.

"In the dark?" I exclaimed, shaking with fear after my hysterical outburst, but still realising our position better than he did. "Sheer madness! The river's in flood, and we've only got a single paddle. Besides, we only go deeper into their country! There's nothing ahead for fifty miles but willows, willows, willows!"

He sat down again in a state of semi-collapse. The positions, by one of those kaleidoscopic changes nature loves, were suddenly reversed, and the control of our forces passed over into my hands. His mind at last had reached the point where it was beginning to weaken.

"What on earth possessed you to do such a thing?" he whispered with the awe of genuine terror in his voice and face.

I crossed round to his side of the fire. I took both his hands in mine, kneeling down beside him and looking straight into his frightened eyes.

"We'll make one more blaze," I said firmly, "and then turn in for the night. At sunrise we'll be off full speed for Komorn. Now, pull yourself together a bit, and remember your own advice about *not thinking fear!*"

He said no more, and I saw that he would agree and obey. In some measure, too, it was a sort of relief to get up and make an excursion into the darkness for more wood. We kept close together, almost touching, groping among the bushes and along the bank. The humming overhead never ceased, but seemed to me to grow louder as we increased our distance from the fire. It was shivery work!

We were grubbing away in the middle of a thickish clump of willows where some driftwood from a former flood had caught high among the branches, when my body was seized in a grip that made me half drop upon the sand. It was the Swede. He had fallen against me, and was clutching me for support. I heard his breath coming and going in short gasps.

"Look! By my soul!" he whispered, and for the first time in my experience I knew what it was to hear tears of terror in a human voice. He was pointing to the fire, some fifty feet away. I followed the direction of his finger, and I swear my heart missed a beat.

There, in front of the dim glow, *something was moving.*

I saw it through a veil that hung before my eyes like the gauze drop-curtain used at the back of a theatre—hazily a little. It was neither a human figure nor an animal. To me it gave the strange impression of being as large as several animals grouped together, like horses, two or three, moving slowly. The Swede, too, got a similar result, though expressing it differently, for he thought it was shaped and sized like a clump of willow bushes, rounded at the top, and moving all over upon its surface—"coiling upon itself like smoke," he said afterwards.

"I watched it settle downwards through the bushes," he sobbed at me. "Look, by God! It's coming this way! Oh, oh!"—he gave a kind of whistling cry. *"They've found us."*

I gave one terrified glance, which just enabled me to see that the shadowy form was swinging towards us through the bushes, and then I collapsed backwards with a crash into the branches. These failed, of course, to support my weight, so that with the Swede on top of me we fell in a struggling heap upon the sand. I really hardly knew what was happening. I was conscious only of a sort of enveloping sensation of icy fear that plucked the nerves out of their fleshly covering, twisted them this way and that, and replaced them quivering. My eyes were tightly shut; something in my throat choked me; a feeling that my consciousness was expanding, extending out into space, swiftly gave way to another feeling that I was losing it altogether, and about to die.

An acute spasm of pain passed through me, and I was aware that the Swede had hold of me in such a way that he hurt me abominably. It was the way he caught at me in falling.

But it was the pain, he declared afterwards, that saved me; it caused me to *forget them* and think of something else at the very instant when they were about to find me. It concealed my mind from them at the moment of discovery, yet just in time to evade their terrible seizing of me. He himself, he says, actually swooned at the same moment, and that was what saved him.

I only know that at a later date, how long or short is impossible to say, I found myself scrambling up out of the slippery network of willow branches, and saw my companion standing in front of me holding out a hand to assist me. I stared at him in a dazed way, rubbing the arm he had twisted for me. Nothing came to me to say, somehow.

"I lost consciousness for a moment or two," I heard him say.

"That's what saved me. It made me stop thinking about them."

"You nearly broke my arm in two," I said, uttering my only con-nected thought at the moment. A numbness came over me.

"That's what saved *you!*" he replied. "Between us, we've managed to set them off on a false tack somewhere. The humming has ceased. It's gone—for the moment at any rate!"

A wave of hysterical laughter seized me again, and this time spread to my friend too—great healing gusts of shaking laughter that brought a tremendous sense of relief in their train. We made our way back to the fire and put the wood on so that it blazed at once. Then we saw that the tent had fallen over and lay in a tangled heap upon the ground.

We picked it up, and during the process tripped more than once and caught our feet in sand.

"It's those sand-funnels," exclaimed the Swede, when the tent was up again and the firelight lit up the ground for several yards about us. "And look at the size of them!"

All round the tent and about the fireplace where we had seen the moving shadows there were deep funnel-shaped hollows in the sand, exactly similar to the ones we had already found over the island, only far bigger and deeper, beautifully formed, and wide enough in some instances to admit the whole of my foot and leg.

Neither of us said a word. We both knew that sleep was the saf-est thing we could do, and to bed we went accordingly without fur-ther delay, having first thrown sand on the fire and taken the provision sack and the paddle inside the tent with us. The canoe, too, we propped in such a way at the end of the tent that our feet touched it, and the least motion would disturb and wake us.

In case of emergency, too, we again went to bed in our clothes, ready for a sudden start.

V

It was my firm intention to lie awake all night and watch, but the ex-haustion of nerves and body decreed otherwise, and sleep after a while came over me with a welcome blanket of oblivion. The fact that my companion also slept quickened its approach. At first he fidgeted and constantly sat up, asking me if I "heard this" or "heard that." He tossed about on his cork mattress, and said the tent was moving and the river had risen over the point of the island; but each time I went out to look I returned with the report that all was well, and finally he grew calmer and lay still. Then at length his breathing became regular and I heard unmistakable sounds of snoring—the first and only time in my life when snoring has been a welcome and calming influence.

This, I remember, was the last thought in my mind before dozing off.

A difficulty in breathing woke me, and I found the blanket over my face. But something else besides the blanket was pressing upon me, and my first thought was that my companion had rolled off his mattress on to my own in his sleep. I called to him and sat up, and at the same moment it came to me that the tent was *surrounded*. That sound of multitudinous soft pattering was again audible outside, filling the night with horror.

I called again to him, louder than before. He did not answer, but I missed the sound of his snoring, and also noticed that the flap of the tent was down. This was the unpardonable sin. I crawled out in the darkness to hook it back securely, and it was then for the first time I realised positively that the Swede was not there. He had gone.

I dashed out in a mad run, seized by a dreadful agitation, and the moment I was out I plunged into a sort of torrent of humming that surrounded me completely and came out of every quarter of the heavens at once. It was that same familiar humming—gone mad! A swarm of great invisible bees might have been about me in the air. The sound seemed to thicken the very atmosphere, and I felt that my lungs worked with difficulty.

But my friend was in danger, and I could not hesitate.

The dawn was just about to break, and a faint whitish light spread upwards over the clouds from a thin strip of clear horizon. No wind stirred. I could just make out the bushes and river beyond, and the pale sandy patches. In my excitement I ran frantically to and fro about the island, calling him by name, shouting at the top of my voice the first words that came into my head. But the willows smothered my voice, and the humming muffled it, so that the sound only travelled a few feet round me. I plunged among the bushes, tripping headlong, tumbling over roots, and scraping my face as I tore this way and that among the preventing branches.

Then, quite unexpectedly, I came out upon the island's point and saw a dark figure outlined between the water and the sky. It was the Swede. And already he had one foot in the river! A moment more and he would have taken the plunge.

I threw myself upon him, flinging my arms about his waist and dragging him shorewards with all my strength. Of course he struggled furiously, making a noise all the time just like that cursed humming, and using the most outlandish phrases in his anger about "going *inside* to Them," and "taking the way of the water and the wind," and God only knows what more besides, that I tried in vain to recall afterwards, but which turned me sick with horror and amazement as I listened. But in the end I managed to get him into the comparative safety of the tent, and flung him breathless and cursing upon the mattress, where I held him until the fit had passed.

I think the suddenness with which it all went and he grew calm, coinciding as it did with the equally abrupt cessation of the humming and pattering outside—I think this was almost the strangest part of the whole business perhaps. For he had just opened his eyes and turned his tired face up to me so that the dawn threw a pale light upon it through the doorway, and said, for all the world just like a frightened child:

"My life, old man—it's my life I owe you. But it's all over now anyhow. They've found a victim in our place!"

Then he dropped back upon his blankets and went to sleep literally under my eyes. He simply collapsed, and began to snore again as healthily as though nothing had happened and he had never tried to offer his own life as a sacrifice by drowning. And when the sunlight woke him three hours later—hours of ceaseless vigil for me—it became so clear to me that he remembered absolutely nothing of what he had attempted to do, that I deemed it wise to hold my peace and ask no dangerous questions.

He woke naturally and easily, as I have said, when the sun was already high in a windless hot sky, and he at once got up and set about the preparation of the fire for breakfast. I followed him anxiously at bathing, but he did not attempt to plunge in, merely dipping his head and making some remark about the extra coldness of the water.

"River's falling at last," he said, "and I'm glad of it."

"The humming has stopped too," I said.

He looked up at me quietly with his normal expression. Evidently he remembered everything except his own attempt at suicide.

"Everything has stopped," he said, "because—"

He hesitated. But I knew some reference to that remark he had made just before he fainted was in his mind, and I was determined to know it.

"Because 'They've found another victim'?" I said, forcing a little laugh.

"Exactly," he answered, "exactly! I feel as positive of it as though—as though—I feel quite safe again, I mean," he finished.

He began to look curiously about him. The sunlight lay in hot patches on the sand. There was no wind. The willows were motionless. He slowly rose to feet.

"Come," he said; "I think if we look, we shall find it."

He started off on a run, and I followed him. He kept to the banks, poking with a stick among the sandy bays and caves and little back-waters, myself always close on his heels.

"Ah!" he exclaimed presently, "ah!"

The tone of his voice somehow brought back to me a vivid sense of the horror of the last twenty-four hours, and I hurried up to join him. He was pointing with his stick at a large black object that lay half in the water and half on the sand. It appeared to be caught by some twisted willow roots so that the river could not sweep it away. A few hours before the spot must have been under water.

"See," he said quietly, "the victim that made our escape possible!"

And when I peered across his shoulder I saw that his stick rested on the body of a man. He turned it over. It was the corpse of a peasant, and the face was hidden in the sand. Clearly the man had been drowned but a few hours before, and his body must have been swept down upon our island somewhere about the hour of the dawn—*at the very time the fit had passed.*

"We must give it a decent burial, you know."

"I suppose so," I replied. I shuddered a little in spite of myself, for there was something about the appearance of that poor drowned man that turned me cold.

The Swede glanced up sharply at me, an undecipherable expression on his face, and began clambering down the bank. I followed him more leisurely. The current, I noticed, had torn away much of the clothing from the body, so that the neck and part of the chest lay bare.

Half-way down the bank my companion suddenly stopped and held up his hand in warning; but either my foot slipped, or I had gained too much momentum to bring myself quickly to a halt, for I bumped into him and sent him forward with a sort of leap to save himself. We tumbled together on to the hard sand so that our feet splashed into the water. And, before anything could be done, we had collided a little heavily against the corpse.

The Swede uttered a sharp cry. And I sprang back as if I had been shot.

At the moment we touched the body there rose from its surface the loud sound of humming—the sound of several hummings—which passed with a vast commotion as of winged things in the air about us and disappeared upwards into the sky, growing fainter and fainter till they finally ceased in the distance. It was exactly as though we had disturbed some living yet invisible creatures at work.

My companion clutched me, and I think I clutched him, but before either of us had time properly to recover from the unexpected shock, we saw that a movement of the current was turning the corpse round so that it became released from the grip of the willow roots. A moment later it had turned completely over, the dead face uppermost, staring at the sky. It lay on the edge of the main stream. In another moment it would be swept away.

The Swede started to save it, shouting again something I did not catch about a "proper burial"—and then abruptly dropped upon his knees on the sand and covered his eyes with his hands. I was beside him in an instant.

I saw what he had seen.

For just as the body swung round to the current the face and the exposed chest turned full towards us, and showed plainly how the skin and flesh were indented with small hollows, beautifully formed, and exactly similar in shape and kind to the sand-funnels that we had found all over the island.

"Their mark!" I heard my companion mutter under his breath. "Their awful mark!"

And when I turned my eyes again from his ghastly face to the river, the current had done its work, and the body had been swept away into midstream and was already beyond our reach and almost out of sight, turning over and over on the waves like an otter.

The Insanity of Jones

A Study in Reincarnation

I

Adventures come to the adventurous, and mysterious things fall in the way of those who, with wonder and imagination, are on the watch for them; but the majority of people go past the doors that are half ajar, thinking them closed, and fail to notice the faint stirrings of the great curtain that hangs ever in the form of appearances between them and the world of causes behind.

For only to the few whose inner senses have been quickened, perchance by some strange suffering in the depths, or by a natural temperament bequeathed from a remote past, comes the knowledge, not too welcome, that this greater world lies ever at their elbow, and that any moment a chance combination of moods and forces may invite them to cross the shifting frontier.

Some, however, are born with this awful certainty in their hearts, and are called to no apprenticeship, and to this select company Jones undoubtedly belonged.

All his life he had realised that his senses brought to him merely a more or less interesting set of sham appearances; that space, as men measure it, was utterly misleading; that time, as the clock ticked it in a succession of minutes, was arbitrary nonsense; and, in fact, that all his sensory perceptions were but a clumsy representation of *real* things behind the curtain—things he was for ever trying to get at, and that sometimes he actually did get at.

He had always been tremblingly aware that he stood on the borderland of another region, a region where time and space were merely forms of thought, where ancient memories lay open to the sight, and where the forces behind each human life stood plainly revealed and he could see the hidden springs at the very heart of the world. Moreover, the fact that he was a clerk in a fire insurance office, and did his work with strict attention, never allowed him to forget for one moment that, just beyond the dingy brick walls where the hundred men scribbled with pointed pens beneath the electric lamps, there existed this glorious region where the important part of himself dwelt and moved and had its being. For in this region he pictured himself playing the part of a spectator to his ordinary workaday life, watching, like a king, the stream of events, but untouched in his own soul by the dirt, the noise, and the vulgar commotion of the outer world.

And this was no poetic dream merely. Jones was not playing prettily with idealism to amuse himself. It was a living, working belief. So convinced was he that the external world was the result of a vast deception practised upon him by the gross senses, that when he stared at a great building like St. Paul's he felt it would not very much surprise him to see it suddenly quiver like a shape of jelly and then melt utterly away, while in its place stood all at once revealed the mass of colour, or the great intricate vibrations, or the splendid sound—the spiritual idea—which it represented in stone.

For something in this way it was that his mind worked.

Yet, to all appearances, and in the satisfaction of all business claims, Jones was normal and unenterprising. He felt nothing but contempt for the wave of modern psychism. He hardly knew the meaning of such words as "clairvoyance" and "clairaudience." He had never felt the least desire to join the Theosophical Society and to speculate in theories of astral-plane life, or elementals. He attended no meetings of the Psychical Research Society, and knew no anxiety as to whether his "aura" was black or blue; nor was he conscious of the slightest wish to mix in with the revival of cheap occultism which proves so attractive to weak minds of mystical tendencies and unleashed imaginations.

There were certain things he *knew,* but none he cared to argue about; and he shrank instinctively from attempting to put names to the contents of this other region, knowing well that such names could only limit and define things that, according to any standards in use in the ordinary world, were simply undefinable and illusive.

So that, although this was the way his mind worked, there was clearly a very strong leaven of common sense in Jones. In a word, the man the world and the office knew as Jones *was* Jones. The name summed him up and labelled him correctly—John Enderby Jones.

Among the things that he *knew*, and therefore never cared to speak or speculate about, one was that he plainly saw himself as the inheritor of a long series of past lives, the net result of painful evolution, always as himself, of course, but in numerous different bodies each determined by the behaviour of the preceding one. The present John Jones was the last result to date of all the previous thinking, feeling, and doing of John Jones in earlier bodies and in other centuries. He pretended to no details, nor claimed distinguished ancestry, for he realised his past must have been utterly commonplace and insignificant to have produced his present; but he was just as sure he had been at this weary game for ages as that he breathed, and it never occurred to him to argue, to doubt, or to ask questions. And one result of this belief was that his thoughts dwelt upon the past rather than upon the future; that he read much history, and felt specially drawn to certain periods whose spirit he understood instinctively as though he had lived in them; and that he found all religions uninteresting because, almost without exception, they start from the present and speculate ahead to what men shall become, instead of looking back and speculating why men have got here as they are.

In the insurance office he did his work exceedingly well, but without much personal ambition. Men and women he regarded as the impersonal instruments for inflicting upon him the pain or pleasure he had earned by his past workings, for chance had no place in his scheme of things at all; and while he recognised that the practical work could not get along unless every man did his work thoroughly and conscientiously, he took no interest in the accumulation of fame or money for himself, and simply, therefore, did his plain duty, with indifference as to results.

In common with others who lead a strictly impersonal life, he possessed the quality of utter bravery, and was always ready to face any combination of circumstances, no matter how terrible, because he saw in them the just working-out of past causes he had himself set in motion which could not be dodged or modified. And whereas the majority of people had little meaning for him, either by way of attraction or repulsion, the moment he met some one with whom he felt his past had been *vitally* interwoven his whole inner being leapt up instantly and shouted the fact in his face, and he regulated his life with the utmost skill and caution, like a sentry on watch for an enemy whose feet could already be heard approaching.

Thus, while the great majority of men and women left him uninfluenced—since he regarded them as so many souls merely passing with him along the great stream of evolution—there were, here and there, individuals with whom he recognised that his smallest intercourse was of the gravest importance. These were persons with whom he knew in every fibre of his being he had accounts to settle, pleasant or otherwise, arising out of dealings in past lives; and into his relations with these few, therefore, he concentrated as it were the efforts that most people spread over their intercourse with a far greater number. By what means he picked out these few individuals only those conversant with the startling processes of the subconscious memory may say, but the point was that Jones believed the main purpose, if not quite the entire purpose, of his present incarnation lay in his faithful and thorough settling of these accounts, and that if he sought to evade the least detail of such settling, no matter how unpleasant, he would have lived in vain, and would return to his next incarnation with this added duty to perform. For according to his beliefs there was no Chance, and could be no ultimate shirking, and to avoid a problem was merely to waste time and lose opportunities for development.

And there was one individual with whom Jones had long understood clearly he had a very large account to settle, and towards the accomplishment of which all the main currents of his being seemed to bear him with unswerving purpose. For, when he first entered the insurance office as a junior clerk ten years before, and through a glass door had caught sight of this man seated in an inner room, one of his sudden overwhelming flashes of intuitive memory had burst up into him from the depths, and he had seen, as in a flame of blinding light, a symbolical picture of the future rising out of a dreadful past, and he had, without any act of definite volition, marked down this man for a real account to be settled.

"With *that* man I shall have much to do," he said to himself, as he noted the big face look up and meet his eye through the glass. "There is something I cannot shirk—a vital relation out of the past of both of us."

And he went to his desk trembling a little, and with shaking knees, as though the memory of some terrible pain had suddenly laid its icy hand upon his heart and touched the scar of a great horror. It was a moment of genuine terror when their eyes had met through the glass door, and he was conscious of an inward shrinking and loathing that seized upon him with great violence and convinced him in a single second that the settling of this account would be almost, perhaps, more than he could manage.

The vision passed as swiftly as it came, dropping back again into the submerged region of his consciousness; but he never forgot it, and the whole of his life thereafter became a sort of natural though undeliberate preparation for the fulfilment of the great duty when the time should be ripe.

In those days—ten years ago—this man was the Assistant Manager, but had since been promoted as Manager to one of the company's local branches; and soon afterwards Jones had likewise found himself transferred to this same branch. A little later, again, the branch at Liverpool, one of the most important, had been in peril owing to mismanagement and defalcation, and the man had gone to take charge of it, and again, by mere chance apparently, Jones had been promoted to the same place. And this pursuit of the Assistant Manager had continued for several years, often, too, in the most curious fashion; and though Jones had never exchanged a single word with him, or been so much as noticed indeed by the great man, the clerk understood perfectly well that these moves in the game were all part of a definite purpose. Never for one moment did he doubt that the Invisibles behind the veil were slowly and surely arranging the details of it all so as to lead up suitably to the climax demanded by justice, a climax in which himself and the Manager would play the leading *rôles*.

"It is inevitable," he said to himself, "and I feel it may be terrible; but when the moment comes I shall be ready, and I pray God that I may face it properly and act like a man."

Moreover, as the years passed, and nothing happened, he felt the horror closing in upon him with steady increase, for the fact was Jones hated and loathed the Manager with an intensity of feeling he had never before experienced towards any human being. He shrank from his presence, and from the glance of his eyes, as though he re-membered to have suffered nameless cruelties at his hands; and he slowly began to realise, moreover, that the matter to be settled be-tween them was one of very ancient standing, and that the nature of the settlement was a discharge of accumulated punishment which would probably be very dreadful in the manner of its fulfilment.

When, therefore, the chief cashier one day informed him that the man was to be in London again—this time as General Manager of the head office—and said that he was charged to find a private secre-tary for him from among the best clerks, and further intimated that the selection had fallen upon himself, Jones accepted the promotion quietly, fatalistically, yet with a degree of inward loathing hardly to be described. For he saw in this merely another move in the evolution of the inevitable Nemesis which he simply dared not seek to frustrate by any personal consideration; and at the same time he was conscious of a certain feeling of relief that the suspense of waiting might soon be mitigated. A secret sense of satisfaction, therefore, accompanied the unpleasant change, and Jones was able to hold himself perfectly well in hand when it was carried into effect and he was formally in-troduced as private secretary to the General Manager.

Now the Manager was a large, fat man, with a very red face and bags beneath his eyes. Being short-sighted, he wore glasses that seemed to magnify his eyes, which were always a little bloodshot. In hot weather a sort of thin slime covered his cheeks, for he perspired easily. His head was almost entirely bald, and over his turn-down col-lar his great neck folded in two distinct reddish collops of flesh. His hands were big and his fingers almost massive in thickness.

He was an excellent business man, of sane judgment and firm will, without enough imagination to confuse his course of action by showing him possible alternatives; and his integrity and ability caused him to be held in universal respect by the world of business and fi-nance. In the important regions of a man's character, however, and at heart, he was coarse, brutal almost to savagery, without consideration for others, and as a result often cruelly unjust to his helpless subordinates.

In moments of temper, which were not infrequent, his face turned a dull purple, while the top of his bald head shone by contrast like white marble, and the bags under his eyes swelled till it seemed they would presently explode with a pop. And at these times he presented a distinctly repulsive appearance.

But to a private secretary like Jones, who did his duty regardless of whether his employer was beast or angel, and whose mainspring was principle and not emotion, this made little difference. Within the narrow limits in which any one *could* satisfy such a man, he pleased the General Manager; and more than once his piercing intuitive faculty, amounting almost to clairvoyance, assisted the chief in a fashion that served to bring the two closer together than might otherwise have been the case, and caused the man to respect in his assistant a power of which he possessed not even the germ himself. It was a curious relationship that grew up between the two, and the cashier, who enjoyed the credit of having made the selection, profited by it indirectly as much as any one else.

So for some time the work of the office continued normally and very prosperously. John Enderby Jones received a good salary, and in the outward appearance of the two chief characters in this history there was little change noticeable, except that the Manager grew fatter and redder, and the secretary observed that his own hair was beginning to show rather greyish at the temples.

There were, however, two changes in progress, and they both had to do with Jones, and are important to mention.

One was that he began to dream evilly. In the region of deep sleep, where the possibility of significant dreaming first develops itself, he was tormented more and more with vivid scenes and pictures in which a tall thin man, dark and sinister of countenance, and with bad eyes, was closely associated with himself. Only the setting was that of a past age, with costumes of centuries gone by, and the scenes had to do with dreadful cruelties that could not belong to modern life as he knew it.

The other change was also significant, but is not so easy to describe, for he had in fact become aware that some new portion of himself, hitherto unawakened, had stirred slowly into life out of the very depths of his consciousness. This new part of himself amounted almost to another personality, and he never observed its least mani-festation without a strange thrill at his heart.

For he understood that it had begun to *watch* the Manager!

II

It was the habit of Jones, since he was compelled to work among conditions that were utterly distasteful, to withdraw his mind wholly from business once the day was over. During office hours he kept the strictest possible watch upon himself, and turned the key on all inner dreams, lest any sudden uprush from the deeps should interfere with his duty. But, once the working day was over, the gates flew open, and he began to enjoy himself.

He read no modern books on the subjects that interested him, and, as already said, he followed no course of training, nor belonged to any society that dabbled with half-told mysteries; but, once re-leased from the office desk in the Manager's room, he simply and naturally entered the other region, because he was an old inhabitant, a rightful denizen, and because he belonged there. It was, in fact, re-ally a case of dual personality; and a carefully drawn agreement exist-ed between Jones-of-the-fire-insurance-office and Jones-of-the-mysteries, by the terms of which, under heavy penalties, neither re-gion claimed him out of hours.

For the moment he reached his rooms under the roof in Bloomsbury, and had changed his city coat to another, the iron doors of the office clanged far behind him, and in front, before his very eyes, rolled up the beautiful gates of ivory, and he entered into the places of flowers and singing and wonderful veiled forms. Sometimes he quite lost touch with the outer world, forgetting to eat his dinner or go to bed, and lay in a state of trance, his consciousness working far out of the body. And on other occasions he walked the streets on air, half-way between the two regions, unable to distinguish between incarnate and discarnate forms, and not very far, probably, beyond the strata where poets, saints, and the greatest artists have moved and thought and found their inspiration. But this was only when some insistent bodily claim prevented his full release, and more often than not he was entirely independent of his physical portion and free of the real region, without let or hindrance.

One evening he reached home utterly exhausted after the burden of the day's work. The Manager had been more than usually brutal, unjust, ill-tempered, and Jones had been almost persuaded out of his settled policy of contempt into answering back. Everything seemed to have gone amiss, and the man's coarse, underbred nature had been in the ascendant all day long: he had thumped the desk with his great fists, abused, found fault unreasonably, uttered outrageous things, and behaved generally as he actually was—beneath the thin veneer of acquired business varnish. He had done and said everything to wound all that was woundable in an ordinary secretary, and though Jones fortunately dwelt in a region from which he looked down upon such a man as he might look down on the blundering of a savage animal, the strain had nevertheless told severely upon him, and he reached home wondering for the first time in his life whether there was perhaps a point beyond which he would be unable to restrain himself any longer.

For something out of the usual had happened. At the close of a passage of great stress between the two, every nerve in the secretary's body tingling from undeserved abuse, the Manager had suddenly turned full upon him, in the corner of the private room where the safes stood, in such a way that the glare of his red eyes, magnified by the glasses, looked straight into his own. And at this very second that other personality in Jones—the one that was ever *watching*—rose up swiftly from the deeps within and held a mirror to his face.

A moment of flame and vision rushed over him, and for one single second—one merciless second of clear sight—he saw the Manager as the tall dark man of his evil dreams, and the knowledge that he had suffered at his hands some awful injury in the past crashed through his mind like the report of a cannon.

It all flashed upon him and was gone, changing him from fire to ice, and then back again to fire; and he left the office with the certain conviction in his heart that the time for his final settlement with the man, the time for the inevitable retribution, was at last drawing very near.

According to his invariable custom, however, he succeeded in putting the memory of all this unpleasantness out of his mind with the changing of his office coat, and after dozing a little in his leather chair before the fire, he started out as usual for dinner in the Soho French restaurant, and began to dream himself away into the region of flowers and singing, and to commune with the Invisibles that were the very sources of his real life and being.

For it was in this way that his mind worked, and the habits of years had crystallised into rigid lines along which it was now necessary and inevitable for him to act.

At the door of the little restaurant he stopped short, a half-remembered appointment in his mind. He had made an engagement with some one, but where, or with whom, had entirely slipped his memory. He thought it was for dinner, or else to meet just after dinner, and for a second it came back to him that it had something to do with the office, but, whatever it was, he was quite unable to recall it, and a reference to his pocket engagement book showed only a blank page. Evidently he had even omitted to enter it; and after standing a moment vainly trying to recall either the time, place, or person, he went in and sat down.

But though the details had escaped him, his subconscious memory seemed to know all about it, for he experienced a sudden sinking of the heart, accompanied by a sense of foreboding anticipation, and felt that beneath his exhaustion there lay a centre of tremendous excitement. The emotion caused by the engagement was at work, and would presently cause the actual details of the appointment to reappear.

Inside the restaurant the feeling increased, instead of passing: some one was waiting for him somewhere—some one whom he had definitely arranged to meet. He was expected by a person that very night and just about that very time. But by whom? Where? A curious inner trembling came over him, and he made a strong effort to hold himself in hand and to be ready for anything that might come.

And then suddenly came the knowledge that the place of appointment was this very restaurant, and, further, that the person he had promised to meet was already here, waiting somewhere quite close beside him.

He looked up nervously and began to examine the faces round

him. The majority of the diners were Frenchmen, chattering loudly with much gesticulation and laughter; and there was a fair sprinkling of clerks like himself who came because the prices were low and the food good, but there was no single face that he recognised until his glance fell upon the occupant of the corner seat opposite, generally filled by himself.

"There's the man who's waiting for me!" thought Jones instantly.

He knew it at once. The man, he saw, was sitting well back into the corner, with a thick overcoat buttoned tightly up to the chin. His skin was very white, and a heavy black beard grew far up over his cheeks. At first the secretary took him for a stranger, but when he looked up and their eyes met, a sense of familiarity flashed across him, and for a second or two Jones imagined he was staring at a man he had known years before. For, barring the beard, it was the face of an elderly clerk who had occupied the next desk to his own when he first entered the service of the insurance company, and had shown him the most painstaking kindness and sympathy in the early difficulties of his work. But a moment later the illusion passed, for he remembered that Thorpe had been dead at least five years. The similarity of the eyes was obviously a mere suggestive trick of memory.

The two men stared at one another for several seconds, and then Jones began to act *instinctively,* and because he had to. He crossed over and took the vacant seat at the other's table, facing him; for he felt it was somehow imperative to explain why he was late, and how it was he had almost forgotten the engagement altogether.

No honest excuse, however, came to his assistance, though his mind had begun to work furiously.

"Yes, you *are* late," said the man quietly, before he could find a single word to utter. "But it doesn't matter. Also, you had forgotten the appointment, but that makes no difference either."

"I knew—that there was an engagement," Jones stammered, passing his hand over his forehead; "but somehow—"

"You will recall it presently," continued the other in a gentle voice, and smiling a little. "It was in deep sleep last night we arranged this, and the unpleasant occurrences of to-day have for the moment obliterated it."

A faint memory stirred within him as the man spoke, and a grove

of trees with moving forms hovered before his eyes and then vanished again, while for an instant the stranger seemed to be capable of
self-distortion and to have assumed vast proportions, with wonderful
flaming eyes.

"Oh!" he gasped. "It was there—in the other region?"

"Of course," said the other, with a smile that illumined his whole
face. "You will remember presently, all in good time, and meanwhile
you have no cause to feel afraid."

There was a wonderful soothing quality in the man's voice, like
the whispering of a great wind, and the clerk felt calmer at once.
They sat a little while longer, but he could not remember that they
talked much or ate anything. He only recalled afterwards that the
head waiter came up and whispered something in his ear, and that he
glanced round and saw the other people were looking at him curiously, some of them laughing, and that his companion then got up and
led the way out of the restaurant.

They walked hurriedly through the streets, neither of them
speaking; and Jones was so intent upon getting back the whole history of the affair from the region of deep sleep, that he barely noticed
the way they took. Yet it was clear he knew where they were bound
for just as well as his companion, for he crossed the streets often
ahead of him, diving down alleys without hesitation, and the other
followed always without correction.

The pavements were very full, and the usual night crowds of
London were surging to and fro in the glare of the shop lights, but
somehow no one impeded their rapid movements, and they seemed
to pass through the people as if they were smoke. And, as they went,
the pedestrians and traffic grew less and less, and they soon passed
the Mansion House and the deserted space in front of the Royal Exchange, and so on down Fenchurch Street and within sight of the
Tower of London, rising dim and shadowy in the smoky air.

Jones remembered all this perfectly well, and thought it was his
intense preoccupation that made the distance seem so short. But it
was when the Tower was left behind and they turned northwards
that he began to notice how altered everything was, and saw that they
were in a neighbourhood where houses were suddenly scarce, and
lanes and fields beginning, and that their only light was the stars

overhead. And, as the deeper consciousness more and more asserted itself to the exclusion of the surface happenings of his mere body during the day, the sense of exhaustion vanished, and he realised that he was moving somewhere in the region of causes behind the veil, beyond the gross deceptions of the senses, and released from the clumsy spell of space and time.

Without great surprise, therefore, he turned and saw that his companion had altered, and shed his overcoat and black hat, and was moving beside him absolutely *without sound.* For a brief second he saw him, tall as a tree, extending through space like a great shadow, misty and wavering of outline, followed by a sound like wings in the darkness; but, when he stopped, fear clutching at his heart, the other resumed his former proportions, and Jones could plainly see his normal outline against the green field behind.

Then the secretary saw him fumbling at his neck, and at the same moment the black beard came away from the face in his hand.

"Then you *are* Thorpe!" he gasped, yet somehow without overwhelming surprise.

They stood facing one another in the lonely lane, trees meeting overhead and hiding the stars, and a sound of mournful sighing among the branches.

"I am Thorpe," was the answer in a voice that almost seemed part of the wind. "And I have come out of our far past to help you, for my debt to you is large, and in this life I had but small opportunity to repay."

Jones thought quickly of the man's kindness to him in the office, and a great wave of feeling surged through him as he began to remember dimly the friend by whose side he had already climbed, perhaps through vast ages of his soul's evolution.

"To help me *now?*" he whispered.

"You will understand me when you enter into your real memory and recall how great a debt I have to pay for old faithful kindnesses of long ago," sighed the other in a voice like falling wind.

"Between us, though, there can be no question of *debt,*" Jones heard himself saying, and remembered the reply that floated to him on the air and the smile that lightened for a moment the stern eyes facing him.

"Not of debt, indeed, but of privilege."

Jones felt his heart leap out towards this man, this old friend, tried by centuries and still faithful. He made a movement to seize his hand. But the other shifted like a thing of mist, and for a moment the clerk's head swam and his eyes seemed to fail.

"Then you are *dead?*" he said under his breath with a slight shiver.

"Five years ago I left the body you knew," replied Thorpe. "I tried to help you then instinctively, not fully recognising you. But now I can accomplish far more."

With an awful sense of foreboding and dread in his heart, the secretary was beginning to understand.

"It has to do with—with—?"

"Your past dealings with the Manager," came the answer, as the wind rose louder among the branches overhead and carried off the remainder of the sentence into the air.

Jones's memory, which was just beginning to stir among the deepest layers of all, shut down suddenly with a snap, and he followed his companion over fields and down sweet-smelling lanes where the air was fragrant and cool, till they came to a large house, standing gaunt and lonely in the shadows at the edge of a wood. It was wrapped in utter stillness, with windows heavily draped in black, and the clerk, as he looked, felt such an overpowering wave of sadness invade him that his eyes began to burn and smart, and he was conscious of a desire to shed tears.

The key made a harsh noise as it turned in the lock, and when the door swung open into a lofty hall they heard a confused sound of rustling and whispering, as of a great throng of people pressing forward to meet them. The air seemed full of swaying movement, and Jones was certain he saw hands held aloft and dim faces claiming recognition, while in his heart, already oppressed by the approaching burden of vast accumulated memories, he was aware of the *uncoiling of something* that had been asleep for ages.

As they advanced he heard the doors close with a muffled thunder behind them, and saw that the shadows seemed to retreat and shrink away towards the interior of the house, carrying the hands and faces with them. He heard the wind singing round the walls and over the roof, and its wailing voice mingled with the sound of deep, collective breathing that filled the house like the murmur of a sea; and as they walked up the broad staircase and through the vaulted rooms, where pillars rose like the stems of trees, he knew that the building was crowded, row upon row, with the thronging memories of his own long past.

"This is the *House of the Past*," whispered Thorpe beside him, as they moved silently from room to room; "the house of *your* past. It is full from cellar to roof with the memories of what you have done, thought, and felt from the earliest stages of your evolution until now.

"The house climbs up almost to the clouds, and stretches back into the heart of the wood you saw outside, but the remoter halls are filled with the ghosts of ages ago too many to count, and even if we were able to waken them you could not remember them now. Some day, though, they will come and claim you, and you must know them, and answer their questions, for they can never rest till they have exhausted themselves again through you, and justice has been perfectly worked out.

"But now follow me closely, and you shall see the particular memory for which I am permitted to be your guide, so that you may know and understand a great force in your present life, and may use the sword of justice, or rise to the level of a great forgiveness, according to your degree of power."

Icy thrills ran through the trembling clerk, and as he walked slowly beside his companion he heard from the vaults below, as well as from more distant regions of the vast building, the stirring and sighing of the serried ranks of sleepers, sounding in the still air like a chord swept from unseen strings stretched somewhere among the very foundations of the house.

Stealthily, picking their way among the great pillars, they moved up the sweeping staircase and through several dark corridors and halls, and presently stopped outside a small door in an archway where the shadows were very deep.

"Remain close by my side, and remember to utter no cry," whispered the voice of his guide, and as the clerk turned to reply he saw his face was stern to whiteness and even shone a little in the darkness.

The room they entered seemed at first to be pitchy black, but

gradually the secretary perceived a faint reddish glow against the farther end, and thought he saw figures moving silently to and fro.

"Now watch!" whispered Thorpe, as they pressed close to the
wall near the door and waited. "But remember to keep absolute silence. It is a torture scene."

Jones felt utterly afraid, and would have turned to fly if he dared,
for an indescribable terror seized him and his knees shook; but some
power that made escape impossible held him remorselessly there, and
with eyes glued on the spots of light he crouched against the wall and
waited.

The figures began to move more swiftly, each in its own dim
light that shed no radiance beyond itself, and he heard a soft clanking
of chains and the voice of a man groaning in pain. Then came the
sound of a door closing, and thereafter Jones saw but one figure, the
figure of an old man, naked entirely, and fastened with chains to an
iron framework on the floor. His memory gave a sudden leap of fear
as he looked, for the features and white beard were familiar, and he
recalled them as though of yesterday.

The other figures had disappeared, and the old man became the
centre of the terrible picture. Slowly, with ghastly groans, as the heat
below him increased into a steady glow, the aged body rose in a curve
of agony, resting on the iron frame only where the chains held wrists
and ankles fast. Cries and gasps filled the air, and Jones felt exactly as
though they came from his own throat, and as if the chains were burning into his own wrists and ankles, and the heat scorching the skin
and flesh upon his own back. He began to writhe and twist himself.

"Spain!" whispered the voice at his side, "and four hundred years
ago."

"And the purpose?" gasped the perspiring clerk, though he knew
quite well what the answer must be.

"To extort the name of a friend, to his death and betrayal," came
the reply through the darkness.

A sliding panel opened with a little rattle in the wall immediately
above the rack, and a face, framed in the same red glow, appeared
and looked down upon the dying victim. Jones was only just able to
choke a scream, for he recognised the tall dark man of his dreams.
With horrible, gloating eyes he gazed down upon the writhing form

of the old man, and his lips moved as in speaking, though no words were actually audible.

"He asks again for the name," explained the other, as the clerk struggled with the intense hatred and loathing that threatened every moment to result in screams and action. His ankles and wrists pained him so that he could scarcely keep still, but a merciless power held him to the scene.

He saw the old man, with a fierce cry, raise his tortured head and spit up into the face at the panel, and then the shutter slid back again, and a moment later the increased glow beneath the body, accompanied by awful writhing, told of the application of further heat. There came the odour of burning flesh; the white beard curled and burned to a crisp; the body fell back limp upon the red-hot iron, and then shot up again in fresh agony; cry after cry, the most awful in the world, rang out with deadened sound between the four walls; and again the panel slid back creaking, and revealed the dreadful face of the torturer.

Again the name was asked for, and again it was refused; and this time, after the closing of the panel, a door opened, and the tall thin man with the evil face came slowly into the chamber. His features were savage with rage and disappointment, and in the dull red glow that fell upon them he looked like a very prince of devils. In his hand he held a pointed iron at white heat.

"Now the murder!" came from Thorpe in a whisper that sounded as if it was outside the building and far away.

Jones knew quite well what was coming, but was unable even to close his eyes. He felt all the fearful pains himself just as though he were actually the sufferer; but now, as he stared, he felt something more besides; and when the tall man deliberately approached the rack and plunged the heated iron first into one eye and then into the other, he heard the faint fizzing of it, and felt his own eyes burst in frightful pain from his head. At the same moment, unable longer to control himself, he uttered a wild shriek and dashed forward to seize the torturer and tear him to a thousand pieces.

Instantly, in a flash, the entire scene vanished; darkness rushed in to fill the room, and he felt himself lifted off his feet by some force like a great wind and borne swiftly away into space.

When he recovered his senses he was standing just outside the house and the figure of Thorpe was beside him in the gloom. The great doors were in the act of closing behind him, but before they shut he fancied he caught a glimpse of an immense veiled figure standing upon the threshold, with flaming eyes, and in his hand a bright weapon like a shining sword of fire.

"Come quickly now—all is over!" Thorpe whispered.

"And the dark man—?" gasped the clerk, as he moved swiftly by the other's side.

"In this present life is the Manager of the company."

"And the victim?"

"Was yourself!"

"And the friend he—*I* refused to betray?"

"I was that friend," answered Thorpe, his voice with every moment sounding more and more like the cry of the wind. "You gave your life in agony to save mine."

"And again, in this life, we have all three been together?"

"Yes. Such forces are not soon or easily exhausted, and justice is not satisfied till all have reaped what they sowed."

Jones had an odd feeling that he was slipping away into some other state of consciousness. Thorpe began to seem unreal. Presently he would be unable to ask more questions. He felt utterly sick and faint with it all, and his strength was ebbing.

"Oh, quick!" he cried, "now tell me more. Why did I see this? What must I do?"

The wind swept across the field on their right and entered the wood beyond with a great roar, and the air round him seemed filled with voices and the rushing of hurried movement.

"To the ends of justice," answered the other, as though speaking out of the centre of the wind and from a distance, "which sometimes is entrusted to the hands of those who suffered and were strong. One wrong cannot be put right by another wrong, but your life has been so worthy that the opportunity is given to—"

The voice grew fainter and fainter, already it was far overhead with the rushing wind.

"You may punish or—" Here Jones lost sight of Thorpe's figure altogether, for he seemed to have vanished and melted away into the wood behind him. His voice sounded far across the trees, very weak, and ever rising.

"Or if you can rise to the level of a great forgiveness—"

The voice became inaudible. . . . The wind came crying out of the wood again.

Jones shivered and stared about him. He shook himself violently and rubbed his eyes. The room was dark, the fire was out; he felt cold and stiff. He got up out of his armchair, still trembling, and lit the gas. Outside the wind was howling, and when he looked at his watch he saw that it was very late and he must go to bed.

He had not even changed his office coat; he must have fallen asleep in the chair as soon as he came in, and he had slept for several hours. Certainly he had eaten no dinner, for he felt ravenous.

III

Next day, and for several weeks thereafter, the business of the office went on as usual, and Jones did his work well and behaved outwardly with perfect propriety. No more visions troubled him, and his relations with the Manager became, if anything, somewhat smoother and easier.

True, the man *looked* a little different, because the clerk kept seeing him with his inner and outer eye promiscuously, so that one moment he was broad and red-faced, and the next he was tall, thin, and dark, enveloped, as it were, in a sort of black atmosphere tinged with red. While at times a confusion of the two sights took place, and Jones saw the two faces mingled in a composite countenance that was very horrible indeed to contemplate. But, beyond this occasional change in the outward appearance of the Manager, there was nothing that the secretary noticed as the result of his vision, and business went on more or less as before, and perhaps even with a little less friction.

But in the rooms under the roof in Bloomsbury it was different, for there it was perfectly clear to Jones that Thorpe had come to take up his abode with him. He never saw him, but he knew all the time he was there. Every night on returning from his work he was greeted

by the well-known whisper, "Be ready when I give the sign!" and often in the night he woke up suddenly out of deep sleep and was
aware that Thorpe had that minute moved away from his bed and
was standing waiting and watching somewhere in the darkness of the
room. Often he followed him down the stairs, though the dim gas jet
on the landings never revealed his outline; and sometimes he did not
come into the room at all, but hovered outside the window, peering
through the dirty panes, or sending his whisper into the chamber in
the whistling of the wind.

For Thorpe had come to stay, and Jones knew that he would not
get rid of him until he had fulfilled the ends of justice and accomplished the purpose for which he was waiting.

Meanwhile, as the days passed, he went through a tremendous
struggle with himself, and came to the perfectly honest decision that
the "level of a great forgiveness" was impossible for him, and that he
must therefore accept the alternative and use the secret knowledge
placed in his hands—and execute justice. And once this decision was
arrived at, he noticed that Thorpe no longer left him alone during the
day as before, but now accompanied him to the office and stayed
more or less at his side all through business hours as well. His whisper made itself heard in the streets and in the train, and even in the
Manager's room where he worked; sometimes warning, sometimes
urging, but never for a moment suggesting the abandonment of the
main purpose, and more than once so plainly audible that the clerk
felt certain others must have heard it as well as himself.

The obsession was complete. He felt he was always under
Thorpe's eye day and night, and he knew he must acquit himself like
a man when the moment came, or prove a failure in his own sight as
well in the sight of the other.

And now that his mind was made up, nothing could prevent the
carrying out of the sentence. He bought a pistol, and spent his Saturday afternoons practising at a target in lonely places along the Essex
shore, marking out in the sand the exact measurements of the Manager's room. Sundays he occupied in like fashion, putting up at an inn
overnight for the purpose, spending the money that usually went into
the savings bank on travelling expenses and cartridges. Everything
was done very thoroughly, for there must be no possibility of failure;

and at the end of several weeks he had become so expert with his six-shooter that at a distance of 25 feet, which was the greatest length of the Manager's room, he could pick the inside out of a halfpenny nine times out of a dozen, and leave a clean, unbroken rim.

There was not the slightest desire to delay. He had thought the matter over from every point of view his mind could reach, and his purpose was inflexible. Indeed, he felt proud to think that he had been chosen as the instrument of justice in the infliction of so well-deserved and so terrible a punishment. Vengeance may have had some part in his decision, but he could not help that, for he still felt at times the hot chains burning his wrists and ankles with fierce agony through to the bone. He remembered the hideous pain of his slowly roasting back, and the point when he thought death *must* intervene to end his suffering, but instead new powers of endurance had surged up in him, and awful further stretches of pain had opened up, and unconsciousness seemed farther off than ever. Then at last the hot irons in his eyes. . . . It all came back to him, and caused him to break out in icy perspiration at the mere thought of it . . . the vile face at the panel . . . the expression of the dark face. . . . His fingers worked. His blood boiled. It was utterly impossible to keep the idea of vengeance altogether out of his mind.

Several times he was temporarily baulked of his prey. Odd things happened to stop him when he was on the point of action. The first day, for instance, the Manager fainted from the heat. Another time when he had decided to do the deed, the Manager did not come down to the office at all. And a third time, when his hand was actually in his hip pocket, he suddenly heard Thorpe's horrid whisper telling him to wait, and turning, he saw that the head cashier had entered the room noiselessly without his noticing it. Thorpe evidently knew what he was about, and did not intend to let the clerk bungle the matter.

He fancied, moreover, that the head cashier was watching him. He was always meeting him in unexpected corners and places, and the cashier never seemed to have an adequate excuse for being there. His movements seemed suddenly of particular interest to others in the office as well, for clerks were always being sent to ask him unnecessary questions, and there was apparently a general design to keep him under a sort of surveillance, so that he was never much alone with the Manager in the private room where they worked. And once the cashier had even gone so far as to suggest that he could take his holiday earlier than usual if he liked, as the work had been very arduous of late and the heat exceedingly trying.

He noticed, too, that he was sometimes followed by a certain individual in the streets, a careless-looking sort of man, who never came face to face with him, or actually ran into him, but who was always in his train or omnibus, and whose eye he often caught observing him over the top of his newspaper, and who on one occasion was even waiting at the door of his lodgings when he came out to dine.

There were other indications too, of various sorts, that led him to think something was at work to defeat his purpose, and that he must act at once before these hostile forces could prevent.

And so the end came very swiftly, and was thoroughly approved by Thorpe.

It was towards the close of July, and one of the hottest days London had ever known, for the City was like an oven, and the particles of dust seemed to burn the throats of the unfortunate toilers in street and office. The portly Manager, who suffered cruelly owing to his size, came down perspiring and gasping with the heat. He carried a light-coloured umbrella to protect his head.

"He'll want something more than that, though!" Jones laughed quietly to himself when he saw him enter.

The pistol was safely in his hip pocket, every one of its six chambers loaded.

The Manager saw the smile on his face, and gave him a long steady look as he sat down to his desk in the corner. A few minutes later he touched the bell for the head cashier—a single ring—and then asked Jones to fetch some papers from another safe in the room upstairs.

A deep inner trembling seized the secretary as he noticed these precautions, for he saw that the hostile forces were at work against him, and yet he felt he could delay no longer and must act that very morning, interference or no interference. However, he went obediently up in the lift to the next floor, and while fumbling with the combination of the safe, known only to himself, the cashier, and the

Manager, he again heard Thorpe's horrid whisper just behind him:

"You must do it to-day! You must do it to-day!"

He came down again with the papers, and found the Manager alone. The room was like a furnace, and a wave of dead heated air met him in the face as he went in. The moment he passed the doorway he realised that he had been the subject of conversation between the head cashier and his enemy. They had been discussing him. Perhaps an inkling of his secret had somehow got into their minds. They had been watching him for days past. They had become suspicious.

Clearly, he must act now, or let the opportunity slip by perhaps for ever. He heard Thorpe's voice in his ear, but this time it was no mere whisper, but a plain human voice, speaking out loud.

"Now!" it said. "Do it now!"

The room was empty. Only the Manager and himself were in it.

Jones turned from his desk where he had been standing, and locked the door leading into the main office. He saw the army of clerks scribbling in their shirt-sleeves, for the upper half of the door was of glass. He had perfect control of himself, and his heart was beating steadily.

The Manager, hearing the key turn in the lock, looked up sharply.

"What's that you're doing?" he asked quickly.

"Only locking the door, sir," replied the secretary in a quite even voice.

"Why? Who told you to—?"

"The voice of Justice, sir," replied Jones, looking steadily into the hated face.

The Manager looked black for a moment, and stared angrily across the room at him. Then suddenly his expression changed as he stared, and he tried to smile. It was meant to be a kind smile evidently, but it only succeeded in being frightened.

"That *is* a good idea in this weather," he said lightly, "but it would be much better to lock it on the *outside*, wouldn't it, Mr. Jones?"

"I think not, sir. You might escape me then. Now you can't."

Jones took his pistol out and pointed it at the other's face. Down the barrel he saw the features of the tall dark man, evil and sinister. Then the outline trembled a little and the face of the Manager slipped back into its place. It was white as death, and shining with perspiration.

"You tortured me to death four hundred years ago," said the clerk in the same steady voice, "and now the dispensers of justice have chosen me to punish you."

The Manager's face turned to flame, and then back to chalk again. He made a quick movement towards the telephone bell, stretching out a hand to reach it, but at the same moment Jones pulled the trigger and the wrist was shattered, splashing the wall behind with blood.

"That's *one* place where the chains burnt," he said quietly to himself. His hand was absolutely steady, and he felt that he was a hero.

The Manager was on his feet, with a scream of pain, supporting himself with his right hand on the desk in front of him, but Jones pressed the trigger again, and a bullet flew into the other wrist, so that the big man, deprived of support, fell forward with a crash onto the desk.

"You damned madman!" shrieked the Manager. "Drop that pistol!"

"That's *another* place," was all Jones said, still taking careful aim for another shot.

The big man, screaming and blundering, scrambled beneath the desk, making frantic efforts to hide, but the secretary took a step forward and fired two shots in quick succession into his projecting legs, hitting first one ankle and then the other, and smashing them horribly.

"Two more places where the chains burnt," he said, going a little nearer.

The Manager, still shrieking, tried desperately to squeeze his bulk behind the shelter of the opening beneath the desk, but he was far too large, and his bald head protruded through on the other side. Jones caught him by the scruff of his great neck and dragged him yelping out onto the carpet. He was covered with blood, and flopped helplessly upon his broken wrists.

"Be quick now!" cried the voice of Thorpe.

There was a tremendous commotion and banging at the door, and Jones gripped his pistol tightly. Something seemed to crash through his brain, clearing it for a second, so that he thought he saw beside him a great veiled figure, with drawn sword and flaming eyes, and sternly approving attitude.

"Remember the eyes! Remember the eyes!" hissed Thorpe in the air above him.

Jones felt like a god, with a god's power. Vengeance disappeared from his mind. He was acting impersonally as an instrument in the hands of the Invisibles who dispense justice and balance accounts. He bent down and put the barrel close into the other's face, smiling a little as he saw the childish efforts of the arms to cover his head. Then he pulled the trigger, and a bullet went straight into the right eye, blackening the skin. Moving the pistol two inches the other way, he sent another bullet crashing into the left eye. Then he stood upright over his victim with a deep sigh of satisfaction.

The Manager wriggled convulsively for the space of a single second, and then lay still in death.

There was not a moment to lose, for the door was already broken in and violent hands were at his neck. Jones put the pistol to his temple and once more pressed the trigger with his finger.

But this time there was no report. Only a little dead click answered the pressure, for the secretary had forgotten that the pistol had only six chambers, and that he had used them all. He threw the useless weapon onto the floor, laughing a little out loud, and turned, without a struggle, to give himself up.

"I *had* to do it," he said quietly, while they tied him. "It was simply my duty! And now I am ready to face the consequences, and Thorpe will be proud of me. For justice has been done and the gods are satisfied."

He made not the slightest resistance, and when the two policemen marched him off through the crowd of shuddering little clerks in the office, he again saw the veiled figure moving majestically in front of him, making slow sweeping circles with the flaming sword, to keep back the host of faces that were thronging in upon him from the Other Region.

The Dance of Death

Browne went to the dance feeling genuinely depressed, for the doctor had just warned him that his heart was weak and that he must be exceedingly careful in the matter of exertion.

"Dancing?" he asked, with that assumed lightness some natures affect in the face of a severe shock—the plucky instinct to conceal pain.

"Well—in moderation, perhaps," hummed the doctor. "Not *wildly!*" he added, with a smile that betrayed something more than mere professional sympathy.

At any other time Browne would probably have laughed, but the doctor's serious manner put a touch of ice on the springs of laughter. At the age of twenty-six one hardly realises death; life is still endless; and it is only old people who have "hearts" and such-like afflictions. So it was that the professional dictum came as a real shock; and with it too, as a sudden revelation, came that little widening of sympathy for others that is part of every deep experience as the years roll up and pass.

At first he thought of sending an excuse. He went about carefully, making the 'buses stop dead before he got out, and going very slowly up steps. Then gradually he grew more accustomed to the burden of his dread secret: the commonplace events of the day; the hated drudgery of the office, where he was an underpaid clerk; the contact with other men who bore similar afflictions with assumed indifference; the fault-finding of the manager, making him fearful of his position—all this helped to reduce the sense of first alarm, and, instead of sending an excuse, he went to the dance, as we have seen, feeling deeply depressed, and moving all the time as if he carried in his side a brittle glass globe that the least jarring might break into a thousand pieces.

The spontaneous jollity natural to a boy and girl dance served, however, to emphasise vividly the contrast of his own mood, and to make him very conscious again of his little hidden source of pain. But, though he would gladly have availed himself of a sympathetic ear among the many there whom he knew intimately, he nevertheless exercised the restraint natural to his character, and avoided any reference to the matter that bulked so largely in his consciousness. Once or twice he was tempted, but a prevision of the probable conversation that would ensue stopped him always in time: "Oh, I *am* so sorry, Mr. Browne, and you mustn't dance *too* hard, you know," and then his careless laugh as he remarked that it didn't matter a bit, and his little joke as he whirled his partner off for another spin.

He knew, of course, there was nothing very sensational about being told that one's heart was weak. Even the doctor had smiled a little; and he now recalled more than one acquaintance who had the same trouble and made light of it. Yet it sounded in Browne's life a note of profound and sinister gloom. It snatched beyond his reach at one fell swoop all that he most loved and enjoyed, destroying a thousand dreams, and painting the future a dull drab colour without hope. He was an idealist at heart, hating the sordid routine of the life he led as a business underling. His dreams were of the open air, of mountains, forests, and great plains, of the sea, and of the lonely places of the world. Wind and rain spoke intimately to his soul, and the storms of heaven, as he heard them raging at night round his high room in Bloomsbury, stirred savage yearnings that haunted him for days afterwards with the voices of the desert. Sometimes during the lunch hour, when he escaped temporarily from the artificial light and close air of his high office stool, to see the white clouds sailing by overhead, and to hear the wind singing in the wires, it set such a fever in his blood that for the remainder of the afternoon he found it impossible to concentrate on his work, and thus exasperated the loud-voiced manager almost to madness.

Having no expectations, and absolutely no practical business ability, he was fortunate, however, in having a "place" at all, and the hard fact that promotion was unlikely made him all the more careful to keep his dreams in their place, to do his work as well as possible, and to save what little he could.

His holidays were the only points of light in an otherwise dreary existence. And one day, when he should have saved enough, he looked forward vaguely to a life close to Nature, perhaps a shepherd on a hundred hills, a dweller in the woods, within sound of his beloved trees and waters, where the smell of the earth and camp fire would be ever in his nostrils, and the running stream always ready to bear his boat swiftly away into happiness.

And now the knowledge that he had a weak heart came to spoil everything. It shook his dream to the very foundations. It depressed him utterly. Any moment the blow might fall. It might catch him in the water, swimming, or half-way up the mountain, or midway in one of his lonely tramps, just when his enjoyment depended most upon his being reckless and forgetful of bodily limitations—that freedom of the spirit in the wilderness he so loved. He might even be forced to spend his holiday, to say nothing of the dream of the far future, in some farmhouse *"quietly,"* instead of gloriously in the untrodden wilds. The thought made him angry with pain. All day he was haunted and dismayed, and all day he heard the wind whispering among branches and the water lapping somewhere against sandy banks in the sun.

The dance was a small subscription affair, hastily arranged and happily informal. It took place in a large hall that was used in the daytime as a gymnasium, but the floor was good and the music more than good. Foils and helmets hung round the walls, and high up under the brown rafters were ropes, rings, and trapezes coiled away out of reach, their unsightliness further concealed by an array of brightly coloured flags. Only the light was not of the best, for the hall was very long, and the gallery at the far end loomed in a sort of twilight that was further deepened by the shadows of the flags overhead. But its benches afforded excellent sitting-out places, where strong light was not always an essential to happiness, and no one dreamed of finding fault.

At first he danced cautiously, but by degrees the spirit of the time and place relieved his depression and helped him to forget. He had probably exaggerated the importance of his malady. Lots of other fellows, even as young as he was, had weak hearts and thought nothing of it. All the time, however, there was an undercurrent of sadness and disappointment not to be denied. Something had gone out of life. A note of darkness had crept in. He found his partners dull, and they no doubt found him still duller.

Yet this dance, with nothing apparently to distinguish it from a hundred others, stood out in all his experience with an indelible red mark against it. It is a common trick of Nature—and a profoundly significant one—that, just when despair is deepest, she waves a wand before the weary eyes and does her best to waken an impossible hope. Her idea, presumably, being to keep her victim going actively to the very end of the chapter, lest through indifference he should lose something of the lesson she wishes to teach.

Thus it was that, midway in the dance, Browne's listless glance fell upon a certain girl whose appearance instantly galvanised him into a state of keenest possible desire. A flash of white light entered his heart and set him all on fire to know her. She attracted him tremendously. She was dressed in pale green, and always danced with the same man—a man about his own height and colouring, whose face, however, he never could properly see. They sat out together much of the time—always in the gallery where the shadows were deepest. The girl's face he saw clearly, and there was something about her that simply lifted him bodily out of himself and sent strange thrills of delight coursing over him like shocks of electricity. Several times their eyes met, and when this happened he could not tear his glance away. She fascinated him, and all the forces in his being merged into a single desire to be with her, to dance with her, speak with her, and to know her name. Especially he wondered who the man was she so favoured; he reminded him so oddly of himself. No one knows precisely what he himself looks like, but this tall dark figure, whose face he never could contrive to see, started the strange thought in him that it was his own *double*.

In vain he sought to compass an introduction to this girl. No one seemed to know her. Her dress, her hair, and a certain wondrous slim grace made him think of a young tree waving in the wind; of ivy leaves; of something that belonged to the life of the woods rather than to ordinary humanity. She possessed him, filling his thoughts with wild woodland dreams. Once, too, he was certain when their eyes met that she smiled at him, and the call was so well-nigh irresistible that he almost dropped his partner's arm to run after her.

But it seemed impossible to obtain an introduction from any one.

"Do you know who that girl is over there?" he asked one of his partners while sitting out a square dance, half exhausted with his exertions; "the one up there in the gallery?"

"In pink?"

"No, the one in green, I mean."

"Oh, next the wall-flower lady in red!"

"*In* the gallery, not *under* it," he explained impatiently.

"I can't see up there. It's so dark," returned the girl after a careful survey through glasses. "I don't think I see any one at all."

"It *is* rather dark," he remarked.

"Why? Do you know who she is!" she asked foolishly.

He did not like to insist. It seemed so rude to his partner. But this sort of thing happened once or twice. Evidently no one knew this girl in green, or else he described her so inaccurately that the people he asked looked at some one else instead.

"In that green sort of ivy-looking dress," he tried another.

"With the rose in her hair and the red nose? Or the one sitting out?"

After that he gave it up finally. His partners seemed to sniff a little when he asked. Evidently *la désirée* was not a popular maiden. Soon after, too, she disappeared and he lost sight of her. Yet the thought that she might have gone home made his heart sink into a sort of horrible blackness.

He lingered on much later than he intended in the hope of getting an introduction, but at last, when he had filled all his engagements, or nearly all, he made up his mind to slip out and go home. It was already late, and he had to be in the office—that hateful office— punctually at nine o'clock. He felt tired, awfully tired, more so than ever before at a dance. It was, of course, his weak heart. He still dawdled a little while, however, hoping for another glimpse of the sylph in green, hungering for a last look that he could carry home with him and perhaps mingle with his dreams. The mere thought of her filled him with pain and joy, and a sort of rarefied delight he had never known before. But he could not wait for ever, and it was already close upon two o'clock in the morning. His rooms were only a short distance down the street; he would light a cigarette and stroll home. No; he had forgotten for a moment; *without* a cigarette: the doctor had been very stern on that point.

He was in the act of turning his back on the whirl of dancing figures, when the flags at the far end of the room parted for an instant in the moving air, and his eye rested upon the gallery just visible among the shadows.

A great pain ran swiftly through his heart as he looked.

There were only two figures seated there: the tall dark man, who was his double, and the ivy girl in green. She was looking straight at him down the length of the room, and even at that distance he could see that she smiled.

He stopped short. The flags waved back again and hid the picture, but on the instant he made up his mind to act. There, among all this dreary crowd of dancing dolls, was some one he really wanted to know, to speak with, to touch—some one who drew him beyond all he had ever known, and made his soul cry aloud. The room was filled with automatic lay-figures, but here was some one *alive*. He must know her. It was impossible to go home without speech, utterly impossible.

A fresh stab of pain, worse than the first, gave him momentary pause. He leant against the wall for an instant just under the clock, where the hands pointed to two, waiting for the swooning blackness to go. Then he passed on, disregarding it utterly. It supplied him, in truth, with the extra little impetus he needed to set the will into vigorous action, for it reminded him forcibly of what *might* happen. His time might be short; he had known few enough of the good things of life; he would seize what he could. He had no introduction, but—to the devil with the conventions. The risk was nothing. To meet her eyes at close quarters, to hear her voice, to know something of the perfume of that hair and dress—what was the risk of a snub compared to that?

He slid down the side of the long room, dodging the dancers as best he could. The tall man, he noted, had left the gallery, but the girl sat on alone. He made his way quickly up the wooden steps, light as air, trembling with anticipation. His heart beat like a quick padded hammer, and the blood played a tambourine in his ears. It was odd he did not meet the tall man on the stairs, but doubtless there was another exit from the gallery that he had not observed. He topped the stairs and turned the corner. By Jove, she was still there, a few feet in front of him, sitting with her arms upon the railing, peering down upon the dancers below. His eyes swam for a moment, and something clutched at the very roots of his being.

But he did not hesitate. He went up quite close past the empty seats, meaning to ask naturally and simply if he might beg for the pleasure of a dance. Then, when he was within a few feet of her side, the girl suddenly turned and faced him, and the words died away on his lips. They seemed absolutely foolish and inadequate.

"Yes, I am ready," she said quietly, looking straight into his eyes; "but what a long time you were in coming. Was it such a great effort to *leave?*"

The form of the question struck him as odd, but he was too happy to pause. He became transfigured with joy. The sound of her voice instantly drowned all the clatter of the ball-room, and seemed to him the only thing in the whole world. It did not break on the consonants like most human speech. It flowed smoothly; it was the sound of wind among branches, of water running over pebbles. It swept into him and caught him away, so that for a moment he saw his beloved woods and hills and seas. The stars were somewhere in it too, and the murmur of the plains.

By the gods! Here was a girl he could speak with in the words of silence; she stretched every string in his soul and then played on them. His spirit expanded with life and happiness. She would listen gladly to all that concerned him. To her he could talk openly about his poor broken heart, for she would sympathise. Indeed, it was all he could do to prevent himself running forward at once with his arms outstretched to take her. There was a perfume of earth and woods about her.

"Oh, I am so *awfully* glad—" he began lamely, his eyes on her face. Then, remembering something of earthly manners, he added:

"My name—er—is—"

Something unusual—something indescribable—in her gesture stopped him. She had moved to give him space at her side.

"Your name!" she laughed, drawing her green skirts with a soft rustle like leaves along the bench to make room; "but you need no name *now*, you know!"

Oh, the wonder of it! She understood him. He sat down with a feeling that he had been flying in a free wind and was resting among the tops of trees. The room faded out temporarily.

"But my name, if you like to know, is Issidy," she said, still smiling.

"Miss Issidy," he stammered, making another attempt at the forms of worldly politeness.

"Not *Miss* Issidy," she laughed aloud merrily. It surely was the sound of wind in poplars. "Issidy is my first name; so if you call me anything, you must call me that."

The name was pure music in his ears, but though he blundered about in his memory to find his own, it had utterly vanished; for the life of him he could not recollect what his friends called him. He stared a moment, vaguely wondering, almost beside himself with delight. No other girls he had known—ye heavens above! there were no longer any other girls! He had never known any other girl than this one. Here was his universe, framed in a green dress, with a voice of sea and wind, eyes like the sun, and movements of bending grasses. All else was mere shadow and fantasy. For the first time in his existence he was alive, *and knew that he was alive.*

"I was sure you would come to me," she was saying. "You couldn't help yourself." Her eyes were always on his face.

"I was afraid at first—"

"But your thoughts," she interrupted softly, "your thoughts were up here with me all the time."

"You knew that!" he cried, delighted.

"I felt them," she replied simply. "They—you kept me company, for I have been alone here all the evening. I know no one else here—*yet.*"

Her words amazed him. He was just going to ask who the tall dark man was, when he saw that she was rising to her feet and that she wanted to dance.

"But my heart—" he stammered.

"It won't hurt your poor heart to dance with *me*, you know," she laughed. "You may trust me. I shall know how to take care of it."

Browne felt simply ecstatic; it was too wonderful to be true; it was impossible—this meeting in London, at an ordinary dull dance, in the twentieth century. He would wake up presently from a dream of silver and gold. Yet he felt even then that she was drawing his arm about her waist for the dance, and with that first magical touch he almost lost consciousness and passed with her into a state of pure spirit.

It puzzled him for a moment how they reached the floor so quickly and found themselves among the whirling couples. He had no recollection of coming down the stairs. But meanwhile he was dancing on wings, and the girl in green beside him seemed to fly too, and as he pressed her to his heart he found it impossible to think of anything else in the world but that—that and his astounding happiness.

And the music was within them, rather than without; indeed they seemed to make their own music out of their swift whirling movements, for it never ceased and he never grew tired. His heart had ceased to pain him. Other curious things happened, too, but he hardly noticed them; or, rather, they no longer seemed strange. In that crowded ball-room they never once touched other people. His partner required no steering. She made no sound. Then suddenly he realised that his own feet made no sound either. They skimmed the floor with noiseless feet like spirits dancing. No one else appeared to take the least notice of them. Most of the faces seemed, indeed, strange to him now, as though he had not seen them before, but once or twice he could have sworn that he passed couples who were dancing almost as happily and lightly as themselves, couples he had known in past years, couples who were *dead*.

Gradually the room emptied of its original comers, and others filled their places, silently, with airy graceful movements and happy faces, till the whole floor at length was covered with the soundless feet and whirling forms of those who had already left the world. And, as the artificial light faded away, there came in its place a soft white light that filled the room with beauty and made all the faces look radiant. And, once, as they skimmed past a mirror, he saw that the girl beside him was not there—that he seemed to be dancing alone, clasping no one; yet when he glanced down, there was her magical face at his shoulder and he felt her little form pressing up against him.

Such dancing, too, he had never even dreamed about, for it was like swinging with the treetops in the winds.

Then they danced farther out, ever swifter and swifter, past the shadows beneath the gallery, under the motionless hanging flags— and out into the night. The walls were behind them. They were off their feet and the wind was in their hair. They were rising, rising, rising towards the stars.

He felt the cool air of the open sky on his cheeks, and when he looked down, as they cleared the summit of the dark-lying hills, he saw that Issidy had melted away into himself and they had become one being. And he knew then that his heart would never pain him again on earth, or cause him to fear for any of his beloved dreams.

But the manager of the "hateful office" only knew two days later why Browne had not turned up to his desk, nor sent any word to explain his absence. He read it in the paper—how he had dropped down dead at a dance, suddenly stricken by heart disease. It happened just before two o'clock in the morning.

"Well," thought the manager, "he's no loss to us anyhow. He had no real business instincts. Smith will do his work much better—and for less money too."

The Old Man of Visions

I

The image of Teufelsdröckh, sitting in his watch-tower "alone with the stars," leaped into my mind the moment I saw him; and the curious expression of his eyes proclaimed at once that here was a being who allowed the world of small effects to pass him by, while he himself dwelt among the eternal verities. It was only necessary to catch a glimpse of the bent grey figure, so slight yet so tremendous, to realise that he carried staff and wallet, and was travelling alone in a spiritual region, uncharted, and full of wonder, difficulty, and fearful joy.

The inner eye perceived this quite as clearly as the outer was aware of his Hebraic ancestry; but along what winding rivers, through what haunted woods, by the shores of what singing seas he pressed forward towards the mountains of his goal, no one could guess from a mere inspection of that wonderful old face.

To have stumbled upon such a figure in the casual way I did seemed incredible to me even at the time, yet I at once caught something of the uplifting airs that followed this inhabitant of a finer world, and I spent days—and considered them well spent—trying to get into conversation with him, so that I might know something more than the thin disguise of his holding a reader's ticket for the Museum Library.

To reach the stage of intimacy where actual speech is a hindrance to close understanding, one need not in some cases have spoken at all; thus by merely setting my mind, and above all, my imagination, into tune with his, and by steeping myself so much in his atmosphere that I absorbed and then gave back to him with my own stamp the forces he exhaled, it was at length possible to persuade those vast-seeing eyes to turn in my direction; and our glances having once met, I simply rose when he rose, and followed him out of the little smoky restaurant so closely up the street that our clothes brushed, and I thought I could even catch the sound of his breathing.

Whether, having already weighed me, he accepted the office, or whether he was grateful for the arm to lean upon, with his many years' burden, I do not know; but the sympathy between us was such that, without a single word, we walked up that foggy London street to the door of his lodging in Bloomsbury, while I noticed that at the touch of his arm the noise of the town seemed to turn into deep singing, and even the hurrying passers-by seemed bent upon noble purposes; and though he barely reached to my shoulder, and his grey beard almost touched my glove as I bent my arm to hold his own, there was something immense about his figure that sent him with towering stature above me and filled my thoughts with enchanting dreams of grandeur and high beauty.

But it was only when the door had closed on him with a little rush of wind, and I was walking home alone, that I fully realised the shock of my return to earth; and on reaching my own rooms I shook with laughter to think I had walked a mile and a half with a complete stranger without uttering a single syllable. Then the laughter suddenly hushed as I caught my face in the glass with the expression of the soul still lingering about the eyes and forehead, and for a brief moment my heart leaped to a sort of noble fever in the blood, leaving me with the smart of the soul's wings stirring beneath the body's crushing weight. And when it passed I found myself dwelling upon the only words he had spoken when I left him at the door:

"I am the Old Man of Visions, and I am *at your service.*"

I think he never had a name—at least, it never passed his lips, and perhaps lay buried with so much else of the past that he clearly deemed unimportant. To me, at any rate, he became simply the Old Man of Visions, and to the little waiting-maid and the old landlady he was known simply as "Mister"—Mister, neither more nor less. The impenetrable veil that hung over his past never lifted for any vital revelations of his personal history, though he evidently knew all countries of the world, and had absorbed into his heart and brain the experience of all possible types of human nature; and there was an air about him not so much of "Ask me no questions," as "Do not ask me, for I cannot answer you *in words.*"

He could satisfy, but not in mere language; he would reveal, but by the wonderful words of silence only; for he was the Old Man of Visions, and visions need no words, being swift and of the spirit.

Moreover, the landlady—poor, dusty, faded woman—the landlady stood in awe, and disliked being probed for information in a passage-way down which he might any moment tread, for she could only tell me, "He just came in one night, years ago, and he's been here ever since!" And more than that I never knew. "Just came in—one night—years ago." This adequately explained him, for where he came *from,* or was journeying *to,* was something quite beyond the scope of ordinary limited language.

I pictured him suddenly turning aside from the stream of unimportant events, quietly stepping out of the world of straining, fighting, and shouting, and moving to take his rightful place among the forces of the still, spiritual region where he belonged by virtue of long pain and difficult attainment. For he was unconnected with any conceivable network of relations, friends, or family, and his terrible aloofness could not be disturbed by any one unless with his permission and by his express wish. Nor could he be imagined as "belonging" to any definite set of souls. He was apart from the world—and above it.

But it was only when I began to creep a little nearer to him, and our strange, silent intimacy passed from mental to spiritual, that I began really to understand more of this wonderful Old Man of Visions.

Steeped in the tragedy, and convulsed with laughter at the comedy, of life, he yet lived there in his high attic wrapped in silence as in a golden cloud; and so seldom did he actually speak to me that each time the sound of his voice, that had something elemental in it—something of winds and waters—thrilled me with the power of the first time. He lived, like Teufelsdröckh, "alone with the stars," and it seemed impossible, more and more, to link him on anywhere into practical dealings with ordinary men and women. Life somehow seemed to pass *below* him. Yet the small, selfish spirit of the recluse was far from him, and he was tenderly and deeply responsive to pain and suffering, and more particularly to genuine yearning for the far things of beauty. The unsatisfied longings of others could move him at once to tears.

"My relations with men are perfect," he said one night as we neared his dwelling. "I give them all sympathy out of my stores of knowledge and experience, and they give to me what kindness I need. My outer shell lies within impenetrable solitude, for only so can my inner life move freely along the paths and terraces that are thronged with the beings to whom I belong." And when I asked him how he maintained such deep sympathy with humanity, and had yet absolved himself apparently from action as from speech, he stopped against an area railing and turned his great eyes on to my face, as though their fires could communicate his thought without the husk of words:

"I have peered too profoundly into life and beyond it," he murmured, "to wish to express in language what I *know*. Action is not for all, always; and I am in touch with the cisterns of thought that lie behind action. I ponder the mysteries. What I may solve is not lost for lack either of speech or action, for the true mystic is ever the true man of action, and my thought will reach others as soon as they are ready for it in the same way that it reached you. All who strongly yearn must, sooner or later, find me and be comforted."

His eyes shifted from my face towards the stars, softly shining above the dark Museum roof, and a moment later he had disappeared into the hall-way of his house.

"An old poet who has strayed afield and lost his way," I mused; but through the door where he had just vanished the words came back to me as from a great distance: "A priest, rather, who has begun to find his way."

For a space I stood, pondering on his face and words:—that mercilessly intelligent look of the Hebrew woven in with the expression of the sadness of a whole race, yet touched with the glory of the spirit; and his utterance—that he had passed through all the traditions and no longer needed a formal, limited creed to hold to. I forget how I reached my own door several miles away, but it seemed to me that I flew.

In this way, and by unregistered degrees, we came to know each other better, and he accepted me and took me into his life. Always wrapped in the great calm of his delightful silence, he taught me more, and told me more, than could ever lie within the confines of mere words; and in moments of need, no matter when or where, I always knew exactly how to find him, reaching him in a few seconds by some swift way that disdained the means of ordinary locomotion.

Then at last one day he gave me the key of his house. And the first time I found my way into his eyry, and realised that it was a haven I could always fly to when the yearnings of the heart and soul struggled vainly for recompense, the full meaning and importance of the Old Man of Visions became finally clear to me.

II

The room, high up creaky, darkened stairs in the ancient house, was bare and fireless, looking through a single patched window across a tumbled sea of roofs and chimneys; yet there was that in it which instantly proclaimed it a little holy place out of the world, a temple in which some one with spiritual vitality had worshipped, prayed, wept, and sung.

It was dusty and unswept, yet it was utterly *unsoiled;* and the Old Man of Visions who lived there, for all his shabby and stained garments, his uncombed beard and broken shoes, stood within its door revealed in his real self, moving in a sort of divine whiteness, iridescent, shining. And here, in this attic (lampless and unswept), high up under the old roofs of Bloomsbury, the window scarred with rain and the corners dropping cobwebs, I heard his silver whisper issue from the shadows:

"Here you may satisfy your soul's desire and may commune with the Invisibles; only, to find the Invisibles, you must first be able to lose yourself."

Ah! through that stained window-pane, the sight leaping at a single bound from black roofs up to the stars, what pictures, dreams, and visions the Old Man has summoned to my eyes! Distances, measureless and impossible hitherto, became easy, and from the oppression of dead bricks and the market-place he transported me in a moment to the slopes of the Mountains of Dream; leading me to little places near the summits where the pines grew thinly and the stars were visible through their branches, fading into the rose of dawn; where the winds tasted of the desert, and the voices of the wilderness fled upward with a sound of wings and falling streams. At his word houses melted away, and the green waves of all the seas flowed into their places; forests waved themselves into the coast-line of dull streets; and the power of the old earth, with all her smells and flowers and wild life, thrilled down among the dead roofs and caught me away into freedom among the sunshine of meadows and the music of sweet pipings. And with the divine deliverance came the crying of sea-gulls, the glimmer of reedy tarns, the whispering of wind among grasses, and the healing scorch of a real sun upon the skin.

And poetry such as was never known or heard before clothed all he uttered, yet even then took no form in actual words, for it was of the substance of aspiration and yearning, voicing adequately all the busy, high-born dreams that haunt the soul yet never live in the uttered line. He breathed it about him in the air so that it filled my being. It was part of him—beyond words; and it sang my own longings, and sang them perfectly so that I was satisfied; for my own mood never failed to touch him instantly and to waken the right response. In its essence it was spiritual—the mystic poetry of heaven; still, the love of humanity informed it, for star-fire and heart's blood were about equally mingled there, while the mystery of unattainable beauty moved through it like a white flame.

With other dreams and longings, too, it was the same; and all the most beautiful ideas that ever haunted a soul undowered with expression here floated with satisfied eyes and smiling lips before one—floated in silence, unencumbered, unlimited, unrestrained by words.

In this dim room, never made ugly by artificial light, but always shadowy in a kind of gentle dusk, the Old Man of Visions had only to lead me to the window to bring peace. Music, that rendered the soul fluid, as it poured across the old roofs into the room, was summoned by him at need; and when one's wings beat sometimes against the prison walls and the yearning for escape oppressed the heart, I have heard the little room rush and fill with the sound of trees, wind among grasses, whispering branches, and lapping waters. The very odours of space and mountain-side came too, and the looming of noble hills seemed visible overhead against the stars, as though the ceiling had suddenly become transparent.

For the Old Man of Visions had the power of instantly satisfying an ideal when once that ideal created a yearning that could tear and burn its way out with sufficient force to set the will a-moving.

III

But as the time passed and I came to depend more and more upon the intimacy with my strange old friend, new light fell upon the nature and possibilities of our connection. I discovered, for instance, that though I held the key to his dwelling, and was familiar with the way, he was nevertheless not always available. Two things, in different fashion, rendered him inaccessible, or mute; and, for the first, I gradually learned that when life was prosperous, and the body singing loud, I could not find my way to his house. No amount of wandering, calculation, or persevering effort enabled me even to find the street again. With any burst of worldly success, however fleeting, the Old Man of Visions somehow slipped away into remote shadows and became unreal and misty. A merely passing desire to be with him, to seek his inspiration by a glimpse through that magic window-pane, resulted only in vain and tiresome pacing to and fro along ugly streets that produced weariness and depression; and after these periods it became, I noticed, less and less easy to discover the house, to fit the key in the door, or, having gained access to the temple, to realise the visions I *thought* I craved for.

Often, in this way, have I searched in vain for days, but only succeeded in losing myself in the murky purlieus of a quite strange Bloomsbury; stopping outside numberless counterfeit doors, and struggling vainly with locks that knew nothing of my little shining key.

But, on the other hand, pain, loneliness, sorrow—the merest whisper of spiritual affliction—and, lo, in a single moment the difficult geography became plain, and without hesitation, when I was unhappy or distressed, I found the way to his house as by a bird's instinctive flight, and the key slipped into the lock as though it loved it and was returning home.

The other cause to render him inaccessible, though not so determined—since it never concealed the way to the house—was even
more distressing, for it depended wholly on myself; and I came to
know how the least ugly action, involving a depreciation of ideals, so
confused the mind that, when I got into the house, with difficulty,
and found him in the little room after much searching, he was able to
do or say scarcely anything at all for me. The mirror facing the door
then gave back, I saw, no proper reflection of his person, but only a
faded and wavering shadow with dim eyes and stooping, indistinct
outline, and I even fancied I could see the pattern of the wall and
shape of the furniture *through* his body, as though he had grown semi-
transparent.

"You must not expect yearnings to weigh," came his whisper,
like wind far overhead, "unless you lend to them *your own* substance;
and your own substance you cannot both keep and lend. If you
would know the Invisibles, forget yourself."

And later, as the years slipped away one after another into the
mists, and the frontier between the real and the unreal began to shift
amazingly with his teachings, it became more and more clear to me
that he belonged to a permanent region that, with all the changes in
the world's history, has itself never altered in any essential particular.
This immemorial Old Man of Visions, as I grew to think of him, had
existed always; he was old as the sea and coeval with the stars; and he
dwelt beyond time and space, reaching out a hand to all those who,
weary of the shadows and illusions of practical life, really call to him
with their heart of hearts. To me, indeed, the touch of sorrow was
always near enough to prevent his becoming often inaccessible, and
after a while even his voice became so *living* that I sometimes heard it
calling to me in the street and in the fields.

Oh, wonderful Old Man of Visions! Happy the days of disaster,
since they taught me how to know you, the Unraveller of Problems,
the Destroyer of Doubts, who bore me ever away with soft flight
down the long, long vistas of the heart and soul!

And his loneliness in that temple attic under the stars, his loneliness, too, had a meaning I did not fail to understand later, and why
he was always available for me and seemed to belong to no other.

"To every one who finds me," he said, with the strange smile that wrapped his whole being and not his face alone, "to every one I am the same, and yet different. I am not really ever alone. The whole world, nay"—his voice rose to a singing cry—"the whole universe lies in this room, or just beyond that window-pane; for here past and future meet and all real dreams find completeness. But remember," he added—and there was a sound as of soft wind and rain in the room with his voice—"no true dream can ever be shared, and should you seek to explain me to another you must lose me beyond recall. You have never asked my name, nor must you ever tell it. Each must find me in his own way."

Yet one day, for all my knowledge and his warnings, I felt so sure of my intimacy with this immemorial being, that I spoke of him to a friend who was, I had thought, so much a part of myself that it seemed no betrayal. And my friend, who went to search and found nothing, returned with the fool's laughter on his face, and swore that no street or number existed, for he had looked in vain, and had re-peatedly *asked the way.*

And, from that day to this, the Old Man of Visions has neither called to me nor let his place be found; the streets are strange and empty, and I have even lost the little shining key.

May Day Eve

I

It was in the spring when I at last found time from the hospital work to visit my friend, the old folk-lorist, in his country isolation, and I rather chuckled to myself, because in my bag I was taking down a book that utterly refuted all his tiresome pet theories of magic and the powers of the soul.

These theories were many and various, and had often troubled me. In the first place, I scorned them for professional reasons, and, in the second, because I had never been able to argue quite well enough to convince or to shake his faith in even the smallest details, and any scientific knowledge I brought to bear only fed him with confirmatory data. To find such a book, therefore, and to know that it was safely in my bag, wrapped up in brown paper and addressed to him, was a deep and satisfactory joy, and I speculated a good deal during the journey how he would deal with the overwhelming arguments it contained against the existence of any important region outside the world of sensory perceptions.

Speculative, too, I was whether his visionary habits and absorbing experiments would permit him to remember my arrival at all, and I was accordingly relieved to hear from the solitary porter that the "professor" had sent a "veeckle" to meet me, and that I was thus free to send my bag and walk the four miles to the house across the hills.

It was a calm, windless evening, just after sunset, the air warm and scented, and delightfully still. The train, already sinking into distance, carried away with it the noise of crowds and cities and the last suggestions of the stressful life behind me, and from the little station on the moorland I stepped at once into the world of silent, growing things, tinkling sheep-bells, shepherds, and wild, desolate spaces.

My path lay diagonally across the turfy hills. It slanted a mile or so to the summit, wandered vaguely another two miles among gorse-bushes along the crest, passed Tom Bassett's cottage by the pines, and then dropped sharply down on the other side through rather thin woods to the ancient house where the old folk-lorist lived and dreamed himself into his impossible world of theory and fantasy. I fell to thinking busily about him during the first part of the ascent, and convinced myself, as usual, that, but for his generosity to the poor, and his benign aspect, the peasantry must undoubtedly have regarded him as a wizard who speculated in souls and had dark dealings with the world of faery.

The path I knew tolerably well. I had already walked it once before—a winter's day some years ago—and from the cottage onwards felt sure of my way; but for the first mile or so there were so many cross cattle-tracks, and the light had become so dim, that I felt it wise to enquire more particularly. And this I was fortunately able to do of a man who with astonishing suddenness rose from the grass where he had been lying behind a clump of bushes, and passed a few yards in front of me at a high pace downhill towards the darkening valley.

He was in such a state of hurry that I called out loudly to him, fearing to be too late, but on hearing my voice he turned sharply, and seemed to arrive almost at once beside me. In a single instant he was standing there, quite close, looking, with a smile and a certain expression of curiosity, I thought, into my face. I remember thinking that his features, pale and wholly untanned, were rather wonderful for a countryman, and that the eyes were those of a foreigner; his great swiftness, too, gave me a distinct sensation—something almost of a start—though I knew my vision was at fault at the best of times, and of course especially so in the deceptive twilight of the open hillside.

Moreover—as the way often is with such instructions—the words did not stay in my mind very clearly after he had uttered them, and the rapid, panther-like movements of the man as he quickly vanished down the hill again left me with little more than a sweeping gesture indicating the line I was to follow. No doubt his sudden rising from behind the gorse-bush, his curious swiftness, and the way he peered into my face, and even touched me on the shoulder, all combined to distract my attention somewhat from the actual words he used; and the fact that I was travelling at a wrong angle, and should have come out a mile too far to the right, helped to complete my feeling that his gesture, pointing the way, was sufficient.

On the crest of the ridge, panting a little with the unwonted exertion, I lay down to rest a moment on the grass beside a flaming yellow gorse-bush. There was still a good hour before I should be looked for at the house; the grass was very soft, the peace and silence soothing. I lingered, and lit a cigarette. And it was just then, I think, that my subconscious memory gave back the words, the actual words, the man had spoken, and the heavy significance of the personal pronoun, as he had emphasised it in his odd foreign voice, touched me with a sense of vague amusement: "The safest way *for you* now," he had said, as though I was so obviously a townsman and might be in danger on the lonely hills after dark. And the quick way he had reached my side, and then slipped off again like a shadow down the steep slope, completed a definite little picture in my mind. Then other thoughts and memories rose up and formed a series of pictures, following each other in rapid succession, and forming a chain of reflections undirected by the will and without purpose or meaning. I fell, that is, into a pleasant reverie.

Below me, and infinitely far away, it seemed, the valley lay silent under a veil of blue evening haze, the lower end losing itself among darkening hills whose peaks rose here and there like giant plumes that would surely nod their great heads and call to one another once the final shadows were down. The village lay, a misty patch, in which lights already twinkled. A sound of rooks faintly cawing, of sea-gulls crying far up in the sky, and of dogs barking at a great distance rose up out of the general murmur of evening voices. Odours of farm and field and open spaces stole to my nostrils, and everything contributed to the feeling that I lay on the top of the world, nothing between me and the stars, and that all the huge, free things of the earth—hills, valleys, woods, and sloping fields—lay breathing deeply about me.

A few sea-gulls—in daytime hereabouts they fill the air—still circled and wheeled within range of sight, uttering from time to time sharp, petulant cries; and far in the distance there was just visible a shadowy line that showed where the sea lay.

Then, as I lay gazing dreamily into this still pool of shadows at my feet, something rose up, something sheet-like, vast, imponderable, off the whole surface of the mapped-out country, moved with incredible swiftness down the valley, and in a single instant climbed the hill where I lay and swept by me, yet without hurry, and in a sense without speed. Veils in this way rose one after another, filling the cups between the hills, shrouding alike fields, village, and hillside as they passed, and settled down somewhere into the gloom behind me over the ridge, or slipped off like vapour into the sky.

Whether it was actually mist rising from the surface of the fast-cooling ground, or merely the earth giving up her heat to the night, I could not determine. The coming of darkness is ever a series of mysteries. I only know that this indescribable vast stirring of the landscape seemed to me as though the earth were unfolding immense sable wings from her sides, and lifting them for silent, gigantic strokes so that she might fly more swiftly from the sun into the night. The darkness, at any rate, did drop down over everything very soon afterwards, and I rose up hastily to follow my pathway, realising with a degree of wonder strangely new to me the magic of twilight, the blue open depths into the valley below, and the pale yellow heights of the watery sky above.

I walked rapidly, a sense of chilliness about me, and soon lost sight of the valley altogether as I got upon the ridge proper of these lonely and desolate hills.

It could not have been more than fifteen minutes that I lay there in reverie, yet the weather, I at once noticed, had changed very abruptly, for mist was seething here and there about me, rising somewhere from smaller valleys in the hills beyond, and obscuring the path, while overhead there was plainly a sound of wind tearing past, far up, with a sound of high shouting. A moment before it had been the stillness of a warm spring night, yet now everything had changed; wet mist coated me, raindrops smartly stung my face, and a gusty wind, descending out of cool heights, began to strike and buffet me, so that I buttoned my coat and pressed my hat more firmly upon my head.

The change was really this—and it came to me for the first time in my life with the power of a real conviction—that everything about me seemed to have become suddenly *alive*.

It came oddly upon me—prosaic, matter-of-fact, materialistic doctor that I was—this realisation that the world about me had somehow stirred into life; oddly, I say, because Nature to me had always been merely a more or less definite arrangement of measurement, weight, and colour, and this new presentation of it was utterly foreign to my temperament. A valley to me was always a valley; a hill, merely a hill; a field, so many acres of flat surface, grass or ploughed, drained well or drained ill; whereas now, with startling vividness, came the strange, haunting idea that after all they could be something more than valley, hill, and field: that what I had hitherto perceived by these names were only the veils of something that lay concealed within, something alive. In a word, that the poetic sense I had always rather sneered at in others, or explained away with some shallow physiological label, had apparently suddenly opened up in myself without any obvious cause.

And, the more I puzzled over it, the more I began to realise that its genesis dated from those few minutes of reverie lying under the gorse-bush (reverie, a thing I had never before in all my life indulged in!), or, now that I came to reflect more accurately, from my brief interview with that wild-eyed, swift-moving, shadowy man of whom I had first enquired the way.

I recalled my singular fancy that veils were lifting off the surface of the hills and fields, and a tremor of excitement accompanied the memory. Such a thing had never before been possible to my practical intelligence, and it made me feel suspicious—suspicious about myself. I stood still a moment—I looked about me into the gathering mist, above me to the vanishing stars, below me to the hidden valley, and then sent an urgent summons to my individuality, as I had always known it, to arrest and chase these undesirable fancies.

But I called in vain. No answer came. Anxiously, hurriedly, confusedly too, I searched for my normal self, but could not find it; and this failure to respond induced in me a sense of uneasiness that touched very nearly upon the borders of alarm.

I pushed on faster and faster along the turfy track among the gorse-bushes with a dread that I might lose the way altogether, and a sudden desire to reach home as soon as might be. Then, without warning, I emerged unexpectedly into clear air again, and the vapour swept past me in a rushing wall and rose into the sky. Anew I saw the

lights of the village behind me in the depths, here and there a line of
smoke rising against the pale yellow sky, and stars overhead peering
down through thin wispy clouds that stretched their wind-signs
across the night.

After all, it had been nothing but a stray bit of sea-fog driving up
from the coast, for the other side of the hills, I remembered, dipped
their chalk cliffs straight into the sea, and strange lost winds must often come a-wandering this way with the sharp changes of temperature about sunset. None the less, it was disconcerting to know that
mist and storm lay hiding within possible reach, and I walked on
smartly for a sight of Tom Bassett's cottage and the lights of the
Manor House in the valley a short mile beyond.

The clearing of the air, however, lasted but a very brief while, and
vapour was soon rising about me as before, hiding the path and making bushes and stone walls look like running shadows. It came, driv-
en apparently by little independent winds up the many side gullies,
and it was very cold, touching my skin like a wet sheet. Curious great
shapes, too, it assumed as the wind worked to and fro through it:
forms of men and animals: grotesque, giant outlines; ever shifting
and running along the ground with silent feet, or leaping into the air
with sharp cries as the gusts twisted them inwardly and lent them
voice. More and more I pushed my pace, and more and more darkness
and vapour obliterated the landscape. The going was not otherwise difficult, and here and there cowslips glimmered in patches of dancing
yellow, while the springy turf made it easy to keep up speed; yet in the
gloom I frequently tripped and plunged into prickly gorse near the
ground, so that from shin to knee was soon a-tingle with sharp pain.
Odd puffs and spits of rain stung my face, and the periods of utter
stillness were always followed by little shouting gusts of wind, each
time from a new direction. Troubled is perhaps too strong a word,
but flustered I certainly was; and though I recognised that it was due
to my being in an environment so remote from the town life I was
accustomed to, I found it impossible to stifle altogether the feeling of
malaise that had crept into my heart, and I looked about with increasing eagerness for the lighted windows of Bassett's cottage.

More and more, little pin-pricks of distress and confusion accumulated, adding to my realisation of being away from streets and

shop-windows, and things I could classify and deal with. The mist, too, distorted as well as concealed, played tricks with sounds as well as with sights. And, once or twice, when I stumbled upon some crouching sheep, they got up without the customary alarm and hurry of sheep, and moved off slowly into the darkness, but in such a singular way that I could almost have sworn they were not sheep at all, but human beings crawling on all-fours, looking back and grimacing at me over their shoulders as they went. On these occasions—for there were more than one—I never could get close enough to feel their woolly wet backs, as I should have liked to do; and the sound of their tinkling bells came faintly through the mist, sometimes from one direction, sometimes from another, sometimes all round me as though a whole flock surrounded me; and I found it impossible to analyse or explain the idea I received that they were *not* sheep-bells at all, but something quite different.

But mist and darkness, and a certain confusion of the senses caused by the excitement of an utterly strange environment, can account for a great deal. I pushed on quickly. The conviction that I had strayed from the route grew, nevertheless, for occasionally there was a great commotion of sea-gulls about me, as though I had disturbed them in their sleeping-places. The air filled with their plaintive cries, and I heard the rushing of multitudinous wings, sometimes very close to my head, but always invisible owing to the mist. And once, above the swishing of the wet wind through the gorse-bushes, I was sure I caught the faint thunder of the sea and the distant crashing of waves rolling up some steep-throated gully in the cliffs. I went cautiously after this, and altered my course a little away from the direction of the sound.

Yet, increasingly all the time, it came to me how the cries of the sea-birds sounded like laughter, and how the everlasting wind blew and drove about me with a purpose, and how the low bushes persistently took the shape of stooping people, moving stealthily past me, and how the mist more and more resembled huge protean figures escorting me across the desolate hills, silently, with immense footsteps. For the inanimate world now touched my awakened poetic sense in a manner hitherto unguessed, and became fraught with the pregnant messages of a dimly concealed life. I readily understood, for the first time, how easily a superstitious peasantry might people their

world, and how even an educated mind might favour an atmosphere
of legend. I stumbled along, looking anxiously for the lights of the
cottage.

Suddenly, as a shape of writhing mist whirled past, I received so
direct a stroke of wind that it was palpably a blow in the face. Something swept by with a shrill cry into the darkness. It was impossible
to prevent jumping to one side and raising an arm by way of protection, and I was only just quick enough to catch a glimpse of the sea-
gull as it raced past, with suddenly altered flight, beating its powerful
wings over my head. Its white body looked enormous as the mist
swallowed it. At the same moment a gust tore the hat from my head
and flung the flap of my coat across my eyes. But I was well trained
by this time, and made a quick dash after the retreating black object,
only to find on overtaking it that I held a prickly branch of gorse.
The wind combed my hair viciously. Then, out of a corner of my eye,
I saw my hat still rolling, and grabbed swiftly at it; but just as I closed
on it, the real hat passed in front of me, turning over in the wind like
a ball, and I instantly released my first capture to chase it. Before it
was within reach, another one shot between my feet so that I stepped
on it. The grass seemed covered with moving hats, yet each one,
when I seized it, turned into a piece of wood, or a tiny gorse-bush, or
a black rabbit hole, till my hands were scored with prickles and running blood. In the darkness, I reflected, all objects looked alike, as
though by general conspiracy.

I straightened up and took a long breath, mopping the blood
with my handkerchief. Then something tapped at my feet, and on
looking down, there was the hat within easy reach, and I stooped
down and put it on my head again. Of course, there were a dozen
ways of explaining my confusion and stupidity, and I walked along
wondering which to select. My eyesight, for one thing—and under
such conditions why seek further? It was nothing, after all, and the
dizziness was a momentary effect caused by the effort and stooping

But for all that, I shouted aloud, on the chance that a wandering
shepherd might hear me; and of course no answer came, for it was
like calling in a padded room, and the mist suffocated my voice and
killed its resonance.

It was really very discouraging: I was cold and wet and hungry;

my legs and clothes torn by the gorse, my hands scratched and bleeding; the wind brought water to my eyes by its constant buffetings, and my skin was numb from contact with the chill mist. Fortunately I had matches, and after some difficulty, by crouching under a wall, I caught a swift glimpse of my watch, and saw that it was but little after eight o'clock. Supper I knew was at nine, and I was surely over halfway by this time. But here again was another instance of the way everything seemed in a conspiracy against me to appear otherwise than ordinary, for in the gleam of the match my watch-glass showed as the face of a little old grey man, uncommonly like the folk-lorist himself, peering up at me with an expression of whimsical laughter. My own reflection it could not possibly have been, for I am clean-shaven, and this face looked up at me through a running tangle of grey hair. Yet a second and a third match revealed only the white surface with the thin black hands moving across it.

II

And it was at this point, I well remember, that I reached what was for me the true heart of the adventure, the little fragment of real experience I learned from it and took back with me to my doctor's life in London, and that has remained with me ever since, and helped me to a new sympathetic insight into the intricacies of certain curious mental cases I had never before really understood.

For it was sufficiently obvious by now that a curious change had been going forward in me for some time, dating, so far as I could focus my thoughts sufficiently to analyse, from the moment of my speech with that hurrying man of shadow on the hillside. And the first deliberate manifestation of the change, now that I looked back, was surely the awakening in my prosaic being of the "poetic thrill"; my sudden amazing appreciation of the world around me as something alive. From that moment the change in me had worked ahead subtly, swiftly. Yet, so natural had been the beginning of it, that although it was a radically new departure for my temperament, I was hardly aware at first of what had actually come about; and it was only now, after so many encounters, that I was forced at length to acknowledge it.

It came the more forcibly too, because my very commonplace ideas of beauty had hitherto always been associated with sunshine and crude effects; yet here this new revelation leaped to me out of wind and mist and desolation on a lonely hillside, out of night, darkness, and discomfort. New values rushed upon me from all sides. Everything had changed, and the very simplicity with which the new values presented themselves proved to me how profound the change, the readjustment, had been. In such trivial things the evidence had come that I was not aware of it until repetition forced my attention: the veils rising from valley and hill; the mountain tops as personalities that shout or murmur in the darkness; the crying of the sea-birds and of the living, purposeful wind; above all, the feeling that Nature about me was instinct with a life differing from my own in degree rather than in kind; everything, from the conspiracy of the gorse-bushes to the disappearing hat, showed that a fundamental attitude of mind in me had changed—and changed, too, without my knowledge or consent.

Moreover, at the same time the deep sadness of beauty had entered my heart like a stroke; for all this mystery and loveliness, I realised poignantly, was utterly independent and careless of *me,* as me; and that while I must pass, decay, grow old, these manifestations would remain for ever young and unalterably potent. And thus gradually had I become permeated with the recognition of a region hitherto unknown to me, and that I had always depreciated in others and especially, it now occurred to me, in my friend the old folk-lorist.

Here surely, I thought, was the beginning of conditions which, carried a little further, must become pathogenic. That the change was real and pregnant I had no doubt whatever. My consciousness was expanding, and I had caught it in the very act. I had of course read much concerning the changes of personality, swift, kaleidoscopic—had come across something of it in my practice—and had listened to the folk-lorist holding forth like a man inspired upon ways and means of reaching concealed regions of the human consciousness, and opening it to the knowledge of things called magical, so that one became free of a larger universe. But it was only now for the first time, on these bare hills, in touch with the wind and the rain, that I realised in how simple a fashion the frontiers of consciousness could shift this way and that, or with what touch of genuine awe the certainty might come that one stood on the borderland of new, untried, perhaps dangerous, experiences.

At any rate, it did now come to me that my consciousness had shifted its frontiers very considerably, and that whatever might happen must seem not abnormal, but quite simple and inevitable, and of course utterly true. This very simplicity, however, doing no violence to my being, brought with it none the less a sense of dread and discomfort; and my dim awareness that unknown possibilities were about me in the night puzzled and distressed me perhaps more than I cared to admit.

III

All this that takes so long to describe became apparent to me in a few seconds. What I had always despised ascended the throne.

But with the finding of Bassett's cottage as a sign-post close to home, my former *sang-froid*, my stupidity, would doubtless return, and my relief was therefore considerable when at length a faint gleam of light appeared through the mist, against which the square dark shadow of the chimney line pointed upwards. After all, I had not strayed so very far out of the way. Now I could definitely ascertain where I was wrong.

Quickening my pace, I scrambled over a broken stone wall, and almost ran across the open bit of grass to the door. One moment the black outline of the cottage was there in front of me, and the next, when I stood actually against it—there was nothing! I laughed to think how utterly I had been deceived. Yet not utterly, for as I groped back again over the wall, the cottage loomed up a little to the left, with its windows lighted and friendly, and I had only been mistaken in my angle of approach after all. Yet again, as I hurried to the door, the mist drove past and thickened a second time—and the cottage was not where I had seen it!

My confusion increased a lot after that. I scrambled about in all directions, rather foolishly hurried, and over countless stone walls it seemed, and completely dazed as to the true points of the compass. Then suddenly, just when a kind of despair came over me, the cottage stood there solidly before my eyes, and I found myself not two feet from the door. Was ever mist before so deceptive? And there, just behind it, I made out the row of pines like a dark wave breaking through the night. I sniffed the wet resinous odour with joy, and a genuine thrill ran through me as I saw the unmistakable yellow light of the windows. At last I was near home and my troubles would soon be over.

A cloud of birds rose with shrill cries off the roof and whirled into the darkness when I knocked with my stick on the door, and human voices, I was almost certain, mingled somewhere with them, though it was impossible to tell whether they were within the cottage, or outside. It all sounded confusedly with a rush of air like a little whirlwind, and I stood there rather alarmed at the clamour of my knocking. By way, too, of further proof that my imagination had awakened, the significance of that knocking at the door set something vibrating within me that most surely had never vibrated before, so that I suddenly realised with what atmosphere of mystical suggestion is the mere act of knocking surrounded—*knocking at a door*—both for him who knocks, wondering what shall be revealed on opening, and for him who stands within, waiting for the summons of the knocker. I only know that I hesitated a lot before making up my mind to knock a second time.

And, anyhow, what happened subsequently came in a sort of haze. Words and memory both fail me when I try to record it truthfully, so that even the faces are difficult to visualise again, the words almost impossible to hear.

Before I knew it the door was open, and before I could frame the words of my first brief question, I was within the threshold, and the door was shut behind me.

I had expected the little dark and narrow hall-way of a cottage, oppressive of air and odour, but instead I came straight into a room that was full of light and full of—people. And the air tasted like the air about a mountain top.

To the end I never saw what produced the light, nor understood how so many men and women found space to move comfortably to and fro and pass each other as they did within the confines of those four walls. An uncomfortable sense of having intruded upon some private gathering was, I think, my first emotion; though how the poverty-stricken countryside could have produced such an assemblage puzzled me beyond belief. And my second emotion—if there was any division at all in the wave of wonder that fairly drenched me—was feeling a sort of glory in the presence of such an atmosphere of splendid and vital *youth*. Everything vibrated, quivered, shook about me, and I almost felt myself as an aged and decrepit man by comparison.

I know my heart gave a great fiery leap as I saw them, for the faces that met me were fine, vigorous, and comely, while burning everywhere through their ripe maturity shone the ardours of youth and a kind of deathless enthusiasm. Old, yet eternally young they were, as rivers and mountains count their years by thousands, yet remain ever youthful; and the first effect of all those pairs of eyes lifted to meet my own was to send a whirlwind of unknown thrills about my heart and make me catch my breath with mingled terror and delight. A fear of death, and at the same time a sensation of touching something vast and eternal that could never die, surged through me.

A deep hush followed my entrance as all turned to look at me. They stood, men and women, grouped about a table, and something about them—not their size alone—conveyed the impression of being *gigantic,* giving me strangely novel realisations of freedom, power, and immense existences more or less than human.

I can only record my thoughts and impressions as they came to me and as I dimly now remember them. I had expected to see old Tom Bassett crouching half asleep over a peat fire, a dim lamp on the table beside him, and instead this assembly of tall and splendid men and women stood there to greet me, and stood in silence. It was little wonder that at first the ready question died upon my lips, and I almost forgot the words of my own language.

"I thought this was Tom Bassett's cottage!" I managed to ask at length, and looked straight at the man nearest me across the table. He had wild hair falling about his shoulders and a face of clear beauty. His eyes too, like all the rest, seemed shrouded by something veillike that reminded me of the shadowy man of whom I had first enquired the way. They were *shaded*—and for some reason I was glad that they were.

At the sound of my voice, unreal and thin, there was a general movement throughout the room, as though every one changed places, passing each other like those shapes of fluid sort I had seen outside in the mist. But no answer came. It seemed to me that the mist even penetrated into the room about me and spread inwardly over my thoughts.

"Is this my way to the Manor House?" I asked again louder, fighting my inward confusion and weakness. "Can *no one* tell me?"

Then apparently every one began to answer at once, or rather, not to answer directly, but to speak to each other in such a way that I could easily overhear. The voices of the men were deep, and of the women wonderfully musical, with a slow rhythm like that of the sea, or of the wind through the pine trees outside. But the unsatisfactory nature of what they said only helped to increase my sense of confusion and dismay.

"Yes," said one; "Tom Bassett *was* here for a while with the sheep, but his home was not here."

"He asks the way to a house when he does not even know the way to his own mind!" another voice said, sounding overhead it seemed.

"And could he recognise the signs if we told him?" came in the singing tones of a woman's voice close beside me.

And then, with a noise more like running water, or wind in the wings of birds, than anything else I could liken it to, came several voices together:

"And what sort of way does he seek? The splendid way, or merely the easy?"

"Or the short way of fools!"

"But he must have *some* credentials, or he never could have got as far as this," came from another.

A laugh ran round the room at this, though what there was to laugh at I could not imagine. It sounded like wind rushing about the hills. I got the impression too that the roof was somehow open to the sky, for their laughter had such a spacious quality in it, and the air was so cool and fresh, and moving about in currents and waves.

"It was I who showed him the way," cried a voice belonging to some one who was looking straight into my face over the table. "It was the safest way for him once he had got so far—"

I looked up and met his eye, and the sentence remained unfinished. It was the hurrying, shadowy man of the hillside. He had the same shifting outline as the others now, and the same veiled and shaded eyes, and as I looked the sense of terror stirred and grew in me. I had come in to ask for help, but now I was only anxious to be free of them all and out again in the rain and darkness on the moor. Thoughts of escape filled my brain, and I searched quickly for the door through which I had entered. But nowhere could I discover it again. The walls were bare; not even the windows were visible. And the room seemed to fill and empty of these figures as the waves of the sea fill and empty a cavern, crowding one upon another, yet never occupying more space, or less. So the coming and going of these men and women always evaded me.

And my terror became simply a terror that the veils of their eyes might lift, and that they would look at me with their clear, naked sight. I became horribly aware of their eyes. It was not that I felt them evil, but that I feared the new depths in me their merciless and terrible insight would stir into life. My consciousness had expanded quite enough for one night! I must escape at all costs and claim my own self again, however limited. I must have sanity, even if with limitations, but sanity at any price.

But meanwhile, though I tried hard to find my voice again, there came nothing but a thin piping sound that was like reeds whistling where winds meet about a corner. My throat was contracted, and I could only produce the smallest and most ridiculous of noises. The power of movement, too, was far less than when I first came in, and every moment it became more difficult to use my muscles, so that I stood there, stiff and awkward, face to face with this assemblage of shifting, wonderful people.

"And now," continued the voice of the man who had last spoken, "and now the safest way for him will be through the other door, where he shall see that which he may more easily understand."

With a great effort I regained the power of movement, while at the same time a burst of anger and a determination to be done with it all and to overcome my dreadful confusion drove me forward.

He saw me coming, of course, and the others indeed opened up and made a way for me, shifting to one side or the other whenever I came too near them, and never allowing me to touch them. But at last, when I was close in front of the man, ready both to speak and act, he was no longer there. I never saw the actual change—but instead of a man it was a woman! And when I turned with amazement, I saw that the other occupants, walking like figures in some ancient ceremony, were moving slowly towards the far end of the room. One by one, as they filed past, they raised their calm, passionless faces to mine, immensely vital, proud, austere, and then, without further word or gesture, they opened the door I had lost and disappeared through it one by one into the darkness of the night beyond. And as they went it seemed that the mist swallowed them up and a gust of wind caught them away, and the light also went with them, leaving me alone with the figure who had last spoken.

Moreover, it was just here that a most disquieting thought flashed through my brain with unreasoning conviction, shaking my personality, as it were, to the foundations: viz., that I had hitherto been spending my life in the pursuit of false knowledge, in the mere classifying and labelling of effects, the analysis of results, scientific so called; whereas it was the folk-lorist, and such like, who with their dreams and prayers were all the time on the path of real knowledge, the trail of causes; that the one was merely adding to the mechanical comfort and safety of the body, ultimately degrading the highest part of man, and never advancing the type, while the other—but then I had never yet believed in a soul—and now was no time to begin, terror or no terror. Clearly, my thoughts were wandering.

IV

It was at this moment the sound of the purring first reached me—deep, guttural purring—that made me think at once of some large concealed animal. It was precisely what I had heard many a time at the Zoological Gardens, and I had visions of cows chewing the cud, or horses munching hay in a stall outside the cottage. It was certainly an animal sound, and one of pleasure and contentment.

Semi-darkness filled the room. Only a very faint moonlight,

struggling through the mist, came through the window, and I moved back instinctively towards the support of the wall against my back. Somewhere, through openings, came the sound of the night driving over the roof, and far above I had visions of those everlasting winds streaming by with clouds as large as continents on their wings. Something in me wanted to sing and shout, but something else in me at the same time was in a very vivid state of unreasoning terror. I felt immense, yet tiny; confident, yet timid; a part of huge, universal forces, yet an utterly small, personal, and very limited being.

In the corner of the room on my right stood the woman. Her face was hid by a mass of tumbling hair, that made me think of living grasses on a field in June. Thus her head was partially turned from me, and the moonlight, catching her outline, just revealed it against the wall like an impressionist picture. Strange hidden memories stirred in the depths of me, and for a moment I felt that I knew all about her. I stared about me quickly, nervously, trying to take in everything at once. Then the purring sound grew much louder and closer, and I forgot my notion that this woman was no stranger to me and that I knew her as well as I knew myself. That purring thing was in the room close beside me. Between us two, indeed, it was, for I now saw that her arm nearest to me was raised, and that she was pointing to the wall in front of us.

Following the direction of her hand, I saw that the wall was transparent, and that I could see through a portion of it into a small square space beyond, as though I was looking through gauze instead of bricks. This small inner space was lighted, and on stooping down I saw that it was a sort of cupboard or cell-like cage let into the wall. The thing that purred was there in the centre of it.

I looked closer. It was a being, apparently a *human* being, crouching down in its narrow cage, feeding. I saw the body stooping over a quantity of coarse-looking, piled-up substance that was evidently food. It was like a man huddled up. There it squatted, happy and contented, with the minimum of air, light, and space, dully satisfied with its prisoned cage behind the bars, utterly unconscious of the vast world about it, grunting with pleasure, purring like a great cat, scornfully ignorant of what might lie beyond. The cell, moreover, I saw was a perfect masterpiece of mechanical contrivance and inventive ingenuity—the very last word in comfort, safety, and scientific skill. I was in the act of trying to fix in my memory some of the details of its construction and arrangement, when I made a chance noise, and at once became too agitated to note carefully what I saw. For at the noise the creature turned, and I saw that it *was* a human being—a man. I was aware of a face close against my own as it pressed forward, but a face with embryonic features impossible to describe and utterly loathsome, with eyes, ears, nose, and skin, only just sufficiently alive and developed to transfer the minimum of gross sensation to the brain. The mouth, however, was large and thick-lipped, and the jaws were still moving in the act of slow mastication.

I shrank back, shuddering with mingled pity and disgust, and at the same moment the woman beside me called me softly *by my own name*. She had moved forward a little so that she stood quite close to me, full in the thin stream of moonlight that fell across the floor, and I was conscious of a swift transition from hell to heaven as my gaze passed from that embryonic visage to a countenance so refined, so majestic, so divinely sensitive in its strength, that it was like turning from the face of a devil to look upon the features of a goddess.

At the same instant I was aware that both beings—the creature and the woman—were moving rapidly towards me.

A pain like a sharp sword dived deep down into me and twisted horribly through my heart, for as I saw them coming I realised in one swift moment of terrible intuition that they had their life in me, that they were born of my own being, and were indeed *projections of myself*. They were portions of my own consciousness projected outwardly into objectivity, and their degree of reality was just as great as that of any other part of me.

With a dreadful swiftness they rushed towards me, and in a single second had merged themselves into my own being; and I understood in some marvellous manner beyond the possibility of doubt that they were symbolic of my own soul: the dull animal part of me that had hitherto acknowledged nothing beyond its cage of minute sensations, and the higher part, almost out of reach, and in touch with the stars, that for the first time had feebly awakened into life during my journey over the hill.

V

I forget altogether how it was that I escaped, whether by the window or the door. I only know I found myself a moment later making great speed over the moor, followed by screaming birds and shouting wind, straight on the track downhill towards the Manor House. Something must have guided me, for I went with the instinct of an animal, having no uncertainties as to turnings, and saw the welcome lights of windows before I had covered another mile. And all the way I felt as though a great sluice gate had been opened to let a flood of new perceptions rush like a sea over my inner being, so that I was half ashamed and half delighted, partly angry, yet partly happy.

Servants met me at the door, several of them, and I was aware at once of an atmosphere of commotion in the house. I arrived breathless and hatless, wet to the skin, my hands scratched and my boots caked with mud.

"We made sure you were lost, sir," I heard the old butler say, and I heard my own reply, faintly, like the voice of some one else:

"I thought so too."

A minute later I found myself in the study, with the old folklorist standing opposite. In his hands he held the book I had brought down for him in my bag, ready addressed. There was a curious smile on his face.

"It never occurred to me that you would dare to *walk*—to-night of all nights," he was saying.

I stared without a word. I was bursting with the desire to tell him something of what had happened and try to be patient with his explanations, but when I sought for words and sentences my story seemed suddenly flat and pointless, and the details of my adventure began to evaporate and melt away, and seemed hard to remember.

"I had an exciting walk," I stammered, still a little breathless from running. "The weather was all right when I started from the station."

"The weather's all right still," he said, "though you may have found some evening mist on the top of the hills. But it's not that I meant."

"What then?"

"I meant," he said, still laughing quizzically, "that you were a very brave man to walk to-night over the enchanted hills, because this is May Day eve, and on May Day eve, you know, *They* have power over the minds of men, and can put glamour upon the imagination—"

"Who—*'they'*? What do you mean?"

He put my book down on the table beside him and looked quietly for a moment into my eyes, and as he did so the memory of my adventure began to revive in detail, and I thought quickly of the shadowy man who had shown me the way first. What could it have been in the face of the old folk-lorist that made me think of this man? A dozen things ran like flashes through my excited mind, and while I attempted to seize them I heard the old man's voice continue. He seemed to be talking to himself as much as to me.

"The elemental beings you have always scoffed at, of course; they who operate ceaselessly behind the screen of appearances, and who fashion and mould the moods of the mind. And an extremist like you—for extremes are always dangerously weak—is their legitimate prey."

"Pshaw!" I interrupted him, knowing that my manner betrayed me hopelessly, and that he had guessed much. "Any man may have subjective experiences, I suppose—"

Then I broke off suddenly. The change in his face made me start; it had taken on for the moment so exactly the look of the man on the hillside. The eyes gazing so steadily into mine had shadows in them, I thought.

"Glamour!" he was saying, "all glamour! One of them must have come very close to you, or perhaps touched you." Then he asked sharply, "Did you meet any one? Did you speak with any one?"

"I came by Tom Bassett's cottage," I said. "I didn't feel quite sure of my way and I went in and asked."

"All glamour," he repeated to himself, and then aloud to me, "And as for Bassett's cottage, it was burnt down three years ago, and nothing stands there now but broken, roofless walls—"

He stopped because I had seized him by the arm. In the shadows of the lamp-lit room behind him I thought I caught sight of dim forms moving past the book-shelves. But when my eye tried to focus them they faded and slipped away again into ceiling and walls. The details of the hill-top cottage, however, started into life again at the sight, and I seized my friend's arm to tell him. But instantly, when I tried, it all faded away again as though it had been a dream, and I could recall nothing intelligible to repeat to him.

He looked at me and laughed.

"They always obliterate the memory afterwards," he said gently, "so that little remains beyond a mood, or an emotion, to show how profoundly deep their touch has been. Though sometimes part of the change remains and becomes permanent—as I hope in your case it may."

Then, before I had time to answer, to swear, or to remonstrate, he stepped briskly past me and closed the door into the hall, and then drew me aside farther into the room. The change that I could not understand was still working in his face and eyes.

"If you have courage enough left to come with me," he said, speaking very seriously, "we will go out again and see more. Up till midnight, you know, there is still the opportunity, and with me perhaps you won't feel so—so—"

It was impossible somehow to refuse; everything combined to make me go. We had a little food and then went out into the hall, and he clapped a wide-awake on his grey hairs. I took a cloak and seized a walking-stick from the stand. I really hardly knew what I was doing. The new world I had awakened-to seemed still a-quiver about me.

As we passed out on to the gravel drive the light from the hall windows fell upon his face, and I saw that the change I had been so long observing was nearing its completeness, for there breathed about him that keen, wonderful atmosphere of eternal youth I had felt upon the inmates of the cottage. He seemed to have gone back forty years; a veil was gathering over his eyes; and I could have sworn that somehow his stature had increased, and that he moved beside me with a vigour and power I had never seen in him before.

And as we began to climb the hill together in silence I saw that the stars were clear overhead and there was no mist, that the trees stood motionless without wind, and that beyond us on the summit of the hills there were lights dancing to and fro, appearing and disappearing like the reflection of stars in water.

Miss Slumbubble—and Claustrophobia

Miss Daphne Slumbubble was a nervous lady of uncertain age who invariably went abroad in the spring. It was her one annual holiday, and she slaved for it all the rest of the year, saving money by the many sad devices known only to those who find their incomes after forty "barely enough," and always hoping that something would one day happen to better her dreary condition of cheap tea, tin loaves, and weekly squabbles with the laundress.

This spring holiday was the only time she really *lived* in the whole year, and she half starved herself for months immediately after her return, so as to put by quickly enough money for the journey in the following year. Once those six pounds were safe she felt better. After that she only had to save so many sums of four francs, each four francs meaning another day in the little cheap *pension* she always went to on the flowery slopes of the Alps of Valais.

Miss Slumbubble was exceedingly conscious of the presence of men. They made her nervous and afraid. She thought in her heart that all men were untrustworthy, not excepting policemen and clergymen, for in her early youth she had been cruelly deceived by a man to whom she had unreservedly given her heart. He had suddenly gone away and left her without a word of explanation, and some months later had married another woman and allowed the announcement to appear in the papers. It is true that he had hardly once spoken to Daphne. But that was nothing. For the way he looked at her, the way he walked about the room, the very way he avoided her at the tea-parties where she used to meet him at her rich sister's house—indeed, everything he did or left undone, brought convincing proof to her fluttering heart that he loved her secretly, and that he knew she loved him. His near presence disturbed her dreadfully, so much so that she invariably spilt her tea if he came even within scenting-distance of her; and once, when he crossed the room to offer her bread and butter, she was so certain the very way he held the plate interpreted his silent love, that she rose from her chair, looked straight into his eyes—and took the *whole plate* in a state of delicious confusion!

But all this was years ago, and she had long since learned to hold her grief in subjection and to prevent her life being too much embittered by the treachery—she felt it *was* treachery—of one man. She still, however, felt anxious and self-conscious in the presence of men, especially of silent, unmarried men, and to some extent it may be said that this fear haunted her life. It was shared, however, with other fears, probably all equally baseless. Thus, she lived in constant dread of fire, of railway accidents, of runaway cabs, and of being locked into a small, confined space. The former fears she shared, of course, with many other persons of both sexes, but the latter, the dread of confined spaces, was entirely due, no doubt, to a story she had heard in early youth to the effect that her father had once suffered from that singular nervous malady, *claustrophobia* (the fear of closed spaces), the terror of being caught in a confined place without possibility of escape.

Thus it was clear that Miss Daphne Slumbubble, this good, honest soul with jet flowers in her bonnet and rows of coloured photographs of Switzerland on her bedroom mantelpiece, led a life unnecessarily haunted.

The thought of the annual holiday, however, compensated for all else. In her lonely room behind Warwick Square she stewed through the dusty heat of summer, fought her way pluckily through the freezing winter fogs, and then, with the lengthening days, worked herself steadily into a fever heat of joyous anticipation as she counted the hours to the taking of her ticket in the first week of May. When the day came her happiness was so great that she wished for nothing else in the world. Even her name ceased to trouble her, for once on the other side of the Channel it sounded quite different on the lips of the foreigners, while in the little *pension* she was known as "Mlle. Daphné," and the mere sound brought music into her heart. The odious surname belonged to the sordid London life. It had nothing to do with the glorious days that Mlle. Daphné spent among the mountain tops.

The platform at Victoria was already crowded when she arrived a good hour before the train started, and got her tiny faded trunk weighed and labelled. She was so excited that she talked unnecessarily to any one who would listen—to any one in station uniform, that is. Already in fancy she saw the blue sky above the shining snow peaks, heard the tinkling cow-bells, and sniffed the odours of pinewood and sawmill. She imagined the cheerful *table d'hôte* room with its wooden floor and rows of chairs; the *diligence* winding up the hot white road far below; the fragrant *café complet* in her bedroom at 7.30—and then the long mornings with sketch-book and poetry-book under the forest shade, the clouds trailing slowly across the great cliffs, and the air always humming with the echoes of falling water.

"And you feel sure the passage will be calm, do you?" she asked the porter for the third time, as she bustled to and fro by his side.

"Well, there ain't no wind '*ere*, at any rate, Miss," he replied cheerfully, putting her small box on a barrow.

"Such a lot of people go by this train, don't they?" she piped.

"Oh, a tidy few. This is the season for foreign parts, I suppose."

"Yes, yes; and the trains on the other side will be very full, too, I dare say," she said, following him down the platform with quick, pattering footsteps, chirping all the way like a happy bird.

"Quite likely, Miss."

"I shall go in a 'Ladies only,' you know. I always do every year. I think it's safer, isn't it?"

"I'll see to it all for yer, Miss," replied the patient porter. "But the train ain't in yet, not for another 'arf hour or so."

"Oh, thank you; then I'll be here when it comes. 'Ladies only,' remember, and second class, and a corner seat facing the engine— no, *back* to the engine, I mean; and I *do* hope the Channel will be smooth. Do you think the wind—?"

But the porter was out of hearing by this time, and Miss Slumbubble went wandering about the platform watching the people arrive, studying the blue and yellow advertisements of the *Côte d'azur*, and waggling her jet beads with delight—with passionate delight—as she thought of her own little village in the high Alps where the snow crept down to a few hundred feet above the church and the meadows were greener than any in the whole wide world.

"I've put yer wraps in a 'Lidies only,' Miss," said the porter at length, when the train came in, "and you've got the corner back to the engine all to yerself, an' quite comfortable. Thank you, Miss." He touched his cap and pocketed his sixpence, and the fussy little traveller went off to take up her position outside the carriage door for another half hour before the train started. She was always very nervous about trains; not only fearful of possible accidents to the engine and carriages, but of untoward happenings to the occupants of corridorless compartments during long journeys without stops. The mere sight of a railway station, with its smoke and whistling and luggage, was sufficient to set her imagination in the direction of possible disaster.

The careful porter had piled all her belongings neatly in the corner for her: three newspapers, a magazine and a novel, a little bag to carry food in, two bananas and a Bath bun in paper, a bundle of wraps tied with a long strap, an umbrella, a bottle of Yanatas, an opera-glass (for the mountains), and a camera. She counted them all over, rearranged them a little differently, and then sighed a bit, partly from excitement, partly by way of protest at the delay.

A number of people came up and eyed the compartment critically and seemed on the point of getting in, but no one actually took possession. One lady put her umbrella in the corner, and then came tearing down the platform a few minutes later to take it away again, as though she had suddenly heard the train was not to start at all. There was much bustling to and fro, and a good deal of French was audible, and the sound of it thrilled Miss Daphne with happiness, for it was another delightful little anticipation of what was to come. Even the language sounded like a holiday, and brought with it a whiff of mountains and the subtle pleasures of sweet freedom.

Then a fat Frenchman arrived and inspected the carriage, and attempted to climb in. But she instantly pounced upon him in courageous dismay.

"Mais, c'est pour dames, m'sieur!" she cried, pronouncing it "dam."

"Oh, damn!" he exclaimed in English; "I didn't notice." And the rudeness of the man—it was the fur coat over his arm made her think he was French—set her all in a flutter, so that she jumped in and took her seat hurriedly, and spread her many parcels in a protective and prohibitive way about her.

For the tenth time she opened her black beaded bag and took out her purse and made sure her ticket was in it, and then counted over her belongings.

"I *do* hope," she murmured, "I do hope that stupid porter *has* put in my luggage all right, and that the Channel won't be rough. Porters *are* so stupid. One ought never to lose sight of them till the luggage is actually in. I think I'd better pay the extra fare and go first class on the boat if it is rough. I can carry all my own packages, I think."

At that moment the man came for tickets. She searched everywhere for her own, but could not find it.

"I'm certain I had it a moment ago," she said breathlessly, while the man stood waiting at the open door. "I know I had it—only this very minute. Dear me, what *can* I have done with it? Ah! here it is!"

The man took so long examining the little tourist cover that she was afraid something must be wrong with it, and when at last he tore out a leaf and handed back the rest a sort of panic seized her.

"It's all right, isn't it, guard? I mean *I'm* all right, am I not?" she asked.

The guard closed the door and locked it.

"All right for Folkestone, ma'am," he said, and was gone.

There was much whistling and shouting and running up and down the platform, and the inspector was standing with his hand raised and the whistle at his lips, waiting to blow and looking cross. Suddenly her own porter flew past with an empty barrow. She dashed her head out of the window and hailed him.

"You're sure you put my luggage in, aren't you?" she cried. The man did not or would not hear, and as the train moved slowly off she bumped her head against an old lady standing on the platform who was looking the other way and waving to some one in a front carriage.

"Ooh!" cried Miss Slumbubble, straightening her bonnet, "you really should look where you're looking, madam!"—and then, realising she had said something foolish, she withdrew into the carriage and sank back in a fluster on the cushions.

"Oh!" she gasped again, "oh dear! I'm actually off at last. It's too good to be true. Oh, that horrid London!"

Then she counted her money over again, examined her ticket once more, and touched each of her many packages with a long finger in a cotton glove, saying, *"That's* there, and that, and that, and—*that!"* And then turning and pointing at herself she added, with a little happy laugh, *"and that!"*

The train gathered speed, and the dirty roofs and sea of ugly chimneys flew by as the dreary miles of depressing suburbs revealed themselves through the windows. She put all her parcels up in the rack and then took them all down again; and after a bit she put a few up—a carefully selected few that she would not need till Folkestone—and arranged the others, some upon the seat beside her, and some opposite. The paper bag of bananas she kept in her lap, where it grew warmer and warmer and more and more dishevelled in appearance.

"Actually off at last!" she murmured again, catching her breath a little in her joy. "Paris, Berne, Thun, Frutigen," she gave herself a little hug that made the jet beads rattle; "then the long diligence journey up those gorgeous mountains," she knew every inch of the way, "and a clear fifteen days at the *pension,* or even eighteen days, if I can get the cheaper room. Wheeeee! Can it be true? Can it be really true?" In her happiness she made sounds just like a bird.

She looked out of the window, where green fields had replaced the rows of streets. She opened her novel and tried to read. She played with the newspapers in a vain attempt to keep her eye on any one column. It was all in vain. A scene of wild beauty held her inner eye and made all else dull and uninteresting. The train sped on—slowly enough to her—yet every moment of the journey, every turn of the creaking wheels that brought her nearer, every little detail of the familiar route, became a source of keenest anticipatory happiness to her. She no longer cared about her name, or her silent and faithless lover of long ago, or of anything in the world but the fact that her absorbing little annual passion was now once again in a fair way to be gratified.

Then, quite suddenly, Miss Slumbubble realised her actual position, and felt afraid, unreasonably afraid. For the first time she became conscious that she was alone, alone in the compartment of an express train, and not even of a corridor express train.

Hitherto the excitement of getting off had occupied her mind to the exclusion of everything else, and if she had realised her solitude at all, she had realised it pleasurably. But now, in the first pause for breath as it were, when she had examined her packages, counted her money, glared at her ticket, and all the rest of it for the twentieth time, she leaned back in her seat and knew with a distinct shock that she was alone in a railway carriage on a comparatively long journey, alone for the first time in her life in a rattling, racing, shrieking train. She sat bolt upright and tried to collect herself a little.

Of all the emotions, that of fear is probably the least susceptible to the power of suggestion, certainly of *auto*-suggestion; and of vague fear that has no obvious cause this is especially true. With a fear of known origin one can argue, humour it, pacify, turn on the hose of ridicule—in a word, *suggest* that it depart; but with a fear that rises stealthily out of no comprehensible causes the mind finds itself at a complete loss. The mere assertion "I am not afraid" is as useless and empty as the subtler kind of suggestion that lies in affecting to ignore it altogether. Searching for the cause, moreover, tends to confuse the mind, and searching in vain, to terrify.

Miss Slumbubble pulled herself sharply together, and began to search for what made her afraid, but for a long time she searched in vain.

At first she searched externally: she thought perhaps it had something to do with one of her packages, and she placed them all out in a row on the seat in front of her and examined each in turn, bananas, camera, food bag, black bead bag, &c. &c. But she discovered nothing among them to cause alarm.

Then she searched internally: her thoughts, her rooms in London, her *pension*, her money, ticket, plans in general, her future, her past, her health, her religion, anything and everything among the events of her inner life she passed in review, yet found nothing that could have caused this sudden sense of being troubled and afraid.

Moreover, as she vainly searched, her fear increased. She got into a regular nervous flurry.

"I declare if I'm not all in a perspiration!" she exclaimed aloud, and shifted down the dirty cushions to another place, looking anxiously about her as she did so. She probed everywhere in her thoughts to find the reason of her fear, but could think of nothing. Yet in her soul there was a sense of growing distress.

She found her new seat no more comfortable than the one before it, and shifted in turn into all the corners of the carriage, and down the middle as well, till at last she had tried every possible part of it. In each place she felt less at ease than in the one before. She got up and looked into the empty racks, under the seats, beneath the heavy cushions, which she lifted with difficulty. Then she put all the packages back again into the rack, dropping several of them in her nervous hurry, and being obliged to kneel on the floor to recover them from under the seats. This made her breathless. Moreover, the dust got into her throat and made her cough. Her eyes smarted and she grew uncomfortably warm. Then, quite accidentally, she caught sight of her reflection in the coloured picture of Boulogne under the rack, and the appearance she presented added greatly to her dismay. She looked so unlike herself, and wore such an odd expression. It was almost like the face of another person altogether.

The sense of alarm, once wakened, is fed by anything and everything, from a buzzing fly to a dark cloud in the sky. The woman collapsed on to the seat behind her in a distressing fluster of nervous fear.

But Miss Daphne Slumbubble had pluck. She was not so easily dismayed after all. She had read somewhere that terror was sometimes dispersed by the loud and strong affirmation of one's own name. She believed much that she read, provided it was plainly and vigorously expressed, and she acted at once on this knowledge.

"I am Daphne Slumbubble!" she affirmed in a firm, confident tone of voice, sitting stiffly on the edge of the seat; "I am not afraid—of anything." She added the last two words as an afterthought. "I am Daphne Slumbubble, and I have paid for my ticket, and know where I am going, and my luggage is in the van, and I have all my smaller things here!" She enumerated them one by one; she omitted nothing.

Yet the sound of her own voice, and especially of her own name, added apparently to her distress. It sounded oddly, like a voice out-side the carriage. Everything seemed suddenly to have become strange, and unfamiliar, and unfriendly. She moved across to the op-posite corner and looked out of the window: trees, fields, and occa-sional country houses flew past in endless swift succession. The country looked charming; she saw rooks flying and farm-horses mov-ing laboriously over the fields. What in the world was there to feel afraid of? What in the world made her so restless and fidgety and frightened? Once again she examined her packages, her ticket, her money. All was right.

Then she dashed across to the window and tried to open it. The sash stuck. She pulled and pulled in vain. The sash refused to yield. She ran to the other window, with a like result. Both were closed. Both refused to open. Her fear grew. She was locked in! The win-dows would not open. Something was wrong with the carriage. She suddenly recalled the way every one had examined it and refused to enter. There must be something the matter with the carriage—something she had omitted to observe. Terror ran like a flame through her. She trembled and was ready to cry.

She ran up and down between the cushioned seats like a bird in a cage, casting wild glances at the racks and under the seats and out of the windows. A sudden panic took her, and she tried to open the door. It was locked. She flew to the other door. That, too, was locked. Good heavens, both were locked! She was locked in. She was a prisoner. She was caught in a closed space. The mountains were out of her reach—the free open woods—the wide fields, the scented winds of heaven. She was caught, hemmed in, celled, restricted like a prisoner in a dungeon. The thought maddened her. The feeling that she could not reach the open spaces of sky and forest, of field and blue horizon, struck straight into her soul and touched all that she held most dear. She screamed. She ran down between the cushioned seats and screamed aloud.

Of course, no one heard her. The thunder of the train killed the feeble sound of her voice. Her voice was the cry of the imprisoned person.

Then quite suddenly she understood what it all meant. There was nothing wrong with the carriage, or with her parcels, or with the train. She sat down abruptly upon the dirty cushions and faced the position there and then. It had nothing to do with her past or her future, her ticket or her money, her religion or her health. It was something else entirely. She knew what it was, and the knowledge brought icy terror at once. She had at last labelled the source of her consternation, and the discovery increased rather than lessened her distress.

It was the fear of closed spaces. It was *claustrophobia!*

There could no longer be any doubt about it. She was shut in. She was enclosed in a narrow space from which she could not escape. The walls and floor and ceiling shut her in implacably. The doors was fastened; the windows were sealed, there was no escape.

"That porter *might* have told me!" she exclaimed inconsequently, mopping her face. Then the foolishness of the saying dawned upon her, and she thought her mind must be going. That was the effect of claustrophobia, she remembered: the mind went, and one said and did foolish things. Oh, to get out into a free open space, uncornered! Here she was trapped, horribly trapped.

"The guard man should never have locked me in—never!" she cried, and ran up and down between the seats, throwing her weight first against the door and then against the other. Of course, fortunately, neither of them yielded.

Thinking food might calm her, perhaps, she took down the banana bag and peeled the squashy over ripe fruit, munching it with part of the Bath bun from the other bag, and sitting midway on the forward seat. Suddenly the right-hand window dropped with a bang and a rattle. It had only been stuck after all, and her efforts, aided by the shaking of the train, had completed its undoing, or rather its unclosing. Miss Slumbubble shrieked, and dropped her banana and bun.

But the shock passed in a moment when she saw what had happened, and that the window was open and the sweet air pouring in from the flying fields. She rushed up and put her head out. This was followed by her hand, for she meant to open the door from the outside if possible. Whatever happened, the one imperative thing was that she must get into open space. The handle turned easily enough, but the door was locked higher up and she could not make it budge. She put her head farther out, so that the wind tore the jet bonnet off her head and left it twirling in the dusty whirlwind on the line far behind, and this sensation of the air whistling past her ears and through her flying hair somehow or other managed to make her feel wilder than ever. In fact, she completely lost her head, and began to scream at the top of her voice:

"I'm locked in! I'm a prisoner! Help, help!" she yelled.

A window opened in the next compartment and a young man put his head out.

"What the deuce is the matter? Are you being murdered?" he shouted down the wind.

"I'm locked in! I'm locked in!" screamed the hatless lady, wrestling furiously with the obdurate door handle.

"Don't open the door!" cried the young man anxiously.

"I can't, you idiot! I can't!"

"Wait a moment and I'll come to you. Don't try to get out. I'll climb along the foot-board. Keep calm, madam, keep calm. I'll save you."

He disappeared from view. Good heavens! He meant to crawl out and come to her carriage by the window! A man, a *young* man, would shortly be in the compartment with her. Locked in, too! No, it was impossible. That was worse than the claustrophobia, and she could not endure such a thing for a moment. The young man would certainly kill her and steal all her packages.

She ran once or twice frantically up and down the narrow floor. Then she looked out of the window.

"Oh, bless my heart and soul!" she cried out, "he's out already!"

The young man, evidently thinking the lady was being assaulted, had climbed out of the window and was pluckily coming to her rescue. He was already on the foot-board, swinging by the brass bars on the side of the coach as the train rocked down the line at a fearful pace.

But Miss Slumbubble took a deep breath and a sudden determination. She did, in fact, the only thing left to her to do. She pulled the communication cord once, twice, three times, and then drew the window up with a sudden snap just before the young man's head appeared round the corner of the sash. Then, stepping backwards, she trod on the slippery banana bag and fell flat on her back upon the dirty floor between the seats.

The train slackened speed almost immediately and came to a stop. Miss Slumbubble still sat on the floor, staring in a dazed fashion at her toes. She realised the enormity of her offence, and was thoroughly frightened. She had actually pulled the cord!—the cord that is meant to be seen but not touched, the little chain that meant a £5 fine and all sorts of dire consequences.

She heard voices shouting and doors opening, and a moment later a key rattled near her head, and she saw the guard swinging up on to the steps of the carriage. The door was wide open, and the young man from the next compartment was explaining volubly what he seen and heard.

"I thought it was murder," he was saying.

But the guard pushed quickly into the carriage and lifted the panting and dishevelled lady on to the seat.

"Now, what's all this about? Was it you that pulled the cord, ma'am?" he asked somewhat roughly. "It's serious stoppin' a train like this, you know, a mail train."

Now Miss Daphne did not mean to tell a lie. It was not deliberate, that is to say. It seemed to slip out of its own accord as the most natural and obvious thing to say. For she was terrified at what she had done, and *had* to find a good excuse. Yet, how in the world could she describe to this stupid and hurried official all she had gone through? Moreover, he would be so certain to think she was merely drunk.

"It was a man," she said, falling back instinctively upon her natural enemy. "There's a man somewhere!" She glanced round at the racks and under the seats. The guard followed her eyes.

"I don't see no man," he declared; "all I know is you've stopped the mail train without any visible or reasonable cause. I'll be obliged with your name and address, ma'am, if you please," he added, taking a dirty notebook from his pocket and wetting the blunt pencil in his mouth.

"Let me get air—at once," she said. "I must have air first. Of course you shall have my name. The whole affair is disgraceful." She was getting her wits back. She moved to the door.

"That may be, ma'am," the man said, "but I've my duty to perform, and I must report the facts, and then get the train on as quick as possible. You must stay in the carriage, please. We've been waiting 'ere a bit too long already."

Miss Slumbubble met her fate calmly. She realised it was not fair to keep all the passengers waiting while she got a little fresh air. There was a brief confabulation between the two guards, which ended by the one who had first come taking his seat in her carriage, while the other blew his whistle and the train started off again and flew at great speed the remaining miles to Folkestone.

"Now I'll take the name and address, if you please, ma'am," he said politely. "*Daphny*, yes, thank you; Daphny without a hef, all right, thank you."

He wrote it all down laboriously while the hatless little lady sat opposite, indignant, excited, ready to be voluble the moment she could think what was best to say, and above all fearful that her holiday would he delayed, if not prevented altogether.

Presently the guard looked up at her and put his notebook away in an inner pocket. It was just after he had entered the number of the carriage.

"You see, ma'am," he explained with sudden suavity, "this communication cord is only for cases of real danger, and if I report this, as I should do, it means a 'eavy fine. You must 'ave just pulled it as a sort of hexperiment, didn't you?"

Something in the man's voice caught her ear; there was a change in it; his manner, too, had altered somehow. He suddenly seemed to have become apologetic. She was quick to notice the change, though she could not understand what caused it. It began, she fancied, from the moment he entered the number of the carriage in his notebook.

"It's the delay to the train I've got to explain," he continued, as if speaking to himself, "and I can't put it all on to the engine-driver—"

"Perhaps we shall make it up and there won't be any delay," ventured Miss Slumbubble, carefully smoothing her hair and rearranging the stray hairpins.

"—and I don't want to get no one into any kind of trouble, least of all myself," he continued, wholly ignoring the interruption. Then he turned round in his seat and stared hard at his companion with rather a worried, puzzled expression of countenance and a shrug of the shoulders that was distinctly apologetic. Plainly, she thought, he was preparing the way for a compromise—for a tip!

The train was slackening speed; already it was in the cutting where it reverses and is pushed backwards on to the pier. Miss Slumbubble was desperate. She had never tipped a man before in her life except for obvious and recognised services, and this seemed to her like compounding a felony, or some such dreadful thing. Yet so much was at stake: she might be detained at Folkestone for days before the matter came into court, to say nothing of a £5 fine, which meant that her holiday would be utterly stopped. The blue and white mountains swam into her field of vision, and she heard the wind in the pine forest.

"Perhaps you would give this to your wife," she said timidly, holding out a sovereign.

The guard looked at it and shook his head.

"I 'aven't got a wife, exackly," he said; "but it isn't money I want. What I want is to 'ush this little matter up as quietly as possible. I may lose my job over this—but if you'll agree to say nothing about it, I think I can square the driver and t'other guard."

"*I* won't say anything, *of course*," stammered the astonished lady. "But I don't think I quite understand—"

"You couldn't understand either till I tell you," he replied, looking greatly relieved; "but the fac' is, I never noticed the carriage till I come to put the number down, and then I see it's the very one—the very same number—"

"What number?"

He stared at her for a moment without speaking. Then he appeared to take a great decision.

"Well, I'm in your 'ands anyhow, ma'am, and I may as well tell you the lot, and then we both 'elps the other out. It's this way, you see. You ain't the first to try and jump out of this carriage—not by a long ways. It's been done before by a good number—"

"Gracious!"

"But the first who did it was that German woman, Binckmann—"

"Binckmann, the woman who was found on the line last year, and the carriage door open?" cried Miss Slumbubble, aghast.

"That's her. This was the carriage she jumped from, and they tried to say it was murder, but couldn't find any one who could have done it, and then they said she must have been crazy. And since then this carriage was said to be 'aunted, because so many other people tried to do the same thing and throw theirselves out too, till the company changed the number—"

"To this number?" cried the excited spinster, pointing to the figures on the door.

"That's it, ma'am. And if you look you'll see this number don't follow on with the others. Even then the thing didn't stop, and we got orders to let no one in. That's where I made my mistake. I left the door unlocked, and they put you in. If this gets in the papers I'll be dismissed for sure. The company's awful strict about that."

"I'm terrified!" exclaimed Miss Slumbubble, "for that's exactly what I felt—"

"That you'd got to jump out, you mean?" asked the guard.

"Yes. The terror of being shut in."

"That's what the doctors said Binckmann had—the fear of being shut up in a tight place. They gave it some long name, but that's what it was: she couldn't abide being closed in. Now, here we are at the pier, ma'am, and, if you'll allow me, I'll help you to carry your little bits of luggage."

"Oh, thank you, guard, thank you," she said faintly, taking his proffered hand and getting out with infinite relief on to the platform.

"Tchivalry ain't dead yet, Miss," he replied gallantly, as he loaded himself up with her packages and led the way down to the steamer.

Ten minutes later the deep notes of the syren echoed across the pier, and the paddles began to churn the green sea. And Miss Daphne Slumbubble, hatless but undismayed, went abroad to flutter the remnants of her faded youth before the indifferent foreigners in the cheap *pension* among the Alps.

The Woman's Ghost Story

Y es," she said, from her seat in the dark corner, "I'll tell you an experience if you care to listen. And, what's more, I'll tell it briefly, without trimmings—I mean without unessentials. That's a thing story-tellers never do, you know," she laughed. "They drag in all the unessentials and leave their listeners to disentangle; but I'll give you just the essentials, and you can make of it what you please. But on one condition: that at the end you ask no questions, because I can't explain it and have no wish to."

We agreed. We were all serious. After listening to a dozen prolix stories from people who merely wished to "talk" but had nothing to tell, we wanted "essentials."

"In those days," she began, feeling from the quality of our silence that we were with her, "in those days I was interested in psychic things, and had arranged to sit up alone in a haunted house in the middle of London. It was a cheap and dingy lodging-house in a mean street, unfurnished. I had already made a preliminary examination in daylight that afternoon, and the keys from the caretaker, who lived next door, were in my pocket. The story was a good one—satisfied me, at any rate, that it was worth investigating; and I won't weary you with details as to the woman's murder and all the tiresome elaboration as to *why* the place was *alive*. Enough that it was.

"I was a good deal bored, therefore, to see a man, whom I took to be the talkative old caretaker, waiting for me on the steps when I went in at 11 P.M., for I had sufficiently explained that I wished to be there alone for the night.

"'I wished to show you *the* room,' he mumbled, and of course I couldn't exactly refuse, having tipped him for the temporary loan of a chair and table.

"'Come in, then, and let's be quick,' I said.

"We went in, he shuffling after me through the unlighted hall up to the first floor where the murder had taken place, and I prepared myself to hear his inevitable account before turning him out with the half-crown his persistence had earned. After lighting the gas I sat down in the arm-chair he had provided—a faded, brown plush arm-chair—and turned for the first time to face him and get through with the performance as quickly as possible. And it was in that instant I got my first shock. The man was *not* the caretaker. It was not the old fool, Carey, I had interviewed earlier in the day and made my plans with. My heart gave a horrid jump.

"'Now who are *you*, pray?' I said. 'You're not Carey, the man I arranged with this afternoon. Who are you?'

"I felt uncomfortable, as you may imagine. I was a 'psychical researcher,' and a young woman of new tendencies, and proud of my liberty, but I did not care to find myself in an empty house with a stranger. Something of my confidence left me. Confidence with women, you know, is all humbug after a certain point. Or perhaps you don't know, for most of you are men. But anyhow my pluck ebbed in a quick rush, and I felt afraid.

"'Who are you?' I repeated quickly and nervously. The fellow was well dressed, youngish, and good-looking, but with a face of great sadness. I myself was barely thirty. I am giving you essentials, or I would not mention it. Out of quite ordinary things comes this story. I think that's why it has value.

"'No,' he said; 'I'm the man who was frightened to death.'

"His voice and his words ran through me like a knife, and I felt ready to drop. In my pocket was the book I had brought to make notes in. I felt the pencil sticking in the socket. I felt, too, the extra warm things I had put on to sit up in, as no bed or sofa was available—a hundred things dashed through my mind, foolishly and without sequence or meaning, as the way is when one is really frightened. Unessentials leaped up and puzzled me, and I thought of what the papers might say if it came out, and what my 'smart' brother-in-law would think, and whether it would be told that I had cigarettes in my pocket, and was a free-thinker.

"'The man who was frightened to death!' I repeated aghast.

"'That's me,' he said stupidly.

"I stared at him just as you would have done—any one of you men now listening to me—and felt my life ebbing and flowing like a sort of hot fluid. You needn't laugh! That's how I felt. Small things, you know, touch the mind with great earnestness when terror is there—*real terror*. But I might have been at a middle-class tea-party, for all the ideas I had: they were so ordinary!

"'But I thought you were the caretaker I tipped this afternoon to let me sleep here!' I gasped. 'Did—did Carey send you to meet me?'

"'No,' he replied in a voice that touched my boots somehow. 'I am the man who was frightened to death. And what is more, I am frightened *now!*'

"'So am I!' I managed to utter, speaking instinctively. 'I'm simply terrified.'

"'Yes,' he replied in that same odd voice that seemed to sound within me. 'But you are still in the flesh, and I—*am not!*'

"I felt the need for vigorous self-assertion. I stood up in that empty, unfurnished room, digging the nails into my palms and clenching my teeth. I was determined to assert my individuality and my courage as a new woman and a free soul.

"'You mean to say you are not in the flesh!' I gasped. 'What in the world are you talking about?'

"The silence of the night swallowed up my voice. For the first time I realised that darkness was over the city; that dust lay upon the stairs; that the floor above was untenanted and the floor below empty. I was alone in an unoccupied and haunted house, unprotected, and a woman. I chilled. I heard the wind round the house, and knew the stars were hidden. My thoughts rushed to policemen and omnibuses, and everything that was useful and comforting. I suddenly realised what a fool I was to come to such a house alone. I was icily afraid. I thought the end of my life had come. I was an utter fool to go in for psychical research when I had not the necessary nerve.

"'Good God!' I gasped. 'If you're not Carey, the man I arranged with, who are you?'

"I was really stiff with terror. The man moved slowly towards me across the empty room. I held out my arm to stop him, getting up out of my chair at the same moment, and he came to a halt just opposite to me, a smile on his worn, sad face.

"'I told you who I am,' he repeated quietly with a sigh, looking at me with the saddest eyes I have ever seen, 'and I am frightened *still.*'

"By this time I was convinced that I was entertaining either a rogue or a madman, and I cursed my stupidity in bringing the man in without having seen his face. My mind was quickly made up, and I knew what to do. Ghosts and psychic phenomena flew to the winds. If I angered the creature my life might pay the price. I must humour him till I got to the door, and then race for the street. I stood bolt upright and faced him. We were about of a height, and I was a strong, athletic woman who played hockey in winter and climbed Alps in summer. My hand itched for a stick, but I had none.

"'Now, of course, I remember,' I said with a sort of stiff smile that was very hard to force. 'Now I remember your case and the wonderful way you behaved. . . .'

"The man stared at me stupidly, turning his head to watch me as I backed more and more quickly to the door. But when his face broke into a smile I could control myself no longer. I reached the door in a run, and shot out on to the landing. Like a fool, I turned the wrong way, and stumbled over the stairs leading to the next storey. But it was too late to change. The man was after me, I was sure, though no sound of footsteps came; and I dashed up the next flight, tearing my skirt and banging my ribs in the darkness, and rushed headlong into the first room I came to. Luckily the door stood ajar, and, still more fortunate, there was a key in the lock. In a second I had slammed the door, flung my whole weight against it, and turned the key.

"I was safe, but my heart was beating like a drum. A second later it seemed to stop altogether, for I saw that there was some one else in the room besides myself. A man's figure stood between me and the window, where the street lamps gave just enough light to outline his shape against the glass. I'm a plucky woman, you know, for even then I didn't give up hope, but I may tell you that I have never felt so vilely frightened in all my born days. I had locked myself in with him!

"The man leaned against the window, watching me where I lay in a collapsed heap upon the floor. So there were two men in the house with me, I reflected. Perhaps the other rooms were occupied too! What could it all mean? But, as I stared something changed in the room, or in me—hard to say which—and I realised my mistake, so that my fear, which had so far been physical, at once altered its character and became *psychical.* I became afraid in my soul instead of in my heart, and I knew immediately who this man was.

"'How in the world did you get up here?' I stammered to him across the empty room, amazement momentarily stemming my fear.

"'Now, let me tell you,' he began, in that odd far-away voice of his that went down my spine like a knife. 'I'm in different space, for one thing, and you'd find me in any room you went into; for according to your way of measuring, I'm *all over the house.* Space is a bodily condition, but I am out of the body, and am not affected by space. It's my condition that keeps me here. I want something to change my condition for me, for then I could get away. What I want is sympathy. Or, really, more than sympathy; I want affection—I want *love!*'

"While he was speaking I gathered myself slowly upon my feet. I wanted to scream and cry and laugh all at once, but I only succeeded in sighing, for my emotion was exhausted and a numbness was coming over me. I felt for the matches in my pocket and made a movement towards the gas jet.

"'I should be much happier if you didn't light the gas,' he said at once, 'for the vibrations of your light hurt me a good deal. You need not be afraid that I shall injure you. I can't touch your body to begin with, for there's a great gulf fixed, you know; and really this half-light suits me best. Now, let me continue what I was trying to say before. You know, so many people have come to this house to see me, and most of them have seen me, and one and all have been terrified. If only, oh! if only some one would be *not* terrified, but kind and loving to me! Then, you see, I might be able to change my condition and get away.'

"His voice was so sad that I felt tears start somewhere at the back of my eyes; but fear kept all else in check, and I stood shaking and cold as I listened to him.

"'Who are you then? Of course Carey didn't send you, I know now,' I managed to utter. My thoughts scattered dreadfully and I could think of nothing to say. I was afraid of a stroke.

"'I know nothing about Carey, or who he is,' continued the man quietly, 'and the name my body had I have forgotten, thank God; but

I am the man who was frightened to death in this house ten years ago, and I have been frightened ever since, and am frightened still; for the succession of cruel and curious people who come to this house to see the ghost, and thus keep alive its atmosphere of terror, only helps to render my condition worse. If only some one would be kind to me—*laugh,* speak gently and rationally with me, cry if they like, pity, comfort, soothe me—anything but come here in curiosity and tremble as you are now doing in that corner. Now, madam, won't you take pity on me?' His voice rose to a dreadful cry. 'Won't you step out into the middle of the room and try to love me a little?'

"A horrible laughter came gurgling up in my throat as I heard him, but the sense of pity was stronger than the laughter, and I found myself actually leaving the support of the wall and approaching the centre of the floor.

"'By God!' he cried, at once straightening up against the window, 'you have done a kind act. That's the first attempt at sympathy that has been shown me since I died, and I feel better already. In life, you know, I was a misanthrope. Everything went wrong with me, and I came to hate my fellow men so much that I couldn't bear to see them even. Of course, like begets like, and this hate was returned. Finally I suffered from horrible delusions, and my room became haunted with demons that laughed and grimaced, and one night I ran into a whole cluster of them near the bed—and the fright stopped my heart and killed me. It's hate and remorse, as much as terror, that clogs me so thickly and keeps me here. If only some one could feel pity, and sympathy, and perhaps a little love for me, I could get away and be happy. When you came this afternoon to see over the house I watched you, and a little hope came to me for the first time. I saw you had courage, originality, resource—*love.* If only I could touch your heart, without frightening you, I knew I could perhaps tap that love you have stored up in your being there, and thus borrow the wings for my escape!'

"Now I must confess my heart began to ache a little, as fear left me and the man's words sank their sad meaning into me. Still, the whole affair was so incredible, and so touched with unholy quality, and the story of a woman's murder I had come to investigate had so obviously nothing to do with this thing, that I felt myself in a kind of wild dream that seemed likely to stop at any moment and leave me somewhere in bed after a nightmare.

"Moreover, his words possessed me to such an extent that I found it impossible to reflect upon anything else at all, or to consider adequately any ways and means of action or escape.

"I moved a little nearer to him in the gloom, horribly frightened, of course, but with the beginnings of a strange determination in my heart.

"'You women,' he continued, his voice plainly thrilling at my approach, 'you wonderful women, to whom life often brings no opportunity of spending your great love, oh, if you only could know how many of *us* simply yearn for it! It would save our souls, if you but knew. Few might find the chance that you now have, but if you only spent your love freely, without definite object, just letting it flow openly for all who need, you would reach hundreds and thousands of souls like me, and *release us!* Oh, madam, I ask you again to feel with me, to be kind and gentle—and if you can to love me a little!'

"My heart did leap within me and this time the tears did come, for I could not restrain them. I laughed too, for the way he called me 'madam' sounded so odd, here in this empty room at midnight in a London street, but my laughter stopped dead and merged in a flood of weeping when I saw how my change of feeling had affected him. He had left his place by the window and was kneeling on the floor at my feet, his hands stretched out towards me, and the first signs of a kind of glory about his head.

"'Put your arms round me and kiss me, for the love of God!' he cried. 'Kiss me, oh, kiss me, and I shall be freed! You have done so much already—now do this!'

"I stuck there, hesitating, shaking, my determination on the verge of action, yet not quite able to compass it. But the terror had almost gone.

"'Forget that I'm a man and you're a woman,' he continued in the most beseeching voice I ever heard. 'Forget that I'm a ghost, and come out boldly and press me to you with a great kiss, and let your love flow into me. Forget yourself just for one minute and do a brave thing! Oh, love me, *love me*, LOVE ME! and I shall be free!'

"The words, or the deep force they somehow released in the centre of my being, stirred me profoundly, and an emotion infinitely greater than fear surged up over me and carried me with it across the edge of action. Without hesitation I took two steps forward towards him where he knelt, and held out my arms. Pity and love were in my heart at that moment, genuine pity, I swear, and genuine love. I forgot myself and my little tremblings in a great desire to help another soul.

"'I love you! poor, aching, unhappy thing! I love you,' I cried through hot tears; 'and I am not the least bit afraid in the world.'

"The man uttered a curious sound, like laughter, yet not laughter, and turned his face up to me. The light from the street below fell on it, but there was another light, too, shining all round it that seemed to come from the eyes and skin. He rose to his feet and met me, and in that second I folded him to my breast and kissed him full on the lips again and again."

All our pipes had gone out, and not even a skirt rustled in that dark studio as the story-teller paused a moment to steady her voice, and put a hand softly up to her eyes before going on again.

"Now, what can I say, and how can I describe to you, all you sceptical men sitting there with pipes in your mouths, the amazing sensation I experienced of holding an intangible, impalpable thing so closely to my heart that it touched my body with equal pressure all the way down, and then melted away somewhere into my very being? For it was like seizing a rush of cool wind and feeling a touch of burning fire the moment it had struck its swift blow and passed on. A series of shocks ran all over and all through me; a momentary ecstasy of flaming sweetness and wonder thrilled down into me; my heart gave another great leap—and then I was alone.

"The room was empty. I turned on the gas and struck a match to prove it. All fear had left me, and something was singing round me in the air and in my heart like the joy of a spring morning in youth. Not all the devils or shadows or hauntings in the world could then have caused me a single tremor.

"I unlocked the door and went all over the dark house, even into kitchen and cellar and up among the ghostly attics. But the house was empty. Something had left it. I lingered a short hour, analysing, thinking, wondering—you can guess what and how, perhaps, but I won't detail, for I promised only essentials, remember—and then went out to sleep the remainder of the night in my own flat, locking the door behind me upon a house no longer haunted.

"But my uncle, Sir Henry, the owner of the house, required an account of my adventure, and of course I was in duty bound to give him some kind of a true story. Before I could begin, however, he held up his hand to stop me.

"'First,' he said, 'I wish to tell you a little deception I ventured to practise on you. So many people have been to that house and seen the ghost that I came to think the story acted on their imaginations, and I wished to make a better test. So I invented for their benefit another story, with the idea that if you did see anything I could be sure it was not due merely to an excited imagination.'

"'Then what you told me about a woman having been murdered, and all that, was not the true story of the haunting?'

"'It was not. The true story is that a cousin of mine went mad in that house, and killed himself in a fit of morbid terror following upon years of miserable hypochondriasis. It is his figure that investigators see.'

"'That explains, then,' I gasped—

"'Explains what?'

"I thought of that poor struggling soul, longing all these years for escape, and determined to keep my story for the present to myself.

"'Explains, I mean, why I did not see the ghost of the murdered woman,' I concluded.

"'Precisely,' said Sir Henry, 'and why, if you had seen anything, it would have had value, inasmuch as it could not have been caused by the imagination working upon a story you already knew.'"

The Farmhouse on the Hill:
A Ghost Story

William Beach, surveyor, arrived about mid-day at the small station of a south Dorchester village and shouldered his bag and instruments to walk across to the inn, where he had already telegraphed earlier in the day for a room. His surveying, having little to do with the account of his distressing subsequent adventures, may be left at once out of the story; but the fact that the inn was in the throes of temporary building operations is important to mention, since it led to the landlord's directing him to the only place in all the length and breadth of the scattered hamlet where accommodation was likely or even possible, the farmhouse half-way up the hill.

"That dark old house where you see the smoke 'anging about the trees," he pointed. "Garfit's away, but his missus'll find you a bed, no doubt, if you care for that kind of a place. That is," he added quickly, by way of correction, "if you ain't too partickler."

"Anything wrong with it, d'you mean?" asked the surveyor.

"Oh, I don't say there's nothing wrong with it," said the man, emphasising a word in every phrase. "I'm not one to criticise my neighbours at any time, and I've known of other gentlemen sleepin' there quite comfortable. Any'ow there's no other house to take you!" And he looked savagely at his own dilapidated hotel as though it cut him to the heart to send a customer elsewhere.

Now there was something in the tone of the disappointed innkeeper and in his curiously suggestive choice of words that combined to affect the surveyor disagreeably and make him vaguely conscious of a certain depression of spirits. He slipped at once into a minor key, and when he turned a corner of the sandy path and found himself suddenly face to face with the old grey-stoned Tudor house, massive of wall and irregular of shape, its forbidding aspect produced so marked an impression on him that he instinctively hesitated, trying to seize the actual definite quality that caused gloom to hang about it like a cloud; and wondering rather uncomfortably how, and why, so picturesque a building, backing against a whole hill-side of heather—there in the full flood of mid-day sunshine—should contrive to present so dolorous and lugubrious an appearance. For this first view at close quarters struck the dominant note of the place with undeniable vividness; the impression it conveyed was unpleasant, but "sinister" was the word that at once leaped to his mind.

With the weakness peculiar to impressionable persons, Beach would probably have retired there and then, but while his purpose was still an instinct merely, he became suddenly aware that a figure with fixed gaze had been staring at him for some time from the pillars of the deep porch where the yew trees that lined the approach threw their darkest shadow. A second glance showed him that it was a woman, a woman dressed in black. Clearly this was Mrs. Garfit; and he advanced to meet her.

She was, he saw, a big strong-faced woman, yet with a cast of features somewhat melancholy, and she gave him a formal smile of welcome, which, if not over cordial at first, changed to something a little more pleasant as soon as she learned his errand.

"We can manage something, perhaps," she said in a flat colourless sort of voice, cutting short his explanations about the inn, and turning slowly to enter the house.

"I'm willing to pay the ordinary inn charges," he added, noticing her want of alacrity and smiling to observe the changes produced by his words.

"Oh, of course, if you pay in advance," she said—which he had not exactly offered to do—and signing him to follow her in.

The surveyor no longer was puzzled by the inn-keeper's description. Plainly the farmer's wife was a grasping woman; she bled her occasional customers more successfully than he did; that was, no doubt, where the poison lay!

He followed her through the cold hall, stone-flagged, and up the broad wooden stairs to the landing, noting the dark beams across the ceiling and the curious sudden slopings of the floors; for the odour of great age breathed everywhere about him, and the interior of the building was as charming as the exterior was sinister.

Then Mrs. Garfit opened a door, moving aside for him to pass, and he saw a small room with a skylight window in the sloping ceiling, a cramped brass bed in the far corner, and hooks in the wall from which a number of faded old dresses hung in a dingy row. The air smelt musty, and there was no fireplace.

The surveyor's heart sank appreciably.

"If you have a somewhat larger room—" he began, turning to her, "one with a fireplace, too, as I shall be working a bit in the evenings—"

Mrs. Garfit looked blankly at him, screwing up her eyes a little, while she weighed the possibility.

"The fire would be a shillin' extra," she said presently, "and I could let you 'ave this room for another two shillin' more than the small room." She crossed the landing and showed him the room referred to; it was large, with two windows, an arm-chair, and a deep fireplace.

"Only I recommends the other," she added somewhat inconsequently.

"I prefer the larger one, thank you," said Beach shortly, and then and there clinched the bargain, making the best terms he could with her for breakfast and supper as well.

"Then you holds to the big one," repeated the woman, after counting over the silver in her big bony hands, "because my 'usband— and he'll be back ter-morrer—'e says the little one sleeps in best."

Beach ordered his fire to be lit immediately and then went out to catch the short hour of light still available, glad to escape for the moment from both house and woman. His work took him out upon the open hilltops, where the sight of the sea, dull crimson under the wintry sunset, and the beauty of the hilly country, did so much towards further dissipating the original impression of gloom, that when he returned about six o'clock, with a roaring appetite, he had passed into a more vigorous and cheerful state of mind, and paid little attention to the dour-faced farmer's wife or to sensations of uneasiness and dismay which had at first oppressed him.

He had a high-tea before the kitchen fire, shared—both tea and fire—by a black cat of huge proportions, which insisted upon rubbing against his knees, jumping up on his lap, and at last even putting her velvet paws into the very middle of his jam and butter.

The general servant clattered about the place, waiting upon him, under occasional orders from the mistress; and a young man, presumably a Garfit, lumbered once or twice through the kitchen with noisy nailed boots and a curiosity to inspect the stranger within his gates. But the food was excellent; he had done a good bit of work; and the friendly attentions of the black cat soothed him so pleasantly that he passed gradually into a happy state of indifference to everything but the seductions of a good pipe and the prospect later of a refreshing sleep.

Then, midway in a stream of most pleasantly flowing reflections, his nerves answered to a startling shock, and his sensations of content were scattered suddenly to the winds of heaven. There, at the end of the room, Mrs. Garfit was bending over an open drawer and, through the smoke curling upwards from his pipe, he had caught sight unexpectedly of her face reflected in the mirror that hung upon the cupboard door. She was evidently not aware of being inspected, and her visage, sombre at any time, now wore an aspect so malefic that the sudden revelation positively horrified him. He saw it, dark and hard, with eyes at once terrible yet haunted, the mouth set, and a deep settled gloom upon the features that was quite dreadful. A flicker of fear, like the faint passing of a light, showed itself for a moment there, and was gone as swiftly as it came.

The surveyor gave a sudden start that sent the cat flying from his knee, and when the woman turned again to face the kitchen she had resumed the mask of her normal expression of countenance.

"I'll take my candle and go up to read a bit," he stammered, as though surprised in an unauthorised or guilty act. "And—please let me have breakfast at eight o'clock."

He was disturbed, and not a little alarmed, by the sight of that changed and evil face, and as he slowly went upstairs he could not help connecting it in his mind with the pain of a tormenting conscience. It seemed to turn the face black—black with mental pain—and the pallor of the skin had made the contrast truly horrible. It lived vividly in his imagination, unpleasantly alive.

A blazing fire in his bedroom, a good novel, and a tolerably comfortable arm-chair, he hoped, would soon put to flight, however, the distressing effects of the vision. Yet, somehow, when he closed the door, it did not keep the woman out. That face came into the room with him. It perched on the table beside his book and seemed to watch him as he read. The picture persisted in his mind; it kept rising before his eyes and the printed page. A sense of presentiment and apprehension began to gather heavily about his heart.

Then, as he sat there, half reading, half listening to the sounds below stairs, his thoughts took another turn. He thought of his brother Hubert.

Now, Hubert was the antithesis of himself; practical and keen-minded. They had formerly known great arguments—visionary versus materialist—in which Hubert's cool and logical mind invariably gained the victory, and William, with what dignity he could muster, always fell back upon the quotation that has often helped others in a similar predicament, "There are more things in heaven and earth, Hubert,"—the lines need not be completed, but he wished Hubert were with him now. Hubert might have argued things away perhaps, certain feelings and trepidations, a strangely persistent inner trembling—a slowly growing fear. . . .

Then, with a fresh start, he recognised that it was this very sense of alarm that had suggested Hubert to his mind at all, and that in his subconsciousness he was already groping for help! Plainly this was the reason of his brother's appearance upon the scene. The sinister setting of his night's lodging, the desolate hills, and above all that revelation of the woman's changed face had combined to touch his imagination with unholy suggestion. The idea of companionship became uncommonly pleasant.

His thoughts dwelt a good deal upon these things, but, after all, the strong Dorsetshire air was not to be denied; the fire, moreover, was comforting, and his limbs ached. By degrees he persuaded the novel to possess him more and more until at length he found relief from his inquietudes in the exciting adventures of others.

The coals dropped softly into the grate and the winter wind came mournfully over the hills and sighed round the walls of the house; there was no other sound; downstairs every one seemed to have gone to bed. He would read one more chapter and turn in himself. Good sleep would chase the phantoms effectually. But the new chapter began with wearisome description, and his thoughts wandered again—theodolite—black cat—Hubert—the woman's face. . . .

His eyes were travelling heavily through a big paragraph when a faint sound made itself audible in the room behind him, and he turned with a quick start to look over the back of his chair. The candle threw his head and shoulders, greatly magnified, upon wall and ceiling; but the room was empty; nothing seemed to stir. Yet the moment he looked down again upon his book the sound was repeated.

Instantly, he was in the whirl of a genuine nervous flurry, confused a little, and thinking of a dozen things at once. Perhaps the friendly black cat had followed him up and was hiding in the room; he would get up and search. But before he could actually leave his chair a slight movement close beside him caught the corner of his eye. The brass knob of the door-handle at his left was turning. That was where the sounds came from. There was some one at the door.

Beach caught his breath with a rush. His first instinct was to dash forward and turn the key; his second, to seize the poker; yet he found no strength to do either the one or the other. He glued his eyes to the knob, watching it slowly turn. It stopped for a moment, and then the door pushed gently open and he saw the figure of Mrs. Garfit, partially concealed by a black shawl over the head, and wearing the very expression that he had seen reflected in the mirror downstairs a few hours before. She was staring intently into the empty room behind him. Encircled by both arms and grasped by her great muscular hands, she carried a kind of loose bundle which she held pressed closely into her body.

The woman, thus drawn in patches of black and white, standing erect in the doorway with darkness at her back, and that face of set evil dominating the picture, presented an appearance so appalling that at once the fear in the surveyor's heart passed into terror, pure and simple, and he found himself unable to utter a sound or make the smallest movement.

Without taking the slightest notice of him, she tiptoed softly forward into the room, and Beach then became aware for the first time that she was not alone. A man crouched behind her in the darkness of the landing, holding a lantern beneath the folds of a cloak. He was kneeling; and his face, with red hair and beard, and half-opened mouth showing the teeth, was just distinguishable in the faint glimmer of the shrouded light.

Looking neither to the right hand nor to the left, the woman passed almost soundlessly beside him, brushing the arm of the chair with her black gown, and making obviously for the end of the room. And when Beach, fearing that any moment she might face about and come towards himself, turned his head by a supreme effort and saw that she was already at the far end beside the bed, he made at the same time the further startling discovery—a cold sweat bursting through his skin—that the bed was occupied!

For one second he saw on the pillow the face of a young girl, sleeping peacefully, with masses of light hair about her, and then the black outline of that terrible woman bent double over her, and the loose bundle she carried in her hands descended full upon the pillow with her great weight above it, and remained there motionless, like a tiger upon its prey, for the space of what seemed to him many minutes.

There was no struggle and no sound; nothing but a little convulsive movement beneath the bed-clothes lower down; and then the surveyor, still powerless to move or cry in the grip of a real terror, was aware that the man had left his post of observation in the passage and was already half-way across the floor. He, too, went past him, as though unaware of his presence, but the woman, hearing the stealthy approach, straightened herself up beside the bed and turned to meet him. The lantern carried by the man, who was short and humpbacked, shed a faint upward light upon her features, and the slow smile it revealed coming into being on her fixed white face was so ghastly that it gave Beach that little extra twist of terror needed to release the frozen will, and make speech and movement possible.

With a loud cry he leaped out of his chair and dashed forward upon the fiendish couple still standing beside the bed of murder—and woke with a violent start in his arm-chair before an extinguished fire in a room that was pitch dark and miserably cold.

Whew! A nightmare after all! But the chill in his blood was due to more, he could swear, than a cold room and a blackened grate. With trembling fingers he lit the second candle and saw to his immense relief that the room was untenanted, the bed smooth and empty. The other candle had long ago guttered out, and his watch showed him that he had slept three hours. It was one o'clock in the morning.

He examined the bed, that awful bed where he had seen a young girl smothered in her sleep, and the horror of the nightmare remained so vividly with him that he gave up trying to persuade himself that it had been nothing more than a dream, and that two evil persons, and a third, had not vacated the room. One thing was certain—he could never sleep in such a bed. He would slip across to the other room. The dread of perhaps meeting the woman in the passage gave him pause for a moment, but after all it was a lesser terror, and he softly opened the door and crept, candle in hand, over the cold boards to the other side of the landing. He stood and listened for a moment—the house was utterly still—and then quietly turned the knob. But the door was locked. He was obliged to return to his own room, where he passed the remainder of a troubled night in what sleep he could snatch upon an arm-chair and two others.

The late daylight, cold and grey, brought no such balm to his imagination as the bright sunshine of a spring morning might have done, and the horror of his dream possessed him so painfully that he realised he could not spend another night in that room unless—yes, that was a splendid idea—unless he could get his brother, Hubert, down for the week-end to share it with him. Hubert's cold logic would work wonders. Ah, and another thought! It would be interesting to see if he felt anything odd about the house or room. He would say nothing about his own impressions, or his own experience, and would see what Hubert felt. The idea possessed him at once and he decided to telegraph the moment he had finished breakfast. Then, having arranged for another bed to be moved into the room, he took some bread and cheese with him and spent the entire day surveying the hills until the darkness fell over the country and it was time to meet the train.

And Hubert came; glad of the prospects of walks and talks with his brother, and seduced by the telegraphic description of the "jolly old farmhouse" among the hills. He appeared delighted, too, with the Tudor building.

"You ought to advertise, ma'am, and take in summer boarders," he said briskly to Mrs. Garfit.

"You better tell my 'usband that," she replied with something like a sigh mixed up in her sullen voice. "He'll be here to-night or to-morrer mornin'."

"Surly old cat," said Hubert, when they were alone at bed-time in their room; "she'd have to wear a veil to keep her boarders. Her face is like some of those women in the Chamber of Horrors." He laughed cheerfully, and plunged into the details of his week's work— he was a stockbroker—and of family matters that were of interest be-tween them. William avoided all reference to his own feelings and kept the talk purposely on the most matter-of-fact subjects possible. He had carefully manœuvred that Hubert should occupy the large bed, but he could not repress a creeping sense of horror when the time for sleep came and he saw his brother snuggling down under the sheets and blankets and putting his head upon that haunted pil-low. All through the night, as long as the fire light lasted, he lay awake and watched to see if anything would happen. But, up to the late hour when he finally fell asleep, nothing did happen.

It must have been very early in the morning when he woke with a start and saw some one standing beside his bed in the darkness, and heard his name called softly. It was Hubert.

"I say, Billy, is that cursed woman in the room, or what—who is calling?"

His brother jumped up and struck a light. Hubert's face was blanched. This was the first thing he noticed.

"What's up?" he stammered, still dazed with sleep. "The door's locked; there's no one here—is there?"

Hubert stood there shivering. Then he took the candle and walked round the room, poking into corners and cupboards and even looking under the beds. He went back to his own bed again and pulled the sheets about savagely.

"What did you hear?" asked William nervously.

"I'm not sure I heard anything. Something woke me—I couldn't breathe properly—felt suffocated—and I thought I heard that wom-an calling to 'hurry up.' Been dreaming, I suppose—"

He hesitated a moment. William saw that he had only told half, and wanted to say something else that rather stuck in his gorge.

"You'll get your death of cold standing there," he whispered.

Hubert ceased fumbling at his own bed and crossed the floor; his face was white as chalk.

"I say, old Billy, do you mind very much if I sleep with you? I think, perhaps, my sheets seem a bit damp," he whispered at length.

And when he had crawled into bed William felt that he was shaking all over, and for a long time before sleep again overtook them he kept giving little nervous starts of fear. He knew his brother too well to ask him just then what had really happened, but next morning, when the sunshine was in the room, he pressed him for an explanation, and Hubert admitted that he had never felt so frightened in his life; horrible dreams of being stifled had haunted his sleep, and finally some one had come stealthily up to the bed and tried to suffocate him by putting a blanket over his face. For a wonder, too, when he heard his brother's story, he neither argued nor scoffed, but merely remarked that it would be interesting to find out the history of the house and also to see if Mr. Garfit resembled the man with the lantern.

And the first person they met on going down to a belated breakfast was the farmer himself coming in from a gig standing in the yard. He was humpbacked and very short. Moreover he had red hair and beard, and a trick of leaving his mouth open so that the teeth showed.

The landlord of the Purbeck Arms, when suitably urged, furnished something of the required "history" of the house by stating that, some years before, Garfit's step-daughter had been found suffocated in her bed, and that the couple of them, man and wife, had only escaped the gallows because the circumstantial evidence was weak.

"It was long before I came to these parts," he said, "but you'll find the whole story in the newspapers of that date."

"I remember the Garfit case when I was a boy, now you mention it," the surveyor said.

"You see," interrupted the man significantly, "the girl had money of her own from her mother. The Garfits, of course, got that."

But a thorough search of the newspaper files at the club when they got back to London corroborated all that the inn-keeper had told them of the Garfit murder. The surveyor, moreover, prepared a careful report of the case for the Psychical Research Society and, when it was published, sent a copy to his brother with various annotations down the margins in red ink.

Appendix

Down the Danube in a Canadian Canoe

I.

It was a brilliant day in early June when we launched our canoe on the waters of the Danube, not one hundred yards from its source in the Black Forest, and commenced our journey of four and twenty hundred miles to the Black Sea. Two weeks before we had sent her from London to Donaueschingen by freight, and when the railway-company telegraphed the word *arrived* we posted after her with tent, kit-bags, blankets, cameras, and cooking-apparatus.

Donaueschingen is an old-fashioned little town on the southern end of the Schwarzwald plateau, and the railway that runs through it brings it apparently no nearer to the world. It breathes a spirit of remoteness and tranquillity born of the forests that encircle it, and that fill the air with pleasant odours and gentle murmurings.

There, lying snugly on a shelf in the goods-shed, we found our slender craft, paddles and boat-hook tied securely to the thwarts,— and without a crack! "No duty to pay," said the courteous official, after examining an enormous book, "and only seventeen marks for freight-charges the whole way from Oxford." She was sixteen feet long (with a beam of thirty-four inches), and had the slim graceful lines and deep curved ribs of the true Rice Lake (Ontario) build. Two or three inches would float her, and yet she could ride safely at top speed over the waves of a rapid that would have capsized a boat twice her size. Splendid little craft, she bore us faithfully and well, almost like a thing of life and intelligence, round many a ticklish corner and under more than one dangerous bridge, though this article will only outline some of our adventures in her over the first thousand miles as far as Budapest.

From the yard of the Schuetzen Inn, where she lay all night, we carried her on our shoulders below the picturesque stone bridge and launched her in a pool where the roach and dace fairly made the water dance. You could toss a stone over the river here without an effort, and when we had said farewell to the kindly villagers and steered out into mid-stream, there was so little water that the stroke of the paddle laid bare the shining pebbles upon the bottom and grated along the bed.

"Happy journey!" cried the townsfolk standing on the bank in blue trousers and waving their straw hats. "And quick return," added the hotel-keeper, who had overcharged us abominably in every possible item. We bore him little malice, however, for there were no inns or hotel-bills ahead of us; and uncommonly light-hearted were we as the canoe felt the stream move beneath her and slipped away at a good speed down the modest little river that must drop twenty-two hundred feet before it pours its immense volume through three arms into the Black Sea.

At first our progress was slow. Patches of white weeds everywhere choked the river and often brought us to a complete standstill, and in less than ten minutes we were aground in a shallow. We had to tuck up our trousers and wade. This was a frequent occurrence during the day and we soon realised that the hundred and twenty-five miles to Ulm, before the tributaries commence to pour in their icy floods from the Alps, would be slow and difficult. But what of that? It was glorious summer weather; the mountain airs were intoxicating, and the scenery charming beyond words. Nowhere that day was the river more than forty yards across, or over three feet deep. The white weeds lay over the surface like thick cream, but the canoe glided smoothly over them, swishing as she passed. Her slim nose opened a pathway that her stern left gently hissing with bubbles as the leaves rose again to the surface; and behind us there was ever a little milk-white track in which the blossoms swam and danced in the sunshine as the current raced merrily along the new channel thus made for it.

Winding in and out among broad fields and acres of reeds we dropped gently down across the great plateau of the Black Forest mountains. The day was hot and clear, and overhead a few white clouds sailed with us, as it were for company's sake, down the blue reaches of the sky. Usually we coasted along the banks, the reeds touching the sides of the canoe and the wind playing over hosts of nodding flowers and fields level to our eyes with standing hay, while, in the distance, the mountain-slopes, speckled with blue shadows, were ever opening into new vistas and valleys. Here the peaceful Danube still dreams, lying in her beauty-sleep as it were, and with no hint of the racing torrent that comes later with full waking. Pretty villages appeared along the banks at intervals. Pforen was the first, snugly gathered into the nook of the hills; a church, a few red-roofed houses, a wooden bridge, and a castle with a fine stork staring down at us from her nest in the ruined tower. The peasants were away in the fields and we drifted lazily by without so much as a greeting. Neidingen was the second, where a huge crucifix presided over the centre of the quaint bridge, and where we landed to buy butter, potatoes, and onions. Gutmadingen was the third; and here a miller and his men helped our portage over the weir while his wife stood in the hot sunshine and asked questions.

"Where are you going to?"

"The Black Sea." She had never heard of it, and evidently thought we were making fun of her. "Ulm, then," Ah! Ulm she knew. "But it's an enormous distance! And is the tent for rain?" she asked.

"No; for sleeping in at night."

"*Ach was!*" she exclaimed. "Well, I wouldn't sleep a night in that tent, or go a yard in that boat, for anything you could give me."

The miller was more appreciative. He gave us a delicious drink,—a sort of mead, which was most refreshing and which, he assured us, would not affect the head in the least—and told us there were twenty-four more weirs before we reached Ulm, the beginning of navigation. But none the less he, too, had his questions to ask.

"I thought all the Englishmen had gone to the war. The papers here say that England is quite empty."

The temptation was too great to resist. "No," we said gravely, "only the big ones went to the war. [We were both over six feet.] England is still full of men of the smaller sizes like ourselves." The expression on his face lightened our work considerably for the next mile.

Soon after the river left the plateau behind it and took a sudden leap into the Donauthal. We shot round a corner about six o'clock and came upon a little willow-island in mid-stream. Here we landed and pitched our tent on the long grass, made a fire, peeled the onions, fried our strips of beef with the potatoes, and made excellent tea. On all sides the pines crept down close into the narrowing valley. In the evening sunlight, with long shadows slanting across the hills, we smoked our pipes after our meal. There were no flies and the air was cool and sweet. Presently the moon rose over the ridge of forest behind us and the lights of Immendingen, twinkling through the shadows, were just visible a mile below us. The night was cool and the river hurried almost silently past our tent-door. When at length we went to bed, on cork mattresses with india-rubber sheets under us and thick Austrian blankets over us, everything was sopping with dew.

The bells of Immendingen coming down the valley were the first sounds we heard as we went to bathe at seven o'clock next morning in the cold sparkling water; and later, when we scrambled over the great Immendingen weir no villagers came to look on and say *"Engländer, Engländer,"* for it was Sunday morning and they were all at mass.

The valley grew narrower and limestone cliffs shone white through the sombre forests. It was very lonely between the villages. The river, now sixty yards wide, swept in great semi-circular reaches under the very shadow of the hills; storks stood about fishing in the shallows; wild swans flew majestically in front of us,—we came across several nests with eggs—and duck were plentiful everywhere. Once, in an open space on the hills, we saw a fine red fox motionless in his observation of some duck,—and ourselves. Presently he trotted away into the cover of the woods and the ducks quacked their thanks to us. Then suddenly, above Möhringen, just when we were congratulating ourselves that wading was over for good, the river dwindled away into a thin trickling line of water that showed the shape of every single pebble in its bed. We went aground continually. Half the Danube had escaped through fissures in the ground. It comes out again, on the other side of the mountains, as the river Ach, and flows into the Lake of Constance. The river was now less in volume than when we started, clear as crystal, dancing in the sunshine, weaving like a silver thread through the valley, and making delightful music over the stones. Yet most of our journey that day was wading. Trousers were always tucked up to the knees, and we had to be ready to jump out at a moment's notice. Before the numberless little rapids the question was: "Is there enough water to float us? Can we squeeze between those rocks? Is that wave a hidden stone, or merely the current?" The steersman stood up to get a better view of the channel and avoid the sun's glare on the water, and in this way we raced down many a bit of leaping, hissing water; and, incidentally, had many a sudden shock before the end, tumbling out headlong, banging against stones, and shipping water all the time. The canoe got sadly scratched, and we decided at length to risk no more of these baby-rapids. A torn canoe in the Black Forest, miles from a railway, spelt helplessness. Thereafter we waded the rapids. It was a hot and laborious process,—the feet icy cold, the head burning hot, and the back always bent double. Weirs, too, became frequent, and unloading and reloading was soon reduced to a science. In the afternoon the villagers poured out to stare and look on. They rarely offered to help, but stood round as close as possible while we unloaded, examining articles, and asking questions all the time. They had no information to give. Few of them knew anything of the river ten miles below their particular village, and none had ever been to Ulm. Now and then there was a sceptical *"Dass ist unmöglich* (that's impossible),'' when we mentioned Ulm as our goal. *"Ach je!* They're mad,—in *that* boat!"

From Donaueschingen to Ulm there is a weir in every five miles, and our progress was slow. Whenever the river grew deep we learned to know that a dam was near; and below a dam there was scarcely enough water to float an egg-shell. But there was no occasion to hurry; everything was done in leisurely fashion in this great garden of Würtemburg, and most of the villages were sound asleep. At Möhringen, indeed, we got the impression that the village had slept for at least a hundred years and that our bustling arrival had suddenly awakened it. It lay in a clearing of the forest, in a charming mossy bed that no doubt made sleep a delightful necessity. The miller invited us to the inn, where we found a score of peasants in their peaked hats and black suits of broadcloth sitting each in front of a foaming tankard; but they drank so slowly that a hundred years did not seem too long to finish a tankard. There was very little conversation, and they stared unconscionably, bowing gravely when we ordered their stone mugs to be refilled and regarding us all the time with steady, expressionless interest. In due time, however, they digested us, and then the stream of inevitable questions burst forth.

"You bivouac? You go to the sea? *If* you ever get to Ulm! You have come the whole way from London in *that* shell?"

We gulped down the excellent cold beer and hurried away. The river dwindled to a width of a dozen yards and wading was incessant. We lightened the canoe as much as possible, but, our kit having been already reduced to what seemed only strictly necessary, there was little enough to throw away,—a tin plate, a tin cup, a fork, a spoon, a knife, and a red cushion. These we piled up in a little mound upon the bank with a branch stuck in the ground to draw attention. I wonder who is now using those costly articles.

Another series of picturesque villages glided past us: Tuttlingen, famous (as the dirty water proclaimed) for its tanneries, and where a couple of hundred folk in their Sunday clothes watched our every movement as we climbed round two high and difficult weirs; Nendringen, where a kind and silent miller gave us of his cool mead; Mülheim straggling half-way up the hills with its red-brown roofs and church and castle all mingled together in most picturesque confusion, as if it had slipped down from the summit and never got straight again; and Friedigen, where we laid in fresh supplies, and found two Germans who had spent years in California, and whose nasal voices sounded strangely out of place among their guttural neighbours. "Camp anywheres you please," they said, "and no one'll objec' to your fires so long as you put 'em out."

I forget how many more villages ending in *ingen* we passed; but now that the heat of the day, and the labour and toil of wading are forgotten, they come before me again with their still, peaceful loveliness like a string of quaint jewels strung along the silver thread of the river.

Soon the water increased and the canoe sped onwards among the little waves and rapids like a winged thing. The mountains became higher, the valley narrower. Limestone cliffs, scooped and furrowed by the eddies of a far larger Danube thousands of years before, rose gleaming out of the pine-woods about their base. We plunged in among the Swabian Alps, and the river tumbled very fast and noisily along a rock-strewn bed. It darted across from side to side, almost as though the cliffs were tossing it across in play to each other. One moment we were in blazing sunlight, the next in deep shadow under the cliffs. There was no room for houses, and no need for bridges; boats we never saw; big, grey fish-hawks, circling buzzards, storks by the score had this part of the river all to themselves.

Suddenly we turned a sharp corner and shot at full speed into an immense cauldron. It was a perfect circle, half a mile in diameter, bound in by the limestone cliffs. The more ancient river had doubtless filled it with a terrifying whirlpool, for the rocks were strangely scooped and eaten into curves hundreds of feet above us. But now its bottom was a clean flat field, where the little stream, with its audacious song, whipped along at the very foot of the cliffs on one side of the circle.

It was a lonely secluded spot, the very place for a camp. Though only five o'clock on a June afternoon the cliffs kept out the sunshine. We sank the canoe, to soak up cracks and ease strained ribs, and soon had our tent up, and a fire burning. Then we climbed the cliffs. It was a puzzle to see how the river got in or got out. As we climbed we came across deep recesses and funnel-shaped holes, caves with spiral openings in the roof, and pillars shaped like an hourglass. Across the gulf the ruined castle of Kallenberg stood on a point of rock that was apparently inaccessible, and when the evening star shone over its broken battlements, it might well have been a ghostly light held aloft by the shades of the robber-barons who once lived in it. When we went to bed at ten o'clock the full moon shone upon the white cliffs with a dazzling brilliance that seemed to turn them into ice, while the deep shadows over the river made the scene strangely impressive. Only the tumbling of the water and the chirping of the crickets broke the silence. In the night we woke and thought we heard people moving round the tent, but, on going out to see, the canoe was still safe, and the white moonshine revealed no figures. It was doubtless the river talking in its sleep, or the wind wandering lost among the bushes.

At five o'clock next morning I looked out of the tent and found our cauldron full of seething mist through which the sunshine was just beginning to force a way. An hour later the tent was too hot for comfort.

All day we followed the gorge, with many a ruined castle of impregnable position looking down upon us from the cliffs. The valley widened about noon, and fields ablaze with poppies lay in the sun, while tall yellow flags fringed the widening river. In another great circle, similar in formation to that of Kallenberg, but five times as large, we found the monastery of Beuron with its eighty monks and fifty lay-brothers. We bathed and put on our celluloid collars (full dress in an outfit where weight is of supreme importance) and went up to the gates. A bearded monk, acting as door-keeper, thrust a smiling face through the wicket in answer to our summons and informed us with genuine courtesy that the monastery was not open to visitors at this time of year.

"There are many visitors in summer, I regret," he explained.

"Visitors! How do they get here?"

"By road; they come from long distances, driving and walking."

"But we may never be here again; we are on our way to the Black Sea."

"Ah, then you will see far more wonderful things than this in your journey." He remained firm; so, by way of consolation we went to the Gasthaus Zur Zonne and enjoyed a meal,—the first for a week that we had not cooked ourselves.

It was a quiet, out-of-the-world spot. Monks were everywhere working in the fields, ploughing and haymaking; and it was here I first saw sheep following a shepherd. A curious covered bridge, lined with crucifixes, crossed the river, and we took an interesting photograph of a monk in a black straw hat and gown going over it with a cloud of dust in the blazing sunshine followed by fifty sheep. There was contentment on all faces, but the place must be dreadfully lonely and desolate in winter. We bought immense loaves in the monks' bakery, and matches, cigars, sugar, and meat in a *devotionshandlung* (store for religious articles)!

Sigmaringen, with its old rock-perched castle and its hundred turrets gleaming in the sun, was reached just in time to find shelter from a thunderstorm that seemed to come out of a clear sky. There was a hurricane of wind, and the rain filled the quaint old streets with dashing spray. In an hour it cleared away, and we pushed on again; but the river had meanwhile risen nearly a foot. The muddy water rushed by with turbulent eddies, and the bridges were crowded with people to see us pass. They stood in silent dark rows without gesture or remark, and stared. Suddenly the storm broke again with redoubled fury. Up went their umbrellas, and we heard their guttural laughter. In a few minutes we were soaked, and no doubt cut a sorry figure as we launched the canoe at the foot of the big weir and vanished into the gathering darkness. We swirled between the pillars of another bridge in sheets of rain and the outlook for a dry camp and a fire was decidedly poor. It was after nine o'clock when we landed in despair under a clump of trees on the left bank, and found to our delight that they concealed a solitary wedge of limestone cliff, and that in this cliff there was an arch, and under that arch a quantity of dry wood. A fire was soon blazing in the strip under the arch,—some three feet wide—and the tent stood beneath the dripping trees. Our waterproof sheets and cork mattresses kept us dry, though all night the rain poured down, while outside we could hear the swollen river rushing past with a seething roar.

Next day the rapids began in earnest. Rapids are to canoeers what fences are to fox-hunters. The first wave curls over in front of the canoe, there is a hiss and a bump, a slap of wet spray in the face, and then the canoe leaps under you and rushes headlong. At Riedlingen, while carrying the canoe across a slippery weir, we fell, boat and all, into the deep hole below the fall, luckily with no worse result than a wetting, for our kit was safely piled upon the bank. At Dietfurt we went into an apparently deserted village to buy milk, but the moment we entered the street it became alive. From every door poured men and women gaping, and the moment they spied the little yellow canoe upon the shore they rushed down in a flock shouting '*E' schiff! E' schiff!*'' But, if they ran fast, we ran faster, and were off before the terrible onslaught of questions had even begun. The milk was a mere detail.

At Gutenstein, where we camped in a hay-field, the mowers woke us at dawn, peering into the mouth of the tent. But they made no objections and merely said *"Gruss Gott"* and *"Gute Reise";* and for an hour afterwards I heard their scythes musically in my dreams as they cut a pathway for us to the river.

At Obermarchsthal we left the mountains behind us, and with them, too, the memory of a pathetic figure. As we landed to go up to the little inn for eggs, an old man, leaning on a stick, hobbled down to meet us. His white hair escaped in disorder from beneath a peaked blue hat, and he wore a suit of a curious checked pattern that seemed wholly out of keeping with the dress of the country. At first, when he spoke, I could not understand him, and asked him in German to repeat his remarks.

"He's talking English," said my companion. "Can't you hear?" And English it was. He invited us up to the inn and told us his story over a mug of beer.

"This is my native village. I was born and raised here, and sixty years ago I ran away from Germany to escape military service. I went to the United States and settled finally in Alabama. I had a shop in Mobile, down South in a nigger town, and as soon as I was ready I wrote to the girl I left here to come out to me. She came and we were married. I've had two wives since out there. Now they're all buried in a little churchyard outside Mobile. And this is the first time I've been back in sixty years," he went on after a gulp of beer. "The village ain't changed one single bit. I feel as though I'd been sleepin' and sorter dreamin' all the while. . . . The shop's sold and I'm takin' a last look round at the ole place. There's only one or two that remembers me, but I was born and raised here, and this is where I had my first love, and the place is full of memories, just chock full. No, I ain't a goin' to live here. I'm goin' back to the States nex' month, so as I can die there and lie beside the others in the cemetery at Mobile."

The country became flatter and the mountains were soon a blue line on the horizon behind us. At Opfingen we crossed our last weir, and among the clouds in front of us saw the spire of Ulm cathedral, the tallest in the world. A fierce current swept us past banks fringed with myrtle bushes, poppies, and yellow flags. Poplars rose in lines over the country, bending their heads in the wind, and we camped at eight o'clock in a wood about a mile above the town. While dinner was cooking a dog rushed barking up to us followed by three men with guns. They were evidently German Jäger. Two of them were dressed like pattern plates out of a tailor's guide to sportsmen,—in spotless gaiters, pointed hats with feathers (like stage Tyrolese), guns with the latest slings, and silver whistles slung on coloured cord round their necks. They examined the canoe first, and then came up and examined us. One of them, who was probably the proprietor of the land, a surly gruff fellow, had evidently made up his mind that we were poachers. And I must admit that at first sight there was ground for suspicion, for no poacher could possibly have found fault with our appearance.

"What are you doing here?" he asked.

"Preparing to camp for the night," we told him.

"When are you going on?"

"We intend to go into Ulm in the morning."

"Where do you come from; are you Englishmen?"

"Yes; we come from London."

"Ach was!" (they all say *Ach was* when they want to be witheringly scornful). "In *that* egg-shell?"

"Certainly."

"And where are you going to?"

"Odessa."

They exchanged glances. "Evidently madmen, and not poachers," said the face of the man with the biggest silver whistle plainer than any words could have spoken it. "Do you know these are private preserves?" was the next question.

"No." My friend, a keen sportsman, sheltered himself scowling behind his alleged ignorance of German (somehow he always knew our conversation afterwards to a word); but the penny whistle and the immaculate costume of the hunters in a scrubby wood where not even a rabbit lived, excited him to explosions of laughter which he concealed by frequent journeys to the tent.

"What's in that tent?"

"Beds." The *chasseurs* and the keeper went to examine, while the dog sniffed about everywhere. Our beds were not then untied, and the sportsman untied them; but they found only blankets and cork mattresses.

"You have no guns, or dogs, or fishing-rods?" We shook our

heads sulkily. "And you are only travelling peacefully for pleasure?"

"We are trying to," we said meekly.

"Then you may sleep here if you go on again to-morrow; but don't go into the woods after game." Then the men moved off. Doubtless they were right to ask questions, yet we were so obviously travellers. "Still, our weather-worn appearance and unshaved faces probably made us look more than a little doubtful," quoth my friend, who himself wore a slouch hat that did not add to the candour of his expression.

In the middle of dinner the men suddenly returned from another angle of the wood and examined everything afresh. We offered them some tea in a tin cup which they declined; and at last after watching us at our meal in silence for ten minutes they moved off, evidently still suspicious. Thereafter we always knew them as the *chasseurs*. They were not the only pests, however. Mosquitoes appeared later,—our first—and that night we slept behind the mosquito-netting we had so carefully fitted to the mouth of the tent when we first erected it weeks before in the garden of a London square. During the night some one prowled about the tent. We heard twigs snapping and the footsteps among the bushes; but neither of us troubled ourselves to get up. If they took the canoe, they'd be drowned; and our other only valuables (a celluloid collar apiece, a clean suit for the big towns, and a map) were safely inside the tent.

In the morning we shaved and washed carefully, and put on our full dress for the benefit of Ulm. We intended to paddle down quietly and stop at the Rowing Club wharf of which we had read; according to the map it was a mile, and the current easy and pleasant. We wished our entrance to be sober and in good taste.

The best-laid plans, however, will sometimes go amiss when you're canoeing on the Danube. We were half-way when we heard a roar like a train rushing over a hollow bridge. It grew louder every minute. In front of us the water danced and leaped, and before we knew what had happened we were plunging about among foaming waves and flying past the banks at something more than ten miles an hour.

"It's the Iller," cried my friend as the paddle was nearly wrested from his grasp. "It's marked on the map just about here."

It was the Iller. It had come in at an acute angle after running almost parallel with us for a little distance. It tumbled in at headlong speed, with an icy, turbulent flood of muddy water, and it gave the sedate Danube an impetus that it did not lose for another hundred miles below Ulm. For a space the two rivers declined to mingle. The noisy, dirty Iller, fresh from the Alps, kept to the right bank, going twice as fast as its more dignified companion on the left. A distinct line (as though drawn by a rope) divided them, in colour, speed, and height,—the Iller remaining for a long time at least half an inch above the level of the Danube. At length they mingled more freely and swept us down upon Ulm in a torrent of rough, racing water. Our leisurely dignified entrance into Ulm was, like the suspicions of the *chasseurs,* a structure built on insufficient knowledge, a mere dream. Ulm lies on a curve of the river. Big bridges with nasty thick pillars (and whirlpools, therefore, behind them) stand at both entrance and exit. How we raced under the first bridge I shall never forget. We were half-way through the town, with the wet spray still on our cheeks, before the sound of the gurgling eddies below the bridge had ceased behind us. Where, oh, where was the friendly wharf of that Danube Rowing Club? The second bridge rose before us. There were crested waves under its arches. Already Ulm was almost a thing of the past; yet we had hoped to spend at least a week exploring its beauties.

"There it is," cried my friend in the bows, "on the left bank! That old board,—see it? That's the wharf."

We managed to turn in mid current and point the canoe upstream. Then, by paddling as hard as we could, we dropped down past the wharf at a pace that just enabled us to grasp the rings in the boards and come to a standstill. You'll never forget Ulm if you arrive there, as we did, in a canoe, when the Iller is in flood.

II.

We spent a week in the quaint old town of Ulm, but our adventures there have properly no part in our journey down the river. Only, in passing, I must mention the courtesy of the Danube Rowing Club. Fritz Miller (who rowed at Henley in 1900 for the Diamond Sculls) is the leading spirit in a list of members who showed us all possible kindness. They housed and mended our canoe, varnished it afresh, and gave us better maps. The secret charms of picturesque Ulm unknown to the tourist were shown to us; and in the evenings we used to meet for music and supper in a quaint little club-room that hangs half of its Roman masonry over the rushing river.

Here the navigation of the Danube (such as it is) is said to begin. The fierce current allows no boats or steamers, but immense barges (called *Ulmer schachtel*) laden with merchandise are floated down the current to the Bavarian towns below. On arrival they are sold for lumber, the return journey being impossible.

The Rowing Club takes out eights and fours. Rowing with all their might they move two miles an hour against the current; and it may well be imagined that, with this training, they are well nigh the first rowing club in Germany.

There was a great deal of rain while we were in Ulm and we started again on a rapidly rising river, full of floating rubbish, and rushing at a pace that made it a pleasure merely to stand and watch it from the bank. The Bavarian bank (Ulm is on the frontier line of Bavaria and Würtemburg) displayed black sign-boards with the kilometers marked in white. We timed our speed by one of Benson's chronometers and found it to be over twelve miles an hour. It was like travelling over a smooth road behind fast horses. My notebook gives an average day, the day, for instance, we left Ulm.

> *June 19th.* The members of the Rowing Club came down in force to see us off at eleven o'clock. Flags were flying in our honour and we heard the men shouting *glückliche Reise* as we shot the middle arch of the bridge on the waves of a rather nasty rapid. The bridge was lined with people, but we only faintly heard their cries for the thunder of the waves. This exceedingly rapid water makes awkward currents as it swirls round the pillars of the big bridges. Behind the arches are always whirlpools, which twist you sideways and toss you from them with ridiculous ease. A wrong turn of the steering paddle and the canoe would be sucked in instead of thrown out, and then—! At a little distance below the bridge the eddies of the whirlpool from adjacent pillars meet in a series of crested waves. The only safe channel lies exactly in the middle. The canoe rises, slaps down again, all its length a-quiver; the first wave breaks under the bows and some of the water comes in, but be-

fore enough is shipped to be dangerous the frail craft rises again with a leap to the next wave. Then the race begins. The least wrong twist to left or right and the waves break sideways into the canoe and down she goes. It takes so little water to sink a laden canoe.

To-day, for the first time, we heard the famous song of the Danube,—famous at least to us who had read of it in so many different accounts. It is a hissing, seething sound which rises everywhere from the river. You think steam must be escaping somewhere, or soda-water fizzing out from an immense syphon among the woods on the banks. It is said to be the friction of the pebbles along the bed of the river, caused by the terrific speed of so great a body of water. Under the canoe it made a peculiar buzzing sound accompanied by a distinct vibration of the thin bass-wood on which we knelt.

We swept through Bavaria much faster than we wished, but it was impossible to go slowly. The river communicated something of its hurry to ourselves, and in my mind the journey now presents itself something in the form of a series of brilliant cineomatographs. Delightful were our lunches at the quaint inns of remote villages—black bread, sausage, and such beer!—Lauingen, a town of the sixteenth century, where the spokesman of the crowd said, "I suppose you're both single"; Donauwörth, in a paradise of wild flowers, where the Lech tears in on the right with leaping waves; Neuberg, with a dangerous stone bridge and the worst rapids we had yet encountered. Then a long stretch where the swamps ceased and the woods began to change. Instead of endless willows we had pine, oak, sycamore, birch, and poplar. The river was a mile wide with outlets into lagoons, like Norfolk Broads, that ran parallel with us for miles and were probably empty mud flats at low water. Fishing-nets were hanging up to dry along the shore, and hay lay sunning itself on the narrow strips of the banks. We passed Ingolstadt, a military post, and then the river dipped down before us into blue hills and we came to Vohburg,—destroyed by the Swiss in 1641, and now, apparently, nothing but a collection of quaint chimneys and storks' nests—and, soon after it, Eining, near Abusina, a Roman frontier station established fifteen years before our era. Trajan's wall crossed the river near here and extended north as far as Wiesbaden.

Then the river narrowed between precipitous limestone cliffs and

we entered the gorge of Kehlheim. At its very mouth, between impregnable rocks, lay the monastery of Weltenburg, the oldest in Bavaria. The river sweeping round a bend into the rocky jaws made
landing difficult; but we accomplished it, and entered the old court-
yard through an iron gate with graceful stone pillars. There were everywhere signs of neglect and decay. The monks' quarters formed one
side of the square and the church another; a third side was a wall of
rock; the fourth was the river. It was secluded, peaceful beyond description, absolutely out of the world. The air was cool, the shadows
deep. Fruit trees grew in the court-yard, and monks (there were only
thirteen in all) in black gowns were piling up wood for the winter. A
priest was intoning vespers in the church, which boasted a beautiful
organ, marble altars, and elaborate carving of the usual gilded sort.
The sunshine filled the painted air. Outside over the neglected walls
crept vines, and at the far end of the courtyard a wild rose tree, covered with sweet-smelling blossoms, grew at the foot of crumbling
stone steps that led under shady trees to a chapel perched on the cliffs.
We toiled up in the heat and were rewarded by a glorious view; from
above the monastery was shut in like a nest between river and cliffs.

Later in the day we were driven by a violent thunderstorm to the
first landing-place we could find. It was a few miles below Weltenburg in the very heart of the gorge. With surprising good fortune we
found a cave leading deep into the mountain, and in less than ten
minutes we were dry and snug before a fire burning cheerfully for
dinner. It was a strange camp,—the storm howling outside and the
firelight dancing down behind us into the interior of the cave, which
was unnecessarily full of bats.

At Ratisbon, the Castra Regina of the Romans, we were solemnly
warned not to attempt to pass under the bridge. "The whirlpools are
savage," they told us. "Of the seven arches of this six-hundred-year-
old bridge, all but one are forbidden by the police." Leaving the canoe half a mile above we landed and walked down the shore to examine. "Boats *have* gone through," said a pompous man on the
bridge as he pointed out the worst places to us, "but even if they got
under the arch they have always been sucked in *there!*" He pointed to
a white seething circle of water. "You'll never get through that in
your cockle-shell, and you'll be arrested even if you do."

"Arrested,—how?" we asked. By way of answer he raised his eyebrows and held up a fat hand in eloquent warning. However, we carefully selected our channel from the bridge, and twenty minutes later were coming down stream towards the arches as cautiously as our speed would permit. People ran along the shore waving their hats and shouting to us to stop. The bridge in front was black with the crowd waiting to see the *verrückte Engländer* upset. We reached the arch and recognised our channel. The water dropped suddenly in front of us and the canoe dipped her nose with it. We were off. The bank and the shouting people flew past us in a black streak. I was just able to recognise one man, our pompous friend, standing below the bridge shading his eyes with his hand, evidently determined to get the best view possible. The roar of voices dwindled behind us into a murmur and a minute later we were out of sight; Ratisbon, bridge, whirlpools, and townsfolk were things of the past. We were not arrested, but perhaps the police are still trying to catch us.

After this came a dull spell as we crossed the great wheat-plain of Bavaria, winding for two days with many curves and little current. Every morning here the workers in the fields woke us early, and praised the boat, and asked us the usual questions, and told us the usual falsehoods about the depth of the river, the distances of the towns, the floods of past years, and all the rest of it. We made no halt at Straubing (Servio Durum of the Romans), or at Deggendorf where the Isar adds its quota of mountain-gathered waters.

Another day was very dismal,—cold showers and storms of wind following one upon another. We crouched under bridges, trees, and anything else that gave cover, paddling fast between the squalls to keep ourselves warm. The plain of Straubing affords little shelter. Towards evening, however, the river made a welcome turn towards the mountains, and we camped on a high bank among clumps of willows with thick woods behind them. New potatoes, dried prunes, and onions in the stew-pot were points of light in a gusty and otherwise dismal meal. We pegged the tent inside and out. All night the wind tore at it, howling; but a gipsy-tent never comes down. The wind sweeps over it, and finding an ever lessening angle of resistance, only drives it more firmly into the ground.

Gradually, now, we were passing out of the lonely portions of the upper river. The country was becoming more populated; larger towns were near; railway-bridges spanned the river; steamers and tugs raced down, and toiled up it.

A few miles above Passau we camped on an island, and were visited by an inquisitive peasant, who saw our fire and came over from the mainland in a punt. "Are we trespassing?" I asked. "No; the island's usually under water." This was all he ever said in our hearing, though he stayed with us, it seemed, for hours. He was a surly-looking fellow in the roughest clothes, with trousers turned up to his knees, and bare feet. His curiosity was immense; with arms crossed and legs wide apart, he stood and stared in silence with expressionless features. We had some villainous Black Forest cigars, bearing on the label the words *la noblesse,* which we sometimes used to get rid of obnoxious people. We gave him two. Knowing nothing about the Greeks and those bearing gifts he nodded his thanks,—and smoked both to the very end! Yet he never stirred, his eyes never left us. It was impossible to prepare our frugal dinner under this merciless scrutiny. At length I prevailed upon him to go over for some eggs, and to bring them to us in the morning for breakfast. He left without a word in his punt, and a sense of oppression seemed to go with him. But, just as dinner was over and we were settling round the fire to our tobacco, he suddenly reappeared. He had brought the eggs in his hat, and he was dressed this time in his Sunday clothes! For an hour he stood beside the fire, answering no questions, volunteering no remarks, till at length my friend went up, shook hands, wished him good-night, and straightway disappeared into the tent. I did likewise, and then the fellow took the hint, and went.

This happened at a place called Pleinling. Another thing also happened there. On the smaller of the arms into which our island divided the river was a weir. With empty canoe, and dressed in shirt and trousers, we practised shooting this weir next morning. The day was hot, and our other things were meanwhile drying on the bank. The silent peasant came over to watch the proceedings, and with him came a picturesque old fellow, most talkative and entertaining, with white hair and a face like Liszt's. When he saw us preparing to shoot the fall he was much excited. "Have you wives and children?" he asked shaking his head warningly. I went over first while my friend took the camera, and got his picture a second before the canoe plunged into the foam and upset. The old fellow, whose name was Jacob Meyer, was not in the least put out. He leaned on his scythe and watched me struggling in the water with the overturned canoe without making any effort to help. Afterwards, when we gave him a *noblesse* he took a lean, dirty little purse out of his pocket, and said, "How much am I to pay for it?" And when we promised to send him the photographs he asked the same question again.

Some hours later we reached Passau, a few miles from the Austrian frontier, and this last glimpse of Bavaria, after traversing its entire breadth, was the sweetest of all. But only from the river itself can you see the quaint old houses leaning over at all imaginable angles; the towers and crooked wooden balconies; gardens hanging from the second storeys; walls with ancient paintings dimmed by wind and weather; and decayed archways showing vistas of tumbling roofs, broken chimneys, and peeps of vivid blue sky at the far ends. The picture it made in my mind as we paddled through it in the late afternoon is uncommonly picturesque,—a jumble of gables, towers, bridges, and the swift muddy Danube rushing past it all in such tremendous hurry.

Half a mile below, the Inn poured in from the Tyrolese Alps and carried us into the finest gorge we had so far seen. The new comer brought cold air with it, and we swept into the gloomy ravine between high mountains with something like a genuine shudder. More and more swiftly ran the river as it compressed itself with an angry roar into a few hundred yards' width and swirled into the hills raging at the indignity thus heaped upon it. It became very difficult now to choose camping-places, as the stream fills the entire gorge, leaving only narrow ledges at the foot of the heights where a tent can stand. Upon one of these ledges, broader than the rest, we managed at length to land. A projecting point of rock sent the water flying out at a tangent into mid-stream and formed a strong backwater below it. Into this we contrived to twist the canoe's nose and on a little promontory, covered with yellow ragwort, we pitched our tent. It commanded a view for two miles up the ravine with the sinking sun at the far end. A boy was tending half a dozen cows among the scanty bushes; a queer little imp with wide-open blue eyes, who watched us land and prepare our camp with no signs of fear or surprise. We gave him cherries and chocolate, and he stuffed his mouth with one and his pockets with the other; then he came and stood over our fire and warmed himself without invitation, as if it had been made for his special benefit. A quaint little figure he cut with his pointed, feathered hat and big eyes. He told us that his name was Josef, that he lived two miles further on, went to bed every night at nine o'clock and got up every morning at four. Then he took off his hat, said good-night, and vanished into the bushes after his cows.

The sun set in a blaze of golden light that filled the whole gorge with fire; but when the glory faded, the strange grandeur of the place began to make itself felt. The ravine was filled with strange noises, the wooded heights looked forbidding, and the great river rolled in a sullen black flood into the night.

Next morning we passed a big rock in mid-stream with a shrine perched on its summit; and just beyond it we entered Austria and visited the customs at Engelhartzell, a village on the right bank with an old Cistercian monastery behind it. There was no duty to pay, and we raced on past the mountain village of Obermühl, and out of the gorge into a fertile and undulating country basking in the fierce sunshine.

Neuhaus, with a fine castle on a wooded height, and Ashach, with a view of the Styrian Alps, flashed by. The river from here to Linz is full of history, and its muddy waters have more than once borne crimson foam. There were bloody fights here during the revolt of the peasantry of Upper Austria. Ashach, in 1626, was the insurgents' headquarters where (as also at Neuhaus) they barricaded the Danube with immense chains to prevent the Bavarians from assisting Count Herberstein, the Austrian governor, who was shut up in Linz. When in flood the Danube escapes from this narrow prison with untold violence. Everywhere the villages bear witness of its path, though most of them lie far away from the banks. High upon the walls lines show the high-water marks of previous years with the dates. "A single night will often send us into the upper storeys," said a woman who sold us milk and eggs; "but the water falls as quickly as it rises, and then we come down again." She took it as a matter of course.

The shores became lonely again and our camps were rarely disturbed. One morning, however, about six o'clock we heard some one rummaging among our pans. Then something stumbled heavily against the tent, and there was a sound of many feet and an old familiar smell. We rushed out, to find ourselves in the centre of a herd of about fifty cows. One had its nose in the provision-basket; another was drinking the milk standing in the pail of water; a third was scratching its head against the iron prop of the kettle. Their curiosity was insatiable; every time we drove them off they returned. While my friend was frying the bacon and I was performing ablutions lower down on the river bank, a squadron swept down upon us unexpectedly by a clever flank movement, and one of them whipped up my pyjamas near the tent and ran down the shore with them on her horns. My friend dared not leave the bacon—and I was *in nudis!* It was exciting for the next few minutes.

In blazing heat that day we came to Linz, the capital of Upper Austria. Below it the Traun and the Enns flowed in, and the Danube became a magnificent river rolling through broad banks alternately wooded and covered with crops and orchards; and now, too, we began again to see vineyards, of which Bavaria had seemed bare.

For a long time, strange as it may sound, we had been enforced vegetarians and drinkers of condensed milk. We could rarely get fresh milk, though we trudged many a mile to farmhouses and inns for it; either it was all used for butter, or had already been sent to the towns. Of course it would not keep sweet in our canoe under the blazing heat, and we could only trust to the chance of getting it an hour or so before we needed it. But, when we were lucky enough to get it, how delicious were those messes of boiled bread and milk! Meat, too, was hard to come at, except at certain hours. The butchers in the small towns open their shops at certain times only. Not one of them would ever trouble himself to supply us with merely a pound of meat, and more would not, of course, keep fresh.

We were drawing near Vienna now, but first we passed through another fine gorge. It began at Grein (where the Duke of Coburg's castle, Greinburg, looks down from the heights) and before we emerged breathless at the other end we had come through the famous whirlpools known as the Wirbel and Strudel. The river, narrowed by half its width, plunged with many contortions round sharp corners between high cliffs and past the island-rock of Wörth. Rising in long, heaving undulations the water was alive with whirlpools, twisting and sucking, and throwing us here and there, gushing up underneath us with ugly noises and seething on every side. There was no foam, no crests, no waves or spray; it was like a monstrous snake trying to writhe through a hole too small for it. The shore raced by at top speed, and steering was uncomfortable for a time. In former years these whirlpools were a source of great danger to the navigation; but in 1866 the Emperor had certain rocks blown up and now an inscription on the face of the cliff testifies to the thanks of a grateful people. The traveller in a big steamer might think this description exaggerated. He would not think so in a canoe.

It is impossible to mention, as one would like, all the abbeys, churches, monasteries, ruins, islands, and other points of historic interest that throng the banks. The scenery is enchanting as well as enchanted. There were some interesting castles in these mountains, and grim they still look even in their ruins. Aggstein rose in solitary grandeur on a peak that commanded miles of the Danube in both directions. It was built in the twelfth century by the Kuenings, a robber-race which stretched chains across the river, plundered the traffic, and drowned the owners. We could still see the Blashaus Tower from which the sentinel announced the approach of boats. It was a plundering, murdering family, and was finally destroyed by the great Ulrich von Grafeneck.

Before Ybbs (the Roman Pons Isidis) we saw the wonderful ruins of Dürrenstein where Richard Cœur de Lion was imprisoned. Here, on the very spot, it was interesting to recall how he was recognised when walking through the fields at Erdberg (since merged in Vienna), captured, and handed over to his enemy, Duke Leopold of Austria, who entrusted him in turn to the keeping of the Kuenings. They kept him for fifteen months (1193) in the great castle of Dürrenstein beneath whose grim walls we passed in our canoe. In Austria the story is implicitly believed, whatever we may think of it in England.

The following day we saw the blue hills of the Wiener Wald rising behind Vienna, and before long we were obliged to don our best clothes, and send a porter down from our hotel to fetch the luggage from the bathing-house where the canoe lay below the Reichsbrücke.

We did not stay long in Vienna. Rooms in July seem stuffy after a tent, and a fly-spotted ceiling is a poor substitute for the stars.

The canoe was packed full of provisions ready to start when our first accident occurred. The river had risen a couple of feet and was very swift. My friend had just taken off his shoes and placed them on the top of the other luggage. Several of the crowd, in their misguided fashion, were trying to help us, when I stepped into the little space vacant for me in the stern. How it happened no one knew; some one let go too soon, and she was instantly swept out sideways into the current. The next second I was dropped out neatly into five feet of water, and the canoe, settling till only the tops of the luggage remained in sight, went full tilt down stream. There were fifty yards of clear water, and then came a row of barges tied ten feet from the shore and leaving an inner channel. Into this the canoe luckily was swept; had she careered off into mid-stream probably we should never have seen her again. With boat-hooks and poles we ran along the banks to catch her before she banged into the barges. My friend ran in his socks. The hotel-porter, the bath-house man, and a dozen idlers all followed shouting different things at once. But the canoe and the mad current had the start of us. Crash! with a sound of rending, splintering wood she banged into the nearest barge and turned completely over. A few seconds later the various articles appeared on the surface again, and there began a sort of obstacle-race that might have been highly comical had it not been so serious. Our beds with the cork mattresses floated high out of the water. Jumbo (a huge kit-bag holding our wardrobe) came next, up to his neck. A smaller waterproof bag, tied at the neck and holding bread and cameras, followed, spinning merrily. The provision-basket (filled with the morning's careful shopping and some tea just arrived from England) showed only its nose above the surface. Coats, hats, socks, maps, tent-poles and tent followed in motley array at the end of an idiotic looking procession. Every time an article banged into a barge it went under for a few seconds, and meanwhile the canoe was crashing on among ropes and poles in the van. The heavy articles defied our efforts, and Jumbo pulled one man bodily into the water when he tried to drag it ashore.

In the end, however, most of the things were saved. The men caught the canoe as she spun past a barge, and held her till help came. All the articles, too, were fished out except those that would not float. Thus, we lost our lantern, the prop of the kettle, a pair of my friend's shoes, an odd one of mine, the ridge-pole of the tent, and my town hat and coat. It was wonderfully little. The bows of the canoe, however, were completely smashed in; and to make it worse, the rain suddenly came down in torrents and a cold wind blew from the north.

Then a carpenter appeared on the scene and said he could mend the canoe and make a new tent-pole. The people of the bath-house took our things in to dry, while we jumped into a closed carriage and drove back into Vienna, my friend with no shoes on his feet, and I without a hat on my head. Yet, such was our good luck, that three hours later we were spinning down the river in the mended canoe; the sun was shining brightly, our things were dried, we had a new tent-pole, Vienna was out of sight below the horizon,—and when we landed for camp the place was so lonely that, on climbing the bank, I looked straight into the eyes of a great stag with branching antlers.

For two days at racing speed we journeyed through wild and lonely country towards the frontiers of Hungary. The river was like a wide lake,—no houses, no boats, no token of man except the daily steamer between Vienna and Budapest. We passed signs of Roman days and Turkish occupancy strangely mingled: Carnuntum, where Marcus Aurelius is said to have written much of his philosophy; Theben on a spur of the little Carpathians, with its rock-perched fortress destroyed by the Turks in 1683 when they swept on to besiege Vienna, and again by the French in 1809. At its very feet the March (the boundary between Austria and Hungary) comes sedately in, and the Danube received a new impetus as we passed below its shadow and into Hungary at last.

The Germans had been kind in a negative fashion, the Bavarians courteous, the Austrians obliging; but the hospitality of the Hungarians was positively aggressive. "Nothing is too much," they used to declare when we expostulated with them on the overwhelming nature of their attentions, "nothing is too good for Englishmen. Everybody will tell you the same in Hungary." Kossuth was the magical word, and hatred of the Austrians the key-note of their emotions. We blessed the generation that had welcomed him in exile and went on our way rejoicing. The crowds no longer stood gaping; they helped without being asked. When we landed for provisions they ran down to hold the canoe, while others went into the village to make our purchases more cheaply for us. Even their questions were intelligent. German is of uncertain value here, and we had carefully learned the Magyar words for the articles we most needed. "Now you begin to learn Magyar when it is too late," laughed the woman in a Pressburg shop where we bought milk and eggs and bacon; "but it's no matter: you can't starve in Hungary." The Hungarian name of the town is Pozsony. It was formerly the capital, where the kings of the Hapsburg race were crowned. Below it the Danube branches into three arms, one of which makes a circuit of fifty miles and comes in again at Komorn. The main river is a couple of miles wide and full of islands, separated by rapids and falls. An officer assured us that we should get lost for days together unless we carefully kept to the main channel. The country is utterly deserted, save for the little black landing-stages of the steamers that appear every twenty miles or so, the villages lying far back and protected by high earthen banks. The loneliness and desolation of these vast reaches of turbulent river and low willow-clad islands were impressive; in flood-time it must be grand.

The water escaped into so many side channels and lagoons that the depth of the river was most variable. Grey shingle-beds appeared often in mid-stream, and over and over again we were swept into them before we could cross to deeper water. It was difficult to distinguish them in time from the muddy, foam-streaked river, until we learned that the cormorants invariably used them for fishing-grounds; and then we took the black bodies in the distance as warning signals that saved us much dangerous wading. The velocity of the stream is so great that one almost expects to see the islands swept bodily away. Big grey hawks circled ever over head and grey crows by the thousand lined the shores. That evening, after crossing and re-crossing the river, we found a sheltered camp on a sandy island where pollards and willows roared in the wind. As if to show the loneliness of the spot an otter, rolling over and over among the eddies, swam past us as we landed. About sunset the clouds broke up momentarily and let out a flood of crimson light all over the wild country. Against the gorgeous red sky a stream of dark clouds, in all shapes and kinds, hurried over the Carpathian mountains, and when we went to bed a full moon cast the queerest shadows through the tossing branches. We dined,—prosaic detail!—off tongue, onions, potatoes, tea, and dried prunes which we stewed and ate with quantities of beetroot sugar.

Next day the river grew wider, swifter, and even more deserted. At Korteljes we landed to buy provisions, though only the watchman's hut was in sight. As we stepped on shore my hat blew off and floated down stream. At once the man (who spoke a little German) went into his hut and produced one of his own which he begged me to wear; it was a greasy wide-brimmed felt, but I could not refuse it, and he seemed delighted. He directed us to a farm a mile inland for milk and eggs, and gave us the correct pronounciation of the necessary words. The farm stood on the broad plain in a grove of acacia trees, with snow-white walls and overhanging thatched roofs, forming a square, within which were oxen, buffaloes, pigs, geese, and romping children in brilliant skirts. The older girls had yellow kerchiefs on their heads; one little girl, in flaming colours, was chasing a chicken in and out among the trees and oxen; all stopped to stare as we approached, swinging an empty milk-can. Through the farmhouse door I got a glimpse into a spotless kitchen, and a most courteous woman with brilliant dark eyes sold us what we required very cheaply. I took off my new greasy hat to them when we left, and the children followed us to the river, a motley escort.

On we went down the great rushing stream, ever flanked by a sea of silvery willows swaying and bending in the wind, reed beds, ten feet high, alternating with stretches of grey shingle. Between the wooded islands vistas opened in all directions; narrow glades where the river sent out new arms in patches of sunshine with the faint sound of water tumbling over distant shallows; while down some far blue reach, filled with the afternoon shadows, we could see immense herds of cattle, swine, and flocks of geese, feeding in meadows lined with poplars and birch trees. Horses in vast quantities roamed along the banks, watched by herdsmen who wore cool white skirts instead of trousers. Often, in the backwaters, oxen, horses, buffalo, pigs, and geese were all crowded together trying to keep cool in the great heat.

At Komorn, rising with its fortress just above the dead level of the plain, we laid in provisions. The grocer was inquisitive: "Where have you come from? Where are you going to? How do you cook? Where do you sleep? Are you not afraid of grasshoppers and snakes? What an awful distance you have come—the source of the Danube, where is it? You are both quite young, aren't you? But you are so enormous,"—and so on, and so on.

From here we saw the blue mountains that encircle Budapest,—not more than forty miles away as a crow would fly it, but a splendid loop of sixty-five miles by the river. Budapest draws one like a magnet. There is a suggestion of delicious wildness about it born of I know not what. The very name seems set to some flying fragment of the wild national music,—a bar of the *csardás,* or of the wailing Hungarian songs that thrill with such intense virility. The West, too, sinks lower on the horizon when Budapest is reached, and the Danube sweeps you on through the Iron Gates to Turkey and the Fekete Tengerig (Black Sea).

Willows, reeds, and islands have all vanished now, and there were no sudden whirlpools in mid-stream. With majestic dignity that disguised the real speed, the mass of water, a mile to a mile and a half wide, swept steadily down under that fierce heat towards the mountains. We kept to mid-stream and were never tired of watching the banks slip by with their ever changing pictures: open shore; fields with barley standing in sheaves; vineyards coming down to the water's edge; cottages with thick thatch and white walls; villages full of wild, over-grown gardens, and groves of acacia trees of brilliant washed green. We landed for milk at a farmhouse on the right bank and found that the proprietor spoke English and had travelled in England and Norway and studied in Vienna. "It's only twenty-six kilometers to Budapest," he told us. Later on we overtook some peasants in a boat full of vegetables, and kept pace with them for a little, while we chatted in German. "It's a little over forty kilometers to Pest," they said. Boats became frequent after this, broad, flat-bottomed, laden with farm-produce, and rowed by men and women who took their hats off to us and asked many questions in bad German. All agreed on one thing,—that the Austrians were a poor lot of people compared with the Hungarians; and all differed on another thing,—the distance to Budapest. It varied with every boat, and at length we became so confused with the arguments of the spokesman in German and the mocking chorus of the rest in Hungarian, that we almost expected to hear that we had already passed it, or were perhaps on the wrong river altogether.

To avoid calamities we increased our speed and left the string of boats behind. In the afternoon we came to Gran. The dome of its huge Italian basilica dominates for miles the plain we had just traversed, but looks like a round gleaming pebble beside the mountains that rise behind it. The charms of this quaint little town made us realise that time is after all but a form of thought; in other words, we stayed too long. At half-past six we entered the wide deep valley of these magical mountains hoping to find a camping-place so soon as we were beyond the town. The sun was hidden; the mountains stood outlined in purple against a wonderful sky, with long thin clouds just touching some of the higher peaks; the water glowed as though fires burned beneath the waves. Mile after mile we followed the windings of the valley, the hills folding up behind us, but opening ever in front again into new and darker distances. But no camping-place appeared; one side was too steep, the other treeless. The shadows lengthened and grew deeper; the hills changed from purple to black; the lights of villages twinkled across the river as across a wide lake. They fairly lined the base of the hills, and secluded camping-spots were evidently things of the past; there was not even an island.

Eight, nine o'clock passed; it became too dark to cross or recross with safety. We hugged the left bank, eagerly scanning the shore under the steep hills and waiting for the moon to rise. It was ten o'clock when the moon topped the mountains of the other shore and filled the valley with silver. We found a level yard or two below some vineyards, unpleasantly close to the abode of the proprietor, and there made a small fire and dined late off eggs and cocoa. The scenery was more thrilling than the meal: the dim hills rising through the moonlight; the white river filling the space between as if the whole valley were sliding noiselessly past, the fragrant air, warm and still, shot here and there with fireflies,—and Hungary,—wild, musical, enchanted Hungary! The fire had died down and we were smoking at the mouth of the tent when sounds of music floated to our ears, and presently a barge of peasants towed by three men along the shore came slowly up the stream. Cymbals and violins were playing a national air and a few low voices were singing. The barge floated past as if no one had seen us, and the music died away in the distance.

And on the mere the wailing died away.

Several hours later the returning voices and violins woke us in the tent as the party went down again too far from shore to be visible to the eye.

A man fishing woke us early and asked if the *weinhüter* (watchman of vineyards) had not disturbed us. Luckily he had not. "That's because it's Sunday and he's overslept himself." In spite of this warning we breakfasted leisurely, and then paddling down stream in blazing sunshine landed a mile below at Visegrad on the opposite bank. This little town, with its ruined castle, and fortress destroyed by the Austrians, nestles among the mountains, and here the good folk of Budapest come in summer to their villas among the acacia trees. Everybody spoke to us, helped to pull up the canoe, told us what to see, where to get good coffee or cooling drinks, described (with painful detail) the remaining twenty miles to Budapest, and showed themselves in all ways most courteous and obliging. Gipsy-music sounded everywhere among the trees, and the peasants in bright Sunday costumes lent colour to the scene.

Below Visegrad, which we left with much reluctance, begins an island which stretches the whole twenty miles to Budapest. Taking the inner channel we paddled peacefully all day under blue mountains in a haze of delicious heat, past villages, ferries, churches, castles, private villas, acres of vineyards over the slopes of the hills, and vast herds of horses and oxen standing in the water, till we camped at sunset on a treeless bit of plain at the extreme point of the island, only a mile from Budapest. It was like camping on the Brighton downs. With difficulty we collected scraps of wood enough to make a fire that would boil water. It was a windless night, and our candle stood tied to a stick in the open air with a motionless flame. The moon, rising late, showed rounded curves of bare hills behind us,—and then, two figures approached us cautiously from the river. They came to the outside of the firelight circle and stopped; but at our invitation they came within and smoked the last of our *noblesse* cigars—poor fellows! Night-fishermen they were, short, thick-set, dark-faced Huns. They drank our cocoa and explained their strange-looking nets to us while waiting for the moon to rise higher. All night long they fished, and on their way home to bed at five next morning they looked in to give us a hearty good morning and the information that the cows were coming.

The thunder of hoofs confirmed this, and we got up in time to protect the tent from a herd of several hundred cattle. A herder followed them, a dwarf-like creature with a pole-axe as big as himself, and a badge which proclaimed him Government keeper of the plain (Crownland) where all men's cattle might feed on certain conditions. He spoke no German, but he understood the meaning of a plate of veal, and he finished our meat (two pounds) in about ten minutes. Then he drank some cocoa, asking, with a wry face, if it were *paprika* (Hungarian pepper).

It was piping hot on the treeless plain, and Budapest lay waiting for us. We shaved and donned our town suits. The herder, grateful for his meal, helped to carry our things to the canoe, and, long after we were off, stood shading his eyes with his hand and staring after us. We drifted lazily down another mile of steaming hot river and landed at the wharf of the Hunnia Rowing Club on the right bank,— nearly a thousand miles from the sleepy little village in the Black Forest where we had embarked six weeks before.

Author's Preface to *Tales of Algernon Blackwood* (1938)

The body, they assure us, changes its atoms every seven years or so, being therefore totally different at twenty-eight from what it was at twenty-one, but science does not commit itself with regard to mental changes, such changes being doubtless incommensurable. At any rate, Mr. Martin Secker's request for an introduction faces me with a question: Am I the man who wrote these tales so many years ago, or am I some one else? This considerable period of time is involved, but as I cannot step back to the platform from which I viewed the world in 1906, the question finds no answer. Neither Dunne's *Serial Universe,* nor Ouspensky's other-dimensional time, nor even a book like Forrest Reid's *Uncle Stephen,* can help, while the recent exposé of the Versailles Adventure suggests brutally that thirty or one hundred years are precisely what they say they are, no more, no less. Moreover, a polite request from an intelligent publisher being in the nature of *force majeure,* if not an Act of God, this introduction, whoever writes it, must be written.

It is, none the less, a dour job, for I have not read these stories since I first wrote them; physically, mentally, spiritually I must have changed more times than I care to remember; they introduce me to some one I now know but slightly, so that it is almost like reading the work of another man. Any desire to cut, to alter, entirely to re-compose is, of course, inadmissible; tinkering is worse than useless, it is dangerous; the tales stand, therefore, as they were first set down. Far from apologising for them, however, I must admit that most of them thrilled me. "I wish I had known the fellow who saw things in this way and thus expressed himself" is the kind of comment my twentieth-century mind suggests, since behind the actual tale I discern hints of an adventurous philosophy. "I wonder whether his

505

queer, observant, questioning mind travelled further!" But what I myself honestly think of the stories to-day not even Torquemada could extract from me.

It is, of course, extremely interesting to look back across the years questioningly, wonderingly, objectively, without detachment, though seeing "objectively" does not necessarily imply seeing truthfully. It ought to imply seeing with self eliminated, yet self obstinately intrudes, whether it be the self of to-day or the self of 1906. I recall, anyhow, that these tales poured from me spontaneously, as though a tap were turned on, and I have often since leaned to the suggestion that many of them derived from buried, unresolved shocks—shocks to the emotions; and by "unresolved," I mean, of course, unexpressed. These "shocks" had come to an exceptionally ignorant youth of twenty who had drifted into the life of a newspaper reporter in New York after a disastrous cattle-farm and a hotel in Canada, and the drifting had included the stress of extreme poverty and starvation. Having told some of this in *Adventures Before Thirty,* I must not repeat, but it holds this psychological interest for me to-day: that the New York experiences in a world of crime and vice had bruised and bludgeoned a sensitive nature that swallowed the horrors without being able to digest them, and that the seeds thus sown, dormant and unresolved in the subconscious, possibly emerged later—and, since the subconscious always dramatises, emerged in story form.

Others are, of course, ghost-stories, so called, for the classification of ghost-stories has stuck to me closer than a brother, and even when the B.B.C. ask for a story it must be, preferably, of the "creepy" kind. Yet this alleged interest in ghosts I should more accurately define as an interest in the Extension of Human Faculty. To be known as the "ghost man" is almost a derogatory classification, and here at last I may perhaps refute it. My interest in psychic matters has always been the interest in questions of extended or expanded consciousness. If a ghost is seen, what *is* it interests one less than what *sees* it? Do we possess faculties which, under exceptional stimulus, register beyond the normal gamut of seeing, hearing, feeling? That such faculties may exist in the human being and occasionally manifest is where my interest has always lain. Such exceptional stimulus may be pathogenic (as duplicated in the Salpetrière and other mental hospitals), or due to some dynamic flash of terror or beauty which strikes a Man in the Street, but that they occur is beyond the denials to-day of the petty sceptic. If this is more certain to me now than it was when I wrote these tales a generation ago means merely that I have since studied more of the increasingly voluminous evidence. Thus in most of these stories there is usually an average man who, either through a flash of terror or of beauty, becomes stimulated into extra-sensory experience. A wide gap may lie between a common-place mind that became clairvoyant and clairaudient from a flash of terror in "The Empty House," to the Man in the Street in *The Centaur* whose sense of beauty blazed into a realisation of the planetary bodies as superhuman entities, but the principle is the same: both experienced an expansion of normal consciousness. And this, I submit, travels a little further than the manufacture of the homespun "ghost-story."

These early stories, though I did not know it at the time, seem to me now to have been practice-flights for more adventurous explorations or, as Eveleigh Nash, my first publisher, phrased it, "trying your hand on a larger canvas." That idea of a "larger canvas" scarified me at the age of thirty-six, but seeing my first book in print, I remember, scarified me even more. It is an experience that must surely intensify any hint of inferiority complex that lies hidden. I well recall my intense relief that *The Empty House,* my first book, enjoyed, if that be the word, a gentle, negligible press until the *Spectator* of that day, half to my distress, half to my delight, chose it as a verse for a special sermon and, later, a scholarly article in the *Morning Post,* analysing the "ghost-story" as a peculiarly Anglo-Saxon form, based its remarks on this particular book and became traceable to Hilaire Belloc, to whose subsequent encouragement I owe much.

What I may call left-handed compliments, at any rate, flew wildly across a barrage of "faithful criticism," and I remember that, while accepting the blame as deserved, I cuddled the compliments, deciding therefore to try again—so that *The Listener* in due course appeared. And, such are the tricks of memory, I can still see the grave expression on the faces of Eveleigh Nash and his gifted "reader," Maude ffoulkes, while we discussed together whether a large Ear might be printed on the cover (picture-jackets had not yet come in), and whether the title-story was not perhaps of too pathogenic a character to be included, my own vote being in the decided negative despite the personal origin of that horrible tale.

It is, at any rate, true that to this persuasive suggestion of "trying a larger canvas" I owed a later *Centaur, Julius Le Vallon, The Human Chord, The Education of Uncle Paul,* and many others. Thus, I both blame and bless Eveleigh Nash for a stimulating hint which, if its results have afflicted others, provided relief to an author who found himself more overcharged with material than probably his talent was competent to express adequately.

The origin of some of these stories may be of interest to a reader here or there: this not only sounds egotistical, but is: it interests me, as I look back to revive old memories ... of a journey down the Danube in a Canadian canoe, and how my friend and I camped on one of the countless lonely islands below Pressburg (Bratislava) and the willows seemed to suffocate us in spite of the gale blowing, and how a year or two later, making the same trip in a barge, we found a dead body caught by a root, its decayed mass dangling against the sandy shore of the very same island my story describes. A coincidence, of course! Of that unfurnished haunted house in a Brighton Square where I sat up to see a ghost with a woman beside me whose rather wrinkled face suddenly blanched smooth as the face of a child, frightening me far more than the ghost I never actually saw; of the Moravian School in the Black Forest (Königsfeld), where as a boy I spent two haunted years and revisited later to find a compensating Devil Worship in full swing and called "Secret Worship"; of the Island in the Baltic where the Were-wolf Legend materialised as "The Camp of the Dog," yet whereof our happy party of six campers remained ignorant until they read my tale; above all, of that old French town of "Ancient Sorceries," where the slinking inhabitants behaved as cats behave, sidling along the pavements with slanting gestures, twitching their sleeky ears and snakey tails, their sharp eyes glinting, all alert and concentrated upon some hidden, secret life of their own while they feigned attention to tourists like ourselves—ourselves just back from climbing in the Dolomites and finding the train so boring on its way from Basle to Boulogne that we hopped out at Laon and spent two days in this witch-ridden atmosphere. The "Auberge de la

Hure" was the name of the Inn, and it was not Angoulème, as some fancied, nor Coutances as John Gibbon thought (*I Wanted to Travel*), nor elsewhere as variously attributed, but Laon, a lovely old haunted town where the Cathedral towers stand up against the sunset like cats' ears, the paws running down the dusky streets, the feline body crouched just below the hill. Yet who should guess that so much magic lay within a kilometer of its dull, desolate railway station, or that from my little bedroom window I should presently stand enthralled as I looked across the moonlit tiles and towers, jotting down on the backs of envelopes an experience that kept sleep away till dawn? Then the awful "Wendigo" comes shouldering up over a hill of memory, a name I remembered vividly in *Hiawatha* ("Wendigos and giants" runs the line), yet hardly thought of again till a friend, just back from Labrador, told me honest tales about mysterious evacuations of a whole family from a lonely valley because the "Wendigo had come blundering in" and "scared them still"; of the "Haunted Island," an island I lived on for an autumn month alone in the Muskoka Lakes north of Toronto, where Red Indians flit to and from when the summer visitors have left; and of a dreadful house I once lived in (New York City) where unaccountable noises, voices, slitherings at night and so forth seemed a commonplace setting for the "Eavesdropping" re-enactment of a gruesome murder of twenty years before. . . .

Memories, indeed, of where each story was written are clearer to me to-day than the conduct and details of the plots themselves, but clearer still is the vivid recollection that in each case an emotion of a very possessive kind produced each tale. To write a ghost-story I must first feel ghostly, a condition not to be artificially induced: and there was a touch of goose-flesh down my back as I watched my "Wendigo" in a mountain inn above Champéry and heard the November night-wind crashing among the pine-forests beyond the window; shivers down the spine, too, as the horror of that "Willows" island crept over the imagination. I think, indeed, the majority of these tales were accompanied at birth by what may be called a delicious shudder. The true "other-worldly" story should issue from that core of superstition which lies in every mother's son of us, and we are still close enough to primitive days with their terror of the dark for Reason to abdicate without too violent resistance.

There has, however, been one striking change in knowledge since the generation when these tales were written—matter has been wiped out of existence. Atoms are no longer minute billiard-balls but charges of negative electricity, and these charges, according to Eddington, Jeans, and Whitehead, are themselves but symbols. What these "symbols" stand for ultimately Science admittedly does not know. Physics remains silent. Jeans speaks of a "world of shadows." "Phenomena," Professor Joad reminds us, "may be merely symbols of a Reality which underlies them. The Reality, for all we know to the contrary, may be of an entirely different order from the events which symbolise it. It may be even mental or spiritual." The Universe, thus, seems to be an appearance merely, our old friend Maya, or Illusion, of the Hindus. Possibly, therefore, Reason might to-day encounter less need for abdicating than thirty years ago, and the *rapprochement* between Modern Physics and so-called psychical and mystical phenomena must seem suggestive to any reflecting mind. All alike conduct their researches in a "world of shadows" among mere symbols of a Reality that may conceivably be "mental or spiritual," but is unknown, if not unknowable.

Let me leave the stories to speak for themselves. They are printed here in the chronological sequence in which they were written between 1906 and 1910.

Bibliography

I. Collections

The Empty House and Other Ghost Stories. London: Eveleigh Nash, 1906. New York: Donald C. Vaughan, 1915. New York: Knopf, 1917. London: Eveleigh Nash & Grayson, 1930. New York: Verry, 1965. Holicong, PA: Wildside Press, 2005. [*Contents:* The Empty House; A Haunted Island; A Case of Eavesdropping; Keeping His Promise; With Intent to Steal; The Wood of the Dead; Smith: An Episode in a Lodging House; A Suspicious Gift; The Strange Adventures of a Private Secretary in New York; Skeleton Lake: An Episode in Camp.]

The Listener and Other Stories. London: Eveleigh Nash, 1907. New York: Vaughan & Gomme, 1914. New York: Knopf, 1917. London: Eveleigh Nash & Grayson, 1930. Freeport, NY: Books for Libraries Press, 1971. [*Contents:* The Listener; Max Hensig—Bacteriologist and Murderer; The Willows; The Insanity of Jones; The Dance of Death; The Old Man of Visions; May Day Eve; Miss Slumbubble—and Claustrophobia; The Woman's Ghost Story.]

Ten Minute Stories. London: John Murray, 1914. New York: Dutton, 1914. Freeport, NY: Books for Libraries Press, 1969. [*Contents:* Accessory Before the Fact; The Deferred Appointment; The Prayer; Strange Disappearance of a Baronet; The Secret; The Lease; Up and Down; Faith Cure on the Channel; The Goblin's Collection; Imagination; The Invitation; The Impulse; Her Birthday; Two in One; Ancient Lights; Dream Trespass; Let Not the Sun—; Entrance and Exit; You *May* Telephone from Here; The Whisperers; Violence; The House of the Past; Jimbo's Longest Day; If the Cap Fits—; News *v.* Nourishment; Wind; Pines; The Winter Alps; The Second Generation.]

Ancient Sorceries and Other Tales. London: Collins, 1927. [*Contents:* Ancient Sorceries; The Willows; The Return; Running Wolf; The Man Whom the Trees Loved; The Man Who Played upon the Leaf.]

The Dance of Death and Other Tales. London: Herbert Jenkins, 1927. New York: Lincoln MacVeagh/Dial Press, 1928. London: Pan, 1963. London: House of Stratus, 2002. [*Contents:* The Dance of Death; A Psychical Invasion; The Old Man of Visions; The South Wind; The Touch of Pan; The Valley of the Beasts.]

Strange Stories. London: Heinemann, 1929. New York: Arno Press, 1976. [*Contents:* The Man Whom the Trees Loved; The Sea Fit; The Glamour of the Snow; The Tryst; Transition; The Occupant of the Room; The Wings of Horus; By Water; Malahide and Forden; Alexander; The Man Who Was Milligan; The Little Beggar; The Pikestaff Case; Accessory Before the Fact; The Deferred Appointment; Ancient Lights; You *May* Telephone from Here; the Goblin's Collection; Running Wolf; The Valley of the Beasts; The Decoy; Confession; A Descent into Egypt; The Damned; The Willows; Ancient Sorceries.]

The Willows and Other Queer Tales. London: Collins, 1932. [*Contents:* The Willows; Ancient Sorceries; The Return; Running Wolf; The Man Whom the Trees Loved; The Man Who Played upon the Leaf; The Tryst; By Water; The Occupant of the Room; The Decoy; Dream Trespass.]

Tales of Algernon Blackwood. London: Martin Secker, 1938. New York: Dutton, 1939. [*Contents:* The Empty House; A Case of Eavesdropping; Strange Adventures of a Private Secretary; With Intent to Steal; Keeping His Promise; The Wood of the Dead; A Suspicious Gift; The Listener; Max Hensig; The Willows; The Insanity of Jones; The Dance of Death; May Day Eve; The Woman's Ghost Story; A Psychical Invasion; Ancient Sorceries; The Nemesis of Fire; Secret Worship; The Camp of the Dog; The Man from the "Gods"; The Wendigo.]

Selected Tales of Algernon Blackwood. Harmondsworth, UK: Penguin, 1942. [*Contents:* The Empty House; Strange Adventures of a Private Secretary; Keeping His Promise; The Woman's Ghost Story; Ancient Sorceries; The Camp of the Dog.]

Selected Short Stories of Algernon Blackwood. New York: Editions for the Armed Services, [1945]. [*Contents:* The Willows; The Wendigo; A Psychical Invasion; The Woman's Ghost Story; Max Hensig; The Wood of the Dead; The Listener.]

Tales of the Uncanny and Supernatural. London: Peter Nevill, 1949. London: Spring, 1962. [*Contents:* The Doll; Running Wolf; The Little Beggar; The Occupant of the Room; The Man Whom the Trees Loved; The Valley of the Beasts; The South Wind; The Man Who Was Milligan; The Trod; The Terror of the Twins; The Deferred Appointment; Accessory Before the Fact; The Glamour of the Snow; The House of the Past; The Decoy; The Tradition; The Touch of Pan; Entrance and Exit; The Pikestaffe Case; The Empty Sleeve; Violence; The Lost Valley.]

II. First Appearances of Individual Stories

"A Case of Eavesdropping." *Pall Mall Magazine* 22 (December 1900): 558–68. In *The Empty House* (1906), *Tales* (1938).

"The Dance of Death." In *The Listener* (1907), *The Dance of Death* (1927), *Selected Tales* (1938).

"The Empty House." In *The Empty House* (1906), *Tales* (1938), *Selected Tales* (1942).

"The Farmhouse on the Hill." *Evening Post* (London) (21 December 1907). *Adelaide Chronicle* [Canberra, Australia] (21 December 1907): 19.

"A Haunted Island." *Pall Mall Magazine* 17 (April 1899): 445–56. In *The Empty House* (1906).

"The House of the Past." *Theosophical Review* 34 (15 April 1904): 145–50. In *Ten Minute Stories* (1914), *Tales of the Uncanny and Supernatural* (1949).

"How Garnier Broke the Log-Jam." *Boy's Own Paper* 27 (31 December 1904): 216–20.

"The Insanity of Jones." In *The Listener* (1907), *Tales* (1938).

"Keeping His Promise." In *The Empty House* (1906), *Tales* (1938), *Selected Tales* (1942).

"The Last Egg in the Nest." *Boy's Own Paper* 24 (23 August 1902): 743–44.

"The Listener." In *The Listener* (1907), *Tales* (1938), *Selected Short Stories* (1945).

"Max Hensig—Bacteriologist and Murderer." In *The Listener* (1907), *Tales* (1938), *Selected Short Stories* (1945).

"May Day Eve." In *The Listener* (1907), *Tales* (1938).

"Miss Slumbubble—and Claustrophobia." In *The Listener* (1907).

"A Mysterious House." *Belgravia* 69 (July 1899): 98–107.

"The Old Man of Visions." In *The Listener* (1907), *The Dance of Death* (1927).

"Skeleton Lake: An Episode in Camp." In *The Empty House* (1906).

"Smith: An Episode in a Lodging House." In *The Empty House* (1906).

"A Strange Adventure in the Black Forest." *Blackfriars Magazine* (November 1889): 253–63.

"The Strange Adventures of a Private Secretary in New York." In *The Empty House* (1906), *Tales* (1938), *Selected Tales* (1942).

"The Story of Karl Ott." *Pall Mall Magazine* 10 (October 1896): 189–200.

"A Suspicious Gift." In *The Empty House* (1906), *Tales* (1938).

"Testing His Courage." *Pearson's Magazine* 18 (September 1904): 250–53.

"The Willows." In *The Listener* (1907), *Ancient Sorceries* (1927), *Strange Stories* (1929), *The Willows* (1932), *Tales* (1938), *Selected Short Stories* (1945).

"With Intent to Steal." In *The Empty House* (1906), *Tales* (1938).

"The Woman's Ghost Story." In *The Listener* (1907), *Tales* (1938), *Selected Tales* (1942), *Selected Short Stories* (1945).

"The Wood of the Dead." In *The Empty House* (1906), *Tales* (1938), *Selected Short Stories* (1945).

Appendix:

"Down the Danube in a Canadian Canoe." *Macmillan's Magazine* No. 503 (September 1901): 350–58; No. 504 (October 1901): 418–29.

"Author's Preface" to *Tales of Algernon Blackwood*. London: Martin Secker, 1938. 7–12.

www.ingramcontent.com/pod-product-compliance
Lightning Source LLC
Chambersburg PA
CBHW061030030726
47504CB00002B/312